I0597096

Produced by BookCreate
bookcreate.com
Seattle, Washington USA

Published by LebowDean

Printed in USA

ISBN 978-0-9991389-1-5

____

Cover Art by Ronnie Leibofsky

She Came in Lit

Susan Lebow

NOTE: All italics are not the author's words

FOR THE READER:

"We make our destinies by our choice of gods."
  - Virgil - from the Aeneid

"Character is fate."
  - Heraclitus

"Something about your self always remains the same."
  - Susan Lebow

FOR RICHARD:

"Ah, Love! could thou and I with Fate conspire
To grasp this sorry Scheme of Things entire.
Would not we shatter it to bits – and then
Re-mold it nearer to the Heart's Desire."

  - from the Rubaiyat of Omar Khayyam

WHO ARE THE SWEET SISTERS FATE

Clotho - spins the thread of human life, which creates the web of cause and effect in which a life plays out.

Lachesis - determines the length of that thread.

Atropos - cuts the thread of human life.

THE PROTAGONIST SPEAKS

And now, looking back at that shallow girl in the mirror, her tangled journey of insolently turned down opportunities and split-second decisions, the people she loved, and lost track of, the disappointments and adventures, I would have changed some things, but to have so fully lived in a time that is now legendary, I couldn't have been any other way.

- Shoshannah Leibofsky

Thank you thank you to:

Richard Dean for keeping me going,

Jeffrey Beals for advice,

Joni Flame for listening,

Jess Lebow for editing,

Ronnie Leibofsky for painting,

Dr. Ida Rose Barber for her friendship and wisdom.

TABLE of CONTENTS

Chapter One

WAKING THE SLEEPING DOG

The Voice possessed absolute authority and seemed to be coming from the heart of the mystery. "Do you know who you are" boomed through mind's untended edge and caught my eyes in the mirror, just an innocent last glance to make sure I look perfect. I locked the apartment door. Who am I, what a question to ask of my perfect life. I had my first good paying job, good for 1966 anyway, charge accounts at Nordstrom, I.Magnin and Fredrick & Nelson, each maxed so I looked like I just stepped-off the cover of Vogue, or maybe from one of the inside pages cause I was too big-chested and too short for a cover model. Guys were crazy for me, two already proposed. And I had been picked to run for Seafair Queen by the very respectable Cirque Playhouse, whose owners Janice and Gene Keene knew me since I was the pretty little girl down the block that came to play in the yard with their Saint Bernard. But who am I, I could not shake it from my seventeen year old head.

I took the bus to work, my secretary job for Boeing, in their downtown Seattle high-rise. I could not type but looked the part, sexy and perky. They needed someone decorative to check security badges at the front desk, an empty head who could pass a level-8 security clearance because the 7th floor was the Strategic Air Command division, and with a spotless record, never even a traffic ticket, I fit the profile. When taking typing my junior year at Mercer Island High School, I made sure to fail and therefore never get stuck behind a typewriter, the typing pool being the direction most girls of little promise were herded till we snagged a husband, and yet here I was, a secretary who could not type, a living cartoon. Once a week my Boss would hand me an inconsequential letter, and glad for something to pass the time, I did my best, full knowing his private secretary would put it in proper form later. To fill the rest of my days, I'd call Penny in Hawaii on the company's free W.A.T.S. Line. Two years ahead of me in school, Penny and I had grown-up across the street from each other, on a small island in Lake Washington, connected to Seattle by the Lake Washington Floating Bridge, the country's first. Though they really couldn't afford the life-style, my Folks moved me and my two brothers from our working class Mt. Baker neighborhood in Seattle to Mercer Island in the summer of my fourth-grade year, because The Island had the best schools in the State, and they were willing to tighten their belts to provide their children with a better education than they had. My Dad being a jeweler on a fixed salary at Zedick's on 3rd Avenue in downtown Seattle, while the other Island kids fathers were doctors, lawyers, business owners and chiefs, it was a real struggle to compete with classmates who had their own charge accounts by 5th grade. It seemed so unfair that money was such an advantage, but I was resource-full and tried hard, buying into the idea that The Island represented the best and was worth the struggle. And I didn't know much more till high school, when I began to get off The Island, and realize though it seemed so conspicuously advantaged, it was really a golden prison much as Seattle's Central District ghetto was a disenfranchised cellblock. This restlessness rustled quietly, I thought of Mercer Island as a Golden Ghetto, beyond that my discontent was still to gilded to comprehend.

One month before my high school graduation Penny broke-up with her long-time beau Nick, moved to Hawaii and would not say why. At first she begged me come live with her after graduation, and I considered it. But only three months in paradise and she was painfully homesick, finding Oahu claustrophobic and way too expensive, she was trying to save money to come home. Hungry for any news, I'd fill her in while re-painting my nails if I'd smudged them the night before. Then I'd read the morning Post Intelligencer, flirt with the pilots and engineers, go to lunch, read the afternoon Seattle Times, flirt with the pilots and engineers, and work the mandatory half-hour overtime every night for time-and-a-half pay. In my ignorance-is-bliss I thought I had it all, but today my own eyes in the mirror haunted me, I couldn't shake-off the feeling I'd built my life so far in quicksand, and that Voice, felt like a challenge to my whole being. After a brief pre-occupied conversation with Penny, and unable to concentrate on the morning paper, except an ad for Ray Charles at the

Seattle Center Coliseum, I called my roommate to see if she wanted to go, Katey would meet me in the ticket line. Then I sat back and looked my self over. Square-toed black patent-leather Charles Jourdan sling-back pumps with three-inch block-heels that made me look almost five-six, sheer smoke-colored Dior silk stockings, fastened to a white lace Dior garter belt, matching bra and bikini-panties underneath a sleeveless white piqué mini-dress and short-sleeved fully-lined matching jacket with black patent-leather buttons. My nails were long, filed blunt, painted Fabergé flat white and always perfect. I repainted them often in bed and fell asleep with my hands carefully placed atop the quilt hoping they'd dry before smudging. Joy by Jean Patou my daily scent. There wasn't a hair on my body I didn't shave, wax, pluck, trim, color or style. I loyally subscribed to Vogue, copying the latest make-up exactly, and wore my hair in a tasteful beehive tied round with a scarf, the ends falling strategically next to my left eye. Good with hair, I created my own do, and bought into the pretense of wrapping it in an ensemble matching designer silk scarf to set me apart from the crowd, like an expensive man's tie. And yet, for the first time in my life I was consciously questioning if looking perfect was the entire definition of who I was. I thought I knew who I was, wore all the right labels, but today I knew for sure, for unshakably sure god-damn-it that I did not. With one glance in the mirror I'd fallen down the rabbit hole into another reality, felt startlingly awake, disturbed, the questions in my head remaining solid instead of drifting off into the just to be forgotten. And I could not go back, the mirror had broken, I was in free-fall, and could not think of where else to start but on the outside.

After work I walked to Nordstrom, charged a paisley long-sleeve wool challis smock-dress with yellow cuffs and big pockets, the skirt ten-inches longer than any I owned. Instead of silk stockings and a garter belt, I chose golden-yellow Danskin dance tights, and matching spaghetti-strap sling-back Capezio shoes with one-inch squashed heels. Once home I took my hair down and washed it. Having discovered that detaching the hood from my hair-dryer and using the hose as a blower, the blasting hot air and a stiff brush were enough to straighten my curls. For according to the Golden Ghetto Girls' bible Vogue, anything but straight was totally out, and though I did not live on The Island for the time being, Vogue still dictated the fashion-slave rules for anyone aspiring to high society, and I understood only too well the consequences of not following the rules. Before the blower method, my oldest friend Rachel and I used to iron our curls pin-straight, and though unable to avoid creases close to the head, fried ends that resembled steel wool, and static electricity that made those ends float, even electric steel wool was better than showing our ethnic curls in a Doris Day world. The hose-blower method made my hair look naturally straight, when it wasn't undone by the damp and rain in the Pacific Northwest. I put on my new outfit, and stood infront of the mirror, looking more like a designer Hippie than Barbie doll. Head and hands the only things uncovered, my hair hung down to my shoulders, covering my long neck, the smock shrouded my tits, waist and hips, thick tights covered my legs, no fuck-me high heels to make my legs seem longer and tip my rump up for that ready look. All the assets I'd been taught to use to catch that man who would sweep me off my feet safely back to the Golden Ghetto were hidden.

I took a cab to the Ray Charles concert, cruised the line for Katey, and not finding her went to the end. Minutes later she walked by, I had to call out, she did not recognize the new me. Nearing the ticket window, Penny's ex-boyfriend Nick spotted me and asked to cut-in with us. Although he'd gone to school in Seattle, I'd known him nigh on six years, since he started dating Penny, and though he'd been a real jerk to her, and made me nervous, I had always been drawn to him. From her body-language, Katey was too, I introduced them. There were enough boys in my life at the moment, and in my mind even flirting with Nick would betray Penny's and my friendship. He pulled a thin marijuana joint from behind his ear, boldly lit it, drew a long toke and held it in, stifling exploding lungs, and passed it to me. Having smoked marijuana only once less than a month ago, and experiencing a super self-consciousness, I was afraid someone might see me in such a public place and tell my Folks, or the police would haul me off to jail. I passed it to Katey, who took a greedy hit, and coughing passed it to Nick. Taking another long drag, he extinguished the cinder in a pool of saliva on his cupped tongue, swallowed the roach, and smiling as if he'd just exposed himself offered to buy our tickets. Thrilled, batting lashes, Katey eagerly accepted. I did not want the obligation or complication and declined, and once inside, slipped away into the crowd. Ray Charles with his beautiful lips and the Raelettes in their pink feather tops were my absolute fav, I'd been to four concerts in two years, and danced the entire three hour show, the new me attracting a different kind of boy, the ones with long hair.

Nick drove us home. Katey invited him up, and we all got stoned. Still a neophyte, I began laughing and could not stop. Reminded of their first times Nick and Katey enjoyed me. We lived in one of the many apartment buildings on Capitol Hill in Seattle, $50 a month, one bedroom, everyone young, lots of cute boys. Through gales and convulsing I heard a pounding, crossed the room to turn-down the record player, and the door busted opened. My neighbor Jake came flying in, red-faced and raging at me for smoking dope, it would ruin my life, Katey and Nick were low-lifes and I'd be a stupid junkie before I knew it. If I wasn't stoned, I would've been scared of him. But this seemed more a slow-motion version of Reefer Madness, the anti-drug movie shown in high schools. And though no one at my school did drugs till my senior year, when two girls started smoking marijuana and stopped wearing panties and bras, I thought the movie was a joke. Jake plainly did not, getting into a hot-head vocal shoving match with Nick. Fearing eviction, I stepped in-between, instinctively shaking a Mother's finger, scolding. Jake retreated, and I pursued, indignant, demanding what right he had to invade my life, he wasn't my Dad, all the way into his bedroom, where an eight-by-ten color photo of my Big Brother's girlfriend Marlee stood on a wooden box by his bed. Jake sank down on the bare mattress and just looked at me. Marlee worked at Boeing and tipped me off to the open job. I pressed what was he doing with her photo, then realized he must be the poor schmuck she dumped for Big. Staring at his feet Jake apologized for interfering, promised to fix my door, and then confessed to being inlove with me and sometimes following me. Lights and sirens went off in my head, I fled without another word. Nick was strutting round the front room pissed. Katey food-tripping on Darigold chocolate ice cream. And I was no longer high but exhausted and went to bed, having an interview in the morning before work with the Seattle Times, they were talking to all the girls in the Seafair Queen Pageant, I needed my beauty sleep. Nick and Katey's voices faded as I slid over sleep's threshold, confused as to how things could get so complicated so fast. Except for once, nothing violent ever happened in my life, my nicely arranged life, lived till now mostly on the surface.

Standing on a sandy beach, massive cliffs jutting-up behind me, it was near high tide and huge breakers were crashing in quick succession, each foaming crest taking flight as a rabid white bat. My friends were huddled at the base of the cliffs with no escape, while I frantically tried sweeping the ocean back with a push-broom. I woke tired, the sinking feeling of being overwhelmed in the pit of my stomach. And still I aced the interview. If The Golden Ghetto had taught me anything, it was how to say all the right things, make all the proper moves. Word was whispering round Pageant contestants that the daughter of the president of the Chamber of Commerce had already been chosen to win. I refused to believe the crown so many girls dreamed of wearing was rigged, and shrugged it off to deliberate rumor-mongering designed to demoralize the rest of us. When I was tired, work seemed endless. I caught a nap on the couch in the ladies room during lunch, and nodded-off again on the bus ride home. My heart leapt against my chest finding Nick's blue Volkswagen bus parked infront of my building. He'd come to invited me on a Lysergic Acid Diethylamide-25 trip. I'd lived with Katey just two weeks when she asked if I wanted to get stoned. Thinking she meant drunk I said sure. And never having smoked even one cigarette, inhaled an entire marijuana joint, getting so high I was afraid to stand up, Frank Zappa and The Mothers of Invention on the record player singing Susie Cream Cheese, and suddenly my skin was breathing from each individual pore, and I understood another kind of life went on under this fragile covering, while my consciousness viewed it from the outside. I felt split-in-two yet solitary, exposed and self-conscious, and fell inlove with Zappa's mind, his lyrics infecting my head, hearing music as if for the first time, pulsing and swelling it took me on a covered wagon ride over a vast rolling landscape and rescued my soul like music had so many times before. Then I was ravenous. Katey called it the munchies. We pulled skirts on over our jeans, put our coats on backwards, fastened clothes pins in our hair, and walked across the street to the little corner grocery. The clerk tried not to notice us. We giggled at his trying, bought Mountain Bars, Hostess chocolate cupcakes, Snowballs and Doctor Pepper, took them back to the apartment and devoured every last crumb. And now, I was considering LSD. Nick assured me it was safe, the pure stuff, dropped on a sugar cube and stored in the freezer, that I shouldn't worry, though LSD had been recently criminalized in some states it was still legal in Washington. I said yes way too casually. Nick licked his bottom lip showing me his tongue, and said he'd be over on the weekend, we could trip in Volunteer Park.

Sometimes things happen all at once. My sixty-two year old maternal Grampa Joe was rushed to Group Health Hospital. I went every day after work. Soon he wasted-thin and curled into a fetal position, supposedly in a coma, unable to hear anything. But sometimes when we were alone, the rhythm of his breath as I spoke or read, I knew he could hear me. In a bitter and sweet way I coveted this time alone with my Grampa, imagining if I was him, I'd still want to know what's going on, so I'd bring the Seattle Times and read to him. One day I brought The Prophet by Kahil Gilbran. Grampa would never read anything this far-out, and I felt as if I was breaking some unwritten rule, I never knew him to read poetry or have much interest in the Arts. He worked hard his entire life, loved to fish, play poker and drink whiskey, though I never saw him drunk. He was the well-respected spiritual patriarch of our large Jewish family, and this was my first chance ever to let him know who I really was. Maybe if he heard what I found profound, maybe we could know each other better.

Time folded in on itself till Grampa woke-up. The family gathered round his bedside, and he told us he heard every word that had been said. My heart swelled knowing I connected with him in a grown-up way, and collapsed as he went on to say he would die soon. With everyone talking at once I had to go before the room closed-in on me, taking motionless refuge in a small waiting area till everyone went to dinner. As Grampa faded in and out of consciousness, I held his hand and spilled my guts, about catching my eyes in the mirror, feeling lost, my foundation sliding from under me, the Seafair rumor, and how much I loved him, pleading please don't go now, just when I'm old enough to have an intelligent conversation with you, and begging forgiveness for my selfishness, if he had to die he could, there had to be something better than the terrible pain he was in even if it was nothing. And when I was willing to see Death on him, the weight of it crushed me. I went crazy, ranting how it made no sense someone I love so much had to leave me, why did God make bodies so fragile, He should be smarter, have better timing than to take my Grampa when I was just wise enough to learn from him, argue with him, maybe be friends, it wasn't fair. Feeling Gramp's hand tighten round mine, I couldn't bear seeing him struggle yet raised my eyes to meet his. They were piercing blue, he whispered "Shoshy, promise me you'll have a Rabbi marry you". I was stunned by this displaced request "I promise". Then he spoke in a clear quiet voice to some one I could not see "Death takes its own time, makes you wait". His wrists were tied to the side-rails with Ace bandages because he'd tried pulling the IV from his arm several times, he pointed with his eyes towards the needle and calmly said "Pull that out". I was paralyzed "No Grampa, I can't". Clutching his hand, feeling the grip pain had on him as he fought for breath through the growing edema, the damn doctors were being stingy with the morphine, I needed to do something and could only sob. With the little he still had Grampa whispered "It's okay Shoshy, I shouldn't ask you". My heart burst, he was trying to comfort me when he was the one, I ran to the nurses' station, demanding a doctor, who insisted Gramp had enough pain medication and that I was hysterical and must keep my voice down. I would not "He's dying. He's not gona be a junkie. If you have a heart, please give him a break". To my surprise the Doc instructed the nurse to give Grampa more, and almost immediately his pained face and body relaxed a bit and his eyes closed. I sat by the bed watching his chest rise and fall to each death-rattle, tears rolling off my face though it felt like someone else's, till Granny, Mom and Dad, and the rest of the family came back from dinner. Kissing Grampa good-bye I walked home. The phone rang at 1:06AM. Grampa died in his sleep, Granny held his hand till it was cold.

My brain turned to fire, and I needed to knock God's teeth out. It was past 4AM when I entered the synagogue, the front door was unlocked. I went straight to the pulpit, never having seen a female up there I was sure this sacrilege would demand Yahweh's attention, that He would show Himself, nothing happened. This God of the Jews scared the salt out of me. He was known to smite if you did something He didn't like. He cursed Cain for offering the best vegetables from his garden when He wanted blood, commanded Abraham to sacrifice his only son, made slaves of His people in Egypt for 400 years, then parted the Red Sea to let them go. No matter, I burned rage that He'd given us dying bodies, taking my Grampa in the reckoning, and did not seem to care. I just wanted Yahweh to show Himself to me, right now, let me know I mattered. Nothing happened. In synagogue you sit or stand, never kneel, so I knelt on the pulpit, nothing happened. I said Jesus Jesus Jesus, nothing happened. I opened the curtain of the Ark and took out the Sefer Torah, removed the beautiful silver finials and bejeweled breast plate with twelve precious stones representing each tribe, slipped the blue, white and gold embroidered satin mantle off the parchment scroll, laid it on the podium, unrolled and began to read. Having gone to Hebrew School every Monday, Thursday and Sunday for seven years preparing for confirmation, I could read Hebrew, and was surely the only female to have ever read from this holy scroll on this pulpit. Though there was never anything said aloud, I knew it was not okay for me to do this, knew it was a violation Yahweh ought to notice. I looked up at the painting of hands on the vaulting ceiling and waited, expecting lightning to crack the roof and kill me, ready, glad to die at least knowing there was a God. Nothing happened. The synagogue was deafeningly silent, just a big empty room, Yahweh wasn't there, didn't care I was, He had not come when I needed Him most. I carefully placed the covering on the Torah, put it back in the Ark, closed the curtain and left the building. Yahweh didn't give a shit about me so I did not him. I felt empty and cheated and alone, walked home, and waited for two days.

Grampa's funeral was jerky disjointed snapshots. According to custom, the Shomrim watch the body from the time of death till burial. Jews believe human beings are created in God's image, each endowed with a special holiness and dignity that does not dissipate with death. Though death may destroy the body, the soul housed in it must continue to be respected, so great care is taken to prepare the body. It's washed and shrouded in clean white cotton or muslin linen, hand-sewn specifically for this purpose, and must be buried within 48 hours of death in a plain pine box. Judaic law forbids embalming or cremation, or any form of ostentation or display at a funeral. Simple burial rites assure equality in death despite the material wealth a person may command in life, so no family no matter how poor will be shamed in death by the simplicity of their coffin or shroud, and that the rich can not attempt to out do one another in death. I sat next to Mom on the newly recovered front bench, feeling too big for the little chapel, noticing every snag and tatter on the carpet, the Rabbi infuriating me, going on and on about Grampa till everyone dissolved in sobs. I refused to cry, staring at the pine box, visualizing my Grampa's withering dead body inside dressed in white, I could hardly sit there. His five brothers shouldered the coffin, and I followed too quickly, too close, stepping on Granny's sister's heel, nearly causing her to fall. And standing on a grassy plot already reserved for my Mom and Dad, I stared at the remarkably vertical sides of Grampa's hole, feeling out-of-body like the raven perched on the phone wire above, remote-viewing my Dad restrain Granny from throwing herself in as the casket was lowered, noting the clods tumble when the Cantor removed the tarpaulin from the dirt mound, how the Rabbi used the back of the shovel to scatter the first measure of dirt on Grampa's box, the hollow bang of pebbles on pine as one by one family stepped forward to take their turn, first with the wrong side of the shovel to show their unwillingness to let go, then the right side as a final act of compassion, a giving that had no way of being repaid. I did not know how to behave. This was my first human loved one buried in the ground, and I was never comfortable revealing private wounds in public, didn't think it was anyone's business how vulnerable and broken I was, so I stood tall and silent, pretending to be Jackie Kennedy, achingly dignified and composed at her husband's funeral. Mom was absolutely destroyed, a zombie, unaware how public her private was, for she lost her Daddy, one of the good ones, and she was her Father's daughter. I wanted to comfort her but the words on my tongue screamed Fuck You God, so I bit hard, and softly held her elbow as we walked from the hole, watching Dad holding her other arm, thinking he was diabetic and how great-full I was that insulin had been discovered and could help him cheat Death, for he too was one of the good ones, and I was definitely my Father's daughter. The overwhelming emotion etched on faces was grief, but guilt and fear were there too. I hadn't said I love you enough to Grampa, though I knew he knew, and hadn't said it much lately to Mom or Dad, wasn't sure they knew. Grampa's death transformed me clear down to my deoxyribonucleic acid, and walking away from his grave I made a vow, in his honor I would not leave any unfinished business, just incase something unexpected happened. Everyone gathered at Granny's, Brenner Brothers catered with a feast of traditional Jewish food, eat eat, herring, chopped liver, lox, bagels, rye, and I stayed till my composure would no longer hold. Granny was well attended by her five sisters and two brothers as I kissed her on the cheek. She stared at me with helpless blood-shot eyes and a crooked grin of dim recognition. Dad had ahold of Mom's hand, and smiled tenderly at my sincere "I love you Daddy". Still a zombie, Mom did not seem to register words. I could not tarnish my sparkling-new vow with a lie, so simply nodded to Big Brother. Little Bro returned a hesitant, surprised "I love you too".

Nick's blue VW bus was parked infront of my building, he'd taken Katey to the downtown Eagles Hall last night to see Jefferson Airplane and I assumed he'd come for her, but he'd come for me, to see was I all right. Aching to cry in private, I told him I needed to be alone. He followed to the door anyway and tried to hug me. I pushed him away hard, needing to keep this all-I-had-left-of-my-Grampa visceral gnawing pain, and quickly slipped inside locking the door. I could not sit, could not stop, round-and-round in tight circles, feeling like a shark, needing to keep moving, to run water over my gills to live, tears falling silent on the carpet, talking to my self outloud till Katey came home. I was never so glad to see anyone, but she did not once look at me, rushing, stuffing a suitcase for the annual family reunion in North Dakota, her Dad honking out front, she didn't say goodbye or shut the door. Sleep refused me, near daylight I laid down on the couch, mind looping round-and-round, cursing God.

Functioning on automatic, yet watching myself make all those good-mannered moves, my bloody underbelly carefully hidden, I let no one know how scared I was losing my faith, how grief consumed me, none of my co-workers noticed the frozen smile as I checked their security badges, no one knew me. The Seafair Pageant seemed like some past life, I couldn't make myself care about the coming television interview. Home was an empty box to wait in till the next obligation, I felt like running into the wall just to feel some other kind of pain, and I worried because I'd begun to relish the torment that kept me close to Grampa, the only one who knew my secrets, the only one who had ever listened. Days passed un-counted, then a knock and hello at my door after sunset. It was Nick. My heart leapt at some one to talk too, I took a deep breath, let it out, cracked open the door and asked if he'd come to see Katey. He said they agreed to just be friends, he'd come to see was I all right. Wholly exhausted, wanting to believe it wasn't really the big bad wolf, I opened, wary, having never been alone with him, his uncanny way of knowing when I was vulnerable made me nervous, yet he seemed to see the inside me, and I needed to be seen or I might disappear. Again he tried for a hug. I stepped back, and desperate to fill the awkward silent moment offer him some of the cheap whiskey I sipped. More silence pushed me to ask without thinking it out, could he get me some Crystal methedrine, Katey raved how it pepped-her-up, and I was having trouble staying awake at work. Licking his bot-tom lip Nick smiled, told me to give him ten bucks, tossed down a gulp of the whiskey and left. Inside the hour returning with a small baggie of white powder he called a dime-bag, and a pint of orange juice, he poured the powder into the juice, shook it hard and offered it to me with a wry grin. Holding the bottle, considering, reasoning maybe this would finally wear me out and bring on sleep, I gulped the bitter brew, gagging on the grainy accumulation at the bottom. Nick urged me finish it off. I did.

Self-control running away so fast I could not regain any safe men-tal ground, staying-up all night blabbering to Nick, who seemed an old friend though I did not really know him. My thoughts a roaring freight train, body in constant feeling of falling, it struck me I didn't really know Katey either. Nick offered to drive me to work, but I felt buoyant, float-ing, not a bit tired, and left early to walk in the beautiful morning light, Crystal an effective high, pushing the pain off my body. At work I talked too much, no one suspected drugs, I was so naturally strait and perky. Sitting at my desk was not possible, I couldn't concentrate on the news-paper, Penny wasn't home, I invented excuses to run errands, fetch things, the day was endless. Finally free, walking home I felt filled with helium, floating up Capitol Hill. Nick was waiting, hungry, wanting to take me to the Hasty Tasty for a bite. I was thankful for somewhere to go, someone to talk too, and in what seemed seconds pulled on my paisley dress, ready. He drove to the District, a three-block section of University Way NE, the main business district close to the University of Washington, also called the Ave, where the Hippies and Flower-Children hung-out. Nick ate a steak rare and fries with lots of ketchup. I watched the blood run from the meat, Crystal wiping-out any interest in eating. Then we paraded up and down the Ave, he seemed to know all the street people. I'd been up 24 hours, my neck stiffened as if someone had ahold of it, and again outside myself, this time out of control, showing more than I would, jabbering to people about nothing, I felt like a puppet and Nick the puppet-master, exposing me, making me a fool, it was not fun and I wanted to come down. I asked how long before the Crystal wore off. He grinned, seeming delighted "You'll be up at least two more days". I freaked, there was no way out, this was not how a Golden Girl acted, or how I wanted to, I screamed at him "Take me home now". He pulled a thin joint from behind his ear on the way. I smoked the whole thing, it did not get me high or slow me down. Once home, I threw back three quick shots of whiskey, hitting my empty stomach like boiling water. They did not slow me at all, and from the grin on Nick's face he was enjoying this way too much. Katey had mentioned Crystal and paranoia went together, maybe I was paranoid, I didn't exactly know what paranoid was, but just thinking I had it freaked me even more. Nick tried to hug me, always wanting to comfort me, again I stepped back. He smiled wide, or was it a grimace, and slowly nodding his head yes whispered "A dime bag's enough to get three people off". What a cruel fucking jerk, urging me to drink the whole thing, yet it was me who trusted the big bad wolf. I shoved him toward the door. He did not resist and left. For effect I slammed and locked it, still, hearing his bus drive off, I panicked, this trip was way too much alone.

Jake's record player seeped through the wall, Bob Dylan, I went next door and knocked. Surprised, he welcomed me. I was plainly short-circuiting, probably looked as if I'd stuck my finger in a light socket, tears flooded my eyes as I told him Grampa died and I could not sleep. He offered me a beer, politely listening to me blubber while drinking the rest of the six-pack, nodding off and on, sitting-up pretending to listen. Every apartment in the building was dark, the whole world was dark, when Jake passed-out I went to the pool, stripped and swam laps till sunrise, readied for work, walked downtown looking in every window, catching my reflection, thinking who is that, wanting to eat enough to slow me down, my throat choking-off the first bite of fresh onion bagel from the Three Sisters Bakery at Pike Place Market, thoughts so scrambled I stood at green lights and walked through red, and though freshly showered, I smelled of burning flesh and could not get away from the nose stinging stench, my heart banging so hard against my breast bone I was sure it shook me for every one to see. Once at my desk I could not sit, on first break I told the boss I was sick, an easy excuse, and no where to go, walked home, pulled on my jeans and headed for Volunteer Park, to sit on the back of the Big Stone Ram infront of the Wing Luke Asian Art Museum, something I'd done countless times growing-up, hoping this would put a tail on my kite. No rest there, I marched home like a puppet soldier, forced down a banana that came right up, Katey was still gone, Penny didn't take drugs and would only be angry with me, my Folks would freak and want me to do something I did not want to, there was no one to call, I felt like a mongrel chasing her tail, round-and-round, my mind a closed system chanting run run run run, where, I could not save my thoughts from rushing into the dark, what if I never come down, what if I get brain damage, what if I never find my self again, then the Ave, the Ave, Hippies take drugs, maybe someone would know what to do. I caught the bus, was not able to stay seated, the driver made me get off, and I ran ran ran ran nine blocks, then pacing up and down the sidewalk peering in the Eiger, the Hasty Tasty, the Coffee Corral, every head shop, into Hippies face, mine frozen in a tight smile, no longer able to form words or ask for help, Crystal was illegal and I was on the outside of the law, an undercover cop could put me away, was this paranoia, every last beat of life rushing out, I might just disappear, and there was Nick. A knowing smile he took my hand and turned it palm-up, placed two small oval golden-orange tablets in the center, said they were Thorazine, what doctors give patients after a heart operation so they won't move, what shrinks give psychotics. I cared only they worked, gulping them down dry. He drove me home. And I began to slow, like a 45 record spinning at 78 and suddenly switched to 33 1/3, I could form words again, demanding to know why he would do such a cruel thing to me. He said I was the type to get strung-out on speed, that he cared too much about me and needed to make sure I had a bad trip so I'd never want more. How dared he do my thinking for me, and all too wrecked to be indignant, too grateful to have someone to talk too, I mustered as warm a voice as I could and assured him I was not the addictive kind, learned lessons much easier than being thrown from a plane without a parachute, that he could have just told me. Against better judgment, and for reasons I did not want to think about, I let him come in, made it clear he would be sleeping on the couch, and went to bed.

Gently rocking my shoulder, Nick woke me, I slept through the alarm. Driving me to work, he offered a thin tightly rolled joint, the one that seemed always hidden behind his ear. And he drove too fast for holding dope, and I smoked the joint pretending it was a cigarette incase a cop noticed us. I could not stand this wolf, nevertheless he wasn't like any other human I knew, yes he was dangerous, even frightening, but he fascinated me. Work seemed an unending unthinking unpleasant something I used to do for money, now an exquisite waste of vital essence, this nothing of consequence all day. After lunch I hatched a plan to amuse my self, stopping every pilot and engineer, even the ones I knew well, making them show a security badges even if theirs was properly clipped on, a little power-trip to compensate for my suddenly humiliating ornamental position, which barely alleviated the slow grind. A few of my victims asked was I okay, and seemed genuinely concerned. I knew they were not. One of the engineers constantly trying to bed me, leaned on my desk and asked too loud, would I like to go to dinner at the Space Needle, and for dessert we could watch the submarine races from his bedroom window over-looking Lake Union. I knew he thought this clever, I knew if I let all this new-found contempt out on him he'd probably burst into flames, and this poor guy didn't deserve it all, he couldn't possibly know what had happened to me, just a few days ago I thought him cute for a 32 year old, so without meeting his eyes, I flashed a perky grin and said I already had a date for the races. We'd gone out once, and he spent the evening infusing everything with clumsy sexual innuendo, but now his stale little jokes were insulting, and I was embarrassed ever having laughed at them. The work day finally expired, I hurried home to crash, who I thought I was a constant leaking away, and no one to talk too, the Golden Ghetto had not prepared me for this leaking. I closed my eyes, tomorrow after work I had a Seafair interview at the Olympic Hotel.

My first time on TV and I could not relax shoulders or jaw, could not shake it out, felt put together with spit and if I dried-out would fall apart. I'd worn the only appropriate things I owned, my senior prom gown, a sheer ankle-length form-fitting sleeveless delicately flowered silk number with a flesh-tone silk slip beneath, hair up in my trademark beehive, wrapped with a matching green silk scarf, green kidskin three-inch pumps and dyed-to-match above the elbow gloves, on the middle finger of my right hand glittered the showy black pearl and diamond ring Dad made for my 16th birthday. I thought I had a chance if I could only relax, for I knew what was expected in this type of a thoroughbred race, sexy and ready yet virginal, docile, altruistic, patriotic, smart but not wise. There were twelve of us. I had not made friends with any of the Girls, had little in common but the Pageant, knew them mainly by their prattling conversations about custom-made gowns, backstage make-up artists and hairdressers, where they'd gone abroad for summer vacation, and how much Daddy made.

As the television crew arrived and began to set-up, Pageant Director instructed us on the questions, and to my surprise on the answers. I was instantly drawn to the camera man, a pouty-faced Badboy in well-worn blue jeans and shoulder length dark brown hair, a resounding anti-establishment statement. It wasn't easy to get any job in long hair or jeans and he proudly wore both, telling me he must be good at what he does, I was smitten with his nerve. We picked numbers from a hat for interview order, the Pageant Director showed us where we would be sitting, advising us not to fret, the interview was being filmed for later broadcast and any mistakes would be edited out, he gave us 15 minutes to primp. Walking passed the Seafair Commodores and this year's King Neptune, I felt like a lamb chop on a plate and thought from the sick feeling at the pit of my gut how old these men were and how juicy the Girls were, and since I had no backstage attendants, decided to go on to the hospitality table for tea and a few moments alone to try and gather my self.

Badboy walked over as I drank my cup, poured a coffee and grinned "Hi". Just plain heart-throbbing up close, I was light-headed simply inhaling the same air and smiled back "I've never been on TV. I just can not relax. All those people watching me". He smiled "The trick, don't think all of them at once, just one person watching one TV set at a time. That's all. There's only one person watching you. You're a big girl, you can handle that". He smile warmed "If you want the camera to love you, look through the lens to me, and think of me cause I'll be thinking of you". I finally engaged his shockingly green eyes "I am a big girl. I can handle that". He asked "So, how old are you". I looked down "Almost eighteen". Shaking his head no he murmured "Such delicious jail-bait". Our eyes touched again, I protested "Only two more weeks". He ran a big hand through his mane to take it off his face. I ached for this man, no submarine jokes, no innuendo, this man did not insult me.

And then it was show time. Having picked number nine, I took my designated seat, kept statue-still trying to breathe evenly, deeply, calmly, watching Badboy run his camera, listening to the Girls pre-chewed answers, pure saccharine, simpering morons, I would not be a moron on TV even for that one person watching, having been hired cute and dumb at Boeing was the last time. When my turn came, I looked through the lens and talked to Badboy "Yes I plan on going to college. Seattle Community". "Yes I'm planning on a career. I've always dreamed of being a criminal lawyer". Why am I running for Seafair Queen. "Emotional ties made me say yes when the Cirque Playhouse asked me to represent them". What emotional ties. "I've been hooked on Seafair since I was five years old, when I won a Tradewell coloring contest and a ride on their float in the Torch Light Parade. I spent my first nine years in the Mount Baker neighborhood, walking distance of Stan Sayres Pits, and when summer and the races came, first I would sell parking spaces infront of our house and driveway, then I'd wheel my lemonade wagon down to the Pits and sell all I could get my Mom to make. In high school my friend Steve Reynolds often took me screaming across Lake Washington in his limited hydro. And, I sometimes baby-sat for the neighbor kids, whose father had been a tenor sax player with the Guy Lombardo Band, has his own local band now called The Kings Men, and just happens to be champion unlimited hydroplane driver Bill Muncey. So you see I have emotional ties to Seafair". Then came the question "What do you think of this new fad, men wearing long hair". The previous eight obliged with the suggested, it looks dirty, criminal, you can't tell if it's a boy or girl from the back. I thought they must be blind, Badboy didn't look anything like a girl, so I smiled through the lens and spoke to him "I think long hair is sexy". Suddenly I relaxed, I'd become a real person, I was no longer one of the Girls. The Pageant Director's booming voice halted the interview and ordered me into the adjoining room. Without looking round I followed, and did not close the door. He demanded "Sit down". His red-face angry loud and accusing "What's a matter with you. Can't you follow simple instructions. The other Girls are smart enough to listen. You're a trouble-maker and I simply can not allow your kind in this Pageant. You're not Seafair material". I should have been shaking, embarrassed beyond articulation, but he was wrong, the Girls were dumb enough to listen, and he was right, I wasn't Seafair material, time had slowed down for me to think, I had nothing to lose here except my self, and to my surprise and delight boomed back "Last I looked Sir, honesty is still a virtue". I paused to watch already swollen neck veins bulge over his starched white collar, and giddy at my own calm, stood, and went on in sure tone "I heard the daughter of the president of the Chamber of Commerce is going to win anyway". I was glad the door was open. Mr. Director's hands tensed, he involuntarily leaned toward me, instantly caught himself and cleared his throat "Now there Little Missy. You don't know what you're saying". I threw him a triumphant smile, said nothing and left the Hotel, head high like the thoroughbred I'd been taught to be, don't look back you could turn to salt singing in my head, realizing from Mr. Director's reaction the contest might really be rigged, that the Girls were being used though I wasn't clear how or why, and that I'd probably been approved by the committee for the most part because Mercer Island was a safe bet, my family must have money, and I surely would obey the rules.

Feeling iridescent neon on the street in my long silk gown and gloves, I caught the bus home, leaving Badboy behind, there was no one to talk too, my friends and family saw running for Seafair Queen as a golden opportunity, how could I explain the exhilaration of purposefully blowing it, or that I was freaking-out at a job they all thought was so great, that my boy-friends seemed exactly that, boys, that Grampa's death had taken the bottom out of my life, that I thought God was fucked, didn't know who I was now that I wasn't who I used to be, and that I was considering taking LSD. But the question that fired my brain, why wasn't there any one to talk too. I had friends and none ever mentioned these things happening to them, none of the magazines mentioned this feeling of being outside my self looking-in. I put Dylan on the record player and crawled into bed still wearing my prom dress and gloves, laying on my back, arms close to my body, feeling like a rocket waiting to be shot into space, too emotionally fatigued to cry, wishing Katey would come home, I could sort of talk to her, playing the day over and over like poison rolling round in my head, till sleep showed some mercy, Dylan singing *when you ain't got nothing, you got nothing to lose.*

Was Nick the only human on earth I could talk too. Friday afternoon I called from work, asking did he still want to take LSD. He was chilly, saying I'd brushed him off. Desperate for any mooring I submitted how messed-up I'd been lately. My tone must have salved any hurt feelings, he would be over at 7PM with Donna and Gabriel. Uncomfortable with the strain of strangers, I said okay.

Gabriel and I were instant friends, he did not come on to me, no pressure, no innuendo, I could relax. Twenty-four years old, a University of California at Santa Cruz quantum mechanics grad student till he was busted for small-time marijuana dealing, he ran before sentencing, went underground, changed his name, and was playing bass in a local band. Donna was gaga for Nick, finding any chance to brush up against him with her tits. Embarrassed for her rawness, her desperation, her seem-ing unawareness of any of this, for her humiliation, and for making me an unwilling participant, I needed to say something "Katey 'll be home tonight". Nick nodded, more telling me to fuck-off than acknowledge my words, running that pointed tongue quickly back and forth along his bottom lip. For some reason they reminded me of animals, this smooth game that went on between male and female, all run by some unthinking program that no one thought about, just did, like it was inevitable, that's what embarrassed me, I was a very private person, yet could see my own desire in Donna, because I was unthinking about it too. Katey's thing for Nick made me a little uneasy having seen him while she was gone, but I had not crossed the line, we were just friends, I'd been care-full not to lead him on or tease. Taking my attention back, Gabriel sat down on the couch, took a small round ornate silver-framed mirror from one coat pocket, a small bundle in tin foil from the other, unwrapped four innocent little sugar cubes and placed them carefully on the mirror, promising this acid is pharmaceutically pure, no need to worry it's cut with anything, promising we'd have a good trip. We gathered round. This felt somehow sacred, and scary, I felt totally unprepared "So what'll this pharmaceutically pure LSD do to me". Gabe smiled "If you're blessed, you'll see God. I did once". His smile grew "He was Buddha". I smiled too, for me Buddha was a green statue Granny had on her mantel and if you rubbed his belly it was supposed to bring good luck, but Gabe seeing God definitely interested me, not Yahweh, Buddha. He went on that most people have similar experiences on acid, it was mainly the individual details that differed. I was deeply excited by this sameness, maybe I could see God too, I needed to, I was pretty sure he wasn't there. Gabe placed the cubes on our tongues, each time saying something in Latin and crossing himself. Nick and Donna laughed. I didn't know much about Christian ritual.

We walked to Volunteer Park on a balmy summer night, the LSD was tasteless and I let the sweet cube dissolve on my tongue, holding it there, considering swallowing or spitting, thinking how funny it was this drug coming on such an innocent vehicle. Gabriel put his hand lightly on my shoulder "You're a brave girl dropping acid for the first time. Stepping into the unknown". I swallowed hard. And when my mouth began to taste of tin foil, the initial sign this was more than a sugar cube, I felt I'd jumped off the Smith Tower and would have to figure out how to fly on the way down or die. Gabe seemed to sense my stiffening, talking in a low soothing tone he confided "Going on someone's first trip is my favorite thing to do. I'm honored to be on yours. And don't worry Shoshannah, I'm here for you". Telling me this only made me stiffen more, knowing there was something I would need someone to be here for. My connection with Gabe drew Nick, and his interest sparked Donna's automatic competition, she glared hard at me. He would be just so very flattered, bitches vying, but my world had begun to warp, and the game appeared so clear, and stupid. I would not automatically compete with Donna, the bitch-rule, win-lose, being played-off each other for a man's favor no longer roused me, I returned the rivalry without defense, telling her she looked beautiful. Having nothing to bark back at disarmed her, she went with me instead of against, we both won. Could it be so easy to dissolve this game that left so little room for personal dignity. At once we were girl-friends, on an acid glide through the park, into the sparkling glass conservatory, modeled on London's Crystal Palace, greeted by a room full of orchid blossom shamelessly showing their privates, bobbing on long gracefully stems, the narrow blacktop walkway absorbing our footfalls as if we road on silent wheels, seeing this familiar botanical garden as if for the first time. Gabriel, Donna, Nick followed me through the five rooms, each a different temperature and humidity, lush cartoon flora reaching for us, Venus fly traps open, waiting, pitcher plants, hibiscus, gigantic mums, palms, cactus, ferns, flowers throwing their perfume snares, not one bug in sight, time irrelevant, casually noticing I stepped outside my self, again. The glide emerged, sun setting behind sapphire Olympics, sky streaking fire-burnt-orange and blue-hot-pink fading to violet, an epiphany sky, tears ran down my cheeks, tasting of the sea, and I knew I was the same. I had silently been chosen guide, and feeling the weight of responsibility turned to Gabe to be there for me, he'd done this before, what more was suppose to happen, when would I see God. He was sure by my response to the sun set I already had. Meandering the grounds, still following me, I wondered aloud could it be so straightforward, could such intense awe at such beauty be God, could something that wasn't male be God, could lowly nature, so often called Mother be God, did it even need gender. Gabe tried to explain quantum physics, how we were all connected yet individual, even Buddha, Yahweh, Shiva being individual manifestations of the whole. I noticed his lips were not moving, and yet I heard him. Nick, Donna too, their thoughts so carnal, was this why Gabe said he would be there for me, was this a bad trip, I could not bear being in-on Nick and Donna's pornography, what if they could hear me too, what if my new ears were permanent, I would eavesdrop this vulgar soap-opera for ever, and it was beginning to have a smell, like rancid fried chicken without the chicken. I had not found my wings, spinning, falling fast, when a full grown Robin landed light on my shoulder, staying my fall. Never having been this close to a wild animal, I did not to flinch, slowly turning my head to get a moonlit look, thinking this bird should be asleep by now. He lingered, tightening his grip, and I heard with these new ears "I don't sleep till I know who's in my yard". It struck me that he spoke English. Robin ruffled "I'm an all American bird, so well fed here I no longer need to migrate". Satisfied with the last word he flew to a near dogwood. I could hear everything in his yard, worms worming, bugs chewing, grass growing, air currenting, trees rustling, squirrels whispering, mice, snakes, raccoons showed themselves, every thing opened and we were all here, individual and connected, acid-here, weightless, bigger than before, again I became aware of the thinness of this skin I wore, how easily torn to bleed-out my life, everything rushing and smooth, reality layered beyond my dearest hope, and my company swept along in my awe, following, in my train. I wondered if the exquisite streaming paisley patterns crawling over everything was the thin film of liquid covering my eyeballs or the life blood of every thing I had never slowed down enough to notice. No one answered, my ears were mine again. The train pulled-up at the Big Stone Ram guarding the entrance to the Wing Luke Museum. We sat on the stairs at its feet. Donna began pounding her fist on her knee, hating her Dad for coming into her room, never stopping at the good-night kiss, she'd run away at fifteen, living on the street was safer. We planned her revenge, planned a new identity for Gabe to get back into school, figured-out the entire universe, and still I was not satisfied, I wanted at least one big hallucination, one I could be sure of. Gabe laughed at me. I laughed at him. We all laughed. Nick lit the joint he'd been carrying behind his ear, promising it would make the ride down easy. Taking long luxurious puffs, not bothering to hold in the smoke, we decided the bathroom at my place was the next stop. Walking away from the stone behemoth, shivering but not at all cold, I looked back at his familiar horn curling round the right side of his big head. He turned and look square in my eyes with that same who are you that caught me in the mirror, and suddenly there was so much more to believe in than I had ever been given to imagine, I knew that if there was God, I had just seen it, outside any boundary of my expectations. And I must have been jumping round, laughing loud, for Gabe found my hand, warning me to calm down. Breathless I whispered "Did you see it look at me". He shook his head "No sweet girl, it was a special gift only for you". I knew this was true, so deep down it salved a place nothing else had touched, for it meant I counted for something, meant I could fly, meant I had some freedom, this was a million times bigger than winning the Seafair crown.

Coming down was for the most part lovely, a passenger in the backseat of a stretch limo on a lazy country road, watching the scenery, newold reality slowly surrounding me again with the mundane, a slight stiff neck from the intensity of the trip, a very dry mouth, I made tea. Gabriel proclaimed this the best trip he'd ever been on. Nick rolled another joint, and in an out-of-character open moment admitted to some really bad trips, calling this one magical, and me remarkable, divine, words never said about me, seductive words every girl of little promise longs to hear. I asked why he would chance another if his were so bad. He said there was always a chance for one like tonight. Donna rubbing up-against him. Relieved they took it to the bedroom, I stacked Dylan, the Beatles, Crosby Stills and Nash on the record player, not wanting ears in on their fucking. Gabe and I sipped tea and talked, and talked, morning arrived, we were not tired, this coming down wonder-fully free of that, he was meeting his guitar player at the Hasty Tasty for breakfast and invited me along. The first morning of my life, everything fresh, clear, clean, calm, less complicated, more complicated, more real, like I knew every thing personally and it knew me, I wanted to take acid again, today. Gabe's face went dark "Don't be so cavalier sweet girl. If you abuse the acid God, you'll sacrifice its gift. The adventure's just begun, and could expand way beyond your imagination if you're wise about taking the magic cube". He confessed "I'm speaking from experience here. I made the mistake, didn't respect it, broke my spiritual connection. Now I can only get there on someone else's trip. You're my Acid God now, my Acid Queen." Gabe was wise and dangerous, a bit silver-tongued, and much too needy, to be his God or anyone's was not my idea of a relationship, and it was beginning to really bother me this warning stuff, I was capable of thinking for my self. My family brought their Little Girl up to marry, hopefully a nice Jewish doctor or lawyer, I would settle down, be content raising at least two kids, be a good mother like my own. But my third-grade year at John Muir Elementary School, their plans for me perished. We were all made to hide under our desks at noon every Wednesday when the air-raid siren screamed. I knew a wooden desk could not protect me from the Red Threat. And we all were told the Russians could win this Cold War, whatever a Cold War was, and come here and make us slaves. I said nothing about this to Mom or Dad, and they never said anything to me, we just looked passed it, lived with it, seeping-in, scaring me. I decided under my desk the last day of third-grade grade, that bringing children into a world that could explode at some evil whim was not something I would do, for how could I bear their eyes looking so frightened, and me helpless to do anything about it, helpless as my Folks. I thought down to the end of my life, their eyes still looking at me, on my death-bed, accusing, how could I leave them behind in such a terrifying world, I should never have had them, it was my fault, they would not forgive me. Walking home I decided to seek adventure, true love, no kids. And as for every guy that fell for me, eventually they wanted to own me, marry me, put me on a pedestal, a throne, to me just fancy words for prison. They wanted to do my thinking for me, decide my life, protect me, girls were prey to boys, we needed one, preferrably one of the good ones to protect us from the others. Gabe making me Queen or God was just a twist on the same old song.

My mind blazed at what LSD had done to me, super-aware of objective consciousness, knowing for sure inside was not all of it. I had found my way out, again, inside and outside at the same moment, subjective holding onto objective, with enough time to pluck individual thoughts from the quicksilver river, and consider. And finally, I understood the Golden Ghetto's implicit dictate, do not dare think beyond it parameters, for everything a pretty little girl like me could ever hope for dream of or aspire to was already inside the Gate. And as payment for this asylum, this protection from all the riff-raff that feed on each other, I must freely mortgage-off any natural confidence, in-trade for the best clothes, jewels, views, cars, food, schools, society, investment art. And while thievishly checking each other for labels, which was easy now they were worn on the outside of our clothes, we're always on-edge, maybe I haven't pulled-off the masquerade, getting caught faking-it, eaten alive. And if some one did by chance think beyond the Golden Gate, the penalty was banishment to the working class, neon shame, don't you dare say the Emperor is naked, or that long hair is sexy. None of these mattered to me now, my own mirror had peeked at me from the other side, there was no going back, and had there been even a chance, LSD popped me like dry corn, I could never again stuff into the slot marked pretty little Golden Girl. This was fine with me. I liked Gabe, but made it clear I was not his God or Queen. He laughed and called me profound. I liked being profound.

As we walked into the Hasty, Gabe's guitar player called-out. They talked band and we ate omelets. I couldn't listen, my mind wandering the room, resting on each face, feeling for the first time like I fit in some where, this hang-out for acid-heads, pot-heads, smack-heads, mescaline-heads, peyote-heads, LSD was such a trip I wondered what all these other drugs would do to my head. Breakfast plates cleaned, Gabe invited me to band practice. I was interested in how a band worked it out and went along. The only furniture, a brittle red naugahyde couch with no arms, I could not get comfortable. Gabe and his guitar player waited for the other band members, talking just below my ability to eavesdrop. I gathered-up the Post Intelligencer from the floor, Lenoard Alfred Schneider, Lenny Bruce found naked and dead of a morphine overdose. A smack-head, good name for it. Three girls came in with the drummer and bass player, rubbing-up-against-kinda-girls, who took their places on the floor infront of the band, legs open, no panties. Feeling like the stuffed salmon entrée at the naugahyde buffet, while the boys worked-up appetite, preening, posing, playing their instruments, I wanted to escape the primitive ritual, yet was held-fast in polite need not to hurt their feelings by leaving unexplained. Finally a smoke break, I excused my self to Gabe saying I was tired. With his charming grin he offered me his bed. I said no, and caught the bus home. Katey would be back today, I was relieved she had not found Nick and Donna still in her bed, thanking Nick for the acid I pushed them to go. Glad to see me home, and alone, he pressed his middle finger to my lips as he left.

Laying her suitcase on the bed Katey woke me. So happy for someone to talk too, I gushed about my trip while she unpacked. Somehow she got the idea Nick and I had been together. I said plainly, emphatically "No, I was not with him". She hissed such venom "You're a liar". I shrank under the quilt "Nick told me you guys were just friend". She slammed the suitcase lid "I love him. How could you go behind my back". Nick seemed to excite this kind of crap, and I did not want any part of it, maybe I could get her to lean in like I had Donna "I wouldn't do that to you. Come on Katey, this guy's not worth our friendship". She heard what she wanted "He's not some guy. I love him. You're just a jealous fucking liar". I knew I did not know her, but this was a mean Katey I never imagined was there, maybe if I gave her all the power, maybe she would soften "Well then I guess I should move out. I don't want to be here if you think I'm such an awful person". Too late I saw ultimatum is a win-lose, the ultimate power-trip, demanding sides be taken. She folded freckled arms across her double-D bosom and stared me cold "Good riddance to bad rubbish". Nick's timing was uncanny, just then knocking loud "Hi in there. I can hear you guys". Katey rushed to answer. I closed the bedroom door and dressed. And they argued, what does she mean he betrayed her, yes he likes her, but just as friends, no nothing happened with Shoshannah. Then he said he was falling in love with me. My stomach dropped. Katey slammed-open the bedroom door, tears in her eyes "You're just a slut and I hate you". She ran from the apartment. I ran after. She would only scream "Get away from me, just get away from me". I did not know what to do but go back and order Nick out of my life. He was already gone. I hoped Katey would see the truth, and when she came home tried talking. She only hissed "Jealous bitch". Not one more word, erased, I slept on the couch.

Waiting for the bus to work, needing to find a new place, I bought the morning Post Intelligencer from the machine, the headlines read, Communist East Germany building a wall to divide Berlin. I hated a friendship ruined over misunderstanding, especially over a jerk, but Katey was so hurt, she never had a serious boyfriend, it was easier to think I took Nick than he did not want her, I could see so clearly I wasn't even mad. My job if possible had become more absurd. I wore the paisley smock dress, squashed heels and tights, my hair down, as loud a statement here at Boeing as Badboy's long hair and jeans. It made me feel completely exposed. No one noticed. The first few hours I leaned back in my swivel chair hardly moving, grin glued on, no need to paint my nails, I had cut them short and removed the polish. Calling Penny would only lead to Nick. I was still somewhat outside my skin, maybe would forever be outside, watching the pilots and engineers file by, thinking how funny it would be to take this decorative job literally. Hmmm, I needed a prop. The push-broom in the storage closet would do. Shouldering the long handle, I marched up-and-back infront of my desk. When someone came off the stairs or elevator, I pointed the handle at them demanding to see a security badge. No doubt this was bizarre, yet seemed absolutely necessary as I waited for something to happen, for someone to say the Emperor is naked. No one did till lunch, when my Boss came out "Are you okay". In my head I sounded like a robot, automatically saluting "Yes Sir. Fine Sir. Just doing my job". His brow pinched tight, he spoke in a fatherly tone "I want you to take the rest of the day off, with pay, and go to your doctor. Your attitude is jeopardizing your job and future advancement in the company". Doctor, what doctor, I didn't have a doctor, my top lip curled "Right Sir. Advancement in the company. To what Sir, perky little call girl". He seemed genuinely shocked "Just go home, now". I returned the push-broom to the closet. Again it was not enough to hold back the huge waves crashing in on me.

Walking home, thinking I should have my tail between my legs, instead I felt the same liberation leaving the Seafair contest, alive, listening to my own breath. Katey left several roaches in the ashtray, I smoked them all and tried to grasp why was I throwing over foundations I built my life on, and more important, why none of it seemed important. The only words Katey had for me when she came home "You still here". Though seeming passive, I thought ignoring my existence was as aggressive as a beating, and saw no need to stay for more undeserved punishment. A perfect summer evening, one of those few you don't need long sleeves, there was no where better in the world than summer in Seattle, I walked slowly up Broadway, bought a payday candy bar and went to see the Big Stone Ram, hoping lightning would strike twice. Nothing happened. I stayed till midnight, and went home to sleep on the couch.

There was no where for me to go but work, and just to push it, I wore the smock dress again. Boss acted as if nothing had happened, handing me a letter to type. I sat quiet, playing secretary till 10AM when two men stepped-off the elevator and asked for me. Instantly, viscerally repulsed I questioned "Who wants to know". The bigger one looked me over and smiled "Reps from Playboy magazine". This did not make sense, how would Playboy know me, I glared "You're looking at her". The littler one moved-in pressing his thighs against the front edge of my desk "Well then, we have the opportunity of a lifetime for you doll". I didn't get it "How do you even know me". Mr.Bigger moved-in too "We know you through the Seafair Pageant. It would be Playboy's treat to take you to lunch and talk. That is if you haven't already eaten". These were predators, and they thought I was dumb prey, still the unexpected always peaked my curiosity "You already know I haven't gone to lunch yet. Come back at eleven and I'll think about it".

The elevator spit them out exactly on time. I left with one on each flank. They opened every door, spoke politely, made sure to walk on the traffic side, gestures that seemed more herding than chivalry. Before LSD the fawning would have flattered me, before I had been called divine, remarkable. Now it made me certain of my initial repulsion, I decided to buy my own lunch, to not owe them more of my time than I wanted to spend. I learned to be cautious who I ate with after reading the hymn to Demeter in high school mythology class. Demeter's daughter Persephone, while gathering flowers, was raped by Hades, and then kidnapped to the Underworld. Demeter raged over the earth, halting the annual death and rebirth cycle of the soil, causing permanent winter, starvation, till Pan revealed where her daughter was, and Hades agreed to let her go. Nevertheless, while captive, Persephone had eaten six pomegranate seeds, and the consequence of taking-in even these small bits made the Underworld part of her, dooming her forever to spend winter underground, coming-up with a herald of forget-me-nots, the first flowers of spring, named for her. We walked to the Olympic Broiler on the corner of 2nd and Pike. They tried to maneuver me between them into the booth. I excused my self to the ladies room. Upon return, Mr.Little slid-out and stood waiting. I insisted on sitting at the end. It was a stand-off. He looked to Mr.Bigger and reluctantly slid-in. The waitress came for our orders. They waited for me. I smiled at her "a dinner salad with Thousand on the side, and a chocolate coke. Oh and my check is separate please". Mr.Bigger instructed her "No no, put it on my tab". She looked at me. I continued smiling "Mine is separate". She nodded. They both ordered martinis, French dip sandwich on grilled sour-dough, chili fries, hot apple pie, vanilla ice cream on top, and coffee. Dripping au jus on his tie, Mr.Bigger did not notice, and be-gan "You have to know how beautiful you are. The Pageant gave us all the contestants' names. We're interviewing each of you". He gulped down his martini "This is the offer of a life time for a girl like you". I picked at my salad but did not eat a bite "How many have you interviewed so far". He seemed surprised by the question "You're the first. We'll call on the others after the Queen's been crowned. We'd like to fly you to New York City, put you up in a nice hotel. You'll apprentice three months at the New York Playboy Club, and either you're hired or sent home depending on talent". I wondered how someone could fail a job like that, but then it was probably the same way I failed the Pageant and Boeing job. Bigger ordered another martini. Mr.Little continued the pitch "All your costumes are provided free. Lodging's free for the trial period. You eat at the Club free, and make $1.25 an hour". He leaned toward me and winked "Plus big tips. And if you're hired on permanent, you'll get to visit the mansion. You know what could happen if you catch the boss's eye". He winked again and sat back. I hated to be winked at, forced my face to relax, it was none of their busi-ness how bad it stung to be solicited for the very magazine my Big Brother hid under the rug in the closet when he wasn't using it to masturbate. I asked Mr.Bigger "What do you mean an offer for a girl like me". His cold stare burned my eyes "You know exactly what I mean little missy". This lit-tle missy thing always enraged me, I held his gaze more with my chin than my eyes "Yeah, stacked". He snorted "Yeah missy, a luscious little cupcake like you". Suddenly I could not breathe, these men scared me, being food made me less than human, they could just as well eat me as their French dips, I coughed to clear my throat, to catch my breath "I can't think why I would go to New York for minimum wage when I make $2.50 an hour here". Shaking his head side-to-side, smiling, Bigger stared openly at my tits "With those you'll make huge tips". He sprawled back, legs spread "It's an offer of a life time". Feeling molested without ever being touched, my head screaming go now, run, it's time, get out of here, I was again unable to walk away unexplained, and stood, smiling polite "Thanks for the offer of a life time. I have to go to work now". Little stood too "We're heading to New York in three days". He handed me a card from the Sorrento Hotel "Room number 106. Think it over and call". I could not stop my polite hand from taking the card. Walking away, their eyes crawling on my back-side, I paid for lunch, feeling I had just purchased my own humiliation.

Again at my desk, nothing to do, head spinning with why didn't I say this, I should have done that, I called Penny. She thought I should seize the offer with both hands while it was hot. There was no one else. Katey had erased me, my oldest friend Rachel had moved to Israel, Mom and Dad would only worry about me alone in this big bad world and want me to move home, Marlee would jump at the chance, and I could just hear Big Brother, it's your opportunity to be someone. He carried a centerfold in his wallet and probably could not imagine any thing better a girl could do than be his wet fantasy, even if I was his Little Sister. And yet, what burrowed in me like an infected tick, I actually might have considered the offer, when surface was all I knew. Now I could sort of smell the shit masquerading as caviar, beauty queen, pair of tits, somehow the scent was the same. If this was the best I ever got, so be it, this offer of a lifetime for girls like me, be a beautiful body, smile, be a body part, a public pair, no need to worry your pretty little head with thinking, underline the little, we'll take care of that for you, just relax lay back and do what you're told, and you will be loved, adored, sought after, which sounded just like the offer of a lifetime for boys, be a jock, a sports star, a brute, get the girls, tempting glittering offers. I was not interested in being Boobs and the Brute.

There were two promising ads in the paper, walking home I stopped at a phone booth to call. The first sounded perfect, I went, a big house on 16th and Republican, divided into five separate living spaces, twenty-five dollars a month, no last or deposit, close to Volunteer Park, move in tomorrow, I paid the rent. When I told Katey, she would only give me a nod, an improvement I was satisfied with. Still I was so bruised and her silence so heavy I could not bear the weight of it and fled to the Ave, taking refuge in the Hasty Tasty for dinner and plans. I knew I had to quit my job or be fired. Boeing's profit sharing program would refund me 240 dollars. I'd saved another 140, giving me some room to find what's next. As for Nick, I had a certain thirst for him, and never wanted to see him again, maybe if I disappeared Katey would have a chance. Yet it wasn't just Nick, I wanted to disappear from everyone I knew. Today was my 18th birthday, as I ate the cheese omelet, I ached for the freedom to find who I really was without all the entanglements, from everyone who thought they knew me, thought they knew what was best for me.

Katey's ice melted as I packed, now it was real, she wanted to work it out, tried to change my mind. Grateful as I was, I needed to go. I didn't have much, a few plates, bowls, glasses and utensils, one mug, one pot, one frying pan, bathroom things, radio, record player, a good record collection, some books, clothes, shoes, fabric, and my Singer sewing machine. All fit in five boxes and two suitcases. It struck me how few books I owned.

In the morning I phoned Boss, asking how he would like me to quit. He gave me no argument, no need to come in unless there were personal items to retrieve. He would lay me off so I could collect unemployment, and arrange my profit sharing check be sent. He said I should see a psychiatrist, job stress had obviously gotten the best of me, and when I felt well, he would hire me again. I thanked him sincerely for such generosity and hung-up. Sick, I was sick, I needed a shrink, maybe, but I didn't think so, I was just beginning to answer the question. I called a taxi.

The first night in my new place KJR's Pat O'Day announced the daughter of the president of the Chamber of Commerce had been crowned Seafair Queen. My first night ever living alone, stomach a burnt-out house, no heat just empty, waiting to fall at any unfamiliar noises, playing the if might and could game, if someone breaks in, he might, he could, more scared than I wanted to think, alone, waiting for day light, when an old pal called my name, my Singer, a friend I could rely on to deliver me. A main Golden Ghetto must, having the right clothes, a constant devotion, that by 6th grade was suffocating me. Clothes clothes clothes, money money money, I needed money for clothes, and there was never enough, never relief, and every month a new Vogue issued, and perfectly good things lost their glow, and there seemed nothing but more and more, all you needed to be royalty in the Golden Ghet was every thing money could buy. From the desperation to breathe came unexpected natural ingenuity, I taught my self to sew, never telling anyone at school, for home-mades were as damning as Sears. I discovered a romance with the feel of cloth, and for the process of engineering and constructing, and I had a good hand for making things look store bought. By 7th grade, advanced Vogue patterns were elegantly easy. By 9th I could copy any garment in the magazine. Sophomore year, over Thanksgiving weekend I dared a leap and made a navy and white wool hounds-tooth hip-hugger skirt. Tucking my white crepe blouse into my bikini undies would not stay, so I attached the blouse to them, borrowed Mom's wide black belt, curved and long enough to lay on my hips, dyed brown knee boots black, and wore the ensemble to school. No one had seen any thing like it, I was a sensation, and I had broken the Rule, daring to wear something not in the magazine, something home-made, some thing no one else could buy, and worse, I dared hold my head high. Mean-spirited competition to get and keep popular was blood sport at my high school, lacking the taste for it, I became the object of vicious aspersions, for I had cut my self from the pack, trumping the competition. Who does she think she is whispered just loud enough as I walked from class, only boys wear their clothes low on the hip, intended to maim the soft under-belly of an unsure teenager, meant to shame her head since chopping it off was no longer legal. Instead of question my sexuality, I wondered why it was considered such a tool of dominion, why should my sexuality make me controllable, was this maybe the specter these Archons feared cast on them selves, I knew the self-righteous moralized from their pulpits how shame-full to be queer, which only brought to mind how they called me Christ Killer. But mostly this punishing made me mad, so each night I washed and carefully ironed that blouse, and wore the whole offense again, every day, all week, parading in their faces. I knew I wasn't a boy, knew a hip-hugger didn't make me one, infact if it was so bad this girl/boy question, why would I want to reveal my self, why would I want to signal the punishers. I was beginning to appreciate how political clothes really were, they dressed the idea or power that had sway, the tighter the skirt, the tighter the control, clothes were more than some fashion dictating how I spent, breeding anxiety when I couldn't, which suddenly seemed funny since these coveted rags had to be identical or they weren't the right ones.

The week was brutal and long, what made it interesting, some dark unexplored part of me was completely enjoying her self. Monday, I wore it again, and four more wore boy-skirts, home-made hip-huggers, they sat with me at lunch, we tanned in the warmth of numbers, even five shut-out the aspersions. I will always applaud these girls holding their audacious heads up with me, and saw clearly that challenging the status-quo with an a original idea meant continuing to stand under crushing pressure to conform, and that others who for many reasons were not so sturdy, for whom the first blows might flatten, could be emboldened to take their not so beaten path. Forty-two days later, the afternoon Jack Ruby murdered Lee Harvey Oswald in the garage of Dallas Police Headquarters, Vogue featured a boy-skirt on the cover, and Golden Girls who could went shopping. Vindication tasted sweet, and left that dark part of me, the part I suspected gave me backbone, the part nice girls were not suppose to have, vindication left me hungry for more face-time. I stood checking my self out in the full-length mirror on the back of my bedroom door, and rolled my bobby-sox up to see how it looked. I had the legs of a ballet dancer, and this made them seem longer, slimmer, more flattering than the prescribed knee-sox, and, only the boys wore their sox up. That dark part compelled me, would this bring the on-slought and outcome of the boy-skirt, sox up I walked to school. The casting began, spilling out of rolled down car windows, even from the school bus. First period, girls rolled-up their sox. Twenty or forty on the way to second period. Some jocks rolled their jeans up and sox down to mock us. No matter, ups were the majority at lunch, not because of me, because it made most legs look better, which was the point of all this wearing the same rags, beyond can you afford to buy, a given for so many Golden Girls, it was the competition, who looked best, easy to judge since we dressed alike. Upon graduation, needing full time work, needing money for college I took the Boeing job, which called for business dress, and having secretly envied those who could, now I could, and eagerly opening all the charge accounts offered to Seafair Queen contestants, I went shopping. I had not thought of my Singer once, and unlatching the cover I threaded it up on the dining room table and spread my meager stash of fabrics on the wood floor.

Days I hunted, materials often sparked my imagination, often told me exactly what they wanted to become. Mostly I hunted thrift shops for orchid flowered drapes, finely embroidered tablecloths and napkins, silk ties none with stripes, scarves, handkerchiefs, crocheted pot holders, tatting, handmade lace, jeans, woven blankets, plaid wool skirts, anything silk or unusual to cannibalize. Nights I worked, stretching-out in the open-space of a sleeping city, feeling my mind travel freely as far as I could think, unbound by the constraints of day-time rote, making a blanket-wool poncho of deftly woven blacks browns and goldens, lined with antique silk kimono panels. I loved the design and construction of kimonos, how they respected the silk by making so few cuts, and how easily taken apart, to become yards and yards for any idea I might need. Well-worn Levi 501's, I cut off the legs just below the pockets, and added a patchwork of rich wool plaids falling to a long soft skirt. Another skirt bloomed from neckties invisibly hand-stitched together at the edges, wide parts at the bottom, flaring like a calla lily. The orchid flower curtains became an ankle-length gown with capped-sleeves fashioned from ivory-silk crocheted pot holders. To respect the handiwork in an exquisitely embroidered linen tablecloth, I cut once, opening only enough to pull my head though, hand-sewing, tucking the blouse into shape, respecting the artist's discarded prowess.

And I bought used books and magazines, and when not sewing or reading, made collages from street findings and Vogue. Some particularly lonely afternoons I would smoke a joint, catch a bus to the Ave, take a seat on the brick wall infront of the Post Office, or the stone wall edging the University of Washington campus, and people watch. Especially interested in the resident Hippies and Flower-Children, some would sit down beside me, lonely too, often interested in my raiment, some wanting to buy them right off me. I reluctantly sold my children, the orchid flower gown and neck-tie skirt, earning first money with my own hands, just too delicious to resist. And I thought, back to 5th grade Sunday school class, listening to the teacher explain Cain and Abel, raising my hand, wondering why did God prefer Abel's bloody dead ram to the best vegetables from Cain's garden, and my teacher's chilling reply, Cain shouldn't have questioned God and neither should you. That was the exact minute a small rift split the surface of smooth blind-faith, I could not understand what was wrong with questioning, what was God afraid of. The only person I talked to then was Penny. She'd been raised Catholic, and on her way to catechism peeked through the hedge surrounding St. Monica's Convent, seeing the nuns' wash on lines, bras hanging in plain sight, big ones, something about big white cotton bras and nuns made her dare ask during class if starving African babies who died never having been baptized could go to heaven. The nun said no, and that was her moment, her rift, she would not, could not believe in a God that punished the innocent. Now with time to think, I wondered how anyone could look up to, how any one who actually thought about it could aspire to up when God was so callous. I wondered if there might be more who had that terrible minute when religious dogma seemed too preposterous to believe, when what was preached no longer rang true and they wondered, and fell through the riddled foundation that could not support the weight of wondering, and like me were in free-fall. I wondered if killing animals to wear, to eat, to sacrifice was just another unquestioned tenet, another inevitable blind-faith, Abel's ram and God, innocent blood everywhere, I wondered if there might be an other way.

Early evenings I nested in the teddy-bear-brown over-stuffed velvet chair on my covered porch, hand-sewing, reading, watching neighbors come home from work. Loneliness a welcome companion, I was not desperate to be involved, and then this couple moved into an upstairs unit of the four-plex cross the street. Their routine was just so curiously precise,

the woman arriving home on work-days at 5PM exactly, the man 5:30. They never went out, even on weekends, dressed so unremarkably it struck me as remarkable, and their faces, vivid, adept, and so paranoid I found my self eagerly anticipating their predictability. One Thursday the woman crossed the street and invited me to dinner. I went without hesitation. Bonita-Kay and Jeffree Johnson from Dallas, and I had to pry that, were gracious Texans who talked of Karma, the Tao, Zen, Alan Watts, of nothing personal, and in-between asked so many personal questions, where did I go to school, how come I wasn't working, where did my parents live, all of which I felt surprisingly comfortable answering. We talked every thing but them, drank dark beer in the kitchenette while Bonita-Kay cooked onions and okra in a fragrant red sauce, added fresh shrimp and lemon at the last minute, and ladled it over large flat dumplings simmered in a cast iron frying pan. After this southern ambrosia, we listened to Sam & Dave, Howling Wolf, Robert Johnson, and I lit the joint stashed behind my ear. Bonita-Kay smiled as I passed it to her, drew in a long deep drag, coughed and passed to Jeffree. Who inhaled deeply and held the smoke while Bonita-Kay clocked him outloud tick tick tock, one-minute six seconds, allowing the tetrahydrocannabinol maximum absorption. He exhaled slowly, leaned back in his chair and declared I must be one of their Karass. Bonita-Kay's head bobbed up-and-down, yes yes, Kurt Vonnegut, Cat's Cradle, I must be one of their cosmically linked family. Maybe being illegal together made them trust me, maybe intuition, may be like me they recognized a friend, and their secret came spilling-out. Fugitives on the run, driving a dark green 1962 Volkswagen Beetle, so very common on the road, dressing to be invisible, staying to themselves. I had to speak the obvious, it had not worked. We all laughed. Jeffree supposed I must see something the people chasing after them did not, so far I was the only one who'd ever taken notice. I knew he was right, I was still on the out side, so far the only one of my kind, and from this perspective people just looked strange, were so unknowingly revealing, showing without any one even having to ask. Mrs. and Mr.Johnson, with bail bondsman banging on their San Francisco front door, climbed down the apartment fire escape and drove north. It wasn't the first time, they'd been running four years, sought the anonymity of big cities, learned to rent places with easy escape, to leave everything important in the car, and when they were able, they would cross the border into Canada. Jeffree had been a photographer of bright note in Dallas, shooting record album covers and promo-shots for rock'n roll band, actors and models. Bonita-Kay sang in clubs and did back-up vocals in the local recording studios. Now she waited the down-town Woolworth lunch counter, and he worked for Tall's Camera Shop in sales. They'd been busted in 1962, with Faylene, a 17 year old white friend, and Arthur, an 18 year old black friend, and the Dallas County Prosecutor Henry Wade decided even though they'd been arrested with 2 thin joints, he was going to make an example of them. A minor, Faylene was convicted and sentenced to one year probation. Bonita-Kay, Jeffree and Arthur were also convicted, and the night before sentencing met with their lawyer, who warned they would probably get twenty-years in the Federal Penitentiary, and as a friend suggested they disappear. Arthur went North, they went West. It wasn't police hunting them but bondsmen wanting the bail money back. They didn't stay long anywhere and did not make friends. I was grateful they broke their rule, and again spoke the ob-vious, had they called their lawyer lately, maybe something had changed. Jeffree lit-up like he faced a blazing fire, no they had not, and this was a very good idea. We talked till they could not stay awake. And I went home too excited to sleep, for joy, something had changed, there were others, people I could talk too, people who could talk to me. I picked through my cuttings and findings and built them a collage, art seemed the only vehicle to celebrate this first contact, I had every thing I needed, and finished closing my eyes after 10AM.

Already nesting in the teddy bear chair by 3PM, I waited chirp chirp chirp, embarrassed at being so needy. Bonita-Kay's 5PM exactly welcom-ing smile as she waved me come over, a benevolent feeding. Off-the-ground excited and lips sealed, she needed Jeffree to hear the news first. Five-thirty PM he took the stairs two and three at a time, tequila, limes, and a dozen red roses in hands. We convened in the kitchenette, toasting every detail of Bonita-Kay's phone call to their lawyer, the state of Texas wanted the case off the books and were offering ten years probation, the offer due to expire in six days. Arthur had already surrendered, and they decided to leave in the morning for Dallas. Bonita-Kay hugged me close, called me their good luck charm, and invited me to come along, to meet the others of their Karass. I could not wrap my mind around such an offer, Texas was somewhere I had never imagined going. We smoked a little golden ball of purified resin from the flowering female cannabis plant, my first taste of hashish, a pungent mellow high, and I listened as they talked-over their possibilities. Jeffree vowed if he must stay in Texas ten years, making a million dollars would be his sweet revenge. Bonita-Kay missed her Mom, was aching to sing again, to live a more steadfast life.

When morning lit the room, they packed while I cooked-up the last of their eggs and toast, and helped carry belongings to the dark green Beetle. Then ran cross for the collage, a big oak tree, branches of arms and legs plundered from Vogue, curled Madrona tree bark glued to the trunk, plaid wool leaves with edges frayed, and crowded round the trunk, magazine advertisement people, with broken shards of mirror glued over their faces and hearts to make them look like empty holes. And I copied a poem across the bottom, composed in 8th grade after nearly inhaling Ayn Rand's The Fountainhead, the first I ever read of a woman using her head instead of her body to get what she wanted, who didn't need a man to be whole yet still sought true love, who could take care of her self. Jeffree read aloud.

The Big Oak

A tree can grow in many ways
All sinew and columns of raised up fists
Or all hunched over like a gremlin sits
But once it's grown – it always stays

The wind may blow in a mighty way
And scatter the leaves everywhere
But a few will remain in tender care
Of the robin in the tree that will always stay

But what of that wonderous tree one day
When now not a robin but a flame does sit

Licking the branches where the lightning hit
That mighty tree I thought would always stay

And now I come to look as I may
Into the hollow trunk of that fallen tree
As hollow and false as people might be
That mighty tree I thought would always stay.

Bonita-Kay kissed my cheek, yes there were many empty shells posing as real live people. Jeffree kissed my other cheek, and asked me to always keep a tender-heart, tender and open enough to be fooled, for ending up stone-cold cynical would be the worst possible out-come. They presented me with their wooden cigar box stash, the label long worn off, marijuana, hashish, mescaline, LSD, and the dozen red roses. I promised to find a way to Texas, and sat in the teddy bear chair, roses and box in lap long after the dark green Beetle turned the corner.

Chapter Two

THE GOLDEN GOSPEL

Again I withdrew, people seemed only out for them selves, it did not matter that I was me, they said whatever nicety to get my ear, my time, my soul. And guys, they wanted a girl's body, any girl, I wondered were they all dogs in heat, sniffing the scent, ever on the hunt, always coming on, sniffing. I wanted connection, friends, true love, my libido was hungry as any, I just thought it should matter it was me and not a convenient life-size cardboard cut-out. I wondered if I propped-up that cut-out and walked away would any one notice, no one so far but Jeffree and Bonita-Kay. A necessary new force had surfaced, the National Organization for Women, NOW, demanding legal abortion and contraceptives, and considering luck and rubbers were it for birth control, and most guys wouldn't wear one, because it was all about them, how a rubber cut down on their pleasure, and depending on how desperate a girl was to have him love her, if he knocked her up, a safe abortion was only available to the Golden Girls whose family could afford the trip to Europe for a 'vacation' to get the little mistake neatly and safely taken care of. The rest of us paid with our lives, either raising the little mistake, or bleeding to death from a back alley abortion. NOW's appearance caught my imagination, I began to consider how life would be if I didn't have to worry about getting pregnant.

I was often stoned, sampling all the wooden cigar box held, grooving on music, sewing, reading Alan Watts, eating mostly vegetarian, solitary pink dawns following star bright and still short nights into long days, then stormy nights becoming warm September afternoons perched on the wall infront of the Post Office watching Humans parade down the Ave in all their noisy conditions, when he sat down next to me, and not too close. He didn't sniff me, didn't come on, didn't try to act cool, we didn't even speak, he just kept my company watching the parade, with his long thick mane of gleaming raven hair, sun-tanned big hands, steady chocolate black eyes, and fresh laundry scent. And then he was gone.

All night I stitched a new dress, and he occupied my mind as if we were connected on some cosmic thread. Mid morning I slipped the frock over my head and went to the wall. And he appeared at the curb on a white Vespa. My eyes for one heart-beat met his, and woosh I was inside my own body again, solid, and too self-conscious to hold the intensity of direct connection dropped my notice to his welcome mouth. He sat close but never touching, the clear noon sun our continuity, watching the parade, watching. When he spoke, his big soft voice sounded old friend "I'm Casey. Would you drop acid with me today". I simply said "Yes". A gentle tilt of his head invited me come on. Scooting in close on the Vespa's black leather seat, I held him fast as we waltzed along the back streets to his place on Queen Anne Hill. This was the first Hippie house I'd ever been in. Much like me it looked normal enough on the out side, inside the walls were hung with black-light posters, paisley tapestries covered most of the furniture, a cloud of marijuana and incense hugged the ceiling. In the kitchen a considerable brass hookah dominated the table, and I met Fast Eddy, and Marlon the biker who for the time being drove a 1958 Mercedes, and his Seatcover Kitty and her not quite tame raccoon Euphoria.

Casey took my hand and climbed the stairs to his corner room, tall windows on two sides, a wooden crate holding candles, eagle feathers and books hugged the arm of an over-stuffed faded green brocade couch spread with beautifully woven blankets, mahogany highboy against the wall. He opened the middle drawer for a pouch, poured the contents into his hand and showed me the little purple pills "Pharmaceutically pure Owsley". He smiled "Thank you Augustus Owsley Stanley the 3rd". Placing one on his tongue and one in my hand he slipped the rest into the pouch and drawer. Casey did not assume, did not make my choice, did not take charge of me, I felt safe, placing the coming trip on my tongue. And having some notion what would happen next, we sat on the couch, facing, waiting the taste of tin foil to signal threshold, quietly exchanging bits of our selves, the afternoon sun streaming in the windows, full of warm promise. His steady solid gaze embraced my whole self, not just the individual parts, making me feel seen and beauty-full in my new dress, cut from a sky blue Egyptian cotton table-cloth, scoop-necked with one inch box-pleats fitting the bodice, left loose from just above the waist to bell into a dirndl skirt trimmed in finely tatted white lace. I'd taken to not wearing underclothes, having been brought-up so good-girl it made me feel naughty, my hair was long, and the weight settled most of the curl. Tasting tin-foil Casey suggested we go downstairs, turn on the black lights, trip on posters and listen to music. He stacked three albums on the turntable, and we fell back into the big soft couch.

My fillings turned to liquid tin. Fast Eddy's voice swelled "It's the cops. Shit, it's a bust". Gravity released me, time and space too, I blew through the living room, the kitchen where Eddy, Marlon, Kitty and Euphoria were still gathered round the hookah, out the back door, over the fence into the next yard, down flights of steep concrete stairs, and finally noticed my feet in my shoes walking a narrow quiet lane, acid Alice in her little dress, wondering was this the wonder she felt as her rabbit hole opened. Unable to resist the pulling I slipped-off my shoes and followed a covert talcum-powder path into the woods, into a clearing, vaulted, thick with flowers, faces swaying to the celestial symphony, casting their scent my way, a ovation that attracted some fat day-glow bugs floating heavily on their fevered wings, ushering me to a swing, hung from the mighty limb of a towering Madrona, plainly Her Majesty of the Realm, I hopped onto the wide worn seat, whose ropes disappeared into an emerald canopy, the resident breeze laid gentle hands to my back, pushing, gliding long lazy sweeps, Flora and Fauna and me, in concert, breathing the melody in and out, in and out, in and out. When time and space weighed on me again, the sun was setting, and I found my self in a secluded park or maybe vacant lot on the West side of Queen Anne Hill looking over the Sound. I followed the talcum path to the lane, my shoes were gone, cold and a bit confused I walked for bearings, and though curious and worried what might have happened to Casey, it was best to go home. No shoes no money, I saw headlights and put out a thumb, acid has its own private frequency, good acid anyway, the driver stopped, rolled down his window and passed me a lit joint, he was coming down too. I climbed in the passenger side of his VW bus, took a courtesy toke and handed it back, for I was savoring the smooth ride down, this was Owsley after all. We spoke of directions and nothing more, at my curb he asked to come in, I said no, and he did not make me feel obliged for the ride. Locking the door I sat down with the hill of magazines on my front room floor and began snipping and pasting, a dark-haired Alice came to life, her big bare feet standing in the dirt, and it occurred to me, my trip couldn't be so unique if Lewis Carroll took his Alice on a similar one, and that Gabriel might be right, on acid it was only the individual details that differed. I slept finally, on the couch, my last thought was of Casey.

Late-afternoon I rode the bus to the Ave. Finding Casey sitting on the wall I smiled and frowned "Who got busted. I heard Fast Eddy and had to go". Casey's eyes twinkled in amusement "Oh Eddy loves to tell his war stories". Being taken lightly burned my skin, I could not look at him "The thought of losing my freedom freaks me out". Still smiling, he stood, coming close to my face so I could smell the coffee on his breath, and confided "Eddy's a junkie. He dresses-up in white coveralls, rents a white van, drives to a department store delivery bay, loads as much as he thinks he can get away with, and takes it to that pawner near Pike Market, who pays 20 cents on the dollar. He was probably just bragging on a close call". I'd been so free of human tangles, worrying about some one grabbed every loose muscle in my body, especially when that one considered my concern mere trifle. And this enthusiasm for Eddy's sly tricks bothered me even more. I did not think stealing for drugs was glamorous or amusing or a worthy motive for crime, just a desperate addict's need. I needed to cool and asked Casey to meet me tomorrow. His dark brows pinched in confusion, still he let me go without question.

Every noon after, we'd meet at the wall. And often hard-faced police swarmed the Ave, and we would head to campus, to talk and walk through the pampered trees. It was a haven, as only campus cops were allowed to patrol UW grounds, and these were not so hard-faced and didn't carry guns. Or we'd browse the ID Bookstore, have a beer at the Century Tavern, the Roach or the Rainbow, which ever bartender would look away that day from my under-age. Most dinners were the Hasty Tasty, Coffee Corral, the Pancake House. Four years older, Casey was Apache and half Italian, born in New Mexico, raised in Long Beach California. He could be so much deeper than he knew, and I did not entirely trust him, still our friendship blossomed, and leaned, for he wanted more than friends, and I was only in-like. The more leaning, the more vigilant in word and deed I became, though secretly flattered, I did not want to lead him on. An LA trip was in the planning, Marlon and Kitty and Euphoria, in the Mercedes. Casey wanted to visit his Folks and invited me along, we would camp in the Redwoods and tour Haight Ashbury on the way. I promised to consider this, and then could think of nothing else.

Marlon and Kitty were not like any I had ever spent time with, bawdy, uninhibited, vulgar, brutally offensive to my Golden stalk, fortunately a new root was taking hold that wasn't so uppity, so superficial, so needy of the Golden Masquerade. They too were owed by their tastes, and still they took me in, did not draw battle lines, maybe because they liked me, more likely they wanted to study me up close. The thing that bothered me most was Marlon's shameless domination of his Seatcover and her willing, obedient submission. When a private opportunity came to ask, Kitty seemed surprised at my concern, assuring me it was a real turn-on. I cringed, not quite but somewhere inside knowing how that could be. My teachers came in odd disguise, lessons from dubious souls, it took me a full week deciding to join this checkered gang, to put myself in their hands for a while. Going became real when I told the landlord. My hole-in-the-wall had been such fertile ground, so creative, safe, and now I was going on my first adventure, first real in-the-body adventure, I ached and sobbed through the night for my coming losses.

Leaning and leaning, Casey subtly and not so subtly wanted to bed me, and suggested it more often. I was less and more attracted to him and sometimes tempted, but definitely not in-love. We were getting stoned, getting ready for a Happening in Ravenna Park, going to hear The Daily Flash and Grateful Dead when he brought this up infront of Marlon and Kitty. Mortified to blushing, this was way too much pressure, I thought better of the whole thing and got-up to leave. Kitty grabbed my arm "Hey now Miss Prissy Girl, don't be such a prude. I fuck all the time. Am I knocked-up". Marlon smiled big, took two foil packets from the leather pouch tied to his belt and handed them to Casey. Who smiling big held the Trojans up to me "And I'm not ready to be a dad". I sat down, amazed things so private were such pubic talk. Marlon grunted his agreement, and taking a light brown nugget of hashish from that same pouch, placed it in the hookah bowl. We smoked, then oozed smoothly into the Mercedes.

The Daily Flash's rich sweet harmonies and inventive blend of folk and rock drew us down the stairs into the ravine, along the wide pathway leading to the park, and in to a multi-colored kaleidoscope of not so solid life-forms shifting though banks of marijuana smoke. I had never dared go to Love-ins Be-ins or Happenings and felt the thrill of stepping over a dangerous line. There were rumors of Ken Kesey, The Merry Pranksters and their traveling psychedelic bus coming to Seattle for an acid test, there were flyers shouting the formation of the Oakland Black Panther Party by Bobby Seale and Huey Newton for the purpose of self-defense, and reports of the budding student resistance to the Vietnam War, and the first issue of the San Francisco Oracle with its headline, Newly Elected Governor of California Ronald Reagan Makes Possession and Use of LSD a Felony. People like me were being arrested.

Soft drugs, hypnotic music, peace and love in mortal bodies raised a whole, criminals-inlaws, outlaws breaking the rules together, openly high, girls and boys, girls and girls, boys and boys, all kinds and colors equal, the social-economic structure designed to separate and elevate the few with education, money, power, access and class had no weight here, we were a potent new creature, making it safe to throw-off the old chains, for we were too many, too big to arrest. And the Grateful Dead played their signature free-flowing jam. And I committed my first public crime, smoking a peace pipe that was passing along, recalling my fear when Nick offered the joint as we waited in line to see Ray Charles, it seemed a life-time long ago. Casey tried to stop me "Hey, you don't know what's in that pipe." I would not be controlled or dominated. And we all danced and swayed as one to the long Dead jam, in the warm breath of an autumn afternoon, Casey's beauty-full body, his scent intoxicating me. And we went to my place, and made Trojan love. I did not orgasm, and did not fake it, and Casey did not seem to notice, saying he loved me, like that was enough. Terribly disappointed in my self, I could feel regret laying in my belly like a hot stone, and vowed never again to let my body make the sole decision, never to make this miss-take with a friend again. I could only hope it did not spoil things, complicate them too much two days before leaving.

My hill of magazines filled two trash cans. I called a cab to Mercer Island, all my possessions fit in the trunk. Mom and Dad were fine with me leaving these in my room, still just as I left it. And I lied to them, that I was going with some girl friends, for they would never understand my need for this adventure, and if they caught sight of Marlon and Kitty, or Casey, they'd worry themselves crazy. I had really good Folks, but little Shoshy was all they wanted to see, someone they'd seriously under-estimated and seriously over-protected, giving me few opportunities to go wrong while living at home, in a safe place to crash and burn.

Dad grew-up on Creston Avenue in the Bronx, a valued member of the Jewish gang because of his Golden Gloves right hand. Every block was commanded by another, Italian, Irish, Negro, Puerto Rican, Catholic, and Dad needed his crew just to make it down those blocks to school. Then like so many without a future, he joined the Army to escape. One year later, December 7, 1942 Japan bombed Pearl Harbor, America went to war and Dad was sent to Seattle to protect Boeing, where he met Mom at a Hadassah Sisterhood dance to entertain Jewish servicemen. It was love at first sight. Mom missed the first months of her senior year at Garfield High School after an emergency appendectomy. She fell far behind, struggled to catch-up, and because it was such an effort concluded she must be stupid. And I was the girl between two brothers, the Big one barely graduated high school. My turn came three years later, and Mom and Dad were so relieved by my Cs and Bs they assumed this was all I was capable of, didn't pay much attention as I was not a problem, didn't take seriously my passion for writing, my evident talent for design and sewing, never suggested I take these further, college was never mentioned, no money was saved. Their fondest hope for me, a 1950's wife and mother. I left home one week after graduation. Seattle Community College had just opened, I signed-up to go, took the Boeing job to pay for it and the apartment with Katey. And still seventeen and raring for freedom, put my right foot on a new road, to claim my capacity, my capability. Mom and Dad feared harm at my every step, questioned every judgment, criticized every choice. And they were mostly right, I had little experience. Still if I bought into the cultural canon that females were not trust-worthy outside the role of daughter-wife-mother, if I accepted the underlying disgust for independent women, the implicit thought that a girl who was not wife-mother-daughter must be whore, I would have to live in those constraints, die my whole life in those taints. I knew instinctively it would suffocate my fire, tame me, that I would never find an authentic life. So I needed some trouble, some bad judgment, and needed it to happen far from the fears of Mom and Dad. The road was mine alone, maybe California would be the place, so I lied.

On the same crisp autumn morning that Cream debuted their album, four humans and a raccoon left Queen Anne Hill. The Mercedes was such a splendid traveling car. Marlon drove through Washington and most of Oregon, stopping at the Wolf Creek Cafe, we were starving. An oatmeal connoisseur, I had the finest bowl on the planet, steamed light and creamy, dressed in butter and maple syrup. The Cafe was mostly truckers, with a small hive of Hippies buzzing in and out for these magnificent freshly baked enormous cinnamon rolls called zuzus. I ordered two to go, and we continue on in the twilight to Grants Pass, and headed southwest onto Highway 199 toward the Pacific. Marlon turned into the next rest stop, we hiked not 50 yards into the woods, to a small level clearing, the moon near full, Casey and Marlon pitched the tent, we slid into our sleeping bags. Late October was still warm here and though weary from sitting so long, I could not sleep, the romance of adventure, vivid possibilities dancing cross my mind. I was actually in California, maybe I would meet someone and fall in love, some one I could have this conversation with out loud, maybe I would find a way to stay in this fair land, maybe a poisonous insect will creep into my bag, bite me, paralyze me, deposit eggs in the wound, leave me to die a slow death without ever having lived, I loathed camping, sleeping on the ground, who could relax considering what might crawl in. Ears on full radar, I listen to the sounds outside, where Euphoria was tethered to a tree, imagining her sitting on haunches, using those fastidious long fingers to pick her dinner kibble delicately one piece at a time and dunk it in the water bowl. Having no saliva glands, she needed the liquor to digest her meal. And hope-fully those purring-giggle sounds were other raccoons, not pregnant insects. I laid still, the top of my bag clutched tight round my face, trying to focus on the even breathing in-an-out in-an-out nin-an-nout of my companions, breathing along with them, nin-an-nout nin-an-nout trying to relax. When Casey whispered "You wake. Wana zip our bags together". I didn't and did "Okay, but nothing's going to happen". His warm body next to mine made me feel safe. My muscles let go, and I was grateful for the dark hiding this humiliation, this appalling need for protection screaming from some unknown unreason deep in the well of my cells. I don't recall falling asleep.

I do recall being rousted at dawn by an eager-beaver park ranger threatening us with fines and tickets for camping in an unauthorized area, if we didn't go immediately blah blah blah. He chastised me and Kitty, not a week earlier a girl, a menstruating girl attracted a bear with her scent and was mauled in these very woods. I wanted his mind out of my pants, but noting how contrite everyone was, bit my lip and lowered my eyes. Promptly, obediently, silently we packed-up. Mr.Eager tapping his foot on a rock in the dirt, threatening to search the Mercedes, we were an irregular looking bunch to be driving a Benz. He followed a few miles in his official white Ford truck and gave-up. Casey and Marlon howled like coyotes, confessing to five pounds of Lebanese hash and a shot gun in the trunk. I was too angry to form words, traveling with contraband that could get me busted and no one thinking I need to know, these were selfish rascals who did not care one whit for me. Marlon kept the speed limit as we rode 199 into northern California, connected with Highway One, and once again into the majesty of giant Sequoias, we voted three to me to camp and drop acid among these towering ancient tree. Marlon turned onto a narrow fire road he knew, we covered the Mercedes with a camouflage tarp, took all the gear and hiked maybe a block into a grace-full natural meadow he and Kitty camped many times. Coleman stove, lanterns, fire-grate, cast iron pans, bowls, mugs, whistling teapot, food, water, blankets, pillows, hammocks, a tent. After all the set-up, Kitty made pancakes and coffee, and I strung-up a hammock and napped the afternoon, in these Redwoods in the warm daylight, being off the ground, now this was camping.

Near sunset we gathered round the campfire, dropped Owsley and waited. It was a mild fragrant night the likes only California offers, the moon rising in its full glory, Casey and Marlon took their shirts off. Before a thought, I had mine off too, the only time since young and flat-chested I'd been bare outside the bedroom or bathroom, and it seemed usual, ordinary, till my nipples stood-up, and suddenly sexual, the unwelcome blush of self-conscious lit my face. I did not cover-up, and let no one see me squirm, boys could take theirs off any time any place without consequence, what was the big deal with tits, I would take this liberty no matter how provocative. Tasting the tin foil, Owsley came on like silk, I had to be alone and slipped away, Luna's topaz face lighting my way up a gentle slope along the side of the meadow to a ridge over-looking the forest. I felt native, brave, bare and wholesome, surrounded by these eminent tree spirits, every one feminine, welcoming me into their order. I stood tall and bold, in stark contrast to living clothed in human society, making so clear the pervasive and mostly unquestioned fear I felt constantly, unthinkingly, of bad men, monsters in every shadow, the few who did the terrors, the violence and rapes, were enough to make me fear all. Some men gave all men a bad name, there were none here, I let my self open, join these nymph spirits, some 2000 years old, and thick, soaring 300 feet, my big sisters, basking in Luna's fullness. Casey and Marlon had dropped two little purple Owsleys, Kitty one and a half, and I took the other half, certain this woodland would carry me the rest of the way, I did not want to disappear. Casey had completely buried the spiritual side of him self, the side that attracted me, a closet Apache in a very white dominated society, I didn't blame him for hiding. Being Jewish in a Christian nation, I knew what it was like to be other, but I had come to the end of him, and my traveling buddies, learned enough of what they had to teach, and was still starving. I needed to know the whole thing and felt a constant tugging in every organ of my body to get on with it. As if a fragrant hot pink rose grew in my heart, I saw, smelled, knew I had always needed to know everything, and amid these grace-full Dryads felt quickened, as though maybe I could. Luna's face began to cave on one side, darken, an eclipse, slowly turning her into a Fire-Horned Goddess, beoming a Great Horned Gate, opening, and I walked through into the Universe, too riddled with poison, too insubstantial to fly, it was in my blood, and I heard that lame excuse echo, I need I need just incase I must impress, more things, more. These never satisfied me, never soothed the craving for more than sometimes a moment, and then I needed again, what I could not answer. And though I made many of the things myself, I still needed new bras in my drawer, never worn, and panties and shoes and jeans tucked away, just incase I needed. I had want and need so confused, that was the double-cross of the Golden Gospel, I did not need more to live but to disguise that I was not. I'd been luckier than most, a working class family income didn't let me buy-in so thoughtlessly, forcing talent, ingenuity. But the poison seeped-in anyway, and manifest an arrogant snobbish attitude that having things and knowing how to act made me better. This was the Golden Ghet mindset that steals a life, as destructive as having no access to opportunity, because it made most openings seem too common, too peasant for a fragile inflated ego to take. And I couldn't flush-out this poison even with Kitty and Marlon. My swell and filigree bumped into people, they loved or hated me, no one was lukewarm. Walking through the Great Horned Gate did not liberate me, I couldn't get away from what was part of me, I'd have to live with it, teach it, some how embrace, transform frothy bloat into sound healthy substance. And now that I could momentarily see my self, one of the wonders of Owsley, I absolutely needed more people to learn from, more trouble to get into, if I was to ever stop wanting and take wing. Suddenly appearing then disappearing, a sparkling star caught my eye, rotating round-and-round, dark-light-dark-light, and contrary to the synagogue, to needing Yahweh to show him self and finding no one there, the Fire-Horned Goddess near full-faced again was so much kinder. I took the whirling star as an exclamation point that walking though the Gate would be met with some regard. When I was eight years old, on a warm summer night I set-up the chaise lounge and my sleeping bag in the back yard to sleep out, though I was never able to sleep outside. Looking up at the Big Dipper, for a moment the sky was no longer flat but yawning with dimension, and I thought if I was on another planet the Big Dipper wouldn't look like the Big Dipper at all. And I remember saying aloud, if a flying saucer lands on earth, please let it land in my back yard instead of NASA or I'll never be able to meet you. I thought there might be others out there, living beings, probably not like me, probably not even in bodies, and as I watched this sparkling star roll on-an-off on-an-off till dawn's pink fingers reached into the sky and it abruptly shot away, I was left with the sure sense I communed with one.

A curious Spotted Owl shadowed me to camp. Coming down enough to feel the morning chill, I pulled on my blouse. Kitty was rocking Euphoria in her arms. The boys seemed settled old men swaying in their hammocks puffing weed from corncob pipes, they had eaten my zuzus. Casey's sheepish smile was all teeth, he offered his cob. Coming down on Owsley didn't want help, adding anything would overwhelm the subtle long glide, I passed with a quiet grin, and kept my adventure inside, only for me. By 9AM we were packed, all set but Kitty, struggling with, deciding to let Euphoria go free. A handsome and persistent male raccoon had come a-courting, Euphoria was smitten, tears washed Kitty's face as she removed her baby's collar, Euphoria scamper, they disappeared into the forest without a look back. I too was eager to get on with what ever came next. We headed to LA.

Marlon drove all day, Highway One to San Francisco then South I-5. I was deee-lighted to be in California, my eyes feasting on the palms and oaks, hills that seemed covered with blonde shag carpet, dark green bushes tucked in the folds, perfect cottonball sheep. The Golden Gate Bridge did not impress as I hoped, but the view and the Eucalyptus and Jasmine on the breezes did. And the broad flat freeway, as many as eight lanes and six ramps stacked on the other, a monstrous octopus wonder. Luna's face was near full when Marlon dropped us at Casey's Folks off South Willow Street in Long Beach. He and Kitty were going on to his brother in Garden Grove, who had a buyer for the hash, and with the money they would score a trunk-load of Acapulco Gold to deal in Seattle, and come back for us in a few days. Casey's Mom rushed from the house, a delicate Apache, high cheek bones, eyes a bit slanted like mine, dressed in June Cleaver's white cardigan sweater and pearls. She covered his face in kisses, her only child home again, and I loved Casey for letting her. She hugged me too, and graciously showed me the guest bedroom and bath. I showered, and slept atop the hand-crocheted spread till Casey knocked to say breakfast was on.

Opening the bedroom drape I stood still, eyes squint against the intense morning light, gathering my self before joining the others round the kitchen table, a mug of coffee waiting and one empty chair. Casey's Mom treated me without pretense, like family, and I found it uncomfortably unusual, but then this was California where the latest things began. She set me a plate of link sausage, scrambled eggs and toast that had my mouth watering. When I drank only black coffee, she rolled her eyes at Casey and asked was I watching my beautiful figure. This was as polite a reason as I could invent, and I let it stand with a shy smile, not wanting to be rude to this lovely woman, but I could not eat, Persephone's law, I could not so easily become part of this family even if it was the latest thing. I needed to think, what was I even doing here. Casey's Dad, a handsome Irish Pan American pilot announced he was trading-in the Ford Fairlane, picking-up his new 1967 Mustang convertible, today, after breakfast. In the surprise and excitement I excused myself and went out into the sunshine for a walk. Casey was clearly in with Marlon on the deal and I would not go back to Seattle with dope in the car. It was good reason to stay in California, this well-lit Hollywood show-ground, looking as if intended for my own personal adventure film. Walking through the neighborhood, lawns that did not need a trim being manicured by a troupe of brown-skinned men, wailing blowers strapped to their backs, rounding-up every stray blade of grass. And the red tile-roof and white stucco homes immaculate in the clear light, tidy cactus and rock gardens, neon bougainvillea climbing porches, showy flowers that as far as I knew grew only in the

Volunteer Park Conservatory, and conducting the whole show, eminent palms flourishing their fronds. The world had turned on its head for me, all this outside abundance had no reference point, even the parking strips were decorated, with a plant I believed some glass artist's fancy. Mom kept a clutch of it in a cloisonné on the kitchen window sill, and here it was for real, sizzling pink ice-plant, common ground-cover dressing the roads and freeways. I wondered what else I could have only imagined and might find matter-of-fact here in California. For me, the crush of Golden Ghet was an insidious censure of imagination by implication, you have every thing you could or should ever dream of, we will tell you what to want, what you need, black-listing to pressure you in-line, banishment for those who will not submit, will not obey, and like Adam's Woman I did not heed the warnings, I ate the apple.

The thought of apples ignited my hunger, I turned West onto Willow and saw a bold lettered sign, Food for the Soul in the front window of a gaily painted house. Climbing the broad porch stairs, amused how oblique California restaurants could be, I enter open French doors, walked through the foyer into the dining room, and took an arm-chair at the head of a long-long table, the only customer. A waitress came right away, asking what did I want. Since she had no menu, I ordered tea please and two grilled cheese sandwiches. She hurried to the kitchen, and I looked round at the walls hung in posters of the Beatles, Krishna, Buddha, Gandhi, Che, Bob Dylan, Joan Baez, and the duel Golden Retrievers lazing on the rug in the foyer who had not twitched an ear or lip as I passed-by. Only in California would dogs be allowed to hang-out in restaurants. I felt odd, stiff being the only one, and leaving seemed the thing to do when a waiter brought my food. Perfectly grilled sliced tomato and cheddar sandwiches, the fresh-baked whole-grain bread spread with sweet hot mustard, a fat kosher dill and grapes on the side, Earl Grey tea. I was too hungry to enjoy, wolfing the feast in greedy bites, hiccupping, waiting for the check, looking toward the kitchen to let someone know. Several faces peeked, no one came, the odd intensified, I laid three dollars on the table, thanked the empty dining room aloud, hurried by the hounds, and the two human-size statues guarding the French doors, Mary holding a radiant baby Jesus and the Statue of Liberty, galloped down the stairs, and lingering on the sidewalk, recognized this was not a restaurant but a church, Food For the Soul their statement of purpose not advertisement to eat. I waved and smiled at the faces peering through the curtain, how kind they had been to feed me, and just as promised, I did feel fed.

Everything in California was faster, louder, sooner, slicker, warmer, a dazzling carnival. I wanted to lie in cordial sand on a sun-baked beach in winter, see Disneyland on acid, and straight-away found myself at Walt's door, looming high above me, a giant glowing glass clown-head on a towering metal pole, glaring over a construct called Jack in the Box. And people dressed for work, waiting in-line in their cars, motors running, to place an order with a lesser glass head. This was a real restaurant, and someone's job had been lost to this gloating God of the machine. All the swirling, spinning, clamoring distractions, what did I want to do here in California, what cut through it all was going to Haight Ashbury, and, the truth, if I stayed with Casey it would become my fault he presumed us more than friends. This gave me little wings, I flew back to the house, so far away from knowing eyes I could be any one I wanted, no one to meddle, no one knew me. Waiting on the porch, Casey was anxious, excited, his Dad had given him the Fairlane, he already called Marlon to head for Seattle without us, we were leaving soon, for Haight Ashbury and then Ensenada, he wanted to show me the coast from San Francisco to Malibu. I no longer felt weightless, though Haight Ashbury was exactly where I wanted to go, Casey had simply informed, done my thinking, no discussion, like his father had informed the wife about the new car. And I was also still too mannered to say.

Rising before us and dressed to her girdle and pearls so early, Mom made sure we had food to go, and were hugged and kissed. She was so affectionate to me I thought there must be some Mad Hatter in her. Casey drove North. Late afternoon we came into San Francisco over the Bay Bridge and parked on Masonic Avenue just off Haight Street. I was far more excited than I wanted him to know, and surprised he had never been here. After high school he went to Lane College in Eugene Oregon, near the end of junior year met Marlon at a party, dropped-out and moved to the Queen Anne house, and lost his heart to a girl, who left him seven months ago for a guitar player. I had never fit-in anywhere easily, and was beyond thrilled to feel right at home with the Flower-Children in their bell-bottoms, colorful rags, beads and fringes, using the sidewalk as a community club-house, sitting cross-legged in small circles, some with backsides propped against the many store fronts, uncombed unguarded smiling faces, smoking dope, musicians drumming and strumming, saffron Hare Krishnas tinging their finger cymbals, a take what you need Free Store, $2.00 a night rooms above most of the shops. And dealers trading on the street, an illicit market backing this spirit-of-the-time, right out in the open. I was welcomed by a tall beautiful man, leaning against the jamb of the Psychedelic Shop, wearing faded jeans, llama fur coat and no shirt, offering me his carved soapstone chillum, a peace-pipe I happily received. The cone-shaped smoker held a lot of grass, I offered it to Casey, who refused with an angry wave of hand.

Crossing Ashbury he started his sermon "Are you stupid, the dope could be laced with something". And he was right, however the resonant selfish possession in his tone made me entirely certain he was jealous and controlling, and trying to make me feel guilty for relating to another Human Being. His Mom converted before the wedding at her Irish mother-in-law's insistence, and raised him Catholic. Casey had confessed to me feeling guilty all the time, even after confession. And he seemed to need the guilt, and need to fabricate it daily to feel God's eye on him, guilty was the holy drug, Casey was addicted, and the Church was his Pusherman. I was raised without the taint of Eve's supposed sin, felt guilt when doing some thing mean or hurt-full, something intentional, premeditated, not just for making a miss-take, or for breathing, or being born of a woman. I said nothing and mulled-over the thought of simply slipping away, when he steered me into a cramped silver-smith shop. I bought the small hand-carved marbled-green soapstone chillum calling me from a black velvet shelf in the display case. Casey a sterling ring with a peace symbol cut into it. Again on the sidewalk, he pressed me up-against the shop window, took my left hand and tried to slide the ring on the third finger, so intense he could only whisper "Marry me". I closed my hand, relief nearly bursting-out as laughter, not because this was funny, it was not. I managed to cough and clear my throat, he had shown him self in a way I had never seen, and still the question was too absurd for him to truly believe I would say yes. Compared to the others I'd known Casey was nearest a man, but I was not in-love and told him many times, in many ways. I had plumbed his depth, and the places I needed into, all their locks had rusted shut, this opening was a single exception, and not enough for me, there was little left for us but to keep using, and I would soon consume him and did not want to become a cannibal. I should have recognized this coming and left in Long Beach, was furious how witless I could be, furious because I felt the guilt, the signs were there before my eyes, if I hadn't been so distracted by what I wanted to do, where I wanted to go, my eyes burned a hole in the sidewalk as I slowly, firmly replied with all the tenderness I was feeling "No Casey, I'm not the one. You know I'll make you miserable. We're better-off friends". He stared down as well, our eyes meeting on a crumbled Blackjack gum wrapper, I could feel his hard-on soften against my hip-bone, he stepped back and exhaled a deep sigh "You're so wrong. We're way passed friends". He raised my chin gently, the ring still in hand, and surveyed my face with such sad eyes "Make me happy, say yes". Once more he was right, I shouldn't have slept with him, and I ached to hold him, comfort him and did not dare "No, it won't work. I'm sorry". And I was, having been selfish too, wanting to be in San Francisco, and still guilting, for once here all I wanted now was to rent a room and find a way to earn enough to stay. Casey insisted we leave for Mexico. Knowing he was manipulating my guilt, feeling like a real jerk, knowing I should not, I agreed to go as friends, and could see in hind-sight this had been planned, and somewhere in Mexico would have been our wedding.

We walked to the car in silence, the driver's door ajar, we had been robbed, everything. Casey leapt up onto the Fairlane's hood looking for the thief, while I stood in frozen disbelief, my hand-made poncho and clothes were gone, my sleeping bag, and Moroccan shoulder bag with all my make-up, gone, how could I brave the world without paint. I hadn't stepped-out bare-faced since junior high school, it was Golden Gospel, a girl, a good girl, a proper girl would not be seen in public without her face on, and I had swallowed this without question too young to know I could opt in or out. Thinking to check the trunk and finding it secure slowed the sinking, my wallet, my sewing and jewelry kits were safe inside, tools I hoped to use for a living. Casey's stuff was gone too, yet he seemed indifferent to our loss, there was no damage to his new ride, it was our fault leaving the doors open, he conveniently ignored the passenger and back doors still locked fast. Disaster can be interesting when it cuts both ways. I did not want to accept something so cold-hearted could exist in the New World, in the Promised Land of peace and love and co-operation, nonetheless it thawed the chilly stand-off between us by making someone else the enemy. Casey jumped down from the hood snarling "Probably junkies. God damn fucking junkies". I hoped this had changed his plans "So, let's go back to Long Beach". He shook his head "No way. We can get what we need at the Free Store, then head outa this shit hole for Ensenada". Still sinking, and now spinning, I needed to hang-on to him for a while and took his arm. Burning incense beckoned from the open door, shameless scented tentacles that lock onto your nose and float you into the Free Store, run by a group called the Diggers. Dazed, stunned, wondering was this how shock feels, thinking how high-pitched and far-away my voice seemed as I ranted the robbing to a girl, reaching at rational for some solid ground to land on, reasoning since my things were hand-mades, they should be easy to spot, maybe I could recover them. She smiled, her tone far too cynical and knowing for her years "Nothin's gona show up. Street people don' steal less they're strung-out. Yer stuff's gone". Casey gathered a regulation Navy pea coat with two missing buttons for me, a faded tan western-shirt with black snaps and red piping, worn through the knee bell-bottom jeans, near new Acme ruff-out cowboy boots, white sox, a Hawaiian muu muu for sleeping, and a brand-new sleeping bag. He took one for himself saying it was all he needed. And he rented a $2.00 room above the Haight Street Bakery, rolled our bags out on the hardwood floor. I folded the pea-coat under-head and went to sleep hungry, without words, our stand-off re-freezing.

The mouth-watering aroma of fresh bread roused me before dawn, from another dream of the ocean threatening to swallow me, I was running hard for safe ground, holding tight to a key in my hand, monster breakers crashing-in, grabbing at my feet, when the tide unexpectedly turned, and a final mighty wave left behind a gift, a battered old wooden treasure chest whole on the sand, 106 newly engraved on the lock, the gleaming rust-free lock, I opened my hand to look at the key. Casey woke too, in a hurry, rushing to compel things his way, he never mentioned showing me the coast road, and I went along, compelled. Traveling East on the Bay Bridge, we stopped for food at Denney's, where Highway 580 meets I-5. Freshening in the bathroom, I was far too grateful my long-lasting water-proof mascara and eyeliner had lived-up to their promise, I still had a face. Over waffles, hash browns and eggs, unspoken, we agreed to carry-on as if all was as it should be.

To fill the frosty silences we sang to the radio, ten hours, the border no longer just a line on the map, my first time in a country that wasn't mostly white, I would not be a snobby American Pig. Casey had been many times, and chose to pass-by Tijuana, saying I wouldn't like it, we'd go on to Ensenada, doing my thinking for me, which at this point made no difference. The Baja was sizzling brown earth swept in hot winds, cactus that seemed more whimsical sculpture than native plant-life, and the biggest blue sky and dazzling ocean white-caps I'd ever seen. The beauty simply overwhelmed our stand-off, we began talking and laughing, and arrived just after 8pm. This far South a rusty-orange and turquoise extravaganza still lit the sky. Casey parked infront of a small fonda at the end of the main street, a woman throwing tortillas in the open kitchen deftly tossing each on top of a brick oven to bake. Casey spoke fluent, and without asking me, ordered dark beer, tortillas, fire-roasted lobster tail, peppers and corn-on-the-cob, sliced alligator pears, wooden bowls of pinto beans and rice, and thick red sauce brewed from lobster nectar, crushed tomatoes, green onions, chilies, cilantro, garlic and lime. All six tables and ten stools filled, tortilla woman cooking, serving, we ate, lingering to give such a feast its due. The only milk-skin here, being Jewish I never felt my white deeper than surface, here I was whole milk, daunting whether paranoid or real, I thought maybe some of each.

Fading rust still held the horizon as we strolled the two blocks of baked-dirt street on raised wooden sidewalks, each shop a color-full bouquet of local wares, most quick-made for tourists, but some achingly elegant, all impossibly inexpensive. I found a hemp sack with sturdy handles, just right for the few things I had left, and a pin-tucked bleached-muslin wedding shirt. Casey insist on buying a shoulder bag for me, hand-woven in serape stripes, his taste superb, this was one of the achingly elegant, having it would soothe the shock of losing my Moroccan bag, if I had only seen it first. I bought him a fine-tooled brown leather belt with a hammered-silver buckle so there could be no strings. Assuming we would be leaving, driving to Long Beach, instead Casey arranged to sleep the night in the fonda owner's guest room, a five dollar deal. My head screamed as we followed Jesus home, God damn you Casey, I will not share a bed with you. The house was a boxy three-story concrete structure, painted sunshine yellow, with a flat roof and big windows, and when Jesus showed us upstairs, and I saw twin beds with crisp fresh sheets, I thanked the Sweet Sisters Fate for smiling on me.

The smell of late morning coffee and bacon woke me. Casey was up, steaming mug in hand, trying to hurry me. I took it and went to wash, care-fully preserving the mascara and eyeliner that remained, touching-up with a Maybelline dark brown eyebrow pencil laying by the sink, and then went down. Jesus other half Oola the tortilla woman giggled as I came in. Her teenage daughter sashaying round the kitchen in my pea-coat, impersonating, saw me, shoved the coat into Mom's hands and fled the room blushing to crimson, younger brother at her heels. Casey giggled with Oola, no language barrier in this, I giggled too. Still flush from dinner, I ate enough of her gorgeous food to be polite, scrambled duck eggs, thick crunchy bacon, fresh tortillas to wrap it in, bananas, and hot chocolate that tasted of cinnamon and vanilla. Oola packed the remains in a wax-paper-lined cardboard box and offered it to Casey. He thanked her. I left the pea-coat hanging over the back of my chair.

Casey no longer seemed so angry. As we neared Tijuana, I asked, please let me see it. Walking mainstreet we were besieged, four-year-old beautiful little girls begging for money with their eyes, out-stretched hands offering one candy-covered Chicklet in return. A mingle of leather goods and grilled meat from the open-air stands fought for my nose, blankets, baskets, jewelry, painted clay pottery on every peg and sill, good and garish the street was intoxicating, and I wanted to have a beer at one of the outdoor tables and be part of it. Casey made plain he was still punishing me for turning him down "No". Just north of town, families lived in outsized cardboard boxes and wooden packing crates on the dirt lip of the road. A simple line on the map and circumstances were so different, I would never again under-estimate my privilege growing-up in the Golden Ghet, or allow the image of people living in crates, the haunting eyes of little starvelings peddling gum, to fade from mind. And I waited, till the Fairlane turned onto Willow "Casey, I'm leaving in the morning". He didn't seem bothered, saying only "We'll meet again". Mom and Dad fast asleep, I went directly to the guest room.

Dad starting up the Mustang woke me. I showered-off the remnants of mascara and eye-liner three days stuck to my face, center parted my long wet hair, care-fully avoiding that naked face in the mirror, packed the hemp sack with all but the sleeping bag, and took them downstairs, to Mom, and her pearls and coffee. She was shaken by my leaving, asking had I broken-off the engagement, her head moving side-to-side, admonishing how perfect I was for her boy, I should think hard before such a decision. Ah, the grounds for making me instant family, Casey must have told them we were getting married, I burned with anger at him leaving me out of this in, felt duped, and so foolish I could not make eye contact, saying only her boy would explain. Mom and I sipped coffee in prickly silence, she offered no food, and when Casey did not come to the table, I thanked her for the hospitality, kissed her cheek, took my things, and was stopped cold at the front door, unable to step-out into the day-light. Dread, persecution, death, I withdrew to the guest bath, unplucked eyebrows, unmascared eyelashes, unlined lids, unblushed cheek-bones, no under-eye concealer, no lipstick, the world would see me as is. I braved a glance in the mirror, too terrible to be seen without her face on, she flashed me a chin-up grin and whispered "But this is who you are". And for some reason it was okay. We gathered our selves, once more meeting the door, sure the world would shrink in disgust, for I had not grown much from that perfect one who caught her eyes in the mirror just four months ago, all this self-indulgent self-disgust waiting transmutation was mostly unnamed, and needed names, so I could call on them. Clutching the sack handles for resolve, thinking how bizarre a toothbrush didn't matter so much as eyeliner, because cavities don't show, I decided to stop thinking, and stepped across the threshold into the day.

Blood heated my face, here I am world, exposed, unadulterated lashes, dark circles, and it struck me how insignificant this daring to show my real mug in public and live really was compared with the Vietnam war, civil rights, poverty, yet it was such a personal victory, and swept me shiny and bold to the Thrifty by Jack-in-the-Box, for toothbrush and paste, Blistex, Jergen lotion, brush and comb, and Jean Naté after-bath splash. Casey had followed me, sitting on the bench outside, arms resting along the back-board, he yawned as our eyes met, and smiled as if nothing was ever wrong "I'll drive you where ever you wana go". I shook my head no "I can't do that". Hurt bleeding through his casual, he demanded "Then tell me where you're going. You owe me that much". Satisfied his duplicity severed any strings, and worried he would keep after me, I lied "Some friends in Santa Cruz have a place for me, and I need to go alone". He threw me a tight-lipped smirk "You'll never make it alone. The road's too dangerous for a girl like you". Quickly tucking-away the acrimony, and smiling big he offered "I'm heading back to Seattle in a few days. If you need anything, ever, call me at the Queen Anne house and it's yours". I wanted to hug him good-bye, wanted to tell him how deceived I felt, that he was a fraud, and just said "Thank you". Walking away, I squeezed the sack handles tight, ready to prove a girl like me could make it alone.

Chapter Three

ONLY BAD GIRLS SWEAT

Riding the Greyhound to San Francisco, too excited to sleep and short on funds I stared into the night and worried how to keep my self. It was just light walking from 4th on Market Street and along Haight. I rented a small corner room up the back-stairs of the Cornucopia Bead Shop, it had a window and good light for sewing. After washing in the community bath that serve all the rooms, I unrolled my bag on the clean wooden floor and laid-down, brain spinning, Casey this, I should have that, what a foolish girl, was I conning my self, did I use him, lead him on, did I owe him, round and round and round. Morpheus could not summon through the din, I packed my shoulder bag with scissors, thimble, needles, a hoop, silk embroidery floss, the Free Store jeans that were too big, and went out to the street, I had an idea. The sun designating a warm spot on the sidewalk infront of City Lights Bookstore, I took a seat, cut the denim into five-by-six inch patches, and began stitching a fanciful butterfly perched on a peace symbol. People stopped, asking how much. Thinking two, three-dollars slid over my tongue, no one balked. Three would buy my room for the night, a sandwich and tea. Another and another sold before the first was finished, all offering extra to have theirs sewn on a torn-knee or worn-bottom.

Mostly street people inhabited the Haight, and tourists on sight-seeing buses coming to observe the Freaks. It felt just splendid sitting there, being part of this New Nation, this tribe looking-out for each other, Flower-Children smoking weed, dropping psychedelics, Hippies into harder drugs, all believing peace love and music would change the world, that we could make this a better place for everyone. Too soon I saw it was ideal but for one awful thing, and one awful person who seemed the only one to notice that guys ran it all, strutting round so entitled, behaving as if something was wrong with a girl like me who wasn't fucking at lease one of them, as if that was my job. Sadly this wasn't the elephant in the room to any one but me. Us girls were more props than contributing citizens, all the posters had us naked, none were of real women anyway, men's fantasy drawings, emphasis on the tits. And when I did not act accordingly, I was quickly chastized with that chilly fraternal high school mind-set attempting to control me by questioning my sexuality. It had not worked then and would not now. Even with the pill newly on the street, attending this free-love masquerade, I wasn't buying-in. Fucking did not equal sexual freedom for me, there were consequences, I saw them everywhere. For me to spread my legs there had to be someone there, someone I was into, and I was not in to into right now, the way guys wanted to own me, rule me, do my thinking, they seemed more like jailers. I was on my own for the first time in the big bad world, not too scared, supporting my self without compromise, hoping to build an ego that could endure the truth, though talk on the street was of killing it.

City Lights Bookstore was the center of the counter-culture here. I found a small paperback on Siddhartha Gautama, causing a look over my own life, and karma. And it wasn't so bad, every time I'd fallen, it had been against the hill instead of tumbling down and over the cliff, giving me some faith in my self, that even if bruised, I would live through what ever came. Next, a study on black holes, something impossible to see, predicted in 1916 by Einstein. I was fascinated how light-energy was sucked in toward the gravitational center of a collapsing star, and just at the threshold, called the event horizon, where light begins to be pulled in faster than it can escape, there is still a chance to step back. But, once the invisible threshold is crossed, there is no escape, no choice but to take the ride no matter the consequence. This seemed a perfect metaphor for my own life, learning when, how to step back and think. And in the time it takes for a shooting star to flash, my mind opened enough to grasp a oneness with the universe, a sameness in things as different as a black hole and me. Maybe the similarity was a god I could believe in, something innate, the same kind of underlying structure that lets the birdie know how to peck its way out of the egg. Maybe I could learn to recognize the event horizons of my own personal black holes before I had no choice but to take the ride and the consequences. Maybe I could learn to see the threshold, for each new one had fooled me so far with a seemingly different face. Circumstance has an amazing wealth of disguise and deception, maybe I could grasp the pattern beneath, maybe it was noise and not sight, maybe the sucking at the threshold, the feeling of my insides rushing-out of me, maybe the vast sound. I needed more experience to recognize the sameness, more adventure to go along with my seemingly reliable karma, more than an adolescent ego, more than a self-centered I want to save my self the awful price I saw so many paying.

Most days were lived on nut-butter sandwiches fruit and tea while sewing. I was never without work, and my sunny spot became a hang-out for on-going discussions on Vietnam, the anti-war movement, Che Guevara's execution in Bolivia, Stokley Carmichael, the Student Nonviolent Coordinating Committee, Star Trek, astrology, how to kill your ego, and what the lyrics of Sergeant Peppers Lonely Heart Club Band really meant. No one but me considered their ego a vital necessary psychic body, none were comfortable talking about the reality of God, no one thought women's rights were civil rights, I was still having most of my conversations alone. Haight cops turned a blind-eye to nearly all street business, acid was common as aspirin, weed smoked like cigarettes, plenty of cheap homegrown available. When a dealer came through, I swapped a patch for some fancy smoke, Ganga pollen, a staggering high, too high, this expensive stuff was way too potent for me. I was not a connoisseur, preferred to pack my chillum with homespun, a lovely mellow trip, the kind that let me connect. While so many others sought the big wallop, wanting to get wiped-out, trip solo, I wondered what they were so keen on wiping-out. The Haight was filled with live music that defined the street the shops and Golden Gate Park, though most players covered tunes off the radio or albums, there were inspired jams. Jerry Garcia and Janis Joplin were said to live near-by, I never saw any knowns except on stage, though one evening royal ravens Margot Fonteyn and Rudolf Nureyev fluttered by. I liked musicians, from afar. Some were pioneers with something to say, most were wana-bees, minor talents who thought music would get them over. Some bizarre equation was at work, the less the musical gift - the more fragile the ego, the more arrogance as disguise - the more a wana-bee believed he was God's gift to women, aiming at attracting some chick to fuck him, worship him, work for mere money to take care of him, give-up her life while he devotes his inadequate talent to art and groupies on the side. I believed music like any art was a way to live-up to your self, and if you got the opportunity to do it, and to get good, it was a privilege that did not require conceit.

The Tribes gathered at Golden Gate Park to welcome in 1967, and Owsley himself brewed a batch of LSD called white lightning just for the occasion. I joined the congregation, and only after much observation, determined the acid was sound and dropped a hit. Since it was usually cut with extenders like speed, talcum powder, heroin, even strychnine, I had not taken much here. Sandoz, Owsley or window-pane made by a friend or friend's-friend the only assurance of safe return, I would not chance my head on made-for-profit street shit. Casey's warning about drugs from strangers stubbornly in-mind, I had promised my self no matter how much I wanted to join-in, I would only take acid that had already been taken by fools, who made it back home. Too many good people were too trusting, and once sucked over the bad-acid event horizon, on a rocket-ship-ride beyond forth-dimensional reality, they sometimes never found their way back, unable to re-adjust to three-D. Some were taken by their folks, some institutionalized, needing to be fed, bathed, wiped, dressed. This was so clear I could not understand why others would chance it, Gabriel was right, acid was a spiritual journey, not frivolous entertainment or distraction. I tasted the tin-foil and melted into the sea of thousands, Allen Ginsberg the dancing Shiva, Timothy Leary trailed by devoted little duckling, I could not stop staring at his clean-shaven face, not one hair mussed, so deliberate, so out-of-place in this plumed flock, our flags flying, god's eyes floating, bodies in tribal rhythm, drums, babies, Hell's Angels, and Gracie Slick's voice soaring over it all. The celebration continued for weeks in the Avalon Ballroom, the Fillmore Auditorium, one dollar entrance fee to be part of the scene, part of the meaning.

On a smooth day I could finish five patches with customers waiting, abundant opportunity to get good, earning more than a Playboy Bunny or Boeing-job-with-a-future, without sacrificing self-respect, without panhandling. The Helix, Seattle's original underground paper made it South, hometown news gave me perspective on how forward it was here, the first place in my life where I felt complex, cultured, knowing my way in this remarkable city. I mostly roamed the Panhandle, Lincoln Park, and Golden Gate, where I met Mona Lisa at the DeYoung Museum, spent hours mesmerized by the perpetual motion display, and felt compelled to keep the family of Crocodiles company. Reading the Egyptian Book of the Dead, their pantheon of Gods, I would smoke a bowl, and go lean across the railing round the great lizard prison, trying to catch an eye, to connect. I knew these ancient creatures carried something unchanged, knew they knew something I needed to know. Lightning speed when provoked or feeding, otherwise stone, seeming sculpture, one finally fixed an eye on mine, Sobek incarnate, turning me stone sculpture, frozen in his cold stare, incarcerated by the likes of me, this fearsome Crocodile God who carried the body of Osiris to shore so Isis could raise her brother from the dead, 2,400 years before the Christian myth. According to the Jews right now was the year 5,727. And still to nearly every one I knew it was 1967, time counting only since Jesus.

Coming from Seattle, Eucalyptus was the exotic whiff in Halls throat lozenges. When ever walking I'd fill my pockets with the fragrant seed pods, treasure locals did not value, free all over the ground. Accumulating a heap, I bought copper-wire, crystals and jade-stone beads, and opened my jewelry kit. Each try at nailing a hole shattered the pod. I was frustrated, till brewing a few in hot tea for flavor, the taste akin to gasoline, the consequence, they softened enough to pierce. I had a wealth of natural bell-shaped beads in days, their pretty little star-faces, rugged jackets and coffee color suited the copper wire. I'd thread it through the hole, twice to form loops, twist spirals, pounding some flat, add crystals and beads, leather tassels. Twenty-four pieces, primitive, aromatic, elaborate tribal breast-plates, regal headbands, earrings fan-dancing the shoulder, I worked each till it spoke to me, till it said when. Then as if preparing for initiation, I bathed and dressed, and took them to the street. Every one sold before noon, to women and men, hailing me avant-garde, artist, I thrilled to the proclamation. Much as I loved Gabriel's profound, artist tickled me more, I had never been named for what I do only what I look like and how I acted. For me, ordinary life had always been thinking some thing up, some times a vivid picture in mind, and gathering the necessaries I would begin. And perhaps this made an artist of a dreamer, doing more than thinking, pushing passed the abstraction, having the dogged determination to finish, and then braving public verdict.

Four days I hole-up in my room, totally possessed, 30 pieces this round, each seemed to build itself, to have momentum, more intricate, ornate, related, one birthing the next till inspiration spent me and I slept. When I took them to the street, a predatory hawk-woman sat down next to me, too well-dressed, too metropolitan to sit on the sidewalk, her perfect skined pointy-face too close to mine when she spoke, a buyer for Bullocks, would I be interested in making jewelry for her. I knew of the place, and from her looks did not want to "Why do I need Bullocks to sell my stuff". Her perfume gave me an instant headache, her laugh a cynical bay, she leaned away as if far-sighted, needing to see her prey "Why money of course my dear". The bid made me queasy, made me want to shower in whiskey and disappear into my sleeping bag. She leaned-in to close the deal, this was my lucky break, my big opportunity, I was in the right place at the right time, sounding just like Mr. Bigger offering to make me a pair of tits. I knew I never wanted to be sickened by what I did with my years, have people like this own my time, become part of my day. And I had some sight into the artist business, seeing ideas burst here on the street, burn hot, fashion, dance, music, attracting attention, the hand-to-mouth quarry were prowled, flattered, seduced on the cheap, swallowed whole by the juggernaut, and now I burned bright, now I was the burst. Happily, fortunately I did not need money, letting my chin lead, looking down my nose, wishing it was longer, sharper, voice rich in Golden disdain, I announced "Flower-Children don't shop Bullocks". Still she insisted on buying my wares. I wanted to take them and run, needing to lie down, and yet it felt too rude, I would get rid of her being too costly "Fifty dollars each. And you buy them all". She did not hesitate scribbling a check. I tried to wriggle-out demanding cash. Smiling, so charming I knew I was finished, she tore the check in-two, dropped the pieces in her Gucci bag, pinched fifteen crisp one-hundred dollar bills that did not diminish her wad, laid them in my lap, seized her spoils and evaporated into a waiting cab. I sat, stilled by so much money, people with good jobs made $8,000 a year, stunned having been sucked over the event horizon without realizing I stood at the threshold. Being polite could be deadly.

Eight months in the Haight when Bullocks ran a Here Comes Summer display in the San Francisco Chronicle featuring my designs, faithful copies. Mainly I stayed in the neighborhood, venturing to the Monterey Pop Festival where Jimi Hendrix electrified us, then drenched his guitar in lighter fluid and struck a match, to Jim Morrison at the Whiskey-A-Go-Go, Moby Grape at Winterland, Mamas and Papas the Family Dog, and the vaulting ceiling, high stage and brass railings of the Fillmore for Janis and Big Brother. I rode the cable car to the Wharf, sipped espresso at Enrico's Sidewalk Café and never saw a single star. Peeped in the Condor Club, curious to see the lauded topless dancer Carol Doda lowered from the ceiling on a grand piano dancing the Watusi, her bouncing bare tits the biggest, I could never have imagined these notorious twin 44's, adamant, bulging bouncing silicone bowling balls on her petite frame, and the giant provocative likeness of her outside, reclining, body outlined in neon, nipples blinking red lights. I was heart-sick for anyone so publicly stripped of their dignity, in doing this to her somehow they had done it to me too, tits a public commodity, and not even real ones but some grotesque male fantasy, the more unnatural the better, bought and sold for a drink at the bar. And I could not understand why women co-operate. Big Al's next door was no less degrading, Al him-self conducting the topless spectacle in his fancy blue silk suit, red silk stuffed in the handkerchief-pocket, and fancy cigar stinking-up the place, covering a worse stink, parading the girls round, promising live bottomless coming soon, meat for the hounds, and they could smell it for miles. And, I walked the Golden Gate Bridge, and went to the southern edge of Chinatown, curiously afraid to go-in, and often sat in Golden Gate Park listening to the latest reigning guru, and except for my books, no one lit my imagination, no teacher appeared, more likely this student wasn't ready. I was bored and decided to take my savings, my two-thousand-three-hundred-and-fourteen dollars and fly to Texas, if Jeffree and Bonita-Kay would have me. She was delighted to hear from her good-luck charm, my welcome still fresh, I bought a ticket to Dallas on United Airlines, and called back with flight number and arrival time. Jeffree would find me infront of baggage.

I'd been allowed to make my way with some self-respect in the Haight, and the mythical quality of this City drew enough Hippies and Flow-er-Children to provide cover, I was not the only Freak. And I might never come here again. For me, living had to be more, I needed teachers, not the kind you dedicate your life to, and give your money, like gurus some were following, but some one who knew some thing I had not already thought, some one I could talk to out-loud about the things I had, things no one here wanted to. I bought a used suitcase with a sturdy lock and key, and packed a now $4.00 a night room, surveying life in my belong-ings. Carl Jung's biography Memories Dreams and Reflections among the paperbacks, more jewelry and sewing tools, the shoulder bag that kept Casey near, a new purple mini-dress from the head-shop on Geary Street, that I wore with Navy surplus cotton bell-bottoms I'd embroidered up the right leg with vines flowers butterflies peace and yin-yang symbols. Sew-ing every day had fostered my hand, my work had grown more delicate, complex, distinctive. Four day, strolling Golden Gate Park, farewelling the crocodiles, sea-gulls, and my friends, most known only by their street names. As the taxi pulled from the curb, I saw a young man leaving the

Cornucopia wearing my blanket-wool poncho lined in antique kimono silk.

Not having thought-it-out well, tools and books too heavy, I lugged the load through the airport, anticipating my first physical ride into the air with fickle confidence. The United ticket agent advised my flight would board in 40 minutes. I stashed five-bucks and change in my jeans, stowed all else in the suitcase, secured the lock and checked into baggage, then walked to the gate, somehow taller, more worldly among the ranks of the flying. My seat was over the wing, I had not thought to choose where, couldn't see much, and the engines began to whine, then scream like monster dentist drills, I had never been so near the authority of a machine that could shred me, the sheer might, I stiffened waiting to rush into the troposphere wrapped in a roaring metal tube, strangers at the control, and I did not understand the physics, how could this massive thunderbird climb into the sky and remain. I began to hum and breathe, filling my mind with something else, reasoning the pilot wasn't any more eager to die today than me, elbows locked stiff, hands white-knuckling the ends of the arm-rest, faster, faster, forcing me back into the seat, I was certain tail-feathers would drag, ignite the fuel, I closed my eyes, humming louder, a wanting distraction. Upon leveling, the stewardess took pity and offered me a cocktail. At nineteen my head delighted being served, while my stomach begged for club soda. The stew obliged. I gulped it, cracking the clear plastic glass in my grip, every muscle strung tight, my total concentration was absolutely necessary for this bird to remain afloat.

Landing, how could behemoth fly this slow and not drop like a gun-shot goose. Again I closed my eyes, shutting-off some stimulus, teeth throbbing from one long grit, my feet pushing into the floor to help brake, and the back wheels made the ground, and the front, and we slowed enough, and I filled my lungs with a whole breath. Gravity no more the enemy, soles kissing solid ground with each foot-fall, I wended the airport, my arrival earlier than anticipated, I would pass time in the café with a jelly doughnut and tea, charmed by the waiter's Southern drawl. Looking for United baggage claim, I noted William P.Hobby Airport Houston Texas printed on a porter's badge, I wasn't early, I wasn't at Love Field, I was not in Dallas, panic grabbed hold, the floor seemed to stick to my feet as I sought United's ticket counter, and another sugary drawl, the second half of my flight had departed fifteen minutes now, there were no others till nine in the AM. Dismissed and dizzy, I sank into the nearest row of chairs, nothing familiar to reference, every one seemed unfriendly, staring, I could not think but to call home. Mom accepted the charges, and initially content with her Little Girl's voice, on hearing my situation she lost it, oh-my-god, oh-god, oh-my-god, and then as always turning authoritarian, insisting I go to the YMCA, or better, Dad was a Mason, I should go directly to the nearest Masonic Lodge, explain my father is a 33rd degree Mason and they would help me with whatever I need. I so regretted calling, Mom managed to make this about her being the one in trouble, needing my soothing. And I accommodated, automatically, using a soft calm consoling voice, tender, pledging to go directly to the Masonic Lodge, assuring I would be picked-up in the morning, begging please don't worry, and on pretext of getting going, left her with I love you and hung-up.

No way would I tuck my tail to the Lodge, or Young Men's Christian Association, by default Mom had done the right thing, calming her had restored my wits, transforming lost and forlorn into delicious challenge. My mind lit-up, Jeffree was heading for baggage, his phone number was in my shoulder bag in the suitcase, I used the near pay phone and called Dallas information, he was unlisted, I asked for Love Field, for United, and pleaded my case to the agent who answered, please have Jeffree Johnson paged, I will call again in thirty minutes, she gave me the number at her station, maybe I would get lucky. Watching the clock, I called, no one had answered the page, so I left a message, I am at the Houston Airport, don't have your phone number, will call this number again in a half hour. The agent promised to keep paging. Sitting close by the phone, the only Flower-Child in the Houston Airport, fending-off suspicious, scrutinizing, sly glancing eyes, my knees tucked-up tight in my arms, waiting, when a heavenly man with brilliant long brown hair simply materialized asking "May I sit". He felt familiar, comfortable, as if we knew one-another, and he and no drawl, I flushed warm and nodded yes. Following traditional introductions, Joshua Strange invited me sailing for a week in the Gulf of Mexico with his family. I was taken completely by surprise, searching his glittering deep-blue eyes for a clue, finding an open gentle soul, my circumstance tumbled-out. Josh suggested I return to the ticket counter and see if mine could be transferred to another airline. The agent checked, no flights till 9AM, she offered a voucher good for ten days. I asked after my suitcase. She explained it surely went on to Dallas, would remain there three weeks, then be sent to storage. I took the voucher. Josh whispered "Fate will have its way" as we walked to where we met, and sat quietly, content, people watching. When he leaned near to ask "Have you waited long enough". I caught my breath, flew to the phone, dropping coins on the way, connected to the same agent, no one had answered my page. Feeling I stood in mid-air and dared not flinch or would fall to my death, I asked her please keep paging, she promised, and I left a new message, Jeffree I need your phone number, please leave it with the agent. Josh gave me his hand "Let's go home. I live with my Mom, her husband and my little sister Sean". I had to know "Why were you here." He smiled "I was looking for you". Taking his hand, he led me out of the William P. Hobby Airport.

Suffocating humidity swallowed us on leaving the terminal. I'd never known such mean heat, could only imagine what day-after-day did to the inmates, and as we sped the freeway, I could see it had driven them mad "How come everyone has their windows rolled-up". Josh chuckled "Air-conditioning. You have to keep the windows closed to stay cool". His jeep didn't have it, every window open including the back, the roasting air rushing through, I asked again "Why were you at the airport". His face turned-up in a wide closed-mouth grin "Never been out of Texas. The airport's a great place to see folks from all over. I go and watch. You know, dreaming of adventure". I did know. Just North of Rice University, on Autry Street we coasted under the automatic garage door into his well-fixed three-bedroom family home, into instant air-conditioned relief, like some relentless ear-splitting siren suddenly stopped screaming at me, cooling in the South even in the Fall as indispensable as warming a Northern winter. Josh took me up to a grand bright living room, where he formally introduced Shoshannah Leibofsky to Ben and Marigold Hill, absolutely gorgeous human beings, who did not seem at all ruffled by my unexpected arrival. Marigold patted a place beside her on the raw silk sofa. All the furniture was white Victorian, I obeyed like a good girl. She had no drawl "You see, Ben and I have been together five years now. We decided to marry last May Day. Strange is Sean and Joshua's father's name. You see, I was

Margo Strange for 20 years. Just think what a mighty influence your name has on you. So you see when Ben and I wed, I changed my first name too". She smiled golden sunshine at Ben "Marigold Hill suits me don't you think". I had never considered how a name might shape its holder, and yes Marigold Hill was miles from Margo Strange. She stood and headed for the kitchen "Now just make your self at home sweet-pie, dinner's almost ready". Sean who had been near invisible, followed. Ben leaned back in his white armchair with the Houston Post. For once indebted to my Golden roots, I felt comfortable and uncomfortably at their mercy, this family of stunningly beautiful laid-back rich Flower-Children. Josh suggested I phone the airport once more. No one had answered the page.

Sean appeared in the yawning archway to the dining-room, summoning us to dinner. Ben and Josh took their places at the heads of the table. I sat with them quietly, as Marigold and Sean brought bowls of steaming miso soup with chopped scallions and mushroom filled dumplings to this table, as big as President Johnson's new Lincoln stretch-limousine, dressed in linen, Tiffany silver and Limoges china. As we waited, Ben admired the embroidery on my jeans and guessed I won a living with thimble and thread. I gave the short version of work on the Haight, adding Boeing-Front-Desk-Girl for relative perspective. He suggested I may still be eligible for unemployment. Josh offered to take me in the morning if I wanted, while he picked-up supplies for their maiden voyage on the Great Water. Marigold and Sean set the final bowls, brown rice, crisp snow-peas mixed with roasted pine nuts, steamed red chard and cilantro drizzled in walnut oil and lemon juice, napkins were spread on laps, we began the feast. Josh explained, each food has a Macrobiotic designation of one two or three yang or yin, and when combined in the ratio of one yin to three yang, is a means of nourishing in yin-yang harmony, enhancing ones mind/body balance, quickening the road to enlightenment. My little ears perked, Josh was right, Fate will have its way, if only by the looks of this sublime family I knew they knew something I needed to know. For me, life had to become more than an ego's design of what I wanted and who I thought I was. Along with karma and will, something inside and out of my conscious control also decided for me, whispering judicious words in mind's ear. I never thought of food as an instrument of enlightenment, but maybe Macrobiotics could hasten the way, I was willing to try.

For three years the Strange-Hills had lovingly built a 40-foot trimaran sailboat and were eager to cross the Atlantic for Rishikesh India, to study Transcendental Meditation with the Maharishi Mahesh Yogi at his Ashram on the Ganges. A test run was planned. I knew this was not my route, perhaps it was theirs, and in the going, the Sweet Sisters Fate would take them somewhere as unexpected as they had taken me today. Marigold and Ben met at Rice University studying Anthropology. She on scholarship, eight years his senior, Mother Demeter incarnate, and a flute player. Now 32, Ben played the tabla, and had inherited the family fortune, an only child of a Texas oil baron whose corporate jet went down off Key West ten years past, Mother and Pop were never found. Newly teenage with all the attending hormones, Sean looked like Ali McGraw, and played violin. And Joshua was 20, graduated Rice in three years with a Bachelors in Music, and played the 12-string. The main thing though, they simply glowed with health, thick shiny hair, flawless skin, compelling charisma, level clear eyes radiating a palpable serenity, the very air a fragrant lily, I filled my lungs and announced intentions to become Macrobiotic. Sean began to clear the table and we moved into the living room. Ben invited me to pick an instrument from the many gilding the room, and join their evening jam. I begged-off that I only played the sewing machine. Josh placed a beautiful beaded Shekere at my feet and a book by Georges Ohsawa, the person who brought Zen Macrobiotics from Japan to America. I curled into the white winged chair, as they engaged their instruments. A fusion of classical-jazz-blues-country-rock-and-roll, a winding seamless ride over mountains and hills and down long smooth valleys, Josh called it playing the day. He was a gifted music man, without the fragile ego and disdain for girls I'd seen in lesser talents, I was embarrassingly drawn. Bedtime, Josh gave me his room and slept on the couch, a spare clean room, single bed sweet in his scent.

Morning Thunder tea, fresh-baked sour dough whole-wheat bread, almond butter, honey, apples and strawberries. After, Josh and I left air-conditioning for the unemployment office and to gather supplies for tomorrow's departure. I was surprised still being eligible for a claim on Boeing benefits and took the papers with. We drove through Houston, by the

Reliant Astrodome, world's first domed sports stadium, nicknamed the 8th wonder, even this early the humidity and heat were relentless. I was born between brothers, raised to be a good little girl who kept her nose clean and knees together, still I loved playing hard, till summer of 6th grade when I bitterly left the field to the boys. I was in my usual wide receiver position, our neighborhood-kids Saturday football game on the elementary school play-ground. At eleven years my bosom had blossomed beyond doubt, and one of the fathers who often came to watch just had to shame me scarlet, shouting I was asking for trouble, that I was far too developed to still be playing with the boys. It seemed this was on his mind and no one else till he made the game about sex, made my tits public spectacle, everyone knew he was a creep, no one challenge him, no one stood by me. Golden Rules, good girls don't play hard, good girls don't sweat, and good girls can not wear muscles that show. Having witnessed this cost to a friend, she was junior AAUW champion butterfly swimmer in the eleven/twelve age-group, and this build her arms and shoulders, and made the boys go rabid, biting at her sexuality, scaring us girls who were active into silence, fearing we were next. No one stood by her including me, I would not find courage for three long years to confront these fetters. And she, wore sleeves even in summer, and by high school no longer swam competition. I was a back-stroker, care-full not to over-build myself, and still I excelled, swam into high school for the Mercerwood Shore Club, regularly winning. The Club's charter did not allow Blacks or Jews to join, so I swam exhibition and the team could not count my winnings, with them they would have taken championships. I did not sweat swimming, and ever after my public shaming, never again did with any poise. The unmistakable implication back of the Rule, only bad girls sweat, any trace of perspiration, any hint of odor and you were a vulgar girl, an ugly girl, a bad girl, how could that be when we were made of sugar and spice and everything nice, and this was burned in my brain. Slowly I'd begun to understand vulgar and ugly were code words to keep me down, that daring to embrace them was a breaking loose. And I was grateful for my freedoms, high heels, girdles, make-up, the typing pool, and yet no amount of idealistic reasoning could exorcise my immediate humid agony. I was slick with sweat, hair stuck to my face and neck, blouse soaked where it touched my body, jeans strangling my thighs, I felt ugly and vulgar and bad infront of this divine man, and his cool composure only magnified the misery. Reading me Josh smiled, he was taking me back home, promising when Macrobiotic for a while my body would be more in-tune with the climate. And he kept me distracted, laughing, talking till we came to a stop inside the ice-box garage, and kissed, just a light brush of lips that made every cell in my body stand attention. A broad grin lit his whole face "How many colors embroidery floss do you want". Avoiding eyes for fear mine would give too much away, I hopped from the jeep and cleared my throat "Twenty-five". He laughed, backed-up the driveway, gunned his engine and roared away.

Too excited to be seen, I stood in the dark till wet clothes made goose-flesh, then slipped into Josh's room, struggled them off and stood under a cool shower. Marigold knocked before coming in, and laid a lovely sun-dress on the bed, saying she had so many it would ease some of her aristocratic guilt if I accepted, leaving me no choice by taking my clothes away to wash. I pulled the carnelian and cobalt Egyptian-cotton batik over my head, it's shirred spaghetti-strap bodice nearly unfolded entirely across my blossoms, full-skirt ruffled at the hem grace-fully brushing mid-calf, something I might have made my self should I stay long enough for genuine Southern-belling to inspire me. I swung and swayed the slow moving skirt to Sean and Marigold's genial appreciation, and proffered help mustering tomorrows gear. Marigold gave Sean a darting look, and smiled at me "No thank you sweet-pie, it's not necessary, you don't know where anything is". Politely telling me stay out of it, I was not offended, for I had landed on her from nowhere, and she seemed a bit stung by jealousy, by sudden loss, no longer leading lady in her son's world. I thought any mom should feel this way about her beloved boy's affection, something the good ones can get passed, so I would respect the position she needed from me, till she regained her equilibrium, till she could determine was I moth or sustenance to her son's flame. Retreating to the living room I settled into a white winged chair with Georges Ohsawa. And day-dreaming heard her beloved boy delivering the whole grains and beans, the oils, fruits, vegetables, bottled water to Mother Marigold. Then he sank down on the floor at my feet, cross-legged, facing me, smiling, showing me color by color the embroidery floss, reading from the Houston Post how last night police were directed by Governor Ronald Reagan to come down hard on the Haight, hundreds had been arrested for drugs, shops were closed. I watched Joshua's intelligent face as he read, my body shrinking in the loss, then a rushing filling thrill, the some thing that so quietly whispered in my ear, maybe it was intuition, maybe I was hearing voices, maybe my imagination, it did not matter, I had listened to it, heard, and instead of letting it drift away or be uncertain, I moved to it, knowing when to go and where to go, I could trust my self, and this was the most wonder-full of knowing. Josh set the Beatles Revolver on the hi-fi, took the matching winged chair across the room, and we looked each other over in appreciation, till the space between us disappeared and desire lowered our eyes, silently agreeing to close them and listen to Tomorrow Never Knows. The album clicked-off and he sighed "I'm gona miss my records on the water". I nodded yes "Music's been my best friend. The place I go for comfort. Government lies, teachers lie, preachers, parents, friends lie, lovers lie. Dylan and John Lennon don't". The afternoon was spent preparing, and Josh and I keeping to opposite sides of the room, ardor needing space, needing some disguise, it was so embarrassing having others in on it. There was some talk of the ravaged Gulf Coast and hurricane Beulah over dinner sandwiches. We were all bedded by nine, Josh on the white Victorian couch, me in his soft scented sheets, I lay there imagining sailing far from land, hoping my swallowed-by-the-ocean dreams were just dreams.

Five AM clocks rang in another already too hot day. Ben and Josh let me help pack the air-conditioned Mercedes station wagon, while Marigold and Sean made steamed oatmeal with dates apricots walnuts and molasses, and Morning Thunder tea. My body really liked this food, how clean it burned, how easily digested, I looked forward to the coming close-quarters allowing me to watch Marigold cook. At the limo-table she advised me to look through the library, there would be plenty of time for read, suggesting the Tao Teh Ching as a good place to begin, explaining Tao was the unifying principle in the universe, the great uncarved block, the idea that everything is one, a common thread through Hinduism, Buddhism, Confucianism. And as companion to the Tao, I should take the Bhaga-vad-Gita, calling it the beautiful poem of Hinduism, Krishna's instruction on the many things and events around a person which are all made out of the same stuff, all manifestations of the same reality. I understood being part of everything from my LSD trips, from Gabriel's explanation of Quantum Physics, even Sobeck the Alligator God, and took Georges Ohsawa's book and the I Ching too. A few days with the Strange/Hills and I'd learn more than my time on the Haight. As we ate, Ben mused that Macrobiotics was another manifestation of Tao. I listened quietly, content being student, when a shadow darkened my mind, maybe I was in a swoon and these people were some mind-sucking cult. The way I met Joshua, like he was cruising for myrmidon, the disciplined way they eat, the books in their library, how unearthly beautiful they are, and we were leaving on such an isolating trip. Wasn't I searching desperately for something to believe in, just the kind of vulnerable soul easily snatched-up by a cult. And yet as I listened inside, for even a faint warning signal, my alarm bells were silent, I let the paranoia fade into another cup of Thunder. Ben and Marigold were discreet in watching Joshua and I do the stay-away-from-each-other waltz, Sean not so much, and I was nearly always a-blush.

Windows rolled-up tight, five hours, 225 miles, Ben drove us to Corpus Christi, Marigold snugged-in next to him, Sean in the mid seat, Josh and I aft, enjoying the cool ride, brushing knees, Ben and Marigold's eyes on us in the rear view mirror. Where it was not in ruins from Beulah, Corpus Christi oozed a slow-moving Southern romance, old money scenting the air, Ocean Drive's landmark mansions, their leaded windows wide-eyed virgins keeping watch on the Gulf's sugar sand coastline, more sedate than Washington or California, if San Francisco was the King of laid-back, Corpus Christi was the King's charming Father. Moored in Oso Bay, when I saw the trimaran, a new admiration for these four gentle souls washed over me, having built so spare and grace-full a craft, teak decks, sails trimmed in turquoise, and no name. Marigold thought a boat need not be named her, or for that matter hurricanes even though they start with hur. She believed if Earth was designated female, and God male, female could not be God, and God could not be female, and for her this was not possible. I welcomed Marigold's perspective. By some biblical mode of thinking I had been made to feel responsible for hurricanes because they were hurs, and for the innate character of Mother Earth, of Eve, and I was happy to shed this skin. Russell and Kiki met us at the dock, they'd build a trimaran like No Name, planned on sailing to India with the Strange/Hills, took it for a final test-run, were caught in the sudden turn of Beulah, lost their mast and most rigging, spent eleven hours in the cabin tossed and bruised. Russell still wanted to sail, believing their vessel, believing they had survived the test, endured the worst and lived. Kiki refused to ever set foot on the water again, he had not repaired the boat, they would fly to India. This talk freaked me out as we unloaded the station wagon, which Russell would take to their near by home. And yet the moment I stepped aboard, No Name was so steady my trepidations hushed. Josh proudly explained it didn't lean much due to the three hulls, and could sail near thirteen degrees off straight into the wind.

We motored through Corpus Christi Bay and Port Aransas, sails unfurling in the gentle wind of the turquoise Gulf. Release from devil-heat quelled a growing nervous frenzy on leaving land behind, on being so small. Ben and Josh tended the maps charts and rigging. Marigold and Sean tended them. I was profoundly disappointed in this old-fashioned arrangement, still here I was, and undertook being one of the Girls. Then an ill-considered mention of these boy-jobs girl-jobs had Marigold set a brittle perimeter, I had stepped on sacred ground, they did what each did best, things worked that way, that was that, no questioning. Sean kept eyes on her tennis shoes. Ben and Joshua had the fun jobs, the big decision jobs, like the paradox of Haight's New Nation, tradition and male domination ruled even in these beauty-full people, and was enforced by Marigold. But then being Macrobiotic was a lot of work, everything made from scratch, and Marigold was devoted, toasting whole grains in dry cast iron pans, grinding them course or fine depending if flour or cereal. Yeast being too yin in hot weather, she employed a sour dough starter, which must be kept warm and fed fresh flour every twelve hours or it would starve to death. And she made pancakes and bread with such care, I recognized feeding was her way of loving her family, that humans like all creatures must eat, most of us often. And it wasn't just cooking, but the gathering, preparation, and thought time, the creativity, this constant work made her essential, valuable, powerful. My Mom was the same, they were both trying with best intentions to pass-on, to prepare their daughters for the authority given women. From Sean's ungebluzen face, I could see she did not have the taste for girl-jobs and was becoming a predicament for Mom. Rumblings of a Women's Movement in America had my attention. The newly founded National Organization for Women, named by Betty Friedan, was demanding equal access and pay in the work place be given to women and minorities just the same as it was to white men, and they were pushing for something called the Equal Rights Amendment. I saw little of it in real life, in the newspapers, on TV, but here it was in the tension between Sean and Marigold. I had wanted things to be more fair since the stings of Mom and Dad giving my Brothers more liberty and trust growing-up than me. The Boys could do and try as they please, succeed and fail on their own, while I required supervision, help. And when old enough to become a problem, was told it's for my own good, for protection, after all I was a girl. This was suppose to satisfy my outrage. No, it bred fierce defiance and anger. I knew I was smarter than my Brothers, deserved more autonomy not less, and the implication by those I trusted that there was something intrinsically wrong with being a girl, and this meant fewer rights, bewildered me. In life so far, no one had spoken to me of Women's Equality, I wondered where the Women Libbers were, wanted bad to meet one, talk to some one who thought liberation was more than free love, more than spreading legs, maybe getting pregnant, and wished desperately for Marigold to be that some one. But I consciously held my tongue, and proffered help in the galley. And was told indirectly, it was her body language, becoming so big for a small woman, there is no room for three in the galley.

Fear and thrill so similar, I was sure now this persistent inner frenzy was thrill, all landmarks gone, the endless Gulf water, perspective changes, I dissolved into nature, embracing my tiny insignificance. We did not fish, did not eat animals, nothing but sunrise and sunset, so breath-takingly overwhelming they were worth waiting all day and all night. I spent my time embroidering everyone's clothes, and reading reading, the Tao so deceptively simple on first glance, the same one or two page story in slightly different form, over and over. Josh encouraged me to think of it as a poetic mantra, to plumb its depth by reading again and maybe again before passing judgment. Already understanding this process from my own writing, the third time through usually lead me near or to the heart of what I was trying to say. So I took his advice, and the Tao revealed its complex simplicity, taking me deeper as each chapter folded back onto the previous and crossed-over itself, opening my mind to infinity of possibility. The grand breath of the Gulf mirroring this, sameness, Tao manifest in nature, inside and outside, the Great Uncarved Block, once you say you know, you don't know, because it has already changed and remained the same, beginningless, incomprehensible, indescribable, the ever transforming core of all things, unifying, underlying. Tao was something I could believe-in, welcome, a connectedness already known to me through LSD. I too was the Great Uncarved Block, fashioning the first consciously intended deliberate face on my self. No Judeo-Christian expression with a divine all-knowing all-seeing God above and sin-full wretched human below. No wicked Eve giving poor innocent Adam the apple, or as I preferred to think, a perfectly ripened Bartlett pear from the Tree of Knowledge of Good and Evil. And not exactly the Yin-Yang principle either, for I thought the line between male and female fuzzier than up or down, left or right, hot or cold, dark or light, I thought each possessed more or less of both. Consciousness was dawning on me, and that insidious question, do you know who you are had been the nudge awakening my sleeping dog. The priced so far, isolation, otherness, being that little fishy who jumped-out of the bowl, realized she could breathe air, and jumping back in to tell of a bigger world, was not believed, you're crazy, go away. The question now, what else would this consciousness bring to me, this loss of idyllic innocence and unconscious paradise, no one to talk too. I could not know, and still wanted it no matter, had it no matter, for once having seen the light, how great the darkness if I slipped again to sleep. Catching eyes in the mirror had been my Rubicon, there was no going back.

Maps and charts consumed Ben, the Boys sailing, the Girls kitchening, Sean a reluctant sous-chef when not working on her tan. Joshua had time to play guitar and dive into the liquid turquoise, completely at ease in the water. I wanted to but just knew something unknown lurking in the bottomless would grab my ankle and pull me down. The cabin too claustrophobic for me, I napped in hammocks strung between the main hull and pontoons, read by lantern through some nights. The threshold between sleep and wake unlocking, I was high, buoyant, the benefits of Macrobiotics, sea-sick never knew me, skin becoming flawless, smelling sweet like Josh, my eyes clear and shining, feeling the ease of a natural animal, mind charged with nonstop energy, running fast in new thoughts. Being far from land and all its human trimmings, I was untangling, and began to trust there was room for every thing I wanted to know, all at the same time in this one lifetime.

Josh the only one to bring an instrument, took such joy in composing melodies. And I would make-up lyrics, and we sang. It was t-shirt weather day and night, happily my mates were not so eccentric as to go completely naked. Ben and Marigold trying to get pregnant as discreetly as possible on so small an island. Josh and my romance mostly in our minds, a brush of arms, a momentary look into eyes, erotic fantasy consumed me, mentally extending each occasion, achingly sweet, like holding honey in my mouth, as if we made love again and again. In passed affairs, always monogamous on my part, the guy tried to bed me soon as possible, only interested in his own satisfaction, I felt cheated, like any body would do. In high school my friend Penny slept round whenever she and Nick were broken-up. She was known as easy, and I often over-heard her called cunt, pig, slut behind her back. She knew this too, yet could not seem to help her behavior, and made very sure drilling in my head, I was never to sleep around, because those boys acted like they didn't know her in public, took her straight to bed when they took her out, never anywhere else, never getting to know her, just her body. She told me her Dad had been coming into her room since she could remember, that she had no self-respect, and made sure I knew not to give my self away like she felt compelled to. She hated her Dad for teaching her to fuck as the way to be loved, felt dirty, guilty, and hated her self for enjoying it, for letting him, hated her Mom for not hearing when she told, for looking the other way. I hated them too, loved her for being generous enough to let me see her pain, and learning from that pain, felt I owed her for showing me. Josh wasn't like those boys, thought love should not be done in haste or on the emotional cheap, falling inlove with some one as a friend before falling inlove with their body. I was charmed by this virtuous talk, speaking to my higher self and all, but it was also a power-full aphrodisiac and only made me want him more.

The third night Ben gave Captain's duty to Josh so he and Marigold could work on a baby. Sean finally went to bed, we were alone, hearts thundering, listening, listening. And when they were quiet long enough, Josh roped the wheel and we undressed each other, too shy to speak, feasting eyes, this tender thought-full man, those deft musicians fingers, kindling, aching, waiting, erect and wet enough, sliding in me, rocking, riding, faster, he leaned away to watch the pleasure on my face, my first ever orgasm, nuclear explosion, chocolate cream éclairs, thump thump thump, and he kissed and licked and thrust and filled me, whispering, declaring "I love you. I love you. Oh god I love you.

Josh was certain of his life, wanting to spend it making music, though he admitted terribly lonely till me, I was the one he had been waiting for. And he'd completely swept me away, I never knew feelings like these, deeper than any I had imagined, maybe I was in love too, I really could not think, it was so fast. He returned to the wheel, and I leaned against him, my eyes following the Milky Way cross the sky, such a wonder, and I worried aloud "What if I got pregnant. We didn't use anything". He promised "A baby only makes life more complete". This was waaay too fast, I whispered "I don't want a baby". He laughed softly "Oh come on, you want one. How could you not want our baby". Troubled he did not hear me, wanting the enchantment to linger, I said no more. Dawn lit everything on fire. Ben and Marigold made morning noises, signaling. And we agreed not to act as if nothing happened. Josh confessing he already told Mom how he felt about me, and anyway what were they going to do, throw us overboard. Ben was first on deck, giving me a knowing grin. Embarrassed to crimson, I fled to the galley to make tea, to hide from his eyes, his imagination, the feeling of being so exposed. Marigold came too soon to begin breakfast, and Sean, and there was no room. Days were marked simply by nights, Josh offering to Captain, Ben yielding, and we made love, Ben and Marigold enjoying our romance, vicarious flame for theirs.

We motored through Port Aransas, Corpus Christi Bay, and into Oso Bay late on the ninth morning, No Name proven fit for the coming voyage. I was never so glad to set foot on land, removing my shoes, kissing it with my toes though it did not quite feel solid under-foot. And then the boiling heat again took me hostage. Josh was eager for my commitment to India. Absolutely sure I was not a sailor, manifest in such pure delight standing on terra firma, I asked him to stay behind instead, knowing full well if his Folks were to realize their dream, he must go. Marigold's attempt to persuade seemed somehow the contrary, oh the adventure, the enlightenment, the opportunity to study with the Maharishi. Josh suggested "Ben could marry us on board". Ben twinkled "Yes, Captains have the legal right". Startled by this sudden proposal, before I could respond, Marigold added "Marriage is better when there's babies". I felt my face blush in panic, mind freaking, I could be, what a fool, what a fucking fool, what if I am, maybe this was a trap. And yet as bad as Marigold wanted another little one, I did not have heart to say I did not, and said nothing. Ben took my silence as final "Well then, what are your plans. We should be leaving this week". I supposed "Aa. I guess I'll go to Dallas for my luggage, and call my friends there Bonita-Kay and Jeffree. They're probably worried sick what happened to me". Marigold spun round and fixed me with her eyes "Now now my sweet pie, do you mean Jeffree and Bonita-Kay Johnson". I could only nod yes, as she shook her head slowly side-to-side, looking at the sky, mouth wide, laughing. Ben laughing too "This is unbelievable. They're our best friends". I was surprised and not entirely, their friendship made perfect sense. Josh wrapped me up in his arms "You're their good luck charm". He held me close and long and I knew I would miss him.

Securing No Name, excited, talking about Bonita-Kay and Jeffree, Russell and Kiki arrived. They were all close friends, and agreed Fate took Joshua to the airport to find me, there was no doubt I belonged to their Karass. We were spending the night at their Ocean Drive home. Kiki had the Johnson's unlisted number, they were also not entirely surprised, deciding to come get me in Houston. These Texans seemed to value this species of relationship beyond all, believing it was due a great deal too some larger authority over their choices, connecting a family beyond blood, a spiritual family, their Karass. And maybe they were right, maybe I was one of them, it just seemed sort of religious to me, without all the religion. Ben and Russell fell into rapt discussion about the coming study with Maharishi. Kiki and Marigold cooked supper and began listing what to take along. Sean helping. And Joshua and I were in our own world, concupiscence painfully public, we retired before dark to the hammocks in the backyard. I was as lonely as he, and savored the relief of having some of my inner conversation with a real live person. He was more than I thought a man could be, and the power of the Sweet Sisters Fate hard to resist, yet I knew, Fate or will aside, we wanted different things, and I would necessarily have to be the one to give-up.

Corpus Christi to Houston in the back-seat, Josh told me not to wear panties. Three times he wet his fingers in his mouth, slipped them under my skirt, spread my lips, and patiently, steadily stroked my clit, and we laughed and talked and acted like nothing else, so delirious, I had to feign coughing to mask each orgasm.

Laying my eyes on Bonita-Kay and Jeffree was emotionally overwhelming. I had last seen them in Seattle and was wholly unprepared to feel so homesick, to ache for what I'd been running away from. Suddenly I was wounded, needing my Mom and Dad, and the Northwest rainfall and drizzle that routinely bathed every thing so clean. And all the green, and Autumn leaves with their mushroomy aroma as they pile-up, and the snow-capped Cascade and Olympic mountains that seemed to float on their usual horizons, and the blue water everywhere, Lake Washington, Elliot Bay, Alki, the Straits of Juan de Fuca. And I needed some familiar vernacular, the humor and style of home, and the comfort of knowing my way round, for I was constantly disoriented in this endless plane of flat-scape, seeing only what was near, distance disappeared. And the relentless claustrophobic, polyester heat, always sticky, always dirty, always aware of my skin. I could not judge what-time-of-day by this hell-sun, this dreary bright blaze, till it sank a ruthless twin to its glorious reflection on the Gulf. Bonita-Kay and Jeffree gave me some bearings. They looked wonder-full, rested, and had been able to openly continue their friendship with the Strange/Hills since it did not violate probation. Not so with Russell and Kiki, the terms forbid people or places where drugs might be present, and if caught, no explaining, go directly to jail. This had taken Bonita-Kay's singing career from her, and Jeffree shooting album covers, on which they had raised solid reputations, the supposition being, all things music involve drugs. Ben and Marigold were old-money pillars, charitable contributors of the Houston Golden Ghetto, beyond suspicion, we would stay two nights.

Joshua and I spent the evening lying on the nineteenth century Kashan silk rug in the living room, listening to music and talking soft. We agreed love should be held close, away from prying eyes, even as Marigold and Ben and now Bonita-Kay and Jeffree gave us little confidentiality. Peacock-parents whose children had fallen inlove, how they just knew I was part of their Karass, how beautiful our kids would be, how our love would surely persuade me to sail away with Joshua. This gush and confabulation upset me, planning my life before I lived it, no surprises no regrets. I found my self begging a God I no longer believed in, please, oh please, I'll be good from now on, please don't let me be pregnant. And onion skin by onion skin, pulling-away from Joshua, I did not want to be anyone's Mother, thought there were plenty of babies on the planet already, and was certain, absolutely positively that India was not my direction. Jeffree and Bonita-Kay took Josh's bedroom. We dozed on the white Victorian couches, I was glad for the separation. And before any one had risen, we left with a cooler of ice and lemonade. Joshua was different away from Mom, driving to his favorite cafe for eggs, toast, hash-browns and coffee. We talked of dropping acid if he could find someone trusted to get it from. No luck, we drove North to the tree lined grassy bank of Cypress Creek. Spreading a patchwork quilt and pillows under the dappled canopy, he cautioned, far too blasé, I should be on the look-out for Cottonmouth Water Moccasins, they were deadly, known to pick-out a person and go after them. I did not feared snakes, there were none deadly in Western Washington, but down here they could kill me. I immediately felt that loathing nagging vulnerable need to be protected, by a man, and wondered did he do this on purpose, maybe not intentionally on purpose, still it felt somehow calculated. We lay on our backs, and I fought sleep, worrying snakes, giving way to heat and heavy food, and the lull of his body close to mine. Joshua strumming a thought-full melody called me back, to cold lemonade and a fat joint of local home-grown. These and a slender breeze rustling the canopy took some edge-off the heat, but not our gravitational attraction. We made love in the open, in-sight of the road, so dangerous, so erotic even with a Trojan. And I told him I could not go to India, and he said he loved me and he understood. And we cried for the coming loneliness.

To every one but Joshua's surprise, I was ready to leave with Jeffree and Bonita-Kay. Trying hard to hold my composure, tears came anyway, maybe I would never see him again, he could drowned on the crossing. Joshua promised to write. Me too. I could not look as we drove away in the invisible green Volkswagen. Some insight surfaced along the 245 miles to Dallas. Yes Josh was tied to his Mom, she was so intensely traditional, and yet a real freak, and he was too, there were few he could relate too. I thought he was more like me than her, yet if I went with, I did not believe he could cut the apron strings. Marigold was a jealous mother, would compel a choice, and I would lose and have to reside in her shadow.

Driving in on the Central Expressway, Dallas rose from the flat marsh like a lonely goose, still reeking of John F. Kennedy's murder, a bitter undertone to the terrible heat that set me strangely quivering, shivering. Jeffree and Bonita-Kay had rented a small house North of downtown on Stratford Avenue in Highland Park, my Big Oak Collage hung in the en-try-hall, framed, welcoming, the rest of the place was in boxes. Sentenced to ten years probation that must be served inside Texan borders, they could not mentally stand Dallas any more than I seemed too physically, we were moving to Fort Worth in days, and in the meantime Bonita-Kay would take me to Love Field for my things. Despite weeks of Macrobiotics, the heat was still relentless, and now I quaked. Bonita-Kay swore it was un-usually hot, but words do not save, I felt sticky all the time, drenched in briny sweat, breaded in fine dust, my brain pan-fried whenever I stepped from air-conditioning, and the night a laughable relief. Wanting to live in the shower, cold water raining on my head, easing every anxiety, petting, soothing, smoothing, magically even shivers and quivers ran away, I could not live in the shower. And yet, as insufferable the heat, were the people, brutally intolerant at every encounter, blunt to indelicate, all smothered in syrupy Texan de-meanor. I could not yet copy their entitled, inhibited, color-full slow-moving tongue, making me instant-suspect. And then of course Flower-Children were the dregs of the chow-chain, but only after draft dodgers and perverts. And yes, it was unusually hot and maybe this was cause, but Bonita-Kay and Jeffree could speak syrup and they were not treated much better. I longed for going home, hoping staying was the right thing. I would do as Carl Jung teaches and *wait and let things develop*, for Bonita-Kay and Jeffree were like no-one else, I wanted some time to learn from them. Jeffree's stellar photographic credentials won him a plum position with a progressive Fort Worth advertising agency that did not flinch at his criminal record. Infact, busted in Texas with a black man and living to tell was virtue in some places. Bonita-Kay had an idea of what she wanted to do, it would have to wait till we settled.

Arthur came to dinner, lanky six-foot-five with blue-black skin, china blue eyes, neat afro, a sculptor in the local art scene, he had been sentenced to ten years probation with the same restrictions. I liked him right away, he laughed at my jokes. In the next days he took me to the Poly District to visit his Grandmam, a celebrated seer who's Mother had passed the ancient wisdom on to her. Over Linden flower tea she held my hand, saying my soul was young here, its inexperience left me without much psychic protection, fortunately my body had its own native intelligence, signaling danger with cold chills and such, danger that could raise to misfortune if I did not listen and act. Her seeing gave me a sureness in trusting these chills, these hairs standing-on-end, these neon lights in my head, I had always known without knowing they were simple truth revealed. And she knew too, and I was grateful and humbled, and promised to listen, and to act. Arthur took us to a near-by roadhouse bar-b-que for supper, the floor inches deep in goober shells. We sat on bar-stools at one of the heavily lacquered wire-spool tables set with two baskets of fresh roasted peanuts, and ordered ice-frosted pint mugs of dark beer, crackling corn-bread and ribs, the best bar-b-que I had ever eaten. At her insist we took Grandmam home, and went on to a local night club, Arthur tipping the doorman to ignore my age. We were there to hear a man in his 50's, wearing a fedora and dark glasses in a dark smoky room, sitting on a worn wooden chair, on a small bare wooden stage, playing acoustic guitar, his foot a thundering second, talking, singing the Southern country-blues. He acknowledged Arthur by name as we sat down. And during break came by our table, Arthur introduced me to Sam Lightnin' Hopkins. I had not heard of him, but immediately recognized his mainline to the pure stuff. I didn't even like the Blues, did not resonate to the life they sang of, yet his spoke to me, included me, called my name, his Blues were so unpretentious, so authentic, such sweet profound privilege. He kissed me on the cheek and went back to the wooden chair for a second set. After, we went on to a local gallery, where black and white could without repercussions. Arthur was a noted sculptor, and keeping quiet his showing, let me have an unaffected experience, have my unedited say regarding the elegant elongated ebony warriors reaching for the sky, for their weapons, for each other, before owning-up. Sweet profound privilege.

And Bonita-Kay took me to the unemployment office, and I used our new Fort Worth address to file a claim. Then we went to Neiman Marcus. Not to shop, to view the heights of fashion, a modern museum where you could touch, try on, even turn garments inside-out to see how the consummate construct their art. Four stores, the latest in Fort Worth, but this first here in Dallas was the mother-ship. A glittering chrome and marble palace, two-story crystal chandelier filling the grand atrium, live elephants parading the main floor, led by six-foot blondes in orange silk harem-pants and sparkling purple beaded bras, just to launch a new fragrance inspired by the spices of India. And there was clothing designer Teal Traina showing his little black evening dress, Twiggy modeling the mod edition. I felt I came to worship on the fashion altar, the most excellent and expensive clothes in America. My Golden Roots were giddy, there was even a junior fur department for little rich girls, though it was hard to imagine wearing another skin in this heat. Bonita-Kay assured me it would get cold, that Texans loved their furs. This was a country unto itself, and Neiman Marcus served the royalty.

No speed limit, we flew the Dallas Fort Worth Turnpike, 30 miles, leaving the scene of the crime gave me some psychic peace, I did not believe the reeking would ever leave Dallas, thankfully we were. Fort Worth was not so much better, still Grandmam was right, no more shivers and quivers, the frozen grip that had me by the scurf opened its hand, my shoulders relaxed, my neck grew long again. Our new place on Crestwood Drive, a two-bedroom air-conditioned garage-house near the Trinity River, was built over a four-car garage, housing a 1955 Rolls Royce Silver Wraith and a 1955 Phantom VI. We would be living in what had been the servants' quarters, the big house some 200 yards up the driveway, its massive white marble columned porch and manicured gardens made me wonder why they bothered to rent. Arthur had come with us to help move-in. Spending time with him allowed me to experience, in the same league as the inhuman heat, the near constant mistreatment he endured with such grace. He told me prejudice was not exclusively White, that no matter his artistic acclaim, many light-skinned Blacks treated him down, for he could not pass the brown papar bag test. Lighter that a bag, you are acceptable to upper class Black Society, for they have their caste system too, and their private summer camps, debutantes and cotillions. And it wasn't only money even if you were light skinned, it was also where you went to school, where your father and mother and their mother and father went to school. Despite the Southern canon, we relished each others company, going for rides into the countryside round Fort Worth in his 1965 air-conditioned black Mustang. A bit lost on a two-lane between Millsap and Cool, two men standing on the road by a mail box, he stopped for directions. Their faces went dark, one growling "God damn coon wid yer hippie whore". Not a hairs hesitation, throwing-up a cloud of rubber, Arthur stood on the gas peddle. I heard a pop, too loud for a fire-cracker. In a calm deep voice Arthur ordered me "Get on the floor now". I held my breath listening for another, Mustang tires screaming under us, rubber burning my nostrils. He kept his foot down, voice pitched high, repeating sarcastically "Where the cops when you need um". I finally took a breath, and could not help but laugh at the irony, the unbelievable reality. Arthur laughed too, solid and long, shaking-off the fear. Unfolding, I tucked-in close to him, and we argued as he drove to the garage-house, I for going to the police, he certain it was a waste, that small towns were viper nests, the cops would smile and take-up our time, and ultimately we'd get no where. Having never lived in a rural town, I guessed this was the case in most, South and North. The incident left me infuriated and frightened, questioning maybe leaving San Francisco was a miss-take, maybe I should go back, or go home. The only redeeming worth I found in Texas was a few people. Maybe cruel climate and brutish disposition were the crucible that made them into such diamonds, and maybe growing-up in Seattle blinded me to what Black people face. Us Northerners were proud of our comparatively liberal attitude, our polite facade masking the prejudice beneath, whereas Southerners let you know exactly where you stand. I thought the mostly unchallenged unconcealed Southern ignorance was worse. Arthur went home to Dallas where he was a bit safer. Ché Guevara's murder dominated the evening news.

Morning's arrival of a $55 unemployment check seemed a sure sign to stay, and, I wanted to work at Neiman Marcus, there was no place on earth like it. Borrowing an appropriate dress and shoes from Bonita-Kay, I went to apply. They were hiring, still the interviewer said no, I spoke too Northern, Fort Worth would not buy from a Yankee, and worse "Bless your little heart, you shoulda worn make-up. Didn't you notice, Neiman Marcus sells glamour". Even so, the part of me that knows best needed to stay, to soak-in what Bonita-Kay and Jeffree knew by spending time, for it wasn't so much what they said, but who they were. Too-hot-to-go-outside-days Bonita-Kay and I went to the market early, sewed and cooked, listening to music all day. I painted the mailbox with psychedelic flowers and butterflies, waiting on a letter from Joshua, waiting, waiting on my monthly bleed, that thankfully came on the usual day, and I was pardoned. And we read, me the Egyptian Book of the Dead, Rudolf Steiner, William Blake, the 17th century King James version of New Testament Revelations. Wow, never having even heard of Revelations, these dream-like symbols, a woman clothed in the sun, the moon under her feet, her head crowned in twelve stars, a great red dragon with seven heads upon his, whose tail swept a third of the stars from heaven and cast them to Earth, the woman with the white wool hair who in travail birthed the baby, four horsemen and their chariots, mountains dancing like lambs, the Apocalypse, I could not really believe any one took these literally, imagery so psychedelic. I was beginning to believe a small g god might exist, very other from the Yahweh I weaned on. At fifteen my questions began in earnest, I noticed Gods on the 9th page of my confirmation study book, and this initiated a long and intense discussion with my Dad about there being more than one God or none at all. He maintained there was only one true God, Yahweh. I recited the first Commandment, Thou Shalt Have No Other Gods Before Me, as proof there were more, otherwise would He bother to demand Thou Shalt Have No Other. Dad said this referred to idols. I said no or it would have said idols, and anyway what kind of Yahweh would let the Holocaust happen. Our friendly impasse still continued. I always eagerly anticipated continued.

Bonita-Kay and Jeffree were well-read, well-thought, open-minded, and ever reminding they were are not the last word on anything. We talked and talked, they urging me to have my own mind, to find more information, lots of it, study many sources. And time and again they differed in their opinions and conclusions. Married people comfortable with, relishing contrary views, sometimes intense, good intense, no fighting, no one having to be right, no one having to win, no power-tripping by walking out the room, friendly impasse, continuing, someone to talk too. The Egyptian Book of The Dead lit my imagination, reincarnation, the transmigration of the soul seemed an explanation that made sense of my life. Where else did I get all these thoughts, how else could I sew so well, things never taught, it made sense that experience and talent have a cumulative affect, that I came in with some of it. Jeffree said he intellectually believed in reincarnation while his heart just could not. Bonita-Kay had come to my conclusion, it was the only explanation that made sense to her. And in the long hot days while Jeffree was away working, we talked of mirrors having been significant in both our lives. She saw people as hers, if she liked some thing she saw in some one, or disliked, she knew it was recognizable in them because she had it in her self, and in knowing this, she could do something to grow it or begin to dig-up the roots. From reading Jung she understood her human-mirrors reflected the projections of her own unconscious, allowing her to see what she could not in the looking-glass, that projection was the normal function of a healthy unconscious, all humans do it, and if one could recognize their projections, realize it's their own stuff they're seeing, and withdraw that projection, they would create an awareness, a personal consciousness of what moves them, drives them, infects them. Jung said, *in withdrawing the projection is where knowledge begins*, that the unconscious projects, and consciousness reflects.

Arthur's friendship had given me new eyes, I saw prejudice and racism in every mirror, and wondered to what degree I was seeing my own unconscious shadow. Bonita-Kay counseled me not to be so harsh on my self, I could not escape being prejudice, racism was a powerful institution in America, seeping into me from every where. Something as seemingly innocent as crayons, only one designated flesh, Caucasian flesh, implying other flesh illegitimate, children getting the message too young to question. She showed me the label on a box of panty-hose, nude, the color of her skin not Arthurs. And she read me Webster's definition for black - soiled, dirty, wicked, hateful, disgraceful, full of sorrow, dismal, gloomy, disastrous, and for white - morally pure, spiritually pure, spotless, innocent, honest, honorable, fair, decent, happy, fortunate, free from evil intent, harmless, white magic. If Webster wasn't institutionalized racism she didn't know what was, so yes I was prejudice at the very core of my cultural education, but since I thought it was wrong, since it was not in my heart, I could use human-mirrors to see it in my self, and face it, admit I was infected, and then begin to work on it, for working on it was the best I could do. And, to remember that lessons take time to learn. I loved this woman, this wise mother-lode, and still I could not bear Texas much longer. Bonita-Kay said she would leave too, soon as her probation was up. And that when I did go, distance would have a magical mirror affect/effect, that the long-view helps digests things, making them easier to take-up.

My Golden was determined to try Neiman Marcus one more time. Buying an appropriate dress and shoes at the downtown Salvation Army thrift store, I glamored my face with too much paint, employed a budding drawl and Nordstrom credentials and went again. My senior year in high school, I worked Monday and Wednesday after, and all day Saturday selling shoes on Nordstrom's 2nd floor in their Seattle flagship store, the largest shoe store in the country. I was putting away dead-wood in the labyrinth stockroom on a rainy afternoon, when one of the Nordstrom sons, manager of the floor came in, and noticing me wearing shoes from their main competitor Fredrick & Nelson, demanded "Why aren't your shoes Nordstrom's". I said matter-of-fact "Because you don't have these sling-backs that match my new dress. Fredrick's did". And just to be a snot, added "There's nothing in my work agreement saying I have to wear company shoes". A wire hanger in-hand to hang his raincoat, he shook it hard in the air and fired me. I could not stop myself putting hand on hip "I'm no fool, if you had the right shoes, I'd buy them here and use my employee discount". This struck him funny, he smiled, unfired me, and from then on called me by name, and even occasionally drove me home, for I lived two blocks up the street. Later that year Nordstrom made their initial move into apparel, buying Best Department Store next door. While remodeling and building access between the stores, they opened a small boutique on the 2nd floor, brought in Miss Barbara to preside. Being the only other female employee on the floor, when she wasn't there, I tended shop for my same salary plus 7% commission. A very good arrangement as these clothes were the hippest in town, sold without selling, and most wanted shoes to match. A different Neiman's interviewer saw me. I was hired to start in two weeks. With most of the money I had left, I shopped for strait clothes, planning to work six months.

Mixed into the heat, humidity and hard-bitten racism, were shrill screaming Katydids feverishly shaking their gourds, biting Horse Flies with blood-sucking serrated mandibles, Spiders monstrous enough to leash, I could not relax. A ticket to Seattle on the red-eye was $106, when my Golden Ego had her fill of Neiman Marcus I would go home. The butterfly mailbox finally delivered a letter from Joshua. The Strange-Hills made a safe crossing, were staying in Rishikesh close-by the Maharishi's Ashram. Having flown, Russell and Kiki were already there. He said India was like landing on another planet, the intense smells, countless people, sights, sounds, major culture shock. He loved it, missed me desperately, and was sure he had done the right thing going, for now it was where he belonged. He offered to send me a plane ticket. I wrote the news, finishing with I am not pregnant, and slipped the letter in a book, not yet sure ending us was right. Days of thought, I sent it off.

Jeffree's less than parochial point of view made him a creative monster at the advertising agency, whose biggest client was Alka Seltzer. Because her probation made singing rock'n roll impossible, Bonita-Kay decided to raise Afghan dogs. She loved animals, there was some money to be made, Arthur had a prized bloodline female pup for her to begin, she would need bigger digs to breed them, which Jeffree's success would accommodate soon enough. The Johnsons were newly Macrobiotic, and though Bonita-Kay was currently the Goddess of the Hearth, her relationship did not pivot on the Mother role, there was no risk letting me in, she could afford to be more generous than Marigold. She was by nature more generous than Marigold, we spent time every day concocting, talking, grinding flour, talking, baking, talking. This feeling high all the time, the intensity and clarity I knew lately was only partly sailing the Gulf. A change had taken in me, likely Macrobiotic enhanced, I was able to retain the big ideas we cooked-up with the food, even contribute to the discussion, sometimes feeling my mind grow new rooms to house them. And I was drug free. But all the staying-inside, I had grown claustrophobic-stir-crazy, and soft from languid sultry days, counting hours till Neimans.

Two weeks soared and crept into 7:30AM Monday morning, dressed as the perkiest glamour-puss I could conjure, Jeffree had to take pictures before dropping me on the way to his office, my maiden-day apprenticing the Junior Fur Department. Neiman Marcus was cool, like walking into a stone-floor cathedral. And I was a quick study, by ten all details of my job were down. Three sales by eleven, I knew I had simply grown too far-out, that paint and a knee-length dress were not enough camouflage, I would be discovered anyway and fired. Neiman's junior fur clients expected complete subservience. Just budding in their adolescent egos, they want a grinning monkey to perform as if being paid far more than miminum wage, while they freely insult working-class, implications deliberately loud, oh giggle giggle did you know monkey is one letter away from money, should we go back to school after lunch or get our nails done, aren't knee-length dresses so last month. These Golden Princesses, more savage than any I remembered from the Island, recognized me as one of them fallen-away, they saw me as food, and pecked like eager baby chicks. These were painfull blunt mirrors to look-in, seeing my own younger self-important self-absorbed self, appreciating how universal Golden Ghetto was, how it spawned the same suffocating cruel elitism wherever it breathed money. I felt so fortunate to have other choices, kindness, compassion, openness, too have friends beyond status, beyond competition, and not just a need to feed, no bottom in the bucket, an ever hungry starveling. And I was quite willing to pay whatever price to get away. Noon, half-hour lunch break, I did not tell the overseer, fled cool church, and took the bus home.

Sipping sweet tea with Arthur, who'd brought her a little wiggle, a long-faced nine week old puppy-girl, Bonita-Kay pleaded guilty to wagering Jeffree a fin I would not last the day. Jeffree bet I would. As she poured me a tall glass over crushed ice and bruised mint, I asked how she knew. She said it was plain the Golden in me wanted to work Neiman's, but that Girl didn't occupy enough of my soul anymore to keep me there for long. It felt good another human being had some sight into me, and good to see Arthur, there was little else holding me, I could go home had I not spent all that money on clothes. Working three hours and walking-away was a mistake, it killed my unemployment. I had 35 dollars and would need a temporary job.

Early morning I went for newspapers, searched the want-ads, interviewing three jobs, three rejections, even Whataburger. After a long shower, I phoned Casey at the Queen Anne house. He answered first ring, as if waiting for my call. Some trivial banter and he asked what do you want. I said a loan of $106 to fly home. He sounded smug, no problem, he'd send it right away. I regretted immediately, for again I had allowed a bogus impression, and used his feeling for me to get what I wanted. What a selfish fucking shill, I was disgusting and immediately began to rationalize, no one will hire me, it's not my fault he miss-read the call, I made it plain the money was a loan, I absolutely must go home or die. Jeffree and Bonita-Kay wanted me to wait till Joshua's return, wanted me to marry him. Lying in bed in the dark, listening for bugs, the little voice that speaks the truth was unequivocal, my destiny was not Texas, I was 19 and had to believe there were more adventures, someone to talk too, a true love ahead. Jeffree and Bonita-Kay understood, their four years running forced them to be resource-full, to learn what was intrinsically important, to depend on their intuition and each other, become quick judges of character, they would settle down, appreciate their reprieve, follow the rules, make the best of it, and leave Texas as soon as probation was served. Bonita-Kay confessed to just being selfish wanting me to stay. I would miss her sorely, Jeffree too. Three days the money arrived, taking Casey's letter from the butterfly mailbox, the reality of leaving Hell lifted me off the ground for a moment. Bonita-Kay would not let go hugging me good-bye at Love Field's departure. The invisible green Volkswagen Beetle disappeared round a curve, and I had the sinking feeling, maybe living in Texas might not be too high a price for a Karass, what if these were the only ones.

Chapter Four

THE BEIGE LADIES

Knowing what to expect, flying still scared me, check suitcase, a small one as I left behind the new clothes for Bonita-Kay, keep the shoulder bag with me. I bought a new music paper called Rolling Stone and the Seattle Post Intelligencer from the international newsstand, found my gate, and settled to read of a shoot-out in Oakland California between Blacks and Police, one cop killed, Huey Newton arrested for murder. Flying at night was like getting into a magic closet for 3 hours and stepping out in another world. I decided to store my stuff and bus home. Walking through a near empty SeaTac to the lockers, a porter offered to carry my bag. I smiled "No thanks. I don't have money". Eyes gleaming he purred "Someone beautiful as you, I'll carry it for free". Instead of flattered, his words called-up that selfish little shill who used Casey asking for money. And I used more, my youth, my charming, my smile, my flirt, my knowing I was pretty would get what I wanted. And every time I cashed-in, I would have to own it even if I never faced Casey, for now I saw what I was doing, I was no longer innocent. Another claiming of self-respect, consciousness was a heavy companion, demanding responsible, demanding response-able, for each act, no matter how small, no matter how pain-full to my ego. Mr.Porter purred softly through an injured smile "I meant beautiful like Jimi Hendrix says". Realizing his eyes gleamed cause the pupils were totally dilated, that he was zonked on acid, I dropped my defense "Thanks, but I need to do this my self". Lockers were a quarter, I stowed my bag and waited for the shuttle.

Stepping onto the street downtown, driver questioned was I sure I wanted to get off on 2nd and University. I nodded yes, the cool Puget Sound morning mist caressing me like a lover, walking quickly one block to Pike where I caught the Mercer Island bus so many times. Across the street, the old Showbox theatre, newly refurbished and named The Gathering, advertising Seattle's Daily Flash opening for Country Joe and the Fish.

But it was past 4AM, streets deserted, and I was more than apprehensive in this part of town, trying to be unseen, standing back against the inside wall of the JC Penney entrance, waiting, when a cop car stopped. He got out, walked slowly up to me, standing too close, shining a flash-light in my face, inquiry so I knew he would not believe me no matter what reply "Why're you downtown this time of the morning". I did not use my cute, or my smile, or a soft voice "Waiting for the bus". Ambivalence clouded his face "Where you from little lady". Oh shit, he thought he was John Wayne, maybe I needed cute, then as if hearing someone else speak, I was surprised by the syrupy Southern drawl dripping from my lips "Mercer Island". He smirked "Buses don't run so early. I'll take you home". Every muscle stiffened, this little lady was not going anywhere with a guy carrying a gun who assumed me a whore, I said firmly "No thank you. I'll wait". Cops crave control, he pointed to my feet "You stay right there missy, I'll call you a cab". I felt like a dog being told to sit "I haven't done anything wrong. This is America. I have rights". He scoffed "You better wait in my cruiser". The authority to so casually suspend my civil rights infuriated me, I folded arms cross my chest, elongated my neck and stood tall. Shaking his head, he reached in for the two-way and called a cab. And we stared each other down till it arrived. I felt no more comfort with the creepy cab driver, would have rather waited for the bus, but he dropped me at my Folks just after 5AM.

Mom was up making blintzes, and happily paid the fare. My Mom, ultra-intuitive about her children to the point of being omniscient, when we were little, she always warned there were eyes in the back of her head, and I always believed her because I nearly always got caught. And she let me believe her being up was sheer Mom's intuition, till sitting cross the kitchen table sipping hot cocoa, she let slip Bonita-Kay had called. I was glad to be home, though mentally long gone and slightly paranoid, Macrobiotics, LSD, a new consciousness had carried me far outside the strait places, including being Mom's Little Girl. And what I had become evidently showed, Mom kept giving me the microscope-eye, as if closer would expose some hidden script on my face revealing the truth. And, she loved my drawl, and I laid it on thick to lighten her up. Hair tousled, sleepy eyes, Dad ambled into the kitchen for a hug. We sat, content to rest eyes on one another. I asked to stay till I knew what to do next. They said yes in unison. We laughed. And in his grand sweeping I'm the king of everything and you can have whatever you want way, Dad assured my room was just as I left it, I could stay as long as I wanted. Mom heated him some 1% milk, and caught me up on family matters. Dad could have two more hours before work, kissing me on the forehead he went back to bed. Mom kissed me too, and followed. And I sat there, relaxing in the light of well-known surroundings, then went to my room, yes exactly as I left it. I was great-full to have a relative place to gauge my changing, while wishing they would let me go, Dad could turn it into a dark room instead of this shrine to some one I used to be. Closing the door, I studied my self in the full length plate-glass mirror on the back, the one I'd looked in 29 million times. It would be so hard for Mom more than Dad to recognize or approve of what I was becoming, and once my welcome wore thin, they would want their little Golden Girl and their rules in their house. I needed to make some money and get my own place, and doubted I could do what I did in San Francisco. Though acid was still legal here, and the last time I was on the Ave, Albert Hoffman lives was spray-painted on buildings, the Ave was years behind the Haight, with scant market for sitting on the street selling patches or jewelry. I lay atop the quilt remembering how uncomplicated life had been when I was little, I didn't really wonder if God was still up there, words had a way of being exactly what they were meaning, life had a way of being exactly what I was seeing, I didn't know the meaning of corrupt, and Mom and Dad took care of every detail.

Morning coffee tickled my nose. Dad had gone to work. Mom poured me a cup and offered, one of the girls she played Pan with owned an exclusive dress shop in Madison Park and needed a sales-girl she could trust, I should call. I knew she set this up thinking she was doing me a favor, never imagining she was taking care of every detail as usual, controlling my future, erasing my adult, but it was done with love, real love as motivation and that mattered, that obliged me. I called and was hired on the phone, not just because she knew Mom, but I was Golden, and that fit with her moneyed clientele. What made me say yes, the offer of in-house alterations, I could sew here too, and agreed to start first of next week. Hanging-up, I couldn't help thinking what ease in life when you have family connections.

My first day out and about, nagging unease swiftly turned to paranoia, isolation, I felt alien, exposed, like going to school in a dream without clothes. And when I saw my face in the human-mirrors, my strangeness in their eyes, it was clear I was naked. Paranoia is an uncanny and won-der-full dis-ease, forced inward for protection I began to journal…

LONELINESS
LONELINESS IS A GROTESQUE MONSTER
SITTING ON ITS HAUNCHES WITH ITS MOUTH OPENED
WAITING TO TAKE A BITE OUT OF YOUR LIFE
LONELINESS IS SILENCE WHEN YOU WANT NOISE
DARKNESS WHEN YOU DESPERATELY WANT TO SEE THE SUN
AND SOLITUDE WHEN YOU'RE LONGING FOR COMPANIONSHIP
LONELINESS IS A LOVE FAR AWAY
A LOVE CLOSE YET FARTHER AWAY
OR NO LOVE AT ALL
LONELINESS IS WALKING INTO A ROOM AND NO ONE NOTICING YOU
DANCING IN A CLUB FULL OF EMPTY STARING FACES
OR WALKING DOWN A HALLWAY OF LAUGHING PEOPLE ALONE
BUT LONELINESS - LONELINESS IS MY FRIEND

The solitude held me close, I ached for Joshua, and often let my mind loiter through our love affair, wanting to send him my poem, which would only be cold and selfish, using him like I had Casey, I could not be that shill ever again, no matter the isolation. So I reached-out to my oldest friend Rachel, her Mom said she was not home. Called Bonita-Kay with-out answer. Wrote her a letter, how right she had been about going home, things were clearer at a distance. By dinner, my shine had dimmed. Mom poo-pooed any suggestion of Macrobiotics as ridiculous, contending with-out meat I would die of protein starvation, that she was my Mother and she knew best. Dad had been diabetic all my remembering, in our home, meals were a matter of him living longer, and instead of separating him, Mom made the family menu diabetic. Like Marigold, feeding was her way of loving, her fiefdom, and she took personal affront when I passed on a thick slice of tongue, an old family favorite, she laid it on my plate anyway. I knew her motivation was love, but I did not want food to be so important anymore, I wasn't sick, did not think my death would be protein starvation. Food was fuel, always fighting my weight, I got plenty of fuel, and believed Macrobiotic suited me better, though in discipline both diets were remarkably alike. I tried to explain. She would not budge, was not ready to learn from her Little Girl, I was not grown enough yet. And it became a power struggle, ultimately to end in some one being wrong, I did not want this battle with her, gave-in and ate the cow's tongue, realizing why many of my contemporaries were embracing Jack Weinberg's words, *You can't trust anyone over thirty.* They could be so stuck in their ways, some solid as cement, I wondered if this was the reason olders got old, not because of their age but their concrete thinking.

Sitting at the dinner table, eating the oh so tender tongue, Mom was a wonderful cook and I still loved the taste, watching body-bags and flag-draped caskets coming home from Vietnam on the six o'clock news, I tried to talk about the anti-war movement, civil rights, Hippies, drugs, the emerging Women's Movement. Mom acted as if I was attaching her way of life, the conversation degenerated into argument. I did not have right words, or understand my own thoughts well enough to explain that I was not attacking, no defense necessary, I was just trying to exorcise a burning desire to understand and know, and could read her apprehension in bold type, maybe her Little Girl had gone crazy and would throw her life away on uninhibited ideas, Golden Girls weren't suppose to be interested in politics, or Macrobiotics, or Womens Lib. As I cleared the table, Mom asked would I talk with our cousin the doctor, he wasn't a head-doctor. To placate I said sure. Next day Dr.Cousin and I had a lively conversation over lunch at Denny's. I was forthcoming but for drugs and my thoughts on god. And he reported back, I was bright rational inquisitive and though searching in rather unusual places, not to worry, it was normal for my age. This pacified Mom, for she gave nearly blind credence to people with credentials, doctors, lawyers, rabbis, politicians.

Preserving amity meant moving-out soon a possible. Everything in the paper was more than I could pay. Borrowing Mom's car, I went by the old place on Republican, finding no vacancy and double the rent. I needed a roommate, and called Rachel again. Her Mother always thought me a terrible influence on her lily-white little girl, mostly to do with all their money and the middle-class means of my family, she would only say Rachel was not home. Katey's face came to mind, her number was in the phone-book, I took a chance time had gone-by, maybe we could be friends all over. I found a sure connection, she had come to appreciate what a stinking jerk Nick was, she had called my Folks months ago only to find I had gone South. She had such an amazing boyfriend now, who just moved in, they were planning a wedding, she would love me to meet him. I suspected she was looking for some corroboration and went to visit, her rented Rainier Beach house. And we talked as if no one had come between, and I stayed hours beyond where Mr. Wonderful should have come home.

The Daily Mirror, a pocket-sized ultra-elite dress shop in the long-pursed beach community of Madison Park, trimming the western shore of Lake Washington and catering to Broadmoor, a Platinum Ghetto, with iron-gates, stone-walls, private golf course, no Jews, no Blacks, 24 hour guards, and moneyed middle-age valium wives, whose husbands callous and indiscrete ego-thirst for youngers was ferociously placated in alcohol and shopping and alcohol. My Boss wanted me to wear store goods, and I happily obliged, avoiding another squander on strait clothes. These Beige Ladies hunting the Mirror, ash blonde hair, dewy pinkless liquid foundation, creamy silk blouses, camel hair pantsuits, real tortoise shell buttons, real alligator loafers and belts and matching handbags, tennis court tans, blinding wedding rings, diamond stud earrings big as headlights, champagne Mercedes 250SL convertibles, they instantly trusted, relied on me to dress them and do the necessary over-night alterations, for those often affairs where every one pretended to an immaculate marriage. And they came back the next day and the next, drinking lunch at the Red Onion, sad-eyed, frantic spending, bitterly complaining their husbands would probably just charge it to the company anyway, probably never even notice. And they made me sick, heart-sick, these lamentable if unwitting whiskey Platinum thralls, believing that trussed-up in the only-one-of this particular gown allotted by the designer to the area, would somehow transform them into authentics, into youngers, somehow alleviate the pain. I never took advantage, when they came frenzied, when they came plastered, making sure they went home with something appropriate, something not too short or too young, something that would not contribute to their desperate humiliation.

A busy Saturday morning and noon, no one after 2PM, Boss closed at three, handing-over my first week's pay in cash. I caught the bus to the Ave and perched on the Post Office wall, hoping to score some weed in an Yves Saint Laurent mustard and brown pin-striped wool pants-suit that did not exactly make me recognizable as one of them. No luck, no one trusted the deal. Hunger took me to the Hasty Tasty, a back booth quietly enjoying the atmosphere, picking most of the cheese from my omelet, Gabriel slipped in next to me. Sultry green eyes, California surfer long hair, he smelled yum, and it hit me, I was attracted to musicians, this was not good. Ordering a French dip, he invited me to band practice. I went along. He rolled a joint. I settled on the tattered orange Naugahyde couch in the living room to smoke it. Getting stoned after so long laid me back, relaxed my shoulders, took me home to that ahhh related gentle knowingness that links rational with instinctive, to kinship with every living thing, I could hear the cosmic chorus singing, feel isolation release me, paranoia fade. The band worked-out one tune, then began the head-spinning hype-talk of a possible record deal. Exciting stuff this making it big, however Casey was heavy on my mind, and with more cash than expected from alteration, I could settle-up, there would never be a good time.

I used the kitchen phone. He answered first ring, inviting me to the Queen Anne house. Determined not to give wrong signals, I asked to meet at the Hasty. Casey did not resist. Telling Gabriel I would come back, walking quickly to the Ave, I stopped in the Esoterica for Blanco-Negro rolling papers, the ID Bookstore for Kerouac's Desolation Angels, took the same booth at the Hasty, ordered tea, paid for it, counted 106 dollars into my lap, and opened the book. I did not see till he slipped in across from me, and had to smile at his simmering face, automatically reaching to touch his hand. He drew back like I was a disease "Keep your money". I laid it on the table in a neat pile and pushed it to him, being intentionally soft "No Casey. I pay my friends". Giving it a passing glance, he showed me a full-faced truly insincere smile and boomed "You are not my friend". Fleeing the booth, his leather pants shrieking against the plastic seat, everyone looking as I flew after, money in-hand, pleading "If you don't take it, I'll leave it here on the ground". I knew he wanted me to feel bad as he, and the thing was, I did "I'm sorry Casey. All I can say is I'm sorry". Sincerity stopped him just out the door. I tried putting the cash in his hand. He slapped at it, growling more a challenge than a threat "Fuck you Bitch". Not wanting to win this, I looked in his boiling eyes and whispered "I lost too you know". On the sidewalk, I laid the money down, turned and ran away like a thief, ashamed of my self, vowing never to sleep with any one ever again from loneliness or a desperation for human contact. Casey's voice followed me, bellowing gall "You lost too. Fuck you Bitch".

Slowing after half a block I looked, Casey was gone. My heart thundering, I headed to Gabe's, absorbed in recrimination, physically bumping into Nick, or maybe him into me, for he had this uncanny way of appearing when I was vulnerable. I was not glad to see him. It seemed he did not recall why "Wow, hell-o". He stood too close "God, you're a fox. Hey, I'm living at my Folks right now, looking for a roomy. Wana get a place". I stepped back and put my feet flat on the ground "I don't think so. You hear anything from Penny". Face darkening, he closed the gap between us "I don't wana talk about her". I thought, this is a bad man, finish this right now, and didn't "Okay, then maybe you've seen Maryjane". Face turning sunny, he spoke louder than necessary "Just happened to have 'er on me. One lid, sifted. To you ten bucks". His loud, his unnecessary tempting Fate made me seasick, I folded-up a ten and concealed it in a handshake, grudgingly remembering how compelling he could be in his narrow-eyed Roman-nose way. He jotted a number on a matchbook cover, handed it to me with the lid, no circumspect, not clandestine, in plain public, ostensibly oblivious. I dropped them into my shoulder bag, Nick took such pleasure exposing him self, in jeopardizing, I forced a smile "Thanks. Got to go now". He held my arm and my eyes, reading the pretense "Call if you wana get a place. Promise, just room-mates". I hurried to Gabe's, the boys already gone home to prepare for tonight's big gig at the Rainbow Tavern, record company reps would be there. Gabriel invited me along.

Needing diversion, thinking it might be fun going with the band, a really good band, I sat down at the kitchen table and rolled a fat joint, mentioning I literally ran into Nick. Gabe took a long drag, holding-in only a few seconds, rolling his eyes, testifying on the exhale "Bad Dude. Good dope". Excusing him self to the shower he grinned all teeth "Hey pretty girl, come get clean with me". Ignoring him, I set the debut Moby Grape album on the record player and tripped to their rich harmonies.

Gabe's band had done the work, playing anywhere they could, often free, practicing, writing songs, practicing, becoming a celebrated local favorite. The Rainbow had a line down the block, fans wall-to-wall inside, I danced all night, alone, shooing all comers, feeling the prestige of sitting at the band table, and the awkwardness of an Yves Saint Laurent wool pantsuit, drinking too much free beer, going to the after-party, I'd never been to one and thought it might be fun. Hashish, tequila, cocaine, every one wasted but me, and it began, a groupie pulled-down the drummers jeans and blew him right there in the kitchen. I blushed hot understanding, chicks were here to fuck, and Gabe was looking my way. I had gravitational attraction to him, but this was not for me, I needed to matter, and shook my head no. Not missing the beat, boosting the nearest girl onto the kitchen counter, he threw her skirt over her face, no panties, spread her legs and lips and ate her like melting ice cream, all the while looking at me. Wanting to run, it was 3AM, I found a chair on the porch, arms wrapped tight round my tucked-up knees, waiting, listening to the record player, as much as possible shutting-out the spoils of musicians in a noted local band on the verge of making it big.

Dawn glazed the sky, I slid-away, caught a-first-of-the-morning bus downtown, and one home. Dad was in the kitchen preparing an insulin needle, trouble sleeping, upset I had been out all night without calling. It never occurred to me to phone home, I should have let it go, balking anyway "Daddy, you know I've been all over on my own. I'm a big girl now, you don't have to worry so much". On the surface, being worried-over seemed a caring thing, underneath it was mostly imagined dangers, control I had never challenged, still it was a tired-eyed dispute with a loving Father whose job it was to worry over me. He reacted with the dreaded "When you're in my house Shoshannah, you follow my rules". He was right, this was his house and I was in it, the difficulty, I had lived freedom from this loving custody, and yet it was quite clear my Folks were not willing to take their eyes off me when they could, they would fret and agonize, and that was that, I simply said "Sorry Daddy. I should have better manners. I promise, it won't happen again". Apology accepted.

Again the Sweet Sisters Fate took the reins of my life. I did not resist, phoning Nick when I woke just after noon, telling myself maybe roommates could work. He passed me a lit joint as I climbed in the bus. Wishing he waited till we were at least down the driveway, knowing Mom was looking, knowing any complaint would only foment more blatant, I let the pencil thin, perfectly rolled MaryJane burn-down without a taste. He took it from my hand. And I picked-up the Post Intelligencer laying on the seat between us and read the headline, *Beatles go to India to study with the giggling Guru Maharishi Mahesh Yogi*, my body hungered for Joshua. Nick had circled the possibilities and made appointments before coming to get me. First was a badly abused and beautifully furnished two-story on Charles Street in Seattle's Central District. Built 1914, the front door opened to a generous living room, red brick fireplace and sitting hearth taking one wall, this alone would cozy the winter. Through a broad archway, a formal dining room, holding a great table, and the kind of good Southern light I would need to sew. Into a considerable kitchen with an open pantry and three yawning windows. The bathroom happily accommodated its graceful footed-tub, two equal-size bedrooms shared a common wall, hardwood floors ran throughout. And, up the stairs just inside the front door, a mother-in-law apartment complete with small kitchen, bedroom, bathroom and living room. A thick laurel hedge near seven-feet surrounding on three sides, enclosing the backyard, where a one-room house stood, what people used to live in while they built their big house. Landlord said we could use it for storage, and rent upstairs if we wanted. Plainly in need of restoration, the house was not available for thirty days, sixty-dollars a month, we would be the only whites in the neighborhood. Nick excused us onto the back porch. We loved the place. He instructed me to go along, telling Landlord we were newlyweds, signing a month-to-month rental agreement, paying first, last and $30 damage. To celebrate we went to the Last Exit on Brooklyn, where radicals intellectuals and artists hung-out, deep in philosophical conversation that would surely send them to the gulag. The owner sought-out anyone new and bought their first cup. From his age and New York accent I guessed Greenwich Village coffee-houses, Beatniks and artists passionately discussing politics, reading Beat poetry aloud were his muse. Nick knew near everyone there, some came by to score. Over carrot-cake and coffee I gave him 75 dollars. He said no. I insisted we split all costs or the deal was off. He took the cash, and we talked about subletting the upstairs. I never mentioned Gabriel or Katey.

And still, if relations with my Folks were to remain smooth, I needed to go soon. When Nick dropped me home I called Rachel again. This time her mother grudgingly gave me a phone number. Renting a two-bedroom apartment in West Seattle right on Alki Beach, Rachel quickly mentioned her eight months pregnant roommate just moved home. I proposed sharing for a month. She welcomed the company and the money. Rachel was eight, me seven, and we were instant best friends from the moment we met in Sunday school. Both Eastern Eurpoean Ashkenazim, we looked remarkably alike, probably the same tribe, and for all we knew from our decimated lineage, probably kin. Her family had the best seats money could buy in synagogue, front-row balcony just above the pulpit, where everyone could see them in all their finery. I would often sit with her during the holidays, holding court, pretentious little ingénues reigning above the congregation. When hormones began to rule, we pledged never to compete, never to mess with each others boyfriend. And since the only cute one in our Conservative congregation had a steady girlfriend, and the rest were skinny pimple-faced nudniks who were sure they already owned us because our Folks forbid dating Gentiles till we were sixteen, we decided to go-out only with boys from the Reform Temple when obligatory events required. Even so, girls in our class were maliciously jealous, for we had most of the boys attention anyway. And we remained tight as twins till senior year high school, when Rachel broke our competition pact. Slender rills she would never admit to crept-in, flirting with my boyfriend, the betrayal made me bleed, my teenage brain had little faculty to challenge this directly, so I made-up plausible excuse. Her Mom had been rounded-up and experimented on, she escaped to China, met her Dad, they were able to immigrate to Canada, and in 1944 allowed into

America. Like many first-generation children Rachel inherited the trauma, always afraid of that knock on the door, living at the mercy of Gentiles who reluctantly let her kind in, the Holocaust shadowing her, and the burning question, why God, how could you. I was second-generation and not so fear-full, and maybe that seemed naïve or unfair to her, maybe this was why whenever we were anywhere together, I would some how get to the door first to open it. And she was so skinny, one illness following another, likely consequence of her Mother's ordeal. Rachel never missed an opportunity to point-out how big and healthy I was, in restaurants handing me the Ketchup bottle to open, look how easy you can manage that. Walking, I was somehow maneuvered to the traffic side. At the tender advent of our budding womanhood, badly needing self-confidence, I felt like her beefy bodyguard, and though this appeared to be all so innocent, so happenstance, it felt quite deliberate. Rachel's Folks blamed me for everything, her poor grades, school skipping, coming home late, drunk, speeding tickets, even when they found her pregnant in 11th grade and sent her to Paris for a weeks wink-wink vacation, my wicked influence was to blame, no matter I was a virgin and Rachel had not been since 9th grade. And despite the fact they bought her every thing and more, they called her stupid, useless, slut to her face. Once I tried talking about this, how mean they were to her. She accused me of being jealous, insisted I was crazy, they never hit her, and later that day drove over in her brand new 1964 white Buick Electra with a black convertible top. I freely admitted being jealous of what money could buy, still it did not change the awful price she paid. So it was not a surprise we drifted away senior year. After graduation she was sent to Israel to live on a kibbutz for a year, and we lost touch.

I called a cab, cruising Harbor Avenue, gazing across Elliott Bay to downtown Seattle, I was hope-full Rachel had woken to the dishonesty, to the abuse of things as pay-off, maybe gained some self worth, enough to quit her job as family scapegoat before it completely murdered her soul. Throwing open the door, she hugged me tight as those frail arms could, and I saw in her shameless hazel-blonde eyes, she was not dead. Rachel did not help carry my few things into the empty bedroom. We took to opposite ends of the front room couch, floor to ceiling windows looking cross the street to Alki Beach, a waning sun turning the salt water to molten gold. I stuffed my green soapstone chillum with some of Nick's weed, and we began to catch-up. Every Spring Rachel went to Israel to buy Bedouin dresses, she was earning good money re-selling them to boutiques. She read Gurdjieff, was reading Ouspensky, and had done a small dose of LSD, not enough for hallucinations, but it helped her see that she was her parents link, she spoke flawless American, and how much they depended on her. Dad had her collecting rent from their properties at ten, she was their cover, and in many ways their parent, she understood they were jealous of her liberty, of her uncomplicated life, so they complicated it. And she had forgiven the tyranny, as long as the abuse came to an end. And in confessional whisper, she admitted to having being jealous of my Folks, my home life, too ashamed to tell till now.

The bus stopped at my front door. Every day after work, to shake it off I walked Alki beach, no matter the October weather, quickly learning the more it blustered the more the place was all mine. I would bring home any unfinished alterations, and Rachel, also an excellent seamstress, when she did not have an appointment or date, we would get stoned and sew and talk, and talk. Nick came over only once, only for a few minutes, leaving four hits of purple Owsley behind. Rachel took an instant visceral dislike, thought I was meshuggeneh to move-in with such a trayfnyak, wanted me to stay with her. I said I would think about it, but never intended to, and could not explain why even to my self, it was as though I had already stepped over the event horizon and had no choice but to go on the ride. I tucked the acid in the freezer behind the ice cubes, and it began its haunting, calling my name. Friday night Rachel's date came for her at 7PM. Soon as she closed the door I gave-in, those purple tablets so deceptively small, somehow akin to the crystal I had naively accepted from Nick, and still I placed two little pills on my tongue to melt, and on swallowing considered sticking fingers down my throat, fearing I would permanently fuck my mind like some I knew in the Haight. Instead I stacked Dylan's Hiway 61 Revisited, Big Brother and the Holding Company, and the Doors on the record player, went into my room and sat on the edge of the bed, facing the mirror, staring at my reflection, right eye to right eye, left to left, transfixed by an empty space opening just below the right, some of me was dissolving, disappearing, I freaked at the taste of tin foil flooding my mouth, too late, mercurial rush, too much LSD flooding through, I took my eyes from the mirror, gliding cross the silken wood floor into the front room, looking through the window I saw her, she was me, my self, my doppelganger standing across the street on the sand in the light of a street lamp, and she saw me, knew me, staring into my eyes, right to right, left to left. I must go to her, breezing though the suddenly cavernous apartment, fumbling a door knob that spun round-and-round and seemed to take a small bite of my palm before opening into the hallway, I stepped onto the raised wooden sidewalks of Ensenada, hall light a burning high noon sun, blinding me, I could only lean against the door, slide to the ground and lower my head, just as the manager oozed down the stairs, she became a Macy's Thanksgiving Day balloon, filling the hallway, over-flowing her black Wrangler jeans and short-sleeved white cotton t-shirt, I could not tell bosom's end and midriff's begin, a half-smoked unfiltered Camel in her right hand, Tasmanian She-Devil tattooed on the inside forearm, certainly not a Jew, we did not tattoo ourselves willingly, and she was already pissed at me for moving in without permission, Rachel neglecting to tell me till today. Halting between me and the sun, She-Devil snarled "What're you doing on the floor like that. You a crazy woooooo". I could only look, no longer able to make-out words, as she became a barking barrel-chested hound with spindly legs, I could not contain laughing, gravity finally re-leasing me, I sprang like a spring, made for the exit, opened by an invisible hands, the night air embracing me, freezing clear, full-moon bright, shin-ing on the face of a bus pulling to the curb, and away, unending inching caterpillar, holding my breath, She-Devil in thundering pursuit, I slipped into the narrow alley between buildings, too slim for her, and became Dylan's lyrics *When you're lost in the rain in Juarez/And it's Easter time too/ And your gravity fails you.* Restored on a side street where I could see in the lamp light my doppelganger had gone, I panicked, racing across the street, concrete Sahara, each foot-fall whirling the dust of an early snow that fell no more, neon diamonds rubies sapphires and emeralds swirling round my huge big feet, LSD truth, earth's intrinsic natural beauty, its ordinary opulence. And in the twitch of a cat's whisker my proportional world dis-appeared, I was Leviathan, pure Tao, divine P'an Ku, Gayomart, immortal Purusha, the secret desire of every heart, embracing, containing, filling the cosmos, planets, suns, black holes, solar systems were now the mere cells of my body, and still I did not forfeit individuality, my consciousness had not thinned, time and space and relativity were disappeared, yet I wiggled my toe and it responded without delay, the sensation of universal oneness overwhelming me to tears, the sanction of personal divinity, I could hear every one and each individually, the spiral symphony of heavenly bodies, the inhale of gravity and each human breath, even She-Devil calling the police, her anger amused me, didn't she know I was far too big to put in a squad car. Another whisker twitch and I drew back the Wizard's curtain, the unknowable secret whispered in my ear, proclaiming "It's as simple as one". And every kind of natural element sprang from my body in brilliant sun-burst understanding, and I was ordinary once more, walking the sand of Alki beach, low-tide, full moon at my back, casting a long shadow before me, I always dreamed of being tall and grace-full and followed this shadow up the beach, feeling the sway and flow of her glorious stature, even as my attention was drawn to the gull walking along side. It flew-off, and I went with, hollow-boned, rising on the shoulder of Aeolus toward the city lights, and when I fell back to my self, knee-deep in the dark water of the Bay, I fell again from the weight of my body, thinking, feeling I must be freezing, crawling from the salt-water, seaweed dressing my body, hurrying to catch my lissome shadow-self, maybe she knew the doppelganger. And where was that terrible screaming coming from, not these lovely men, long flowing hair, two glowing Angels inviting me to come along.

The material world gently re-assembling, my parts re-integrating, wrapped in a soft brown chenille robe, in the lap of a wicker peacock chair, a fragrant mug of jasmine tea in my hands, and the Angels. We'd met on the bus, Oscar and Sebastian lived one stop before mine, and were walking the beach too, coming-down on acid when they heard screaming, went to see, and surprised, found me on a bad trip, having assumed from my work-suits I was strait, they took me home with them, dried my clothes, and attended my coming-down. I sipped the tea, and thanked them. They giggled in harmony, there was no need, neither had ever disrobed a girl, it was their pleasure. Being undressed by these Angels held no discomfit, I smiled and declared my trip was amazing. Sebastian said it sure sounded bad, the screaming. So it was me, my mind swam in what might have been had I flown all the way with the gull, or if they had been bad men, I could be dead or worse. Quickly another part of me rang-in, do not play the if might and could game, given I had not, they were not, I was not, for this epic budding element in me, that was becoming in me, this ache for living and adventure managed so far to fasten a secure foot even when other constituents could be so irresponsible. The blessing of these Angels being there, salvaging me, this feeling of tremendous inclusiveness, grace that was not religious, not personified, or judgmental, or terrible, I knew I was a part of this wholeness, and was certain the real peril of venturing so far-out into a consciousness I could not have imagined till arriving, this frivol, was a Faustian bargain I would risk again.

First light, Angels walked me home. Rachel waiting up, worried, angry, She-Devil was threatening eviction. Oh shit, I hated being the cause of trouble for any one but my own self. Apologizing for the pickle, and not pointing-out she should have asked before letting me moved in, I promised to see Devil when I had my wits again. Rachel went to her room in a dark huff. Thinking, I'll get stoned, listen to some music and come-down all the way, I went to mine, undressed, put on a long kimono, and opened the top dresser drawer. My chillum was where I left it, MaryJane was not, I hurried to Rachel hoping she had indulged. No. We both freaked, looking everywhere, two times, three, four, the front door flew opened, with her pass-key Devil spilled in and headed for the living room. We beat her to the couch, leaving one too small chair. She stood over us, eyeing me bare-feet to eyes, barking "Why you dressed like a whore. Spectin' a trick." She stuffed her ham-thighs into the chair. My robe an antique hand-painted silk ceremonial kimono, I uncrossed my legs and let it slide open, there was nothing to lose here, she would evict me no matter, a wayward smile took my face "You interested". Her intention to push my buttons, and I had turned the tables, she went defensive, threatening "Rachel can stay. But you. I came in here before calling the fuzz. Found your weed, an the acid in the icebox. They're in my safe keeping, an I'll call the cops again, have you busted if you aren't gone tomorrow". Folding arms over her loose bosom, she tried leaning back into the small chair. My mind screamed, you do drugs, how else would you know to look in the freezer or even recognize LSD, then I thought better of the game, Rachel was doe-eyed in the headlights, there were only six days till Nick and I moved-in, and She-Devil made a serious miss-take showing her cards. I spoke plain and purposeful "So, you're holding drugs. It's me who can have you busted". Her jaw loosened. Again I smiled "Just so you know, Rachel didn't know, so here's the deal. I'll stay six more days. That's it. And if you leave us be, you can keep the dope". She wrenched from the chair "Six days". I stood too. Thundering from the room, shaking the floor, she slammed the door.

Rachel softened into the couch, her perfectly arched dark brown eyebrows knit together, she loved her place and was relieved to stay. I apologized, again. She grinned. I knew that grin, and grinned back. Opening her cigarette case to a fat joint, she lit-up. Flower tops, the best of highs, we laughed at the bizarre movie we had just been in, and laughed till we were laughed-out. She kept an endless eye on me six days, staying home at night, worried I had lost my mind. I tried to talk about my trip, about the divine wholeness. She vetoed every attempt, saying I should just forget it, maybe hoping this would return me to the girl she knew, the one of us who never caused trouble for her till now. But I had escaped from the separateness, heard some one in me announce "I'm sorry, you've gotten too big, we're going to have to let you go". Rachel and I were back on that hard surface again, loved each other like family, always would, promised to keep in touch, but she was no longer some one to talk too, and tried not-so-hard to hide her oh so glad when Nick came for me. I hoped this bargain would work. If not, I made enough money, I could move away.

Chapter Five

SOULMATE CELLMATE

I knew Nick played guitar, but not what a really good musician he was, and began looking forward to coming home from the Daily Mirror, getting stoned on his perpetual stash of primo weed, doing alterations in the dining room where I set-up my Singer, listening to him jam in the front room with Andy Aldridge, William Paten, and Rich Dangle. Our Charles Street home fast became known as the music house, and though Nick forbid me in the front room while jams were on, living where the music was made infinitesimally appeased the insufferable affront. A casual friend of Nick's, William and his girlfriend of one month Tara were looking for a place to move-in together. I liked them and agreed with Nick to sublet the upstairs, expenses split four-ways. Tara was starched, soft-spoken and mostly passive, five-foot-seven, 120 pounds, cornflower blue eyes, thick natural straw-blonde hair that swaggered down her long poised neck and porcelain shoulders. The only child of a Garden Grove California couple who began her ballet at five, voice lessons at seven, modeling school nine, finishing school twelve, nose, chin and tits by seventeen, full mouth of caps eighteen, and then she ran, to Seattle, from their loving smothering control. I admired her courage, force-fed the entire Golden menu, constructed into an ideal fabrication, something I had escaped in not being rich, in not being the plaything of my parents. And William, her clean-shaven square-jawed dreamy-eyed six-foot Ken doll, proper as an English school-boy, gentle enough to mitigate his white princeness, clothes so clean they smelled of sunshine, long thick honey-brown hair tied neatly in a simple leather thong, he played Tony in his high school rendition of *West Side Story*, was a good poet, good musician, good singer, and quite shy but for his music. They moved in. And Nick took possession of me, becoming inhospitable when Gabriel or Katey came by, taking my phone calls, never passing on the message. If my work schedule varied 20 minutes, he would grill who was I with, and began showing-up every evening in his blue bus outside the Mirror to take me home. Though I railed inside and out at this encroachment, some one in me was flattered and powerless to stay the slide. And he came to my bed. For me it was carnal, a guilty pleasure, nothing like Josh. Nick was experienced, deliberate, satiating, and always wore protection.

Tara and William spent most of their time downstairs, William jamming, Tara allowed in the front room, draping her long body over the couch, silent muse, not allowed to speak. I'd come home hungry, and she took to joining me in the kitchen, interested in Macrobiotics. Tara was part-time waitress at the International House of Pancakes, wages and tips barely covered their expenses. William worked on nothing but his music. Nick's dealing seemed small-time, I suspected more as he always had money, but he never let me see it, leaving me to pay for the groceries. I felt used, and did not protest. These self-interested arrogant musicians thought they deserved taking care of, and most girls would bear-up just to be close to the flame. Tara was one of those, and apparently to my sorry surprise, I was one of those. I did not think music was more sacred than other arts, and though Nick and William were certainly good, they were not great, for greatness fostered a graciousness and ease, an inclusive nature their preening egos had not realized. I fledged my own reputation at the Mirror, clientele hailing me Golden Fingers. And I earned enough in alterations, all cash under-the-table, to make my hourly wage near insignificant, enough to have a stash to move-out, enough, one-hundred and six dollars enough to replace the Singer with a Pfaff free-arm 297-1, the first zig-zag on the market. This machine, my own private robot-slave, saved me so much time, I made much more, Pfaff paid for itself easily, and left me with juice enough for designing.

Nick the first beneficiary, a white Egyptian cotton poet's shirt, generously ruffled at the cuffs, making him look more pirate than poet. He was completely thrilled with the image it created for him, and benevolent and open-handed for many days. And then Tara, my tall enough, blonde enough, thin enough with just enough bosom, my own private Vogue model, I made a finely woven paisley tapestry into an ankle-long halter-dress, that made her feel lilting and grace-full and look like Faye Dunaway. Seeing my work walking round the house gave me a needed objective perspective, I remembered I was good, and remembering made me feel good. Nevertheless, Nick's dominion escalated into imagined jealousy. He took possession of my voice, my words, I was not allowed to speak to an other male, girls spoke to girls, boys to boys, unless the boy owned you, these were the new rules. If I had something to say to William, I must look at Tara and say it to her, even if William was sitting right next to her, then Tara would repeat it exactly to him as if he had not heard, and if there was need for a reply, he would speak keeping eyes only on her, for it was forbidden for him to look at me, she would then relay to me as if I had not heard, and she was to follow this same rule if she had something to say to Nick. I protested what I called second-speak, hoping Tara or William would back me up. They were so sexually repressed, to them this felt safe, a fun game, even a noble experiment, for none of us knew how to live to-gether, marriage was the norm, there were no rules for living-in-sin except don't do it. Nick was happy to prescribe, using their compliance to sustain his continuing. And I ceased any verbal protest, loneliness my close friend again, inertia, isolation, melancholy my touchstones, Nick was in control, of my eyes too, and somehow I had become too emasculated to challenge the course, feeling if I did I would miss some primal key to my life, while my mind raged in an active resounding looping colloquy, I do not love this guy, why am I letting him run my life, I felt impotent, I felt obliged, like I had to stay to find out why I was staying. I knew now why Penny remained so long with him, breaking-up time after time, swearing on each she would never go back, finally moving away to Hawaii.

Working the Daily Mirror did not threaten Nick's control, no man ever came-in. Now he drove me to and from. I was not allowed on the Ave without him, or in the grocery store without him, he waited outside Pacific Iron Fabric Store, and watched me, and listen to my phone calls. And I had no answer to the constant inner screaming, WHY WHY WHY only made me crazy. And shame had joined the mix, for I prided my self on becoming my own person, left Josh to live an original life, and here I was, dominated, rationalizing, and too over-ruled to move-out, too ashamed to go home, too confused to write Bonita-Kay for advise, too disgraced to tell anyone, but Tara, the one I was allowed to talk too. She was not interested, in liberation, in divine wholeness, in an original life, only in William, in pleasing her Prince. She complained thinking such big thoughts, thinking so far out-there into the universe made her anxious, made her feel like she was too small. And Nick, raised stern Roman Catholic, any discussion about God, about a divine wholeness, trampled on his sacred ground, his don't you dare ground. For he was convinced God was omnipotent, omniscient, and afraid He could hear. In-fact any thing that interested me, he would put-down as not worthy of his time, unless he initiated the conversation and could later take credit for my ideas too. I mentally fractured, started having three and four way head conversations, lively and actual.

Nick neglected to always censor the mail, often too stoned to remember. An invitation arrived for my cousin's Bar Mitzvah, temporary parole. I quietly made a dress akin to Tara's, and while the Saturday jam whirled, and Tara lay draped over the couch, I painted my nails and face, pinned my hair-up in a casual Gibson, called a cab and slipped-out the back door. Feeling the wide-open rush of freedom, as in high school when I could not sleep and would sneak-out my bedroom window, one or two PM, just to have a stroll, to have the whole place to my self. My Folks were furious with me living-in-sin, especially with this particular man, their anger melted when they saw me in the flesh. I danced with my Dad, as always at family gatherings. He reminded me how I learned to dance standing on his shoes, then looking long and deep into my eyes said softly "Shoshy, you come home any time, no questions asked". I flashed a deceivingly carefree smile and kissed his cheek, my Dad, I had one of the good ones, I knew what a good man could be, I knew better, Nick was not a good man, if only I could go home.

And I danced with Little Brother, and confided "I feel like neon. Is it my imagination, or is everyone really looking at me". Little laughed "Duh they're looking. You're not wearing a bra". Reluctantly, obligingly I danced with Big Brother, who came with Marlee. He and Nick were the same age, knew the other from inter-mural baseball, knew because it was common knowledge how badly Nick treated Penny, knew because Big always had a crush on her, and, always believed he could simply order me around "I want you to stop living with Nick". Growing-up, naïve to my handsome Big Brother's shortcomings, I realized more every year, Big was oblivious to other's feelings, and controlling, there seemed to be some essential piece of him missing, and thus he wielded the license of being first-born boy-child in a Jewish family, the sort of boy I would never choose to have anything personal to do with. Paroled from Nick, I relished a small but delivering act of defiance to this unmerited prerogative, declaring in chin-out bravado "It's my life. I will live it as I see fit". He pushed me away and exploded "You leave him now or else". He would never back down, I'd never seen it even cross his mind, riposte mattered only to me "You're not my Father. You can't tell me what to do". This only fueled outrage, he boomed "Then you're not my sister anymore". Everyone turned toward the commotion, he strode-off the dance floor. Neon, braless, I followed, arms out-stretched, hands open, entreating, mostly for effect "Come on. Here's my hand. Take it". He disregarded me, left the room, and my dear protective Granny was magically by my side, taking my hand, leading me to our table. Still I did not own the poise to bear family scrutiny right now, Big had this trick of making our confrontations look like I was the instigator, and I wasn't clever, or maybe wasn't devious or cunning or wily or sly or bully enough to ever prevail. I was thinking I never would, and that I did not want to try anymore, he was my brother, but did that mean I need have any further obligation. I called a cab, parole annulled.

Sitting in the kitchen, waiting in the dark, Nick sniffed the air as I came-in, then accused me of sneaking-out to fuck Gabriel. I took the Bar Mitzvah invitation from my purse, laid it on the table and bid flatly "Call my Folks if you want". The insubordination, the lack of engagement pissed him off even more "Right. They'll just lie for you. Jews lie. God damn fucking liars, don't feel any honest guilt. I need to watch you all the time or you'll cunt every fucking dick". With a thumb he flipped-on the light switch behind him "Look at you, parading around with your tits out, advertising whore to the whole world. You should be flattered I'm jealous". I was not, only frightened at the latest hostility, toward me being Jewish. This was plainly about way more than me. I did not get why I should feel guilty, he knew I wasn't a whore. This had to be his Catholic sin stuff, no matter how good you are, you're still bad, the born-of-woman crap. So clever to make this something to be guilty of, some thing a human had no choice in. And the jealousy, Katey and Rachel considered it a demonstration of indisputable love, Tara too, if their man wasn't green-eyed, they would deliberately do some thing to elicit the monster. I was the white crow in the flock, insisting they had love and jealousy mixed together. And yet I was not exactly sure, this was my first cohabitation, I was not certain how things were suppose to go. Dad never treated Mom like this, my mind was spinning, screaming fuck you jerk, my mouth spoke in fear and apology "I promise I won't do it again". Nick was not appeased, tore the invitation in half and threw it at my face. Rods of steel shot through me into the floor, I planted my feet and softened my body, he was going to hit me for the first time, and I wanted him to, tangible proof this was wrong, solid, good reason to leave. Knocking on the front door broke the moment. Nick left to answer. It was William's brother, who had been drafted, and flying to Fort Benning in the morning, had promised little brother Billy the keys to his VW bus. Nick went upstairs with him. I went to bed.

Tara immediately wanted to move into the bus, take the load off her meager earnings, it would be such fun traveling around like gypsies, pure freedom. William soon agreed, at the end of the month, one week. Without their distraction, days and nights folded in on themselves, while my looping mind-conversation repeated, spinning. The axis, I hoped, even prayed to the vague unknown, this can not be love, this wretched miserable thing, I did not feel this helpless hopeless bondage with Josh, and I left him, maybe that wasn't love, maybe this was the real thing, maybe this was how love feels, maybe there was only one true love for each person, maybe I would only fall in love one time, maybe it was better to love once and lose than never love at all, I had no other answer for this towing, thralling fascination for Nick, it was crazy-cliché, moth to a flame crazy, so extreme I wished he would strike me, and worse, if this was love, I was intolerably disappointed. Nick was master of the dark side, his higher nature wasted, and yet he could be so bright. I believed he would pay a sorry price not being open to learn from me, discounting all I said as trivial, stupid, not worth his time. He went down on me often, I thought ultimately to control me, make me gasp in orgasm, care-fully grooming me into a polished practiced lover, totally responsive. And he was a promising composer who only in private called me muse. And so I remained, confused, immobilized, Nick making all decisions. I purposely failed typing to avoid getting stuck behind a typewriter, and that somehow took me to a Boeing typewriter, and my headstrong quest for illumination, for an original life, for love somehow took me again, to incarceration, and again I must wait for change.

One week into 1968, Howard and his girlfriend Lizabeth sublet upstairs, he knew William and heard the place was available, and brought the new Beatles Magical Mystery Tour album. Howard was a junkie, dealing small-time to keep himself in smack, Lizabeth a student of cello at Cornish School of Music, neither would participate in second-speak. Lizabeth was never invited to join the boys jam. She, Howard and I would frequently get stoned in the kitchen while they played. As Nick's insults and insinuations escalated, he began reading my diary, threatening to read it to the boys. I had the nauseating feeling he already had, and from that minute no longer wrote my real thoughts or feelings, no more a safe place to talk too my self, the one I had left. And he began calling my cooking garbage, me a monotonous mechanical lover, that I had too much hair on my body for a girl, scoffing at my poetry, my sewing, my collages, and my playing guitar, never letting me touch his 1955 Epiphone Texan flat top, boasting it had better curves, that I wasn't worthy. Self-esteem nearing annihilation, still I refused to be sucked-into competing for curves with a guitar.

And then the Sweet Sisters Fate offered refuge in a new neighbor, Maya, Jamaican by way of Louisiana, single Mom of three girls, ages five, six and fourteen. We were instant sisters, and she immediately began trying to convince me I would be better-off alone than with a man who put me down, that I had no marriage, no kids to keep me, and should get gone before I did. I didn't know where to go or what to say to people, too proud, too embarrassed, and I felt dazed from the cacophony banging in my head, promising her, when I knew what to do, I would leave. She understood, having stayed herself, having two more kids. Nick did not regard Maya a threat, her place became my sanctuary, as long as no men were there, and there were never men there. When the 45th Governor of Alabama, George Wallace, announced his candidacy as 3rd party challenger to LBJ and Eugene McCarthy in the presidential election, we decided if Wallace won we would move to Canada together. When Martin Luther King Junior gave his February 4th sermon from Atlanta Georgia, we watched on her 13 inch Sears television and dreamed of going South to help, to be part of something so inspiring. In her cozy kitchen, kids on our laps, we talked of a better world, and what we could do to make it happen, believing our friendship was a good beginning, for I was her first White, she my first Black. Maya cook limas and ham-hocks, red beans and rice, mustard greens, cornbread, jambalaya, gumbo, and though I was Macrobiotic, I ate with relish. I cooked potato latkes, raisin noodle kugel, blintzes, eggplant pot-la-john, and cold beet borscht with chopped green onions and sour cream, and she ate with relish. Her Girls, like me as a child, turned-up their noses at the borscht. And we talked of White privilege in America. From Arthur I knew access was the key that made the difference. She lovingly smiled as I went on how I understood dis-crimination growing-up Jewish on Mercer Island, how my neighbor was cousin to a well-known Christian singer and would not allow me to put even one toe on their property, somehow I would contaminate it by my Jewness. I proudly told of sneaking-out my bedroom window at night to walk across, to desecrate those very neighbors tennis court. We laughed and laughed at my way of payback. Many neighborhoods on the Island would not allow Blacks or Jews. Even school-mates parties were segre-gated, pretext blamed on their parents, some invited me anyway, please go to the back door and I will let you in, I never went. Maya agreed I had suffered, still if I hid any sign of being Jewish my white-skin allowed access impossible to her. And she was right, I could hide, she could not, the thing was, I did not have it in me to hide. Maya was raped by a 22 year old chum of her older brother, who blamed her for enticing him, and when she began to show, Dad threw her out. She never finished high school, gave birth at 16, and lived with that chum for 11 years, having two more kids, leaving when she walk-in on him molesting their eleven year old daughter. He stalked them, threatening killing for her leaving, she disappeared, he wrested her address from welfare under the guise of wanting to support his kids, take the burden off the state. Her chance, her 7 month escape-window came when he was busted a year ago, convicted and sentenced to three years penitentiary, seven months on good behavior, she sold everything and moved here. Maya never had a paying job, and could not afford one now, there was no way for her to make enough to pay a baby-sitter, pay her children's medical and have any food or rent, and though it would be easier monetarily with a man around, especially collecting welfare and him working, and there had been offers, she refused to subjugate herself or her kids ever again. She was also always on hight alert incase he found her again. Maya loved my White, and especially my Jewish, wanting to know all about customs and rituals. And I loved her Jamaican and Rastafarian and wanted the same. Neither were experts, neither practiced. We found our samenesses not surprising, our differences endearing, fascinating, never cause for distrust or separation. We found when the unknown or unfamiliar came known, it was no longer other, strange, unpredictable, no longer frightening.

Working the Mirror was refuge too, I never missed a day, till Robert Kennedy announced his challenge to Eugene McCarthy and President Johnson for the Democratic nomination, I came down with the stomach flu, and took the rest of the week off. Feeling better, I decided to check-out the little house in the backyard. Built of one-by-five unpainted pine, light shining through all the knot-holes fallen out over time, it had a concrete floor, and was full of stuff. I picked through the old whiskey bottles and rusted tools, and found a long wooden box, a single barrel shotgun made by Harrington & Richardson inside, so beautiful I needed a deep breath just to take it in. And another box with a shell making machine stamped Remington, and a cardboard box full of brass bottom shell casing, a round can of gun-powder with a measuring spoon inside, a paper bag marked felt wads, and a canvas bag filled with little dark gray metal balls. I lifted the machine onto a wooden bench, and followed the instruction booklet, pushing a casing into the proper slot, one scoop gun-powder, one felt wad to cover, buckshot to the line, I pulled the handle down that packs and closes the top. Making five before one looked right, I always wanted to and never had fired a gun, opening it, loading the shell, closing, I pointed at the wall and pulled the trigger. Wham, the barrel slammed into my shoulder, spinning, knocking me down, head banging on a whiskey bottle, then concrete, ringing like a church bell, I saw stars. Suddenly sick to my stomach, shoulder numb, my eyes focused on the sun-light streaming through a new big hole in the wall. Rolling over, panicked, I pushed to my knees and crawled to see my neighbor, who refused to acknowledge the existence of White people in his neighborhood, taking flight up his back-porch stairs. Irony curled my mouth with what might have seemed a smile, Mr.Neighbor could not ignore my blowing the pickets off his fence. Overwhelmingly relieved he seemed physically fine, my wits recovering, I stood, banshees screaming in my head, made my way to his front door and knocked. After what seemed too long, I heard the lock slide shut and a voice demanding what do you wanted. I must have boomed to overcome the banshees, begging his forgiveness, explaining what sounded so preposterous. He cut me off, shouting get off my porch or he would call the police. I went home and barfed, resigned to wait my Fate, wait for Nick to come home, wondering where he was all day, I had not been home weekdays to know he was gone, waiting, afraid to tell him, afraid we'd get busted. No one came knocking, no one came home, and wholly, utterly, completely exhausted, shoulder aching, neck too, my head at last un-ringing, stomach unsettled, I went to bed.

A rapping on the front door with morning coffee. Nick looked at me accusingly and went to answer. I followed. Mr.Neighbor handed him a pencil-thin joint and asked could we be friends. I understood, it was my choice to expose this or not, I invite him please come in for coffee. Mr.Neighbor followed us into the kitchen. Loaded silent. I poured him a cup. Nick struck a match to the joint, took a drag and passed to me. I showed Mr.Neighbor the rectangular bruise on my shoulder, giving explanation not excuse, asking forgiveness again, and relighting the peace-joint, took a small toke, and passed to him. He leaned in further than necessary, took the joint lightly touching my fingers, and looking me friendly in the eyes leaned back, inhaled a short puff, smiled at me as he exhaled and stood-up, nodding to Nick, he was on his way to work. Nick nodded back. Mr.Neighbor left the roach in the ashtray and was gone. We never spoke again. This was the proof Nick had been waiting for, substantiation, irrefutable confirmation I was incompetent, that he must do all my thinking for me. He never missed a chance to repeat the story to anyone who would listen. And my head spun round-and-round, maybe he was right, I did such a brainless, potentially deadly thing, did not mean to, but I did it. But this also painted me in new adjectives, unpredictable, dangerous. I rather liked how they made Nick seriously cautious. And I did not protest.

To work again, bruised shoulder yellowing round the edge, goose-egg back of my head going away, headaches remained. I mentioned nothing to Boss, knowing she was an express conduit to Mom. Saturday night, Nick celebrating his parents 25th wedding anniversary at Kim's Broiler with dinner and their favorite entertainment, the Gil Conte Trio, I was not invited, and under orders, do not leave the property. Sitting down to work at my Pfaff, Howard knocked at the back-door. Lizabeth was out too, practicing with her promising new four-piece chamber group, he invited me to do some smack with him. Head aching, I was game and followed, technically obeying Nick's command.

We sat at one corner of the chrome and pink Formica table, too big for the small kitchen, bare but for an army-issued olive-drab metal strongbox, **CHEST AMMUNITION CAL.50 M17 D 39106** stenciled in black on the front. Howard opened the latch, took out a cherry-size red balloon and set it on the table. I chaffed at heroin coming in a child's toy. He mentioned it was a dime balloon. I offered to split the cost. He smiled "Absolutely not. When I stop sharing with my friends, then I'm strung-out. This is on me". He was strung-out, this was his disclaimer. I sat quiet, watching the ritual, worrying, wondering if the terrible was true, that I would be hooked after just one time, not caring. A small aluminum pot came out of the box, which Howard filled with an inch of water and set on the gas stove to boil. A white linen hand-towel carefully laid on the table, a shot glass he filled with water, a small glass eye-dropper. And a red velvet lined silver box, he opened to reveal a well-worn cloudy glass syringe he called a fit, with two reusable needles and a needle cleaner, he placed neatly on the linen towel. A box of cotton went next to the shot glass, an ivory-handled strait razor, round hand-mirror, needle-nose pliers, small wooden board, and a burnt-bottomed silver soup-spoon with its flat wide handle curled back and under to make a stable foot. Tools laid precisely in their well-known places. Howard switched on a second burner to low flame, slit the balloon and carefully poured the smack onto the mirror. It sparkled in the harsh kitchen light as he chopped the crystals with the strait razor, scooped one-third into the spoon, adding exactly five drops of water from the shot glass with the eye-dropper. Pliers held the spoon over the flame till the contents bubbled light brown with dark specks. He set the spoon on the wooden board to cool, dark specks settling to the bottom. Hands trembling he pulled a bit of cotton from the box, rolled it between thumb and fingers to caper-size, and dropped it in the spoon. With pliers he laid the syringe and needles gently into the boiling pot, thirty seconds he turned off the gas. Lifting one needle and the syringe onto the towel to cool, washing hands, he deftly attached the syringe to the needle, laid the tip at an angle on the cotton caper, and slowly, smoothly pulled the plunger, sucking-up light brown liquid, cotton filtering out the dark specks. Holding the needle up, gently flicking the glass cylinder with his finger to jog any air to the tip, saying it would not feel so good to blow air into my vein, then slowly pushing the plunger till a small bubble formed at the tip and burst. Laying the fit on the linen, he asked me to roll-up my sleeve, removed his belt, wound it twice round my arm just above the elbow, cinching tight, gripping the ends securely in his left hand. It pinched, I surrendered my arm to the table, palm-up. Howard instructed make a fist, and with his free first fingers lightly slapped just at the bend of my arm. Raising a fat blue vein he picked-up the fit, slid the needle in bevel-side up, careful not to pierce through the other side, allowing a tinge of blood into the cylinder to make sure it was in, he let go the belt and slowly injected the muddy liquid. I watched him withdraw the needle, a small bead of blood covering the exit, moaning rushing waves of heat running though my body, orgasm in every cell, brain swamp, unable to move, solid as fudge, I was the Wholeness, the Beatles Fool on the Hill, disconnecting from physical and mental pain, I realized how much I held now it was gone. Howard gave me a fraternal smile. I could only nod. He rolled-up his sleeve, showing track stained pale skin, and repeated the ritual with the remaining two-thirds, using the other needle in the pot, wrapping the belt round his arm, one end held in his teeth, buckle between his knees, his near invisible veins rolling away from the needle, trying again, blood tinging the dark liquid, opening his mouth he let go the belt, smack in, Howard exhaled slowly.

I felt a real intimacy using needles. We sat in mutual silence, submerged in very low vibration, together on the same plate, queasy, pupils completely taking our eyes, trying to shrink from the kitchen light. When he stood,

I did, and followed to the living room. He lit the candle on the coffee-table, stacked John Coltrane and Miles Davis on the record player, we took to opposite ends of the couch, Coltrane the perfect compliment. And Howard told me his story. Special Forces, a Green Beret, discharged five months now, the unexpected unbearable incongruity of coming home to civilization made it clear what a killer he had become, made it impossible living with him self, knowing how capable he was. He'd been in the Secret War, code named Operation Phoenix, ordered into Cambodia by LBJ, over-seen from Vietnam by William Colby, ordered, silent into the jungle, to garrot the gooks. I didn't know the words garrot or gooks, and did not ask. His recompense, crisp one-hundred dollar bills for proof of kill, for ears, and all the drugs caviar and whiskey he could swill in 36 hours leave. He took the numb oblivion, blotting-out the job, too horrible to imagine, too horrible to live with, then back to work. And because Operation Phoenix was illegal, because LBJ was lying to the American people that we are not in Cambodia, there was no help for Howard when he came home, since it never happened. Now, haunted when he wasn't wasted, when he could feel or think, he wasted him self daily. I'd never heard of Operation Phoenix, and totally believed, for something had him, something so awful he needed numb just to live in his skin. With parental blessing, Nick acted crazy and queer and dodged Vietnam. Howard's Father, Colonel Aloof, expected his son, his only son to carry on family tradition, without regard for an introverted, sensitive boy who craved Dad's love and approval enough to obey. They were estranged now, and Howard was a junkie, thin, pale, hollow-eyed, he nodded-off. I did too, enjoying the deep hum of smack, peace-full parole, till I heard Nick's bus, spilled down the stairs and into bed, disappearing into a dreamless bog.

Nick woke me with morning coffee, and noticing the track on my pristine arm, wasn't bothered by the smack, marching me upstairs to accuse us of fucking. Unlike William, Howard was not intimidated by Nick, he laughed, asking who could fuck on smack, challenging Nick to grow-up, that only a sissy pushes his woman around. Nick took me downstairs, and humiliated, threatened with a raised open hand. It had been all mind game with us till right now, I dared not cower, eyes glaring into his. He lowered the hand to his side, closing it into a fist. Without striking he won my fear, because he might. I did not make a noise, withdrew to the bath-tub, daring to lock the door. Nick and Howard were high school buddies, being smaller men bonded them. A deep chill grew between Howard and me, not of my making.

Lizabeth and Howard came down to watch LBJ address the nation. His startling closing statement *"Accordingly, I shall not seek, and will not accept, the nomination of my party for another term as your President"*. I flushed exhilaration, Robert Kennedy had captured my imagination, he brought such intelligence to the national political debate. Yes he was a rich-kid, still I believed in my heart he wanted to, that he could make things better for everyone, somehow make my life better too. LBJ had just opened it wide for Kennedy to challenge Eugene McCarthy for the Democratic nomination, and to contest Richard Nixon, the clear Republican front-runner to Ronald Reagan. And for Walter Cronkite to speculate, would Vice President Hubert Humphrey now enter the race. After the broadcast, Howard announce Lizabeth was pregnant, and they were moving to a thirty-acre farm in the Cascade Foothills, twenty-five miles east of Seattle, to have the baby. Thrill turned to dread, I would be left alone with Nick.

April third, Nick offered his bus to help them move, the farm was a really good place to grow a baby. We smoked Howard's entire stash of opium. I nodded-off on the ride home, and went to sleep in my clothes as the sun came up. Stepping over rocks to the white sand beach of an ocean front estate, Cesar Romero standing on the deck watching the surf roll in when he saw me. Smiling, greeting a dear friend, he came to give me a hand. We went to water's edge. And the Mothers, Grandmothers, the Great Grandmothers came walking from the waves, dressed in Victorian, completely dry woolens and lace, cotton gloves, hats. These were my Mothers, my Sisters, I was over-joyed, and knew in my heart they had come to claim me. A high-pitched constant piercing through abducted me, crossing sleep's threshold, opening my eyes, wondering why was I dressed, wondering why Mr.Neighbor was mowing his lawn on a Thursday afternoon when he should be at work. The Mirror had closed for a few days, Boss gone to market in New York City, I planned on sleeping all day, and when the mower stopped at last, tried to regain the dream, wondering why Cesar Romero. Kidnapped awake again, this time Nick taking me to the kitchen window to see the laurel hedge surrounding our house butchered to stubs. Deep in my Jewish blood I knew it was time, whispering loud, urgent "Nick, we need to go, now". His grip on my arm tightened "Where to stupid". I could see he was afraid, pulling him to the front room, turning on TV. Robert Kennedy was standing there on a flatbed truck, heavy husky voice saying Martin Luther King Jr. had been murdered in Memphis. Gasping crowds, disbelief, anguish and violence crossed the county, fifty cities under siege, in flames, eight dead in Chicago, four in DC, four here, flames burning here, police overwhelmed and acting badly, LBJ threatening to call-out the National Guard. I felt the same fury as when Grampa died, for no one had moved a high school sophomore more, sitting at the dinner table, watching Martin Luther King Jr. leading the August 1963 March on Washington DC, listening to him speak his Dream. I was marked Christ-killer in a Christian country, and also dreamed of being judged by the content of my character. The hedge an unmistakable messenger Nick could not ignore, not even to prove me wrong, he phoned Grandma, matriarch of their tight-knit Roman Catholic family and explained our circumstance. Grandma Tortoise knew of a house, two doors up the hill from her on Holly Street, the owners had built a new one on the same property, moved-in and were considering renting, she would arrange it. We filled every grocery bag, garbage bag, pillow-case, sheet and box. Nick packed the bus, and I went to see Maya. She opened the door an inch and warned "Go 'way li'l sister". I reached for her hand, she took mine, such loss between us, no use swapping promises, no matter how we had wanted our friendship to matter, it was small comfort to the wreckage that had happened. I hurried over the butchered hedge, one jagged stump tearing my shin, bleeding through my sock, blood sacrifice every where. Nick viewed the murder as inevitable, my tears as weakness, he showed no emotion. I left them on my face, and road to the Holly Street house, silent.

Thirty-dollars a month, completely furnished, beautifully furnished. Unpacking in the morning I found thieves in the wreckage, many cherished belongings were missing. My 13th birthday ring, a white-gold sunflower with a two-carat peridot at heart. My black pearl ring, a delicate bird's nest of spun-gold cradling the imperfect orb. Dad acquired the large pearl while serving in the South Pacific, made it into a tie tack, and ever since I could recall, I shamelessly coveted that ample wonder over breakfast, pinned to the center of his tie, ready for work. For my fifteenth, Dad made it into a ring. The party was at the Bleu Dolphin restaurant. I wondered why such a fancy place would set the table with a crumpled napkin, picked it up to investigate, and was speechless for maybe a whole minute when the ring tumbled onto the table. And my sterling silver sixteen-charm bracelet was gone, sweet-sixteen gift from Granny and Grampa. Most expensive, my twelve-charm gold bracelet, Dad made one for each year I was in school, my favorite, a miniature bicycle with moving handle-bars and wheels, he fastened it onto my wrist high school graduation eve. Least valuable and most dear, the silver candelabrum passed down to me from Granny's Mother, the only thing she dared hide under her coat when fleeing the Kishinev pogrom. I rarely wore the jewelry, having them was the wealth, imbued with such precious meaning, irreplaceable memories, this was the real worth, these belongings, these treasures I just knew Howard took, and probably already sold to feed his habit. And, I knew it would do no good, but had to tell Nick, I had to tell someone. Oh surprise, he took Howard's side, insisting I was stupid and misplaced them, warning me not to dirty a man's reputation when I didn't know what I was talking about. Outrage displaced heartache, Nick knew I never misplaced, maybe he took them. But then Howard had become so suddenly distant. Yes, I was stupid, a stupid fool to leave precious things round, to have been so naive.

Our landlords, Fred and Kumi Yamasaki, and his Father had been rounded-up and shipped to the Puyallup Relocation Center during World War II, then to Idaho, the Minidoka Japanese American Internment Camp, imprisoned there two years. Fred's Father made his name as a landscape artist in Seattle, using their half-acre property as nursery for hundred year old Bonsai trees, and uncounted exotic flora. Fred learned well from his Dad, and was selected in 1959 to do the stone-setting for the Seattle Japanese Gardens in Washington Park Arboretum. Now their property was surrounded in tall bamboo.

I liked Fred and Kumi right away, could have been content living in their garden alone, for I was beginning to think there was great dignity in being alone. There were no jams here to grant me private time, and though Tara and William found living in his brothers VW bus not so idyllic as they imagined, needing a place to bathe and eat and shit, they parked in our driveway on nights they were not staying at Howard and Lizabeth's farm. And even with the constant stream of quick buyers in-and-out to score, Nick's grip on me tightened. One morning I woke with a loud commandment in my head, you need a wave. I completely understood, sitting too long on my surf board waiting, it was time to start swimming. In a stolen moment I solicited Tara, did she have any good LSD. She gave me windowpane, a small clear gelatin square, cautioning, only take half.

Stashed in my sewing basket, I waited for Sunday, often after church Nick and his family would brunch at Ray's Boathouse, and weather permitting, take their 42-foot Christ Craft Constellation out for the day. I was relieved never to be invited, my Jewish made them uncomfortable after mass. A gentle dry Spring day, I cleaned the house, bathed in symbolic purification, donned the blue-and-red batik dress Marigold gave me, and by 2PM, confident Nick was on the water, placed the windowpane on my tongue, stacked Nilsson, Simon & Garfunkel, Cream, and Tim Hardin on the turn-table, sat cross-legged on the azure living room carpet, cup of Oolong cooling on the low black lacquer table inlaid with abalone dragons, waiting. There was no hint of tin foil when the walls blew-out. I went streaking though the stars, melting glowing colored ribbons, coming to soft land at the feet of a tremendous entity, holding the sun in its right and moon in its left hand. I was relieved it had hands, some thing I could relate to, this was Diabutsu, the great Buddha at Kamakura. Tears of joy running my cheeks, emotionally overtaken, I dared look-up at the face, feeling completely whole and precious simply being in its presence, understanding as if I always knew, my purpose was not instinctual animal hungers, survival at any cost, perpetuation of the species, but to grow an immortal seed, innate, living, to foster depth of character, courage, humility, consciousness. Suddenly Diabutsu look down on me with glowing red diamond eyes and decreed "I am not for you. Seek the Gate of Horn elsewhere". Rivers of molten fire gushed from those eyes, sweeping me with such force, hurling toward the earth, off kilter, and space and time again holding me, I sat where I was, cross-legged on the azure carpet, records done, tea cold, remembering Gabriel had seen the Buddha.

I did not know what to make of the decree to seek the Gate of Horn elsewhere, or the ferocity in which I was swept away, but the living room walls were too close, and I hurried into the sweet evening, perching on a small grass knoll in the lower garden, over-looking Rainier Valley. The yard abuzz with Grandpa Yamasaki's ghost tending the Bonsais, and me so still the critters did not mind. A brown bunny sitting very still too turned her lovely slender pink ears to me as the light left the sky, the stars coming on with a flick of a switch, and the sparkling one I saw in the Redwoods, again rotating. This time I knew there was no one inside, that the light was a projection from some other source, like an image on TV. Maybe the same light Jews followed in the Ark of the Covenant as they wandered through the Sinai, that lit the star leading Balthazar, Melchior and Caspar to baby Jesus, that lit the Diabutsu's diamond eyes, and my Sweet Sisters Fate. My mind suddenly outside my body, strangely small, eight-inches long, seven wide, one-inch thick, thinning to naught at the rounded edge, made of solid silicon, the ideal conductor of electricity, for stacking like pancakes to make love, for telepathic communication, friction free, able to travel at the speed of thought, there is no time or space in thought, I could think of being a child and be there instantly, fast as if it was right now, and I was not actually physically in this disc shaped vehicle, more of it, mind not brain the traveler, this new body of the future. The very thought of body, I was heavy in mine again, and the rotating sparkling star shot away, gone, leaving me amazed how improbable, how precarious and thin-skinned my carbon-based medium was. And like good acid always did for me, a wave arrived, I must find the Gate of Horn, maybe the stone ram with its horns curled round its ears, I must find others so I am not so alone, so vulnerable, maybe go back to Texas.

Nick and me had good times too. He was generous in his way, amusing, charming, and loved to show me off in public, making me feel the fairest of them all. And he had this compelling quality I could not name, some potential that I wasn't sure was love. However, LSD nor Macrobiotics had initiated any real quickening in him, and I found my self considering, maybe the potential I saw was really my own, maybe Nick was an imperceptible mirror, maybe staying, loving no-matter-what did not help him realize any potential, maybe it was really my own reflection. I wished the way to awake was as simple as drugs and eating the right Ying/Yang balance, neither had done much for William or Tara either. The sound of his bus did not register till he parked at the front steps, it was too late to steal inside, I sat still in the dark. He saw me, outside, in the dark, and the charging began "Hiding some dog in heat". He took his time, looking round, eyes darting, growing increasingly paranoid, he seemed to make-up what he wanted to believe, steadily leaning on me to quit the Mirror, after all he made good money, and it didn't look right his woman working. Finding no hound in the yard, he stood over me "Why shouldn't I take your clothes and lock you out. Your lover 'll keep you warm, right. Maybe I'll make a scene at the Mirror tomorrow. Get you fired. How'd you like that". He knew this was my sole-link to the outside. I'd been secreting money away for when I could leave. Summoning what I had, sure he could read the dissemble in my eyes, chin jutting so little I could protest not, a hint of sass "Would that make you feel like a big man". Not sure he would raise a hand, no, I took a slow deep breath, noting a whisper of Emeraude perfume, tell-tale mention, I sniffed the air, chin unmistakably jutting "Do I smell a dog in heat". He looked surprised "You Bitch. I went to the Black & Tan after lunch. Jammed with some cats. Time got away. I don't need to tell you anything". I could see the dissemble in his eyes, knew he knew I won this small victory, one tick-tock in the bigger game, allowing me to slipped by into the house.

Nick could not bear the power shift, the loss of control, wrapping his arms round and wrestling me to the carpet. I did not struggle when he sat on my stomach, or when he raised my arms above my head pinning elbows down with his knees, I did not struggle, would not struggle, I did not recognize the face on his face. Disappointed in my surrender, anger blazing his eyes, his nose sharper, he slapped my face, not slapped, more pushing it side to side, repeating "Stupid Bitch. Say it. Stupid Bitch. Say it. I'm a stupid Bitch. Say it Bitch". I did not, would not, and left my body, quick like smoke through the front door, into the Labyrinth, knowing I would not find my way out, that it was better inside, safer than being sane, taking a portion of me Nick could not degrade, corrupt, taint. And I began to laugh, uncontrollably, like a loon. And he knew, and rolled off me, knew he pushed me beyond his control. I stood, still laughing, and went to my room.

Before work, I always took my coffee into the bamboo garden and sat for a while on the bench, enjoying the beauty and peace. This morning I came upon the Yamasaki's Siamese cat savaging a young robin. Throwing my coffee, scalding Cat's haunch, she flew straight-up in the air screaming, and ran, leaving a bloody little fledge. At first I was afraid to touch, then, he did not struggle as I carry in both hands to the kitchen, and laid him on a soft dish towel. Fledge was quiet, ripped open, one eye on me, one anguished eye on me. I knew he could not live, and that I had the power, the mercy to be Death's hand. Waking Nick, I pleaded for a pinch of smack. He obliged, recognizing from my resolve he could appease no other way, taking his time, underlining his control. And though each second hurt my heart, I stood, patiently, hands open, giving him no ground to change his mind. After crushing the crystals to fine dust with the bottom of a glass, and dissolving in a tablespoon of warm milk, I used an eye-dropper, Fledge took willingly, tears falling on his feathers, stroking the side of his head with my baby finger, the light in his brave eye still fixed on me, fading, his tiny heart stopped beating. So fragile, inconsequential, so easily lost, I felt a terrible release, wondering where life goes as I swaddled him in a crimson silk scarf, consecrated with tears, and opened a small grave beneath the dwarf flowering plum tree in the bamboo garden, Cat watching. Nick took enthusiastic advantage of my vulnerable, shadowing every move, deriding my compassion as if it was a failing, demanding I pay for the smack. I felt a visceral satisfying symbolic vindication from the powerlessness of my Grampa's death, washed tears from my face, I gave Nick ten-bucks, and said nothing as he drove me to work. We brawled verbally whenever we were in the bus. He would accuse me of the impossible, like having been with a guy that looked at me while we stopped at a light, and then hound me about it for days. There was no defense to such irrational charges, so I stopped looking, and now he owned my eyes. I never thought a person could own your eyes.

One more week and we were evicted. From the transient comings and goings Fred figured Nick was dealing, and did not want our kind around, if we were gone in twenty-four hours, he would not tell Grandma Tortoise. Nick called Howard, was there room at the farm. Tara and William had moved into the empty trailer on the property, we were welcome to park and use the main house kitchen and bath. Our things again went into bags. I hated slinking-off with the stink of Nick's business on me, but did not protest, even knowing I would have to quit the Mirror, public transportation stopped miles from the farm, and Nick would certainly not take me. From her tight-lipped response, Boss was pissed at my leaving without notice, saying she understood, I knew only because of her long friendship with Mom. Howard had done detox, three weeks voluntary in-patient at Harborview, still struggling with the mental craves. And though his larceny enraged me, I did so admire his love, his respect for Liz, for the coming baby, and the courage to own, too deal with his habit, reasons for a new friendship. We were all Macrobiotic now, it was the hip thing to be, and if nothing, Tara had to be the hip thing to be. She'd taken the power of the kitchen, Muse abandoned for Earth Mother, and like Marigold, allowed room for no one. Lizabeth was uncomfortable pregnant, and fine with this. We ate together in the big open kitchen. I was quite surprised to find how unfettered I felt, no more Beige Ladies, no house to keep, meals to prepare, I set-up my Pfaff on the farmhouse porch and began sewing for everyone and the baby. And I resumed my journal, this time as fiction, certain Nick did not suspect I knew he was reading it, writing what I dare not say aloud to him. When I needed the truth, privately, like a poem called The Rutabaga I Live With, I wrote, and then lit it with a match. Howard had strung yards of wire, putting speakers on the roof and in near-by trees, so Lizabeth could laze outside in the hammock listening to her favorite music. Sergeant Pepper playing, I packed my green soapstone chillum in Nick's best weed, and tripped along the over-grown trail into twenty-acres of second-growth alder, maples and cedar. A sunny afternoon that took me to an abandoned dirt-floor shack, on the shore of a small clear lake covered in water lilies, that butted another 400 acres reaching into the Cascade foothills. No one to hear me scream.

Howard's warning ignored, Nick and William decided to get into smack, the hip thing for serious musicians to do. Tara wanted along for the ride, and I went too. We shot-up at sundown, sharing a balloon, using disposable syringes, Nick doing the honors. A quarter balloon not near the same rush I felt with Howard, plastic syringes could not excite the same shared intimacy, did not solve my pain, taking only the edge off, leaving only despair. We sat like wet clay in the trailer's rusted kitchenette, pupils fully dilated, candles lit, muttering our strange second-speak, sipping Chamomile tea to calm the nausea, listening to MoonGoose, smack-head Hippies favorite album, marveling at Delroy Bogave's virtuoso guitar, making empty talk.

Eight sun-downs and I was done, quarter balloon no longer getting anyone off, I wanted more too, more to get to the same miserable place. The new arrangement, half-a-balloon each. The voice in my head screaming absolutely no, you my dear are already a big fat tuna with a big fat hook in your mouth. And when I said no, Nick called me coward, liar, traitor, chicken-shit, stupid Bitch, threatening to force me. And the lovely quandary of how psychotic was I really, if he pushed too far he could lose his quarry to madness, end the deadly dance, he did not want to end the dance. And me ever so slightly madd, not really sure it was an act, I was happy to be chicken-shit, better than stealing from friends. Sundown, lingering in the trailer doorway, watching them divide my share, I felt such desire, withdrew to the bus, monotonous ache creeping into my low back, wailing for relief, begging to be smacked. Taking four Excedrin Extra Strength, a shot of Nyquil chased with a Coors, throwing up, I could not be still for the pain, shivering, sweating, dehydrated, dry heaves, even water would not stay with me. Tara and William too stoned to do anything. Nick claiming it was just an act to get some after all, regarding me an unwelcome stray. Not one pinch of kindness, compassion, no human beings there really, just players in this devious rambling game and doing drugs, no one having fun, no one mentioning the game. It struck me, maybe no one knew, maybe it was so automatic, so inevitable that no one questioned, the cruelty, the control. Maybe I was the only one who saw it, maybe I was some other species, maybe I could get out of my body for a while and leave the pain, jump off the earth. June nights mercifully six hours, Howard was up at dawn, saw me, knew, and took me in. Lizabeth too, tenderly through the next day, till I could suck on ice and keep it down, till I was nearing my self.

Half a balloon was soon not enough. My ordeal may have moved William, then Tara into yikes this is enough. Their ride down not so raw, they had each other. Nick kept going, short-fuse, ashen-face, losing weight, impotent, stubborn too a whole balloon, somehow believing this made him the winner, made him the hippest of all. It was Howard who suffered his poisonous withdrawal, rocking him in his arms most of two days. I did not, his cold-heart killed mine, delivering my own dark-side, Nick the unwelcome stray, and with no grounds for grievance, for I was merely following his lead, his deeds, being his mirror, my head saying go now, take only what you can carry, quick while he's down, while you can. The decision to leave Casey had not been this certain and I did it. I knew to leave Boeing, the Haight, Texas, in hind-sight all right choices, all seeming individual disjointed choices till this minute. I could see my continuity, see a real foundation for trusting my own judgment, feeling solid for the first time ever. This moment was the perfect, face-saving, pride-saving, ego-saving time to go, Nick had treated me so bad infront of witnesses, and I did not go.

Howard's friend Monty West moved into the shack on the lake. Professor of Anthropology, dismissed from the University of Washington for conducting LSD experiments with his students, his well-publicized escapades established him reining, sought-after counter-culture Guru. But the notoriety was interfering with his new vocation, organizing an accredited Experimental College with a Metaphysical curriculum, he needed sanctuary to work. Scientology, Dianetics were just as central to him. He was becoming what they called a Clear, freeing himself from engrams, from his emotions, clearing the way to personal salvation. And compared to his diet, Macrobiotics was pure decadence. I'd taken to mushroom hunting the woods, and he seemed to know and pop out of the air, casually picking licorice ferns from the cedars, eating flowers, weeds, shrooms, harvesting water lily roots from the lake. My interest in him aggravated the shit out of Nick, who resented Monty's natural authority and charisma, and forbid me ever speaking to him. I went anyway, in my latest creation, made from buckskins Howard gave me, although never spoken, bare ransom for his thieving. The skins repulsed me, but they were already dead, and I could only respect them by making use, making my self bell-bottoms that laced-up the sides, and moccasins for all. One morning at the bathroom mirror, weaving wild-flowers into my long braids, looking back at me, an ancient Hebrew face, Asian face, Arab, even Native American face, high cheekbones, slightly slanting eyes, olive skin, a tribe-girl dressed in her buckskins, I was pleased. And no matter when or where in the woods, Monty was waiting, flirting just enough to make me nervous, make me self-conscious, I would chatter politely trying not to show. Fifteen years older, plainly enjoying the unease, he would show his perfect teeth, and point direction to the Chanterelles or Morels, reminding me there were Amanita Phalloides, death caps on the property, advising, telling me, maybe hinting, never feed anyone anything that grows on decay, even by mistake, and he would vanish, fungi always where he said. My hunts bountiful, consistent, Nick began to encourage me.

June 5, just after midnight from the Embassy Room of the Ambassador Hotel in Los Angeles, Robert Kennedy had already claimed victory in the California and South Dakota Democratic Presidential Primaries and was addressing his camgaign workers. I was rich in hope this lovely late warm night, sitting on the porch steps alone, listening to the radio broadcast, feeling so connected. What, he's been shot. What. I found myself walking in a slow circle, biting my lips, holding my ears, what, another Brother, no not another Brother. And I found my self pledging God I will be good forever if you just let Bobby live, begging that on-high I no longer be-lieved in, killing John and Martin was too much already, too many blows, making a simpleton's petition to an at best inadequate deity whose prom-ises were never kept, who could not stop this from happening any more than He could slow or speed Grampa's death, wishing to die my self than endure this excruciation again, this unexpected, this vulnerable, there was no solid ground, no safe place. Bobby was the hope I could see for that better world Maya and I dreamed of. The Malignant knew this, instinc-tively, knew murdering hope again and again, killing the light-bringers, that murdering the one murders the many, making us fear the pain, and worse than losing hope, making us fear hope.

I could not sleep, waiting all day and night by the radio. Frank Mankiewicz announced, *Senator Robert Francis Kennedy died at 1:44AM today. June 6, 1968.* A wail from every cell, sobbing, broken. And Nick just had to mock me, wringing his hands and moaning. Howard told him lay-off. No matter, he was in league with the Malignant, I had to run away, in the dark, into the woods, and Monty, tears gleaming his eyes too. He held my chin, blotting the wet with his thrumo t-shirt sleeve "You're so much smarter than Nick. Why're you wasting your time". I wanted the tears on my face, but let him, aching for comfort in sympathetic arms, my head warning no, he's a lawless werewolf, one little bite and like Persephone you are forever doomed. I took a step back "Don't know. Wish I did". He let me and the moment go "Wow, people aren't usually so honest. Make up excuses. Hey, I'm working on a method of psychic healing, a course I want to offer at the Experimental College. Would you let me try on you. Won't take long. The technique should settle any short circuits in your Chakras electrical field". I knew some of what he was saying, and not wanting to be alone, followed to the shack. A Hudson Bay blanket already spread on the ground outside, Monty gestured with his hand "Just lie down on your back, resting your arms by your sides". I did as told. He sat close to my right elbow, barefoot, legs folded in Lotus position, hands resting on his knees, palms open to the sky, and instructed in a kind unhurried voice "Now shut your eyes Shoshannah, and breathe in through your nose, deeply, evenly, and then breathe out the same way. Think about your breath going in, and coming out, evenly. Relax your muscles, soles of your feet first, then your ankles, legs, hips, back, shoulders, neck, and your head". He paused "Now clear your mind, of everything. Let it all go. If a thought comes in, just let it drift away, do not engage". He smelled moldy, I settled. When our breathing synchronized, he placed his right palm lightly on my solar plexus, and shot straight to his feet, shaking his hand, yelping "Holy shit. No one ever did that". I stood too "What. Did what". He walked round me still shaking his hand "You had a substantial shock in your 4th, in the Heart Chakra. Probably Nick. I took it off, held it in my electrical field so you could feel your heart free of it, feel the peace, know what to strive for. When I fed it back to you, gradually, people will only take it in small doses, you took it all in one gulp. Literally sucked it out of me. I could feel the electricity". I did not know what to say "Sorry. I didn't notice anything, just calm from the breathing. But you're right, when I do something, I go after it". Standing face-to-face, suddenly his equal, I put-out my hand "Well, thank you". He took it in both his "And thanks for being my guinea pig. Psychic benefits are subtle. You let me know if you observe anything, even if you don't think it's connected or important". Looking intensely into my eyes, his grip tightened "There's someone you must meet. Her name's Dr.Ida Rose Barber. She would absolutely love you. I own the home next door. I'll make an appointment for you". I nodded yes, preoccupied, bodies have a proven electrical field, an electrocardiograph machine measures it, maybe he did do something to me "You know, I do feel better. Maybe it's just someone to talk too tonight, this awful night". He smiled, wolfish, letting me know it was time to reclaim my hand, or stay. I did, thanking him again, and followed the trail to the farmhouse.

June 8, we watched Little Brother Edward Kennedy's eulogy from St. Patrick's Cathedral. And the flag-draped African mahogany casket, carried through the bronze doors, into a gray hearse, 75 vehicles moving slowly through fifty-thousand mourners, to Pennsylvania Station, where the box was lifted onto a twenty-one car funeral train bound for Washington DC. Bobby would be buried close to his Big Brother, on a hillside in Arlington National Cemetery. Days later, Hubert Humphrey announced for the Democratic nomination, and Lizabeth's water broke in the shower. Her yoga-teacher-midwife came, to coach her breathing, and the unhitching of her pelvic joints to ease the birth. Two hours like ten, without drugs or tearing, Lizabeth delivered a dainty baby-girl into Howard's drug-free hands. Laying her on Lizabeth, waiting for the cord to stop pulsing, carefully cutting and tying, he carried the girl-child to the kitchen sink, cleaning her in 98.6° water, while yogi-midwife delivered the afterbirth. Lizabeth was amazing, resting half-an-hour, she showered, ate some macaroni and cheese, and laid down with Howard and child to breast-feed. This was the one human birth I witnessed in-person, miraculous, breathtakingly courageous, easy by any standard, and terrifying, I was horrified, revulsed, the pushing and groaning, the fluids, the grunting, I knew I would not do this, knew again leaving Josh had been right. Tara and William were intoxicated, proclaiming they must have their own. Nick stayed away.

Visiting my Folks was the one reason Nick allowed me off the farm. Our relationship was strained because of heavy-handed pressure to leave him when ever I went home. Of course they were right, and I did not argue, only saying I would leave when I was ready, that what I needed from them was to listen, their constant judgment did not help. They did not listen, and visits became fewer, Nick waiting in the bus. I had no channel save my own creativity, sewing and beading kept me from losing grip, especially the small inexpensive colored glass beads with nothing to hide. I loved them, I could look right through, hold their honesty in my hand, mingle hues with rhythmic stitches, embellishing baby moccasins, leather pouches, vests, hours and days with some feeling of accomplishment, satisfaction, my work celebrated by all but Nick. Who was an even bigger dealer, with a motley collection coming to score, always guys. If one looked at or spoke to me, no matter how far-fetched, Nick accused me of knowing him, flirting, fucking. To escape persecution I would disappear into the woods, for mushrooms, hoping Monty would appear. A week and no one saw him. I was giving-up the hunt when he showed "You have an appointment little Red Riding Hood, Ida Rose will see you tomorrow, 11AM". This sounded so strange to me, an appointment for what, why do I need an appointment, who is she, this person Monty holds in such esteem, I worried aloud "Nick'll never let me go alone". Monty smiled those perfect teeth "Just bring the little shit. No one can cross Ida Rose's threshold that isn't suppose to". Still smiling, twinkling really, he handed me a matchbook with her address written on the inside, and knowing I needed cover pointed me to a flush bed of morels. I had to beg, and beg, and detail how I happened to run into Monty on the hunt. First came the usual accusations, lying, flirting, fucking, threats to take away my Pfaff, still he took his time, there was a glimmer of intrigue, he would never admit to being curious about Monty's friends. I did not defend the allegations. Nick agreed to take me.

Chapter Six

THE WOMAN WITH THE WHITE WOOL HAIR

We parked infront of the three-story white brick house, 2214 East Crescent Drive, Seattle, on the hill. Nick grumbled he would not stay long, as we walked the flagstones through an exuberant blooming yard, flowers simply bursting with joy to be in this particular garden, up two stairs to the green slate porch. I knocked on the white door, and thought this must be the house of the wise pig, the one Big Bad Wolf could not huff and puff. An elegant slender woman opened, clear hazel eyes, hair of white wool, wearing ivory pleated-trousers, ivory silk blouse and cashmere cardigan to match, black velvet flats. Dr.Ida Rose Barber's genuine smile erased more than a score of her 70 years "You must be Shoshannah, and Nick. Please, come in children". I could feel Nick's ego bristle, and carefully did not look at him. Ida Rose raised the Grandmothers and Great Grandmothers in me, she had that stature, that grace, I floated cross her threshold. Steering us right of the door, she embarked on the requisite tour "Some who come here have trouble with my message. The white brick house, the precious things give me standing in their eyes". The front room boasted a Victorian couch of tufted emerald-green brocade, rumored from Teddy Roosevelt's private office, two black-lacquer cabinets reported belonging to Napoleon Bonaparte at Fontainebleau, a Louis XV burgundy brocade chaise-longue and matching wing-chair, a striped pink and burgundy satin Victorian divan, Tiffany lamps all, Tiffany figurines and vases lining the carved white marble fireplace mantel, a pipe organ, the pipes built into the walls, a Steinway Grand amid the panoramic windows looking East and North, eighteenth century Kashan rugs, and larger nineteenth century Sarouks. We followed her passed the wide staircase, someone standing at the top, along the hallway she pointed among many treasures mounted on the wall, to a primitive Egyptian metal plate, said to have rested on the mummy of Amenhotep's elder brother. And into the dining room, another fireplace, Sarouks, floor-to-ceiling bookshelves, a seventeenth century excellent fake of Titian's Sacred and Profane Love, and The Three Graces maybe done by a student of Rubens, far beyond what my Golden roots could soak in one sightsee. Ida Rose invited us take seats at the mahogany dining table, large enough for a dozen, facing another Northern panoramic view, over-looking the backyard rose-garden, she mentioned as she went into the kitchen "Many of those extraordinary things are gifts from my students". Nick was dead silent. It took stubborn effort not to peek at him. Happily she returned near at once, with a silver tray, Limoges coffee service, sterling spoons, white linen napkins and four gold-rimmed Limoges cups and saucers. She poured, taking hers black, and the chair cross from me, her back to the window. I was overwhelmed, and wondering why was I here. Ida Rose graciously put me at ease "Did you make that beautiful jacket Little One". It was my best, a Mao style, chocolate-cake brown moiré, quilted along the shadings, lined in blood-red raw-silk, trimmed in blood-silk quarter-inch piping, I stood and turned round to model. Her eyes twinkled "It's some of the finest needlework I have ever seen". Nick slurped coffee, his attitude embarrassing me. Ida Rose seemed not to notice. My shoulders had loosened enough to ask for a second cup, when a sandy-haired man in his forties came in from the hallway. Ida Rose fondly invited him to sit, placing one sugar lump in his cup, pouring, she properly introduced "I would like you to meet Edward Floyd. This is Shoshannah Leibofsky. And Nick Baller. Eddie's my chief auditor. When we finish our coffee, he'll audit you. I want to find out who you are. If you're part of my old crowd". I had no notion of what she was talking, and it did not matter, she had me, and so did Eddie.

When they stood, I did. Clearing his throat, Nick glared my way. I ignored him and followed into the front room. Eddie stretched-out on Roosevelt's couch. With a sweep of her hand Ida Rose said "Please, make your selves comfortable". She took her place in the winged-chair to the right of the couch, turned on the torchiere Tiffany, reached for the yellow legal pad and pencil waiting on Bonparte's lacquer cabinet. Nick sat rigid on the edge of the striped divan. I the chaise-longue, formidable furnishings, not easy to settle on, Ida Rose and Eddie looked comfortable, I took their lead. Nick unflinchingly stiff, detached, for him it was not the furniture, but an effort to control me. My eyes clung to Eddie. Ida Rose asked him "Are you comfortable". He sat-up, removed his shoes, and laid down again "Yes Dr.Barber, I'm ready".

Ida Rose: *"Master. Please take Eddie into whatever valence, stream of consciousness, point on the time track necessary for what you may wish to say to us. When I count from five to one you'll be there. 5-4-3-2-1."*

Eddie closed his eyes. The hair on my arms stood, who was this Master. I had no idea who Ida Rose was summoning, yet someone deep within me knew I had nothing to fear.

Ida Rose: *"Master what have you for us. I present* Shoshannah Leibofsky and Nick Baller."

Eddie spoke in his own voice, but the style and manner were not his: *"I can see* Shoshannah *in Palestine. She has been a Jewess in all her human incarnations. Always picking the same face and body.* Shoshannah *wears a white robe, firmly tied at the waist with a turquoise and gold braided cord, to distinguish her as a daughter of Israel. She is weeping as she stands watching Jesus crucified. Her heart is breaking at this tragedy, for Jesus was suppose to live.* Shoshannah *is a skilled potter, and makes Jesus' Mother a pot, a symbolic gift in sympathy. As she is not rich, it is a small but beautiful blue and white pot. Mary does not appreciate its beauty or meaning, has only contempt for its humble size and smashes it to shards.* Shoshannah *is deeply hurt. In the coming Kingdom of Heaven, where everyone will want to live, but most will only visit,* Shoshannah *stands inside the gate, and as the visitors leave, she will give each a small blue and white pot as a memento of their visit. This is an honored position."*

Ida Rose asks: *"Why has* Shoshannah *come here. Where did she come from."*

Eddie: *"She is from a realm so distant, the only visible colors are blues and greens. An unwilling representative from her group.* Shoshannah *did not want to suffer the consequences of a physical body. She was thrown down here with such great speed, that when she hit earth, she split in two, male and female halves. She has been the female half in all her human incarnations. Nick the male. They came for the birth of Jesus, as did representatives from many other realms, to witness the New Covenant of Love, for Jesus came to bring us ongoing life by mutual cooperation and empathy. And like many of these representatives, she has suffered greatly, for Jesus did not live to deliver the promise of his message. Instead the Great Whore of Revelations, the cruel hoax of vicarious atonement was foisted on humanity."*

Ida Rose looked across the room to me: *"Do you have any questions."*

Only able to shake my head no, I looked at Nick. The veil still drawn down tight over his face.

Ida Rose said to Eddie: *"Please ask the Master if Clarence's terrible arthritis can be helped."*

Eddie: *"Clarence has turned away and is punishing himself. He can't be helped as long as he is in this frame of mind."*

Ida Rose: *"Is that all."*

Eddie: *"Yes, that's all I have."*

Ida Rose: *"Thank you. When I count to five you will be in present time. 1-2-3-4-5 present time."*

Ida Rose turned to me *"You see, Clarence was Jesus' Mother. She was such a haughty woman, Jesus never referred to her as Mother, only as that woman*". Eddie opened his eyes "Was the audit okay Dr.Barber". With sweet affection she said "Yes dear. Thank you". And again too me "I'm taking this down in shorthand and will type it up for you later". She continued jotting. Eddie slipped into his shoes. I sat still watching her, so it was Dr.Barber, not a medical doctor, I could just as easily be in the presence of the Devil or God in the guise of this sublime white-haired woman. Suddenly Nick bolted from the room, fumbled the front door handle, flung it open, and went out. This did not seem to disturb Ida Rose, who placed the yellow legal pad and pencil on Bonaparte's cabinet, and smiling invited "Come children. I've made Danish and there's more coffee". Passing the open door she encouraged "Nick, won't you join us". Reeking insolence, standing on her porch smoking a fat joint he scowled "No". She closed the door. And I remembered Monty's words, no one could cross Ida Rose's threshold unless they're suppose to, and I understood, it was not Ida Rose who barred them, it was their own demons.

Fifty years between us, vital, essential, someone who had learned from experience instead of just experiencing, some one who did not judge me, try to parent me, tell me what to do, who knew something for real, a palpable living wisdom, not someone else's theory or rhetoric regurgitated, she actually knew something, so big it terrified me. Maybe she was the Devil's own spawn calling on her Master, maybe I had fallen under her spell and would forfeit my soul, be eaten, I did not care, for the first time in my whole life I did not feel crazy, who ever she was, what ever she was, what ever she knew, I must know too. Eddie had to go. Ida Rose wrapped his Danish in a linen napkin. He kissed her tenderly on the cheek. She sat tolerating, uncomfortable in this display of affection. Undissuaded, he left by the back door, saying good-bye to me with a broad smile and nod. She poured coffee, and warmly interested, wanted to know about me.

I was beyond my self having some one to tell, beginning with the Golden Ghet, Boeing, Seafair Queen, the Playboy proposition, Haight Ashbury, Bonita-Kay and Jeffree, Josh, Macrobiotics, Grampa's death, my profound disappointment, disaffection, dismissal of God. She thought I had a perceptive mind, and cautioned me pay attention to eating Macrobiotic "You must get enough protein. Those amino acids your body does not make on its own. A soul can be driven from the body if it doesn't get enough protein. Now tell me Little One, why you left Nick out of the story". I flushed hot "Because I'm such a fool still being with him. I feel compelled to stay, and didn't understand why till I heard the audit". She nodded "Yes. He's your other half. The male side. Your Soulmate. Jung would say you Animus. You're taking in everything, all of his knowing, while he has grown callous from unexamined unconscious prejudice devaluing his female side. Alas, he is not able to learn from you. Missing his best hope this incarnation to become whole. You are not". This lit me up "What you say makes perfect sense. I am learning from him, mainly by observation. But he just puts down everything I know or say. I'm not just some stupid girl staying with some jerk. I need to take what he has. Then I can leave. And if he doesn't learn anything from me, I still don't have to stay". Ida Rose was smiling "I'm glad to hear you're thinking of leaving him. You must take care not to lose your self in the mean time. And you must be discrete when you intend to go. Leaving is the most dangerous time". I felt a physical rush, this was better than smack "It's like I was starving, and now I'm fed. I'm full of energy, and I know what to do". The phone rang, she was expecting the call, some one named Tommy, and what time he was coming for dinner.

I took the occasion to turn the conversation, wanting to know about her. Ida Rose smiled "Well, let me see. My maiden name is Smallette. I'm Northern Irish. Have four sisters. I went to the University of Chicago in the 40's, and earned my Doctorate in Comparative Religion. An honorary Doctor of Divinity too. Then *I sought out Count Alfred Korzybski, hoping to find some formula which could explain me to myself. I was searching for the roots of my being. Korzybski used to call me his little divine. It was 1945 when he asked me to undertake a study in human regression, using some technique other than hypnosis. To discover what I could about the silent level, the part of mind that works before words, the realm of feeling and sensation. He wanted consciousness to monitor the events, to see if mind knew anything about itself. This is what propelled me. With a few really dedicated students, it took some twenty-years of exhaustive research and experimentation to develop a way of tapping the unconscious consciously. We were searching for pattern. Auditing was the result".* I asked "Is auditing the same as General Semantics". She smiled, a warm kind smile *"It's the next step. Not yet accepted by the Institute of General Semantics. Often a person's hang-ups come long before this incarnation. Traditional GS is a blueprint, disciplines discovered by Korzybski for teaching the nervous system to be whole and healthy. Enabling humans to discriminate among words and symbols that continually bombard their minds and emotions, to process and organize the information, to make better choices. General Semantics is something we learn to use, it is not something done to us.* It's quite natural really, and effective when you know how the brain/mind works. That's what Korzybski discovered, the process. You will be able to think with more confidence when you learn the disciplines". She went to her book-selves and returned with a small red book called The Pink Elephant, Something About General Semantics. Opening it to the title page, she wrote something, and presented it to me. Reading the dedication, To Shoshannah with love Ida Rose Barber, I looked up in surprise. This made her laugh "I wrote this little text *out of loyalty to my students.* To distill General Semantics to a primer, something high schoolers could understand. Korzybski was a brilliant mathematician. But his masterpiece *Science and Sanity* was too long, and erudite for the general population, and certainly beyond children's comprehension. *I don't think he actually wrote* his second book, *Manhood of Humanity. It didn't have the scientific objectivity of Korzybski. I think Marjorie Kendig wrote it, with his blessings.* It's absolutely crucial for the survival of humanity to teach General Semantic to children. Give them a foundation for sound decision making early. Auditing is the method I developed at Korzybski's request. One *audit some fifteen years ago, a student revealed that Richard Nixon, at the time a young senator, had been Nero.* And went on to say, *when a man with an X in the middle of his name became president of the United States of America, he would be the last duly elected president of a united America.* Auditing allows me to review past lives from the mouths of the people who lived them, hear the truth from the unadulterated source, go to the original scene of the crime. *I can vividly remember when I was three years old, standing and holding a tattered New Testament in my little hands, I was suddenly in some kind of reverie and told that my destiny was to discover what happened at Palestine. That there would be great changes in the human scene during my lifetime and I must prepare myself to prove that there is a "core" of caring, a God if you please, that we are responsible, intelligent beings with a purpose.* Auditing has provided me access to that story from the time-tracks of those who were there, in their own words". Wow, I actually understood this, but only as she spoke, it was too big for my little head to hold on to whole. And I had a sinking feeling, maybe I wasn't, maybe I could never be smart enough, and was about to promise to study her book, and if it was okay come back, when everything around her turned pink, intense Bazooka-bubble-gum-pink, a spectacular transparent starburst radiating pentacles six-feet in all directions from her body. I thought the sun streaming in the window from behind her must be playing tricks, but the corona grew even more resplendent, maybe this was The Pink Elephant "Ida Rose, everything around you just turned hot pink". She smiled "You must be seeing my aura Lamby. Pink is the color of love. They must have shown it to you as a gift". I knew about these gifts from when the Big Stone Ram turn its head and looked at me "Can you see it too". She shook her head slightly "No. I'm not psychic. Though I am empirically certain it's going to rain soon. I must do some weeding in the garden while I can". I wanted to stay here forever, but she was a busy woman, I needed an appointment "Me too. I mean I better go before I don't have a ride. I'll thank Monty for introducing us". She walked me to the door "I know you must think highly of Monty, he certainly is some-one, nevertheless he was Saint Philip, and has lost his way again in this life. Like so many of my old crowd, he wants to follow a religion. Blind faith instead of thinking for himself. Many have begged me to set up a doctrine based on my work, dogma they could follow. Like Hubbard did with his Dianetics. But I refuse to play God". She opened the door "Please come back when you've read my book. We'll talk about General Seman-tics". Sitting on the top step, Nick jumped to his feet "It's about time". Ida Rose ignored him, instructing me "Remember Lamby, always look for the hidden factor. What is not seen or said can often be of great importance. And, come back. You're always welcome here". The mischievous glint in her eyes told me she repeated her welcome to make clear to Nick that she valued me. Standing on the porch, not even slightly diminished by the scale of the big white brick house, Ida Rose waved as we drove away. I held her book tightly over my heart, aching that I might never see her again, waving with my other hand.

I had fallen down the rabbit hole once more, this time the main-burrow. Ida Rose was so elegant, witty, so dangerous, the kind of full-flower woman that repeals all dread of growing old and dull. Her confidence in me filled my heart and lungs in a way they had never been. But what thrilled more was her calling me Lamby. I wanted a tail, so I could wag. And there was Nick, I was seeing him with fresh eyes, a petty tyrant, spoiled only-child, trying hard to stifle me with a don't-you-dare-speak-or-else look, as if silencing what happened would make it disappear. And his foot was too heavy on the peddle, knowing it stressed me, he spoke after all "Monty's a fucking idiot if he thinks that evil old witch is worth shit". This was sour grapes, making plain how much Ida Rose upset his sacred ground, my head raced free, it's easy to be smart when you know the truth, Nick was my Yang, the irresistible attraction, for both of us. I felt a rising emancipation, and relief, for this was not love, more a wounded echo of the past. For me to be free, for me to have my life, I must learn everything from him, fast before I was too damaged, and then go. On the long cold ride, I recalled a curious twelve year old girl, on Sunday walking to St. Monica's church with Penny, I wanted to know how Christians worship. Entering the front lobby, there was this bigger-than-life highly-polished wooden figure of Jesus, nailed hands and feet to a towering black wooden cross, stickers wrapped round his head. I caught my breath, how much this gruesome graven image affected me, my hands trembled at the nails, tears welled my eyes, if I believe the audit, this reaction had been authentic. Maybe I had been there. It explained so much to me. I felt blood coursing in my veins. This was it, Ida Rose was my Rubicon, evil or angel, I would study her little red book, and go back when I could.

Nick parked the bus, and went straight for his guitar, playing to shut me out, his way of punishing, music made with cruel intent. This time I wanted to be shut-out, wanted to read. When Tara knocked, requesting the Great Mushroom Hunter ply her talents to enrich our evening meal, I gladly put on my leathers and went to find Monty. When deep into the woods and he did not appear, I hiked the way to his shack, coming upon his Land Rover, engine idling, passenger door open, and Monty, I hoped sleeping on his side across the front seat. Laying a timid hand on his back, my heart thundered. His breathing was even, I shook him by the shoulder. He would not wake. Remembering Grampa say he could hear in the coma, I shook hard "Monty, wake up. Come on, wake up". He did not. And I freaked, turning to run for help, coming face-to-face with a man Monty's age, dressed in a crisp white shirt and tie, who said he was a Thetan from the Church of Scientology. Mr. Thetan was far too collected for the situation, telling me Monty was fine, this was expected beharior when ascending to becoming a Clear. That I must not interfere. I was afraid of this man, could not accept comatose as the way to enlightenment, and yet bound by some damning compulsion to be polite, just stood there with a stupid grin on my face. Monty sighed. And I ran, finding a clutch of Chanterelles on my way, delivering them to Tara. I did not mention the bizarre encounter.

Still playing, Nick used the bus as an amplifier. I sat outside in a lawn-chair listening, he was a struggling composer and I wanted to love his music, but he cast all desirable female qualities on his Epiphone, inanimate object he could completely dominate, demonstrating this is how he would love me if I would just let him. On the surface I was obedient, subdued, but I was not broken. And though he painted wicked on me, siren, devouring, castrating, deceiving whore, hoping I would compete with strings and wood for his love, his Catholic-head could not understand I had been brought-up Old Testament, I was already chosen, and would never embrace the ignominy of Eve, female infamy, intrinsically disgraced, never accept that being born of woman permanently stained a person, guilt was not my incentive to obey, he could not imagine being free of this original sin shit, this convenient power-trip, everyone being born of woman. When he finally consummated his sprawling dithyramb, I went in to retrieve my green soapstone chillum, and the little red book. Nick lovingly stroked the guitar's waist-curve, hoping to provoke some jealousy. This gave him away, I was safe, he thought I was still playing the game, could not see how Ida Rose had kindled me, shown me a way off the melodramatic Ferris-wheel ride. My chillum was no where, and after the obligatory interrogation, where I had been, admitting only to a successful mushroom hunt, I left him to his wooden lover.

Hearing Ida Rose's voice in my head reading to me, I devoured the Pink Elephant. General Semantics had its own language, and trying to grasp it, Differentiated Activation, Delayed Reaction, Aristotelian Logic, Dating and Indexing, the Structural Differential, and for fleeting brilliant moments my brain expanded to accommodate, letting me know I could. But, making a lasting mental structure of these diciplines would take more than one transient mind expansion. Josh taught me to read the Tao as many times as it took, and like the Tao, General Semantics was common sense, though not very common. I would need time to learn, make it more than words on pages, become familiar with the language. And I could not wait, and by some miraculous feat of the unconscious, some building process, on a second reading, it was easier to retain, allowing me to actually think of what I thought of Differentiated Activation, choosing to act different than usual to a stimulus, Delayed Reaction, counting to ten to let the brain have time to differentiate its activation, Dating and Indexing, saying to myself, you are not five you are nineteen years old and do not have to react like a five year old. I felt my brain actually growning. And I was literally aching to see if Monty was still breathing, to talk about Ida Rose, and why he'd gone the way of Dianetics when she was his neighbor. Searching again for my chillum, I asked Nick had he seen it. He swore "No". And warned me off while he measured a pile of cocaine into little plastic bags, for an Oregon dealer who'd come days earlier to arrange the score. I smiled inside at the convenient excuse, and took my leave.

Finding Monty in Lotus position on the Hudson Bay blanket outside his shack, a rock-rimmed fire and scent of burning sage greeted me, he smiled, gesturing to sit. I would have liked to just quietly happen with him, but he was such a wily unstable element, made me so uneasy, silence left too much to the imagination. In a high-tense voice I recounted finding him comatose in the Land Rover, and Mr. Thetan's attempt to convince me coma was the way to enlightenment. Monty took a deep breath and let it out "It's been a fantastic journey becoming a Clear. When I lost consciousness, my mind just sailed out of my body, out beyond Pluto. You know, there's no life as we know it on any of the planets". For an instant, I could see it, as if watching a movie "I believe you. But don't you think there's a better way of finding your self then blacking-out and leaving your body. It just doesn't seem right. Leaving an empty shell has to be awful tempting. What if some thing noticed you were gone, moved-in and refuse to leave. You'd be possessed". Monty chuckled dismissive. I knew instantly, instinctively that I had been right to distrust this Dianetics. Defending, he touted Mr. Thetan as so advanced, he could take energy directly from the sun to feed his body, no longer needing solid food, he could live up to 30 days on water. I wondered aloud "Wow, how did I mistake a plant for a man". Monty was not amused, seemed to have lost his sense of humor and looked away. And I felt the power shift, he was uneasy with me, I went on with conviction "Being a plant can't be any more kosher that getting enlightened through a coma. There has to be some value in being human, in having to live in a body with all that demands. It levels the field for everyone. Escaping the consequences of being human seems to just degrade the terribly legitimate, courageous struggle we all have to go through". Never having been so articulate, I was blown-away at what had come from of my mouth. Monty closed his eyes and closed me out. And I remembered Ida Rose say he had been Saint Philip and lost his way again. I could see for my self what she meant, and walked back to the farmhouse.

Nick's Folks expected us for dinner 6PM sharp. My first invite to his Mom's house. I did not want to go, but I had sewn a beaded leather shoulder-bag for my Mom's birthday gift, we would be driving over the Island and Nick promised to leave early so I could deliver it. Mid afternoon he changed his mind, the Oregon dealer was coming at four, if he took me, we'd be late for dinner. My Mom would be heart-broken if her Little Girl did not pay homage, nevertheless it was Nick's palpable enjoyment in taking something away from me that really burned. When he went to the main-house for a shower, I asked Howard could I borrow his '62 Mercury Comet. Nick would be furious, Howard smiled and tossed me the keys "Gas tank's full. Enjoy". I knew there'd be a price as I wrapped the buck-skin purse in green silk, and tied it with antique-lace. Another power-shift, Nick did not like me taking anything away from him "You're putting me in a fucking position. I can just hear my Mother. So, that Hebrew girlfriend of yours, is there something wrong she didn't come. Too good for us. Are you fighting. I fucking hate having to explain. It's hard enough for them to swallow you". I knew exactly what to do "Okay, then I'll go". The flush of conquest washed his face. I knew that winning the moment was only a moment and did not really matter, and I waited the count of ten "If we stop on the Island". Honk, the Oregon dealer parking his green Nash Rambler station-wagon by the lawn-chairs. Nick glared daggers, and went out to meet him. I started Howard's car.

Driving the country two-lane to Interstate 90, I longed to go home, not only a physical place, somewhere I could just get on with it, where there were none of these cruel games. And I had to smile, as far as eating my way there through Macrobiotics, it was excellent discipline to live by, but could not enlighten me any more than drawing food directly from the sun. And, I would be not so vegetarian, make Mom happy, eat what she fed me today.

Their eyes always lit-up on me, though all too soon talk turned to Nick. Mom could not stand him, worrying for all the wrong reasons, how could I live in a car, without a bathroom, was I pregnant, God forbid don't you marry that boy, and the relentless are you still eating that crazy diet. I wanted to say, I must walk through Nick not run away, that I was not just drifting no matter how it seemed, that the Sweet Sisters Fate took me to people and places she plainly saw nothing in, that I must have all these for my brew, for my brew was not her brew. I wanted to tell of Ida Rose and the audit, that I was the Yin-side, in the act of claiming my Yang, redeeming that part of me living in Nick's darkness, that I must do this to break the bond, that I was willing, eager to pay the price of staying for my freedom. She already suspected my sanity, I would not stoke new fears, instead reminding Dad how our lively discussions had encouraged me to think, and that I was doing just that. He looked down at his hands "I'd like to knock that boy's head open and see if there's any brains inside". This was so like him I did not respond, regretting my life gave them such distress. Dad looked at me "I know only too well, if you play, you have to be willing to lose to win. I have always believed you are a winner Shoshy. But I have to confess I'm worried about you". Little Brother walking through the front door, and the 6PM news took the heat off me. A police raid here on the Black Panther's Central District office, civilians and police wounded.

I set the table and made Thousand Island dressing. It was Mom's day, she fixed her favorite dinner, in-season salad, falling-apart-tender brisket, baked with carrots and prunes, natural gravy and Kasha. I was relieved to hear Big Brother was too busy to come, his predictable way of making himself consequential, making him the poignant focus of attention. Nevertheless, all was right with the world when Mom fed her family, she was smiles and laughter, the food delicious, and all forgiven when I finished every morsel she put on my plate. I knew to be home before Nick, and cleared the table into the dishwasher after dinner. Mom refrigerated the leftovers. Dad brought in a New York cheese-cake hidden in the car, no one should make their own birthday cake. Mom wished, blew out the 44 candles with no help, and opened her presents. From Dad, her favorite, a large bottle of Chanel No.5, and 44 red roses. From Little, a hand-written gift certificate to detail and tune-up her car. Soon to be a high school senior, Little was self-employed, in the business of home car repair. And from me, the shoulder bag. Tears welled in Mom's eyes "I love you all so much". I knew she really meant it, and it sounded so automatic, inevitable. Ever since I could remember, I had her unconditional love, her eyes lit-up when-ever I came into the room, it gave me enduring confidence, but this love was for her Little Girl, not the creature I had become, and she dared not look any closer. Whereas Dad had good insight.

Nick was home, waiting, furious I made him look bad infront of family. He cut dinner short, drove by my Folk's, saw an unfamiliar car, and demanded to know who I was fucking, refusing to believe it was Little Brother's repair business. I dared him to call. Triggering the silent-treatment, rancor for one more imaginary wrong, aggressively ignoring my existence, taking-up all the air in the bus. This was far more volatile than words, I made my self small, still, another tenterhook night. Howard's knocking delivered me. Dear Howard inviting us in for a celebration, they had a phone installed. A cool night, Nick demanded I wait while he lit a christening coal-fire in the small pot-belly stove he spent days putting-in.

They were watching the Miss America Pageant, and a group called Radical Women picketing outside. Wow, there they were, the Libbers I read about and hardly seen, staging their own Pageant on the sidewalk, feminists protesting *the commercialization of beauty,* the *intrinsic degradation of women as objects,* crowning a live sheep as Miss America. I was elated, validated, vindicated, having deliberately blown running for Seafair Queen, recognizing the manipulation of little girls dreams in big girls bodies, the exploitation of docile minds and tits, having felt like meat. Lizabeth scoffed, it must be a guy who thought-up high-heels and bikinis. Tara had that glaze in her eyes, she loved wearing heels, they made her legs look longer. William adoringly agreed. And Nick, could no longer hold his animosity "Look at 'em. Fucking dykes. They hate men, couldn't get one if they begged on their knees. Dried-up old cunts, hairy bitches, they're just jealous of the pretty girls inside". Howard put a match to a bowl of Acapulco Gold, passed it to me with an uncomfortable wink. I took the pipe, dismissing his convenient camaraderie, for only a man's opinion out-loud would mean anything to Nick. The Boys implicit bonding in hostility toward women who did not conform to the Playboy icon, women who were not controlled by what men thought of them, their bodies not owned, no they did not want it bad, did not need it, women who were not ready-to-fuck, Howard's silence complicity lent the weight of the moment to Nick's rant, to my detriment, and Lizabeth, and their baby-girl, even Tara though she likely would beg to differ.

I decided to walkout in mute protest, just as Monty came through the front door, calmly informing Nick his bus was on fire. Black smoke bursting from the seams, Nick threw open the side doors, soot billowed, and despite Monty's strident advice not too, he ran for the hose, extinguished the pot-belly, water fusing the oily soot to everything inside. William noticed the flue was closed. I stood quietly, shaking inside with laughter, sure Nick would somehow blame me. He did, this wouldn't have happened if I hadn't made him so mad, so distracted going to my Mom's. It fell short with every one, this face-saving at my expense made him look a fool, and he knew it. I remained outwardly obedient, following him in to phone Grandma Tortoise. She detested me, a feeling I fully returned. Just after moving to the Holly Street house, she invited her darling boy and his little Jew Girl to the family dinner, wanting to finally get a look at who was living-in-sin with her precious Grandson, wanting to see my horns close-up. Before dessert I asked to use the phone to call my Mom, we had none and I knew Nick would not refuse infront of the family. He showed me to the one in Grandma's bedroom, where I could have some privacy. A snap-shot of him and me lay on the night-stand, strips of white adhesive tape covering my eyes and mouth. I did not dial, took the photo to the dining room and held it up for all to see. A seasoned foe, Grandma Tortoise was solid composure, putting-on surprise, peering at both sided of my head, raising hands just above her ears, fore-fingers curling into horns, nodding knowingly to her daughters, claiming I put the tape on myself, to cause trouble. Nick, an only little prince Mom and Auntie and Grandma fawned and slavered over, could not lift a pinkie in their company. They cut his food, kissed his cheeks, smoothed his hair, complaining it was too long, that he needed a shave. And Nick basked in the dominion. I could see how he had been taught to treat females with such contempt, and why they regarded me a thief, stealing the light of their lives. I peeled the strips from the photo, stuck them to the the table top, ripped it down the middle, separating me and Nick, pushed the pieces into my pocket, and sat down, back straight, shoulders relaxed, head high, hands folded in my lap. No one spoke till Nick ordered "Let's go. Now". He snatched the tape from the table, and we left without one more word. From then on, I refused no matter what threatened penalty, to go to Grandma's house. But she owned a furnished log cabin, seventeen miles East of the farm, one-mile outside North Bend, on the Snoqualmie River's South Fork. Grandpa's Getaway, used wink wink for trout fishing, in-fact to bed his mistress, vacant since his demise, the key hung above the outhouse door, Nick was welcome to it as long as he wanted. We cleaned the bus best we could, and went.

One room, oak buckets for hauling water, cast-iron coal-and-wood cook-stove with chrome foot-rails, cords of wood, a bin of coal, kerosene lanterns, six full kerosene cans, luxury compared to the bus. When we fled to the farm, I kept near all my things packed, no room for them in the bus, and stowed them in cardboard boxes in the barn. I left them there, Howard promising to take good care, escape money rolled in my shoes. We slept sound in the twin-beds, fully clothed.

No food, no place to bathe, first business of the morning, in too town, the North Bend Grange and Hardware Store, finding a blue plastic kid's swimming pool in the likeness of Shamu the Killer Whale, a perfectly fine bathtub. The over-6-foot, over-300-pound store manager, and there was no doubt, as manager was sewn front and back of his khaki work-shirt, took our money, and gave me a ravening look up then slowly down. We raised Shamu upside-down over our heads, me infront. Manager's maw ran foul "Dirty Hippies. Don' ever come in here again when there's decent Americans in the store". Nick's lip curled to his nose, eyes narrowed, he rested Shamu on his head, turned and flipped-the-bird with both hands. A kissing sound sputtered from Manager's pursed-mouth. Something really bad could happen, I pulled Nick toward the exit and felt him relent, he might enjoy intimidating me, but I never saw him do it to a man. The glass-exit-door swung open, some one outside holding it, I towed Nick through, the awful moment passing, and I knew there would be no appreciation, that somehow this too would be my fault. Shamu lashed atop the bus, I looked at us in the sparkling morning light, Manager was somewhat apropos, we were tousled and crinkled and schmutzig. Nick ordered me stay in the bus while he shopped Safeway for groceries, I would eat his decisions. And, he built a fire in the cook-stove. And I fetched water, some to boil in two large kettles, enough for shampoo, rinse, and a shallow bath in the Whale. Nick sat cold-eyed, smoking hash in the brown leather recliner. I considered how erotic bathing for a lover might be. He made it sordid, still I knew I must make those eyes welcome, carefully orchestrating the sponge over my body, while he beat-off, cuming in the tepid bath water. Only then could I wrap in a towel.

And the soot work began. What a mess. For some hours I tried-on the romance of back-to-nature, pioneer-woman-in-the-woods, fetching from the fast moving river, heating, wiping, washing the grimy towels again and again. No romance, just hard labor, Nick directing, sitting on the porch, strumming his wooden lover.

Days with Nick. When dealing took him to Seattle, or wink wink to jam with friends, I was not allowed along, sure to slink-off and fuck someone. I never let my pleased show, feigning scared to be alone, leaving me a certain punishment. I'd lock the door and windows, relentless tension gone, space to think, to study General Semantics. The Pink Elephant – Chapter Two - *This idea of unity of process is a part of the discipline called organism-as-a-whole-in-the-environment-as-a-whole.* Ida Rose's way of describing the cosmic connectedness I realized on acid, Gabriel's quantum physics, George Harrison's - *life goes on within you and without you.* Chapter Seventeen - Delayed Reaction - I was learning to recognize my own consciousness relative to my unconscious, beginning to act instead of re-act. This discipline taught, in waiting after a stimulus occurs, for at least the count-of-ten, in permitting the stumulus to travel from the thalamus, where all inbound is first received and viewed, Ida Rose called the thalamus *the foyer of the brain*, the keeper of programs and reactions, and theis keeper could be quite irrational, but this counting-to-ten allowed the information to travel to the cortex, the cerebral cortex, the seat of consciousness, where a person could have the opportunity to think it over, walk round it, reflect, and maybe choose to act differently, to act instead of re-act.

Tara and William came to call. Boys jamming, Girls cooking. We still practiced second-speak, and I did not complain, a waste of energy, I had no allies. After dinner, the plan, take our sooty laundry and theirs to the 24-hour Wash'n Dry, Nick was sure no one would be there after 11PM. Tara had cramps and stayed behind. We took Nick's bus, drove the dark two-lane into North Bend, a rural cliché Redneck town, on Interstate 90, the sign read - Elevation 440 feet - Population 1106. The town business, gas, booze, burgers for skiers on their way to Snoqualmie Pass, and a truck-stop offering under-age run-aways to long-haulers heading for Eastern Washington. We were unwelcome Hippies, and stayed clear except late when no one was around. Nick had finished renovating the bus and parked under a bright light to show William his latest invention, a fold-down table fastened to the back of the driver's seat. He locked the doors as William and I shouldered pillowcases full into the Wash'n Dry. A no muffler black Ford pick-up roared into the parking lot, Baby Huey and his twin brother, necks fat as their heads, jeering out the windows "Hey girls. Wana fuck". Nick and William were slim Longhairs, but patently male, I dismissed the pubescent testosterone, went in and started filling a machine with towels. William too. But Nick came flying through the door, ripped a pipe for hanging clothes off the wall, and holding it like a bat, ordered "Shit, run across the street ta the Police Station. Those bohunks are shit-faced and wana shove a shotgun up my ass." We darted cross I-90 into the Station, the two cops playing Gin, not in the least anxious to help us. The taller one asked "What're you girls doin' up so late". The smaller stood, rested a hand on his gun butt and looked at Nick "What're you doin' with the metal pipe." Nick's mouth curled-up. I was scared enough to put my hand on his arm and try explaining. Smaller listened impatiently, a smirk spreading his mouth, interrupting "Yeah, yeah. Have they actually done anythin' to you. I know 'em. They're good boys. Just havin' some fun. Where as you have destroyed private property". I pleaded "But they will do something". Nick growled at me "Shut-up". Delighted, Taller resonated "Yeah, shud-up". And then dismissed us "Boys will be boys you know. But then you girls wouldn't un'erstand. Yer more 'en welcome ta come back though, file a complaint if somethin' does happens". It was far to quiet as we crossed the street, pulled laundry from the washers, and hurried to the bus.

The good boys no where to be heard, Nick decided we should head back to the cabin. I did not think it safe, they could be waiting, follow us home, find where we live, but I bit my tongue, knowing anything I said, Nick would automatically need to go contrary. William kept quiet too. We were blocks from town when head-lights were following, the Ford soon alongside us, a good boy bellowing "One a you queers is gona die tanight". Nick took the next turn, onto a one-lane dirt road. All I could think, what a waste if I die now, before ever living, before my chance to break into the open and run full-speed. Nick's machete handle peeking-out from under the seat, I unsheathed and held it tight in both hands, what to do with it a blank, even so I felt better, Athena born full-grown, bursting from the head of her father Zeus, fully dressed in battle armor, weapon in hand. Nick was sure he knew where the road led, thinking aloud "They're shit-faced. I could lose them". We dead-ended in a barn-yard. The lights were coming. Nick ordered "Stay in the bus. Lock the doors". He grabbed the machete from me and threatened "Shut-up. Lock the door". We were sitting ducks. I at least wanted a chance, and bolted from the side door into the dark barn, staying close to the wall, fighting a mighty urge to run as far and fast as I could, counting to ten, I could not believe my sudden calm, looking round for something, any thing to use, adrenaline rendering X-ray vision, the glint of glass, gallon jugs lining a concrete bulkhead, I broke one on it, formidable weapon, someone certainly heard, please let them be too shit-faced to find me. A silhouette in the doorway. I smelled the booze. He whistled "Cumon liddle Hippie dippy. Be a goood liddle bitch. Come ta yer Daddy". Part of me stepped out of my body and floated-up to the hay loft, everything slowed, as I watched my body step from the shadow, raise the jagged weapon face high, a voice I did not recognize growled low "So you think I'm a Hippie dippy little bitch. Come here Daddy and this bitch will cut you bad". He looked at me in total disbelief, and ran away. Suddenly in body, my knees went-out from under, I sank down on my feet, stomach queasing, heart thundering, ears ringing, and wholly exhilarated, even smiling, thinking how mad, how proud Dad would be of me. Two shots cracked the night air. Trying to stand, I rolled onto my knees and crawled to the door. The Ford was leaving, a good boy shooting in the air three more times, bawling "Hippie queers ain't no real man's game. We own this town. You bedder ged out 'r else".

They were gone, no muffler fainting, and no trace of light or sound from the nearby farmhouse. When my knees could hold me, I walked slowly to the bus, dreading what might be. The driver's wing-window was smashed, left front tire shot flat, and William blanched and frozen in the passenger seat. Nick came from behind me, no words. William opened the door and slid out to the ground. Nick kicked the flat twice, and began to change it. William stared at me so intense, sympathetic, and still would not violate second-speak. And I was drained and laid down on the grass, needing to be held, needing some one to say I'm so glad you're alive, you showed such courage, needing my story told and repeated till it became legend, trying to breath through queasy, thinking how small-town-Texas this was. Nick ordered me into the bus. I curled-up on the floor. He drove slowly, cautiously to the two-lane, to the cabin. No one spoke. My mind whirling, this has to be the finale, I might not survive the menace that so often met Nick, attracted to his darkness, as long as I was near him, I would by default pay some of it. Ida Rose warned to be vigilant around other people's Karma, for there certainly would be collateral damage, that paying their Karma would not lessen your own, only reduce what is rightfully theirs, robbing their occasion to pay, delaying their emancipation. She said I would know when to leave Nick, that contrary to the popular notion that we are all searching for our one-and-only Soulmate to spend the rest of days with, we should not stay with them, learn from them absolutely, remain no, for the same would happen again, life after life.

Opportunity came with the morn. Nick took me along to report the shooting. Again Taller dismissed us "More likely you busted yer own window. Shot yer own tire. You wana get those good boys in trouble don't ya. It's yer word aginst theirs. Bet you ten-ta-one you lose in my town". Smaller knew these boys, one belonged to Manager. Boiling, Nick took me back to the cabin, and immediately left for Seattle, Bowwow Volkswagen, to buy a replacement window, a new tire. I waited ten minutes, not sure he wasn't just fucking with my head, then walked and ran into town, fear feeding a new-born strength. I called Katey from the bus station payphone, no answer, Rachel, no one, and then called home though it was Saturday and my Folk's were at work. Little Brother answered, he would come straight-away. I ran to collect what I could, knowing I should not. And the bus engine proved should not. Nick quietly walked-in, looked at the bloated pillow-case by the door, then at me "You leave with nothing". I plucked my shoulder-bag from the door handle and darted outside. He followed, hammering my back with household epithets "Fucking Kike. Cunt. Rancid fucking pussy. Ugly. Fat. Hairy. Stupid fucking whore. Bitch. I should've fucked you pregnant. I promise you this is not over. No one wants a used-up fucking cunt". I had never been more scared for my life, remembering Ida Rose warn that leaving was the most dangerous time. Suddenly sweat soaked, legs too heavy, I pleaded with them, keep going, come on, one foot, breathe in, and out, don't listen to him, concentrate on breathing. Little's car came into sight, jumping-out he swung open the gate. Nick melted into the shade. And I walked, slowly, a voice in my head calmly directing "Don't look back, you could turn to salt", hoping I had learned, had earned what must be for autonomy.

My Folks welcomed, no questions. I slept through Sunday afternoon, then called the Mirror Boss at home, asking for my old job. She had not found another Golden Girl willing to work minimum wage, able to do nimble flawless alterations, report in the morning or no deal. My days were an exhausting sham, and Mom and Dad in denial, going along as if nothing had happened to me in the last two years. I rode the bus to work, smiled at the Beige Ladies, small-talked, ate Mom's food, watching without critique the on-going parade of flag-draped caskets on the six o'clock news, did alterations, did not call my friends, went to bed early, yearned to see Ida Rose, and could not find the energy. And I noticed the sound of Nick's bus, that familiar engine driving by the house at night, or one street up from the bus-stop in the morning, and parked outside of the Mirror. Certain and not so, the '66 Volkswagen bus so common, I needed to know, and called the farm. Tara picked-up "Wow Shoshy, I was just thinking of you". I did possess the uncanny knack of tuning-in on people "Yeah, I can be a fly on the wall. You know I left Nick". She sounded concerned "Well, he didn't say anything". I was not surprised "Have you seen him". She hesitated enough I knew her allegiance was with him "Well, you know he jams here with William most days". I wasn't sure I should say, and needed to tell someone "I think he's following me, and it scares me. He made some ugly threats when I left". Her airy preoccupation took sway "Oh, I wouldn't know about that. I'm just sooo glad you called. You'll never guess what. William asked me to marry him. Can you believe it. I said yes. And now his Mom's throwing a party, this Sunday at her house, to formally announce our engagement. You're my best friend, you have to come".

Wearing the white Eqyptian cotton poet's shirt, hair tied-back, Nick looked like the best of him self, and I ached for that part. My composure, my carefully constructed house-of-cards quivered as he moved-in too close, so solicitous, so charming when I wasn't his, promising "I've changed. You'll see. I'll never accuse you again. Never control you. I'll buy you a car. I'll buy you a diamond ring". So he knew all along, every thing, and I knew better, and still persuaded to believe, wooed to bite the worm, surely reeled-in, struck unconscious, gutted and consumed, I heard Ida Rose in the air "Remember Lamby, count to ten". Ah yes, slow things down, and there it was, I saw the flicker of a hook, my feet firmed, surprising my self by stepping back, I took a breath, counting aloud on the exhale "1-2-3-4-5". His influence let loose, I took another breath, a long one, exhaling "6-7-8-9-10". Nick crowded me to the wall, purring a monotone "You know you're mine. No one can ever satisfy you. You belong to me. We're the same. You need me. Dream about me". He sucked the air from the air, smiling so loving, so considerate, like we were still together, knowing my polite would not want to stain Tara's party. Lungs straining, I moved from the wall, clear of him, and kept circulating, breathing, biding time, trembling. Tara and William could have been the original wedding cake ornament, their stunning good looks enchanting all. She gave me the lovely engagement announcement, which included both parents phone numbers, and presented me to William's Mom and Dad, and to hers, just in from West Garden Grove California, which had to be important as it preceeded the introduction. Nick talked to every one I did, joining the conversation as if we were the happy couple. When it seemed respectful, I called a cab and began good-bye, kissing William on the cheek, I was fond of him regardless, and disappointed circumstances had not allowed us to know each other more directly, this was likely the last I saw of him, and Tara, and Howard and Lizabeth. Nick disappeared. I slipped-out the back door.

Rain a soft mist, I stood on the parking strip close to the trunk of a prosperous old maple, certain I could not be seen from the house, lit a Marlboro, and heard the familiar engine. Nick drove right up to me on the parking strip, window down, a penitent rogue "Hey there pretty girl, can I give you a ride home". I did not look at him "No". The heart-felt-sincere in his voice embellished "Promise, I'll take you straight home. I just wana talk". I bit, the hook sunk-in, I got in the bus. And he took me East on I-90 to Grandpa's Getaway. I was furious with my self, mind rushing in every direction, mouth screaming every obscenity and damnation. Nick's stoic cool filled the bus as loud as me, and out-living. Energy used-up, my voice refusing more sound, a throbbing headache kicking bass drum behind my eyes, I leaned against the chilled window, shivering in a sunshine-yellow cotton mini-dress and matching squashed-heel spaghetti-strap sandals. Now raining hard, Nick swung the gate open, a Golden Retriever came running, barking, yipping, following us to the cabin door. I went in, wrapped my shaking self in a blanket, and stood in the middle of the room needing to gather wits. The retriever sniffed my legs, wagging and huffing, kind eyes, mouth agape, plainly laughing. Nick lit the cookstove and sat down at the kitchen table. I took the opposite chair. Shining a murderous enmity, he leaned-in, eyes drilling me through, finally breaking silence in a slow mechanical monotone "If I can't have you, no one can. I'm goin' to make you take ten hits of windowpane. Blow your mind so far out the other side of yer head, you'll never come back. But don't worry, I'll take good care of you fer the rest of yer life". I believed him, and daring no delay, flew out the door, up the driveway onto the road. Dog stayed at the gate. There was no moon, and terribly frightened of the dark, I ran, spaghetti-straps splitting from soles did not slow me, cursing aloud, so enraged I did not appreciate my purse left behind till the glow of North Bend brought me to the moment, I had no money for a call. Cops not an option, I walked passed to the bus station, washed the mud off my legs and shoes in the warm bathroom, blotted dry as I could with paper towels, finger combed my hair, no need to act as if waiting for a bus, there was no one here. And no Nick following, he knew how scared I was of the dark, so I must be somewhere close to the cabin, he could just wait my return. I considered the possibilities, panhandle change for a call, there was no one even on the street, hitch-hike home, not from here where I would be taken for an under-age runaway, and these were reasonable excuse, but then the show would be over, and I was far too strung-out on the drama-of-the-drama, could not bear to let it end with me slinking away, no matter how obviously foolish, I must go back and collect my dignity.

The rain evaporated, a thick darkness swallowed me as I walked the two-lane, spent-anger no longer loud enough to blot-out hungry night-terrors, cougars, wolves, raccoons, hawks, snakes, rats, spiders, vampires, were-wolves, all pretenders to the real darkness that stalked me, my Soulmate's need to dominate, to prove he was the right half, and ideas like compro-mise and co-operation were not in his vocabulary, he wanted one thing only, control, and would obliterate my consciousness, kill me without kill-ing me to get it. I was damn-right to be afraid, and began singing *Zippity doo dah, Zippity aye, My oh my oh what a wonderful day*, when I heard the familiar engine, and turned round as if walking to town. Nick rolled down the window, offering the first note of respect I ever heard in his voice, and not one single I promise "If you get in, I'll take you to Mercer Island". Dignity collected, I got in.

Nick rescued the retriever from the pound days after I split. Dog was greedy for pets, put a big head in my lap, and I gladly stroked his willing fur. When he whimpered a short high-pitched signal, Nick pulled onto the highway shoulder. I urged, please be safe, drive to the next exit at least, do not let Dog out on the Interstate. He insisted Dog obeyed him absolutely. A nightmare I was powerless to affect, Dog freaked at a logging truck's sudden air-horn, stampeded into the road, a car swerved and could not miss his big head entirely, and kept going. I would always remember that thud. Dog shrieked and fell. Time and matter stood still, allowing me between the traffic. Nick too, carrying Dog to the bus. I sat on the floor, cradling that big head in my lap, stroking his neck and ears, cooing what a good boy, his fear burning my nostrils, blood soaking my sunshine dress. Nick sped a seeming endless road to the Veterinary Hospital in Issaquah where he had taken Dog for shots, and carried him into the back emergency door. A vet rushed them to a room. And I sat stalk-still vigil in the lobby, till news, Dog had a dislocated jaw, broken teeth, lacerations, x-ray showed no internal injuries, he was sedated, being re-adjusted, sewn, nothing we could do for now. Nick took me home. We said nothing more. Mom and Dad were asleep, I could shower-off dried blood and dirt no questions. Shoes and dress ruined, I stuffed them in a pillow-case, and went to bed.

Feeling crazy-brave on waking, yesterday honed and demented me, the line between them gone of late, I knew I must go for my purse and few other things, even recognizing this was the rationale of an addict. Borrowing Little Brother's car, I took the yellow shoes and dress. Relieved and disappointed to find Nick gone, I did not hurry, straining to believe this collecting would take away the material part of me, so he could not look at, could not psychically connect through them, and wanting him to show-up before I was gone. Leaving dress and shoes on the kitchen table. He called Mercer Island just after dinner, telling me Dog was okay, that he had rented a house in Rainier Beach, I should move-in with him, he could not live without me, sleep without me, eat without me, promising if I gave him this one more chance, I could keep my job, see my friends, whatever I wanted. Promises, soul-sucking promises. I knew better, saying no, never call me again.

My Folks tried to make-believe I was their pristine Little Princess who never let her panties down. And I could abide the role while dazed, leadened. But now, I desperately needed someone to talk too, some one who would listen, who would not judge me, or tell me what to do. Mom believed a good mother made her children's problems her own, mine were not mine but hers too, making me responsible for how they upset her. I had learned it was best to keep them to my self. And Dad, at this turn if he knew the whole of it, would be so mad, he would go find and knock that boy's head open and see if there's any brains inside. I could not bear one more complication. It was clear, even if I wanted to, I could no longer live here, and squeeze into the narrow gilded space marked Little Shoshy. I knew they wanted only the best for me, but it was their best, they would never really know me, or get passed how they wanted to see me, what they wanted me to become. All this was exaggerated by fears of what if-might-or-could happen. Their life worked fine for them, but it was their rules, their hallowed taboos, and to live under their roof I must obey. I called Katey. Who kicked-out the cad she had been so hot for, was five months pregnant and too scared to get an illegal abortion or try her self. She was glad for someone to talk too, welcomed help with the rent, I could have the basement. Mom and Dad made no attempt to talk me out of going, singing the good parent refrain in harmony, our door's always open, use your key and come home, no questions asked. I knew in private they were relieved to have their life without all the complication. Boss gave me a three-day weekend, Mom lent me her 1959 Ford Fairlane station-wagon. A load of trepidation in my gut, I drove to the farm and collected my boxes, money still safe in my shoes, no one home, I left a note.

After patiently listening to my story, Katey was far too smug, recalling her good sense not to stay mixed-up with Nick, conveniently forgetting he did not want her, that her immediate x-boyfriend had not treated her any better. When the conversation came to Ida Rose, Katey thought auditing was a-crock-of-shit, the far-out raving of a lunatic, she'd been raised Catholic, God was God and should be left in His heaven or He certainly would do something about it. Though I felt a terrible lonely in my heart, in my innards, even in my hands, teeth, nose, tongue and feet, there was some of me that had emancipated, and was determined, thrilled to be going on alone to meet my life. A Soulmate was all about the past. I would sight the blue bus, hear the familiar engine, and it began to rattle me, because it eased the lonely, because we were not yet done.

Dreaming of a childhood friend whose face was not quite human, still I thought how wonder-full and knew exactly who she was. We were

172

walking hand-in-hand to John Muir Elementary School, she showing me how to change the color of trees and sky at will, when something crashed through my window onto the concrete floor. I jumped-up, not knowing where I was till Katey threw open the door and flipped on the light. A mason jar lay shattered, big brown Wolf Spiders scrambling for every shadow. Frozen, I knew it was Nick. Katey did too, and started stomping on them, fearless, calling him a fucking coward who had to do his fucking crimes in the fucking dark, punctuating each stomp with fucking. The staccato stomp, the way she made fucking a benediction thawed me. We hunted the spiders we could find, swept the glass, and taped cardboard over the window. Katey wanted to call police. I had enough callous cops. Reluctantly she said okay. I showered, and went to work. Brown Wolf Spiders were not killers, but at thirteen, one bit the bridge of my nose, the thing was on my face while I slept in my own bed, and left a lasting trauma. Like a fool I told Nick the story, so he knew this deed would steal my sleep, dreading his eight-legged emissaries patiently waiting on me to close my eyes. I had to stop judging, stop being so proud I was not like him, I had to absorb some of his dark-side, become terrible enough, and welcome, hope, even be grateful this sinister act would infect me with a cold detachment, with his ability to be utterly egocentric. In this he was my teacher, and I his loathe student. The alternative, an ever-engrossing intimidation and control by him and his ilk, a fly trapped in spider's silk, waiting the inevitable. Embracing the dark would grant me power to initiate. I had once hurt another person, I had it in me. Good girls were not supposed to be snakes and snails, only sugar and spice, I must have some puppy dog tails.

So, I phoned Howard for Nick's new address, and borrowed Katey's car. Finding him only six blocks away. I knocked. He seemed waiting, invited me in "I knew you'd come. You can't live without me". Stepping over the threshold, I heard Maya's voice and mentally patted my own back, for I had not married him, did not have his kids, there was nothing physical, nothing legal holding me. And he plied his charming persuasion, promising there would be no more controlling, no more suspicion, that we belong together, had to trust each other, that I must take him at his word. I did not resist the seduction. And did not tell Mom or Dad, paying an extra months rent to Katey, and for the window replacement, there was no reason she should get burned in this deadly dance. Moving all my boxes that night, I had to be all in, this had to be real to tell the tale. Dog was no longer with Nick, he would not say why.

Four days in, deliberately catching the bus to the Ave after work, I dined at the Hasty, and came home before dark. Nick was on the couch playing his wooden-lover. I said "Hi". And deliberately hanging my shoulder bag on the door handle, hurried to the bathroom. He followed, sniffing the air, demanding "Who you been fucking Bitch. You can't wash it off". No use responding, futile promises, I closed the door, sitting down on the toilet seat. Nick barged-in and smacked my face, so fast I had no time to relax. Lightning flashing, stinging, tears welling, and murder in my eyes as I looked-up, met his, and kicked his crotch hard as I could with my pointed-toe boot. He face turned gray, pupils fixed on me, lips taut across teeth, holding his groin, falling to his knees. Time stood still, out-of-body I moved easily and had the wits to take my bag on the way out. This was it, I knew in my bones, running down the middle of the street, unexpectedly buoyant, quarreling out-loud "I should go back, see if he's okay. No way, why am I making excuses. But what if I really hurt him. No, fuck him, he hit me first. God damn it he hit me. What if he calls the police. Ha, right, wouldn't I love to see that. He hit me. I have the right, I have the fucking obligation to defend my self".

Once before I'd physically hurt another human being, struck her over and over, leaving an irrevocable stain on me, because it was premeditated. I was twelve, and she was the daughter next-door, three years older, five inches taller, 50 pounds heavier, accusing my Little Brother of stealing her bike. There was bad blood between the families already, building their fence eleven inches on our property, Dad made them move it, and the war was on. Next came their basketball court, the hoop too close to the fence, any shots missed, the ball could not help but come down into our yard, and one of them would happily trample our rockery to fetch it. Dad insisted they be more considerate, and they were only if he was home, however crushed flowers, shrubs and loosened rocks told the truth. Then came this bike stealing accusation. Little Brother's birthday gift had been a shiny-black Schwinn. Big Bully Daughter swore he stole hers, good pretext for a sneak-over, and finding him alone, she shoved him hard to the ground.

He and I pleaded assault, let's call the police. Dad said no, accepting her father's promise to ground Miss Bully one month, and justifying to us, these were the only other Jews in our neighborhood, people were already quick to believe the worst of us, he did not want to fuel more prejudice by making it public. But this had nothing to do with Jews, just people, these were the ones in the neighborhood hurting us, and even when her bike magically appeared the following day, her parents never made her serve time or apology. I began stalking her after school, for weeks. She rode a Raleigh English Racer, the kind with really thin tires. I had a full-size blue Schwinn, and learned her route, up to the high school, twice round the parking lot, down the hill to Mercer Crest Elementary tennis courts, where she circled, hunting for prey. Fridays, 4PM there was never anyone. I waited by the gym, hands wet on the handle-bars, heart pounding in my throat, and gaining full-speed, mowed her to the ground, she rolled onto her back as I leapt, mounting her, knees pinning her arms, they could not ward-off my fists hammering her shoulders and chest, bouncing my whole weight on her paunch, knocking-the-wind-out, and that wiry black hair, I grabbed at the temples, jerking her head side-to-side, more in-control than I had ever been in my whole young life. Dismounting only because I was exhausted, I stood over her, stunned and staring at me, there was no blood. My arms hung like hams, I spit in her open mouth, kicked her leg with all the juice left, bent close and whispered "If you ever even look at my Little Brother again I'll kill you". Shaked from the violence, feeling justice done, I turned my back in final insult, picked-up my bike, and rubber-legged home, slowly, stinking of adrenaline, physically unmarked. A power-full fatigue owned me, I could just shower-off the stench, eat some home-made peanut-butter cookies, turn-on TV, and crash on the couch. I am certain Miss Bully told her parents, though nothing was ever said to mine. And I never told, any one. This capacity for violence freaked-me-out, premeditated, planned, stalked, I beat her, and found my self capable. Power-full revelation, and I had come to this tribulation again with Nick, though it was passion not premeditation, and technically less criminal. I ran to Katey's.

Nick's bus pulled to the curb, gunning the engine on seeing me, he was okay. And Katey opened the door. A quiet neighborhood, his threat rang-out "If you leave me, you leave empty-handed". I regretted moving my boxes, Great Grandma Monya's precious Tiffany Lily Lamp and Giltwood mirror, the clothes I made, books, beads, the Martin D28 Dreadnought guitar, I was sad and willing to lose these precious things for freedom, ransom for my life, and carefull not to look his way testified "My things will only haunt you. You'll never be free. Never have a chance to hit me again". He laughed "You think it's over. It's not". I realized he took my nerve as a challenge, an invitation, I faced him, no longer a small-time dealer, he could not stand the cops glaring his way, the irony of them do-ing my bidding made me smirk, I commanded "Katey, go call the cops". Nick drove up over the curb "It's not over Bitch". Tires burning ruts in the grass, dirt and grass flying he roared away. I was queasy for days. He hunted me openly. Too vulnerable to stay with Katey, the stress too much in an already strained pregnancy, she should not pay one more rupee of my Karma, I moved to Mercer Island. Nick would not openly come there, he feared my Father.

Chapter Seven

LOOKING OVER BOTH SHOULDERS

Nick sank into the scenery, and I embraced what liberty that allowed, taking the bus to the Ave after work, sitting on the Wall infront of the Post Office, eating a meatless meal out. These did not make me free, I was on constant look-out, tense, anyone I might want to know picking-up on such paranoid-vibes left me alone. I knew I had to make a new life or slide back, the habit-canals Ida Rose wrote of in her book, dug so deep in my psyche, and I ran in them so easily, without thinking, it would take a vigilant consciousness to remember to climb-out and keep digging the new ones. I wrote notes to re-mind, put them everywhere, even on my hands, wake-up Shoshy, remember who you are. And when I thought to, would reach for some things with the other hand, brush my teeth with the other hand, eat, cross my legs the other way, anything to dislocate the old ways, to remember to dig. I pictured my self with gold leather gloves and a golden shovel, and avoided looking down the way too far. The important thing was to begin, it did not matter where, the Sweet Sisters Fate made all roads the same, my task was the digging. Right now, the hippest place-to-be was Gerry Kingen's Red Robin Tavern, at the South end of the University Bridge. Some place I would never go, I decided it was a good place to start. Getting ready, reeking of here I am alone and all that meant going to a bar, no matter what I put-on felt neon, vulnerable, exposed. Okay Shoshy, stop thinking or you won't go, putting-on my jeans, a high-necked deep-purple brushed-rayon blouse with long full sleeves, wide chocolate-brown leather belt buckled at the small-of-my-back, and cowboy boots. I stood infront of the bedroom mirror, totally covered, thinking how much money people would assume I spent to impress, and they would act accordingly, unfortunate since the blouse and belt cost me so little to make. Mom reluctantly lent her car, all the while thrilled to see me going, gushing how beautiful, what a good figure, have fun, be careful.

Nearing twenty, with the right make-up and flirt, Doorman let me pass, while two old men standing just inside, icky old men were busy mentally undressing me. I walked toward the bar, wishing I had not cinched the belt so tight, suddenly remembering no girls allowed at the bar, any bar, there, a small table, the guy leaving a tip, defendable spot with my back to a wall, no one could sneak-up. I lit a smoke to give my hands something to do, to put a fire infront of me. Washington State Blue Laws banned females sitting at the bar, or even going up to order a drink, except if you're an employee, the barmaids could legally attend. Why State Government was in the business of because you have tits and will not sell them it's not okay for you to sit at the fucking bar, I did not understand. I would have to wait on the barmaid, hers spilling over the man-datory naughty wench bustier. She saw me, and made me wait two more cigarettes. Ordering a Rainier, I lit another. One beer doing little to pull my shoulders down from my ears, when she finally came round again, and did not lean-in to hear my request as she had all the men, I asked for two more, and please bring me a glass. I understood why she did this, bigger tips from the men, but what if I wanted women, I might give a bigger tip too. The Red Robin was smoky sticky sardines, an instinctive Lonely-Hearts-Club, and one after another these meticulously trimmed beards and mustaches came asking for a dance, buy you a beer, light your smoke, the motive always unsaid, oh yeah and can I get-in your pants later. The perfectly-trimmed were not my type, to easily angered by polite rebuff, like I had no right to say no, some mouthing Bitch, some making certain I could read their lips, some spitting it out loud. Public pussy, cheap as a beer, easy as a light, for these preening cocks any hole would do, I had to wonder if it showed, that I had almost been tamed, had already done what they want me too. But being here made me fair game, all trussed-up, glowing neon, girl alone, a usual precept, incomplete without a man, needing her hole filled, standard male fantasy, empty and waiting.

Beginning was the important thing no matter where, for I knew it would take me somewhere I could not imagine. Holding my last Marlboro, I crumpled the pack, having given the hippest-place-to-be a three-beer try, I would go home and wait for tomorrow. A big hand with a lit stick match neared the end of my smoke. Turning, I glared into Gabriel's green eyes and unshaven face, immediately searching for a flinch, a slight squint, a look away, was he spying for Nick, and finding none, I smiled and leaned into the flame. He lit his with it too and just stood there, not trying to claim me or talk over the music. When the jukebox arm took Iron Butterfly from the turn-table and reached for another album, Gabe asked "How about some fresh air". I nodded yes, grateful, following him out of Hieronymus Bosch into a fragrant evening. We walked arm-in-arm across the University Bridge and up the Ave. I was thrilled to find him absolutely furious at nightly news body bags, at local cops murdering Black Panther Welton Armstead, and at President Johnson ordering the National Guard to Columbia University to put-down a student take-over of campus buildings. We shared excitement at a world-wide uprising, French, Czechoslovakian, Polish students taking to streets and campuses, protests so powerful they all but shut-down their counties. And we both wished for a way in, not knowing where to find the door. There was no word of Nick, and little catching-up, Gabe still played bass, the band's record deal never materialized. I could feel he was on the prowl, some one to talk too so very seductive, I could have easily fallen, never ever wanting any thing to do with a musician again. And still, wanting to say yes when he invited me home, a small but firm constituent compelled me, you are way too vulnerable, remember this is the guy who wanted to make you his God, and I listened in sorry disappointment to my voice say "Maybe next time". Looking way too crushed, he took my left hand and printed in ball-point pen a phone number slowly cross the palm, just below remember who you are. My body thrilled to the symbolic ravishing though I did not let on. He kissed the numbers as if sealing them in, leaving ink on his bottom lip, and walking away, slowly, backwards down the sidewalk toward the Robin, putting his palms together, raising them in prayer to the moon "Call me beautiful". I appreciated the next move was mine "Maybe I will". Gabriel turned, and with enough night ahead resumed the prowl. Ink hand resting safely in my lap, I merged onto the I-5, enjoying the budding feeling of confidence, headlights coming too fast on my bumper, VW bus in the rear view, Nick's eyes boring into mine, I panicked, floored-it, aiming to draw the cops. He understood instantly and took the Mercer exit. My foot twitching on the gas-peddle, self-confidence gone, Nick only had to show him self. I often thought I saw him, always in the shadow, always a wondering, why make it real now.

Two days, I went to and from work, sitting duck at the bus stop, staying away from windows at home, never another sighting yet he was in every shade. Then it dawned, his cunning move made me prisoner of my own fear, for as long as I'd been unsure, I had some naïve liberty. Dad often said turning a paralyzing thought into action would break the spell. This was a battle for deliverance, to save my ego's life, I had to initiate even if I was scared. Catching the bus to the District after work, I perched on the concrete bulkhead edging campus, NE 42nd and 15th AVE NE, here I am in plain view, lighting a smoke, when a Longhair came running, plunked a brown paper lunch-bag in my lap and kept going, two uniform cops not far behind. I set the bag next to me and took a long drag, trying to relax my shoulders. They ran by me too. And when the pursuit turned down 43rd, I took the bag and my purse onto campus, where only campus cops were allowed, walking North on Memorial Way, crossing 45th to 17th, up Frat Row, heart thundering in my ears, lunch-bag so heavy I was afraid what it might be, feeling eyes on my back, not daring to look. I let my purse fall stepping-off the next curb, peeking behind, scooping it up, seeing no one, unrolling the bag. Black and yellow gel caps, hundreds, I kept on going, casual as possible.

A breezy early August evening, cool enough to wear the chocolate knee-length suede coat and matching boots I bought junior-year high school to go see the Beatles, costing three-months pay from Dairy Queen, and a designer chartreuse sweater-dress from work, so Golden Ghet, yet I felt it no disguise, deciding to walk to 50th and catch a bus downtown. Half way down the block, seeing an open trash-can at the curb, I thought to get rid of this bag, no, there was a woman standing on the sidewalk watching me. She was maybe 5 years older, thick rusty-brown hair, a badly cut shag, faded bell-bottoms, skin-tight tie-dyed t-shirt boasting her A-cup braless bosom, she seemed to be waiting, smiling, showing her chipped front tooth "Hey, hi. I'm Keely". I half-smiled "Hey". She continued smiling, pudding-brown eyes concerned, inviting me "Come on, let's go sit on the porch". Recognizing a rabbit hole I followed, relieved to be off the street, heart slowing as we sat on the top step, I set the bag and my purse down between us. Keely put her hand on the bag "So, what's for lunch". I could not breathe or speak. Lifting, noting the weight, she placed it in her lap, unrolled, and laughed too loud, looking at the house across the street "Well, certainly not lunch. They're Yellow Jackets". Her laugh seemed a signal, the screen door opened, an Irish man stepped-out, and sat too close on my other side. Six feet, slim, a mop of coarse black hair, freck-led milk-glass skin making his blue eyes bluer, Keely introduced Dancing Bear, recent UW Journalism Grad, and passed him the bag. He laughed to loud too. Re-igniting my paranoia, if I had been followed, they were being so deliberately conspicuous. Wanting to run, held-fast by an over-whelming need to see where the rabbit hole went, I whispered "Please you guys. Could you be more discrete". Both instantly obliged, pressing me to tell the tale of the bag. I began. Looking across the street, Keely frowned "Come on, let's take this inside".

I knew crossing the threshold, though it had the trappings of a Hippie house, this was way more serious. Following Dancing Bear into the dining room, he pointed to a chair at the enormous rectangular oak table, put the bag on the seat, walked round and sat opposite. I set the bag on the table, sat and lit a smoke. Keely next to Bear, shoved a full ashtray cross the table for me, slouching, picking at cuticles, not taking her attention off a bleeding snag she confessed "I've been waiting for the Welfare Lady. Only met her on the phone. When you came looking so business, I thought you were her". Strained disbelief never left Bear's face, he lit a hand-rolled smoke, took a few long drags, and began the questions, where did I live, who did I live with, where did I work, what was my Boss's name, where was I from, where did I go to school. I did not mind, they gave me sanctuary even if mistaken, but his tone was not sarcastic enough, far too harsh, I could hear Ida Rose in my ear - *always look for what is not being said. Look for the hidden factor* – I wondered why he didn't just ask me to leave. Silent, Keely watched the exchange, arms folded tight over her chest, hands tucked captive in arm-pits, she could not get at those cuticles. I envied her ability to fold so easily cross her chest, and the not-in-the-least-bit-worried-for-her-femininity demeanor, when three little Boys blew through the room to the kitchen, all with Keely's exuberant rusty-brown hair. She went after them, to attend their Mooom I'm thirsty demands, asking me over her shoulder "You want some Tang". I leaned back in my chair, grinning childish-polite "Yes please Mom I would". These little cosmic allies had come to my respite, I was duly impressed by their splendid timing.

Gulping their glasses, squabbling who has the best orange mustache, they paraded in to inspect me. I could hear Keely on the phone to Welfare. Robby was just five, dirty-face, Mickey Mouse voice, he brought my glass of Tang. Scottie, baby-fat three-year-old, pouty-mouth permanently stained raspberry jam, did not speak but smiled greedily as he stroked the soft suede of my coat, I was his new pet. And Lance, the little man, introduced himself the biggest because he was seven, his six-month-old brother Sundance was asleep upstairs, he could go get him right now if I wanted to see. This seemed the starting gun, they scampered off on a mission, Keely following, devoted, solicitous. They so completely cleared the room of paranoia, I felt okay asking Dancing Bear "What kind of house is this". He stiffened "Hydra's a political collective. Five resident adults. We organize anti-war protests. Next one's on campus". My jaw actually dropped, here was the way in Gabriel and I hoped to find "Wow. Cool. Can I help". Bear cocked his head "Are you against the war". I nodded "Yes I am". He cocked his head the other way, "Why". I copied his move "Just know in my heart it's wrong. You know, watching the body-bags on TV while your family eats their dinner, never missing a bite. Bodies counted-up like a basketball score. And government, and the news aren't telling us the truth. People all over the world are daring to say so, and I want to be one of them". Bear's mouth was smiling, his eyes were not "You're welcome to demonstrate with us. Anyone can". An uncomfortable silence, we smoked our cigarettes, and I read the poster on the wall behind him, quoting Mario Savio, initiator, leader of the Free Speech Movement 1964 – *There is a time when the operation of the machine becomes so odious, makes you so sick at heart, that you can't take part; you can't even passively take part, and you've got to put your bodies upon the levers, upon all the apparatus and you've got to make it stop. And you've got to indicate to the people who run it, to the people who own it, that unless you're free, the machine will be prevented from working at all.* I understood this completely, it was how I felt about my own freedom. Bear leaned forward "So what're you going to do with the Yellow Jackets". I recognized an offer and went along "Maybe take them home, now I know what they are. Though I don't do speed anymore". He was all business "How much you think the bag's worth". I smiled "Twenty-bucks". He asked "How come so cheap". I smiled bigger "Simple. I'm not greedy". He pulled a wallet from his back pocket and laid a five and ten on the table. Keely appeared with Sundance on her hip and added two crumpled dollars. A tall lean man close behind, freshly washed blonde hair, zits pocking an otherwise handsome face, put three more on the pile. Bear flattened the bills neat, pushed them to me and asked could he have one of my store boughts, his smile was genuine. Mine too, I pushed the bag across and reached out a Marlboro. Taking both he quickly left the room.

I put the money in my purse, as the tall blonde slid into Bear's chair and introduced himself. I liked Mark right away, and thought these guys must be dealers, probably not big-time, and I must seem so unbelievably suspect showing-up with a bag of speed. Keely let Sundance slide down her leg onto a satin quilt spread on the floor. Another man suddenly appeared, dead serious dark brown eyes, mustache, goatee, unkempt wavy black hair, small, wiry and still he filled the room. Keely presented her husband Ric. Who made me holy uncomfortable as he turned round a chair, straddled it, legs wide, face relaxed, and in a steady blunt tone simply dismissed me "Now it's time for you to go". Feeling the darkness of Nick, but not the conceit, and his palpable charisma, I curbed a polite automatic smile and looked directly into his eyes "It's been a real honor meeting you". His mouth corners turned-up. My mien disarmed him, I smiled too, snuffed my smoke, and stood just as the Boys gusted into the room with bouquets of dandelions and daffodils for Mom. Keely took me to the door, sounding frustrated "You can come back another day". The Boys echoed her words as they flew by us outside "Come back. Please come back". Believing Keely sincere I said "Thanks. I'd really like to". The Boys stopped pursuing me at the end of the block, still chanting "Come back. Come back. Please come back". Walking two blocks to 50th, I took the bus, closing my eyes, making a move never took me where I thought, trusting the Sweet Sisters Fate ever more than I could anticipate, connecting with Keely as magical as meeting Josh in the Houston airport. I sorely missed him and Bonita-Kay and Jeffree, people I could talk too. And now possibly some new ones, intent on stopping the war, something I wanted too. I could not sleep for thinking, almost called Gabriel, such a good excuse.

After work I went, hoping it wasn't too soon, that I didn't seem too desperate, hoping Keely's invitation was real. She answered my knock, warm and glad to see me, coming out on the porch, closing the door. We sat on the top step, and I could hardly hold my tongue through amenities, asking the questions that kept me awake. Keely answered without hesitation. Their political collective was Hydra, named for the mythic nine-headed serpent. If any head was lopped-off in battle, two more grew instantly. They chose Hydra because every one in the collective was a leader, a head, and if the Man thought he could take one by arrest or murder, and that the collective would fold for lack of leadership, they were wrong, there would always be more heads to carry on the struggle. Nodding hers to the house across the street she confided "They're watching right now. FBI rented it two months ago. Probably bugged us then. I'm sure they're gona plant something and arrest us". My eyes involuntarily fixed on the house, stomach falling, they surely took my photo yesterday with the paper bag, oh shit was I that girl who fucked once and got pregnant, while the likes of Nick dealt without consequence. I whispered "Why's the FBI watching". Keely's jaw clinched in firm futility, her head shaking slowly side-to-side. My question went unanswered as the door swung opened, and a girl-woman softly stepped-out, followed by Mark and Arnie.

Keely introduced Carolion, a fifteen-year-old waif in too-tight tapestry hip-huggers, wrinkled white-cotton tuxedo-shirt unbuttoned and tied midriff, sleeves rolled above her elbows, no bra, no make-up, long dishwater blonde hair so fine and clean it defied gravity. Smelling of Sensemilla, lingering only for the introduction she floated on her way. Mark smelled of Sinsemilla too, flashed a mischievous grin, sat down on my open side and glared defiantly at the window curtain moving across the street. I asked "Where you from". Without pause he answered "Originally Ithaca New York. Dropped-out of the UW here a few months shy of an engineering degree". He smiled affectionaltely at Keely "To join the cause. I'm Hydra's resident electronics wizard. Getting my degree where it really counts". His willingness encouraged me "Is Hydra the only collective". Putting hand over heart, eyes fixed on the now still curtain, talking as if being recorded by a directional microphone he said "No. There's collectives everywhere. We're strong. Sundance was the first. Mike Lerner, Chip Marshall, Jeff Dowd, and ah, Joe Kelly. There's three more houses on the west-side of Capitol Hill. Great view over-looking Lake Union. Seattle Liberation Front's the umbrella for all of 'em. We are the mighty SLF. Berkeley Liberation Front inspired us, but we're the first West Coast off-shoot of the Students for a Democratic Society. You know, the infamous SDS. Not long after Sundance collective formed, Mike Abeles organized the Rebels. Then Ric and Bear started Hydra. And there's Mother Jones, the Country Doctor, and the Grodes. Each collective works on what's close to their heart. Workers rights, welfare rights, health-care for all, legal birth-control, day-care, the war". Keely added "There's the Fortress too. But they don't consider themselves SLF". She giggled "The Weathermen think they're weenies". Mark voice took an irritated defense "And the SDS thinks we're weenies. Some kind of stupid ego trip, like what degree of militancy sets the standard, what's the measure of a true revolutionary. You know, competition for who's got the biggest dick. And the Weathermen are the worst". He amplified his irritated, speaking to the curtain "I believe it's really all Big Brother, in bed with the propaganda press machine. They hope to divide the movement through internal dissension. You know, divide an conquer. But every one of us is necessary for the people to win this. We all have our place and function. We have to stand together to be strong enough. And far from weenies, the SLF is probably best suited to engage middle class student's who are not ready to be as aggressive as the Weathermen or SDS in the name of revolution. We need the Proletariat and the Bourgeoisie if we are going to succeed". The Boys came tumbling onto the porch, pulling Mark down to the lawn, a willing bucking bronco. Keely took the opportunity to ask more questions. And flattered someone was interested, I drew Nick only in sketch, and how Gabriel and I had been wishing to find a way in to the anti-war movement, but had no idea where. Her face shifted from curiosity to paranoid preoccupation "Look, can I come home with you. Spend the night". I thought wow what a bold request, maybe she needs a break from the Boys, maybe she's fighting with Ric, whatever the motive I was happy for company "Well, yah, sure. My Folks 'll be glad I have a friend". Asking me to please wait on the porch, she was back in minutes with a small knapsack slung over her shoulder. We took the bus home.

Mom and Dad liked her. To my surprise Keely enjoyed them too. We went to bed early, and she told her story. Raised by a single mom on welfare, oldest of five, she married Ric at seventeen, a proper Catholic wedding, had three boys before moving here from Modesto for Ric's new job, science teacher at Holy Names Girls Academy. She was four-months pregnant with Sundance when they dropped-out to form Hydra and work for change. Demonstrating against the ROTC recruiting on high school and college campuses, organizing speak-outs for free speech, sit-ins protesting racism, street dances for under-age kids to have somewhere to go at night. And, Hydra was looking for a way to buy enough land to constitute a township, a place residents could vote-in their own town laws. She talked of the other collectives, Mother Jones was a four-bedroom house at the corner of 23rd and South Judkins Street, in the Central District, just three blocks from where Nick and I lived on Charles Street. They opened their door at 6AM every week-day morning for any kid to come eat a good breakfast, no charge, no indoctrination, because full-bellies let them concentrate on school instead of hunger. The Country Doctor, kitty-corner from Mother Jones, were busy writing a grant for Federal start-up money to open a free medical clinic, *the Walk-in Clinic*. The Grodes, Rebels, the Fortress were in-general anti-war collectives. And Keely, was no longer in-love with Ric, maybe never was, had kids before she could think, Ric's Catholic refusing to wear a condom, she felt trapped living everyone's life but her own, and since she was being honest, it had been marry or run-away, anything but remaining Little Mommy to her four younger siblings. I could see the deep sadness in her eyes confessing to bitter envy for what she saw as my perfect unencumbered life of freedom and privilege. In the morning, on the bus downtown, she revealed why the coming home with me. Ric thought I might be an undercover cop, my expensive clothes, the way I came along just when she was expecting the welfare lady, and if that wasn't enough, there were the yellow jackets. He wanted to see, was I for real. It amused me being taken for a cop. Keely said she was sure I was not the moment she saw me, exactly because of how I was dressed, but cautioned "Spies come in the most unsuspecting disguises". Thanking me for the lovely sleep-over vacation, she invited "Come to Hydra anytime. You will be welcomed". She transferred to the District, and I caught the Madison Park.

I went every day after work, doing whatever was asked, mimeographing flyers for the coming anti-war protest, distributing up-and-down the Ave, and on campus. Inside a week Hydra unanimously sanctioned me, each having an equal vote, I was invited to join in meetings. Ric, Mark, Bear, Keely all had four and more years on me, the men had degrees, and I was in awe of their political savvy, listening, learning. And, not one Nick sighting or shadow, my paranoia began to ebb, feeling protected among comrades, I phoned Gabriel. His voice ragged, throaty, hard-earned, smoking, drinking, singing rock'n roll all night, and delighted to hear from me. I asked to meet at Hydra. Paranoid Ric believed a band was perfect cover for an FBI agent, Mark was a fan of Gabe's band, and his friend Arnie just-in from Ithaca, interviewed, interrogated Gabe on the porch. I sat silent, watching them taken as I had been by his authentic stuffing, substance that could not be faked, the kind of true quality an artist must innately have beyond talent to be good enough to have something to say. Mark asked most of the questions, same ones asked me. And I realized how smart this was, my self not really knowing much about Gabe. Soon Ric and Gabe were rapped in conversation, the draft, Vietnam, Sky River Rock Festival, Gabe's band maybe playing a street dance Hydra planned on next Friday. And then Lance Robby and Scottie spilled-out the door, pulling Mark and Ric down to the lawn. Gabriel and I took-off. Ric calling after "Hey man, if you pass the smell test, Shoshannah'll let you know". Gabe was euphoric meeting someone like Ric, eternally grateful I called him, I could feel a heat when he took my hand, walking. We coffeed at the Last Exit on Brooklyn, he pressing to spend time together, inviting me home to band practice. I hesitated outside the Exit, what he wanted I wanted, but I was way too emotionally unsteady to let desire rule, looking at the sidewalk so he could not see the heat in my eyes "I'm going home. See you Friday". Disappointment owned his voice "Yeah, right, Friday". I turned to go. He grabbed me from behind, big hands on my tits, finding erect nipples, rolling them in those gifted fingers, pulling me against him, hard-on at the small of my back, kissing my neck. For one stunned moment, indulging an unwilling submission fantasy, wanting him to take me right there, I pushed those hands away and spun round to slap his face. Hopping-back, his green eyes smiling innocent as if nothing unusual happened "See you Friday".

Next day Ric informed me Gabe was a big okay. I decided to call and give-in. His chilly-tone was confusing "We can't play your street dance. I forgot we're booked at the Rainbow Friday night. A&R people, agents're coming. Could you tell Ric I'm truly sorry". I didn't believe him "Wow, sure. That's so great your band gets another chance. We can play records. And I'll walk over to the Rainbow after the dance". He dropped the pretense "Look, right after you left yesterday, Nick confronted me on the street, claiming you belong to him, that you're Soulmates, and if I don't keep my hands off, he'll break 'em with a hammer. There's something wrong with his head. He freaks me out. I think he would do it and don't want any part of this". Anger, fear washed over me "Oh god no. I haven't seen him in weeks. I'm so sorry". Gabe cleared his throat "I'm sorry too sweet piece. Maybe sometime. For now, I'm staying far away from you, and you're staying far away from me and my band. He's a psycho". I promised "Yes. You're right. He is". I eased the blow with some truth, that Gabe had nearly as little regard for women as Nick, and I would have been just another belt-notch Groupie. Nick still determining for me, there was no ease.

I took Friday off work. My first public act of civil disobedience, Hydra and friends were marching, downtown, down the middle of 4th Avenue from Pike to Lenora at high noon. I counted 26 of us, stopping traffic, calling for President Johnson to tell the truth about the war, demanding legal birth control. And in a flicker I saw my place in history, from the nameless suffragettes dressed in white, marching, campaigning, demanding for 70 years the right to vote, I was another unknown soldier, carrying a metal hanger raised high, dark-red poster paint spilled down white pants, down my inner thigh, showing the only sort of abortion available, illegal, unspoken, deadly, unless you came from a gilded-bed. When police arrived, we scattered. I wore two pair of pants and quickly shed the painted ones and coat hanger into a public trash can. No one got caught. Radio and local evening TV carried the news, 15 of us, our numbers always under-reported, spontaneous gorilla theatre, burning a flag, and draft cards, we were heard and seen. It was a win, heady stuff, intoxicating, power-full, and I was beginning to believe we could change the world.

Walking with Mark to the street dance, high on success, he offered a square of windowpane made by a chemist friend. Safe, uncut with any junk, just my kind, I did not indulge, feeling neon vulnerable, keeping a sober eye for Nick. And he was there, in the shadow of a building edging the dance. I confided to Keely, who told Ric Bear Mark and Arnie, and they surrounded him. Ric was loud in his low steady voice "Creeps are not welcome at Hydra events, at Hydra House, on Hydra streets, hassling Hydra chicks. We know your face, and will be looking for you". Nick was stone still and silent, till Ric stepped aside, opening the circle to let him go. A swaggering sad soul, he promised me "I ache for you. Need you. Can't sleep without you. And I won't bother you again". I believed, and did not "No matter how true you sound, I don't believe anything you say. You see, I have friends now. Something you made sure I didn't. And they believe me, not you. I'm not afraid of you anymore". My quivering lip revealed the lie. He smiled and disappeared. Keely and Mark stayed close to me. The street dance was a blast even with records, hundreds of under-age kids had somewhere to go, and all the collectives, some SDS, Weathermen, Black Panthers, more revolutionaries in Seattle than I imagined, came to celebrate our win today. Keely warned the FBI, undercover cops, spies were among them, and week-end Hippies in long-hair wigs, playing it strait during the work-week, partying, getting stoned on weekends, wanting the best of both world without paying the price. That was kind of me too, working a strait job, living in the Golden Ghetto, but I was not in disguise, and not just partying, and the Man knew exactly who I was. Keely and Mark walked me to the bus, waited till it came, and invited me to move in.

> Lies
> Everything I hear rings hollow
> All conning me to follow
> But it's lies lies lies
> Coming through my ears and my eyes
> Burning and tearing up my brain
> Leaving me in so much pain
> With no shred of sanity or humanity
> But lots of profanity
> And I wonder what's the use
> All this abuse
> Then I look in your eyes
> An see no compromise
> What else is there to do
> But try for you
> So glad there's you
>
> Everywhere I look its lies
> Everywhere except your eyes

I put down my journal and closed my eye, savoring the freedom to write without Nick's censure, wondering would some one real ever fill the you in my poem, some one I could reveal my self to without fear of crushing them. Some one I could talk too about every thing.

Chapter Eight

HYDRA

Dad forbid me "Moving in with those hoodlums causing all the trouble". I thought he was wrong "But we're not the ones lying, or dropping bombs, or turning our face away from poverty and racism". I knew this was his thin-skin of fears, he could not protect his Little Precious Girl out in the big bad world, that feeling helpless made him mad, but these were his fears not mine. I knew he planned on me going safely from his house to a husband like Mom had, and thought my indomitable determination to do and be every thing was some tomboy quality I would out-grow, that I would soften into a young woman's delicate sensibilities. What he considered headstrong, our clashing of wills, was really my own budding ego's curiosity, ingenuity, an aching desire to count for something. I knew he loved me maybe more than his sons, we were more alike, and they more like Mom, nevertheless his mind was fixed, I was not as capable as a boy, there was something missing. I knew this mad was the unexpected realization that it was too late, that I was already out there, and all he could do was use some father-clout to try and coerce. Nick tried telling me what to do, I rejected my Soulmate for liberty, and would do the same with Daddy's Good Little Girl. He huffed "Those revolutionaries are no-goods, troublemakers. Getting involved with them will ruin your life, your future. You're a smart girl Shoshy, I can't believe that's what you want". The system worked for him, madly in-love with his wife of twenty-four years, living in a fine home, actively considering going into business for themselves, this was success beyond his dreams, his treasure, and I was an integral part of it, about to ruin the prefect picture. He did not get how seeing his girl inadequate to be out there on my own, making my own decisions, wounded me so deep, warped my picture. I loved my Dad, hated being his distress, and needed him to understand "Do you thrust the politicians, the lawyers, teachers, the merchant chiefs. They don't have our interest at heart, only theirs. I'm not putting down what you and Mom work so hard for. I'm more grateful then you'll ever know for my life. I need to be the hero in it now, not some maiden waiting for rescue". Dad suppressed a proud smile, his mad dissolve "I fought in the war to stand for something beyond my own personal interest. You can get lost in doing for everyone though. You have to think about yourself too". Silent tears ran Mom's face. Dad put his arm round, giving her a tender squeeze. I said gently "Come on Mom. Look at me. I'm fine. You did a really great job. I have to finish it for my self. Win my dragon fight". She heaved a sighed "I don't know why you have to fight a dragon. What dragon". I smiled "Yeah I know, and I can't explain cause I don't really know myself. It's the thing I have to do. Like you raising me, being as good a parent as you could". She didn't get it. Mom often would say she wasn't smart, I knew she was a bit naive, sheltered, and plenty smart when she made the effort. But she did not and looked away from me. Dad got it, still warning "You picked the wrong battle. You can't fight City Hall". I folded my arms across my chest wishing to do it easy as Keely "But Dad, I'm not alone. I have to fight the fight that's right here on my plate or miss the moment, like Hitler was your fight". This begot the inevitable last-ditch "I'm older than you, and I know better". I looked at him and grinned my chin out. His eyes twinkled, satisfaction spreading into a broad smile, these endless battles we fought over my choices, his way of teaching me, if I can stand-up to all-powerful Oz, I can stand-up to anyone.

I called a cab. Did not need much for work, Boss had me modeling the latest arrivals. I took books, shoes, jeans, dainties, sewing kit, all but the sleeping-bag and pillow fit in my backpack. I kissed Mom's cheek "I love you". She sighed her resignation "I love you Shoshy, no matter what". I kissed Dad's cheek "I love you Daddy". He shook his head slowly side-to-side "I love you too Shoshannah. Be careful, and keep your nose clean". Crossing the bridge, sun setting in every hue of pink and blue clouds, I felt my self on a one-way ticket, shooting into outer space with no way back.

Sharing Mark's bedroom, kept me awake the first night, our attraction went both ways. He acted as if sharing was no big deal, and it worked, we were polite private respectful and neat, out-mannering the temptation.

One week at Hydra and I gave notice to the Mirror. Altering designer clothes, engineering them to fit bodies so disproportionate, the challenge and the pay was good, still I desperately hated retail selling, and, Boss played Sunday afternoon Mahjongg in the same club as Mom. Having known me since birth, she was soon on my case for moving-in with those dangerous Hippies, it was a close-quarters shop, she and me eight hours a day, her impertinent questions, prying eyes, invasive, scrutinizing, and the daily phone call to Mom. When Nick and I moved to the farm, I quit without notice, she never mentioned it on hiring me again, so I wanted to finish right this time, offering two weeks and all the waiting alterations complete. She countered with a raise and benefits, ten-dollars-more-a-day, 60% on alterations, I could work in my jean, and do only alterations if I didn't want to sell. Nearly disarmed by these never before perks speaking to my worth, and why wait till now to give it to me, I said no. She cold-silenced the balance of the day, and on closing said I need not come back, ever. I left it there, the bigger reason not something for her daily phone call, Mom and Dad would freak if they knew I sought refuge from Nick, openly stalking me, standing hours across from the Mirror, waiting in his bus as I waited for mine. I was too public, far too accessible, he was capable of everything, and scared exactly what he wanted in me. I never saw him near Hydra, maybe he was scared too.

My new free days went to reading, hand sewing, hanging-out with the Little Ones, and soaking-up the continuing, evolving political discussion on the benefits of Socialism, the consummate adjective to Democracy, planning for the up-coming Democratic Convention in Chicago, and the heated argument around Sundance maybe going to be raised by Ric's Parents. Arnie, Mark and Bear were adamant, only a bad mother could be so selfish. Carolion and I adamant, what great courage it took to give-up a beloved child. Ric was habitual Catholic, though not practicing, he refused to use birth control or let Keely. She did anyway, and when he found her diaphragm and freaked, she kicked him out of her bed. As punishment, raising the Boys became her sole job, while he had more important man-things to do, like running the revolution. His Folks in their late 40's, wealthy, harshly disapproving his politics and the life-style their grand-children were being raised, offered to take Sundance. They saw him as a last chance to salvage one, take him while he was young enough to bond with them, to adopt, give him what they considered a good life. Having been pregnant and raising infants for eight years, Keely was considering the quality of attention Sundance would get as an only, and the reality of her life. Ric insisted his Folks would turn Sundance against them. When Keely threatened to make him do the rearing, he folded. She conceded to a trial, no adoption, no question if she changed her mind. Folks readily agreed, flying-in the next day to claim their boy. That minute, unanticipated melancholy, a more than usual reticence took hold of Keely.

High noons, Hydra gathered round the big oak table in the dining room, the War Table, planning how to expose the lies government was feeding America, mobilize the middle class, stop the war, disrupt the Democratic Convention, hopefully getting Eugene McCarthy nominated, and of course how to amuse ourselves. Out of respect for the seasoned players at the Table, I held my tongue, noticing Keely and Carolion were constantly stifled. When finally daring to speak, I met the same stifling, where did I get my information, what proof did I have, put on the defense, foiled-off in a direction I could not remember in-the-heat-of-the-moment not to go till already there, and never effectively finding my way back to the point as things moved-on. I knew this tactic, this supposedly benign and impartial maneuver most guys did not use on each other, a destructive, discounting, diluting, negating of any influence I might legitimately accrue, shutting-me-up without saying shut-up. And I tried calling foul long before living here, but like hardened cynics the foulers always deny anything was happening, insisting I was being treated exactly the same as the guys, that I was over-reacting, too emotional, and then of course asking for proof of this imagined foul. There was never anything specific, no way to turn defense into discussion unless the foulers acknowledge the game. And I knew they believed it was justified, boys know better, this stealthy way of maintaiing power, shutting me up exactly what the game was designed for. And the arrogant unwillingness to even hear about this power-trip, a coordinated and skilled conspiracy, denying the silenced full democratic participation. And the voracity for winning the game that seemed only to whet their appetite. I voiced none of this, stopped attending the War

Table, frustrated how entrenched male chauvinism was, a secret society, savvy little boys gleaning at the knee, little girls not privy. And I felt deeply betrayed, behavior-as-usual was here even at the heart of the Revolution, male comrades effectively erasing females while happily claiming our ideas for their own. I thought it might be so automatic and unconscious that they did not even know. I made a mistake moving-in, and could not bear going home to Mom and Dad so wrong, did not dare live alone. When I tried explaining, Keely and Carolion did not get my complaint, continuing the War Table, falling for the proof-trap every day, dogs chasing their tails, every day. I burned indignant, this egalitarian collective was male rhetoric, empty-talk and no walk, and spent my time with the Little Boys, still largely unskilled at this insidious sport.

It was 1968, free love supposedly liberated from Victorian constructs, and Arnie was pressing me hard, emancipated chicks should open their legs freely for the cause. I was not a prude, glad to make love without getting pregnant, but I saw no love, just fucking on male terms, and the chance to get pregnant if the condom failed. To me free love was a contradiction in terms, more a sport, devoid of love, trivializing love. I was an idealistic romantic, determined to find my one true, and while I sought, would channel any libido into hand-sewing hats for sale. As usual, this was unacceptable behavior, unrevolutionary to be unavailable, too serious for a girl, and punishable. I was a tease, a prude, a frigid bitch, a dyke. Labeled all these in the past, my femininity called to question, to control me, just never by those who were suppose to be comrades. Victorian constructs conveniently thrown-out for sex, and fully implemented when it came to other behavior, I responded to each verbal assault calmly and evenly "Fucking for fucking sake does not interest me. Deal with it". This held sway only days, for a girl did not really mean what she said, I must be playing a game, playing hard-to-get, how could I not want to fuck. Inscrutable, uncomfortable and yes flattered by the attention, I knew I had the power in this, for Arnie had some principles and would not take me unless I said yes.

The Seattle Liberation Front was a primary destination for revolutionaries from all over, some staying a few days, some longer, like Arnie, coming West to help us strategize for the Chicago Democratic Convention. And we categorically had the press, and the City's attention. John Hinterberger of the Seattle Times, Mike James KING TV, Walt Crowley and Tim Harvey of the Helix, all knocking on Hydra's door when ever something happened, whether we did it or not. Our in-house freelance journalist Dancing Bear would go out and talk to them, or Ric, or Mark, and now Arnie. Never Keely, never Carolion, never me.

And despite FBI across the street, perennial small-time dealing went on to pay rent, utilities, phone, food, gas, leaflets, under-writing the Revolution. I began to indulge in a little deliberate experimentation with drugs I had not tried. First came psilocybin mushrooms, known as the Magician of Psychedelic, I brewed a tea, not too strong, preferring to be in some control, and meandered to Volunteer Park for a long-winded communion with the Big Stone Ram. I loved this gentle high, more tea, and to Ravenna Park for a day-into-night Be-In. Another brew, and the Seattle Center outdoor hootenanny, a shining new voice there, Jimmy Page, the other performers left no impression. More, and downtown to the Fraternal Order of Eagles Hall, dazzled by the fledgling Joffrey Ballet, borne aloft by the Chrome Syrcus. I was always on vigilant look-out for Nick. The thing with psilocybin, it can cut both ways, the mind merely thinking magician and flowers would pour from my sleeve, a swooning fragrant bouquet. I could reach into my pocket-full-of-stars and fling them into the night sky, giving light to my bare feet rooting into the soft earth, the other tree nymphs whispering how absolutely lovely, sap running in my veins too, I was their Sister. Any thought made manifest, I reminded my self aloud "Be care-full where you head goes Shoshy. Be care-full who you trip with. Thoughts can stray. This can just as well turn nightmare". So I tripped alone.

Tetrahydrocannabinol, the get-high part of Marijuana and Hashish, recently synthesized by some shrewd entrepreneur, marketed as THC, came to Hydra when Ric scored two-dozen small brown vials from the same Oregon dealer in the same green Nash Rambler station-wagon that bought cocaine from Nick at the farm. All my defenses screamed, I made certain he did not see me. Twenty-three little brown vials to sell, one for us. We dipped our cigarettes in the colorless odorless liquid, and let them dry. Walking to the Roach Tavern with Mark and Keely, lighting-up, always extra delicious getting stoned in public, committing crime in the open. One toke of this shit and it was too late, a toxic-metal taste, not like tinfoil acid, stunning the cilia in my lungs, too heavy to exhale, suffocating for a deep breath, poison, nausea, dizzy, I laid down on the sidewalk to die, a freight train barreling through me, shivering, coughing, gulping in air, I was a logical fool having reasoned, hmmmmm, let see now, THC, derivative of marijuana and hashish, ahhh the heavenly rhythmic connected nature of these substances I regularly risk liberty to smoke, and I get this wretched imposter, I should have waited for some one to try it first, too late sucker you're dead. Keely, Mark floated over me, comical bobbing puppets, dangling till I could stand. They went on to the Roach, THC agreeing with them. I went home, found my sleeping bag, crawled inside the long silky gullet, satin touching me, calming the whole of my body, all parts contained, anxious, waiting, trying to control a gushing swaying thought-fountain, this vulnerable, never again this out-of-control, I wanted to drive the car not have it drive me, listening to a part of me bargaining with old Yahweh, pleeease pleeease oh pleeease let me come to rest with an unbroken mind. And when gravity began to stick, obliging relief came in waves, oh thank you thank you thank you, promising this was the one time I would ever use THC, that I learned my lesson big-time, another part smiling at this still obstinate inclination.

When MDA arrived, a three-day acid-like super-high, I waited on a fool going first. It was one of the Grodes, who never made it entirely back, never sleeping, growing thin and pale, hardly eating, wetting himself and his bed, talking constantly, spinning tales of astral travel to regions beyond disguised as the Red Knight, of worthy alien adversaries, honor winning battles, a hero unable to claim his own body, unable to tend to its needs. His Mother came and took him away. He did not resist. So it was no to MDA, and cocaine, and methamphetamines. I was not hard-core enough anymore for smack and opium, or interested in the ubiquitous black-market prescription downers, Codeine, Percodan, Quaaludes, Librium, Valium, Seconal, Demerol, Dilaudid. My only penchant now, marijuana, hashish, mushrooms, and still sacred to me lysergic acid diethalamide-25. Temptations newest name was DMT, touted the supreme summit psychedelic thrill-ride without after-price, able to reach enlightenment at the speed of thought.

DMT initiation came scouting shops on the Ave to sell my hats, running into Oscar and Sebastian, the Angels invited me come to their newly purchased home in the District to smoke some. A fine old white two-story, fancy wrought-iron fence, over-grown garden, generous porch, leaded windows, window seats, wooden floors, rich tapestries hugging stucco walls, carnelian glass-beaded curtain dripping cross the broad archway that separated dining and living room, bongos, tambouras, congas, gourd-shakers, lush sitting-pillows populated the floor, in the corner a black-light shining through the salt-water tank of electric blue and yellow fish, silver framed photos of Eleanor Roosevelt, Rock Hudson, Errol Flynn, Judy Garland, percolating lava lamps, boston ferns, the room centered with a Sarouk underneath brown velvet couches facing each other, glass-top coffee-table in-between, holding a tall green glass hookah. I decided to try only a taste. We took opposite couches. Sebastian rolled two fat joint, dipped them in a small brown vial, laid both on the glass-top to dry, lit the hookah and passed its black mouth-piece to me. I took a long drag of friendly water cooled homegrown, exhaled without holding, passed to Oscar, and considered how many drugs came in small brown glass vials these days, synthetics, so far I had not enjoyed any of the trips. Sebastian brewed a pot of Jasmine tea, put Ravi Shankar on the record player, and poured our cups. The joints dry, he put a match to one, took a big hit, held the smoke in and passed to me, nodding yes with a broad closed-mouth grin, slowly leaning back into the couch. I took a modest hit, passed to Oscar, and wham, I slow-motion leaned back into the couch, everything warping fun-house mirror, instant hallucinations, so intense and exquisite they blotted any ability to speak or move, I rested my eyes on Sebastian and Oscar, what stunning creatures, faces day-glow poster-paint, Oscar blue, Sebastian hot pink, loud in the black light, and their hair, bright white owl feathers, just like Edie Adams in the White Owl Cigarillo commercials on Ernie Kovacs show, the beaded curtain and tapestries swaying to Ravi, drums and shakers playing themselves, lava lamps rainbow volcanoes outside their glass, velvet growing like grass on time-lapse, carpet pattern swimming, the fish were bored, the pores of my skin breathing air, again making me aware of how permeable I was,

Rock Hudson winked at me. I came down fast as I went up, straight-up, no concept of time, straight-down, a soft-landing, the contrast stunning, thrilling, I could move again, leaning forward for the cup of warm tea, a mild tinny after-taste in my mouth. DMT was not a spiritual high, more atomic explosion, a cheap-thrill-ride, nothing akin to LSD but the hallucinations, nothing sacred. Sebastian lit the remaining joint, graciously offering me first hit. Their body language wishing to be alone. I made a lame excuse, having to be somewhere. Walking to Hydra, I wondered how many cheap-thrill-rides a brain could survive intact.

The Grode's scored a little brown vial of DMT and threw a party. The only one at Hydra who fancied psychedelics, I told none it was my twentieth birthday and went, wanting to try DMT again, it didn't let me create hallucinations like Psilocybin, more exaggerated what was already there, and I rather enjoyed the ride. Ten chairs round their War Table, sixteen people in the room, five 100 watt bare bulbs in the chandelier, talk drifting while joints were rolled, dipped and dried. I took a very modest hit, and shot directly into alter-world, glad I had a chair to slowly lean back in, eyes resting on the others. Bulbs glaring, unforgiving on day-glow faces, animal-natures peeking through, some feral under-faces, teeth sharp, laughing. I leaned further into my chair, eyes looking down for certainly to my own hands, knuckles exaggerated, this was not getting high but low, really fucked-up, and I was a little scared, wishing for instant magical transport into the satin-throat of my sleeping bag. Another dipped joint came by, I could not have reached for it if I would, and another, everyone two-hits beyond anywhere I wanted to imagine. I must stay-still, invisible till I can go, my eyes only on the elaborate castle covering the War Table, built with single-serving cereal boxes, paper cups, pop bottles, beer cans, plastic knives and forks, popsicle sticks, dominos, rubber bands, home to lead soldiers, Civil and World War, plastic baseball players, Native Americans, cowboys, horses, tiny guns, cannons, all their faces silently turning to meet my gaze. I concentrated on breathing in-and-out, waiting for straight-down. An unstable landing, taking more intentional breaths, I slipped in-between and out the front door, staying on the porch till my legs were steady, walking to the bus stop. I could not trip with people so willing, so needing to rocket so far-out of their own company, beyond any gravitational pull, too easy to come apart, never return whole. In weighing the supposed either/or of nurture and nature, I came away from this knowing it was both. Without doubt a good trip depended on the purity of drug, but also and even more, on the character of the user, and users with, for as Ida Rose had said - *the air between us is not empty.*

Discussion quickened at Hydra, what action would we take to the Chicago Democratic Convention. Seduced, I began to occasion the War Table. How to get McCarthy the nomination, discredit Humphrey who would certainly rubber-stamp LBJ's Vietnam War policy. We talked of buying milk trucks, home-delivery near a thing of the past, they could be gotten cheap, driven to Chicago, we would put Humphrey signs on the sides, and then disabled them at major intersections round the Conrad Hilton Hotel, home-base for the Convention, throwing Chicago into chaos, all blamed on Hubert. Our electronics genius, Mark unveiled his latest invention, a black box he spent the morning attaching to the phone. Why, how it worked he never said, but using it was simple. Flip the red toggle switch for delete, flip the black for free long-distance calls. When both were in the off position the phone worked normal. But when a phone number was dialed and rang once, if you flipped the red toggle to on, it deleted that number from the phone company's data-bank as if it never existed, no one could call the place again till a new number was issued. Or dial a number, and after one ring flip the black toggle to on, and it tells the phone company computer the number just dialed is already busy, not registering the call as going through, giving us free long distance. Suddenly organizing beyond Seattle was free of charge. Keely and I went to the library for phone numbers, the Pentagon, White House, members of the House and Senate, Chicago police, the phone company.

I did what pleased me, not having seen or sensed Nick, he had no opportunity to know where I might be, get to me, I was getting long for the first time in a while, like a cat who lays down all curled-up, and soon stretches-out her hind legs, and her front, and then they stretch as far as possible, her back a bit arched, she is as long and relaxed as a cat can be. There was so much music to hear, the hometown Daily Flash, Floating Bridge, Child. Jimi Hendrix and Janis Joplin with Big Brother and the Holding Company came for one night to Sick's baseball Stadium, Keely and I talked our way in backstage. And there was Janis, opening a bottle of Southern Comfort on her way to the stage, downing it like apple juice, tossing the empty aside, strutting-out to a standing screaming crowd. She was not a beautiful woman, but when possessed, soaring, raw, she was. Hendrix we missed, fleeing the Roadies who let us in, wanting to claim payment right there on the backstage floor. And I went to sit-ins, street dances, and every band playing the downtown Eagles Hall, Iron Butterfly, Quicksilver Messenger Service, the Youngbloods, Vanilla Fudge, It's a Beautiful Day, Pink Floyd. I never intended going to the Democratic Convention, Bobby Kennedy's murder snuffed my last honest hope any politician could or would fix anything, or tell anything but lies lies lies, I could not chance putting a true stake in McCarthy or McGovern, another man-of-the-people, maybe bang, dead, and me too. In the end no one from Hydra went. We gathered round the television, silenced by the violence on screen, the National Guard and guns, and Mayor Richard Daly's police force in Grant Park, with mace, and guns, and sticks breaking bones, unarmed bodies dragged to waiting paddy-wagons, tear-gas drifting into the Hilton. I was awed by such individual courage in the face of crushing force, bravery those fighting for freedom must find to push-back against overwhelming might, and felt an intense and tender regret having missed the battle alongside these resolute soldiers. Humphrey got the nomination anyway, and Daly's police riot extinguished any stubborn flicker of hope I had for a solution by peace-full process. Violent over-throw now seemed justified, in the same way murdering Eldridge Clever and Doctor King had turned the Panthers' struggle.

I plunged into the deep, sleeping 12 hours and more, some invisible sucking malaise, and then rocket-ship rides, up all-night, wired, obsessed, beading hats to sell at the Arabesque and Esoterica boutiques. Arnie's un-employment check, Keely's welfare, food stamps, dealing, my little earnings, we were covered. Then one long late August afternoon, sewing at the War Table I looked-up and saw Max. Golden-green eyes, soft curly brown hair, milk white skin, clean-shaven chin, six-feet tall and lean, faded bell-bottoms, waffle-stompers, embroidered llama skin coat, fur on the inside, and no shirt, he was the most beautiful man I had ever seen in-person, and re-minded of Josh. A member of Arnie's SDS chapter, Max hitched West, curious to see what the Seattle Liberation Front was all about. Arnie's stubborn pressure to fuck me, and my stony celibate refuge, made him want me now more for sport than appetite. Regardless, I did not shy from this joy-full magnetic pull, falling openly for Max, and he for me. He sat there smiling, beaming really, obliging Ric's every question. And he and Arnie caught-up. And, I took him to my room and locked Mark out.

He wore protection without asking, and we made love on his fur coat, taking turns on-top, slowly, satisfying, nourishing on every levels. And we went everywhere together, most nights to the Century Tavern, where the SLF, SDS, Weathermen, and FBI infiltraitors mingled. One evening, ripped on Sinsemilla, sipping beer, shooting pool, I walked right-out of my body and over to the window, so unexpectedly, so easily again on the outside, and there she was, Shoshy the pool-shark, common barfly, so far from who I aimed to be, her voice defensive and loud in my head, but the Century's the People's Bar, it's the only place to be, these are the only People worth being with, accusing my sudden objectivity as haughty, stuck-up, so Golden Ghetto, and me of still needing some humble. I was not persuaded, this out-sight was a gift, for I had no problem coming to the Century for a beer with the Gang, but leaning over the pool-table with a cigarette hanging from my lips made me feel vulgar, cheap. Drifting for too long now, I did not respect who I had become, and could not get out of there fast enough. Walking back into my self, I leaned the cue against the wall, set the beer on the window sill, absconding smooth and quick. Max followed. I tried explaining as we walked to Hydra. He thought I was being too hard on my self. And I knew sadly that he would never see me, never be more than a transient sweetheart.

We found the door open. Max shot up-stairs to the Littles room. Fearing what I might find, inching through the main floor, I could hear Carolion whimpering. In the kitchen, under the shelf in the pantry, seeing me she wiggled-out and sat cross-legged, in enough light for me to witness her split lower-lip, blood-crusted nostrils. I was too scared to move. Max came-in relieved "The Boys are sound asleep". Seeing Carolion, he reached to help her up. Shrinking-away, shoulders slumping, legs twitching, she began to talk, not to us but some one, how her father raped her so many times, but she fought back this time. Momentarily shocked, how could a father, but then Penny's father, fuming at my self for not noticing some thing, any thing, broken-hearted she had such a father and kept the secret, I sat down and barely touched my foot to hers. She began to sob quietly at the connection. Max sank to his knees, hands together as if in-prayer "I'll go get everyone". Like him I would have fled her anguish, instead gently coaxing her upstairs, I bathed her porcelain body in a warm tub. She sat still, limp, staring at nothing, confiding how Mom abandoned her at nine, how he'd been fucking her ever since. Letting me pat her dry, rub her arms with Jean Nate, plait her long wet hair, dress her in my favorite jeans and Mexican wedding shirt, promising "Your Father will never touch you again".

We gathered round the War Table after 1AM, a solemn council. Carolion kept her eyes and hands in her lap. Arnie volunteered far too enthusiastically to chop-off the asshole's dick. Squirming her shoulders she did not look-up. Keely told Ric "We're going to adopt her". Carolion raised her eyes "Thank you". Ric prompted "What else do you want". She roared without hesitation "I never want him to touch me again". Keely and Ric argued who would stay with the Boys. Ric prevailed. We took Bear's 1965 Ford Fairlane 500 Station wagon to Carolions. She unlocked the apartment door, and we ambushed Dad sitting at the kitchen table, tossing down a shot of Dewar's, having just come from the Firelight Lounge, one of Frank Colacurcio's notorious topless joints. He was not the drooling misshapen miscreant I pictured, but a well-dressed, clean-cut, 35 year old Boeing engineer. Ric warned him why we came. Too drunk to be scared, even seeming somewhat amused, Dad scoffed "You can' tell me wha' ta do with my own girl. Now ged outa my house er I'll call the cops". Carolion stood tall. Recognizing this man had the same infection as Nick, I moved to her side and did too. Ric, Mark, Arnie, Bear and Max swarmed, taking him down on his back, Arnie sat on his chest, Mark and Bear his legs, Ric and Max pinned his arms. Carolion put the Beatles on the record player. And Dad struggled and spat and cursed and bayed and threatened and wailed and bawled for help, a little man in more than stature, soon drenched in sweat, barely grunting and groaning his menace. Color flushed Carolion's cheeks, she put her foot on his neck "It's the weekend. No one can hear you. And no one will think twice about the loud music". I knew she was repeating his words. We sang the White Album, and near all Sergeant Pepper. Dad peed his pants, panting, begging "I can' breathe. Oh God, ged off me. Please. I'll do anything ya want. Anything". We kept singing. He began pleading Carolion "I'll led you go baby". She walked slowly to the telephone table for a tablet and pen, handing them to me. I wrote a contract, Carolion is hereby free to emancipate, free to be adopted. Ric and Keely witnessed. Arnie threatened to sit on him till a heart-attack if he didn't sign immediately. Dad nodded yes. Max freed his right arm. I put pen in his hand, and held the tablet. He signed, and went limp in his puddle. No one got off till Carolion collected her belongings. We had not broken-in, done no damage, left no mark on him, just drug-crazed-pinko-commie-Hippies promising to hunt him down and kill him if he ever looked at Carolion again.

One more honey kiss, swearing to see each other again, Max went home. The very same autumn morning, September 30th, Boeing rolled-out their first 747 jumbo jet, immediately dubbed the *Crowd Killer*. This double-decker would carry 374, and could take 490 with the right seat configuration, while its predecessor, the 727 carried 131 tops. And the very minute Max went out the door, Arnie resumed his pressing, I slept with Max, why not him. I did not bother an answer. Movement guys were for the most part boys with patriarchal hang-overs. Just because the Pill was available now with a prescription, they wanted to believe there were no consequences to fucking. But it did not protect from the clap, gonorrhea, syphilis, and was not fail-safe. And then what, an illegal abortion you could die from, or have a baby. And no one mentioned the emotional cost of sleeping round, which was the unofficial right of passage for movement chicks to be considered real revolutionaries. Revolutionary or not, these were guys rules not mine. Yes there were VD consequenced for them, but they seemed to think getting pregnant was all on the girl, her problem, deal with it. I would here them tattle who they'd done and how, and it did not sound any different from high school. I respected how they went after Carolion's Dad for raping her, but fucking them was not my idea of revolutionary initiation. And still, I missed the fleeting end of hungry restless physical loneliness, Max was an ardent imaginative lover, never through till I was. And I missed the public refuge, the courtesy extended him from other men who would have came-on to me were I was alone, fair game, like it was their obligation to trespass my space, like there was something aberrant, deficient about a lone woman that screamed fix me I am not whole. What conceited princes, I was nauseated by their song, you're so beautiful, why aren't you smiling, come on give me a smile, like smiling all the time was my obligation, like there was something wrong with me not smiling, I could not possibly be okay, or happy without the required sub-missive non-threatening grin frozen to my face and their dick in my cunt. And there was no winning, if I smiled to placate, they took it as an invitation, if I did not, it was a threat, and if I acted the least bit offended by their invasion of my personal space, they called me frigid bitch, dyke, yet they would never dream of going round smiling all the time. With Max, they let another man's woman alone, some unspoken ownership code of respect. Nevertheless I had my liberty again, to do exactly what I wanted when I wanted without having to explain or tell anyone, even Max, who maintained all this was paranoia, though I knew he knew.

Thousands crowded the Ave for the *Love-U-District-Festival*. Keely and I took the Littles to a free concert to see the Youngbloods, Santana, and the Floating Bridge. One week later, Mark and I and two-thousand plus sat-in at the UW Faculty Club, protesting the lack of tenured Blacks and Women. Campus police flocked, we must leave immediately, voluntarily, or be arrested. Mark stayed. Scared, I ran-away, humiliated, demoralized, sulking for weeks, tussling such want of courage. And then another blow, though not unexpected, Richard Nixon won the election, invoking Ida Rose's chilling anecdote from a 1952 audit predicting - *When a man with an X in the middle of his name becomes president of the United States of America, he will be the last <u>duly</u> elected president of a <u>united</u> America.* In my wayward drift I thought of Ida Rose every day, re-read and re-read her book, my brain rocking between paranoia and not. There was such power there, she must be evil, waiting to capture my soul in a jar if I put one toe over her threshold again, and, she's the most inspiring human being I ever met. Back far as I could think, I ached for something till now unnamed, to see my self in others, out there in the world, living proof I was okay to exist, as is, even do something important, for I needed reason and purpose beyond biology and breathing air, and there were no real live role models.

Mom was struck down with appendicitis early her senior high school year, emergency surgery right there on the kitchen table to save her life, recuperating for months, she fell far behind and never caught-up. Her dream to be a nurse, revised by the school counselor to take-up typing, settle for secretary. Another girl of little promise no one encouraged to follow her dream, no one believed-in, no one offered catch-up help, she began thinking herself incapable, even stupid, and never shook it off. Her Mom was four-years-old when the Family fled pogroms in Odessa to Constantinople. In 1912, when Granny was nine, freighter passage had been saved-up and they sailed to America, Papa, Mama, five sisters and two brothers allowed in though Ellis Island. Speaking Yiddish only, Granny entered 3rd grade, could not catch-on to English quick enough to keep-up, and dropped-out after 4th grade. I loved my Mom and Granny, they were fine wife and mother role models, with real courage and ingenuity, but where was one American Stateswoman, one philosopher, even Will Durant's Story of Philosophy did not contain a single female. And sports, oh yes there was one champion golfer, Mildred "Babe" Didrikson Zaharias, who died when I was eight. And where were the visible spiritual leaders, in private, at home women were keepers of the rituals. I had discovered Ayn Rand in 9th grade, a revelation, the Fountainhead, Atlas Shrugged, it wasn't the stories but her female characters, smart, strong, self-determined, and public. And there was Dale Messick's comic-strip heroine Brenda Starr, and on screen Katherine Hepburn, and Audrey who never wore high heels. Bonita-Kay was the first role model I could have a conversation with, who believed smart was a valuable, normal, necessary female pursuit, opening in me a space for something between mother or whore. And then, proving Bonita-Kay was not an incongruity, Monty made the appointment with Ida Rose, and she opened that space into a universe, the domain of spirituality and philosophy no longer exclusively male voiced. Nick tried hard to discount her, unable to accept authority in a female. I knew better, for she generously gave me tools to learn to think for my self, to understand Nick would do all my thinking for me if I let him. Often feeling desperately lonely, I was content all the same, for it was my choice, to be in the world, to try and make a difference, not just take-up space. I needed to resolve the ambivanence and go see her, thank her for helping me name the ache.

Word was spreading out of New York of the coming Woodstock Music and Art Fair and Aquarian Festival, and we caught the fever. Walking to the Reserve Officers Training Corps office recently opened at the UW, in Clark Hall, Arnie, Mark, Carolion, Ric, Bear were ready, eager to protest the University of Washington sanctioning military recruitment on campus. I found the stuffing to go along, and we began seriously planning our own festival. It was national turn-in-your-draft-card-day, a jailable offense, 106 brave souls turned theirs in to the ROTC office. So far I had not done more to jeopardize my freedom than get high in public, regarding the criminalization of Maryjane the Establishment's political weapon to create felons of good kids by making us outlaws. This did not come close to turning-in a draft card, witnessing these fearless soldiers really moved me. I needed to do something too, so I made a new poncho, from a finely-banded brown-and-grey hand-woven wool blanket purchased at Hadassah Thrift Shop on Broadway for one-dollar because of the large burn-hole, conveniently where I cut the head-hole, trimming it in burgundy velvet, putting large pockets on the inside so I need not carry my shoulder bag. Keely and I were the regular food-shoppers, and I began swiping cheese and cookies for the Littles in those big pockets, rationalizing feeding the revolution by ripping-off the big-profit grocery store chain was a noble act, that food, shelter, education, health-care were basic human rights, and should be at the very least not-for-profit. The adrenaline rush getting away with it was an unexpected surprise. To me the Establishment was a massive cannibalistic grey blob, who murdered the Kennedys, Dr. King and our hope, who were now rabidly after the Black Panthers, especially Eldridge Clever who narrowly escaped to Algeria though the Underground, who conspire to take and take and take for themselves without regard. Feeling this blotting-out the sun, I contrived an even bolder personal attack.

I knew big department store charge-account policy. As a courtesy, a show-of-good-faith, when a charge was under ten-dollars, clerks were instructed not to ask for identification or check the account balance, a customer only need sign their name and address on the sales slip. Dressed to my Golden nines, tickled to get some use of my former self, I spent time casing the big three, Fredrick & Nelson, Nordstrom, Bon Marché, deciding Fredricks the most unsuspecting. I filled three of their large shopping bags, each item under ten, clerks never questioning the bogus names and addresses, signing slips with superior off-handed confidence. Toys and clothes for the Littles, knit hats scarves and gloves for everyone, nothing for my self, taking from the Man for personal gain would be a desecration. I could carry no more, flying high, when a mannequin wearing a black felt broad-brimmed hat whispered my name. I absolutely had to have that hat and took it to a clerk. With tax $10.38, oh shit, I forgot to add the tax. Clerk picked-up the phone calling for authorization. Lips quivering, ears gone deaf, I wanted to run, holding my composure standing in mid-air, flinch and fall to my death, waiting, over-confidence, knee-jerk selfish desire had made me stupid. Clerk hung-up, her brow questioning, voice thick in accusation, eying my bags "There's no account here in that name". Smiling to smooth the quiver, hands quaking I lifted one of the bags-full in my arms, steadying it to my bosom, heart banging, time to think, knit your brow like hers, tilt head slightly back and to the side, look down nose, clear your throat "Oh, right. I guess I haven't opened one here yet. I'll pay cash." Setting the bag down with the others, looking in my wallet for money, preparing to say oh, I must have spent it all, please hold the hat for me, and these bags, I'll go open an account now, and then I would vanish, and, there they were, two crisp twenties, payment from Arabesque for beaded hats, my smile beamed, I laid one on the glass counter. Visibly taken aback she wrapped the hat in tissue, shoved it in a bag, and laid it on the counter with my change. Mustering all the Golden I had left, I demanded extra "Put it in a shopping bag". As she did, I collected the change, and the bags, and casual as jitters would allow, moseyed toward the nearest exit, idling to consider things I could not even focus on, ex-iting the 4th Avenue door, a bus-driver lingering at the stop, door open, I got on. Hydra's Christmas Eve had a Jewish Santa, the only one with gifts, all but the Littles surprised at being included in my caper, at the rich booty. Lance, Robby, Scottie pulled on their new clothes over pajamas, and fought over every toy. The rest put on their hats scarves gloves and wore them all evening in my honor. I waited till the Littles went to bed before telling the tale, in less than full detail, basking in the glory, the take $151.06, dangerous, premeditated, cool and smooth till nearly caught, I left out the quivering and stupidity, knowing full-well I got-away because the Sweet Sisters had not sealed my Fate. I was no fool, adrenaline rush and glory, my Robin Hood days ended when the bus left the curb. I gave Carolion the black felt broad-brimmed hat.

The Seattle Times and Post Intelligencer reported on what their owners, editors and advertisers deemed important to them. Ida Rose had cautioned in her book – *all maps are self-reflexive*. The underground papers were mostly in-keeping, owners, editors, all white men with maps, the Helix supposedly far left, Federalist and Spotlight far right, and least worst, the Wonder Wart Hog Believe it or Leave it Time. Only the Hog reported on the Women's Movement without cracking the obligatory jokes, while the rest sold anything to do with tits as hard news whenever they could make it seem even sorta legit, often headless close-ups, no names, we were regularly disembodied-parts. All the papers covered the woman, never named, no credit, who in protest went topless on Alki Beach, Lady Godiva, arrested even at such a reasonable place as the beach, jailed, fined for indecent exposure. Making me realize I could be too, in my own home, just walking by a window, some neighbor or passer-by sees, parts of me legally indecent, offensive, I was a crime just having a she-body. While industries earned fortunes on this titillation, the press too, I'd never thought it further, that the tit business was not all of it, that making them publicly illegal gave the business even more titillation, made them even more money. A righteous anger brewed in my heart, how dare they make parts of my body indecent, laws I assumed inevitable till now thanks to this one courageous provocative nameless woman, even as many men had tits bigger than many women and could take their bare-chested freedom without consequence. The Hog announced a meeting, called by two Movement women forming a Women's Lib collective in Seattle. Keely, Carolion's had no interest. I was thrilled, could hardly wait to talk out-loud, put words to shared outrage, my expectations felt like beacons of neon shooting from the crown of my head into the sky, imagining what power in coming together, discovering the roots of our indignation, focusing it, maybe on a demonstration infront of the men-only Rainier Club. The SLF hierarchy and really the whole movement was one whopping male power-trip. Yeah we worked side-by-side toward the same goals, but the men did zero shopping unless for personal smokes and beer, zero cooking, cleaning, washing clothes, typing, mimeographing, many of our legs were spread wide, getting pregnant, getting dishpan hands, never getting any of the credit, never talking to the press, never given the blow-horn at marches and rallies, never asked to go with them on clandestine night reconnaissance, getting fucked.

My beaded hats sold fast as I could make them. I delivered three to Arabesque on the way to meet. A large room full of women sitting on the floor, leaning the walls, filling chairs and couches, I was last in, nodded to the few I casually knew, nervously lit a smoke and took a space on the floor by the door. Someone I had never seen stood "We'll go around the room to the left. Introduce yourself and say something about what you're into". She pointed to the one left of me, who sprang-up boasting "My name's Mama-Laid. I'm a Plaster Caster, and I got a perfect cast of Delroy Bogave's dick for my collection". Next, "My name's CC, short for Candy-Cunt. My goal's to sleep with a hundred lead guitar players before I'm legal to drink". Then, Sugar who hates men. Angel wants to kill Nixon. Holly fucks Vietnam Vets as her personal crusade to help with their rehabilitation. GG only fucks Black men as a way to drive her Dad nuts. Debbie fucks Black men because she believes white girls owed them for being the cause of so many lynchings. Head reeling, my heart sank as this continued round to the one on my right, very pregnant, she had trouble getting off the floor "My names Tricksee, an I'm into tidbits". I stood, barely able to find legs, speaking to my shoes "My name's Shoshannah, from Hydra". Clearing my throat I repeated what I had practiced "I'm honored to be here with you. I believe together we can take our credit due, take power publicly, refuse to be just cunts and caretakers. Can you imagine what a force we will be". Embarrassment flushed, I sank to the ground, having gone over-and-over these words, so unexpectedly misplaced they hushed the room, these women came to bitch about men. A beginning for sure, certainly I had my resentments, but the meeting had been called to form a Women's Action Collective, to fight for our rights, take power because it was not being shared, the possibilities excited me, now it was clear this would come only after enough anger vented, and even more clear and cold that what I said was not welcome. Over-expecting, wounded by a freeze I did not really understand, the meeting turned to enthusiastic man-bashing. I slipped out and walked home, realizing I was not angry as they were, well maybe just-as but for other reasons, since I had no babies, did not spread my legs for the cause, lived at Hydra, and seemed really fancy free, I guess it looked like I could not relate, maybe I didn't. Either way I was alone again, the possiblilty of some Sisters to talk too, not yet.

Hydra's kitchen full of people. Mark was coming down on acid, lounging the living room couch smoking a joint, I slumped in next to him. He slipped a friendly arm round my shoulders "Man this is really mellow windowpane. Want some. Looks like you can use it". Smiling at being called man, the human contact made me feel better, I turned-up my palm. He put a transparent square on it "One's all you get". I did not hesitate placing it on my tongue, waiting to taste the tin, something Ida Rose said that I had not appreciate at the time unraveling – *Minor expectations. Try to have minor expectations Little One.* This was excellent advice, I'd flown too high in anticipation, and would not have fallen so far had I not, it was my own fault. They plainly saw me through the lense of Hydra, known as the most chauvinistic house, I must have sounded condescending, and so princess, and should have be satisfied, women gathering without men, I should have said hi my name is Shoshy and I'm into tripping. Tasting tin-foil, I went out on the porch, sky bright in more than half-moon, found my place on the top step and stared across the street at the moving curtain. A little painted doll-face five-year-old girl joined me. Mom and Dad had come by to score, and were in a loud argument over who goes to the New Year's party and who goes home with the kid. She snuggled in to me close and quiet. I put a friendly arm round her little shoulders, touched by such an artless spirit, but then I felt that way about most kids, they were still mostly unaffected, unadulterated, not yet so good at the games, no need to talk, leaning-on each other for comfort enough. Without noticeable approach a stranger appeared at the bottom of the steps, fixing his stare on me, strained watery eyes boring into mine, I was unable to look away. He reached our way with both hands, mouthing "Help". Almost peaking, I could not have helped even my self, and couldn't tell was he offering or needing. Painted Doll shrank into my side. I heard my words as if from afar "Are you hungry". No answer, more reaching, his arms far too long and getting longer. I whispered not sure if aloud or just thought till it echoed down the block "Sorry". His mouth did not moved "My first acid trip. I'm lost. Help". Like Painted Doll, I knew one touch of him would infect me too "I have nothing for you, but you are here, I see you". He took back his hands, and whisked away into the unseen. Painted Doll scampered into the house. And gravity let me go, off the porch, scattering molecules evenly in all ways, beyond consciousness, extreme velocity the only sensation, time, memory gone, and shivering, hands clutching the lip of the top stair, I am here too, whole and freezing, feeling something important had been lost without my knowing, without consent. Gabriel warned of taking acid for the wrong reason, I had been too anxious for escape, now go inside Shoshy, where did this coat come from, I'm freezing, duh it's Winter. Everyone had gone to the party but Ric staying home with the Littles. Stretched-out on the couch watching Johnny Carson, he handed me the joint from his mouth "How's your trip". I took a long grateful drag, holding till I could not "Don't know, I was gone". He chuckled "Yeah. I came out couple a times. You seemed okay. So, happy New Year". It was so heavy being whole again, I needed to lay down "Thanks for the coat. Happy you too". Taking the joint to my room, I crawled in my silky bag, clothes and shoes on.

The Wart Hog's first issue of 1969, had a list from the new Women's Lib Collective titled The Seattle Liberation Front's Biggest Chauvinist Pigs, all Hydra men were named, most of the Grodes, Sundance, the Rebels, and me. How chauvinistic pig could apply to me, and yet there was my name in bold-type, spelled wrong, an insect under a microscope, larger, more alarming, bloated, exposed. I had planned on going to the next meeting, be a part of the budding movement, my speech a misunderstanding I would try and right, but if wanting more than a good bitch session made me chauvanistic, so be it, I was unwelcome. I decided to walk to the District, grab up all copies of the Hog that I could find, and took them home to burn. Hydra men saw the list as a badge of honor and power, framing, hanging it on the War Room wall. And ironically, a new camaraderie flowered, they sanctioned me an honorary man, the only way a chick could be acceptable as more than pussy or wife, making manifest why they deserved the listing. From then on I was in on every clandestine reconnaissance, treated like one of the guys, Arnie laid-off me, and every time I went along, the intoxicating thrill of action compensated for my unwelcome. Keely had thoughts on my infamy, having seen it before, with Hydra's national profile, fame, and popularity in the Movement and press, it made people jealous. I was being punished because they could get to me, it was the reason she had no interest going. I knew she was right, admired her smarts, and was so glad she opened-up, showing me she was a Sister.

Outwardly so very indignant at supposedly unwanted list notoriety, Arnie and Ric grew pompous egos, complaining their anonymity had been irreparably compromised, they were actually the good guys, had the best interest of Movement chicks at heart, and proof, they let me in on the action. Oh great, now I was their token testimony, isolating me even more. Two Black Panthers, party leader Alprentice Bunchy Carter and aide John Huggins Jr. were assassinated on UCLA's campus. And here, Seattle Urban League Director Edwin Pratt was shot in the head in the doorway of his own home, three men fled in a Buick Skylark and so far had not been captured. We sat round the War Table brain-storming a symbolic act in solidarity with Edwin Pratt. Jack-in-the-Box had come to the Ave, Washington's first automated fast-food drive-in, with its icon giant glass clown-head. Workers being replaced with robot clowns, making fools of them as they ordered from the greedy corporate evil that took their jobs. Someone suggested assassinating the clown-head. Perfect. The vote was unanimous.

Ric drove. I went along in the back seat with Mark. Arnie brought his Smith&Wesson traveling companion, everyone else in prickly overload having a pistol in the car. Thoughts of jail scared me crazy, the intoxication of outlaw avenging angel steadied crazy, having already mentally crossed the violent line, I was about to in real life. Jack was seven blocks from Hydra, 11:30PM we drove-thru, ordering from the incorporeal voice. Greasy tacos, three for 99cents, we cruised round eating, singing to the radio, laughing, smoking, pretending to shoot everything abhorrent with finger-guns, naming ourselves, Che Guevara, the Lone Ranger, Captain America, Annie Oakley, till the early morning streets were asleep. And as easy as pretend, Arnie rolled down the passenger window, a single shot to the giant luminous head. I was awed by his accuracy, did not flinch at the bang, and explosion, pulverizing glass, backlit in the street lamps, floating down, a sparkling mist, dead in the doorway of its own home. Ric headed West on 50th to I-5. Now Arnie was prickly "Don't speed man. Please don't speed". Ric offsetting "I'm cool man. You be cool too". Thirty-miles north to Everett, we bought gas. Ric carefully folding the alibi receipt into his wallet, taking 99 South, throwing Smith&Wesson off the Aurora Bridge, obeying all traffic laws. We smoked the joint I had stashed behind my ear. Knowing we would be suspect, the main one, deciding not to take credit, even anonymously, increasing the speculation and mystery, letting public imagination make this bigger, we were content, our comrades would know.

No one slept. March 20, 9AM morning news, Jerry Rubin, Abbie Hoffman, David Dellinger, Rennie Davis, Tom Hayden, John Froines, Lee Weiner and Bobby Seale, branded the Chicago Eight, were indicted for conspiracy. And we had clown confirmation. KJR radio DJ Lan Roberts was first to report. KOL's Robert O.Smith next. Then the afternoon Seattle Times. Mike James KING TV local evening news. Even the 6PM Walter Cronkite national. Symbolic connection to Edwin Pratt's murder was missed, however, the working-class feared automation was taking their jobs, and Arnie's one shot ignited their imagination, we championed their cause, expressed a deep and till now unspoken fear. And this scared their Masters, some one other than corporate and State sponsored terrorism had come to parochial little nowhere Seattle, now it could happen any where. Media speculation went wild, and they came to Hydra first, for our expert opinion. Of course it was Ric who gave his, underscoring Edwin Pratt. Insisting after, he did not want to be seen as the head of Hydra, and continued assuming the position. The house across the street no longer pretended casual scrutiny, but Arnie's gun was untraceable, the bullets hand-made, no evidence, no witness as long as we kept our mouths shut. And in the afternoon mail, a lovely gift for me, dear Max thoughtfully sent the inaugural issue of Off Our Backs, an underground Women's Lib paper from DC, he circled an exposé on the copy-cat patriarchal power structure in the Movement, and how it conveniently keeps females in their place. I mimeographed, and left a few neatly on the War Table. They were gone in the morning.

The exhilaration remained, the headiest ever without drugs, a power-full righteousness bolstering me in the face of big paranoia, unlike anything I ever felt. I had always mattered as an individual to the sly monsters lurking in a little girl's bedroom, and to Nick, and while this current stalker had those same close-set dark piercing eyes, intent on domination, feeding on fear, it also had the shiny badge of the law, and did not give a shit it was me. Crossing the line had raised the stakes, impersonalized the hunt, I was not sure how else yet, but there was more to gain, and more to lose, and I needed to be very sure this heady high did not tempt me to frivol. Victory had similar affect, we were all wired, sleepless nights and days brainstorming how to strike another resonant chord, quietly care-full to say nothing that could be over-heard.

The FBI had many ways of hounding us. No matter where we legally parked, the City impounded our cars, knowing it cost money we did not have. Waking-up to all three gone, and there it was, we voted unanimously to blow-up a tow truck, symbolic harassment not only to us but every working-class nobody. Ric loved reading comic books to the Littles, and had recently and surprisingly come upon a simple bomb recipe, and being a scientist he understood it was for real. Fill a large wine bottle two-thirds with gasoline, carefully float Fells Naphtha powdered laundry detergent on top, leave room for a gas-soaked wick stuffed in the neck, shake, light, throw and run like hell. The prospect of shopping for a bomb at the grocery store proved endless ad lib theater, being caught red-handed with laundry soap at the check-out counter, pleading innocent to the judge, too drunk on the wine to throw the bomb far enough, lighting ourselves on fire, lightening our underlying unspoken mix of fear and dread, for none of us had bomb making or throwing experience.

A dry and moonless night, we ceremoniously drank the near gallon of Cribari Chianti, put the bottle, a full gas-can, box of Fells Naphtha, and cheese-cloth for a wick in a basket of towels, along with two more baskets of laundry in the car, we were off to the 24 hour Laundromat. Ric and I took the back seat, Mark front passenger, Arnie drove. And Ric prepared the bomb, spilling gasoline on my shoe while dowsing the wick, handing me the finished product to hold steady, ditching the gas-can and soap box in a Safeway store dumpster. There I sat, very still, smiling a fear frozen face, feeling every curve, every little bump in the road, bomb between my legs, gasoline fumes coating my tongue and throat, stinging my lungs, thinking, considering how absolutely calm I was, how brave and stupid, and how unstable was this bomb, as we cruised Capitol Hill for just the right target, checking-out where the Pigs might be hiding. I became curiously nonchalant, unattached. The Boys agreed on a white Ford tow-truck parked at 15th and Cherry near the City impound lot. Arnie rounded the block three times, and seeing no one, pulled to the curb six car-lengths infront of the truck. Ric hopped-out, came to my door, gently took the bomb from my lap. I thought him brave and stupid, none of us knew how long after lighting the wick, tip-toeing toward the Ford like a cartoon villan, shaking the bottle hard, he set it in the truck-bed by the winch, lit the wick and ran. The truck thundered to a fireball as he dove into the backseat. Arnie sped away, door slamming with the momentum. We caught our collective holy shit breath at the might of a comic book bomb, and then a second blast. Arnie went West on Madison toward downtown. I was suddenly dizzy, and laid my head on Ric's leg. He stroked my hair and arm, half teasing as Arnie took the on-ramp to I-5 North "Don't speed man. Please don't speed". Arnie laughed "I'm cool man. You be cool too". Again to the Everett gas station, again Ric putting the alibi receipt in his wallet. I had a terrible gas-fume headache, and explosion after-jitters, Ric could have been burned, or killed, repercussions far beyond one single shot to a clown-head, and I was convinced the Pigs would soon stop us, smell gas on my shoe, and blame only me to prison for life. I said nothing, panic, paranoia would not be well received from an honorary man, we did not speak our fears, did not speak most of the round-about way home. When I removed the implicating footwear and dropped them out the window onto Highway 9, no one seemed to notice. Arnie parked infront of Hydra. Cross the street two men in suits stood under the porch light. We acted drunk and loud, 2AM coming home from the Laundromat and bar loud. Suddenly, unexpectedly on the porch Mark grabbed me up in his arms, and set me down in the dark entry hall, close to his warm body, I did not resist the kiss.

Just after sunrise we took our places at the War Table, sleepless, exhausted, radio loud to garble any discourse, each admitting being freaked by the power of the bomb. The SDS and the Weathermen liked calling us uncommitted wimps for shunning violent, we voted to let them keep thinking, and waited anxiously for the morning Post Intelligencer. Front page above the fold, 33,000 dead American soldiers, no mention how many Vietnamese, they were not full human beings worth counting. Below the fold, Berkeley Hippies take-over a neglected vacant lot belonging to the University of California, refurbish it with saplings, flowers, benches and swings, and call it People's Park. Not a tow truck word. Ric was sure authorities were keeping quiet till they arrested us. Then a morning DJ broke the story, and another, and we breathed a collective sigh of relief realizing the PI had gone to press before we struck. Again we resonated big with the people, they totally got it, all afternoon local radio beat the drum, Seattle Times and local TV asking who did this, and what might be next. There was no question among us, the Reserve Officers Training Corp office on campus had to be next. We swept the house of drugs and accoutrements, weapons, anything written that could be used against us. Mark removed the toggles from the phone, a brilliant and well used invention. And the men across the street began to openly follow us, everywhere. Word or deed by those hanging round the Movement fringe took on exaggerated meaning, even those I barely knew seemed suspect, insignificant details charged with meaning, my paranoia geometrically expanding. Now I understood how sinister and seductive the thrill of power could be, how quick and wide the gap in right and wrong, how innocuous anything in-between.

Without warning, California Governor Ronald Reagan sent 250 Highway Patrolmen in to clear People's Park, to stand guard while City workmen built an eight-foot chain-link fence round the entire block. According to the Post Intelligencer, the University had *"to make sure that the land was recognized as University property"*. By noon thousands had gathered in nearby Sproul Plaza, chanting *"Take back the park"*. And they flooded down Telegraph Avenue to the chain-link, now ringed in Pigs wearing gas-masks, carrying shotguns and tear-gas canisters. Undaunted, people swarmed into the stinging white smoke, hurling the burning canisters back on the Pigs, Berkeley Police Captain Charles Plummer was quoted saying to his troops, you are *"the last stronghold against commies, and today we are going to crush them"*. The longest battle of its kind in American history, 33,000 people demonstrated round the clock, round the fence, facing Alameda County Sheriffs armed with shotguns loaded in bird-shot and double-o buckshot. The first ever used against students, 153 wounded, often in the back, one James Rector killed. Hundreds of Berkeley faculty boycotted the University, calling for the Chancellors resignation, the Daily Cal student-newspaper demanded the University close. Major General Ames, commander of the National Guard sent in a helicopter to released tear-gas on James Rector's funeral procession, calling it *"perfectly logical"*. And in a speech to the Council of California Growers, Reagan commented *"If the students want a bloodbath, let's get it over with"*. Reagan united us in solidarity and purpose with Berkeley. No matter how often, I was always stunned and sickened that my own government would wage war against, that the Terrible Father would devour his own children.

Our next mission began percolating, with a civil right the FBI had not yet stop, we would throw a street dance infront of Hydra, enlisting newcomers, and affording us some respite in this dead serious battle. Followed the next day with another ROTC march, against University sanctioned recruiters on campus who shrewdly preyed on the untested impatient macho of young men. Bear managed to get a permit from the City, closing the street from 7PM to Nine. No one but me thought this was way too easy. Carolion knew a band eager to play free for the cause. Mark and Arnie rented a sound system. Ric composed a NO-ROTC-ON-CAMPUS street dance flyers. Keely and I mimeographed and taped them to every possible shop window and pole in the District.

Nature offering a warm-enough dry March night, most of the neighborhood frat and sorority houses came out, the street a friendly over-flowing, maybe two-hundred-plus when the band cranked-up the amps. Standing on the porch across the street, the usual white men with binoculars, taking notes. The band was really good, and soon wed the crowd into one, neighbors coming-out, joining-in. Just after 8PM, standing on the proch I saw maybe twenty Pigs marching from the North in full riot-gear. We invited the press, we always did just incase, as witness, none had come. I took Lance and Robby by the hands, Lance fighting me all the way up to their bedroom, Robby not, Scottie sleeping peacefully. Lance would stay only if I did, their window over-looking the street, he hung-out too far, waving, screaming. Gas-masks were on the porcine faces, there was no warning, canisters hit the ground hissing poison, batons raised high, jackboots into the flock, the music died, and for one long moment all the little lambs froze, bewildered, then scattering chaos, some falling under clubs, under each other, some just falling, bleating. We saw Carolion battered to her knees on the parking strip. Robby clung to me, then Lance, I held their heads, rocking side-to-side, humming, powerless to look away. And then it stopped, silent, Pigs gone without bust or arrest, gas-fingers floating through the window, Keely ran in breathless, crying, slamming it shut, cracking the pane full length, grabbed Robby and Lance to her, Scottie still sleeping. I hurried out for Carolion, still on her hands and knees, dry heaving, more terrorized than injured. No one had been broken, the assault a show of force to scare the shit out of anyone considering joining the cause, to scare us to cease and desist or else. But it worked for us, galvanizing many to enlist who might have only come for the party. Hydra never could have turned them so surely on our own.

The morning PI reported Nixon's attempt to appease the growing anti-war movement by proposing a draft-lottery. While 20,000 rallied peacefully in Berkeley, protesting the disgraceful disrespect of James Rector's funeral, and the dismantling of Peoples Park. And there we were, front page, supposedly Hydra had provoked a police attack by refusing to shutdown a wild illegal street-dance when ordered. Since the underground political scene put Seattle on the national map, most conventional press told the story as they saw fit. We should have been scared enough by this police storm, instead it brought us new clarity, boldly underscoring how desperate they were to crush us, making us more determined not to slow, or be silenced. And nine-thousand strong, way more than we imagined, way more because of the press, at high-noon we marched against the ROTC on campus. Our numbers could not be ignored, local and national news carried a story, Hydra got credit. Our momentum was a rocketship ride, huddling round coffee at the Last Exit on Brooklyn, wondering what next, and right there laying open on the table, a article in the Seattle Times, Boeing's newest 727 jet-airliner would be officially unveiled April 15th, by invitation only. A major war supplier, builder of the Minuteman solid-fuel intercontinental ballistic missiles for the Pentagon, B-52 bombers and Chinook helicopters for use in Vietnam, most Washingtonians had no idea Boeing manufactured more than commercial airplanes, that war toys were being built in their back yard. We decided it was our duty to inform them. We decided to crash the party.

Ric and I went to Goodwill for strait clothes. Mark and Bear scouted the route to Boeing Field. The morning of, we took our costumes in grocery bags, left Hydra at different times, in different directions, in two cars, driving around, slipping tails, rendezvous at the Texaco station in Georgetown, blocks from the party, parking on the street. Dressing in the bathrooms, guys in business suits, stiff collar shirts, silk ties, shined wing-tips, black sox, long hair secure underneath seemly wigs, except for Ric, who had his cut short and goatee shaved, stripping his sinister, baring an unexpectedly sweet face. I knew exactly how to camouflage for Boeing, 3-inch black leather pumps, sheer smoke stockings, long-sleeve tight gray sweater-dress, long black-and-white checkered silk scarf tied round my neck, hair-up in a French-knot, fire-engine red lipstick, gobs of mascara, tasteful fake pearl earrings, a small black leather shoulder bag. The spike-heel-red-lipstick-long-neck affect on my somewhat-evolved men-children should not have surprised or shaken me so, but they did not even try hiding the leers. These reputed leading-edge revolutionaries, symbol to the world of change I was risking freedom and future for, wore very thin-veneer. Sex had its place, but certainly not in such a serious escapade, and not used as persistent pretext to steal-away legitimate rank, discount my mind, relegate me to body, object for use, not some one to be trusted. I wanted power-with, not sexual power-over, and knew well how the tired-old disagreement went if I voiced affront, a girls allure is her immutable power over the Gods and mortal men, an effortless exclusive tool, and since I have it, why not use my best weapon for the cause. My best weapon was my mind, their prurient not my cause "You guys are such pigs. Just go fuck-off in the little-boys room and be done with it". Sadly, regretfully, despite the thrill of inclusion, this gross humiliation repeatedly wounded me and was no longer tolerable, it had to be the last of only-girl-honorary-man-accomplice, Hydra men could no more use my company in defense of their Neanderthal, a chronic disposition forcing me near hating them all, at the same time admiring their dedication to the cause. Right now the situation demanded clear focus, I would save my boiling disgust for later.

The plan was simple, be creative, be keen, who ever sees an opportunity, take it. We brought our regular clothes with and went in one car. There were so many at Boeing Field, invitations not carefully checked, we blended-in the hanger door. Effortless access, hiding in plain sight, stalking opportunity, thrill making my blood rush and mind sharp. I could see and feel the suits following the curves of my sweater dress, yes being a girl was wily subterfuge. Ric and Bear went their ways. Mark squired me round the absolutely awesome up-close 727 in the center of the hanger, we browsed hors d'oeuvre tables, petit fours, sipped coffee, and there it was, a perfect, to scale miniature 727 all by it self on a table by the wall. Swapping wicked grins, we drifted over. As if flying on a clear plastic stand, seventeen-inches long, wing-span a bit wider, Mark plucked the model from its perch. It was heavier than anticipated, tucking it firmly under his right arm, offering me the left, we walked evenly toward the gaping hanger door, no one seemed to notice, or maybe could believe, or made a move to stop us. Ric and Bear were on their own, we crossed the parking lot to the car, guard smiling at my smile as he raised the gate. In minutes we were on I-5 North, taking the next exit to Beacon Hill, and down McClellan to Rainier Avenue, stopping at Tradewell for beer, stopping for gas, changing in the bathrooms, ditching our costumes at the Goodwill donation drop-box on Deaborn, going home.

Ric and Bear already there. I brought the beer. Mark wrapped the plane in his jacket, and swaggering in, set the 727 on the War Table, turning the radio loud, grumbling "Thrill's already gone. So big deal, I copped a model plane. Dangerous one for sure, but it's just a fucking toy". Convenient bystander to the action, I knew my decision was right, when I went along, it was at a discount. All of us sat, solemnly staring at the plane, drinking beer, knowing we dare not keep it. Ric proposed "Let's set it on fire in front of the ROTC office. Send 'em a message. It'll drive 'em crazy exactly what it means". An instant unanimous yes vote. Invited along, I wanted to go and almost did. The model was wrapped in old Wonder Warthogs, soaked in lighter fluid and set ablaze on the steps of Clark Hall, with a clean getaway.

Ric's idea was absolutely brilliantly convoluted, and made the morning PI front-page. They had no clue what to make of the flaming stolen scale model turning-up at Clark Hall. And played right into our hands, filling the story with facts and figures of Boeing's military contracts for missiles, bombers and helicopters, broadly drawing the Vietnam connection and considerable military profits. Gloating, whooping, stomping, smiling round the house till our cheeks hurt, Littles happily joining in the dance. We done it again, feeling numinous, sublime, glorious, edifying, addicting, no drug, nothing came close. And we waited, sure across the street knew, even if there was no proof. Never before, and just at dinner time they came over, twin short hair-cuts, twin suits, twins knocking hard on the door. Ever the doyen, Ric opened inches, his sage non-sequiturs and fain innocence-of-the-heart responding to their questions and thinly veiled threats. They went away dangerously irate. Unlike smack, tolerance for the thrill of victory had no build-up, and now, paranoia again became my only constant companion, tangled in with righteous invulnerability, as if idealism had armor to save me.

We were not the only ones, a ready train of events roared through the Summer of '69. Seattle Community College and the Black Student Union clashed over Black representation on campus. Six fire-bombs exploding there in six days. The UW administration building was bombed too. Pigs brawled daily with kids over premise and turf on the Ave, community volunteers came in to walk the streets, restoring calm and commerce. The City's first worker-owned cooperative, Morningtown Pizza opened on Roosevelt Way, boasting a vegetarian pizza, becoming my new hangout. Nixon doubled the draft. Mayor Wes Ulman sent in Pigs to gas an outdoor Alki Beach Peace concert across from Rachel's apartment. And the Manson Family, absent Charles was arrested for savage murderings, Roman Polanski's eight-month pregnant fiancée Sharon Tate, Hollywood hair-stylist Jay Sebring, Voyteck Frykowski and his coffee heiress girlfriend Abigail Folger, all staying at Tate's Hollywood Hills estate. The Family looked like Hippies, making every one of us frightening and suspect, precisely how the Establishment wanted us to be seen. Invading Hollywood's Golden Ghetto, the Family's ferocious brutality rang chilling alarm through exclusive bastions everywhere, their hallowed walls were not high enough. Neil Armstrong and Edwin Buzz Aldrin rode Apollo II to the moon, Neil took a walk. And in-keeping with its mission, the Underground Community entered a Peace Float in the Torchlight Parade. I was happy to be part of Seafair on my terms, vindicated Princess, crowned in daisies, smiling, waving, floating pre-folded paper airplanes into the five-deep crowding 3rd Avenue, announcing a rally on the Ave in support of the Chicago Eight.

I kept my 21st to my self, planning to challenge the Washington State blue-law prohibiting anyone with tits sitting at the bar, or even ordering drinks at the bar, tits must sit at a table or booth and wait to be served, or have a prick go for them. No one at Hydra was interested in this confontation. Choosing a small neighborhood tavern on Roosevelt Way where no one knew me, walking in resolute, I took a stool at the long wooden bar, spine steadfast, head high, jaw set, hands gripping the edge, ready. Mr.Bartender came over smiling "What's your pleasure". Dumbfounded I barely mumbled "Miller". Quick with the bottle and frosted mug, he asked "Have some ID". Wits gathering I laid my expired drivers license on the bar "How come you'll serve me". He looked at it "Oh those blue-law. Voted-out as of today, an good riddance". Providentially spared the skirmish, and so relieved my spine nearly let me go, I put three dollars on the bar and smiled "Thank you. Please keep the change". Leaving the money, he pointed to me and broadcast for all to hear "Hey everyone, she's legal today. First one's on the house". A cropped-hair women I had not noticed next to me raised her mug "Happy Birthday Sister". In my tunnel vision I had not noticed the whole bar was full of women, I raised my mug "*That's one small step for man, one giant leap for* womankind".

Woodstock Music and Air Fair dispatched the Country's imagination in both directions. On its heels, Sky River Rock Festival and Lighter than Air Fair, 40 miles South of Seattle, outside the small town of Tenino. Produced by John Chambless and the New American Community, who also did the first Sky River at Betty Nelson's organic raspberry farm on the Skykomish River, the one the Grateful Dead showed-up for, outside the even smaller town of Sultan. Sky River II was a young nation, a peace-full nation, an alternative notion, and totally freaked Governor Dan Evans and his cronies into banning these subversive events. Rock'n roll, rock festivals by nature were political, as was the New American Community, although only by nature of long-hair and blue jeans. Essentially they were business investment looking to make a buck not a battle, and when interviewed after the ban, after they did not make any money, proclaimed "*Sky River is dead*". We talked a lot of doing our own festival, making it the political event we knew it could be, and thanks to the Governor, and the New American Community, there was an opportunity for us to take-on Sky River III, if we could find a way to get around the law. It just tickled me when Government tried preventing us, beating, gassing, arresting, murdering us, escalating the war, closing Peoples Park, banning festivals, how circumstances also went in our favor. But for right now, the Chicago Eight conspiracy trial had our attention. America and the world were about to get a civics lesson on how free we really were, for conspiracy was a thought crime.

This trial more than any previous event created a National Underground Community, giving us martyrs who managed to stay alive and in the country. And the American people, effectively kept compliant under the whip of patriotism, afraid to take a stand against the war, afraid of becoming suspect, being labeled Pinko Commie like us, afraid of losing what privilege they had, were beginning to make themselves heard. Our ranks swelled. I remembered Ida Rose saying "*If you're not for me, you're against me*". The vast middle-class when silenced could be counted with the government. But daily demonstrations somewhere in America's front-yard, and now in America's front-room on the nightly news, a trial starring their nephews, their brothers, their sons, charged with thought-crimes, looking a lot like Russian totalitarianism, tyranny to silence the intellectuals and dissidents, keep the status quo, fill the gulags. They could see their own sons in the Chicago Eight.

The Seattle Liberation Front was a main artery in the Underground Railroad, for draft-resisters and other political fugitives needing to flee their homeland, we smuggled some of them through the Blaine crossing into Canada. It was my turn to be someone's bride, heading to Vancouver on our honeymoon, Niagara Falls of the West. The Committee to Aid American Objectors, consisting mostly of conscientious objectors who successfully fled into Canada, provided all the necessities. The day the

Weathermen destroyed the ROTC office at Clark Hall, and the SLF led an anti-war rally of 4000 though downtown, I dressed in a short-sleeved geranium-pink linen blouse and matching shorts, pulled my hair into a ponytail high on the back of my head, tied a pink and black striped scarf round the rubber-band, spackled my lips in geranium-pink lipstick and met my anxious Hubby for lunch at the International House of Pancakes on 43rd and Brooklyn. As we ate and acquainted, a churchy looking middle-age woman passed by the table, leaving us an envelope. Car keys and registration, drivers and marriage license, fake diamond solitaire wedding ring and plain gold band, 300 dollars, and instructions. We found the 1968 white Lincoln Continental in the parking lot, gas-tank full. Hubby drove just under the speed-limit to Blaine, we practiced our story, getting there with peak traffic as instructed. The Canadian border guard asked the usual, why are we traveling to Canada, how long did we plan on staying, did we have anything to declare, seemed satisfied with our honeymoon answer, and still wanted to check the trunk. Pushing a button on the dash, Hubby popped it open, whispering "Stay cool". Mr.Guard went for a look, and slowly walked back to the driver's window, shining his flashlight in the back-seat and on the floor, demanding "Where's your luggage". Whoa, serious mistake, feeling Hubby freeze-up, I draped my body and arms round him, making sure Mr.Guard could not miss the sparkling rock on my ring finger, and lilted "Baby wants to buy his Mommy everything new". I kissed his ear and cooed "This man knows how to take care of me". Hoping to sound innocuous newly wed, I giggled the pride of tasteless nouveau riche. Mr.Guard looked at our licenses again, shined his light in our faces, warned Hubby to declare all purchases on re-entry, and let us pass. Hubby so relieved he drove a block and had to pull-over and barf.

Hyper-alert, rushing yet calm, I took the wheel and found the right spot on Robson Street, where two men waited. Hubby thanked me, they thanked me and disappeared into the street population. I drove into Gastown, parked as arranged infront of the Golden Empress, locked the documents and rings in the glove compartment, went into the restaurant, asked for a man called Mun, and gave him the car keys. He showed me to a booth where Keely and Ric were eating dinner, a welcome sight, they were my ride home. The food looked delicious, had me salivating, I was too fatigued to eat. The American border guard searched our car for drugs, regularly smuggled out of Canada. Expecting it, Keely had meticulously cleaned the car before leaving Hydra. Ms.Guard found nothing. Passing the Peace Arch into Washington, Keely took a joint from behind her ear, well hidden in that thatch of hair, lit and passed to me "You're a brave girl Shoshy. I'm proud of you, even wearing that awful geranium-pink outfit". I admired her nerve too and wished we had a deeper friendship, wished she had interests in spiritual things, Women's lib things, I took a toke and passed to Ric.

The Chicago Eight Conspiracy Trial became the Chicago Seven all-white-men Conspiracy Trial when Judge Julius Hoffman ordered Bobby Seale, Black Panther National Chairman, carried into the courtroom gagged and shackled to his chair, because he would not obey the rule of speaking only when on the stand. Three days the nation watched a Black man treated like a dog, and still Bobby could not be silenced. Judge Hoffman ordered a rubber plug forced into his mouth before gagging, but nothing could silence his rocking and jerking his chair, his screaming through the plug-gag. Hoffman did not seem to understand America was watching, charging Bobby with 16 counts of contempt and calling a mistrial in his case only. Next morning, bombs went off at General Motors offices in New York City, the RCA building and Chase Manhattan Bank, Weathermen were arrested, Jack Kerouac died at 47, and Hydra announced to the Warthog and Helix we would be putting on next years Sky River. The War Table became Festival Central. We decided ours must be big enough to bring in enough to buy 150 acres, enough land to constitute a legal township in Washington State, allowing residents to make their own town laws. Bear researched the festival ban, and determined using private or Indian land would get round it.

November 16, 567 Vietnamese civilians were reported massacred by American Soldiers at My Lai. That day Ric, Bear and I drove South to the Puyallup Indian Reservation, hoping to see the Chief about Sky River. He liked me, my Jewish heritage, pointing-out I too belonged to a tribe. And we walked, Ric explaining the situation, the Chief patiently listening, even considering our plan worthy, but did not see any benefit to the tribe having our festival on their land, wishing us good luck, he said no. We would keep looking, maybe a big farm, one we could purchase afterward with ticket sales profits. First we needed seed money, and that night round Festival Central, Mark came-up with an idea, throw a New Years Eve bash at the downtown Eagles Hall, get great local bands, maybe one from out of town, ask all to play for expenses only, promising featured spots at Sky River. A unanimous yes. Ric contracted with the Eagles under a bogus name, the Washington Planned Community Association, we could proceed in peace, the press would not know it was us. Carolion booked the Dr.Zarkov Liquid Projection Light Show, the Daily Flash, the Wiz Kids, and from Santa Cruz California, the band One Hand Clapping, all happy to play for the bargain. It was on.

Always up-against police, FBI, the strait press, every little accomplishment was a victory. In less than one year attitudes had fundamentally changed within the Movement, revolution becoming more violent on both sides. Chicago police murdered Black Panthers Fred Hampton and Mark Clark in their beds. Wounded and dead American soldiers topped 300,000, Vietnamese still were not counted. College kids were regularly gassed, injured and arrested during campus demonstrations. And the press uglied, exaggerated, inflated every move our side made. I learned as a Junior in high school how a notion could swell, when I persuaded four of my sophomore American History classmates to boycott school lunch by bringing our own. Studying the Boston Tea Party and Colonial boycott, I thought it would be interesting to see if boycott still worked. Day-one there were five, I made flyers. Day-two caught fire, over half brought a bag lunch. Mr.Principal addressed us over the intercom, asking the ring-leader to come forward with his demands, never imagining me, a girl of so little promise. Day-three the original four urged me take credit, make demands, and while weighing what those should be, two senior boys appropriated the boycott and issued theirs. The story was featured in the Mercer Island Reporter, calling it *"The opening round of a boycott the cause of which is unclear"*. And they published the demands, hot dogs and hamburgers on the menu every day, and a statement by Mr.Principal *"I'm not awfully upset, it's a lawful form of civil disobedience. However, I am concerned with the food being wasted"*. Having influence lit the student body to almost total participation, holding-fast against daily pressure from teachers, and administrators threatening to make this part of our permanent school record that would haunt us through-out our lives. But Mr.Principal had already informed us the boycott was lawful, and it continued. Day-eight, burgers and dogs were added to the daily menu, except on fish Fridays. I saw boycott was still an effective tool. And learned how history is warped and re-written by bold pretenders, opportunists, boys who usurp ideas and deeds and take the power and the credit. And, how a notion could become a blazing monster, when powers-that-be stoke the flames with false assumption that things are as organized as they would have organized them. Any simple day-to-day Hydra activity was reported as a sinister and carefully thought-out exploit. So there was nothing to do but fuck with them too. We gave interviews, casually, intentionally naming an elitist organization or oppressive corporation as an ally, attending their public meetings, creating suspicion by association, reputations were vulnerable to press investigation, creating paranoia. And I was continually amazed how word-on-the-wire came-up with such wicked reasons for our every day routine. Three of us strolling Volunteer Park, certainly a planning meeting to pour LSD into the reservoir there. Shopping at Safeway, we must be laying-in supplies for a siege. Just for fun, we all went to Saint Marks Cathedral Sunday mass. The headline, Seattle Liberation Front in moral and ethical crisis, seeking salvation.

Every element began falling in-place for the New Years bash, as if they occupied those same places so many times already they knew without direction exactly where to go, like snow falling on the ground. Thanksgiving, we toasted Charles Manson's arrest, and the National Democratic Party voting delegate quotas into their platform requiring proportional amounts of women and minorities. And, for fear of hexing ours, we said nothing of Altamont Speedway's Free Festival in LA, where the Hell's Angels Oakland Club beat a man to death while the Rolling Stones played *Gimme Shelter*. Chanukah, Christmas passed without presents. And One Hand Clapping arrived on the 28th, in a big yellow school bus from Santa Cruz California. Carolion promised them free room and meals. Mark and I had the largest, and gave it up to them, I would bunk in Carolion and Bear's, Bear and Mark with Arnie. Carolion and I decided to make our new arrangement permanent. As they were affectionately or maybe not nicknamed by fans, The Clap was a hometown cult-sensation, ambitious for a record deal, for national fame, they thought Sky River would help. Erik played guitar, pretty-boy Joey harmonica. All but unapproachably self-important, the usual clichéd musicians, we play and you don't, God touched us with a heavier finger, on your knees peon. I considered ego-grande most necessary to do a job big, as long as mine fit skin-tight it was solid and strong, affording me unassuming confidence, conviction, poise. As I gained experience, who I am, what I am, what I will and would not do, I needed more space, and my ego amended, I could feel the substance and size necessary for fight. But when my thinking leaned to righteous, and it often did, my ego inflated, bloated, became fragile, vulnerable to any imagined offense, and defensive, easily bruised, angered, it would burst back down to skin-tight, initially hurting bad, but becoming solid again, and safe. Josh showed me talent with the necessary ego was not threatened, that genuine ability was not angry, haughty, defensive.

Erik and Joey had no shame singing the spoils of rock'n roll, of wholesale groupies raring to lay their bodies on the altar of music. A fish-eyed exaggeration shared by most Gona-Bees enjoying a small taste of fame, their self-indulgence a pathetic ruse, fragile egos inflated in the wiles of hype, dangerously exposed to the slightest bump, always on guard. Erik was the band leader, wrote the songs, his lyrics the best part, he played respectable guitar, could only just carry lead vocals, and good-looking Joey the soulful harmonica player, they made no effort to veil their fucking expectations, presuming me and Carolion would, and should. I felt sick when she serviced both over night, and so terribly angry with my self for not making sure this did not happen, angry at Keely for the same. And the Hydra men, and their little grinning exchanges at the rock'n roll stories, bonding in the degradation of chicks, and their Little Sister's in her own home, I expected more of them than they had. Erik never failed a juvenile innuendo or double-entendre, his form of romantic foreplay, plainly he assumed I was next, though I did not think his interest was sex, more virility testimony, power as leader. It came to a pitch over hot dogs and beans round the War Table. I bit into mine. Erik smiled "Plump and juicy enough for you". Joey sniggered like a naughty pre-teen. Everyone else kept their eyes on the food. The conjured image made me retch, I spit the wiener out on the plate and took a sip of Coke, Erik left me no longer willing to play polite host, I wanted to burn him down "For your information Erik, when I take a lover, he won't be a little weenie. Women like men not boys. And if you ever manage to grow up, call me, my answer will still be NO". I had expected to weather these five days, would have borne the indignity, not thrown a punch if he had not insisted on degrading me to cock-sucker at my own supper table. I needed him to know I could deliver a blow, needed to back him off, and I hated this whole thing. Insulted infront of his pack, he laughed that laugh "You sure can put a nasty twist on an innocent remark". Everyone knew bull-shit, so I let it go, thinking for the moment I had some protection in his high regard for what Hydra did politically, in his desire for bigger band notice. I was wrong, he made his mission making my life miserable, at every opportunity, Joey too, I guessed it completely escaped them they already treated me like another bitch-in-heat. When any one was there, they were sweet, respectful. If by chance alone, no matter how I tried to avoid, Erik became bulky, unpredictable, intimidating, whispering without moving his lips "I know you want it". Like Nick he didn't get it, probably never would, believing I was flattered by the physical pursuit, and ever hungry, needing him to fill my hole to be whole, therefore I must be playing hard-to-get, and would happily surrender when he found the right abracadabra, or else I must be a Dyke. My solace, he and Joey would be gone in days. And then there was oh so shy or maybe it was reserved Andrew, who played flute, trombone and jug, and went walking alone smoking cigars. I liked him right away, asking can I come along, and took him with to the Ave to sell hats, over the University Bridge for a beer at the Red Robin, Volunteer Park to meet the Big Stone Ram, smoking my first cigar, enjoying it, and his company. He told me Erik was not dangerous, and that he had a wife, Colleen.

Like any party, we worried no one would come. The sweet rush of relief filled me as Mark and me slipped in the Eagles Hall side door, 6PM, New Years Eve, thousands lined-up for an 8PM opening. A massive November riot happened on this very spot, demanding concert promoter Boyd Grafmyre lower ticket prices, we took notice, admission three bucks. Opening act, the Daily Flash, and Dr.Zarkov's Liquid Projection Light Show pulsing the fifteen-foot screen back of the stage, this wonder-full ornate hall, sweeping wide staircases, balconies, lobby all overflowing, and the sidewalk, and no rain, the party was on. Mark and I spread-out on velvet couches in one of the plush back-rooms, he had psilocybin, gel-caps filled with pure brown mushroom powder, and whiskey swigs to chase.

Almost against my will, I floated-out into the tribal ball. Dr.Zarkov had escaped its screen confines, throbbin, oozing colors, pictures, claiming the walls, balconies, ceiling, every-body gestating in the same womb. The claustrophobic intimacy was suffocating, I began to freak for a full breath, squeezing my way through the heated body, floating-up a graceful undulating staircase, caught by a face-painter who turned me into a glitter-throated pigeon, I made the balcony, perched on a wide low railing, dangling my too big feet over the steaming groundswelling below, suspended in the same symbiotic serum, individual identity dissolving, Dr.Zarkov our one beating heart, what was left of me regretting the psilocybin, becoming part of the mass, lost, waiting it out. One Hand Clapping took the stage, Erik the conquering general, and we answered his call. And the Wiz Kids Theatre Troup, drag-queens presenting the Miss Wiz Beauty Pageant, fake lashes on fake lashes, neon eye-shadow, glitter lipstick, glitter rouge, glittering beards mustaches sideburns under-arm chest crotch and leg hair, furry-gorgeous, strutting their stilettos, beautiful long legs, narrow hips in sequin bathing suits, satin gowns, twirling fire-batons, singing Over the Rainbow, Why Can't a Woman Be More Like a Man, frenzied cheers and whistles voting the winner, Miss Wiz crowned in rhinestone tiara, green and white sash, full-length purple velvet cape, liquid-gold lining, high white ermine collar, dozens of yellow roses, swanking the stage, singing I Feel Pretty, and a ten-foot hot-pink papier-mâché penis wheeled onto the stage, phallic cannon, stroke of midnight the new Miss Wiz pushing the plunger, whipped cream ejaculation, everyone, ecstatic screaming worshippers, One Hand Clapping playing Auld Lang Syne, Dr.Zarkov pounding liquid light to pagan rite, communal high that felt more like a low, people licking cream off each other. In New Year's reverie, my year of surfing on the front of the wave, I still had the same inner colloquy, that voice I knew at seven, ten, sixteen years old, longing to know every thing, longing for some one to talk too, still just as longing. Mark's tall form, approaching, beaming a wide handsome grin, dressing me in his arms, proclaiming "It's New Years". There were times I could fall for this one, others were sufficient to stop me, we kissed-in 1970, and feeling passion's embrace, and caring too much for his friendship to be more temptation, I pushed him away.

One AM the Bacchanalia unwound without significant incident. Dr.Zarkov and the bands had their equipment in vehicles, floors were swept, garbage in dumpsters, money counted by 2:30. We sold 6,310 tickets, made 18,930 dollars, after expenses 12,106, all cash, enough to seed Sky River, we were beyond thrilled. Ric stowed the dough in his briefcase, all the extra people staying at Hydra made him nervous taking it home, the Olympic Hotel was eight blocks away, and always open, he decided we would walk there first, and stow it in their vault. Mark locked the Eagles front door and dropped the keys though the mail slot as arranged. Harbingers of the New Age, parading deserted downtown, cops had not bothered our bash, made no drug busts, their cruiser escorting us now, keeping safe the funding for our township, this would not leave our tickle bones alone. Seattle's crown jewel, the grand Olympic Hotel, mainstay to titans and their entourage, we proceeded through an empty lobby to the front desk. Ric laid his briefcase on the marble counter. The Concierge hurried from a back-room in quick steps, making no eye contact. Opening the locks and lid, Ric turned it for inspection "I'd like to store this in your vault". Three men strode in the lobby door, marching toward us, they had guns and they were drawn. I held my breath, still high, suddenly coming down into my body like wet cement. We all froze but Ric, who raised his hands over-head, and in calm and slightly sarcastic voice assured the gunmen "Don't shoot fellas. We're harmless. Really. We're only here to put money in the vault not take it out". Pointing a finger to the briefcase he invited the lead gunslinger "Go ahead, take a look". A deep admiration for Ric's clear-head and slightly insane courage swelled in me, I would not question again why he was our leader. Gunslinger cautiously moving up to the briefcase, gun still on Ric, I could see his shiny cop badge as he peered in, and lifted out a yellow squirt-gun, showing it to Concierge. Who turned crimson embarassed "Shit. I guess I made a mistake". Letting his hands slowly down, grinning wry, Ric cracked "Yeah, and it's loaded". Gunslinger holstered his, ordering the other two do the same. Knees giving way, I sat on my feet. Mark sank with me. While Ric breathed fire, holding up the squirt-gun "Any fool can see this is a toy. Three guns pointed at my head, come on". Gunslinger said nothing. Concierge fawning, smoothing "I'm so sorry. When I pushed the silent alarm, I didn't know this would happen. It's the only time I ever did it. I'll be happy to put your money in the vault, no charge. And please let me give you some gift certificates for dinner in the Marine Room. For all of you". Ric said yes to the vault, and no to dinners cheap recompense. Having had their fun Gunmen took their leave. Concierge wrote a receipt for the briefcase and contents. Bear used the desk phone to call a cab. Too weak-kneed to stand, Mark pulled me up. None ever admitted to being scared as me, or as the tale was told and told into legend. New Year's Day, awake and secure in the satin throat of my sleeping bag, Carolion snoring, I smiled at the sound of One Hand Clapping's big yellow school bus leaving the curb, on their way home to Santa Cruz.

Wonder Warthog's headline-of-the-new-year "*Seattle, bombing capitol of the country*". The story recounted 69 bombings in 1969. And there was a notice for a second Women's Lib meeting. Having been called far worse than chauvinist, I would not be run-off by name-calling, would go for another try, in my heart believing women were the civilizers of society, and if we were not involved in creating the future, men, boys no matter how well intended, could not help but set-up the same old inadequate system. Again the room was full, I nodded to a familiar face, and sat on the floor close by the door. Glaring, she scanned mine and looked away, landing the kind of blow that leaves no physical mark, effectively silencing me though-out a meeting called by women for women, to plot our first political act as a group, the idea exactly what I had proposed and was condemned for, women coming together to take power. The plan, demonstrate on the capitol steps while legislature is in session, demanding legal abortion in Washington State. My presence hardly tolerated, my mouth shut, Ida Rose's words barely soothing the aching disappointment "*Minor expectations Lamby. Remember to have minor expectations*". These women had already moved from man-bashing to political action, consoling progress despite the high school clique mentality.

Chapter Nine

REDEEMING GOD

The saying goes, all roads lead to the same place. It was time to go see Ida Rose, I no longer cared she might be evil incarnate, her perception of Nick, her good counsel accompanied me, whispered in my ear, made my life better. And I could not stop thinking of that audit. Growing-up Jewish in a country soaked in Christian Mythology, the mental image of watching Jesus crucified haunted me. I knew no one to talk too of this, no one at Hydra would. God was taboo in a Marxist-Leninist charged milieu, though it was not really godless, for the State simply replaced Church for Ric and Keely, fall-away Catholics craving the lost communion, something to satisfy the gaping loss of the Eucharist. I had put The Pink Elephant on the coffee-table for any to read. Ric the only bite. When I mentioned going to see Ida Rose, he asked to come along. I thought she might like meeting a leader of the revolution, and if he was not suppose to be there, he could not cross her threshold.

We decided to walk, a crispy dry February day through Volunteer Park, salutations to the Big Stone Ram. Not till standing infront of her white brick house did it occur, maybe I was way too presumptuous coming without an appointment, bringing a stranger, would she even remember me. Ric rapped three times. Ida Rose opened, a broad smile washing her face "Why, hello Shoshannah. I'm delighted to see you again. Won't you come in. And your friend too". I could see the awe light Ric's face on seeing her treasures, just what she said they were for. This time I hardly noticed, following her down the hallway, into the dining room, Eddie was sitting at the big mahogany table sipping coffee. He smiled recognition and stood. I introduced Ric. Ida Rose was cordial and pre-occupied, asking Eddie "Would you like more coffee dear". He smiled tenderly at the gentle nudge "I think two cups 're enough". She turned to me and

Ric "Come into the living room children. We're going to run an audit". I could hardly believe my good timing, matching her nimble gate once more down the hallway. Amenable to Ida Rose's palpable integrity and natural authority, Ric followed, not an inkling what he was in for. Eddie slipped-off his burgundy Weejuns, stretched-out on Roosevelt's emerald-green brocade couch, adjusting a matching pillow beneath his head. Ida Rose took her place to the right in the winged-chair, picking up a yellow legal pad and pencil from Bonaparte's black lacquered cabinet, telling Ric "I take down the audits verbatim in shorthand". Sitting on the striped divan, my eyes hung on her, so elegant and intense as she waited for Ric to seat himself on the chaise longue. She asked Eddie "Are you ready". He said "Yes Ida Rose. I'm ready".

She spoke to someone unseen: *"Master, please take Eddie into whatever valence, stream of consciousness, point on the time track necessary for what you may wish to say to us please. When I count from five to one you'll be there. 5-4-3-2-1."*

Ida Rose began: *"A question for the Master: Who were the men in black robes who wore the Egyptian crosses and saw the body of Jesus burned?"*

Eddie closed his eyes and answered in his normal voice, though the style and manner were not his: *"Those were the Essenes. Pretty stern people. They did not take Jesus' death and the burning of the body laughingly. Too bad his soul had to be crucified for the cause. Too bad the King of Wisdom could not have told man the truth then. I say. But would it have made much difference? Remember the Christ Conscious was in charge here. Because of the Holy Spirit this all took place. And has taken place again. After all it was he who let Richard Nixon become President of the United States. To take a place in history to ruin another empire, after all he has been attempting to ruin empires for over 2,000 years. As Nero for instance."*

Ida Rose: *"What is the Arc of the Covenant?"*

Eddie: *"I explain it belonged to the system of Moses. Well the Arc of the Covenant belongs to the Arc Angels. This has something to do with the arcing of light through a prism to break down the rays. The Arc of the Covenant signifies the edge and the Abyss between night and day. The Arc signifies the edge between gratitude and ingratitude in the cosmos. The one who signified both of them.*

The one who takes on them all.
The Arc Angels.
The one who breaks the law for good and for evil to
build them back again.
He who breaks them down.
He who comes from the Arc.
He who comes from the edge of night and day.
He who encompasses them both.
He who takes on the Yin and Yang.
He who fuses the split consciousness.
He who put together the black and the white to form grey.
These are the Arc Angels.
These are the Smoke Grey Entities.
These are the Kings of the Lords of Flame.
Flame and Grey Smoke.

He who put the black and the white, the night and the day, together to form Grey.

Thus the Arc of the Covenant, the task is sealed, between night and day. The fused cosmos lies solid against a once black leaden sky. The Chariots of the Gods fly forward once again, with the white horses conquering. Amen

Between the both of them the white and the black lies the grey. Neither are they good nor are they evil. They are the testers between the black and the white. The day and the night. The Grey between the good and the evil. Them who straightened this out. They who are the messengers and the testers to see whether good and evil when challenged may straighten out and stand upright. The challenge of might and right. They challenged them both. All these things to be brought forward to present time. Like a rush from the tide. All the shells filled with significance, data, rush forward and line the shore away from receding tides. And remedies are pulled out of the shells and are brought forward. And present day that is doomed shall pass unhindered. Amen."

Ida Rose knew this was the end: *"Thank you Master. That was beautiful. I'll have to type this up and get it to my students right away, they need this message"*. She turned to me: *"Is there something you would like to ask."*

I felt sure any thing I said would sound insignificant, yet needed to be a part of this even if just an inconsequential fraction *"Will Sky River be a success. Will we buy the land and build our town".*

Ida Rose to Eddie: *"Master, do you have anything for us regarding Sky River".*

Eddie: *"Shoshannah is safe in what looks like a clear protective bubble. Dark forces attempt to penetrate her refuge but will not succeed. The scene is a hoard of naked bodies and two giant Chinese guard dogs looming from above. They lean down their huge heads and take bites of the crowd. Small naked bodies hanging from their jagged jowls."*

Ida Rose looked to me: *"Of course this is an allegory".* She turned again to Eddie: *"Is that all Master."*

Eddie: *"Yes."*

Ida Rose: *"Thank you. When I count to five you will be there. 1-2-3-4-5 present time."*

Eddie opened his eyes and smiled at her: *"Was it okay Big Mo."*

Ida Rose assured him: *"Perfectly beautiful. Thank you."*

Instead of blown-away, this time my head was bursting in questions, why was Jesus' body burned, who were these background figures manipulating earth affairs, the King of Wisdom, Christ Conscious, I had a vague idea of the Holy Spirit but this one did not match-up to the Christian story, and what right did they have to fuck with us anyway. And Nixon, was he really corrupt as I intuitively understood, again playing the lyre as Rome burned. I turned to Ric. His face deadpan, he stood, and like Nick left the room, and out the front door. I let him go without a word, remembering how overwhelming my first audit, knowing this whole Jesus thing really didn't mean much to me, but to him, a Catholic, yikes. Ida Rose glanced as if seeing this so many times before, finished her shorthand, laid the pad and pencil on the cabinet, and invited Eddie and me to the dining room for homemade lemon meringue pie.

Eddie took to the rocking chair near the smoldering fireplace and reached for the poker, plainly satisfied with him self. I followed Ida Rose into the kitchen, wanting to be where she was, and seeing dishes in the sink, offered to do them. Shining thank you on me she filled a tea-kettle with bottled water, and ground coffee beans for the Melitta. Never had I been near a presence like her, a towering, magnificent entity, beyond the utmost Golden Ghet imagination, yet she was accessible, at ease in her spiritual nobility, obliging the weight of her vocation, like she respectfully acknowledged, accepted the Sweet Sister's hands on her days. I felt privileged just standing on her porch, being remembered, welcomed inside an honor I planned on living-up to, and all this rendered me pretty speechless. The Melitta finished dripping, and I finished the dishes, taking in coffee's aroma, drying my hands, smiling as Ida Rose rinsed a remarkable silver coffee decanter in hot water so it would not rob the brew of its heat. She noted "This was a gift from one of my long time students. There's hand lotion on the window sill if you like". The full decanter went on its tray set with matching creamer, sugar bowl, spoons and forks, she carried it to the coffee-table by the fireplace. I brought cups and dessert plates already on another tray, went back for the pie, topped in five-inches of perfectly browned meringue, and took a seat on the hearth beneath the Sacred and Profane Love painting, still hesitating a word, feeling I might never speak if not right now, and asked after it. Ida Rose qualified "The nature of art is so personal and subjective, I can only say what it means to me". She pointed to the mother and child on the left "I think these figures represent the kind of love that comes from duty". Pointing right to the virginal naked woman "And her, love that frees the heart". I had never consciously thought what it was about some kinds of love that turned me off, especially guys who were fixated on big tits, there was something wrong with them, something missing that made me know they could never be my friend, they had some notion because mine were bigger than small, I must be a certain kind of girl.

Ida Rose cut the pie, Eddie poured coffee, and they talked of his new job. The Washington State prison system had opened an experimental rehabilitation farm called Echo Glen, for first-time youth offenders who committed non-violent crimes. The recidivism rate for kids like these was 74 percent, Eddie had been hired to teach them new life skills based on General Semantics. Ida Rose was so pleased to have her book used in this controlled setting, a fair test, and if the recidivism rate fell, GS would clearly be the reason. Half through my pie, I remembered Ric and excused myself. Finding him sitting on the porch, head in hands, I sat close beside. He whispered "Did you see it". I did too "See what". He spoke in a gush "She turned into a silver skeleton from the neck down". I shook my head trying not to smile "No. I only saw Ida Rose". Something had happened, something he could not explain, I knew the feeling, knew he had to handle it him self, believe what he had seen or not on his own terms. After a short silence he got up and started down the steps, saying as if going for a burger "Catch you later". I remained, watching till he disappeared up the hill, terribly disappointed he would not be someone to talk too.

When I told the tale, Eddie and Ida Rose shared a knowing chuckle. She explained "They must have shown him a vision. Given him an opportunity to trust his own eyes. They do that sometimes. The strictly scientific type is often unable to consider what the rational mind can not explain. I am sure Ric is not one of my people, and won't be back". Eddie nodded agreement. I did too "You're right Ida Rose. He was a science professor at Holy Names. Whenever I try talking about something beyond the material world, he stops me or changes the subject. He's taken lots of LSD, but he's Catholic like Nick. You know, whether he wants to or not, he believes God is watching and listening". I took a deep breath and softly asked "Did you know he saw you turn into a silver skeleton from the neck down". Her eyes smiled "No. I never know when they are going to play these tricks, but I am often told, especially by children who point to my forehead and ask about my third eye". I looked to Eddie "Did you see it". Mouth full of pie he shook his head no. Ida Rose beamed at him "They show people quite a range. Something to cause that particular individual to question, grow, maybe even make better choices. And there's no need to show them a second time. If they don't get it at first, they won't forget. Like the pink star-burst they showed to you". I nodded "Yeah, I knew right away it was a gift, just for me. I didn't see the skeleton either". She held my gaze "They showed you, and you trusted yourself". Something so pure shined though her like sun dancing off the water, too bright to fully behold, I suspected if she let it go I'd be temporarily blind, my eyes watering anyway. I did my best to sound smart "How come you call your book The Pink Elephant. It's not about pink elephants, but human behavior, our nervous system, how to organize and process information better. Make more discriminating choices, right". Her smile warmed my face "You have it Little One. And it thrills me that you do. The principle of The Pink Elephant. Well. Let's take an alcoholic, suffering the DTs, he may see a pink elephant. It does no good for us to ask what shade of pink his elephant is, or call him crazy. But asking what might cause him to see a pink elephant in the first place, that begins to get at the problem". I did not understand "Don't only drunks see pink elephants". Eddie answered "Seeing a pink elephant is a symptom. Simply telling a person they're crazy, that pink elephants don't exist doesn't help. Returning with them to the scene of the crime, finding out what caused the trauma, which now has them seeing a pink elephant, brings the cause of their suffering to consciousness, breaking the hypnotic hold on the unconscious. You see, the recollection raids an engram of its unconscious authority. And the person is born again from this experience, brought up to present time, able to make different choices, to act instead of react. Quoting General George Patton, *A tactic known becomes no tactic*". Ida Rose continued "A woman who came to me several years ago was in constant fear bears were waiting to attack her, even in places bears could not possibly be. Through an audit we were able to go back to when she had been frightened by a bear as a very young child on a family trip to Yellowstone. She had completely blocked out the memory, but the trauma was still active in her unconscious and asking for help, manifesting in an irrational fear that bears were everywhere, her pink elephant, causing terrible anxiety and embarrassment. Carl Jung says that *a neurosis displayed is a neurosis begging to be cured.* When she re-called the origin and realized she was not just plain crazy, the grip of the engram dissolved, and the memory could be brought forward to present time, placed in conscious perspective, integrated, re-dated and indexed". I confessed "Your book, I've read it full-on three times and still can't say I understand". She leaned thoughtfully toward me "Most of my students have never really integrated General Semantics into their nervous systems. They get it intellectually, but it has not taken root in the unconscious where it can help them. It takes hard work to get to the bottom of that little book. People want it done to them instead of doing the work themselves. They want a magic vitamin. But work never goes for naught. Continue stretching your mind Little One. It's like a muscle, the more you exercise it, the more it becomes. Your persistence will be its own reward. I'm always happy to discuss my book with you, anytime". I sighed "Oh good, cause I brought it with me. You know the part about maiming God, I read it over and over, and just don't get it. I can't hold the idea in my mind long enough to even think about it". Ida Rose grinned "Why don't you read it to me".

"The semanticist Korzybski, like most of us, wondered who and what man might be in the scheme of things. Having been a soldier in World War I, he realized that man is not often God-like in his thoughts or behavior, and he thought that anyone claiming to a knowledge of "reality" must long ago have mastered himself and his environment. So he had to assume that men had not found "God" without maiming him, though many claimed to have done so. So he tried to devise some means of sorting out ideas and words-about-ideas, so that students among mankind — and we are all students as long as we live — could judge words and ideas for their meaning and significance for us and for other men."

Ida Rose explained "Most religions and mythologies kill or maim their Gods. For we create our Gods in our own image. Kings, sultans, sons of Gods. Since humans are flawed and mortal, so our Gods. We cut God into pieced and bury him, as the Egyptian God Osiris, to fructify the earth, cattle and crops, and he rises again whole. Abraham is asked to sacrifice his own son. We crucify Jesus to assure the salvation of Christians, and he rises again. Regicide is common thoughout history, as told in the Bard of Avon's Hamlet. The King-God must die young, in full possession of his faculties, his vitality, virility, so all that potency can be transferred to his successor, uncontaminated by the weakness and decay of age. So we bloody our Gods, cast in our own image". Every one of my LSD trips had given me at least a glimpse of, for lack of yet having found a better word, God. Not always human-like, or always a he, and more all pervading and not omniscient or omnipotent, more underneath and through, not over, not maimed, bloodied or blood-thirsty. I submitted "Believing in a maimed God would maim me. I mean I can't look-up to a God that would want that. But I need to believe in something, cause I know I didn't think my self up. My life would be too small, too personal if I didn't have something beyond me. But I can't believe in any of the Gods or religions anymore. I feel more like a witness. Every time I learn something, any kind of god I could believe in, maybe it's a giant cosmic library, would learn it with me". Ida Rose smiled proud "You are absolutely right Lamby. Building consciousness contributes to the evolution of God". I loved this woman, she did not think of me as blasphemous or arrogant or a rebel or

crazy or the label I hated most, a free spirit, a most predictable brush-off when I tried talking my thoughts on God. She didn't seem to fear He would hear and take revenge, making me feel for the first time in a long while, that I am not crazy. It was such a relief not feeling crazy, I always knew I wasn't. She went to the book shelves that covered the entire eastern wall of the dining room for Alfred North Whitehead's Process and Reality, saying "*Whitehead has the only description of God that I can buy*".
She read from page 524:

"*One side of God's nature is constituted by his conceptual experience. This experience is the primordial fact in the world. Limited by no actuality which is presupposed. It is therefore infinite, devoid of all negative prehensions. This side of his nature is free, complete, primordial, eternal, actually deficient, and unconscious. The other side originated with physical experience derived from the temporal world. And then acquired integration with the primordial side. It is determined, incomplete, consequent, 'everlasting', fully actual and conscious. His necessary goodness expresses the determination of his consequent nature.*"

She turned to page 527:

"*In this way God is completed by the individual. Fluent satisfactions of finite fact, and the temporal occasions are completed by their everlasting union with their transformed selves. Purged into conformation with the eternal order which is final absolute 'wisdom'.*"

By my face Ida Rose had no doubt I understood only the ands and thes, and simplified "Whitehead spends most of the book proving his thesis to academics and skeptics, only getting to the meat in his final chapter, God and the World. He's quite an intellectual snob with his language. You see, God is deficient without us humans, we are the process. God is the the potential, and without us, an unconscious idea. We make God conscious reality. For we are God too. We need each other. Like you said so brilliantly in your own way, we redeem God by our being conscious witness, and God evolves". Oh my, she used the word brilliant and me in the same sentence, I could not breathe.

The last sip of coffee gone, we had eaten half the pie. Ida Rose asked Eddie "Would you have time to take me up to QFC. I'm expecting one of my long time students, Marietta Chickeral from Washington DC. She's absolutely gifted. Completely reorganized the Library of Congress. She'll be tired from a long flight. I want to cook her something special for dinner". Eddie stood "Sure. We can go now if you like". Ida Rose was extraordinary and ordinary at the same time, Whitehead to grocery shopping in an effortless stream. She walked me to the front door "I'm sorry we have to end our visit so soon". I had a compelling desire to wrap my arms around her, say how much she meant to me, and remembering her uncomfort offered my hand instead. She took it in both hers "You are always welcome here Little One". I do not remember walking home.

> Oh Pioneer
> There's a trail of broken Karma behind you
> And what's ahead hasn't been written
> It's up to you Oh Pioneer
> To hear without ears
> See without eyes
> Think what hasn't been thought
> Without playing God
>
> Oh Pioneer - Go on
> Greatful for any company along the road
> Bouncing off the walls
> Of black and white
> Left and right
> Male and female
> Arab and Israel
> Wrong and right
> Dark and light
>
> Oh Pioneer go on down the middle
> And fear not the dark shadows
> For they are only you
> You're alone and lonely
> And though the road is long and bloody
> It does lead Home
>
> Oh Pioneer - Go on

Chapter Ten

WASHOUGAL WASHINGTON

February 1970, the Black Panthers brought suit against the United States government for harassment. Subject to referendum in the Fall, Washington State could vote to make abortion legal. And Hydra seriously began planning Sky River, unanimously voting Carolion would contact the bands cause she wanted it so bad. We were waiting for confirmation on a late summer date to set ours. Nixon would be giving the keynote speech at the American Legion National Conference in Portland Oregon, we would stage the festival to coincide, a convenient site in Southwestern Washington, and march on him with a mighty force. Also happening, one or two people from each SLF collective were meeting daily with other groups, planning a February 17th rally at the Federal Courthouse downtown, to protest the war's intensification, and to stand in solidarity with the Chicago Seven. Judge Hoffman could not get them on the original conspiracy charge, so he would try to indict them for contempt. Almost ever day somewhere in the country massive anti-war demonstrations took place, coalitions, groups, all with their own agendas, yet with enough points of unity to put differences aside and join together, we hoped for thousands here. As usual this rally was not real well-organized, no one worried too much, we had learned things tend to solidify in the spontaneous magic of the moment. I did not go to any of the meetings, my interest only in Sky River, and the near daily car-trips with Mark or Bear to possible locations. I was not even going to the rally, having grown paranoid of public demonstrations, always fearing a violent turn, I was not brave enough, or maybe foolish enough. And lately I thought I saw Nick.

The Littles, Keely and I had a night before sign painting party. And in the heat of foolish morning excitement, I took a sign and a bundle of leaflets and went with Keely and Carolion to the courthouse. We smoked a joint in the car, were first on the scene, and had big-fun standing on the steps in tie-dyes and beads handing anti-war anti-imperialism leaflets to the general disapproval of hustling Suits and Skirts seeking only their lunch. I counted forty peace-officers arrive in full regalia, far too many for this demonstration, making me a nervous rumble. Keely and I had a practice of interacting with them, trying to be human beings instead of Pinko-Commie-Hippies. Sometimes it worked, today they had steel in their eyes, seeing just the enemy. Noon we scaled the steps to the top, counting a rough 2000 on sidewalk and courthouse steps as the Boys began their speeches, free healthcare for all, free education for all, tenants rights, stop the degradation of the environment, recognize the institution of racism and end it, end the war, free the Chicago Seven. I saw Nick across the street. Sinking in every organ of my body, I told Keely. She ignored me for a shoving match between a peace-officer and protester insisting on his civil right to stand on a public sidewalk. Then a bull of a man pushed by me with something big under his coat, and hurled a loaf-of-bread size stone at the Courthouse's twelve-foot glass front doors, smashing one completely, just as another bull threw a gallon of red paint on the other door. I'd never seen these guys and wondered, unholy shit, who are the goons. The crowd stampeded, peace-officers pulled on their masks and waded in with nausea-gas, mace and batons, paddy-wagon sirens under-scoring the frenzy. I could not find any reason being clubbed or gassed for some shadowy glass-breaker and paint-thrower, and fled North, long flying gazelle strides, white smoke billowing behind, a uniform chasing me half-a-block, fuel-injected adrenaline, ground never touching my boots, seven blocks to the Pike Place Market. Not even winded I merged into the weekend bustle, found an upstairs booth at the Athenian Café, ordered a Rainier beer, and another, eavesdropping the excited chatter of smashed office building windows, banks, hotels, expensive department stores, luxury car windows, peace-officers clubbing kids, mass arrests.

Afraid to go home, the law certainly waiting, I meandered though the market, through downtown, through Nordstrom, I.Magnin, up Pine Street to Capitol Hill, along Broadway, across the University Bridge, ate a slice of pizza at Morningtown, lingering, unsure what to do, where to go, maybe the Blue Moon Tavern, someone there might know something. Nursing a Miller at the bar, no reliable information, suspiciously nothing on the news, I decided to catch the bus to Mercer Island, when a high school classmate came in, and recognizing me took the next stool, way to thrilled to see me, we had not friends, I could not recall ever even having a word, and yet I was glad to see him too. Lately home from Vietnam, I listened to his gung-ho all American enlisting, and once deployed, adamant turning against the war, and dishonorable discharge. Deciding going home to Mom and Dad was not the best idea, telling him why, I asked to crash at his place. He said yes, promising no strings. The tiny studio apartment smelled like oranges and hashish, we got wasted on them, listened to his favorite bands, Moby Grape and Bob Dylan, talked old times and new hopes, and fell asleep sitting-up.

Just after 6AM, venturing down Hydra's street, the house quiet and dark, I went in. Bear was up, in the kitchen, making coffee, listening to the radio, and gave me good news, none of Hydra had been hurt or detained, still there were 89 arrests, including Grodes and Rebels, we wouldn't know for days who would be charged and who not. Ric brought-in pizza for lunch, our long faces gathered round the War Table, Bear reading us a Post Intelligencer article accusing the Seattle Liberation Front of starting a riot that shattered windows and caused 75 thousand dollars damage to the courthouse. No surprise, not one word of why we were there, the violence always taking the limelight. And, the Chicago Seven were officially acquitted of conspiracy by a Federal jury, and at the same time indicted for contempt, five additionally charged with crossing state lines to incite riot. Ric forecast this was a preview of what we were in-for. I was too depressed to eat, did not want to think on this, only Sky River, suggesting our best revenge was to go on with the plan. Suddenly terribly exhausted, I climbed the stairs and slid into my sleeping bag, letting the satin lining calm my skin and close my eyes.

For thirteen days bombs went off somewhere in the Seattle. Three at the UW to protest the exclusion of Black construction workers on campus, two were duds, one did minor property damage. Ten quiet nervous days, then a small bomb blast infront of the District post office. Three more days, and the SLF and Black Student Union walked hand-in-hand into Thomson Hall with pillows and backpacks full of food and drink, sat down, and issued a demand. The University of Washington must terminate all athletic competition with Brigham Young University for their discrimination against Black athletes. We would sit-in till they did. I went, to break the deep hold despair had on me, with no intention of staying overnight. Endless rounds of We Shall Overcome resounding the hardwood and marble, everyone settling-in, knowing full well we were too many for campus police to do more than manage. And there was Nick, casually leaning against the door jamb smoking a cigarette. I seemed to be scared most of the time anyway, but Nick was personal, panic grabbed hold, I wanted to run, to jump off the earth, but was better with Mark and Bear, and Keely who would be going home to feed the Littles. I waited and went with, Nick vanished. Thomson Hall was occupied for six days, till the University agreed to our demand. Spontaneous and not so, anti-war demonstrations took place daily on campus. There was an arson at Parrington Hall. And, Chicago Seven's Tom Hayden spoke at the UW Hub. On that day, for the first time ever, Seattle police were invited on campus, to do more than manage.

Mid April, conspiracy to riot indictments were issued from a Federal Grand Jury for our own, Chip Marshall, Michael Lerner, Michael Justensen, Susan Stern, Jeff Dowd, Joe Kelly, Mike Abeles and Roger Lippman, for thought crimes. Intended to scare the whole Movement, like one rapist on the loose scares all women, the government wanted to stop dissent from the political Left, sending the message, if these eight can be charged for thinking and talking, because conspiring is not commiting, so can you. The defendants became the Seattle Eight, accused of conspiring to damage Federal property during the courthouse demonstration. At the War Table, I recounted seeing both incidents, that I did not recognize either goon. We all knew absolutely, it was an FBI frame. Next day, Mike Abeles, Jeff Dowd, Michael Lerner and Joe Kelly, were also charged for crossing state lines with the intent to incite riot. Each count carried a maximum five-years in prison and ten-thousand-dollar fine. These came from on-high, Nixon instructing United States Attorney General John Mitchell to initiate the charges, and FBI director J.Edgar Hoover to order the U.S. Attorney for Western Washington Stan Pitkin to present the evidence.

I felt sorry for the defendants, their lives were no longer theirs. And, they became willing celebs, our corner of the country's first famous revolutionaries, for wrong or right the faces and voices of authority. Some Movement kingpins could not contain their jealousy, privately complaining they had been arbitrarily superseded by the defendants sudden rise, fame envied even at the price of freedom. These seven men and Susan were not so arbitrary though, most likely targets all along. Still, the movements self-seeking and back-stabbing further disenchanted me, this nasty underbelly of politics no matter what side, a mean-spirited soap opera of ambitions that had everything to do with wielding power for personal gain. I wanted to believe our side was pure of heart, idealists that liked to party too much, my expectations were way too high, disappointment an enduring fall, for both sides had their ulterior motives. I needed to step-back and take a look at where I was headed, for I had joined in blind-faith, trusting the integrity and innate goodness of the Movement, buoyed by a righteous feeling of doing right, happy to be a small hand in changing the world, surrounded mostly by others with the same motivation. Yes, the Women's Lib collective shunned me, but I was determined to win their trust. And yes, the chauvinism angered me, but I saw the Boys growing-up a little. Even so, I could not afford blind-faith in the face of convenient ethics. Ida Rose said that a person's motivation was an accurate indication of their substance. I had a good look at some substances, and withdrew again, except for planning Sky River. Building a town, people living with dignity, this still held my enthusiasm.

Taking two hats to Arabesque, Nick brushed by me on the Ave. A dark intense dialogue began rolling round in my head, I knew I had to confront him to break the connection. Next afternoon I deliberately walked the Ave alone, and the Sweet Sisters Fate arranged. He came-out of the Hasty at my approach, so very surprised running into me "Well if it isn't Shoshannah Leibofsky. God you're such a fox, and you know it". Standing soft-kneed and flat-footed I was loud enough for the whole street to hear "Quit stalking me". He feigned insult "You don't mean that. Look, I'm big-time now. Have all the shekels you could ever want. So stop punishing your self and come home". Right, I don't mean what I say, and shekels, what, I'm a money-grubbing Kike. I could not help notice he was smaller than the specter haunting me, that I was not so afraid of him in-person, even when he rested his hand on the hilt of a fixed-blade Kabar Army combat knife attached to his belt. More a show of potency, of permanent erection than kill weapon, I could feel his near uncontrollable desire to unsheathe, stab me in the breast, and knew he was too meticulously covert to ever do anything in public. This was pure mind-game, I shook-off the intimidation, smiled and defiantly engaged his eyes "You don't get it, and you never will. It's never been about shekels, I make my own. It's about freedom, thinking for myself, not you doing it for me. It's about my dreams not just yours". He was not listening "Come on Shoshy, can't you see I've changed. You can have all the freedom and money you want. Honest". I was the only one changed here, no longer needing him. Yes I felt a hollowness without him, and alone, and unknown. Maybe he was my one true love, maybe I never would love again, maybe I was making a terrible mistake, but I knew unequivocally that I willingly take love lost over abject degradation, over losing my mind, over being merely a body, and that I would be whole all by myself. I tried to engage his eyes once more. He would not, looking passed my ear. Standing resolute as I could, determined to end this "There's not one chance I'm ever coming back to you. So get on with your life and leave me out". Nick riveted his pupils to mine, so filled with loathing they no longer looked human. I could not look away, my declaration of independence had clearly amplified the deadly dance. He turned abruptly and walked away, showing his back, the ultimate power-trip before murder, leaving me bloody without cutting-off a limb.

Nixon ordered the carpet-bombing of North Vietnam, and rumored bombing of Cambodia, while swearing he did not. The country smelled the lie, near every college campus erupted in turmoil, student strikes commonplace. Americans were tinder and every one had a match. Nixon's keynote at the American Legion Convention August 30th was confirmed. Vice President Agnew might speak too. So, Sky River would open August 28, and carry-on for eleven days, through Labor Day weekend. Most Movement attention went to our new martyrs, the Seattle Eight, planning, raising money for, finding a great defense team. Hydra mostly focused on Sky River, using the Washington Planned Community Association façade to do business behind. Carolion drove to California by her self, interviewing Delroy Bogave at his Boulder Creek ranch and booking Moongoose, the other band he played lead guitar when he wasn't on the road with Moby Grape. Moongoose loved our idea of a Hippie town, and agreed to play for expenses. She went to Santa Cruz, booking One Hand Clapping. San Francisco, to meet with Commander Cody, an art professor at Cal-Berkley, and his band the Lost Planet Airmen, who also resonated to Sky River politics and would play for expenses. She opened dialogue with the Youngbloods to headline, and Doug Kershaw, and Boz Scaggs, hoping to politicize them enough to take the deal. The line-up growing substantial, we were confident droves would come, this was bigger than we thought, Sky River's reputation preceded us, making the way easier. We needed more front money, all nodding silent-yes to a vote, we would do our first big dealing, use New Year's profits to buy product.

May 1st, newspapers confirm Nixon bombing the neutral nation of Cambodia. Spontaneously, we massed in the District, thousands, making the point, making the news, giving many first-timers a real taste of people power. Mayor Wes Ullman showed some restraint, ordering the police to let the demonstration play itself out, nevertheless clubs were used, no gas, nine arrests, two windows broken. That afternoon, the ROTC office at Clark Hall was trashed as thousands more protested, a heady event even with police allowed on campus. We had the numbers, and the moral high ground. And there was Nick, making sure I saw him. Shivers raised my short-hairs, he won, Bear walk me home. Lance had a talent for reading people's immediate state of mind, valuable survival skill in his particular upbringing, one he often used to protect the siblings, and he wanted to know "What's a matter Shoshy". His earnest compassion had me swallowing tears, I took a deep breath "There's a bully bothering me". Looking into his full-fledged eyes I could not help but ask "What would you do about it". He answered, no hesitation "Tell everyone and then they know". This precious little sage made perfect sense, everyone at Hydra knew, Nick did not come here, but William, Tara, Lizabeth, Howard, maybe letting them know would give me more safety.

I called the farm, number no longer in service, even so, maybe they could not afford a phone anymore. I bussed far as the line went, walking the last two miles. Such a knee-jerk decision, regretting not telling anyone where I went, my shoulders crawling, Nick in every approaching vehicle, I was determined, and angry enough to push-on, somewhere inside understanding that putting-up a fight was essential. The farm abandoned, Monty's cabin too, and suddenly so far down a long dead-end, I ran back to the road. Walking maybe a half-mile in light rain, the sky opened, and I put-out a half-hearted thumb for a ride. Two flat-bed trucks, five cars, one tractor, a pick-up loaded high in hay passed without slowing. Then matching my gait, a copper-and-cream 1956 Chevy Bel Air, and two young men, the only Blacks I had ever seen in rural Issaquah. Passenger unrolled his window "Need a lift. We're heading for the Ave". He unlocked the back door. My gut warned this is the wrong ride, guilty urge to be polite over-ruling, I got in. My shoulders stopped crawling, I sat quite, looking out the window, rationalizing my initial reaction as likely stubborn stereotypical prejudice. On reaching I-90, Driver lit-up a skinny joint. I relaxed a little as he took a hit and passed to his buddy, who sucked-up most of it, attached a roach-clip and passed it over his shoulder to me. I knew better than to smoke this, took a seeming hit, holding in my mouth five seconds, exhaling though my nose, passing it back. Passanger opened the clip, dropped the roach in a pool of saliva cupped on his pink tongue, a seed popped and hissed, he laughed in surprise and swallowed. Driver turned the radio on to KRAB. No one spoke through Issaquah, over Mercer Island, the floating bridge, and out the West end of the tunnel. He offered "We're lookin' to score. If ya know a some good weed, I'll take ya right to yur front door". Oh shit they're narcs, my brain flew out the window, laughing to steady my self, sighing "Nope. Sorry. Yours is all I've seen in a while. But, when I get home, I could ask my brothers". Sure bringing them to Hydra was not the best idea, I was seriously wondering would I get home, and given we were dealing, I would let Ric be the judge. Driver parked infront of Hydra, the curtain cross the street opened as I got out, making me feel absurdly safe knowing they were documenting the license plate. I bid them "Wait here. I'll come back soon". My whole body relaxed on seeing Mark, Ric and Arnie round the War Table, I quietly explained. All went out to the car with me, several questions, and Ric asked them in. Music turned loud. Driver wanted a kilo. More questions, and Mark Arnie and Ric went in private discussion. Ric gave them a price. Driver said it was do-able, they'd be back with the money in one hour. I did not like this, no one would listen, exhilaration, desire ruling the first big sale.

I had been reading The Chronicles of Narnia by C.S.Lewis to the Littles, they took me with all six hands to their room for the next chapter in book three, The Voyage of the Dawn Treader. After near or far an hour, hunger ruled, we tramped down to the kitchen, Robby and Scottie taking their usual places at the table, Lance being older, the Captain, opened two bags of potato chips. I made tuna salad and chopped black olives sandwiches. Scottie pulling at my sleeve, up-turned cherub-face asking through a mouth full of chips "What kind of sandwich mine is". Smiling at this pure sweetness I crooned "Tuna fish and black olives my little sugar plum. Is that all right with you". He nodded seriously and went back to his chair. And it hit me, this was the only time I had ever heard him speak, I hurried into the living room for Keely. Their faces were glued to the TV screen, Carolion, Bear, Arnie, Mark, Keely, Ric, watching Walter Cronkite reporting that four students had been killed by National Guardsmen on Kent State University campus in Ohio. I stood some moments, the bowl of tuna in my hands, and went back to the kitchen. This had to back-fire on Nixon, maybe even be the spark to ignite our ready national tinder. Thousands of dead American soldiers, no one would say how many Vietnamese, and sadly for our collective soul, murdering Black Panthers in their beds had not been enough. Now four White kids. Nixon's unmistakable message to all who dare defy him, I am an equal opportunity killer, color will not save you, today's bullet has your name on it too.

Standing at the counter cutting sandwiches in quarters with a serrated steak knife, I saw Driver coming from the living room through the dining room, and assuming he must be here for the deal and needed to use the bathroom just off the kitchen, I smiled and pointed "It's thata way". He kept coming my way, setting-off all alarm bells. Oh shit, now Shoshy don't freak-out the Littles, I faced him, and smiling hard, could think of nothing else "So, can I make you a sandwich". Filling the room, he looked passed me to the counter. My brain scrambled for footing, maybe he wants a drink of water, maybe my alarm is chronic prejudice, no one in the house is making a commotion. Moving fast, he pinned me against the counter with his bulk, reaching, taking the Safeway shopping bag next to the toaster. I simply reacted "You can't have that. It's our groceries". Steak knife still in hand, grabbing for the folded bag top with my other, it was full, dope sifted clean of stems and seeds, I yanked, trying to tear it open, spill it on the floor, my hand slick with tuna and mayo slid free, the bag intact. Driver smiled Cheshire as he backed from the kitchen. I growled "God damn you. Give that back". Shaking his head, he spun and thundered though the house. Knife gripped tight, I went after. He was out the front door, Passenger on his heels. I raced through the living room, everyone strangely still. Driver revved the Chevy as I stood infront, not thinking of anything but getting that bag back. He did not challenge, lurching backing down the narrow street, Passenger struggling to pull his door shut. I gave chase, cursing, waving the serrated blade high in the air, repeating the license plate aloud OLK 106 OLK 106 OLK 106. At blocks end, Driver swung rear to the right, and before peeling-away rolled down his window and blew me a kiss. I hurled the knife at him, hitting his arm with the blade, flipping him off with both hands. The men across the street watched openly as I lumbered-up the stairs, cold, sweaty, breathing heavy from the chase. Everyone strangely still in the living room, I proud-ly announced the license plate number. Ric gave a cynical little snort "Fine detective work Sherlock. Now let's call the pigs and ask 'em to go get our dope". He took a deep breath "Guess you missed the other guy here in the living room holding a shotgun on us". Suddenly wiped-out I shuddered at what had really been, knew why no commotion, how Driver knew where and what was in the bag. Hiccupping, doe-eyed Keely croaked "Wow hic, you should've seen yourself hic, chasing those guys out the door with that little knife in your hand. I couldn't believe it. You were amazing". She went to her Littles and finished their lunch. I did not tell her that Scottie spoke words, she should be first to hear them.

Arnie raged "Those mother-fuckers took our stash right off the fucking coffee-table. No class assholes". Carolion pulled a fat joint from behind her ear. A terrible heavy guilt made me flush "I'm so sorry, bringing them here. Round the kids". Ric's enormous ego or maybe heart would not let me own all the blame "It's not on you. I made the decision to sell". Bear held a match to the joint "On me too. I thought they were okay". Mark in his eternal optimism "All's not lost. We have money to buy more". My friends, trying to make me feel better, didn't really matter, I felt deeply humiliated, immature, far off any path to enlightenment I had fancied my self on. In painful need of redirection, taken by an aloof detachment, I retired to my sleeping-bag, too exhausted to worm in.

The National Guard killing Kent State students William Schroeder, Alison Krause, Jeffrey Miller and Sandra Scheuer ignited the national tinder. University Presidents throughout the country asked Nixon to withdraw from Vietnam and the surrounding area. In protest, many shut-down their schools for the balance of Spring quarter. University of Washington for only one day, and so we organized, 7000 plus students and marched onto campus in peaceful protest. Authorities were caught surprised. Once again Mayor Ullman instructed police to let it run its course. Next morning rallies spread over the District. This time Mr.Mayor ordered tear-gas. Thousands fled, swarming into downtown, the police driving most of us onto I-5 at Cherry Street, stopping traffic both ways. Mayor called-off his dogs, and the demonstration dispersed peacefully on its own. When police did not interfere with weapons and gas, it was usually mostly peaceful. Campus protests continue, buildings were occupied, the campus radio station KUOW, dubbed Radio Free Seattle, gave students an on air-voice. ROTC for the first time in 41 years moved its annual meeting off campus. King County Democrats endorsed Black lawyer Carl Maxey over incumbent Sentaor Henry Jackson, and called for Nixon's impeachment. The UW obtained an injunction to prevent Hydra from holding a festival on campus. We had no intention. Seattle police released alleged private papers from the SLF outlining our plans to close down the UW by crippling phones, electrical and radio services, and contaminating the water with LSD. Hydra had no plans or papers. May 15, police murdered two Black students on Jackson State University campus in Mississippi. UW canceled classes in-memorial. And the American people stayed in the streets, with major demonstrations daily, the middle class was finally engaged, we were jubilant, there was no revolution without the middle class. I slept twelve hours, spending awake mostly sewing and with the Littles, offering to sit for Keely, letting her go to every rally and party, she desperately appreciated the liberty. Starving for anyone's attention, Littles and I were becoming friends. They had a devoted admiration for my chasing down Driver and

Passanger with the now famous serrated knife blade. It was a two-way street, I respected their native good sense and imagination, never trying to parent or tell them what to do, just hanging-out, watching-out, letting them use my experience.

Long as I laid-low, I could manage the Nick nightmare, secretly grateful for the constants across the street, though I could not reason why they had not yet busted us. And then there was Driver and Passanger, such incredibly poor judgment, why hadn't I listened to my gut. Any trust in my ability to make good decisions was badly shaken. And it haunted me, how that violent element of Nick I got away from had come round anyway, maybe it wasn't only him but me too. I even thought Driver and Passenger were out in rural Issaquah because they once scored at the farm and had gone to see if Nick was still there. And then, the Oregon dealer who bought cocaine from Nick, walked into Hydra with Ric to buy some bricks. As if wrapped in spider silk and bitten, waiting my fate, sure this was it, I sat at the War Table during the deal, till Ida Rose whispered in my ear, *One of the few truths you can count on Lamby, is that things change.* Somehow this freed me, I quietly left the table. No one but her really interested me anymore, none wanted to explore below the surface, I was so dead-bored with surface. People seemed marionettes, and I wanted to know who or what pulled their strings and mine. Local politics were the same, the Movement galvanized around the Seattle Eight, nowadays inflated beyond recognition, behaving like rock-stars, although I didn't blame them. So I kept a distance, enduring, alone and falling, the constant heat inside of losing a loved one though no one was lost but me, wanting to end the torment, collecting pills, no one noticed. But for the promise of Sky River, the Littles, and not coming-up with a nice neat plan.

Even with his management refusing to let him sign a contract for less that ten-thousand, and making it clear they did not like our politics, Carolion talked Doug Kershaw into playing for expenses. The San Francisco Mime Troupe, Hot Tuna, Jefferson Airplane said no money no show. The Wiz Kids said yes, and Dr.Zarkov, and Wavy Gravy and the Hog Farm Collective promised to come from New Mexico in their bus and feed the people. The big coup came when everyone was off to the UW Hub, six of the Chicago Seven were there to speak in support of our conspiracy defendants, now called the Seattle Seven, since Michael Justensen had still not been apprehended. I was home with the Littles and took the call from Jesse Colin Young of the Youngbloods, they would play for expenses and hotel rooms. News spread, all the collectives wanted-in, we appreciated the help. Bear, Mark and I had not found a site and gladly turned the search over to Russell Wadell and his real estate agent Mother Georgia. Ric knew them, had solid confidence they could be trusted to keep quiet. Mother Georgie offered to hock her diamond ring for earnest money. Following much debate around the War Table, we settled, each festival ticket would be a deed, automatically making the purchaser part owner, we could pay for the land by selling it to the people for the price of admission. Such beautiful simplicity inspired my heart, lifted the malaise, I stopped collecting pills.

Bear coined our mantra, *Sky River Lives*, after seeing Jesus Lives spray-painted on the side of moving van. All agreed, for Sky River to live well, we should make space in the eleven days for more than music. Workshops on health-food, vitamins, massage, acupuncture, growing food, growing pot, building geodesic domes, and painters, potters, weavers, astrologers, historians, even politicians. We put in another phone line, and as the Washington Planned Community Association, contacted Bastyr University for the Healing Arts, Cornish School for the Musical Arts, the Seattle Symphony, Washington State Senators and Representatives. I called Judge Solie Ringold's office asking him to speak. A friend of my Dad, our families went to the same synagogue, he was the the first ever Jewish and most liberal Supreme Court Justice on the State bench, continually under attack from the right, and I was a fan. We cast an open-minded net, knowing there would be less than enthusiastic response from those who had too much to lose being associated with anything like Sky River, nonetheless we called everyone. And we got no, and NO, and N-O, and I'll think about it, I'll get back to you, maybe, yes, and YES, and Sky River was born. Mark formed the *Kady Grady Fly by Night Construction Company*, to build the stage and light-show towers. When a site was found, it would be kept secret till the very last possible minute, authorities were sure to try and stop us. Water, Sani-cans, lights, sound equipment, lumber, all would be moved only by cover of night. And, to conjure excitement, Ric leak to the Helix from the Washington Planned Community Association, the Youngbloods would headline. Other papers hounded the Association phone number. Ric would say no more than *"People should be prepared for a three hour drive from the Oregon border or the Canadian border"*.

June 22, Nixon signed an extension of the Voting Rights Act, requiring the legal age be lowered to 18 in all Federal, State and Local elections. To celebrate this real victory for boys being drafted without ever getting to vote for or against who was sending them to die, Ric leaked more of Sky River's musical line-up to the Helix. But no site yet, and we were getting nervous. By July all our dope was dealt, we had enough up-front money, planning intensified, taking all our attention off the Seattle Seven, who now had some high profile lawyers. One of them, Jeffrey Steinborn came to some of our events. The trial had been scheduled for October, and a new group, the Seattle Conspiracy Defense Collective formed specifically to raise money for the Seven.

Long Summer days, near 18 hours of light and not a hint of Nick unexpectedly lifted my cynical paranoia. I managed to create a continuous mental loop that ran, minor expectations, minor expectations, minor expectations, which made my judgments less harsh, disappointments less bitter, and fostered some trust again in my ability to make competent decisions. I no longer zombie-walked all the way into the under-world of depression, for on finding my self standing at the door, or some distance down the path already, I would say, okay Shoshy, just stop now, you've been down here enough already, you know where this takes you, a really bad place, you do not need to go the rest of the way, turn around now. When some good psilocybin mushrooms appeared on the War Table, I felt stable enough to risk a mellow trip, just one mild cup of tea. No hallucination, and one epiphany on an Old Testament teaching. After 400 years of Egyptian slavery, Yahweh had the Jews wander in the Sinai almost 500 months, for slaves would certainly re-create a corresponding social order, so a new generation had to be born in freedom to go into the Land of Milk and Honey and build a free society. I could see we all had one foot in the old and one in the new, and began to worry when we bought the town of Sky River what social order we would construct.

Russell and Mother Georgie found a site in Washougal Washington, we all went to see Edwin Tate's farm, and it was perfection. Tickets were printed. And the day FBI fugitive Father Daniel Berrigan was captured in Danbury Conneticut, we called a press conference to reveal most of the festival details, blowing our Washington Planned Community Association cover in the bargain. Ric would do the talking as usual, and Bear and Mark and probably Arnie. I protested Carolion deserved to speak too, since she booked the music. Girls were out-voted by the Boys. All newspapers radio and TV stations were invited. We knew they would read subterranean meaning into any thing we did, so Carolion, Keely, the Littles and I spoke by decorating the War Table, with Lance's high-top tennis shoes stuffed with flowers he made from colored Kleenex, Robby's Stretch Armstrong doll, Scottie's full collection of naked Barbies, most with limbs missing, all their toy swords, knives and guns, a hangman's noose, handcuffs, three hammer, a box of nails, an empty box of bullets, empty box of tampons, empty box of Trojans, empty box of crayons, an empty box of Kellogg's Frosted Flakes, a large glow-in-the-dark crucifix, a God's eye, a carton of broken eggs, a frozen ham, a stack of peanut butter and jelly sandwichs, three tall glasses of milk, and candles lit all over the room. Five reporters and two TV cameras showed. Ric would not let the cameras inside. They were ushered, and seated on one side of the War Table. Ric, Mark, Bear, Arnie on the other. Girls standing behind. Littles banished upstairs and loudly complaining. Bear offered milk and sandwiches, and began *"Sky River is a great name for a city"*. Mark relayed *"Sky River won't be a shuck for sure, it can't help but come off. We expect it to cost $65.000 to get started. There are about 30 bands so far. We plan to avoid legal problems by keeping the site secret until the day before the festival, and sell the land to ticket holders for the price of the ticket. Who ever wants can stay afterwards and live there"*. Bear handed-out a press release *"Location to be announced August 27th. Be prepared to travel three hours from Seattle or Portland. If coming from the South stay in Portland. If coming from the North stay in Seattle. The festival site will be announced in both cities. The site is secluded, with a natural am-phitheatre and river. Water, food, sanitary facilities, etc., will be more than adequate. After costs, profits will go to the Black Panthers, to daycare centers, and the Seattle Seven's defense"*. Mark continued *"Hydra hasn't purchased the site yet. We have part of the funds for that. The rest will come from ticket sales"*.

Times reporter John Hinterberger wanted to know why Hydra thought there would be a profit *"Most rock festivals lose money"*. Mark answered in his typical fuck-you fashion *"There'll be a hundred-thousand people at this one and that's a conservative estimate. I can give you a radical one if you like"*. Ric added *"Everything is going beautifully. There are no legal problems that will stop the festival"*. King TV's Mike James asked if there was any truth to the rumor that Hydra intended to assassinate Nixon during the festival. Not one more word, we started chanting Sky River Lives, reporters were ushered out.

A short two weeks remaining, the chute had been well greased and the ride took us. I volunteered to take on security, after all, I had an actual government top clearance from Boeing, and no one else wanted the job. Negotiations for Edwin Tate's farm finally jelled when he heard why we wanted the land, signing his name to the sales contract, very pleased *"I always wanted to have a festival on my land"*. And Mother Georgie kept the faith, pawning her big diamond ring for one-thousand-dollars earnest money needed to seal the deal. The Washington Planned Community Association could occupy the land right away, Edwin and his wife could stay in their home as long as the wanted for one-dollar a month. Sky River Rock Festival and Lighter than Air Fair III would live in Clark County Washington, 20 miles East of Portland, 160 acres on the North bank of the Washougal River, a shallow tributary of the mighty Columbia. Every County in the State already passed an ordinance prohibiting multi-day gatherings. We believed since the farm was private land, we did not violated any law, building began immediately, care-full as possible to attract little attention. Messages were sent to Governor Dan Evans and Oregon's Tom McCall, asking to let the festival go on in peace. We knew there would be trouble, authorities could not let us do any thing, even legal without over-reacting, duly alarmed at how effectively we destabilize status-quo. I knew well how status-quo kept its rule. All I had to do was walk through downtown in no make-up, bell-bottoms, pea coat, waffle-stompers, and Straits would freak-out, often insulting me, some kind of dirty-girl, mostly under their breath. One woman, round 50, stocky, going to work, in a hurry, in a nice suit and sturdy shoes spit on me. Just eight years past, this proper 13 year-old would never dared go into downtown

Seattle in less than a good suit, hat and gloves, or her character would be called to question. Now I relished being on the front of the wave, and not so terribly alone, for Carolion, Keely, Ric, Mark, Bear, Arnie, the Littles were out there with me. When I began questioning proper, the Golden Ghet turned its cold-eye on me. That insidious mind-trap, where you are required to believe everything you will ever want or need is already there before your eyes, and you must never look beyond the Golden Gate, or deep inside your self, and do not question, never question, for it's all on the surface, in plain sight, you can't miss the right address, club member-ship, symphony seats, investments, the right cars, boat, designer labels, restaurants, wine, friends, the best is yours, you are safe, never ever sus-pect, the law is on your side, just let you originality, authenticity, your god-forbid imagination wither, stay inside the lines, because if you dare don't, you will be shunned, dismissed, and when of-age, dismissed from Eden to live a low-class life and die a low-class life. But I had not died living beyond, au contraire, in my world imagination and differences were celebrated assets not aberration.

On my twenty-second birthday, the Washington State Legislature le-galized abortion.

August 15, forty-five of us descended on Edwin Tate's farm, to help build the stage, light show towers, concession row for the food venders, health-food to hot dogs, head-shops, jewelry, clothes, shoes, kites, books, perfumes. The Country Doctor raised their Open-Door Clinic, for medi-cal emergencies. Next door was a full-service Drug Store, chemists would be on-hand to analysis anyone's dope for purity. We hoped to nip the over-dose, and let people know if they were dropping something that was really something else. Sani-cans were delivered, and water. We needed lodging for the bands. Washougal a one-street town, post office, grange, grocery store and gas station. The nearest accommodations were three miles West, the two-street town of Camas. Mark and I found the Camas Inn, spa-cious, charming, gracious grounds, and booked it for eleven days. The owner wanted five-thousand damage deposit up-front. Mark gave it to him, sure we would fill the place with performers and speakers who were too tender, some too full-of-themselves to camp. And then he tapped-into the farmhouse phone-line, running it into the 32-foot trailer Ric rented for a command center. Ric would stay on-site and manage logistics. I took the task of collecting ticket money from Seattle area outlets, and rode home with Arnie, who would make daily cash-runs back to Washougal, to pay suppliers.

August 26, time had come to publicly announce location. Rick and Mark drove home to conduct a press conference. Not one hour passed and Clark County Sheriff Clarence McKay ordered a road block in Washougal. Ric was finally allowed a word with him, and gee whiz, Sheriff could not explain exactly why a road block had been called for, lifting it soon after. Ric decided to manage things from Hydra. Mark was anxious to get back to building. Carolion wanted one more phone call before going with, to John Lennon's manager. She had been trying to get a message to John and Yoko, please come to Sky River, not to perform, just hang-out with us. Calling daily for 11 days, this time John's secretary put her through. John listened to her, and said only one word "No". Still Carolion was off-the-ground, her hero had spoken to her, tears burst "Wow. I talked to John Lennon. I can't believe it".

Late afternoon, Clark County's Prosecutor sent the Washington Planned Community Association a telegram, informing us Sky River was in violation of ordinances, an injunction would be sought, and, his office could find no record of a firm sale of the land. Edwin Tate was interviewed on the evening news. At the urging of Prosecutor, he was trying to cancel the sale, saying about us *"They're out there. I can't tell just what they're doing, but they keep coming"*. And we were coming, Hippies, Yippies, weekend Hippies, Flower-Children, freaks, radicals, idealist, cynics, dealers, users, outlaws, in-laws, young, not so young, to initiate a new hometown. Keely, the Littles, and I began collecting sleeping bags, pillows, clothes, toys, cooking tools, food, lanterns, a ten-man tent, anything we could think of for twelve days by the river in Washougal Washington.

Early morning the ringing began, reporters calling for the story, and we were thrilled with the publicity. The site had been served with an eviction notice, if we weren't gone by the end of the day there would be legal action. Ric responded the same to each call *"The festival will open in 24 hours. There's no way people will be stopped from coming. Over 6,000 tickets have been sold at $11 dollars each. None of the bands have canceled. It will* *be an interesting power struggle to see what the authorities can do when so many people want to do what the Man doesn't want them to".* Littles had not slept, absolutely crazed with excitement the day had finally come, we were going camping. Keely dressed and fed them. Ric and I packed the car. There was a wooden chest on the War Table he needed a hand with. I asked "So, what's in this". He motioned toward the front door with his head "Come on, help me". Picking it up by the black metal handles we went out on the porch. It was sunny and warm, and it was heavy, we set it down between us and sat on the top step in full-view. His laugh high and sardonic "It's Sandoz". Sure he was kidding I laughed too "Right. Show me". He opened the lid all the way. I was stunned at the wealth of white pills, a light mist of powder rising. Ric said calmly "Don't breath in 'r you'll be gone. There's one-hundred-thousand hits. FBI brought it over last night. Compliments of Bechtel, the perfect cover for Spooks don't you think". I did not understand "Why would they give us good acid". Ric sneered "Crowd control. Since they can't stop us, they hope to control us". I could not believe my eyes, pharmaceutically pure Sandoz, absolutely no chance of a bad trip, impossible to come-by anymore. I ran my hand through, raising the powder, and took two heaping hand-fulls, tying them in my bandana, tucking it in the bottom of my shoulder bag. Ric smiled as if for a photo, waved to the house across the street, closed the chest, and we carried it to the station wagon. I cautioned "You know we're being set-up for a bust. With the kids in the car, you could lose them. Come on, the acid's got to be bad". He shook his head "Government's been experimenting with it for years as a way of controling the enemy. They want it to get to Sky River. Good acid makes crowd control much easier than bad".

Some thirty miles South of Portland, a free two-day festival call Vortex was opening on the weekend in McIver State Park, heavily hyped as *"Just like Sky River"*. And a Labor Day pop festival, also free, scheduled for next weekend in Portland, 30,000 predicted to attend. Rumor was Oregon Governor Tim McCall readily sanctioned the backers and permits, hoping to draw away from us. Ric was delighted with so much publicity, that so many would be drawn to the area, and not the least worried, for Sky River had a solid reputation, even if everyone went to the others, they would come to Washougal, our tickets were good for all eleven days, and we had the Youngbloods. Government machinations aside, we had broken no law, were on private land and had a signed sales contract, there was nothing authorities could legally do to stop us having a party on our own property, unless we got foolish. And so far, only one incident, someone spray-painted site directions on the main road through Washougal. Arnie painted them out, no charges were brought.

Chapter Eleven

SKY RIVER LIVES

High noon radio news, Nixon had cancelled his trip to Portland, no explanation. We knew it was us, affecting the highest office in the land felt deliciously power-full. But Ric was fuming, Vice President Agnew also cancelled, we had no one to march on. Mark called from command central with other news, and Ric made a final statement to the press *"Actions by officials to halt Sky River will not be effective. Some road signs at locations given as guide posts to the site have been removed by officers. It will not work. We put people at the important places to make sure everyone knows the way"*. Ric and I tied a tarp tightly over the station-wagon's loaded roof-rack. He took the wheel. Keely corralled the Littles into the back-seat. I took the middle. And Nick pulled infront of us, blocking the way. Taking my knapsack I stepped out on the street. Ric and Keely too, on my either side. I asked "Please, just go. I can handle this". Smiling, Nick backed-up to let them. Ric made his hand into a gun, shot three times at Nick's head, looked him dead in the eyes, smiled, and then started the engine. Keely did the same, and got in, door wide-open, insisting "Come on Shoshy, go with us". I wanted to but shook my head "No. It's okay. Really. I'll hitch". Her face pinched in doubt "You sure". I did not want this to be their problem right now, a far too cavalier "Yes" escaping my mouth. She was upset "Okay. Fine". My stomach fell as she slammed the door in frustration. Littles said nothing, and I knew it was right keeping Nick away from them. Ric slowly drove away. Littles furiously waving at me from the rear window.

I made my self tall, feet apart, hands open, quivering inside, counting long breaths, in, hold, out, hold, in, hold, out, waiting to see what this was, suddenly thankful the curtain opened across the street. Nick took time finishing his smoke, flicking the butt at my feet "You're such a fox. I thought you might need a lift to Sky River". Resistance would only heighten this, my bells screaming like a grade-school fire alarm, and oh shit, having inhaled Sandoz-mist there was a hint of tin foil in my mouth. I said flatly "Do now". Walking deliberately round the front of the bus, I climbed onto the passenger seat, put my pack between us, having lived in this vehicle, it felt and smelled like an old friend.

A three hour ride to Washougal, I saw no hallucinations, and quietly appreciated acid's perspective, saying nothing as Nick droned a measured calm hypnotic monotone, never looking my way "I'm rich now... You can have it all if you just stop this stupid game and marry me... I forgive you... Forgive everything you've done to me... We can move anywhere you want... I'll buy you any house you want... Do whatever you say... I promise I won't be jealous anymore... I promise you can work if you want too... I promise you can have friends... Men friends and I won't get jealous... I promise... I'll stay away from my Folks... They hate Jews, you know, that Christ killer thing... I promise...". This composure instead of the usual volatile frightened me. He seemed robotic, possessed, I kept still, soft, unclenching when I noticed my jaw stiffen, measuring my breath. One hour South on I- 5, passing Olympia, the State Capitol Rotunda a majesty, Nick waned silent and lit a joint, I seemed properly subjugated. Still it was not done, breathing became the language, a way for him to get inside me. My head leaning against the window, watching pavement speeding by I consider opening the door and just falling-out. Any talk perilous for the conquered, I knew I had to risk "Can I turn on the radio". He did, maintaining control. Oregon Governor McCall was on the defensive, giving an interview, standing-by his controversial decision to approve Vortex *"I was hoping it would attract young people away from Portland and the planned anti-Legion demonstrations. Nixon and Agnew were expected to be a big draw, that's why they aren't coming. And Vortex is working, it's sold 4,000 tickets already. The Peoples Army Jamboree is gathering at Delta Park by downtown Portland, to organize the anti-Legion march. There are less that 100 of them but with people from Sky River there'll be plenty".* He warned *"There's a heavy State preparedness for coming events. Four truck loads of Guardsmen, a first-aid car and four jeeps have been moved into Washington Park in downtown Portland. Guardsmen and police are ready to respond in heavy numbers to any clash between protesters and Legionnaires, and 6,000 more Guardsmen are available on short call".* This sounded like war to me, Hydra was known for its non-violence, I risked "Wow, major over-kill". Nick in his mind-drilling tone "You're crazy you know, living with those Commies. They'll get you killed. I should take you home where it's safe". I would not again speak unless spoken too, he wasn't driving all the way to Sky River just to give me a lift, I could smell the weed, he was going to sell his wares, this was a business trip. Nick believed I would come back to him, that I must be playing hard-to-get, that money would ultimately seduce me. He could not hear anything I had to say, it was beyond him that I was fine on my own, he had not changed at all and I was certain he never would. Suddenly my advantage was obvious, he did not know me, but I knew him, the oppressed need know everything about the oppressor to survive, while the oppressor need only know how to control with fear. While I had plenty of reverent concern, fear did not immobilize me anymore, allowing for moves he would not expect. This was poker, and I had a good hand, held by the virgin deep inside that Nick had never been able to touch, only love could reach in that far. I sat, waiting, quieting my breath, heart unexpectedly breaking for his shipwrecked-soul. He spoke first "You got any smokes". Reaching in my bag I fingered the bandana, mind leaping, he was a connoisseur and Sandoz impossible to get, if the FBI considered it good crowd control, it should work on him. I offered "Kool menthols". He smiled "Yeah. Light me one". I obeyed, lit another for myself, put the pack back in my bag, undid the bandana, collected two tabs and offered them palm-up "Sandoz". He took both with a snide little chuckle as if reading my mind, and dropped them into his shirt pocket. This temporary advantage did not fool me, he was suffering, and I would have comforted him if he were any other human being on earth, but I no longer felt responsible for his feelings.

Finding Sky River was easy, signs were back in place, and there were cops every 50 yards taking down license plates. I was not worried about being busted, but the corners of Nick's mouth winced at every one. I counted 53 cars lining the sides of Keep Road, dead-ending at the big gate to Edwin Tate's 160 acre farm. People sunning on car-hoods, lawn chairs, passing pipes and bottles, playing guitar, harmonica, juice harp, kazoo, ukulele, banjo, waiting for tomorrow morning's open. Arnie had the gate, and on recognizing Nick came round to the passenger side "You okay Shoshy". I nodded "Yes I am". He swung half the gate open to let us pass. Nick coasted the dirt road, parking at command central. I snatched my stuff, hopped-out and went inside. All faces turned, startled, who in the fuck are you. Recognizing no one I asked "Is Mark here or Ric". An older, strait looking man stood "Ric drove by not long ago with his family. Mark's walking some wire down to hook-up a phone line to the stage". Wanting to be light, nimble, I stashed my pack in the bedroom, used the bathroom, and seeing Nick no where, started down the road, following the wire, the dirt worn to pastry flour. Nick materialized by my side, smiling as if we were the happiest of couples, droning his monotone, spinning a faerie-story of thee and me and how good it will be, invading, occupying, hypnotizing, till cresting the ridge, the sight of Sky River wiped it from my mind.

Gentle sloping hills of thick evergreens on three sides, framing good pasture-land maybe 300 level yards to the stage, 100 beyond, dropping not too steep to the River. Light-show towers rising high from the floor of this natural amphitheater. It was pure perfection, and I was surprised, delighted how well organized we were. All my life I day-dreamed of a belonging place, where walking down any street felt safe, everyone resounding a welcome hello. My Folks had the dream too in moving us to the Golden Ghetto, but growing-up there was a merciless nightmare. One 8th-grade Saturday afternoon, at home, enjoying the whole place to my self, lying on my bed reading Ayn Rand, Bully-neighbor-girl's Mother was suddenly in my house, at my bedroom door, puffy-face shining madd, unkempt wire-hair, a bear of a woman roaring something about a basketball, her bulk taking-up the doorway. I scrambled far as I could to the window, bed between us in what had become a very small space. She came round after me. I flew over the top, out the front door leaving it wide, and without thinking across the street to a neighbor's house, rapping hard on the front door, hurting my knuckles, begging "Let me in. Pleease let me in. She's gona kill me". The door never opened, only eyes peering down through the peep-hole, and a stern voice "Go 'way". No welcome for the frightened 12 year old who walked to school every morning with her daughter. I could see Bully's Mom coming out my door, and she saw me. I took-off down the middle of streets, passing doors I could not knock on, they hated my kind, every one seemed as forbidding, legs turning to rubber at the corner, I climbed the very public Lutheran Church stairs and sat there at the top, pretty sure Bully's Mom could not run this far, and if she could, someone would see, witness the murder. Thinking how it did not matter at all her being my kind, she was no more an ally than Peep-hole across the street. I sat there, lost, not knowing where to go, my privacy, safety gone, in my own room in my own home. Sky River could be the day-dream, being built before my eyes, I began humming *The Yellow Rose of Texas*, gliding the gentle slope to the stage, pastry flour billowing every foot-fall, my head full, there was no room for Nick.

Mark's legs dangled over the stage lip, 100 feet wide, 40 feet deep, six feet high to make it hard for the audience to climb on, and not yet done. He was tearing black cloth into three-inch strips, gave me a questioning look, turned dagger-eyes on Nick, and jumped down, hugging me with real affection "Glad you made it. Keely an Ric're backstage setting-up camp. They didn't know if you'd show. Look, people're in the way of construction, so I thought I'd get security started. Pick out some likely suspects to watch the stage, help stop the interference". He held up the strips and smiled "Black arm bands. Should make it official don't you think". I did not have an idea "Good plan. What can I do to help". Mark handed me the cloth "Security's all yours, I have a stage to finish". Taking the red bandana from his neck, he tied it round my right arm "Okay, this officially designates you chief security pig". And lightly placing hands on my shoulders, holding my eyes with his "Look, you got lots a friends all around here. Don't hesitate". He kissed my forehead "I know your gift for improve Shoshy. You'll be a great head hog". Pointing to the phone on stage next to a paper bag "Okay, so all you have to do ta call command central is dial 555. Oh, an there's more cloth in the bag, other colors too if you need 'em". Nick was backing away. Mark spoke louder "555 to the command center. I'll be there for a while, someone will answer. Or you can just yell for help". He faced Nick "Remember Shoshy, don't hesitate if you need anything". Walking backward, daggers fixed on Nick "Any thing". He ran up the dirt road.

Nick was on me immediately, accusing, Mark and I were fucking, in his mind all he need do to make it true was say so. Classic Nick logic, because males can not be friends with a sub-species, every interaction must come to fucking. I knew any explaination or defense, any response would only serve to confirm the indictment in his mind, even so I needed to speak against his will "This is why you and I can never be anything ever again". If he heard he did not let on, accusing, demanding details. Clarity washed through me like a cool river, drowning him out, Mark and I had a better relationship than I ever had with Nick, exactly because we were friends, man-woman friends. It was so simple, I saw my self walking down a hall of mirrors, each reflecting the others image, all the way back to the very core of what I understood relationship to be. I had not yet become friends with my Dad, we had more of a parent-child peace agreement, Grampa died before I was old enough to really make friends, I could never be with my Brothers, Older had that first-born-male entitled notion, which included the right to control me, which I did not find at all friendly, plus his degrading ideas of females made any friendship impossible, Little Brother was heading in the same direction, just too young yet. In high school hormones ruled relationships. Casey had intended to rule me. And though Josh and I came close, I could see he intended too. Jeffree and I had begun friendship, and Arthur. And Hydra men, chauvinists yes, yet all but Arnie, and maybe even Arnie were slowly evolving in the right direction. Ric, Mark, Bear had come to appreciate my merit, and I would not, did not have to settle for less. What a glorious clear evelation, and this time I gave Nick no credit just because he was here, realizing he did not even know something had happened, that I learned this without him, that my freedom had always depended on this exact realization, that I could go on from here without wondering did he hold some key I must go back for. I was free to go. Still, his menace intensified in direct proportion to my pulling away, just as Ida Rose had warned. Walking the length of the stage twice, looking to recruit bystanders for security, I tried to face him down, using the public as protection, demanding in a big voice "You have to leave me alone". Everyone looked. Using public perception too, he laughed like it was the punchline of a joke, and resumed his droning. The sound had begun to bore into my brain.

Only concessionaires and construction workers and Hydra were suppose to be on site. Maybe one-hundred others loitered the stage and grounds, they snuck, conned, muscled their way passed Arnie, or climbed the fences. Most were stoned and getting in the way. I wanted to pick those who would not go too power-mad, knowing I could not tell much with eyes beyond my own prejudices, I would let the acid help. It drew me to a six-foot-three biker, 250 pound in black leathers, Gypsy Jokers embroidered on the back of his vest, in-part because Nick would not mess with him. I came close, looking-up "Pardon me. Hi. I'm from Hydra. We're putting on the festival. Would you be interested in helping with security". He had a charming smile and perfect white teeth "At your service ma'am". Offering me the cigar-size joint curled in his finger. I took it, wanting to show Nick my liberty, thinking this is so fat, it must be home-grown, inhaling, I coughed my lungs out, getting too high too fast for the situation. Biker smiled mischievously at my miscalculation "Premium bud". Fortunately I was good at maintaining, returning the cigar with a sarcastic "Thanks". I now knew he was the kind to spike my beer with bad acid and hang round to enjoy the loss of control, the kind I would rather have on my side. I croaked "So what's your name". "Garrity ma'am". I put my hand out "Shoshannah, nice to meet you". He took it and kissed the back. I could not help be intrigued by his manners and perfect teeth, so contrary to his clothes, pulling my hand free, I showed him a black-band "Let me tie this round your arm, make it official". He offered his left. Needing some power between us "I'll be giving out twelve black bands total. Pick your own partner, and tear this in half. Security will be done in twos. And, we'll be wearing them on right arms". Willing, he offered his. Tying the cloth in a bow round that huge bicep I continued "I'll be the only red band. But if I'm not here, you're the boss okay". Nodding he smiled "Okay". I smiled too "The main thing right now, the stage and light show towers have to get built, and too many people are in the way". I looked into his face "So keep them away, gently, okay". Instantly defensive, folding arms cross his chest "Yes ma'am". I reached in my shoulder bag for a smoke to bring me down some, and fingering Sandoz spilled in the bottom, offered him one to seal the agreement. He genuflected. I place the white tablet on his tongue.

Choosing seven men and four women, telling each to pick a partner, and if I could not be found, go to Garrity. They already knew who he was. I posted three the length of the stage, one at each light show tower, and asked the rest to spread-out along concession row, having all swear on a hit of Sandoz there would be no violence, this was the beginning of a new community and we did not need pigs for police. Garrity worked, Nick faded away, and I took a cautious stroll through the business district. What a spectacle, American flags, Viet Cong flags, peace symbols, free Huey Newton, power-to-the-people banners flying from every store front, most still under-construction, most already doing business. The Country Doctor collective calling themselves the Open Door Clinic was open, and the Drug Store. The Grodes had a kissing booth, the SDS a candy store called Munchies, both donating all profit to the purchase of Sky River and the Seattle Conspiracy Defense Fund. Corn-on-the-cob ten-cents, corn-dogs hot-dogs fifteen-cents, soup twenty-cents, spaghetti, lasagna, tamales, bagels, fried chicken, soft drinks, popcorn, candy cotton, water-melon, pipes, sunglasses, t-shirts, sandals, tarps, sleeping bags, blankets, toilet paper. I knew some, introduced my self to the rest, explaining security as I went, improvising. If a vendor must leave their booth empty, alert the neighbors to keep watch. If trouble, most likely a thief, I would be providing whistles to call the Black-bands. Vendors were to let Black-bands handle any trouble, I reassured they would be posted somewhat evenly. Thieves, no matter how petty, would be escorted out the gate permanently, absolutely no rough stuff. Someone gets too high and freaks, gets hurt, over-doses, take them to the Open Door Clinic whether they want to or not. I encouraged everyone to get their drugs tested at the Drug Store before swallowing. Any fighting no matter why or who starts it, both sides are out the gate permanently, no exceptions. All Black-bands swore on their honor. My plan was so straight-forward I thought it had a chance. As I walked the nearly-done fence separating backstage from the crowd, I could feel Nick's eyes on me.

Keely and the Littles were rimming a fire-pit in smooth river rocks. Ric and Bear raising the tent. They were relieved to see me safe. I reported on security and whistles, saying nothing of Nick. Ric really liked the plan. Bear thought "We might need a separate security team for backstage". He was right. Ric handed me a hundred dollars in fives "Here, go get what you want. I need the station-wagon, so take Mark's car, up at the command center". I found the bag of extra cloth still on stage, all yellow, found Garrity, his troops firmly in-hand, and could not help smiling at how power had shaken-out, all Black-bands had torn their cloth for a partner, Garrity's still in the original bow. I asked him please spread word, Black–bands are front-stage security only. There will be Yellow-bands backstage.

Mark stood in the smoke-filled command center, impatiently listening to the corn-dog concessionaire refusing to understand, since he paid 200 dollar for the booth, and got only three free festival tickets, how come he has to buy tickets for the other six employees who came with him. Mark was matter-of-fact calm and firm, all for-profits agreed when signing-up, three free employee tickets. No one needs nine in an eight-by-eight booth. The Country Doctor and Drug Store were services, Munchies and the kissing booth donating everything to the Seattle Conspiracy Defense Fund and purchase of Sky River. All for-profits agreed to three free tickets period. He ended by inviting me into the bedroom-office and closing the door, amused how many vendors tried to wangle free tickets for all their friends. I told him the whistle plan, the Black-bands, Garrity, and needing Yellow-bands as backstage security, handing over the sack of cloth. He promised to pick some good people, and gave me his car keys. Starting the engine, I noticed Nick's bus was gone. Arnie confirmed he came through half-hour ago, and opened the gate. I felt a watchful optimism.

Mark just bought his ride, a 1950 pea-soup-green Chevy 4-door, $200, that burned a quart of oil every tank of gas. Slow-cruising the Camas business district, tail-pipe smoking, this unsuspecting three-block town no more ready for us than any, I parked infront of the Sprouse Reitz and went in. A really pretty woman my age, yellow cotton sundress and red canvas apron, keen golden-brown eyes, freckles, and long straight hair matching her dress, stood back of the counter, shifting foot-to-foot as she cleared her throat, asking could she help me. Whistles, ribbon, bandanas, scissors, squirt-guns. She seemed relieved and bid me follow, inquiring why so many whistles. I spun the story of Sky River, lighting her imagination as she helped me count 100 blue bandanas, 39-cents each, to be worn by vendors round their neck, 100 stainless steel whistles with rings, 15-cents each, to be tied onto bandanas with 100 yards of satin ribbon at 10-cents each, and three squirt guns. She rang the sale. I placed a yellow Sky River ticket and hit of Sandoz atop the cash. Eyes darting to the man at the back of the store, secreting the acid and ticket into her sundress-pocket before making change, she helped me carry bags to the car, whispering "Thank you soooo much. I'll try an come. Be really careful around here. I'm the only Freak in town". The usual small-town, anyone with imagination was a Freak, if you dare fly your colors, you will be punished. I suspected there were more like her in-hiding "Maybe if you show your self a little, you might find some friends." She smirked "I work for my Dad and he would kill me".

Cars clogging Keep Road, I wound through to the gate, Arnie and a Black-band reluctantly selling tickets, letting people in. It was not a good idea, no music till tomorrow night, nothing for them to do, the atmosphere already rest-less, and Arnie no longer had a choice. Parking at the command center, I went in to return keys, finding a woman-girl with the most beautiful electric-blue eyes, to my surprise she was in-charge, I could not believe it, a woman in-charge, asking did she know where was Mark. Words pushed through tight lips, I guessed her way of being in-charge, uptight, brusque, condescending, Mark and Ric went to the Camas Inn to welcome bands, and dismissing, she turned away. I liked her nerve, pocketed the key, retrieved my pack, gathered bags from the car and merged into the down-hill stream. Progress had grown beyond the bounds-of-time, tents blooming like mushrooms, Santi-cans functional, water trucks filling the 1800 gallon blue plastic swimming-pool we were using as a reservoir, stairs to the stage were done, Dr.Zarkov had most of their equipment up the wooden ladders onto the light-show tower platforms, miles of snaky black electrical cable tamed in silver duct-tape, Black-bands solidly in control, and rather bad-tempered, as they were not allowed backstage. Mark had decided only those needing to be backstage should, only Yellow-bands. And Garrity, smiling, smoking his fat joint, clearly enjoying his clout, leaning against the unfinished backstage gate, had a Yellow-band tied in-a-bow beneath the Black. I stowed my pack in the tent. Keely was roasting hot-dogs on the campfire. Littles wound-up and ravenous, demanded to see what's in the Sprouse Reitz bags. Keely gave me an I would truly appreciate a diversion grimace. On seeing the bandanas and whistles, Lance wanted one of each, and so too Robby and Scottie. I bargained, if they help me tie ribbons to whistles, there was a surprise. Quick and careful Lance measured an arms-length and cut the ribbon, careful too Robby threaded one end through the whistle-ring and tied a knot, and Scottie brought it to me. I folded the bandanas, threaded on the ribbon and knotted them to slip over-heads, and when near done, and the Littles could sit no more, I laid the squirt-guns infront of me. Lance took orange, the biggest. Robby green. Scottie delighted to have yellow no matter it was least, and ran after the bigger Littles to find the nearest water spigot, deluge imminent, war was on.

Vendors, speakers, amps, bands coming in trailers, campers, vans. One Hand Clapping's yellow school bus parked thirty-feet from our tent, I thought how the Sweet Sisters machinations were impossible to escape. Bandanas in bags, I went delivering. The power was finally turned on concession row, twinkling in the twilight, a humming peaceful community, and the ease which every one accepted my authority, I found no need for brusque. Still, the absurdity, the responsibility of being law here made me squirm, Sky River was hanging on a thin code of honor, I had to assume, presume principle would endure, that my expectations were not as high as the crowd. We had all promised not to open the acid chest till things were well established, I was completely down from inhaling the powder, and could feel an electric contact high, plainly Sandoz was out big-time. I hoped the FBI was right, good acid = good crowd control.

Delivering done, every bandana, I was beginning to relax when Nick slipped in by my side, as if he belonged to me, his vibe a glaring contrast to the peaceful hum, pupils pinned, speeding, talking ventriloquist through a fixed smile "You think you're protected with all your fucking lovers here, but they don't give a shit about you. They don't know you like I do. I saw you give that chic at Sprouse Reitz something extra. You can't hide anything from me. I'll fuck with your head like all your lovers fuck your cunt. No one will ever know. And if you bitch, they'll just think you're a fucking Bitch to a nice guy like me. You're my SoulMate. I own you. We'll get married. I'll buy you a car. I'll buy you a house…". His voice a red-hot ball bering rolling round my brain, and once rolling, poison insists, you will have this conversation whether you want to or not. But he could no longer occupy me, anger had proclaim my freedom, I headed for the security of backstage. Nick knew how private I liked to be, how pride kept me from revealing, and counting on this, assured Garrity "Hey Man. It's okay, she's my ol'lady". I was beyond glad for Garrity, and understood without doubt there was no conscience governing Nick, he could and would use any story, his end justifying his means. Lance's wise words - tell everyone and they'll know - flashed neon in my mind, embracing the loss of face as head of security I let Garrity know "It's not okay. I'm not anyone's ol'lady. In-fact, this guy's a bully and I don't want him any where near me". Nick shot me with how dare you break the rules of the game. These rules were his, I never agreed to in the first place, and would not play his way anymore, committing the ultimate unforgivable sin, exposure. Rage, surprise, hurt shaded his face, he said nothing as Garrity ordered two Black-bands, take this guy, walk him up the hill, escorted him and if he has a vehicle out the gate, and make sure they know, do not let him in again. I turned crimson being cause of commotion, taking up time, embarrassing, making myself the focus of attention, awed by Garrity's unquestioned, enthusiastic use of power.

Though gone, Nick won anyway, an emotional vampire, he sucked me dry, fatigue, fainting, I could only lay down where I stood. Garrity's huge arms scooped me up and took me to Hydra's tent, the biggest dog in town, I was grateful having him on my side. Alone in camp, exhausted through the other-side to anxious, Nick's eyes still glaring in my head, his monotone looping round-and-round, owning me as I walked round the camp fire. I had to stop this now, searching my shoulder bag for a smoke, a joint, something, anything to interrupt, Sandoz sticking to my fingers, no, think again, yes, the cigarettes are in you backpack, I went into the tent where the Littles were sleeping and pulled the Marlboros out along with Ida Rose's book. Opening the Pink Elephant by the campfire light,

I could hear her clear quick voice reading to me – *What an existential nightmare. A creator who could not explain or even control his own creation! At that point, it is hoped, some species wiser than we, are willing to take over. Maybe somewhere in the cosmos a bell will ring and someone will begin to notice us. Let us hope it will not be a creator who cannot explain his own creation or control his product. One fun-house such as ours should be enough for any universe.* I absolutely loved her fearless point of view, totally un-afraid God would hear, remembering her tell me - *Just one drop of love or levity will shake a million tons of evil to its very foundation.* I could feel the warmth of her bubble-gum pink aura reach in and neutralize the poison. Anger worked for a moment, but one drop of her love and no more room for Nick, I was again in my own possession, hearing my own voice in my own mind. It was amazing how there was no time or space in the mind, for in just a blink I could travel from here to four years back, standing in the synagogue, broken from Grampa dying, calling on Yahweh to fulfill His promise. This God who intervened for the Jews with such dramatic super-natural miracles, bringing plagues, parting the Red Sea, giving the ten commandments, and six-thousand years later the Jews were still the scapegoat. Having found only silence from Him, I knew even more right now that my life was up to me, that I was by default my own god, creator of my own life, responsible for my own days, and I was determined not to make it a fun-house. I went back into the tent and slipped into my bag.

Littles sweet-snoring-harmony in their sleeping bags woke me. Outside had bloomed in tepees, tapestries, acoustic music, campfire smoke and marijuana floating on the moonlight. What a beautiful night, I washed my face at the water spigot, and aching with hunger went to find food. The stage was done, wiring not. Garrity, who seemed to never sleep, re-ported no problems and no Nick. As I walked though the backstage-gate, Connie from the Country Doctor was coming in, on her way to their van to get high, she invited me along. Such an unpretentious gem, working to make healthcare available for those who could not afford, the one woman who stood with me when Warthog published the chauvinistic pig list, I overheard her defending me more than once, scolding, save your vim and vitriol for the real enemy, Shoshannah is risking her personal freedom for the cause, she respected my commitment, my work and my friendship, and I hers. It was a delicious warm evening that comes only in August, Connie left the van sliding door opened, back seats had been removed, the floor covered in green shag carpet, we sat cross-legged on either side of a large glass hookah. She struck a match, just as Nick dove-in the door, knocking me back, knocking my wind out, holding me down, the Kabar blade just under my chin, growling in low steal "If I can't have you, no one can". I went deaf from lack of air and closed my eyes, strangely calm and amused by the cliché, thinking yes he struck me once before, still I did not suppose he would intentionally slit my throat, it would definitely end the game, he did not want that. Then he was off me, and I could breathe, opening my eyes. Mark held the Kabar, Garrity had Nick on his knees, left hand wrenched behind his back, threatening "Gimme a reason asshole. How did you get by me". I heard my voice as if far away "Not his hand, he's a musician". Garrity released, taking the scruff and back of his shirt "Yes ma'am". This time he personally took him out. Nick made no sound. Mark, tender big brother I never had, hugged an arm round my shoulders "Whoa, that was way too heavy. You're not safe here Shoshy. Go stay in Camas. Use Hydra's room, no one's there". I shoved hands deep in my pockets, pulling-out his car keys "No, I can't let him rule my life". Feeling like this was happening to some one else, dissociated, and resigned Nick could steal into here or the Camas Inn, what difference did it make, he was my incubus, my responsibility, I did not want to burden Mark one second longer, or anyone, I did not want to be thought of as a problem. Connie slipped her quivering arm through mine "I can hardly believe that really happened. It was so fast". Suddenly humiliation burned my skin, I needed to disappear, apologizing to her, and Mark, and those attracted by the commotion, I walked away. Passing One Hand Clapping's tent to Hydra's, unpacked my magic whistling teapot, filling it at the spigot, I put it on the fire-grate, poking embers, and finally present in my body, the seriousness of what happened quaking in the dark. Semi-sleepwalking, Robby came out of the tent and sat by me, wanting a drink of water, feeling my shudders, asking "How do clams walk". His reaction let go fear's grip, I knew he did not like me or anyone to, still I hugged him close, and fetched the water, and carried him back to bed. For me, two cups of Linden Flower tea laid me out on my bag to a sweet-snoring lullaby.

August 28th, 1970, opening day a pink dawn, 5AM, Keely and the Littles rustled me come-with to the river and bathe. Not yet rested, and in surprising good humor, I opened a carton of Dr.Bronners Organic Peppermint Soap, 100 bars donated by Cook's Health Food Store in Bellevue so bathing in the river would not polute with chemicals, I put six in my shoulder bag. Most everyone sleeping, I left my waffle-stompers at the top of the hill, and followed the zig-zag trail down. Naked sprites bobbed in pools of slow water. Longing to wash-away my ordeal in peppermint foam, stubborn modesty precluding, I perched on a long flat rock next to a hand-written sign - *do not go beyond this point our neighbors are armed and dangerous* – eased my feet in the cold liquid, and handed-out soap. Across the river, a lone two-story log house with cathedral picture windows, an older man and woman sitting on the wrap-around deck, and in the deck's under-shadow, one uniformed cop and two young men in gray suits, with cameras and binoculars. Raging from her lounge chair to the deck rail, the woman leaned as far as possible, shrieking at the top of her range "Get the hell out of the river you Freaks". A spontaneous chorus "Take it off and join us". She hurried inside, the man laughing at her. There was talk of a mile long car-line waiting for Sky River's 8AM opening, and young men in dark suits sitting in lawn chairs along the route, with portable tape recorders taking license plate numbers. We never seriously discussed killing Nixon, the FBI was certain we had real plans, that the festival was our straw-man, yet they had not arrested or charged any of us, and Nixon cancelled, and Agnew, and the Suits were reduced to voyeurs with high-powered glasses. I did not hate them, or the cops, for I had come to appreciate the passion that drives anyone no matter which side to take sides, respecting their heart-felt belief, and saved the hate for mercenaries.

Having given-out the soap, I took a Marlboro from my bag, fingering Sandoz, an acid trip would dilute the strain Nick left on me, mental and physical, things seemed to be running smooth, I placed a tablet on my tongue, considered the consequences, and when no alarm-bells rang, swallowed, and wended the switch-back path back to the top. My shoes were gone, my only pair, I looked where I left them again and again, wanting to have misplaced them, and not have some cold-hearted thief afoot, tin foil mouth announcing a soft even ride-up so typical of good acid, shoes and thieves would have to wait. I went for the teapot, and let the Sweet Sisters Fate take me to One Hand Clapping's camp. Cultivating the campfire, Celtic earth-mother, waist-length thick straight golden-orange hair parted in-the-middle, wearing a beautifully embroidered traditional white cotton Mexican wedding dress, I like her right away. Colleen, Erik's wife invited me sit and heat my teapot on the coleman stove, fetching two delicately painted teacups from a wicker picnic-basket, oh goodie a tea party. The sun beginning to show, warming the air, I could smell bacon and weed on little breezes, banjos, recorders, harmonicas, all sorts of hand drums, a communal band bringing in the morning, soft harmony, quantum spirit fledging, shared vision. Joy rolled off my cheeks, Sky River was political to the bone, peace and love counter-culture manifest before my eyes nose and ears, an alchemical melding of class, customs, brown red white yellow black, the mysterious marriage, universal desire to get along, no longer a dream. I looked at my bare feet, there was vermin in town too, some Misdemeanor had stolen my shoes. Colleen touched my arm "You all right". Reaching in my bag, I offered her a Sandoz "Yes, I am. So, do you want some candy little girl". Taking the white tab, reading Sandoz, she popped it in her mouth "Wow. Thank you". We enjoyed a comfortable silence, and each others company. Stepping from the yellow bus, Erik was inches shorter than Colleen, yawning, stretching, lizard eyes half-open, recognizing me he stiffened. Except for new gadgets, I thought past-lives must be little changed from present ones, unless considerable personal introspection initiated some growth. Erik plainly had been a Viking and still was, champion to Odin or Thor - *Everyday they ride out into the court or field and fight until they cut each other in pieces. This is their pastime. But when meal time comes they recover from their wounds and return to feast in Valhalla.* Sure he would say no to anything from me, trying anyway in the spirit of Sky River, I respectfully offered "Does One Hand Clapping need anything". His grin disingenuous "Nope, we're just fine thank you". Joey came out next, and Colleen was not enough to civilize his hostility "Shit. What's she doing here". I had my fill, moving-on without delay. Joey's darkness felt like Nick, when I came down, I would take Mark up on a room at the Inn.

This high had no intrusive hallucinations, more a fluid innocent whispering children's tale, tripping campfire to campfire, joining the circles. A flock of Charismatic Christians reading the Bible aloud, I set my teapot on their fire-grate and listened quietly, pouring tea, pondering what God would have to be for me to believe-on like them. As far as I could see, Christianity split-off evil from the whole, personified it as the Devil, so they had some one to blame for the things God could not possibly do, leaving Jesus all good and perfect and impossible to live-up too. Splitting-off anything from the whole creates exaggerated natures. This Lucifer they called the brightest and most beautiful morning star, who supposedly fell along with a third of heaven, seemed to be an essential ingredient in the whole, like salt and lemon to Tequila, sugar to rhubarb, and when mixed-in it softens the harsh, and strengthens, even sweetens the whole, but then to be whole Christians would have to take responsibility for their own shadow instead of projecting it on a convenient Satan, or Jews, and I did not see that happening. I thought their version of God was not quite as jealous as Jewish Yahweh, and far more maimed and blood-thirsty, eating the body, drinking the blood, cannibalizing to cleanse, becoming one with the Savior. I understood needing something physically impossible, such as a virgin birth, the mysterious lure, and it wasn't the first time this metaphor had been used, per say Athena born full-grown from her father's head, but come on, believing it actually happened. And then this vicarious atonement, privately confess to the priest, eat God, drink blood, and saved again, you can go do the same thing tomorrow, as long as you confess, eat more body, drink more blood, never having to directly admit or make restitution to those you sinned against, only your priest knows and he's sworn to secrecy. And if you happened to be privileged with wealth or connection you can purchase dispensation. To me vicarious redemption was - how can you possibly believe that - unless you were spoon-fed young on virgin birth, and raised from the dead, and dying for someone elses sins, prepare the way and a person will swallow anything. Ida Rose said that we were absolutely not to pay another person's karma, for it would take away their opportunity to pay it down for themselves. But to me, the most insidious of all, Christian heaven, relegating earth and purgatory as mere stop-overs on the way to life-everlasting, trivializing human suffering to beside the point, just blindly follow the dogma, don't ask questions, bide your time, death will take you now or eventually after purgatory to a better place, and those who are not baptized, those who are not going with you, those who do not believe what you do, well they don't matter cause they won't be in everlasting Heaven with you. These were my first Born-agains, they seemed genuine, trying to break with Church tradition, be more like the original Christians. I smelled a cloying beneath their righteous virtue, and moved on.

Evening but a eddy in Sandoz-time, orange sherbet frosting on the horizon, having gently come down, waiting along with most of Sky River for the music to run in our veins, the Kady Grady Fly by Night Construction Company had not yet successfully hooked stage wiring into the power lines, and One Hand Clapping graciously marshaled on stage, waiving egos amps and microphones to play acoustic. Their first song, Get On Board, won every heart, they were christened the People's Band, Sky River was officially born. Looking for some nice homegrown, I stood at the verge of an impressive camp, pony-hide teepee fourteen-feet tall, flag pole flying a Jolly Roger, rugs, cushions on the grass, three fine-looking men lazing by the fire. Invited to sit, I put my teapot on the fire grate, settled cross-legged on a cushion, and considered the trappings, empty bottle of Wild Turkey, well-used carved Meerschaum nestled in a crumbled brick of weed, open packs of Camels, Kool Menthols, cigars, Doritos, graham crackers, marshmallows, Hershey bars, pepperoni, beef jerky, and guitars. I asked "Is the brick designer". The rugged blonde who bid me sit chuckled "No. It's just good ol' Montgomery Ward gooz". I loved that he got me, and bargained Sandoz for some smoke. He sat-up smiling. Yikes, it was Delroy Bogave, monster lead-guitar for Moby Grape, I was duly impressed, turning into Miss Welcome Wagon ambassador, offering a room at the Inn compliments of Hydra. He smiled and said "Thank you, but we just fine here". I picked 2 leafy stems from the brick, and crumpled one into the Meerschaum. Delroy put a match to it, and playing duly impressed with my credentials, very formally introducing his bass player and drummer, this was Moongoose. And he the only celebrity not camping backstage, behind a guarded gate, or safe at the Inn. I admired his willing communality for such an important rock god, his adoring fans coming-up one by one, waiting to be invited close to his fire, paying homage, fawning, beseeching, demanding autographs on their arms, bare tops and bottoms, shirts, jackets, jeans, on their Moby Grape albums. And Delroy graciously obliged, patiently indulging his disciples. I could see they forced him into position, with such talent and fame maybe rightfully a victim of his own magic, he could not help presiding over court, somewhat detached, exempted from the certification needed by mere mortals, exemption that more often fosters aloof cynical contempt for the rules, especially when females throw themselves on the magnitude of his talent, feathers to the flame. Though I was a fan too, of the music not the musician, and he showed me no disrespect, I already had my fill musicians and could not chance being taken for feathers. Slipping the cellophane off my cigarette pack, I dropped in three Sandoz, put them down with the Meerschaum, took my teapot and the other stem of weed and moved on.

Security had eaten yeast and doubled, I did not recognize most Black-bands, while they all knew me as boss. Garrity reported things peaceful, and no Nick. Mark was on stage, maddly wiring with three more, optimistic there would soon be juice. Hungry and tired I asked when he might be going to the Inn. Smelling both arm pits, deciding he needed a shower, the others held their noses urging him go, they would finish soon. Walking arm-in-arm to camp, overcome in silence by what we had created here, gathering our packs from the tent, Keely and the Littles snoring sweet. I had been to one-day concerts, be-ins, this was my first festival, we were creating a permanent town, no others could claim this, Woodstock was beyond amazing, but every one had to physically go home. We climbed the hill against a swell of comers, our land was being settled. More inundating the gate, Arnie alone and in-control, we drove through smiling big, Sky River a triumph. Three-miles to Camas, I counted thirty cops.

Small town pristine, 1920's charming, three-stories, a full roof-patio, sixty rooms, the Camas Inn's open sunny atriuim furnished in white wicker, yellow and green floral cushions, bunches and bunches of fragrant daffodils cut-fresh from the gardens. Management was friendlier, more attentive than I expected, grateful for the business, and uneasy enough to have stationed uniformed off-duty cops in the lobby. Hydra's top floor room was one at the end of each hall with its own bathroom, the rest used a community one. Six tall windows, wooden floor, desk and swivel chair, phone for local calls, oak kitchen table and five chairs, brass and glass coffee-table, brown leather chairs on either side, and strangely for so large a room, one single bed against the wall. Mark offered me first shower, and called for three folding beds. I went in and locked the door. Finding him zonked, arms and legs sprawled over the sides of the small mattress, I sat down at the desk to empty three cigarettes, rolling them gently between my fingers and thumb, loosening the tobacco without breaking the paper, mixing in the leaves off the weed stem, repacking, tamping with a stick match. I lit one, and strolled bare-foot down the broad staircase, remembering there was a Nordstrom at Jantzen Beach Mall in Portland, having eleven dollars with me, I used the coffee-shop pay-phone to call Mom. Authorized on her account, I knew better than use it without asking. After hellos, the guilt-trip, it's been too long since I heard my Little Girls voice, and the quiz, where are you, what are you doing, and the inquisition, are you keeping your nose clean, and my try being believed futile as usual, I listened quietly, and asked could I charge a pair of shoes, promising to reimburse. She reminded in her of-course way, no need to ask or pay back, I trust you, after all I'm your Mother and I love you, and more inquisition. I had not called collect on purpose, when the operator warned time near spent, I simply had no more change, please don't worry about me, I love you and Dad, kiss him for me, honest I'm fine. She pressed, what kind of place was I that steals your shoes, the phone went dead, I did not have to explain what could not be. Yes there were scoundrels at Sky River, like those who threw rocks and paint on the Federal building during what should have been a peaceful anti-war demonstration, that's what grabs the attention, what your enemy counts on to steal away the message, undercover inflitrators. Co-operating newspapers, TV, radio, movies, Nixon and his brigands successfully cast us misguided, unwashed, sex-crazed, drug-crazed, violent, anti-American Pinko-Commies. I did not blame Mom falling for it, her generation trusted their leaders, trusted the news. I was pretty sure she thought herself a failure as a Mother in my case, for I was not safely married-off to a nice Jewish optometrist or dentist, and with kids. Her life more instinct-driven than mine, having a family came first, loving them the main thing to do, and for her perhaps so. I was fortunate to have a good one like her, but we had not matured beyond Mother always knows best, and when I challenged this in any way, it meant only one thing to her, she must have done something wrong and was a bad Mother. If I mentioned Ida Rose, she felt attacked, another elder female in my life unforgivable betrayal, defending with you don't look so well, are you eating right. If I talked politics, she wanted to know why I always put what she believes-in down. If I bought a book, it was how much did it cost, when did I get it, where, and not where generally but the exact location, and how a dress-shop used to be there, when did the bookstore go in, no interest in the content. These made my head-scream, I never wanted to answer one more, yet they were our ground, and I did not want to forfeit or hurt her. I wondered would there ever come time when she wanted to know who I was and not who she wanted me to be, or maybe, maybe she was just avoiding this altogether. In a real way, I had to thank her for imagining so little of me, powerful under-estimation to push hard against, impetus for lift-off.

Mark slept through cots delivered and set-up. I ate the Snickers bar I bought in the coffee-shop, closed the shades and crashed on one, into an old familiar dream. I am eight years old, standing on the street around the block from my house in Seattle's Mount Baker neighborhood, I have forgotten my skate-key. Every day after school I put on my saddle shoes and take my roller-skates there, because the street is newly black-topped, and on my worn metal wheels, this is smooth heaven. The street has somehow sunk down six-feet. Walking along the edge, peering down, something swaying in the shadows, a slender woman, wearing a long gown of fine sapphire wool, waist length wavy blue-black hair, milk skin, 25 carat ruby ring on the index finger of her left hand. She is stirring a large black caldron with a long-handle carved spoon made of some animal's leg-bone, reaching for a pinch of this or that from the carboys and gallipots lining one wall and full of what, she tastes, never swallowing, spitting onto the flagstone floor, the brew hisses, and evaporates in thin bursts of white smoke. Soon as I see her, she sees me and gives no further notice. The more she ignores me, the more I need her to see me, dancing along the concrete rim, far enough away, dangling a toe over, wiggling, taunting, captivated by her grace-full manner, too elegant for the wicked old Baba

Yaga, and too beautiful, my fear dissolving in wonder, her ruby-finger hand, fast as a lizard's tongue, darting, longer that it could possibly be, grabs my ankle, gripping strong and sure, her iridescent hazel-green eyes penetrating deep into mine, my heart stops, I am hers, she flashes a play-full smile and lets me go. Instantly I wake-up, always bewildered, her smile and smooth hands, still feeling the grip on my ankle, wondering why she let me go. Today, on waking, she is no longer a nightmare, for I just finished reading the Mysteries of Britain by the great 19th century psychic Lewis Spense, about the Druids before Arthurian legend and Christianity obscured them, and there I found my enigmatic witch, not an ugly old hag but the beautiful Celtic Ceridwen, Druid Goddess, venerable Crone who brews the caldron of inspiration that the bards and oracles drink from. It seemed in all the fairy-tales the old women were evil, ugly, used potions, ate children, the cannibal-witch of Hansel and Gretel, vain Queen of Sleeping Beauty, Cinderella's cruel step-mother, and assuming the one in my dream must be the same, I was always terrified having her so close, having her on my in-side. Now I knew she was no withering warted old hag, but the exquisite Ceridwen, play-full wise-woman, brewer of the inspiration, Goddess I should have been told of when young, because I could have, would have taken much needed succor, felt my own power-full Sorceress, the wise female I longed for and found so rare on the outside, She was in me all along. Thrilled, and at the same time angry with my own Mom, my Aunties, my Grandmas, all the Mothers who never passed the good stories onto their daughters, stories of confidence and beauty, not dread and ugly and loathing, making girls fear the in-escapable inevitable growing old. I felt an aching sorrow too, Mothers, Grandmothers, and theirs, almost certainly never knew these good stories either, and had their confidence stolen too. I could not, would not believe they did this on purpose, this age-old surreptitious conspiracy that cheats females of our rightful satisfaction, authority, wisdom, treasure that accumulates only with age, poisoning little girls with ugly witches, turning our world unintentionally on its head, making us fear our own authority and wisdom. According to Lewis Spense, a supplicant must be pure of heart to drink from Ceridwen's caldron. When a bard was not, and did anyway, the light was theirs for a long moment, then how great the darkness, for in them the brew turns slow poison, while the pure-of-heart grow wings. Ceridwen, the Mother of God, Sister of Isis, possessed the knowledge to spin spiritual straw into gold, and Spense gives the recipe for her brew. *The ingredients of Ceridwen's cauldron which, according to Taliesin, contained berries, the foam of the ocean, cresses, wort and vervain which had been borne aloft and kept apart from the influence of the moon. Then nine muses warmed it with their breathe.* It was full morning, Mark was gone, I took my shoulder bag and journal, went to the coffee-shop for fresh-baked cinnamon rolls and oolong tea, took them to the roof, and sat near the edge, toes dangling over, looking-out on the lush back gardens, realizing I was the brewer and the brew, that who I will love must be pure of heart. And I was beginning to understand how life imitated art, brew you life pure art and you will flow into it and live. And how, so many times I see something only after dreaming it, writing it, like Bonita-Kay taught me, distance has its effect.

Five New Magic Colors

I always tend to wander
Into the gates of big ideas
And as I'm passing through them
I always know I'm in for it

It's not an easy trip
These dragon size ideas
The struggle it to be big enough
To hold them all inside

And there are always consequences
To taking these inside
I know I won't be quite the same
Don't know how I'll come out

Then things that happen inside
Begin to happen outside

No longer just a wandering
I seem to know my way

Like a waking dream scene happening
I change from grub to gossamer
And if I wonder long enough
I can hear that still small voice

Finding words to tell the tale
Will anyone understand me
I know I look just like before
But everything has changed

The words I use – they sound the same
But the meanings have been altered
This big idea dragon flight
Leaves me at the edge of time

With five new magic colors
Weaving winding spinning
A coat of many colors
For a brave new muse's journey

And so life goes beyond the hero
Half monster and half muse
No longer in the Gorgons' grasp
They had to let me go

Now I am the magic
I belong to the age
With hands of the ancients
Black with rage

Using them with tenderness
Is the alchemy of it all

The treasure's in the work
Heart before my head

It takes so long to find my way
Because I make it up my self
With help from all my wanderings
And friends whose words I heed

But the only place my heart beats
Is in the present time
So I gather all my parts up
And begin to face the day

Why do I wander in these gates
And pay a price so strange
Adventure pure adventure
Seduces me my dear.

Cinnamon roll sticky and delicious, hunger soothed, I laid back on the warm roof, hands under my head, bathing in the soft sunshine, mind running so fast it would not let me still, sitting-up, lighting another weed-laced smoke, looking over the gardens, a young-woman came out the back door, and maybe feeling my gaze looked up. It was her, the one I saw across the street from Rachel's apartment that snowy acid-night, I motioned her come. Smiling she nodded yes. Amanda Boggs, known as Gretchen Fetchin-Fine, we were instant Sisters, carrying on a conversation begun long ago, our struggles akin, the men in them similar, and yet life had given us such contrary points of view. Gretchen believed "Fucking's just the way a girl get's what she wants in this life". I took the liberty of an old friend "So you got what you want yet. Cause I think we're way more than just spreading our legs". She contended "You know it's a man's world. Pet their ego an fuck 'em, that's all they want and they'll give you anything". I pursed my lips "Yeah, so many are like that. But there's got to be some that're way more. I know my great love's out there, an he'll love my head and my body. Anyway, our brains are good as any guy, we can get what we want on our own". She laughed in such a musical way, the sound of the Sister I always wished for. Gretchen had the natural beauty that comes with an ease, comfortable in her skin, long wavy honey-gold hair, freckles showering a perfect nose, apple cheeks and soft shoulders, her breasts medium-size oranges, a long-legged California Girl, with a four-year old daughter named Ava. She came to Sky River by way of Berkeley, with a roady from the Boz Scaggs Band, her first trip out of State, and when I mentioned driving to Portland for shoes, she was game. I offered a Sandoz on the way down to the lobby. She grinned mischief "I will if you will". Since my first trip with Donna, Nick and Gabriel, LSD had been an intimate solo trip, but I felt safe with Gretchen Fetchin-Fine. She broke the tab evenly, blessed me in Latin and put half on my tongue. Taking the other, singing the HaMotzi, I placed it on hers. Ordained High Priestesses of the New Land.

Mark was in the lobby setting-up shuttle service for musicians and staff, I asked for his car. Literally drooling over Miss Fetchen-Fine, he would have said yes to anything, and happily handed her the keys. Lashes fluttering she took them "Thank you Daddy". I could see his blood rising, and promised to leave the keys in Hydra's room by the phone. The lobby littered with bags, instruments, and bands checking-in, Gretchen flaunted her goods, casting the spell, showing me how she got what she wanted. And I had to admire her talent, every male was glued, an audible collective sigh as she left the building. We were the only car heading away. Gretchen giggling, full of her powers. I loved this potent siren, confessing to being tempted, though I did not think it would get me what I wanted, true love. She scoffed at true love, did not trust idealism to bring her anything worth the risk. I knew she acted on impulse, without any self-conscious criticism, without paying heed to the implications of her deeds, conquering for pure power not love, a wanton sexuality that made her irresistible, men willing to close their eyes to cold-blooded selfish for the privilege of spreading her long legs, being close to her fire. And I knew she was a smart girl with a real beating heart, I could feel its warmth, for some reason she wrapped it in barbed-wire.

Jantzen Beach Oregon, the parking-lot Labor Day weekend, crowded, tasting the tin foil, everything exaggerating. As we neared Nordstrom in the mall I wondered aloud "Will they even sell me shoes if I'm barefoot". Gretchen lit on a friendly bench, slipped off her loafers, she would wait and people watch. "What big feet you have", curling my toes I shuffled into the store, passing a display of waffle-stompers, the grey suede ones whispering my name, I took a number and sat near them. Perfumes and powders overwhelming, primped and painted zombies, and employees far too perky for a Monday, fortunately none had noticed my flesh and blood, yet. I began counting-down to run for your life, 10-9-8-7-6 a salesman pulled-up a stool, sitting infront of me, legs spread-wide, he removed my right shoe, and holding my bare foot in both hands, asked what did I fancy. Take your hands off me you creep not quite making it passed my lips, I pulled free and pointed to the stompers. Surprised I wanted to see only one pair, he slid the metal measure from under my seat. I could not bear his touch again and said far too firm "Size six-an-a-half". He was gone and back before I took a breath, giving me disposable cotton footies. I put them on my self, and the stompers, shoes that did not need breaking-in were my idea of being wealthy, I walked round, feeling these satin pillows must have been custom-made just for my own personal pleasure, feeling complete satisfaction, they were everything I could possibly want in the world, I cooed "Perfect. I'll wear them". He put the loafers in the box and carried it to the cashier. Who took an instant dislike, and since I was not the primary account name, made me wait while the signature card was carried down from the office for comparison. Enough Golden in me not to flinch or offer defense, I sat, seeming relaxed, staring at her orange-marmalade lipstick duck bill mouth, thinking how we were more alike than she would want to believe. I understood her having to dress rich on minimum wage to work at Nordstroms, and smile, and be so animated while I leisured in a funky ankle-length blue-jean skirt and no make-up, spending money. In the four years since my Boeing days, Nordstrom had become the epitome of bourgeois, the place I would not shop if I had a choice. Approval conceded, I smiled, and laid a hit of Sandoz and a ticket to Sky River on the counter, for a budding alchemist must use any shit available to spin her gold, and just maybe giving Ms.Marmalade kindheartedness for spite would be so unexpected, it might stop hailing on the poor dear's head. Gliding away on my new grey satin pillows, I distinctly heard thank you, and knew it was not spoken aloud.

Leaving Jantzen Beach I stopped for motor oil and gas, 34-cents a gallon. Too hot in the car, Gretchen stepped-out, hands on hips, forcing those firm ripe oranges high in the air, flirting-up the attendant. On driving away I could not help wonder, since she was in it for what she could get, what did she get for this. Bothered, as if caught at some reflex unaware, turning her face to the side-window, she pouted "It makes me feel pretty". Sandoz peaking, I barely needed to steer, riding a train track road to the Inn. The lobby was a zoo, we went to the roof and hung our feet over, laughing, crying, figuring-out the universe as is always the way of good acid, my soul salvaged in the bargain, some one to talk too, another girl of little promise, no one ever encouraged Gretchen to develop anything beyond her wiles, a well-trained kitten for a rich Daddy's lap. She got pregnant at 17, her Dad threw her out, life turned hard, and all she wanted now was payback. I understood the barbed-wire. And she absolutely did not consider herself the least bit political. I had to laugh, having a child not married, refusing to be shamed or let the illegitimate stigma taint her or the little girl, rejecting the rules made her radically political, why did she think her life had turned so hard, Straits love to talk freedom and hate it flaunted infront of their face, they intend her to suffer, want her to believe love is nothing but a dirty little bargain, that she was just a lazy cunt on welfare, that it's her own fault she got pregnant and life is hard, that she was asking for it. LSD revelation though fleeting, is often compensated by lasting clarity, this one held sway only long enough for Gretchen's bent on revenge to make it proof positive she better get to using before being used. I lit the last weed-smoke, passing to her, gazing down at my precious waffle-stompers, noticing Delroy Bogave grinning up at us, motioning him come-on, wondering how we must appear sitting on the edge of a three story building. Gretchen saw him too, her engine revved "Wow, you know him. Is it who I think". I nodded "Yep". She began rustling, preening, pinching cheeks, fluffing hair, licking lips, sitting tall, back-arched, adjusting her oranges high in the padded black-lace push-up bra. Delroy was gentleman enough to wait till I introduced Miss Fetchin-Fine before completely ignoring me, their attraction so hot I smelled smoke. He just scored some coke and invited us to his room for a snort. I knew he was asking her to bed, went along anyway, curious what coming-down off Sandoz on cocaine would be like, wondering why Delroy was in my life.

Two beautiful men put their guitars down as Gretchen sashayed in and arranged herself on the couch. I took the floor by the glass-top coffee-table. Delroy poured the glittering crystals on it, chopping a fine powder with a razor blade, cutting five lines from the pile. Everyone's proboscis grew big as their heads. Gretchen rolled a dollar bill tight into a straw and handed it to me. I snorted half the shortest line, instantly shooting through the ceiling, too high to deal with giant noses, and giant cocks. One guitar player proposed I rub the rest of my line on his and we ride the range. As if gravity did not exist I sprang-up "Got to get back to the festival". Purring, Gretchen slid her hand between Delroy's legs "Okay little Sister Sunshine, catch ya later". Delroy winked at me "Come on back". Embarrassed I fled to the hall, goof-balled, Sandoz mellow and speeding, angry with my self for doing the line, terrible-anxious for it to wear-down, maybe 20 minutes, thinking I should wait it out in Hydra's room. Cots, chairs, bathroom full of strangers, I left Mark's key by the phone and raced to the lobby, for the shuttle. Dan Hicks and his band the Hot Licks, Good Clean Fun, High Voltage gladly made room, cocaine pushing me friendlier than I wanted, talking to people I don't know, sending the wrong message to a bus full of men, I was grateful when a joint came by, took a greedy toke, not sufficient to smooth the coke, coughing, promising never ever again to be so impulsive, recalling too late the degradation and paranoia of speed.

Without Nixon or Agnew we did not leave the site to demonstrate. The Peoples Army Jamboree march on the American Legions National Conference drew 200, Vortex Music Festival a tame 5000, Sky River maybe 50,000. I walked the talcum powder road down hill, power to the stage was on, the congregation abandoned to an impassioned electric dithyramb by Redbone, a Native American rock band just making it big. The Hog Farm had their painted school bus stage-left cooking porridge. Too high to eat much in days, I felt unsteady waiting in-line for a bowl, 25 cents, and took my perch on one of the trees felled for sitting, breathing-in the Dionysian atmosphere. An older couple, conspicuous among us, sharing a joint, strolling naked but for the man's black sox and brown sandals, and the woman's unbuttoned full-length mink coat and dark glasses, I recognized them from the log house cross the river, oh my how getting stoned, how another reality when you thought there was only one can so totally convert into Wow. A second bowl of porridge, brown sugar and cream, my steady and sense of responsibility in reach, I went looking for Garrity. Security had grown a labyrinth of gates and green and blue and black and yellow arm-bands, though my red bandana still gave me total access through every obstacle. I found him backstage, in supreme control "There's been no trouble ma'am". I took that to mean none he could not handle "So, who are the blue and green bands". Garrity smiled "Everyone knows red's the boss. You gave the venders blue. Black's the same. Yellow's backstage. Green gets you onstage". He must have been some noteworthy general in a previous life the way he naturally understood the dynamics of command, I thanked him for improvising and offered my red bandana. As if to punctuate prowess, he took me round the waist with those ham-hands, tossed me in the air like a child, laughing, catching, setting me down exactly where I had been, leaving no doubt he did not need my bandana to wield power. So public a man-handling and too much porridge made me sick, mustering all possible dignity I excused my self, faltering in the dusky evening to Hydra's tent, finding the Littles in sound slumber, I slipped into my bag and let their snoring lull me. Awakened by someone cuddling-up to my back, a stranger, stoned, smelling good, feeling good, I lingered before ordering him to leave, reality reasoning my ear, if this one can get next to you, so can anyone, you are not safe.

Rolling a log on the campfire, poking embers till it caught, I leaned close to feel the heat, waiting for dawn's light to drive-off the night monsters who came for me long ago, and more recently. Though I had not seen and could no longer feel him in my blood, I knew Nick was not done. Peopled conversations drifted through camp in Sandoz after-life, no trace of the speed, wondering did I really have a protective bubble like Eddie's audit said, feeling burned-out inside, my cigarette tasting really bad, now why was it that I smoked these things, time ticking out-loud, each tick tock counted and accounted for, the devouring seemed to know my location. Sunrise's hot-pink fingers always stopped the ticking, and One Hand Clapping again on stage, their acoustic morning offering comforting as warm apple pie and melting vanilla ice cream. Erik on guitar, Andrew jug and slide trombone, Joey harmonica, not the best players or voices, but Erik wrote relevant songs no one could sing better. I joined the gathering stage front, conceding my ego in heartfelt appreciation. Seeing me he looked away. The snubbing did not smart as intended, I was beyond exhaustion, out into the undaunted realm of weightless cartoon delirium, where all the mean moves and games of wit are just plain funny.

Climbing the hill seemed effortless, I was looking for a ride to the Inn. Command central empty but for the Electric Blue Eyed woman fast asleep on the couch. I expected her anger on being roused for such a trifle. She did not disappoint, snarling, looking at her watch "For Christ-sake, it's 7AM. Shuttle comes at ten. Get the hell out of here". I could not help liking her as I floated on to the gate. Finding Arnie sleeping in a pup-tent with a girl, who on closer look was Yellow-hair from Sprouse Reitz. Opening her eyes she smiled affectionate recognition and closed them. I slipped through the chained-gate contemplating Sky River's influence, hearing an authoritative voice in my head "Your way has been arranged". Sitting down in the tall grass by the road, there were no cars moving, nothing but Goldfinches, Red-wing Blackbirds, Robins, Crows, Dragonflies, Bees, what a lovely place to be. Cracking the air, scattering all the critters, a Harley roared up, my ride to the Inn.

Relieved finding Hydra's room vacant, standing under the shower till it went cold, washing away the weight of ages, I heared men's voices, and dressed quickly. Three sitting round the kitchen table snorting lines off the wood. I asked nicely who are you. A surly reply "Ric gave us a key. Who are you". Kind of freaked, not a word, I grabbed my shoulder bag and left, slamming the door, furious with Ric, and bone weary, needing somewhere to land. The lobby empty but for two thinly disguised FBI agents, I did not remember Delroy's room number in my hurried flight, asking the desk clerk. Several minutes standing at the door, ear straining for what might be inside, hearing Gretchen's sweet giggle I knocked soft "It's Shoshannah". Delroy invited "It's open, come on girl". Gretchen purred from under the covers "My beautiful Sister Sunshine". I sighed "Can I crash here". Delroy smiled "Sure, no one'll bother you. Sweet dreams". I sank into the couch.

Delroy woke me practicing his hot licks, sitting in a chair, no shirt no shoes, smoking a Camel, maybe the best rock guitar in the world. I closed my eyes and lay still, not wanting to make the process a performance, remembering how I loved listening to Nick work-it-out, again feeling the rare privilege. Maybe an hour and Gretchen rose from the covers like Venus, wanting a shower, fretting over having to use the community bathroom. I offered Hydra's. She draped her front on Delroy's back, kissing his neck, arranging to meet later. He seemed glad to be rid of us. Ric was laying on a cot, full dressed, coat and boots, smoking a joint, remnants of white powder and three neatly stacked piles of money on the coffee-table. Gretchen went directly to the bathroom. I sat down on the bed "Hey man, those guys you gave the room too were real jerks". He winced and passed me the joint "That's for sure, speed-freaks are jerks. They bought a shit-load of coke from us, but it's not enough. Look, I want you to take Mark's car and go home for the rest of the ticket money. We need it to pay for water, and clean the Sani-cans. And bring all the unsold tickets back with you. We need them here at the gate. The Pigs are slapping injunctions on all deliveries, trying to stop us. It's such a hassle, drivers want their money up front or they won't risk it. You're the only one with a valid driver's license, they can't stop you". He put keys in my hand and gave the speech "Shoshy, you're a good soldier. This is an important mission. You know how I depend on you". His words were honest, I said yes. Ric was almost never predictable, instead of drooling over Gretchen like every other, he did not notice when she came out of the shower, driving her nuts, which I realized was the intent, turning her into a political groupie would be a power-full coup. These natural leaders have by necessity an enormous ego and compelling charisma that gathers folks to them. Ric was that singular combination of big ego and modest desire for the limelight, intellectually ethical, smart like a fox, a real hero of the people, our own Ernesto "Che" Guevara, and just as illusive, he vanished in the air.

Gretchen wanted to go with, see Seattle if I promised to be back by 8PM, Moongoose was scheduled to play. I kept the speedometer near 70, in three hours rounding the bend on I-5 just North of Boeing Field, seeing the Space Needle, Gretchen squealed her delight. The engine squealed too, and died with enough momentum, rolling us to the side of the road by the Rainier Brewery. Anger, blame, responsibility grabbed me, mouth foaming profanity. Gretchen laughed "Oh Sunshine, just take everything. I'll unscrew the license plates". She was right, and I should have stopped for oil, but the car was a beater, Mark would not fix it, and the irony of a tow truck having to haul it away made me laugh. Hitching illegal in Washington State, we had to walk, hugging the concrete barrier, hoping to get off the next exit before a cop came by. Three cars pulled-over. Gretchen chose the black Cadillac DeVille, wiggling across the leather seat and up close to the driver, who would have taken her to Jupiter if that's where she wanted. In minutes to the Ave, he offered dinner at Vitos, the Space Needle, the Cloud Room at the Camlin, a suite at the Sorrento, clothes, shoes, money, jewelry, anything to fuck her all day and all night. She giggled and clucked, arching her back at each proposition. Though he was not much bigger than me, I felt threatened by this guy, his presumption we were for sale. When he finally stopped at a red light on 42nd and University, I got-out, demanding Gretchen do too. She took her sweet time, using the rear view mirror, fluffing her hair with both hands, letting Cadillac take her oranges in both hands, and beg. Brushing them off, giggling, she scoot-ed-out. Cars honking behind him, gunning the engine twice, he burned the street in rubber. I would be very careful from now on getting in a car of Gretchen's choice.

The Oracle, Arabesque, the Id Bookstore, all outlets sold a total of 2840 ticket in 24 hours, $31,040, the most money I'd ever seen. Collecting the rest of the tickets, some 5,000, instructing please say they are available at the gate, I put them in a double paper shopping bag, stored it behind the counter at the Id, and made the bank in-time to change small bills into large. Thankful Gretchen came with, two with all this dough, I stuffed it in my bag, not feeling so nervous, for who would think I had a purse full of cash, and starving, took her to Morningtown, thinking it would be a good place to find a ride to Sky River. We reveled in the armor of each others company, parading down the street in comfortable shoes, long hair flying. I had come to see the man-woman rules, those we were never asked to approve and expected to follow unquestioning, as deliberate limits to a girl's access, there to make it hard to take care of our selves, forcing com-petition for men who have access. Rules that devalue as too emotional the softer qualities of sharing, caring, communication, empathy, intuition, compassion, cooperation, community, rules that shame our natural smells as disgusting, any hair below the mane as masculine, having muscles or power or an opinion we are branded aggressive, irritating, Dyke, Bitch, especially by men with the strictest rules though not always the most access, and God forbid a woman president men-struating with her finger on the button. Gretchen and I made a pact to break these rules, to openly like each other, to never complete for men, to make Bitch and Dyke the tribute it should be. Our friendship was chain-mail.

The large mushroom olive pizza so good, we ate the whole thing, but no luck finding a ride. Heading back for the tickets, Gretchen decided to stand outside the Id, stop someone coming to buy, and trade for a ride. I sat on the sidewalk, leaning against the building, watching her operate. Three bikers could not resist, one for her, one for me, one to carry the tickets, they were Gypsy Jokers, members of the Tacoma club, Garrity was their leader. The 90 degree afternoon and equal humidity unusual even for late summer, skimmimg the freeway on a Harley welcome relief only after learning against my instinct to lean into the curves, even thrilling when I could shut-out the image of pavement scraping-off my face. We rode to the head of a long line waiting entry to Sky River, I had been thrilled enough, gave tickets and thanks, and Gretchen and I took the bag to the gate. The keepers did not know me, refusing entrance. Opening the bag I waved a hand-full, left the tickets with them, and we hurried to command central with money. The unmistakable voice of Delroy's Gibson L-5 soaring from the amphitheatre floor, Gretchen had to go, promising to find me later. The trailer was packed, sweaty cranky tired self-important sardines, money was already missing, and none willing to take responsibility for more. I phoned Hydra's room, some guy said Ric was not there and hung-up, I called the stage, no one picked-up, so I raised my voice "God damn it. This money's for water and Sani-cans. It won't do any good in my purse. Anyone here got the eggs to take it". Electric Blue Eyes poked her head out the bedroom-office "God damn it, I do and I will". She waved me come in. I laid the cash on the bed and stood there. Counting twice, 31,240, two-hundred more than I thought, she locked it in a metal safe, wrote me a receipt, and business done, lit a joint and passed to me. A not-so-instant Sister, Leda came to Sky River with Russell and Mother Georgie Wadell, and being the only one with any book-keeping skills, set-up a system, that was no longer working so well. The trailer an oven, I needed to go, find Ric, let him know the money's here, make him tell Mark about the car. Leda asked was there a place for staff to clean-up. I placed two hits of Sandoz where the money had been, offering her Hydra's room. Picking one up, reading Sandoz aloud, she beamed at me and popped it in her mouth. Friendship's accord, I felt I must do the same. Dehydrated and way too high already, I did not taste the tin foil, individuality dissipating half-way down the hill.

Nin-and-nout of consciousness, twilight, continuity unraveling in vivid disconnected snap-shots, no sequence, no time, climbing off the back of Garrity's hog at the Inn, too high to speak, wandering the halls, each room another planet, day-and-night flickering on-and-off, there were so many of us, cops reluctant to interfere. The Washington State Patrol Chief howling from a TV screen *"If we're expected to arrest all of them, we'll have to build stockades. There aren't enough facilities to hold masses of people committing misdemeanors"*. Governor Dan Evans scowling *"I've received telegrams urging me to send in the State Patrol or National Guard to clean out the festival"*. Edwin Tate's attorney growling a one-hundred-thousand dollar lawsuit against the Washington Planned Community Association and all Associates. Restraining orders had been issued prohibiting suppliers entering, every delivery vehicle would be cited. There were three natural streams on the property, wells being dug, toilets built, walkie-talkies used for communication, and so many people coming, all authorities could do was take pictures and control traffic. Sandoz a seamless transport, I found myself everywhere, the Open Door Clinic as our first new citizen is born, three over-doses revived, so few certainly a consequence of being able to test your stuff at the Drug Store. In a room-full at the Inn, Ms.Marmalade among the noses waiting to snort a pile of white powder, springing-up so fast I thought she would keep going, thanking me for the Sandoz and ticket, really really sorry for acting such a Bitch at Nordstrom, making room for me at the trough. I felt guilty giving her a ticket, seeing her here like this, it would be my fault if something terrible happened, and without thinking I sniffed a fat line. Oh shit, brain-fire, tasting more like film developer than coke, it was too late, too much over-drive took me, helium filled, no tail, head bumping the hall ceiling, floating down stairs, this drug might not return me whole, I snagged the arm of a wicker couch, pulling my self in beside a plain-clothes agent, who engaged me in conversation, no lecture, no intimidation, he was funny and human, even cute, with a passionate commitment to country that rivaled any on our side, never admitting he was FBI, just in Camas on business, he knew what I sniffed, not coke but a horse tranquilizer known as PCP, Angel Dust, something I would never have knowingly taken, or could understand why anyone would, it did not get you high, just fucked-up. Gratefully engaged, I spun my own banal identity, Boeing, sales-girl at Neiman Marcus, and when I weighed enough to walk, I kissed him hard on the mouth "Wish you were on our side".

Hydra's room for a hot shower, to leach the Phencyclidine from my pores, the door was open, Leda with the Electric Blue Eyes sitting cross-legged on the floor facing a dark-haired handsome man who looked just like one of the Seattle Seven Lawyers, she was rubbing Tiger Balm on his temples in a circular motion, attempting to calm his freaking-bad-acid-trip, someone had laced his 7-Up in LSD cut with strychnine. The bathroom door was closed, a heated arguing inside, I was glad to see Leda again, and could not stay here.

Hearts throbbing as one to the music, some hand in the Sandoz box had spiked the Hog Farm's huge coffee urns, everyone drank the brew, even kids, without a choice, of all freedoms, I held individual choice most sacred, we had become a wild herd, cavorting, raising the dust, the bands encouraging. I needed to jump-off the planet or die trying, scaling a light-show tower to the platform, sitting still, hours maybe days, over-seeing frolic and fornication, nothing to be done but hold onto my self and hope for a safe landing. Redbone did an authentic American Indian rain-dance, chanting, they were the calm, we had been too high too hot too dry too long, they gentled all 50,000, magically opening the sky, turning dust to chocolate pudding, and us new-born mud-baby believers. The rain seemed to avoid all electrical equipment on stage, and the Wiz Kids rolled their giant paper mache penis to center, ejaculating whipped-cream over the flock, what made us human completely annihilated, easy fodder for the temple guard dogs gaping maw, and other disembodied forced that came to feed. I knew many young egos would not survive this high, not sure of my own, the FBI insidiously right, Sandoz was crowd control, too much fracturing, even more effective than mace or baton, there was no further upward escape for me, and the sheer gravitational pull, a throbbing mob calling my name, just swan-dive in, a final act of grace-full self-determination, Garrity's arms and legs wrapped round me, welcome strait-jacket, rocking slowly, focusing on Dr.Zarkov's liquid-projection light show, the one sure thing, pulsing, pounding, and that constancy brought me home, Moongoose on stage, and it rained, Boz Scaggs and it rained, Commander Cody, Albert Collins, unbridled, inspired, riding each to a safe landing.

Youngbloods rumored soon at the Inn, Ric told me go attend. Garrity took me on his bike, letting on how much he wanted me, asking permission. He excited some measure of my soul, the contradiction of outlaw and beautiful teeth, rogue smile, shining knight, educated mien, natural command and control, eliciting vivid fantasy I shuddered to think. Yes this one rescued me, too often, and without permission taking on what was mine to fight, mine to win or lose, mine to learn. I was grateful for the kindness and concern, but he robbed me of full impact, full lesson, full strength, I was absolutely unyielding, we must keep it business. Ever cavalier, he roared into Camas, to the sole restaurant, family-style, seating sixty, over-run in the Hippie Horde, eaten out of eggs, bacon and white bread, our waitress fawning, gushing how much she loved us, apron pockets bulging in tips. Still high I was not hungry, and had the good sense to eat, whole-wheat toast and jam, cottage cheese, strawberries and tea. Garrity, two chicken-fried steaks and gravy, stuffed baked potato, two orders link-sausage, two ham, one large milk. Sharing chow with this man, the naked appetite, the gusto of his feeding was like fucking anyway, his up-town manners took their time, as he pined wistful for his ex ol'lady, who after three years left him for a Hell's Angel named Lonny from Santa Cruz California. For a moment I wondered was I making a mistake turning him away, knowing in my heart after the wooing, he would slowly and totally take control of my life, I liked him too much to lead-on, and was more than a little afraid. We rode to the Inn. Garrity kissed the palms of my hands and returned to the festival, security totally in his. I went to the desk. The Youngbloods had been picked-up at SeaTac Airport and were on their way. Hydra's room empty, beyond exhausted I lock the door, took a cool shower, stretched-out on a cot, solitary quiet refuge.

Boom boom boom. Mane still wet, hesitating I unlocked the door. Mr. Bushy black hair and handle-bar mustache stood in the jamb, outraged his room did not have a bathroom, if he didn't get one fast the band would go home. I knew he was Youngbloods, and wanted to lock horns with the little snot for wielding that same club all demi-gods use on lessers, Ida Rose said their motto was – *If you won't play the game my way, I'll take the ball and go home.* The ultimate power-trip, then again they were the anticipated attraction and had kindly agreed to play for cheap, I covered my self in accommodation "Well then, you can have Hydra's room, and we'll take yours". To my absolute surprise he apologized sincerely for being such a jerk. We traded keys. I wrote a note directing Hydra to our new room number, that the key was at the desk, stuck it to the outside door with bubble gum, left the key at the desk, and caught the shuttle, getting in with Boz Scaggs and his band, tired, aching to go home, rationalizing anything that could happened should have by now and I was still in one piece, fingering a Sandoz at the bottom of my bag, putting it on my tongue knowing I should not.

Sun setting in banks of liquid gold, bruised purple, pink and baby-blue, fading to a moonless night. Tin-foil, no one at Hydra camp, I took my teapot campfire-to-campfire, this magic teapot that was always full though I did not remember ever filling it, listening to the talk, no hallucinations, just a peep-hole through pretense, what, who people were beneath, Janus-faced, Mona Lisa enigma, the right side for public consumption, peace-full, good, kind, smiling, and the private other, the left side, grasping, greedy, selfish, mostly scared. I caught sight of mine in a school bus window, smiling hope-full idealist, fighting the good fight for all to see, and privately, paranoid, lonely, heart-broken, madd, and there were Gretchen Fetchin-Fine and Leda's faces too. I spun round. They giggled like twins, and wiggled for their panting male entourage. Meeting in Hydra's room, they decided to find me, Gretchen christening us the Mothertruckers, offering a half-empty bottle of Southern Comfort in toast and consecration. I swigged, and handed to Leda, envying how natural they were in their sexuality, wasted on layers of drugs and whiskey, bonded in such uninhibited rapture they began undulating for the hounds, swaying, casting their scent, hypnotically intoning "Lure. Lure. Lure". Reaching their hands for mine, I ached too join, desperately alone, but the vibe reeked unholy alliance, and once joined, knowing I knew better, would forfeit my way home, I could not give my hands nor look in their eyes "Goda go do security. Come to Hydra House and find me if I don't catch-up with you first". Running-away, terribly disappointed they flew so low, thinking how much one of the hounds looked like the dealer from Oregon with the green Nash Rambler station-wagon. Gretchen came after me "Hey Sister Sunshine. Can I stay with you a while at Hydra House. My little Girl's with her Dad till Christmas. I have some freedom and wanted to hang-out with you and Leda. Maybe take the Mothertruckers to Santa Cruz". Needing somewhere to go Nick did not know, clueless where to find the rabbit hole, reaching for her warm soft body I nearly hugged Miss Fine off the ground "Yes, come for sure". She promised, crossing her heart, hoping to die.

Somewhere after sunset Mark sat by me at Hydra's campfire, tickled how I left his car for the tow truck. And eventually there was nothing left but to climb the light-show tower again and hold-up the sky, rain ending, not one blade of grass survived the whipped-cream mud-babies. The Youngbloods took the stage, closing Sky River with *Don't let the Rain Bring You Down*, and a long-spun jam of *Darkness Darkness*, riding-out an anthem that released any unspent emotion, they were awesome, world-class, and so wicked, never resolving the song, leaving us too high in the air, and no way down but mass crash-landing. I waited in my protective bubble till dawn.

Chapter Twelve

TRIAL

September 8, 1970, eleven days, 27 drug arrests, none on-site, I guessed Nick's disappearance put him one, the Open Door Clinic delivered three healthy babies, and revived all eleven over-doses thanks to the skill and dedication of Connie, Abe and Ronnie. And there were only two bad fights with minor injuries, firmly establishing my standing as Security Goddess. Keely, Carolion and I packed the station-wagon and the Littles. Ric, Arnie, Mark, Bear, the Grodes, the Rebels, the Country Doctor, and Mother Jones staying to clean-up. Ric's voice rang-out over the soon to be dismantled sound system, echoing-off the dried-mud amphitheater to a hard-core 106 still determined to make Sky River their home "What an amazing trip. Hi out there. So where are we going now my friends. Well here it is, as of today, the Washington Planned Community Association can not afford to purchase Edwin Tate's farm. We have been slapped with outrageous clean-up fines. One hundred-thousand fucking dollars. All ticket money and more will be needed to pay them down. Right now Hydra's considering if we can bring the fight to court. But don't get your hopes up citizens, judges aren't ruling in favor of the revolution these days. So, please help us clean-up. We have three days. Over an out". As Keely drove-up the hill, the stage, light-show towers, fences and concession booths were coming down, toilet trenches filled-in, three huge trash fires blazing, the command center trailer gone, mostly cigarette butts and pull-tabs littered the ground, no legitimate reason for one hundred-thousand-dollars. Keely filled us in "Except for the fine, we'd be good. Everyone's been paid, with just over five-grand to spare. That's five months mortgage on the farm". From the strain in her voice I knew there was more. She turned-on the radio and waited for the warm car and rhythm of the road to lull her Boys to sleep before confiding "If they insist on the fine even if the farm is whistle clean, Ric plans on flying to Costa Rica with the five-grand. He can score coke cheap there, find a buyer here first, no one in the middle, and make enough to pay the fine. His Uncle's the Minister of Justice, it's a convincing cover. But I'm dead against it, and he won't listen. Shit they know every one of us. They're just waiting to bust us for something big". I had been too high too long, not paying attention "The fines are so obviously bogus. We can beat them in court". Keely laughed sarcastic "Shoshy, Ric was kidding. We got no chance in court". I was confused "But he needs a majority vote to use the money". Carolion protested "Yeah, him, Mark, Arnie, Bear. That's always Ric's majority vote". Keely worried "He thinks Hydra's reputation is on the line, and that means his on the line. He acts like it's only his. I know once he decides it never matters what I say". Scottie woke in need of a bathroom. Keely took the next rest-stop. On the road again, I told tale of the MotherTruckers, Gretchen Fetchin-Fine, Leda with the Electric Blue Eyes, the prospect of going to Santa Cruz. Bitter-sweet desire for independence mixed with loving willing responsibility to her young pinched Keely's whole face as she glanced often in the rear-view mirror at them and gnawed her finger-nails. Carolion, newly and madly in-love, was not interested in leaving town. I could see the powers-that-be would never let Sky River become a town, it was all that held me to Hydra, I wanted to disappear somewhere Nick could not find.

Hydra House a decompressing relief, just the Littles and us Girls. I was at the edge of my known being, drug compromised to the point of dissolution, bordering psychotic, promising, vowing no more Sandoz. Two days, Gretchen and Leda arrived, with Leda's charismatic white German Shepherd Amaru, the Ecuadorian name for a female shaman of the Secona tribe, her green eyes engaged mine so earnestly I knew she understood everything. Like me, Keely took to them instantly, listening quietly as we sat round the War Table conceiving our adventure. Only one thing was for certain, Gretchen had to be set-up in a place by the end of December when she got Ava back from her Dad. Leda had recently hitched to Malibu and back with Amaru, and planned on taking her. Gretchen loved the idea of a big dog. I proposed Keely come with. She laughed me off. We made her an honorary MotherTrucker anyway, pricking our fuck-you fingers with the same pin, mixing a blood compact, pledging to be faithful friends, always believe what each other had to say no matter how far-out, and never compete for men. My Sisters had their faults, but were more like me than any I had known, I believed if we stuck together we could compensate for each others short-comings, and was excited to be going South again, a direction that had always called my name.

September 13, the Weather Underground helped Timothy Leary escape from the California Men's Colony near San Luis Obispo. And Hydra voted unanimously to throw a Halloween dance at the downtown Eagles Hall to raise money for Sky River debt. Five days later 27 year old Jimi Hendrix died in London of an overdose. And we were evicted. Moving the next day to a rental at 23rd Avenue South and South Judkins Street, across the little dead-end street from Mother Jones and the Country Doctor, three blocks from Maya's. Two more days, Hendrix was buried in Renton Washington, 27 year old Janis Joplin died in Hollywood from a overdose, and two bombs went-off at the ROTC office in Clark Hall causing $150,000 damage. October 19, conspiracy charges were dropped against Bobby Seale, and Timothy Leary emerged in Algeria. I was numb to everything, warriors freed, champions dead too young, Janis and Jimi were not Dr. King or the Kennedys, even so they were our heroes, rock 'n roll the sound track of the revolution, and I worried I should feel something. Even the Joffery Ballet performing to the Chrome Syrcus at our Halloween dance did not interest me, I would take the Littles out trick-or-treating and give Keely the night with Gretchen and Leda. All Hydra went, and Mother Jones. Connie, Abe, Ronnie staying home, for the Country Doctor was working hard against a deadline to write a grant for newly available Federal funds that could finance their dream of a free Open Door Clinic.

We went there first, Littles and me dressed as Flower-Children, all the beaded necklaces in the house, tie-dyes, faces painted in daisies and peace symbols, laughing every time we look at each other, they were not too young to appreciate the irony of going as our-selves. Connie ooed and awed and gave them kisses and giant-size snickers bars. And we went to every door with a shining porch-light. Holding my breath as Lance knocked on Maya's, she was not there, no forwarding address. The Charles Street house was dark, the butchered hedge a grotesque reminder of Dr. King's murder. And only when their bags were full could we go home. Lance took the War Table, Robby the kitchen, Scottie the living room rug, arranging their loot in mounds, biggest and therefore best, smaller but still good, okay, and will-trade, each picking me one from their good pile, and any thing I wanted from will-trade. Greedy sweet mouths full, fingers chocolate and sticky stuff, chasing round the house, filching the others best, squealing, hooting, squabbling sugar-high delight. And then sirens came screaming into our little dead-end street, yellow and red light show. Me and the Littles spilled onto the porch. One police cruiser had blocked-off the street, two parked infront of the Country Doctor, cops in the yards, at the doors, oh shit, a bust, I ordered Littles inside, never having ordered them anywhere, they obeyed at once, taking all the candy up to their room. Drapes wide open, lights on, doors unlocked, frantic, securing the house, collecting all dope I knew of in a Halloween bag, I slipped out the back door, stashed it in the blackberry brambles under the far south side of the fence, and shaky-scared walked across the street. Ronnie was sitting on the porch staring into the dark sky, not registering me climb and sit down close to him, I rested my hand lightly on his knee. Face pale, tear-streaked, he looked down at my hand, put his over and spoke low and mechanical "Connie opened the door thinking trick-or-treat. These big-guys wearing Nixon masks. One held a shot-gun to her chest, the others duct-taped Abe and me to kitchen chairs. I'll blow your face off if you make a sound. They made Connie take off her clothes. Take them all off Bitch. Hurry up Bitch. Get on your knees Bitch. They took turns in her mouth. Do it Bitch. Suck harder Bitch. No teeth Bitch. Be creative Bitch. I want to believe you love it Bitch. They raped her with a loaded shotgun, and laughed and pulled the trigger. It was not loaded". He took a long shivering breath "They took their time. Not afraid of being interrupted or caught. They spray-painted CUNT on Connie's back. They spray-painted commie pinko on the kitchen wall in red. They took our money and our dope. Warning this is only the beginning. And they left". Ronnie began to sob "I was so scared, I didn't do anything. Connie just there on the floor". I had no words. Stepping out on the porch as the ambulance arrived, a stone-faced Pig ordered Ronnie inside for questions. His docile compliance told me I must go in too, Pigs should not be the only ones with them. Stone-face barred me, pointing, ordering "Go home right now". I ran, fiends were at-large, the Littles alone, checking windows doors, windows doors, I needed a plan if they came here. Arnie's Smith & Wesson, no bullets, my old friend the serrated steak knife. Peeping through the drapes, siren whirling, ambulance carrying Connie away, nausea gave the will-trades and good up to the kitchen sink, it could have been us, I knew people feared, hated us, but never could have imagined this.

The Pigs were gone when Hydra and Mother Jones came home from a profitable Halloween dance. Outrage, fear, intense anger, retaliation. I retrieved the dope, we smoked and sniffed it all right there at the War Table. Nixon masks were an unmistakable message, it suited him to have us scared, and now the battle was no longer only in the street, no where was safe, not even home. This explicit act against the Seattle Liberation Front sent shock waves throughout the Movement, most thinking these thugs were COINTELPRO, the FBI's covert counter intelligence program. Since jail and trials could not stop us, we believed Nixon told his henchmen to finish us by any means, and if we needed evidence, the Halloween thugs were not being pursued. My numb detached distance vanished, I was razors-edge-present and absolutely sure I would soon as possible go South with or without the MotherTruckers. Connie was hospitalized two days, Ronnie and Abe brought her home to a house full of flowers and friends. No serious internal injuries, and so brutally degraded, so emotionally destroyed, she would not see anyone, would not leave her room. Mom and Dad drove-in from Spokane to collect her.

Rightly freaked, Gretchen and Leda fled to her Mom's house in Federal Way. Leda's Mother was so relentless in ridiculing her only daughter's life and choices, two nights three days and they came back, planning for the MotherTruckers departure in earnest. Connie's nightmare blighted our sleep, of all collectives the Country Doctor was most peaceful and caring, and maybe that was the point. Like Black Panthers and Weathermen, Nixon considered us a national security threat, when the attack never made the police blotter, we knew rape, an everyday war tactic abroad, was a war tactic at home. Connie was the victim, but all of us were raped with her, the men too, and it could have been any of us, nothing freaked me more than being a wholesale target. Short-tempered, picking at each other, aimless, what can be done to restore some footing. It arrived on the evening news, Washington had become the 6th state to legalized abortion, sorely needed truimph even if we were not on the front line of this. Out came the Sandoz box, maybe one-thousand hits left, the only dope in the house, government issue. My abstinence vow aside, this was legitimate justification for the sacred potion. Littles sleeping at last, Keely, Carolion, Ric, Mark, Arnie, Bear, Leda, Gretchen and I gathered round the War Table, first time ever Girls out-numbered Boys, one white tablet on each tongue, chased with a cold Rainier. Tin foil, gently riding-up on the Byrds and Jefferson Airplane, it was a mellow healing, we bonded once more as a collective, every thing mystically whole, unwinding the woe and weal of the universe right there at the Table. Peaking near midnight, the phone ringing. Ric managed to answer sounding quite normal. A voice claiming to be drummer Buddy Miles, founding member of the Band of Gypsys with his friend Jimi Hendrix, wanted to stage a memorial here in Seattle, and having heard we were the only one in-town to handle such a big project, he needed Hydra to organize and build the stage, inviting us to the Washington Plaza Hotel penthouse for breakfast. Ric took the number saying he would call back with an answer. We deliberated, this was probably a hoax, how did he get our number anyway, we had other more pressing things to do, and no we did not, Hendrix's song Purple Haze defined what beautiful meant, gliding-down on the morning light, we were beautiful too, and regarded him a fellow soldier that died for the cause, we would be honored to help deliver his due.

Nine AM, Mark representing the Kady Grady Fly by Night Construction Company, Ric and Arnie Sky River producers extraodinaire, and me security goddess arrived at Seattle's newest luxury hotel, raised on the bones of a once grand Orpheum movie palace. The Doorman forbid us entry, calling Mr.Miles for verification, ordering a valet to park that piece-of-junk station wagon beyond the light of day, the Concierge hustling us to a private penthouse elevator. We would not be rushed. Buddy met us at the door, eyes puffy with sleep, wearing a floor-length black velvet dashiki, little round mirrors sewn-in all over, and the biggest afro I had ever seen in-person, I thought at first it must be a wig. We followed him passed two lavish bedrooms, extravagant bathroom, kitchen, formal dining room, table set for seven, into the living room's breath-taking view of blue-ridge Olympic Mountains hovering in the air, Puget Sound ferry boats, the Space Needle, and took our places on white leather couches and arm-chairs. I thought this is how the really rich live so far above our everyday lives, as Mr.Miles called room service, ordering breakfast and drinks. Though designated security, I found my self completely left-out of the discussion, deciding instead of just sitting ignored, I would use the bathroom. Every thing whipped-cream white, save the glorious bouquets of purple dahlias on every counter, mirrors and mirrors, Jacuzzi tub, walk-in tile shower so big it did not need a door, sun lamps, heat lamps, soaps, shampoos, rinses, body lotions, massage oils, bubble and bath salts, after-bath splash, after-shave splash, thick soft towels and robes, and a bottle of Courvoisier. Locking the door, I opened the brandy, what lovely smooth liquid, and off came the Mexican wedding-shirt, long blue-jean skirt and waffle stompers. I turned the giant shower-head on full, and stood long, letting hot water rain on my head, using all the goodies, washing off the insult of disregard.

In high negotiation, the Boys Club barely noted my return or wet hair. Mark and Arnie mostly did not notice me much anymore anyway, drawn to the ego-stroking Gretchen Fetchin-Fine kind. I settled in an arm-chair, and one of that kind swayed into the living room. Cree was a six-foot rare beauty that looked remarkably like Carol Channing, wearing a body-hugging chartreuse mohair mini-dress, perfect compliment to her dark mahogany skin and shiny black hair in finger-waves close to her head, generous mouth slicked in baby-pink, matching nails, huge gold hoop-earrings that pulled at the holes in her ears, sling-back blue-suede stilettos, she had such lovely long thin feet. Demonstrating to the Boys his command of this beauty, Mr.Miles lightly patted the couch next to him. She obeyed without pause, crossing those endless legs, dress just short enough to show the lace-tops of her silk-hose and black garters, just enough there was a good chance to see more. The Boys leaned-in, mouths open more and less, eyes fixed where her thighs met the leather, never on the beautiful face. She used this power, shifting those legs ever so slightly when ever their attention drifted. I was impressed by the unblushing manipulation, her cool composure, her power-full sexuality, and knew somewhere along the way she and Gretchen had sold-out their self-respect, or had it taken. Mr.Miles palmed a fat roll of bills from the folds of his dashiki, peeled-off a crisp 100, creased it in-half the long way, placed it like a canoe on the coffee-table, his hand disappearing again into those folds with the roll, and voila, a not so little brown glass vial. Pouring some of the fine-chopped sparkling white powder into the canoe, he leaned back, and with a slight jut of his chin to Cree "Have your fill Mama". Leaning forward fast, addiction fast, taking hold of the long chain round her neck, pulling a silver coke-spoon from deep inside her dress, she scooped every bit the little spoon could hold for each nostril. Master of this game, Ric made me smile, brandishing a not-so-crisp one-dollar bill from his wallet, rolling it the short-way into a tube, flourishing the red Swiss Army knife from his pocket, opening the main blade, cutting a fat-line onto the glass table, he vacuumed half in each nostril and passed the knife and tube to Mark, who did the same, and Arnie. I was never going to be interested in speed again, or in compromising the gentle Sandoz and delicious Courvoisier for a stupid who's got the biggest dick game, and passed. Speed-freaks are the paranoid of paranoid, Mr.Miles stiffened, looking at me for the first time. Paranoid as I was, and knowing that passing on free drugs was just too bold a move for an undercover cop, I held his eyes long enough, and looking down, let him win. He dismissed me entirely, using the near half-inch-long squared-off pinky nail on his right hand to scoop a load for each nostril. And the predictable coke-spin took hold. I went out on the balcony for a penthouse view, negotiation for-a-guy by-the-guys of-the-guys, period, I did not have the passion or patience to fight for respect already earned and earned, only to be called aggressive Bitch behind my back, especially when accommodating Cree was there to under-score the claim.

September's cool morning, damp hair, breakfast served, I joined the dining room table, none touching their Eggs Benedict but me. Everyone still talking, seeming agreeable, and so fast, till the coke wore-down, and Mr.Miles demanded "Absolutely no drugs or Hippies at the memorial". Silence. He brought the canoe to the table, scooped a heaping nail full and held it under Cree's nose. Her upper lip already powdered in white, she grimaced reluctant, and sniffed. The way Ric cocked his head and scowled, I could see the hypocrisy lodge just above his Adam's apple, waiting, clearing his throat twice, speaking low and calm "Hendrix was one of us. He sang about us. He died on drugs. His fans do drugs. We do drugs. You do drugs". He took a breath "If you insist, we won't build your stage. You can't do this size gig without us". Mr.Miles answered by taking a scoop for him self. On that Ric stood. We flocked with him out the door, into the elevator, down 40 floors, spirits falling with each, how sweet it would have been to honor a fallen soldier, but selling-out was not an option. The afternoon Times carried Mr.Miles interview. No way could he arrange financing without someone to build a stage. The memorial was a no-go. Somehow this did not feel like victory.

Leda and Gretchen were enjoying such enthusiastic attention from SLF men, our Santa Cruz plans kept sliding. Having convinced themselves they are not part of the Movement, therefore not political, and therefore not targets, these beautiful ostriches would not see their flaunting mores alone made them marks, for nothing was allowed to spoil their fun. When three bulky brutes took the place of the Suits cross the street, and I caught sight of Nick's bus, a deadline became necessary, one month to support the impending conspiracy trial, and to sew and save money, and if the MotherTruckers weren't ready, I did not really know what or where but I had to go. Moving home was not possible, though initially welcome, Dad and Mom would insist on their terms and I would not last long, or long enough in the kind of strait-job needed to afford my own place. And then there was Gretchen and Leda's main interest, making me not so comfortable hitching South with them, though I did not entirely blame them, sex the way most males and females related, they were only claiming the fleeting power Society grants young and beautiful, fucking one and another and more. In truth they were trusting easily exploited free-love Flower-Children, leaning on denial for protection, winking at the Clap, Gonorrhea, Syphilis, regularly cured with a dose of penicillin, getting pregnant never mentioned, even as Gretchen had a daughter. I understood the masked desperation in taking such risk, intuitively recognizing neither had a protective bubble, that mine was only as resolute as my own character and vigilance. I so dearly appreciated the longer view, having the privilege of knowing Ida Rose and Bonita-Kay, the blessing of their wisdom whispering in my ear, I would not judge my Sisters against this. They wanted what they could to-day, thought equality meant getting the same size dinner steak as a man, and yet they understood girls could be friends, that we had to love and trust each other. I would make five dresses, five hats and ten necklaces. Gretchen had to be in California by late December, if we did go, I would bring my tools to make a living. Aiming to get this moving, I took Leda and Gretchen to Goodwill on Dearborn Street for traveling gear. The one of us who had actually hitched the long road, Leda urged us carry backpacks. Having always seen the eyes, the way shoulder straps force a girl's bosom out there in the air, advertizing what guys driving by look at first, I bought a fine old tan leather suitcase with big soft handle and sturdy belts round the outside, for two dollars. This act of buying, it somehow eased my anxiety, I was going South, even if I go alone.

Unanimous, Hydra voted to donate the near $4000 profit from our Halloween dance to the Seattle Conspiracy Defense Fund, given it was not enough to make a real dent in Hydra's debt. Back in early September the defense lawyers, Spokane's Carl Maxey, the first Black to pass the bar in Eastern Washington, and UCLA Professor of Law Michael Tigar, both counselors to the Chicago Seven, and Lee Holley, former Assistant District Attorney of Newark New Jersey, now practicing in Seattle, and Seattle's Jeffrey Steinborn, filed a motion to *"Dismiss the defendants on the grounds that there's been too much pre-trial publicity about the Seattle Liberation Front for some of the defendants to get a fair trial"*. The motion was denied by Judge George H.Boldt, appointed to hear the case, who ruled instead to relocate the proceedings 30 miles South, to the city of Tacoma, population fifty-thousand, and then delayed the trial one month to *"Let the effects of the publicity die down"*. Defense argued Tacoma got their news from the same sources as Seattle and appealed to the 9th Circuit Court in San Francisco to move the trial back to Seattle, claiming it was *"Inconvenient for the defendants to drive so far, and a more urban and understanding jury could be found in Seattle"*. This was denied. A final week of delay came when Susan Stern, member of the local Weathermen, Students for a Democratic Society, and lone female defendant took ill.

Michael Justensen had not been found as trial opened, November twenty-third, 9AM. I stood infront of Tacoma's courthouse with 52 others, prevented entrance without a court-issued Press or special pass. Extra benches had been added in the courtroom to accommodate 40, the Press were limited to 25 first-comes, over-flow to halls and outside in the rain with us. We cheered as defendants and their lawyers were escorted in through an armed Deputy secured side-door. Gretchen Fetchin-Fine and Leda with the Electric Blue Eyes disappeared from Hydra before dawn without explanation. They blew me kisses parading in that same secure door on Jeffrey Steinborn's either arm, wearing long black gowns, hands and face glittered, giggling, waving Tinker Bell glow-in-the-dark magic wands. The J.Edgar-Nixon prosecution mob, U.S. District Attorney for Western Washington Stan Pitkin, Assistant U.S. Attorneys Charles Billinghurst and William Erxleben, arrived all-smiles and arrogantly late in separate chauffeur-driven Lincoln Continentals, and were pelted with our hisses and boos. Eight Pigs posted outside to keep us in-line, two laying a white tape line down the sidewalk. We were allotted twelve-inches behind this line, penned against neatly-clipped Rhododendrons trimming the courthouse *"To keep the way clear for pedestrians and others with business at the courthouse"*. We were warned repeatedly *"Stay behind the white line or be arrested"*. The newly formed Tacoma Defense Collective came at ten with coffee sandwiches and signs. And we kept coming, crowding in behind the white tape, over-flow Press with nothing to do but interview us. I laid-low, Mom and Dad would worry sick, and just after noon, shivering and soaked, caught a ride home with soaked and shivering Mark. Keely pleaded to go back with him. And I happily stayed with the Littles, locked the doors, turned on radio and TV, sailing a lovely silly afternoon making signs, *Wake up America the Dream is Over*, *We're All the Conspiracy*, *We Are Your Children*, *Framed by the FBI*. I drew the words in black felt pen, and sewed. They filled with poster paint, and crayons, and their own embellishments, peace-signs, rabbits, horses, monsters, clowns, bugs, American flags, lightning bolts, stars, rainbows, smiles, frowns, question marks. And when Leda and Gretchen came on screen in all their glory, and were called witches, casting evil spells on the judge and prosecutors with their magic wands, we laughed and laughed and laughed.

Day two. Bear having a legit journalism degree, could not be denied a Press pass and one for his photographer, and to my surprise invited me, handing over a Nikon to wear round my neck. Keely sulking effective, I gave the camera to her. The Littles presented our posters, exacting promises to wave and say their names on TV. After breakfast we walked to 7-11 for the Post Intelligencer, and popcorn and Snickers bars and black licorice, and listened to the radio all day, and watched the news. Free the Seattle Seven stickers showed up everywhere, stuck on doors, walls, backs of court room chairs and people. One-hundred-twenty-five prospective jurors reported on-hand. Coverage mostly focusing on angry exchanges in court and on the street, Littles hooting, snorting, falling on the floor, kicking feet in the air when their posters, when Mom came on screen waving. Judge Boldt limited Seattle Seven supporters to 30 courtroom passes.

Someone called for a moment of silence to remember the people killed today bombing Vietnam, all 30 stood raising clinched fists. Boldt expelled three for laughing. Michael Tigar spoke on the noon news to Boldt *"We object to this action. If we are to have proceedings where every little ripple of laughter and every human emotion results in this, it goes far beyond the powers you have"*. And Lee Holley *"This puts a chilling effect of repression upon every human emotion"*. A comic circus, center-ring, attorneys objecting, both sides seizing every little morsel, and Boldt openly disrespected in his own courtroom taking opportunities whether in-fact or imagined, to squeeze and reprimand the defendants, their counsel and supporters. Outside, a belligerent tug-of-war over the white tape line. Day two ending, supporters storm the courtroom chanting *"Stop the trial and stop the war"*.

There were benefit parties at night to raise funds and fervor. I went with Gretchen and Leda to the one a Freeway Hall. Ten PM it was raided, the Pigs insisting they received reports of prowlers. And there was alcohol, and Leda was under-age, Gretchen grabbing her and my hands flew us down the basement stairs and out a side door. We hid in a plumbers van till after midnight, freezing, walking home. Morning news, the arrests of Jeff Dowd charged for swearing, Joe Kelly for hindering police officers by stepping in-between two girls and the Pigs manhandling them, and on checking his drivers license Mike Abeles was arrested for *"Frequenting a place as a minor where liquor is present"*. Harassed, fined, jailed as much as possible, Pigs, FBI, Federal Marshals were methodically picking us off. The odds of jail made my paranoia border hysteria, I was not seeking instant celebrity by arrest, I was not very brave.

And yet, beyond reason and compelled, day three I went with Bear, Nikon round my neck. Waiting at the side entrance to be searched, I counted 53 behind the white tape. Inside was different, I understood the rules, Golden Ghet rules, people knew their position. Defense fought passionately to seat youngers and less-hostile to an already half selected jury. The current prospect wanted a seat, waxing surprisingly sympathetic to Hippies and revolutionaries, but when asked could he be a fair juror, he could not contain a racist bent toward Mike Abeles' lawyer Carl Maxey *"His skin color will bias my ability to judge Abeles fairly"*. I expected intrigue, and a jury of peers, and justice, my experience with court all Perry Mason.

When the prosecution disqualified best possibles without cause, and the jury so far forty years old and older, I was confused. Bear explained each side had a right called Preemptory Challenge, defense could dismiss 14 prospective jurors without cause or explanation, prosecution eight. Both sides excellent poker players, it was interesting watching them play the numbers, but 14 to eight was no real advantage for the defendants. Tacoma and Pierce County were run by a good-old-boys political network with ties to construction and illegal gambling, and the population overwhelmingly conservative. Morning crept technical, defense tearing at any opening, trying to broaden the subject matter of questions they could ask prospective jurors. Judge Boldt parsimonious. Would-be jurors voicing similar condemnation of those insolent young people in general, dirty Hippies and Pinko-Commies in particular. My mind wandered South. From behind Gretchen whispered "Me and Leda are sooo bored. Wana drop some acid". Knowing she meant do you have any, I turned shaking my head no, whispering "Do not bring anything incriminating". Missing what provoked defendant Jeff Dowd to leap from his chair toward Chief Prosecutor Pitkin, shaking his fist, yelling *"I'm going to shoot to kill the next agent I see you on my property"*. Pitkin plainly relished this a win and swaggered-up to Boldt, complaining *"Defendants are going over to my table and reading my notes"*. Dowd stalking after, still shaking his fist *"The FBI, the police come to my house. I am scared. My girlfriend is scared. The Vietnamese people are scared of your bombings. And you're worried about your notes"*. The room exploded in applause. Boldt warned *"If you continue your threatening manner toward the United States Attorney, you're going to be in trouble"*. Ignoring him Dowd got in Pitkin's face *"We're going to come in the middle of the night and show you what it's like"*. Michael Lerner and Chip Marshall jumped to their feet, demanding Boldt have the FBI stop bugging their phones. Pitkin strongly denied any bugging. Pounding his gavel Boldt called a one-hour lunch recess. Gretchen Leda and I walked to the near-by Peoples Coffeehouse, opened the day before by the Tacoma Defense Collective to raise funds, pure windowpane one-dollar a hit listed top of the menu. I bought myself a blueberry scone and coffee, them tea and acid. Gretchen again winding an irresistible tale of white sand beaches and warm Santa Cruz winters. I was lulled in-spite of her lack of solid any things, like when would she be ready to go and who were these quote nice guys we were welcome to stay with. Skirting specifics with such grace, I enjoyed her routine too much to press. The last of my coffee and they were beginning to trip. I walked back to court alone.

Body-searching in the wrong-hands a legal molestation, the armed Deputy was not pure business on me. Inside, waiting till all were seated for afternoon session, Bailiff ordered us stand *"Here ye, here ye. The honorable judge Boldt presiding. God save the United States of America"*. Some one adding *"He better"*. Boldt chose to ignore this and took his throne. Minutes later expelling two for laughing while he reprimanded Chip Marshall for wearing tap shoes with the word phone painted in white on the toes. The courtroom thick in snares and delusions, arrogant and indignant words, supporters were easily sucked-in and kicked-out. At the same-time, defense artfully managed to broaden the questioning of potential jurors as to their views on political activists, demonstrations, anti-war activities, the Weathermen, SDS, SLF, Black Panthers, discrimination against Blacks, and if they had served in the military. Steinborn asked one if he felt *"People with money were better people"*. The answer an unqualified *"Yes"*. Quarter-to-two, prosecution requested a break. Courtroom air exhausted, I needed some fresh, went out the main-doors and down the stairs for a smoke. Signs waving, chanting, our side challenging a wall of Pigs over sidewalk rights. All wars are turf wars, standing attention in black leather jackets and knee-boots, 25 of Tacoma's finest neatly lined the curb, gleaming white hard-helmets, black visors and chin straps, guns hanging off bullet-belts, batons, handcuffs, mace, waiting, all to keep the obviously unarmed, stocking-cap waffle-stomper pea-coat rain-soaked rabble in-line. And maybe David Dellinger, Chicago Seven defendant was rumored coming here today to help raise money for the defense. The players so entrenched, so volatile I lost my nerve, preferring another wrong-hands body-search, knowing the inside rules better, prudent silence, properly thralled comportment.

I took my seat with Bear. Jeff Dowd indignantly wagging his tongue and finger at Boldt *"You just said you've given your life for justice. Well so have we, and we've done it for nothing. You're probably getting $25,000 for it"*. Michael Lerner stood *"I want to point out to the jurors that we have ac-*

cused you judge Boldt of racism and sexism, because of your membership in all white-male organizations". Boldt did not respond, jury selection resumed. Broadening the questioning managed to expose the general issue of racism, something the Movement badly wanted to put on trial. Most jurors knew about the arrest and murder of Black Panthers, and not one could seem to recall hearing or reading a thing about the Weathermen or SDS, most saying they really ought to be disqualified anyway for their unfriendly stance on *"Long hair, beards and Hippies types"*. Three-thirty, prosecution asked another break. Mike Lerner and Susan Stern walked out on the main-stairs to address the crowd. I followed staying just outside the door. The building, the whole block seemed so alien it could just separate from the ground and fly-off into space, the people chanting a rolling thunder of *Freedom Now*, and *We Shall Not Be Moved*. In some kind of magical time-warp where every thing is perfectly co-ordinated, David Dellinger stepped from the back-seat of a green '52 Chevy onto the sidewalk, took the stairs and stopped half-way up. Of the Chicago Seven, he was the oldest at 55, and the real thing. A life-long pacifist, sent to prison in 1940 refusing to register for conscription, and to solitary confinement for organizing protests against racial segregation in the prison mess halls. And when the U.S. joined World War II, he refused to register and went to prison again. This man could have every privilege and chose instead to give it to the people. Coming here today was a no small risk, he was out on bail. The Crowd surged over the tape-line and gathered at the foot of the stairs, Susan Stern and Michael Lerner came down to Dellinger, the people hushed, Lerner presented *"David Dellinger. That famous defendant of the Chicago Trial"*. He stood taller than he was and raised a fist in Black Power solidarity, and we raised ours in chorus of *Power to the People*, the bright light of his integrity making me feel taller than I was, making us feel taller, he motioned for quiet, and we attended him, speaking passion for us, speaking outrage for us, at Nixon resuming the bombing of Vietnam, the police state prosecuting people for thinking, and how honored he was to stand with the Seattle Seven. We chanted *No Justice No Peace*. He walked up stairs, the threat of arrest following if he cursed one more word, Michael Tigar smiling big to see his friend, handing him a guest-pass.

Another aggressive body-search, I took my seat. Dellinger approached the bench requesting to speak. Judge Boldt denied him. He sat down infront, a beacon that could not be denied. Somehow this hit me hard, no heart of justice beat here in this building, I began promising my self never to ever again commit any act that would give my fate into these cold hands of 'Justice', I was not brave as him. Telling Bear I would hitch home, walking careful down the front stairs, the People and Pigs had taken their postures, some snapping photo mementos. As a rule, we used any opening to be seen daughter, son, neighbor, friend, it was harder to beat your friends over the head. Sinking behind the tape-line, and behind the human wall, squeezing across the rhododendrons, edging to the corner of the building, I took the cross-walk with the light, and slow hurried to the Peoples Coffeehouse hoping to find a ride home. Gretchen and Leda were still there, acid-eyes glittering over a square-jaw clean-cut TV reporter with extra court-room passes. Their mischief and spectacle and fun-loving inappropriate behavior a commotion so outside the restraint of the courthouse, embarrassing, a lawyer had to maintain his decorum, so Jeff simply could not afford to take them with to court again, he must keep a credible public distance. And they wanted back-in, needed passes, but the day's court near done, and Square-jaw literally drooling over Leda, offered only a ride home. She snuggled-in next to him. Gretchen and me in back, I used the face-time to ask more on Santa Cruz. When she mentioned One Hand Clapping, I freaked, recounting history with Erik and Joey, swearing I would not go if we stayed with them. She admitted not liking them much either, petting me smooth, cross-her-heart-hope-to-die we would be staying with Andrew the jug player, and Luke the Roady, it was all arranged, I could trust her. I just barely did, but did, making her promise if we stay longer than seven days, we will get our own place, the MotherTruckers house. She gave her word-of-honor. Qualms, reservations, unpredictabilities, still I planned to go South long enough for Nick to believe I was dead. I could see little else, would have to venture, knowing the Sweet Sisters Fate will have their way anyway.

Against my vehement objections, Square-jaw enticed Leda to dinner at the Camlin Hotel, and dropped us at Morningtown. Gretchen had come down enough to be hungry, we ate a mushroom pizza, and she convinced me to go with her to the Dellinger fund-raiser at the District

Tavern, she was dying to meet him and did not like showing-up alone. Needing a hot shower to purge the stink of Boldt's court, my soul craved a little celebration, I let her persuade. Shower at Hydra, primping, we split half a Sandoz. Aside from mercenary sex, Gretchen was a dancing brook on a sunny afternoon, her passion for living so contagious, I decided to wear one of the gowns I made to sell. This one so beautiful I should keep it anyway, the time had come, I needed a lighter-heart, needed to wear something other than my militant uniform, something gay, this sapphire silk velvet, halter-top straps crisscrossing my back, tying through button-holes in the waist-band, a generous bow at the small of my spine, ball-gown-skirt, ruffle-trim fat and lazy, sweeping the floor, topped with a green velvet shrug lined in yellow satin, fastened at the collar-bone with a golden-yellow glass button carved into an open rose. Envious, generous, Gretchen declared me a rare hothouse flower, as she parted my long hair in the center, and with hot curling-iron wound one plump ringlet to cascade down and dance-off my shoulder, all the while trying to reason me out of the dress, please she just wanted to try it on, since I wasn't so much interested in men right now, maybe she could wear it this once. I knew her needy inside-girl hungered for validation, for attention, and was tempted just to watch her sashay, but I too needed, and had a practice of wearing my creations first, explaining how events and people leave permanent finger-prints, with consequences, the gown was a blank-slate and I wanted to write on it first, promising next time. She was not appeased, pouting all the way to the tavern, still Gretchen Fetchin-Fine did not need velvet to strut, the hounds smelling her before she arrived, waiting. I regretted my choice, people came from all over to meet Mr.Dellinger, and presumed me some rich-dressed Bitch slumming, treating me accordingly. Minutes passed 8PM he arrived, Gretchen well established, I could go home.

Paranoia followed me in the form of a cop-car, I could see my self dragged into his cruiser, raped, murdered and dumped like so many girls, trash on the side of the road or maybe Hydra's lawn, one less Hippy chick. I turned-up the next walkway to a dark-lit house, tried the door handle, unlocked, I slowly walked-in, coming face-to-face with a man, my height, in a royal-purple floor-length ceremonial robe embroidered in gold crescent moons and stars down the front, the pointy-sleeves ending in gold tassels. He held my eyes and smiled "Welcome Leo. Follow me". I just walked into this guy's home uninvited, how could he know my sign, but then anything can happen when you slip down the rabbit hole, I closed the door and went along. He pulled-out a dining room chair for me at the seat-twelve-comfortably rectangular oak table, gliding to his place on the opposite. I could not tell, ancient or youth, illuminati or actor, psychopomp or friend, and took the designated seat. Table strewn in Astrological charts, open books, a bowl of half-eaten cat food, green candles burning, sandalwood incense, an impressive crystal ball between us, I was about to explain my intrusion, and thank him for refuge. He hushed with a long finger to thin dry lips "It's fine Little Wren. Be still". Lighting a joint with a stick match, or was it his finger, inhaling half in one long slow drag, losing the fragile ash as he passed to me. Distinctive aromas, flower-tops and pollen, remembering Garrity's potent weed, feeling I must accept, taking a very small toke, getting to high anyway, teetering at the end of the high-dive, those waiting pushing me to go, I could not breathe speak or move, drawn to candle-light reflecting in the crystal ball, suddenly understanding the intrinsic value of focusing energy in one spot, falling-in. As if to rescue, Wizard inquired "Tea". I nodded and just as suddenly could breathe. He vanished. There was a palpable presence here, if smelled, rotting cedar, if heard, dissonance, if felt, comforting and dangerous as lying in the arms of a Biker lover. Wizard brought steaming cups and Lorna Doones. I politely took his offering, thinking how Persephone ate two small Pomegranate seeds in the Nether World and no matter how innocent, was condemned forever to spend Autumn and Winter there, I needed to take some control and asked "Can I hold the crystal ball". Wizard winced, nodding reluctant yes. I hesitated, picking the weighty juju from its silver stand with both hands, carefully setting it on the table infront of me, and not knowing what else to do, swirled my hands over it like some cartoon fortune teller, a booming voice startling me from above, dictating "This is not for you". My hands jerked away as from a hot burner, I put them in my lap, and looked to the high ceiling. The voice thundered "When you look in, I see you. This karma is not for you. You do not want me to know who you are". I sat back in my chair, gripping the seat, looking at Wizard "Did you say that. Did you throw you voice". A wry little grin raised the corners of his thin mouth, eyes blazing "You heard him". I repeated the words. His eyes widening "Wow. My Great Grandmother left the ball specifically for me in her will". Pride beaming his face "She was quite the famous psychic in her day. It's never spoken to anyone else but me. But then no one ever had the nerve to pick it up". I could not stay seated and went to a stack of books on the sideboard behind me, thinking I should run from here right now. A thin green hard-back lay open to a picture of the same pink starburst I'd seen round Ida Rose, excitement swept near panic, someone else had seen the same, and painted it, the exact hot-pink burst, and it was titled Love. Blood rushing in my ears, arm-hair standing, I knew I was exactly where I should be, on the exact spot in the whole universe, at the exact right moment, there was no other way to know but this kind of corroboration, sinking to the floor in my gown like a wilted lily, I felt sane. Wizard floated over "Ah yes, *Thought Forms* by Annie Besant. You've seen that aura before". My tears welling "Yes, all round my friend Ida Rose". The aloof mystical persona fell away, he took my hands, pulling to my feet, gushing "Ida Rose Barber. Dr.Barber. I knew your coming here was no accident. Magic moves in you". He blotted my tears with his sleeve "Good things happen when you're around, right. People don't realize it's you though. Only a few know you're a lucky charm". He smiled excited "So, who do you think I am". I did not want to stand, did not want him touching me even if he knew Ida Rose "Taliesin, Merlin, Mephistopheles, Beelzebub". He laughed "Come on, stay with me Beautiful". At last I could see him, long ash-brown hair, wan face, red-rimmed eyes, I could be anyone from anywhere and this person would know everything, his province the same unwholesome hypnotic magic Leda and Gretchen used in their Lure Lure Lure game at Sky River. I went for the front door "People are waiting for me". He with me as if on wheels not legs "Come on, stay and I'll do your chart". I shook my head "No thanks. I don't want to know what's going to happen". The door had locked itself. He turned the bolt, opening wide, letting me pass. Without thinking I gave him my hand "Thank you for refuge". Holding too tight he kissed the back, as if marking me. I pulled away, looking in his haunted face, probably a Wizard before and before, he needed some sunshine. I gathered my skirt and hurried over the threshold.

His specter followed me into the rainy night, full of consequences and familiars, where circumstances move straining, and anything can loom from between the lines, smelling sweet as it smothers. The cold late November wind pushing, I began to sing *Zippity doo dah* to shake-off the stalking, Wizard reeked of Nick, clinging as rain-soaked velvet, and yet I could not help an almost out-of-body amusement at this grand initiation of my new gown, and how subtle and potent a quarter-hit of Sandoz could be. Reaching my ears, Leda's laughter, I found her with Mark, parked infront of Hydra making-out in his new 1959 Edsel, Square-jaw had become Mr.Hyde, she called from a phone booth, Mark came to the rescue. Her laughter drove-off the stalking, evidence of her quality, together we had more protection. I only hoped she would out-grow the fascination with Lures before they permanently stained her, for like Gretchen she was enough on her own, though I knew she also did not know. Inside Keely Bear and Gretchen sat at the War Table drinking beer, smoking cigars. Gretchen demanded "Shoshy, Jesus shit, where you been. You can't just leave without telling me". Too wet, too wrung to tell, I managed a genuine smile "Just needed a little walk Mom". Everyone laughed. I bid goodnight, content with an empty bedroom for now, spreading all-the-way-out, considering my new chums. I did not keep any high school pals, in their slumbering Golden conceit, partly my own reflection though not entirely, none seemed worth the effort, and I simply had no college friends. Telling this to Ida Rose, she recommended patients, that human beings are fundamentally gregarious, crave companionship, saying I should not fault myself for picking the best of a poor lot when convenient classmates and neighbors were all there were to choose from, that parents decide where their children live and go to school, and now the choices were mine, with all the attending joys disappointments and repercussions that come with deciding, and therefore my task was to learn to discriminate, learn how to make good choices. I knew she was right, hoping I picked Gretchen and Leda with my head as well as my heart, although the decision did not seem entirely voluntary.

Driving on loose gravel, speeding down a barren mountain road at the wheel of a long black sedan, sliding to stop at the rim of a vast inland ocean, feeling desperate to cross the water, looking, certain I will drown. A familiar dream, and I had never once tried to cross, realizing on waking I feared losing my self, my hard fought for individuality in the unfathomable indiscriminate ocean of the unconscious, wondering could I build enough substance, a buoyant vehicle to keep me afloat over such great deeps of oblivion. Leda Gretchen Keely were my contemporaries, but none considered their inner dialogue anything to question or pay much attention too. My interest in dreams, human behavior, my behavior, theirs, Women's Lib, God or none, were shared with Ida Rose and a few Texans, and I had to wonder if I made a terrible mistake trying to wake-up, it was so freezing solitary. This had to be the rub for Eve, eating from the Tree of Knowledge, cut her out separate from the comforting collective buzzing union in that ever-rolling mind-numbing subjective drama that everyone is party-line to. Listening to my self as objectively as is possible, questioning, choosing, this was the real loss of Eden, the beginning of self-knowledge, self responsibility. And I could not just go blithely back to sleep, for having once seen the light, how much greater the darkness. Leda, Gretchen snoring softly through this morning epiphany, I watched them for a while, sweet lovely little kittens, my best of a poor lot. I showered and went with Bear, day four.

Driving to Tacoma, Bear filled me in on yesterday's late afternoon court spectacle. Jury selection was complete when a bomb threat evacuated the building. With 42 reported so far this year, and Seattle's reputation as bombing capital of the country, it was easy to threaten and be taken serious. Bear said he knew it was bogus, no one on our side wanted this trial stopped, it had to be an empty threat, likely COINTELPRO, knowing we would be suspect, taking any opportunity to smear us violent and dangerous. No bomb was found, those who dared were allowed back in, court came to order. Defense opening statements began, they intended to put government policies and establishment sentiments on trial. Jeff Steinborn *"Attitudes toward long hair and hippie types. Attitudes about race, the war in Vietnam, poverty, discrimination, Women's Liberation, groups such as the Weathermen, Black Panthers, Students for a Democratic Society, the Seattle Liberation Front. Demonstrations, violent demonstrations, the right of all citizens to gather, protests and speak freely are the real issues here. The demonstration that resulted in the arrests of the defendants was a protest against contempt sentencing in the Chicago Conspiracy Trial, which resulted from an anti-war protest during the 1968 Democratic National Convention and nothing more*". Just then demonstrators burst-in the court-room chanting "*Order in the court. Here come the judge*". Defendants came to their feet, fists and voices raised "*Power to the people*". The more Boldt pounded his gavel the more resounding the Choir's stomping and chanting. Boldt slowly rose-up on his hind legs "*Be seated. Be silent. Remove those people*". Jeff Dowd thundered "*Make them drag you out*". Boldt hammered "*Your conduct is in contempt of this court. Your conduct has been disruptive of this court*". Susan Stern countered "*This trial has been disruptive of our lives*". Mike Abeles roared "*I charge you with outrageous prejudice*". The Choir accused Boldt "*You are the real criminal*". Boldt threatened contempt again "*I'm at the point where I cannot continue to overlook anything of this kind*". The Pigs swarmed in. Boldt dismissed.

Bear and I took our usual places as the jury was seated. Tension arrived with Boldt, rumbling self-centered arbitrator. A trial no longer about conspiracy but of the times, the clash of protean youth seeking equitable change up-against an entrenched Establishment holding most of the power, for which change was anathema, liberty and justice for all written in disappearing ink, rubber-stamped and appointed to the bench by Nixon to do his bidding. Defense played the game too, assaulting Boldt and Pitkin's egos, hoping to trip them into giving away their real allegiance. Ida Rose's book called this *The Law of the Premises*. Both sides believe they are right, rationalize their conduct, the greater good and God on their side. But the melodrama isn't really going on in the moment, instead old prejudices, and childhood hurts endeavor to play themselves out, *attempting to communicate by force from conclusion to conclusion, forgetting that conclusions are prejudices in untrained humanity, and that they are never rational or complete, but conditioned by some innate patterns not known to Psychology, and by our whole system of abstractions – our total reaction as an organism to its environment.* I needed to see her before going South, even if she knew Wizard. An argument fulminating at the door, Deputy refusing three ousted yesterday from entering, even though they had today's proper pass. Boldt ruled they could be seated, but from now on anyone expelled was permanently out. Michael Lerner distributed a prepared press statement detailing his intention *"To subpoena Vice President Spiro Agnew, Attorney General John Mitchell, and Federal Bureau of Investigation Director J.Edgar Hoover, to show that they are the real conspirators by attempting to discredit the political Left"*. The stone-face jury, 8 men, 4 women, age 26 to 59, one under 30, six over 40, four urbans from Tacoma and Vancouver, two Washougal and Sumner rurals, and five frighteningly reactionary agriculturals from Shelton, Union, Mason and Pierce County. Michael Lerner the oldest defendant at 27, anyone could see this was not a jury of peers, where was their jury of peers, I laughed aloud at my stubborn disbelief. Boldt took no notice, attending Prosecutor Pitkin's opening statement *"The only issue here is unlawful conduct. I will show that the defendants committed acts of violence against the United States Courthouse that caused 6,500 dollars damage. A great many people came to demonstrate peacefully, and were duped by a criminal conspiracy to provide cover for those bent on damage and riot. That police confronted demonstrators only after the violence started. That Mike Abeles gave Chip Marshall a can of tear gas"*. Pitkin took a long inhale *"I will introduce into evidence a photo showing Marshall's arm throwing the can into the crowd"*. He paced quickly infront of the jury *"I will outline the organizational meetings of the revolutionary Seattle Liberation Front, tying the defendants to those meetings. Starting with a January 19, 1970 meeting in Seattle to which Marshall and Lerner invited representatives of various radical Left Organizations"*. He then read *"The Fourteen Point Program of the Seattle Liberation Front"*. I quietly leaned to Bear "Ever hear of this". He shrugged "There's no such thing. But it sure makes us sound well organized and dangerous. And if they publish it enough, it'll become fact just like The Protocols of Zion". With measured breath Pitkin continued *"Chip Marshall stated at the January 19th meeting that the Seattle Liberation Front would launch an attack on the American Fascist Judicial System. At a February 4th meeting he participated in a debate over the use of violent tactics"*. That was the one meeting I went to, it was a free-for-all brain-storm, we considered everything hypothetically, and suddenly the truth hit me, I understood why Keely had been so paranoid, wanting to come spend the night with me, the FBI was more than bugging us, they had people inside or they could not know these things, and unfortunately their Pigeons lacked the brains to understand what was actually going on. Pitkin continued *"Marshall and Lerner urged people to go back to the courthouse after the police had ordered them off. Marshall used a blow horn to incite the crowd: "We've got to close it down, come back and fight". And when everyone began to run, Marshall was seen breaking a police car window, throwing rocks at two banks, yelling at cohorts: "There are plenty of banks around, don't trash the small businesses""*. The prosecutions forty-minute opening statement done, Boldt called a short recess. I went into the hallway, my head screaming, Pitkin has a biased judge and jury hanging-on every word, we can not prevail here, the defendants are food, kill and be eaten, contemptible prey for these big game Hunters. A riveting melancholy held me witness to this State sponsored blood-sport, loath to watch, compelled to stay, again I took my seat.

Spectacle resumed, a beautiful woman wanting in court, Deputy gripping her upper-arm, insisting she does not have the right pass, Chip Marshall charging cross the room, planting himself between her and Deputy, screaming in his face *"You'll be decked the next time this happens. She's been searched and has the right color ticket"*. Boldt seemed preoccupied, allowed her in, and then addressed Chip *"Your remarks constitute contempt of court. I will not cite you at this time, but hold a hearing on the matter"*. We all feared contempt, however Boldt had finally shown his allegiance, springing the tension in the room, this was the leveler Defense hoped for, one I could barely comprehended, there were no objections. Michael Tigar, representing Jeff Dowd and Roger Lippman took the floor *"I will prove my clients were not even in the State on the days they were charged with plotting conspiracy"*. He laid out dates, times, places, and would call witnesses to substantiate. Defiant applause. Boldt let this slide. Carl Maxey stood representing Mike Abeles *"Evidence will show the defendants were charged not for what they did but what they thought politically. Guilt by idea, guilt by drug culture, guilt by doing too much toward ending the war"*. More applause, feet stomping, fists in the air, he spoke for us. Boldt glared, but did not throw anyone out, others would only take our places, delaying, disrupting, we had his hands tied a little, and with the public watching, he wanted to appear in control. Maxey went on *"This was a demonstration called by the People of the United States. There were 30 such demonstrations across the United States that day. These are the only defendants, here in the obscure Northwest that were charged. None of these defendants were among the 89 arrested out of over 2000 who participated in the February 17th court-house demonstration in Seattle, and many of the 86 charged were dismissed"*. He was eloquent, inspired, and I dared believe just a little again. Maxey *"Of the 18 overt acts the government has listed in the conspiracy indictment, 15 are related to speech, only 2 to window-breaking and one to a Karate les-son. Hardly revolutionary in itself"*. He strolled confidently infront of the jury, reminding them of Boldt's instructions *"Advocating revolution is not a crime. You don't have to agree with the defendants to find them innocent"*. Stopping he faced them *"Virtually all of the conspiratorial meetings of the defendants outlined in the government charges were well-publicized public gatherings on the University of Washington campus. The government is put-ting together a case based on happenstance. Evidence will show that Joe Kelly was in Chicago during the February 4th meeting here the government said he was attending. This is part of the government's case to mix the top of the radical movement with others, stir in violence, mix well and convict. Evidence will show Chip Marshall did not throw the tear-gas canister into the courthouse during the demonstration as accused by the government in its opening state-ment. We submit one of the reasons for this prosecution is to crush youth, to put them on notice you can't discuss these things in peace and freedom"*. He proceeded to accuse the Nixon administration, particularly Vice President Agnew of *"Inciting public passions against dissenting youth"*. Still facing the jury *"After hearing the evidence, you will not be like the prospective juror who said he didn't have an opinion on the war"''*. Cheering our avenging angel, we all sat taller. Defending himself, Michael Lerner walked to center ring with a red telephone hung round his neck *"This represents five years of my life. I've been charged with using the telephone, using interstate telephone lines with the intent to incite riot"*. Pitkin objected to the prop. Boldt instructed Lerner *"Take it off"*. Slowly unwinding the cord from his neck he placed it on the podium *"Evidence will show the Seattle Liberation Front to be one of the most undisciplined organizations that ever existed. There could be no con-spiracy, most of us couldn't agree on anything. For the record, John F. Kennedy wrote my recommendation to college. I'm acquainted with several Congress-men but became a revolutionary when I saw the interrelationship between problems and the need for change"*. We all stood, chapping wildly. Boldt warned *"Sit down, this is not entertainment but a courtroom and applause is not in order"*. We sat. Chip Marshall, also defending himself walked to center facing the jury, and accused the government of *"Perjuring itself. Committing little accidents, like saying Joe Kelly was a speaker at one of the meetings when evidence would prove he was in Berkeley"*. He guaranteed *"The photo supposedly showing my arm with the tear-gas will show it was really a blow horn"*. Pitkin objected *"This is argumentative and exceeding the bounds of statements"*. Marshall insisted *"The indictment is politically motivated from Washington D.C. and brought over your objections"*. Pitkin covered his straw-belly *"That's an outrageous lie"*. Marshall smiled at him *"You told me that in our office Stan"*. And turning back to the jury *"I did not lead an assault on the courthouse. Things had gotten out-of-hand before I got there. I threw no rocks"*. We were on our feet rooting. Boldt excused the jury. Michael Tigar standing with us, moved for a mistrial *"because of Prosecutor Pitkin's objection during Marshall's opening statement"*. Pitkin stood *"Marshall's statement was the equivalent of testimony and he should give it under oath as a witness"*. Tigar *"None of the defendants are required to be witnesses and your objection is prejudicial"*. Boldt denied Pitkin's motion. Marshall *"The FBI has all of the defendants under surveillance"*. Pitkin vehemently denied this. Marshall barked *"You're lying"*. We stomped and clapped. Boldt warned Marshall *"To say what your said is very serious misconduct. It's disruptive*. Mike Abeles on his feet *"So are lies disruptive"*. Banging his gavel, finally pushed to stand, Boldt decreed *"Court is suspended for the day insomuch as it seems impossible to have any rational discussion"*. Federal Marshals pushed us from the courtroom chanting *"Power to the people"*. Drained, reconciled, I felt hope flickering. So did Bear.

Day five. Admitted FBI paid informer Horace L.Parker, 23 year-old mercenary without political conscience, or any I could distinguish, star witness for the prosecution took the stand. I respected soldiers of passion, not of fortune. The FBI had given him a total of $7000 to infiltrate us, the Weathermen, and the Students for a Democratic Society, which he obediently detailed in a long prepared recitation for Pitkin. Cross-examination began with Horace-L stating he lived three-months with the Weathermen at the collective called the Fort. Asked by Chip Marshall if that was true. Horace-L admitted *"I only resided at The Fort for three days"*. That he had actually taken an apartment across the street for three months and would go over and try to hang around, boasting proudly "*I infiltrated them the best I could.* And bragging "*I encouraged others to engage in unlawful acts when I worked for the FBI, to protect my credibility with the Underground organizations*". Marshall inquired "*Would you go to any lengths to bring us to justice*". Horace-L "*Yeah, any lengths, including lying to you, anything to protect my credibility*". Marshall swallowed his excitement "*You were willing to lie to get us?*". Horace-L "*Yes*". The court-room had been quiet, testimony riveting, but this, applause shook the walls, in his own words prosecution's darling confessed to being a liar, and to furnishing a loaded tear-gas gun to former Seattle SDS member Robby Stern, Susan's husband, and to supplying drugs to people in the Movement, and taking paint paid for by the FBI to use on the courthouse in the February 17th demonstration. We went crazy-loud. Boldt did little but lean back in his chair and give a sour look to Pitkin. When quiet enough, Marshall asked "*The FBI paid for the paint and you brought it to the courthouse*". Horace-L "*Yes, I provided the paint on the instruction of the FBI. But it was so I'd have an excuse to check the Weathermen's collective for explosives. The FBI also gave me money to buy five pounds of potassium chlorate from a smack dealer, material that could be used for making self-igniting Molotov cocktails. I turned it over to the FBI for analysis, then gave it to the Weathermen*". His vainglorious spilled with the slightest pressure and to no objection. While in Idaho he offered to purchase dynamite and caps for the Weathermen, took the money but never delivered, crowing how he made some of them "*Believe I was a Green Beret and offered to give them shooting instructions*". Marshall asked "*Why*". Horace-L "*Because they represented themselves as urban guerillas and I wanted to find out how well they could shoot. Most couldn't hit the broad side of a barn*". He testified the FBI gave him money to put toward Serve the People, and Stop the Pigs stickers. That he "*Recruited people as revolutionaries, and talked about armed struggle and violence, but it was all part of repeating the Weathermen line*". Beyond incredulous Marshall queried "*Have you ever heard of the concept of police creating incidents so people will be entrapped*". Horace-L "*Yes*". Marshall's face literally shined as he asked about Parker's use of drugs and dealing while working for the FBI "*Did you get the name Speed Parker because you were heavily into Methedrine and*

Dexedrine". Horace'L seemed frustrated "*No, but I was worried at one time about becoming an addict*". Each question begging the next, Marshall "*Did you think it was glamorous being an FBI informant, and maybe exaggerate your report to them*". Parker qualified "*Not at all. But as far as posing as a Weatherman for the FBI, I wouldn't recommend anybody else try it*". A short break called by Pitkin, after which Horace-L could no longer exactly remember much. Cross-examination persisted, little more exposed, defense frequently complaining Pitkin was not giving them "*Complete and timely records*". Each time Boldt instructed prosecution "*The Government has a duty to continually update such records for the defense*". Yet he never imposed a penalty for non-compliance.

Day six I gave Keely the Nikon and stayed with the Littles, sewing between making apple-butter, playing hide-an-seek, all dipping cheese sticks and marshmallows in the cooled apple-butter, playing war, and cooking mushroom and black olive spaghetti sauce for dinner.

Day seven, Horace-L's 3rd on the stand, by mid-afternoon he was dry and dismissed. Boldt dismissed the jury too. Marshall and Lerner came to center ring, Lerner requesting Boldt appoint "*An independent inquiry, or direct Pitkin to bring conspiracy charges against the Government for aiding and abetting and counseling others to commit unlawful acts*". Boldt shook his head "*I am not a prosecutor but have the power, and will present to the Federal Grand Jury information regarding criminal offenses by anyone, if I deem it necessary at the end of the trial. But I have to know a lot more than I know now to do that. Court dismissed*".

December 2nd, day eight a sunny crisp morning, Keely happily taking my court-room pass, Gretchen and Leda would baby-sit the Littles. I dressed warm, and set-out on chance Ida Rose might have time for me, not calling first, embarrassingly presumptuous, maybe she would say no, desperately needing to be near her fire, hear her voice on the outside of my head. Walking down Crescent Avenue I saw her small frame kneeling between the bare rose-bushes, and felt my heart swell, this remarkable woman on her knees in the dirt, Gardener a perfect metaphor. Seeing me she stood, nimble as a 20 year old "Why hello Lamby. I'm so happy it's you. They told me someone would be coming today to help with this mulch. I must cover these rose beds before the coming freeze". I would crawl on broken glass to be so welcome, gladly shoveling buckets and distributing, while she smoothed, and detailed the pedigree of each rose bush, this one newly bred to honor President Kennedy, that one a hybrid for Roosevelt, those glorious old standards. And she invited me in for coffee. And I followed like a hungry stray. We washed in the kitchen sink, she brought a thermo-carafe of coffee and plate of Peak Freans cookies into the dining room, me the cups. Gourmet Magazine lay open on the big mahogany table, her main auditor Tom was coming later to do an audit and she wanted to cook something special for his dinner. We nibbled and sipped and talked food as she perused the recipes. Ida Rose's hair, silver white candy-cotton in need of dressing, I hoped it would not sound an insult, and offered "If you want, I can do your hair. I used to do my friends, starting in Junior High. Invented some really great styles that everyone copied. I even considered going to Beauty School for a minute. My Mom thought doing hair would be a great way for me to make a living. It's in the family. My Dad was a barber in the Army, and his brother has his own beauty shop in the Bronx". As if I offered box seats to see Nijinsky dance, she popped from her chair smiling Cheshire "Wonderful, that would be just wonderful Little One. I'll go upstairs right now and wash my hair". Still smiling she added over her shoulder *"I am the woman in Revelations with the white wool hair who births the baby born in travail"*.

Suckled on the Original Bible, I knew little of Revelations, and went to her book-shelf for the King James Testament, wondering what a woman old enough to have white hair birthing a baby in travail meant, finding Isis Unveiled by Madame H.P.Blavatsky instead, thumbing through it when Ida Rose came back. Her head wrapped in a lush white towel, arms heavy with clear plastic zipper bags of foam and brush rollers, bobby pins and picks, comb and brush, hair spray, Dippity Do, a hand mirror, and Sunbeam hair-dryer exactly like the one I used in high school. She arranged them on the table "I hope this is everything you'll need". Noting the book in my hands she cautioned *"Madame Blavatsky is a charlatan and worse. The truth means nothing to her. She has some things right in her book, but most are far from it. She's after power, arrogant power. I have it on good authority she collaborated with Hitler. Taking him on peyote induced drug trips to the Astral Plane, to read from the Akashic Record. They were trying to find out his destiny*". Ida Rose sat down. I began combing her thick short mane "Who is the Revelations woman with the white wool hair and the baby". When she spoke of her work it was with passion and velocity "*My students are the baby, the third birth on earth of God incarnate. Adam and Eve were the first incarnation, and Yahweh too his credit cared for his people, gave them beneficial laws and justice. Then Jesus, the second incarnation. He came to teach love, which has not shown itself to be strong enough without justice. You see, through auditing the time tracks of those who were there, many of them screaming through the terrors of their past lives, I have uncovered the truth of that terrible murder in Palestine, the murder of love by cutting asunder love and justice, separating Christian from Jew. Finding the truth has freed Jesus' soul to graduate, opening the Books of Life, which was always the intention, ordaining the third incarnation, the Baby, who will become Lords of Humanity, born in travail of the woman with the white wool hair, to inherit the earth from Lucifer. They are the first to look inward and find God. The first able to read the Books of Life, ushering in the Age of Self-discovery, and as Korzybski hoped, the Manhood of Humanity*". Just barely grasping the story, of such scale I had to force the walls of my mind to make room and could not hold for long "Then discovering the truth set Jesus free. And now we can look in and find what makes us tick and grow-up". Her satisfaction radiated so loving I could feel the warm "Yes, you understand perfectly Little One". I was beyond thrilled by her praise, searching desperately for something more worth saying, the walls closing-in, I could only ask "Have you been following the Conspiracy Trial". She nodded "Oh yes. I've seen your friend Ric's picture in the paper several times, but not yours". I was so happy to have said something that carried on "I've been there in court most every day. Laying low. My Folks would freak-out if they knew. That judge Boldt isn't even close to being impartial. And there's no jury of peers. The government means to smash us by making examples of the defendants. I am so totally disgusted with our so-called justice system". She nodded "Justice has no balance without love. Your anguish seems quite legitimate". Siding with me took some of the vinegar out of my wound "That really means a lot to me". Picking up Gourmet, she read aloud the recipe under consideration "*This sounds good don't you think. Bone and skin two whole chicken breasts. Pound flat. Stuff with sautéed mushrooms, leeks, slivered water chestnuts, and seasoned bread crumbs. Wrap in Kosher Lox. Secure with toothpicks. Bake in cream sauce. Serve with fresh asparagus when available or zucchini, and homemade egg noodles.* I think Tom will love it. Would you like to join us for dinner". My heart pounding in my ears, making me know how excited I was by this invitation "Yes, I would".

Being conscientious not to pull hard or wind too much hair on each roller, half-done I excused myself to the bathroom. Ida Rose went to her desk, phoning the nearby QFC, ordering delivery of the necessary ingredients. On return, she was sitting, yellow legal pad in-hand "This new audit is so interesting. I'll read to you while you work. *Six-thousand years ago the island continent of Atlantis had developed their technology to the point where they could bottle and sell the life essence itself. And they genetically engineered mutant-slaves, half-human half-animal, satyrs, centaurs and such, the creatures of mythology. Their capitol, Olympus was a grand palace high on a mountain, Poseidon ruling, attended by Athena, Zeus, Ares, Aphrodite, Hermes, Hephaistos, Demeter, Dionysus, Apollo, Hestia, Hera. Being islanders, Atlanteans were great seafarers, known for their lavish ships and prowess at sea. On long voyages they took their animals and entire families on board. Egypt was the favored vacation destination, accounting for its remarkable and until now unexplainably advanced civilization, and its animal-human Gods. Atlantean technocrats developed the laser, inevitably leading to a huge weapon and the need to test it. Their brilliant solution, aim at the dimly seen planet Venus and pull the trigger. At the time earth was surrounded by what Plato called a "fire mist", steamy fog that shrouded the planet, the result of an ice shell enveloping the Mesosphere, maintaining a very humid 72 degrees over the whole globe. Sun shining through this fog made the sky seem on fire. And the constant temperature made earth a fertile hothouse Garden of Eden, accounting for mammoths with tropical vegetation still in their mouths preserved in polar ice flows. There were no seasons, just one long tropical summer. And the earth spun nearly upright on its axis. Unaware of this ice shell, these technocrats tested their laser beam, shooting at Venus, shattering the shell, which was pulled in by the magnetic poles, creating the polar ice caps, a world wide flood and catastrophe so violent it knocked the earth off its axis 23 degrees creating the seasons, sinking Atlantis except for its highest peaks the Azores, and throwing up the Olympic and Cascade mountain ranges and more, making the mountains dance like lambs. Most Atlanteans perished in the sinking, but those at sea, who put into surviving native villages all along the Atlantic coasts, where the likes of such advanced people were taken for Gods, and where stories are still handed down of the great flood and legendary Noah, Nona, Nodah, Nonana, a God-man who came from the sea with his family and animals, and stayed, teaching them the magic of metals, astronomy, and other wonders. Though Nixon was Nero, the United States is much more than Rome, with our nuclear weapons and history of using them, America is more like Atlantis"*. Ida Rose suggested "If you would like to read more about Atlantis, you can borrow Ignatius Donnelly's book The Antediluvian Flood and the Ice Age. Through his access as a U.S.Senator to Library of Congress manuscripts, he tracked the languages of tribes living on the Atlantic coasts to a single source, and the advanced use of metals by them to the same intrusive source, Atlantis. Even Plato believed Atlantis existed *"below the Azores, beyond the Pillars of Hercules"'*. My spine and shoulders shivered in thrill, Ida Rose would lend me one of her books, which meant I could bring it back, and come again. I had managed as many rollers on her head as possible, carefully pulled the dryer-hood over, folded the towel, set the motor-base on it to dampen the sound, and flipped on the switch. She was surprised and delighted "I can still hear perfectly. This is so clever of you, using the towel as a muffler". Fifty-two years between us a distinction of experience and wisdom more than age, she did not lord it over me, and I began to relax "I'd love to borrow it, but I'm going on a trip and think I will buy my own. I'd feel awful if I lost yours. Is there any more books you could recommend". She surprised me with two on the current New York Times best-seller list "Yes, the Amityville Horror is an excellent and quite accurate account of a haunting. And if you're interested in a first-rate story of how reincarnation and karma cycle from life to life you could read The Reincarnation of Peter Proud". She did not dictate a list of must heavy tomes, necessary to being educated, essential to membership in the elite club. I felt at ease, my thoughts came freely, how grateful I was to have some one to talk too that did not think I was crazy or too far-out, how true Eddie's audit had been about my protective bubble and Sky River, how I watched the players battle in court "It's just like in your book, you know, the chapter called Law of the Premises. These grown men acting like children, screaming at each other from conclusion to conclusion, re-living old contests, wrangling over old injuries that have little or nothing to do with the current situation. I understand, even if I don't get your book when I'm reading, I concentrate on every word, cause it sinks in anyway, and when I'm ready, shows itself right infront of my face". Ida Rose's eyes gleaming gold "You're learning to discriminate, to think critically, using the cortex to review your response to a stimulus instead of allowing the thalamus, *the desk clerk sitting in the foyer of your unconscious mind* to interpret it for you. You're not giving that clerk the last word so to speak, to employ some tired old thalamic recipe that once worked, that was likely useful when you were a child but no more. The way the human brain is ordered, the desk clerk gets the stimulus first, so you must delay your reaction, giving the cortex a chance to receive it. If you remember to count to ten, to breathe, it takes that long for a stimulus to travel to the cortex, the clerk will have to pass it on, and therefore his will not be the final take on the matter. This allows you to think, so you can act instead of react. It's called Differentiated Activation, acting differently, and the more you do it, the deeper you dig the canal, the easier it becomes to flow in. Korzybski found that General Semantics progresses geometrically, that it has a way of working for you once you get started, but it's not easy, thinking is the hardest of all jobs. Many of my students make no effort to study GS. They would rather I start a church like L.Ron Hubbard did with Dianetics and then Scientology, some dogma to do their thinking for them. This is Hu-man's greatest flaw, wanting someone else to do the work for them, their thinking, even if that someone doesn't have their best interests at heart. Again and again as history has shown us, people blindly follow the latest messiah over the cliff. That way leads to terrible demise, just look at Hitler and Germany. You are not one of my old gang, you have no fancy pedigree, no college degrees, and you have seen little of the world, yet you are wonderfully curious and bright, you want to think, and that is so very reassuring to me. It tells me the Greater Cosmos gets it".

I switched-off the dryer to check, her hair was nearly dry "I feel like I would swallow the whole world in one gulp if I could. And I feel so inadequate, so small, and the job so big, like I have too much to learn before I know anything. I didn't know how to learn in school, wasted so much time just sitting there trying to cleverly pass a class with as little effort as possible instead of listening, studying. I wonder if I can ever learn enough to know anything. I've been peeking behind as many curtains as I can, and so far every Wizard of Oz has been just a little man. When I met you, I knew right away you knew something. Even the hairs on my body knew it. At first I thought maybe you were evil, you know, I had nothing to compare you too. Then your advice made such an difference in my life, always look for the hidden factor, consider the source, it gave me real advantage compared to those around me, not to be better than them, but to see what's going on. It's like you gave me glasses for my mind's eye. You even whisper in my ear sometime. I can hear your voice when I read The Pink Elephant. And I don't care anymore if you are in-league with the Devil, for better or worse, I'm on your team". She did not shrink from heartfelt homage or wax saccharine humility "Thank you Lamby. If you are an example of what my work has borne I am truly gratified".

I took down the rollers, teased, sculpted and sprayed. Ida Rose inquired after Nick. I sketched him at Sky River, leaving out the knife and drugs, seeing him late at night drive by Hydra "But I'm not sure it's him. I just have a feeling. He's mostly why I'm going to California. You were right, I learned what I could from him, and feel like I salvaged enough of my self to go on alone. I want to despise him, but all I do is feel sorry". Her thoughts came from long insightful observation that had only a little to do with Nick "It's a tragedy to lose anyone. But his dark side dominates, making it impossible for him to learn anything from you. I'm afraid he's lost". Feeling a sudden stab in the heart I nodded "Yes, that's the sorry I feel. He knows it too, the way he keeps trying to get me back". She consoled softly "You can't change him. He has to do the work himself. Despising only binds you to him. You have wisely chosen sorrow". I suddenly realized I was mourning lifetimes of grief over lost hopes and expectations, that I'd suffered a tremendous loss of soul, that the path to recovery was through sorrow, that I had a way to go and time to mourn "Thank you Ida Rose. I don't think I would have ever understood if you hadn't helped me". Pushing Nick away I changed the focus "You know, I saw the I Ching in your bookshelf. At first I threw it as much as 20 times a day. I wanted to see if it had any integrity or relevance. It fascinated me how sometimes the hexagrams were exactly right. I throw it maybe once a month now, more as a meditation to get in-touch with my inside thoughts. What do you think of it". She thought for a moment "I consider the I Ching one of the great books of wisdom. How people use it is the problem. Consulting it as a divining crutch, to decide what to invest in, who to marry, where to vacation, letting it do their thinking for them. There again the problem is people not wanting to do the hard work, not the I Ching". Her hair done to my satisfaction. And to hers as she consulted the hand mirror "Even the most skilled beauticians have trouble with my hair. None have done a finer job. If you had gone to beauty school, you certainly have the talent and would have been a great success. You've made me look so civilized, I must go change these garden clothes".

Things flowed and conspired with Ida Rose. The groceries arrived as she came down-stairs in a white wool pants suit and silk blouse exactly matching the color of her hair. She tied an apron round her small waist, handed one to me, and commenced skinning, boning and pounding the chicken breasts flat but not too thin, preparing the stuffing, and noodle batter and cream sauce. While I wiped the mushrooms clean with a damp sponge and sliced them thin, washed sand from and chopped the leeks, peeled the asparagus stalks, and cut the fruit for a dessert platter. On cue, the stuffed-chicken went in the oven, and Tom arrived. They exchanged looks of long fondness. An unpretentious and shy smile handsomed his 22 year old face as we were introduced. I liked him right away. Ida Rose eager to get started with the audit, we followed into the living room. Tom adjusted the pillows on Roosevelt's green brocade couch, slipped-off his black-and-white Converse tennis shoes and lay down. Ida Rose took her usual winged chair, yellow legal pad and pencil poised. I sat on the Louis the XV chaise longue, hands tucked under my thighs, staring at Tom's clean white sox, the hairs on my arms at keen attention, this was the best rabbit hole in the world and I felt a great privilege being here.

Ida Rose began: *"Tom dear are you ready."*

Closing his eyes he exhaled: *"Yes Ida Rose I am."*

Ida Rose: *"Master please take Tom into whatever valence, stream of consciousness, point on the time track necessary for what you may wish to say to us.*

When I count from five to one you'll be there. 5-4-3-2-1."

Like Eddie, Tom's rhythm and words were not entirely his: *"There are events about to transpire which will be known in the Cosmos as the Big Split. Those whose loyalties lie with you Ida Rose and those whose loyalties do not. This is primarily due to the fact that Gabriel no longer wishes to hold the boot straps of other peoples programs. This is not of his own choosing. However it is by right of his own satisfaction in coalition with those of us who do not believe that his talent should lie wasting while others scoff. His magnitude is not of being first, the most, the highest, or the supreme being of your work. Rather, as being the first and most, and the greatest in the catalytic affects of your work. True, he has been antagonistic, arrogant and aggrieved in trying to make amends for events and things which have transpired in his own past. But for which he is not totally to blame, for his are not the marks of the one but of the many. And his time-binding spells do not reach back to any one God but rather to the many whose controls he has subjected himself to. Subjects and subjected alike. I see these ants in a volcano. A cone shaped ant hill. The survival of the fittest seems rather innocuous here, for ominous forces lie hovering as black clouds, fire and smoke encompass the skyline and are gathering forever formidable over the horizon, over the earth, this cone shaped ant hill. The giant queen ant is soon to be devoured by the giant spider whose mandibles cannot stand the pressure of the fangs from within and above. The egg sack has been laid, the two sides of the brain have been destroyed, and we wait for the 300 mutants to be hatched, this is nothing but an allegory dealing with the destruction of the Yin and Yang system. The two sides of the mind, the thalamus and the cortex, being eradicated so that neither one or the other shall be permitted to exist without re-evaluation of both systems, these things must all be re-evaluated. I see a great shipping clerk with invoices before him. Tallying up accounts due and accounts past due. These all have names, addresses, and phone numbers of those who enlisted their courage or lack of it into the program of the Great Godhead without really knowing why nor for some, really caring. It is with great dereliction of duty that some of these accounts are past due. And although some of us, and I use the word us loosely, have been thriving upon this credit in past due accounts, there are those of us who are frightened and are now trying to have these abject dues paid. In the advent that these are not reconciled or that the reconciling for these accounts does not transpire, there must be a re-accounting of these names to be put in a large filing cabinet. And I see that there are four filing cabinets, and these names are put in the second drawer of the second to the highest cabinet. For although there are temperaments and dispositions for those second most high Gods, we must remember that there are Over-seers to these. The Great Godhead himself owns the filing cabinets. None are impervious to His judgment and wrath, although wrath does not supply the proper idea here. Anxiety would be a more apt term. For although He is not totally conscious of them in their smaller frames of reference, He has seen through greater eyes with greater expectations than has the Great Father of the Christ Consciousness, He expected more from the Christ Conscious than it could produce. Promises, and promises, and more promises."*

Ida Rose: *"What's wrong with the God of this part of the cosmos, of the Twelve Constellations. Was He immature."*

Tom: *"The Great Father has always been in a state of fatigue"*.

Ida Rose: *"How did the cosmos produce such a weakling."*

Tom: *"It was not ready to expand when it did."*

Ida Rose: *"Who gave it the impetus to expand."*

Tom: *"The Great Godhead."*

Ida Rose: *"You mean the Great Godhead or the Great Father."*

Tom: *"The Great Father and Mother split, a hundred million years ago, which is relatively a short time, but enough to make a difference. They split before they should have. Thus creating a vacuum of confusion. It was therefore an immature cosmos to begin with."*

Ida Rose: *"Are you talking about the Bigger Cosmos or the Twelve Constellations."*

Tom: *"There is a dark area of the Great Father as opposed to the Great Godhead, I see that, I see this wedge in the Great Father's head, as representing the Twelve Constellations, this black area, and this area was never given proper time to fill in, there was a void space that needed more time for creative mind to develop there. All you had were fumes of creative mind in a stagnant situation, seeping though from the rest of this intelligence that surrounded it. And therefore when this exploded and brought in part of the vacuum which lies outside this intelligence, it created havoc among the Fallen Angels, among the Fallen Gods, you see, this wedge was thrown out. This wedge, this Twelve Constellation wedge was thrown out from the Great Father of the; what they call the Great Loving Sphere of Influence, of mind. It would have been as though instead of allowing the cancer to spread through the Great Father it was surgically removed and thrown out, to let it fester on its own. And I see that all the way back from there this information comes spiraling down to us. If you could give out report cards on the various deities or entities, you'd get various percentages, grade points, but for me to expose what they themselves are worth on a one to ten scale or a four point scale would be, would seem astonishing and erroneous. In fact, these entities themselves know who's to pay the piper, not I. And you Ida Rose, from your limited parameter which these others have given you, must decide for yourself according to what you know and what has been offered up to you, what is the truth and what is not. And I cannot challenge your sphere of influence although I must protect you at times from these programmed inadequacies which others would foster upon you, by revealing new aspects of the truth which all of us must pay for. None of us is left alone in a vacuum, unless we are only an organism and then we are nothing but a member of the living dead as far as the Bigger Cosmos is concerned. They call that; living decay. You must search your own soul and seek out the truth in some of these self-instilled parameters, so that others may know. Before it is too late for them to change it."*

Ida Rose: *"What about my long time student Wyatt. He has been very faithful to me as an organism. Don't misunderstand me. Is he a part of this Old Man's system or is he of the Bigger Cosmos."*

Tom: *"These people such as Wyatt, although they have been important in the past, are living in a vacuum. Stagnant in his own mental processes he has become spiritually inept. And dogmatic. And these things do not flatter him."*

Ida Rose: *"Why does he take on that wife, take on that spirit for so many lives. What does she represent."*

Tom: *"It is the same thing that Academia everywhere in your world suffers from, the Intelligencia which Wyatt is definitely a part, although he would not be seen in the same framework. It is one of the flaws of the Hydrogen Era brought forward into Carbon — where abstraction was the only medium of thought. You cannot have complacency toward an idea."*

Ida Rose: *"Who is Wyatt trying to save."*

Tom: *"Beauty with-out its negatives. He thought these cosmic flaws inherent in the Beauty Ray could be destroyed. But instead they ended up running rampant. And they are and always will be suffocating him. His wife has a negative Beauty Ray and shouldn't have been allowed to develop into such a monster. She is a succubus, and has no rightful place next to a man who wears such a magnificent golden crown. He is an example of the monarch who becomes impotent, due to lack of a positive female principal. When a positive male thesis is thwarted by a negative female one, or visa versa, there is no room left for creative thought, positive thought. And each must be eradicated, taken out to let fester on its own. But even so, mentation cannot be destroyed, therefore this thing was used as an example by the Great Godhead to see what could be done with festering cancer. And it too will soon be destroyed because its slow development and progress impeded the rest of the Cosmos for twelve billion years. Which is too long to let the cancer be alive. That's how long the cancer has been in existence. Twelve billion years."*

Ida Rose Demurely: *"What should Ida Rose do with the rest of her life."*

Tom: *"Ida Rose, you have been stifled, and impeded too long. By progress at the cost of hindrance. And this is about to change for the better. So therefore, take heart in the changes, which you see coming in the next years. Although there are times when you will feel things will be catastrophic, they're going to be positive and constructive changes, for the betterment of all of us. And those of whom you worry the most are those of whom will be searched out and if found to be true will live and if not, they will be destroyed. For there are those of us who love you and will continue to serve you, whether within or without your household."*

Ida Rose: *"Thank you Master. When I count to five you will be in present time. 1-2-3-4-5 present time."*

Tom's lids fluttered and his voice belonged to him again "Was it okay Big Mo". Busy writing she did not look up "Oh yes Dear it was beautiful. Thank You". Outwardly quiet, wishing I could speak to my thoughts, what a complicated story and I'd come in so far behind, these great spheres of influence, the Great Godhead, the Great Mother and Great Father of the Twelve Constellations, this Gabriel a great sphere too, partly so arrogant partly not, and the Christ Conscious, and the Over-seers, and Rays, a negative Beauty Ray, Wyatt and his wife weren't any better together than Nick and me. Tom slowly sat up, slipping on his sneakers and smiling at me, boyish good-looking without the innocence, we stole small glances, while Ida Rose finished her notes. When she laid the pencil down and leaned back in the wing-chair, I found my voice "Ida Rose can I ask how an audit works. How you get such important information". She seemed pleased "First and most essential when doing an audit, you must have a guide with spiritual authority and integrity. It was in 1949, *Dr.Southon of the California Testing Bureau and the University of California at Los Angeles asked me and several other professors at the University of Oregon to study human regression and develop a technique to tap the unconscious consciously, without hypnosis.* After studying with Korzybski, this was exactly what he had asked me to go on and do, undertake a study in human regression using some technique other than hypnosis. He wanted the consciousness to monitor the events to see if the mind knew anything about itself, to find out what I could about the silent level, the part that works before words, the realm of feelings and sensation, this was largely what propelled me to accept the opportunity and challenge. The Russians were also conducting this type of research, and when Dr.Southon left, and Major General Douglas M.Kelley of Nuremberg fame, and the United States Government took over the project, wanting to make sure they were not at any disadvantage to the Russians, they code named it MK2ULTRA. After months of intense work I discovered a process which I called auditing. I found so to speak the magic words that gave the auditor permission to speak. That very afternoon I asked a trusted colleague to privately do an audit on one of my co-experimenters L.Ron Hubbard. I was not completely surprised to find him in his most recent past life, with Mary Baker Eddy founder of Christian Science, and Aimee Semple McPherson the revered Pentecostal Evangelist and founder of the International Church of the Foursquare Gospel. They were together in a darkened basement performing a Black Mass. I knew then I was working with the wrong team and must begin to do this work on my own. Sending a copy of the audit to Major General Kelley, one to Hubbard to let him know I was on to him, and one to my house in Portland Oregon, I boarded the train for home that night, never imagining I was in danger until two men followed me onto the train. Fortunately a police sergeant on vacation befriended me, we rode the entire trip together, and he escorted me safely to my front door. The audit I sent to myself never arrived, Major Kelley never received his, and Hubbard continues to threaten and harass me to this day because I know the truth about him. Unfortunately auditing worked all too well, and Hubbard went on to build his Science of Dianetics on it. However, lacking the spiritual authority and integrity to guide an auditor across the Astral to read a person's life written on the Akashic Record, because of who he had been and still is, Hubbard wasn't capable of regressing them into past lives safely, could not protect them from the Astral, where any entity in any disguise can and does interfere and deceive for any reason. Auditing is dangerous business, sometimes taking you back to the scene of a horrific crime or death when you may not be ready or capable of handling it, and in the hands of someone like Hubbard, who could afford you no protection from the Astral, because he is in league with it, these poor people go screaming though the horror with no way home, branding their souls again with the same engram, burning it in deeper, which I suspect is Hubbard's real motive. Soul trauma is how he controls his congregation". Ida Rose looked at me but seemed to be talking to Hubbard "Auditing is not a game, not a party favor to be played with like a Fallen God's toy. The psyche is too precarious, too dangerous, too fragile". Now speaking to me "I am eternally sorry I showed him the way. If earth is a plane of form, the Astral is a plane of force, *a region surrounding earth, a sort of limbo just beyond human perception, but virulent indeed with many forces, an abode of Devils, and these wait for the unwary novice, the unprotected, or even experienced adept to unleash them.* These forces don't have the courage to take on human form, to pay the price that entails, yet they have their premises to prove too, and will gladly plead their case in whatever guise you might believe as you cross the Astral to the Akashic record, where every jot and tittle of your life is recorded. But a guide without the spiritual authority to negotiate these dangerous tides of force, to literally have the purity of purpose and heart to say *Satan get thee behind me*, will usher you as if alone into the demons den, helpless, not only jeopardizing the integrity of the audit with contaminated information, but subjecting you to very real danger, such as possession, from which you are totally unprotected and unprepared, and only by the grace of God can escape. Most people's lives are messy. They're desperate for relief, and naively turn to Dianetics and the like. They take the Dianetics course, join the Church of Scientology with the goal of becoming a Clear, not knowing that becoming cleared of engrams is the real lie, the real what I call Demon Chip. Some are regressed to terrible past engrams, being buried alive in the Spanish Inquisition, experimented on in a Nazi death camp, back to the scene of the crime, which if unraveled with care and a safe guide could free them for its grip even beyond the grave. But Dianetics is evil to it's very foundations, has nothing to protect them from the embrace of the Astral, they get unwittingly stuck in the horror of the moment, with no way out, no way home, replaying the terror and pain over and over. Some simply can not bear the torture. You've read the newspaper stories, Scientologist jumps from window, from the top of a building, anything to stop the agony. There are many out there that will beckon you to follow, but few have the truth. Dianetics plants its Demon Chip in the mind of a follower with false promises that once believed are impossible to extract. Disciples are blinded, much like an infant's baptism where the Catholic Priest closes the eyes ears nose mouth and mind of the child to influences other than the Church, then the poison is administered slowly and surely over a lifetime. Auditing is a powerfully numinous tool even in the wrong hands, and Hubbard's are the wrong hands. Gods need their congregations. He started his Church to play God, never intending his followers to realize their freedom, cleverly mixing in just enough truth to keep them mesmerized, while dripping the poison lie over time, not enough to notice consciously, steadily taking them in a direction they never intended to go. And drip drip as they instinctively jerk away from poison, the Demon Chip hooks deeper in their soul, making extraction seem more deadly than leaving it be".

I told of Monty becoming a Clear. Ida Rose shook her head slowly "Saint Philip was already going in the wrong direction. Dianetics will only hasten that". Tom nodded agreement. And I recounted investigating the Church of Scientology, having heard a high school beau was an upper echelon in the local order, downtown headquarters at the corner of 4th and Pine. Curious to see what this had done for him, I took the stairs by

twos, was greeted, no corralled on the second floor landing by a muscular blonde woman around 30. I asked for my friend. Without checking she assured me he was not there at this time, that she would be happy to talk with me about the Church if I would take their Personality Profile Test first, that she was a Clear, we would go over the test afterwards, and she would explain how Dianetics will help me. Thinking what do I have to lose but some time, I went with her to one of 16 cubicles. Many of the questions did not fit me at all, I chose the closest possible answers to 47, the other 3 any choice would have been so totally misleading I thought it more honest to leave blank, wanting to do my best, just incase Scientology held something for me, however when it came to my name and address at the end, I made them up, feeling more comfortable being anonymous after answering such invasive question for a stranger. Muscles reappeared the instant I put down the pen, taking the swivel chair cross the desk from me, barely fitting in the small space she scanned my test without expression, then jutting her chin and looking down a long thin Nordic nose, she challenged, did I simply miss 3 questions or was I too stupid to answer them. And she picked well, being called stupid always a loaded word for me, fortunately I had listened to the quiet part of me that knows the truth of the moment and was not completely ambushed, firmly stating how I thought giving a true picture of my self was important, that she nor the test said I had to answer all the questions, and since none of the 3 had answers that even remotely fit me, maybe it wasn't me, maybe her test needed fixing. Her brow began twitching, I had turned the table, pushed her button, one Dianetics plainly failed to clear. In a tight pitched voice she damned, how dare I criticize something that has helped so many, and shooting to her feet, ears crimson, wagging her finger like firing a gun, her pitch even tighter, my attitude and answers clearly showed how sick I was, obviously too dumb for their program. She was scaring me, I stopped listening, telling my self, unclench you hands Shoshy, breathe, let the poison pass through without resistance, sit small and still till her wrath is spent, for it is so hot it can not sustain. Finger slowing, she took my silence as surrender, put her gun hand on an abundant hip and waited. I rose like the Phoenix and fled. She followed, threatening we know your name, where you live. I couldn't help but turn on the stairs for a look, thinking if this is what Dianetics does, I certainly did not want it, then ran the rest of the stairs, down to 4th and turned on Pike, proud of my self, I had listened to my intuition, I could trust my intuition.

Tom congratulated me on getting away without repercussions "Big Mo and I know people who've been terribly harassed once the Church got their name". I had to ask "How come you call Ida Rose Big Mo". His eyes twinkled "After the battle ship Missouri. It's got the biggest guns in the Fleet, 16 inchers. And Ida Rose has the biggest guns in the Cosmos". Ida Rose chuckled "Yes Tom, I am a killer". Smiling too, picturing this 115 pound, 74 year old woman a killer, I somehow knew it was the truth. Tom had a dead serious edge to his funny, he'd been drafted to Vietnam, and upon seeing the war up-close, in good conscience could not fight, took a dishonorable discharge, dropped acid, spent time on the Haight, played drums in a band, he still smoked a little weed and played folk guitar. Ida Rose adding in her fashion that which would seem inconceivable bragging coming from anyone else "Tom carries the Arch Angel Gabriel's spirit with him. It's Gabriel who audits". My mind could not accommodate this "You mean he's an Angel". She sat up and gently smiled "No Little One, he carries that spirit much like you would carry a knapsack". Tom seemed very human to me, I could not see an Angel there, still there was something about him, some component formidable enough to hold its own with Ida Rose.

An intense discussion rose around the audit. I had many questions, listening to them talk so wonderful I just did not ask. Conversation moved to a newspaper article Tom read on the latest Quantum Physics theory, and how it sounded remarkably like and seemed to prove one of General Semantics tenets, The Organism as a Whole in the Environment as a Whole. And then too a paper Ida Rose sent for on the newly published conclusions of a 15 year study done on rats by Professor of Psychology David Krech at University of California at Berkeley, proving the brain worked exactly as Korzybski observed 60 years earlier with his theory of Delayed Reaction, counting to ten. Ida Rose spoke in high-speed, Nick and Ric complained after meeting her, somehow they thought this velocity, they both called it fast-talking cast a shadow on her integrity. But she was not too fast for Tom, or for me, I knew she was just keeping-up with her thoughts. As if hearing, she explained "My brain is cortically sublimated. Information goes directly to the cortex, by-passing the thalamus all together". I could not grasp this, thrilled she did not talked down to me and all that implied. Conversation moved to the latest in a steady stream of students from all over the world who came searching Ida Rose out, staying an hour or a day, as long as she would let them, listening to her speak of her work, some being audited to see were they in Palestine, could they contribute a first-hand account of that tragic murder, and, if the audit also shed some light on their personal journey, maybe took them safely to and from the scene of the crime, that was an extra benefit, though Ida Rose said it was not her purpose. She smiled tenderly at me "Very few ever come back".

Talk of Family and friends as we ate dinner and most of the fruit platter drizzled with honey and fresh lime. Without doubt the finest meal and the finest company in the twelve constellations, I wanted to reciprocate and offered to do the dishes. Ida Rose said no, she would take care of them in the morning, and brought two quart bottles of ice-cold Miller beer to the table. Of late I had a worrisome fatigue and sipped only the foam of my tall glass, exactly where I wanted to be anyway, no need to alter my head. The SLF had accepted me but I never really fit in, never really fit in anywhere, not even entirely with Jeffree and Bonita-Kay, or Josh. But here, the dialogue in my head was out-loud, and God, Gods a regular topic though not the only one. Tom started the jokes. A Rabbi, a Priest and a Minister were having lunch, talking about what they do with their collections. The Minister said his method was simple, take the collections outside, draw a line on the ground, throw the money in the air, whatever lands on the right side of the line he gives to God, what ever lands on the left he keeps. The Priest confessed to nearly the same, go outside, draw a circle on the ground, stand in the center and throw the money to heaven, whatever lands inside the circle he gives to God, what ever lands outside he keeps. The Rabbi shook his head marveling at their Christian God, for he also took the gelt outside and threw it up in the air, figuring what ever God wanted he'd keep. We laughed and laughed. Then Ida Rose. Moses and Jesus were playing golf. Jesus decides to use an iron for a long shot over a pond, landing the ball in the water. Moses parts the water, retrieves the ball, and handing it to Jesus advises him to use a wood. Jesus protests saying Arnold Palmer uses an iron on this shot and so will he, and proceeds to hit the ball into the pond again. Moses complains, parts the water and recovers the ball, this time urging Jesus to use a wood for he will not part the water a third time. Jesus insists, Arnold Palmer uses this club on this shot and so will he. Meanwhile two men hoping to play through are watching Jesus hit the ball into the pond a third time, and walk on water to redeem it, they ask Moses, who does that guy think he is Jesus Christ. Moses shakes his head, no he thinks he's Arnold Palmer. Tom and I laughed to tears, the beer helped, still Ida Rose could deliver lines so well, I thought anything she said could be funny. My turn, I had a good one and took time delivering with my best Yiddish inflection. A Rabbi and a Priest were good friends and had arranged to go on vacation. When the Rabbi arrived to pick up the Priest, he still had several confessions to hear. Rabbi offered to finish-up while the Priest got ready. Priest thought that would be okay since Jesus was a Jew, but he wanted Rabbi to listen to a few confessions first, to make sure he got it right. Rabbi concealed himself behind the confessional, while Priest took his seat behind the screen. A man entered confessing he slept three times with a woman who was not his wife. Priest granted him absolution and penance of ten hail Marys and ten dollars in the collection box. Another man entered, confessing he also slept three times with a woman who was not his wife. Priest absolves him with ten hail Marys and ten dollars in the collection box, then goes behind the confessional to his friend. Rabbi assures he understands perfectly, dons the Priest's robe and takes his place behind the screen. This time a woman enters, confessing she slept one time with a man who was not her husband, wanting absolution. Rabbi strokes his long beard thinking for a moment, then advises her to go sleep with the man two more times because the Church is running a special, three sins for ten dollars. I won legitimate laughter, so very pleased to hold my own.

Empty beer bottles and plates on the table, Ida Rose covered her yawn with a graceful hand, wearing a lovely diamond wedding ring, her beloved husband gone 12 years. She walked us to the door, inviting Tom "If you have time for an audit tomorrow, I'll make your dinner". He smiled in pure delight "I'll come right from work, by seven. That okay". She smiled "Perfect. I'll have something delicious waiting". She smiled at me too "You come back too Lamby, anytime. You are always welcome here". Plainly I died and went to heaven, and before I thought wrapped my arms round her small frame in gratitude. She did not exactly return my exuberance, yet from the way she leaned-in and did not stiffen, I knew it was not because she didn't appreciate this spontaneous physical display of affection but more the Victorian manners she's grown-up with that made a public show impolite. Tom and I walked silently to the parking strip. A bit glassy-eyed and tentative he inquired "It's still early, you wana go to the Blue Moon for a beer". I could see the glint of a coy wolf behind the shy invitation and considered long enough to let the invite make me feel good "Thank you, maybe next time. I really want to walk in the night air and be as big as I feel under the sky". He laughed softly "I know what you mean. Big Mo 'll do that to you". I looked at the moon "Yeah. It's like a dream really, and I don't want to take my attention away and have it vanish. Hope I see you again though". He flashed a toothy pirate's grin and got into his '66 Bug "Me too". I spread out and floated home, thoughts traveling into the universe on sliver threads illuminated by Luna's full company. Ida Rose was so much better than LSD.

Leda and Gretchen were fucking some young bucks, all riding to the same rhythm, nothing could bother me, standing at my bedroom door for a moment, such beautiful Sisters, so well formed, so uninhibited, I collected sleeping bag and pillow and went to the living room couch. And fell into the dream, stubborn, persistent, always vivid enough to make it over the threshold into consciousness and linger. A barren mountain, and I am rushing headlong down a winding loose gravel road behind the wheel of an older sedan, brakes iffy, sliding to a stop at the edge of a vast in-land sea, intimately familiar with this place though I don't recognize it. No one but me and not a cloud in the sky, looking across the placid golden green water, sun dancing, far-off blue hills rolling, I hear as if God instructing me "What a good day to die". Inextricably summoned to certain death, I grip the wheel, elbows locked, foot full-throttle to the floor, as fast as possible as far as possible before I sink, the first time ever I have courage to try, throwing a great rooster tail, finding the water only 3 inches deep, I am flying, I am free. My eyes shut tight against the morning light, willing the dream to linger, the feeling of flying staying with me, all these years I had been afraid to try, but something inside had changed, the dark deeps of fear, crossing the Great Waters of the Unknown in a vehicle never intended to fly, and I knew, I knew I did not need Nick's dark side to be whole, that I had my own, a whole inland ocean, and it would not swallow me alive. The feeling remained while I showered, and tiptoed into my room for fresh clothes, all four snoring in rhythm. Day nine I rode with Bear.

Court's drama no longer compelled me, even the body-search did not matter, though as the defendants took their seats, I coveted more than ever my freedom to come and to go. Over night I found my self heading another way, and it felt good, while some of me screamed dilettante, shame on you for abandoning your comrades, I did not have the stuffing for battles to come and all my paranoid phantoms. Ida Rose assured me that *consciousness of all things was the most lasting,* that thoughts were things, we had to think-up the New World and begin to live there if it was to become. I wanted to feel better and maybe it was as simple and complicated as finding what made me feel that way, and then making that happen more often, to incarnate in the New World. Day-dreaming of someone like Tom, some one I could talk too about everything, the jury was seated. Boldt entered in his ceremonial robe, here ye, here ye, and the game was on. Prosecution planned to call witness number 9, another FBI informer infiltrator of our meetings, who was unexpectedly not available, they asked instead to enter Horace L. Parker's personal diary into evidence. Banging his gavel twice Boldt dismissed the jury, saying he needed time to *"Review the diary before determining which if any portions were admissible as evidence"*. There were always those of us waiting for a seat in court. Overnight the fire department determined aisles were suddenly too narrow for safety and removed the extra benches that sat 40, giving rise to protest from the defendants *"Our Constitutional right to a public trial is being violated because of the court's refusal to allow all spectators in to witness the trial"*. Boldt never looked-up from the diary. Defense requested Jan Tissot and Donovan Workman, named as co-conspirators though not charged in the indictment, currently doing-time at McNeil Island Federal Penitentiary for unrelated offenses, be brought to Tacoma for a conference. Boldt granted the request, then abruptly adjourned to chambers. Jeff Dowd followed, pounding on Boldt's door with both fists, demanding spectators be let into the courtroom, pounding and pounding and demanding, the room hung silent. Boldt flung-open his door, brown leather brogues slapping the wood floor, mounting the bench, he did not sit, charging Dowd with contempt, and slap slap back to his chambers, contempt his only way to win. And now we knew the score, conspiracy could not be proven, that we had won the larger game, a sober victory, the cost to some so very terrible. Defendants and attorneys withdrew to strategize. I stepped outside in cold December rain, crowd cheering wild to word of the first formal contempt charge, they knew too we had ultimately won.

Jury and prosecution seated once more, I took mine, wet and chilled. Poised as a scorpion, predator eyes focused, Boldt instructed Deputy to demand the defendants and their counsel be seated immediately. Twenty minutes passed in barely rippled hush, six defendants, Susan Stern was home recuperating for an operation, and counsel took their places. Chip Marshall walked up to the jury and began explaining the delay. Boldt warned him sit down. Marshall continued *"Delay is our way of taking action in solidarity with the spectators being forced to stand in the rain outside the courthouse"*. Boldt held till everyone was seated and court brought to order, then dismissed the jury, and after they filed-out declared a mistrial *"The defendants have prejudiced their own case with the jury by improper conduct and statements"*. He cited each for contempt *"The display today was one of the most degrading and outrageous instances of contempt of court I have ever read or heard about"*. He charged defense lawyers Michael Tigar, Jeffrey Steinborn and Lee Holley with misconduct, adjourned in haughty disgust, ordering the courtroom cleared. This happened so fast we filed-out in stun, spilling onto the sidewalk, into a volatile turf war, Pigs aching for a reason, protesters shouting *"Off the Pigs"*. All anyone had to do was cross the white-tape line, not one did, Pigs had no reason. Riding home with Bear, shaking from the adrenaline rush of near riot, singing to the radio, we did not talk.

Straight to my room, grateful to find it empty, wet clothes off, dry on, I lit a lavender scented candle and stretched out on my sleeping bag with a biography of the first Queen Elizabeth. Coerced by all in court to do the proper thing and marry, she stood fast, refusing to give up power to a man, remaining spinster, the Great Virgin Queen. Finding precedent and corroboration always tempered my mettle, it wasn't that I didn't want a man, I longed for some one, but we had not changed so much toward women's freedom since Elizabeth, I did not want to live through one either, and thought a good man should stand behind him self. Napping when Gretchen waltzed in with a ready boy, I didn't mind, and did not stay for the festivities though they would have enjoyed an audience. Gretchen was a living illusion, miss-taking lust of the moment for more, maybe even love. I hoped she was just naïve and not ignorant, for I had not differentiated them out-loud either till Ida Rose explained her painting of sacred and profane love, still I suspected Gretchen knew and did not care, that I may have picked a friend who lived without personal honor and would not remain. I joined Ric and Arnie infront of the TV for Michael Tigar's interview *"The defendants want to proceed with the trial, did not move for a mistrial and do not feel their actions prejudiced the jury. We will appeal the contempt charges and mistral to the 9th Circuit Court in San Francisco or the Appellate Court, asking for a Writ of Probation against retrial. The charges of Summary Contempt are unusual for a mistrial, usually it's called when the prosecution asks the charges be dismissed"*. I couldn't escape falling down despair, like something precious and irreplaceable, handed in my family for generations had been intentionally smashed. The judicial system I'd been brought-up to believe would protect the innocent, was really a tool of the rich and powerful, conscience looked on as weakness of character, the only real sin, getting caught, little Nixons had been planted everywhere, judges, juries, police, politicians, businessmen, lying, cheating, stealing my soul, and worse, they had taken me down so fast, so low I felt a traitor saving my own life, leaving for California while the defendants fate hung, when maybe one more rooting for them might make the difference, one more quarter in the one-arm-bandit could take the jackpot.

Arnie, Ric heading to the Blue Moon for beer and burgers invited me along, and since Arnie was off my case and into Gretchen though she seemed oblivious, going somewhere fun could brake the falling down. Still, I felt like an alien, like nothing could slow the speed, Boldt and Pitkin were not Nixon's only long-armed puppets, they were locust, a plague, maybe the answer was to think-up a way to amend the arbitrary automatic reincarnation cycle, establish some benchmark for coming back that had to do with consciousness, compassion, conscience, there had to be a point where rubbish was no longer given carte blanche, born again and again. Tomorrow, tomorrow I would push the coward thoughts away and live in my honor, a nameless faceless soldier, I could no longer sit safely in the court room, day ten I would stand outside, transform my hands by taking theirs. Arnie met a beautiful girl, Ric ordered another pitcher, and alcohol ultimately gave me some surcease. I liked Ric, he never came on to me, treating me sometimes an equal when it suited him, we danced and drank and laughed, and held each other up walking home. His inebriated tongue complaining, a commanding anger toward his wife for even thinking of going South with us "I jus' know if she tastes some autonomy, she might never come home to me". Keely left a strict Catholic home at seventeen for a Catholic husband, pregnant right away, she had four, if she came with, it would be the first adventure on her own, and the only time Ric would have full responsibility for the Boys. I did not want to be in the middle of this and kept thoughts to my self "She hasn't said a word about coming with us". Glad for Ric's company, the hairs on my neck saying Nick was near-by. Gretchen and her latest were gone, the room smelled of them, I cracked a window, lit some sandalwood incense and crashed.

Morning hang-over headache and desert thirst, my mind unambiguous, I must get far-away from Nick, from the controlling worry of my family, from the SLF, the FBI, I longed to be on my own again, find out who I had become, there had never been a time like this, where a no-one like me, common-as-dirt-little-dung-beetle who did not belong to any Secret Society or Priesthood could have access, because of some, like Freud who discovered the unconscious, and Carl Gustav Jung who went on to deliver it from Freud's neurotic vision that all psychic energy issued from sexual instinct and repression, that all girls suffered from penis envy. In Jung's daring to challenge Freud's absolute authority and domination of the psychoanalytical hierarchy, he paid the terrible price of being marginalized. And because of Dr.Ida Rose Barber, discovering auditing, recovering the truth of the most current version of the myth, of the murder at Palestine, that Jesus was not suppose to die, consequently freeing his soul to graduate and fulfill its destiny of opening the Books of Life. And in-turn free us from the grip of an unconscious God, opening a way out, through the eye of the needle, for a girl of little promise to self-discover and learn to think, to look inside and read my own Book of Life, revisit the scene of the crimes perpetrated on my soul, have a chance to untangle the skein, reflect, be born-again and again in consciousness, to spend my life building an everlasting character through a consciousness that could give rise to and develop those qualities that can come with me through the needle's eye, courage, charity, ingenuity, integrity, perception, patience, love, honor, compassion, mercy, understanding, whimsy, intrinsically valuable qualities. And maybe without the weight of this life-sucking paranoia that fed on me, because I was so close to snapping the string of my kite, the slightest thing would do it, maybe I could grow-up, maybe I could live an original life, maybe I could matter if I got away.

Day ten. I dressed for rain and rode with Bear and Ric. We hoped contempt charges would flock people to the street, it was the only way prosecution could jail the defendants, we hoped for outrage. Bear handed me a pass as we walked the gauntlet, 30 Pigs standing shoulder-to-shoulder along the curb, 300 demonstrators crammed behind the white-tape line chanting Power to the People. I decided to go in first, the body-search especially invasive, there were twice as many deputies in court. First to speak Carl Maxey stood *"The legal questions to be considered are whether United States District Court Judge George H.Boldt acted within his discretionary authority in declaring a mistrial yesterday and contempt-of-court citations against six of the seven defendants"*. Boldt bristled *"The defendants will have to show cause why they shouldn't be held in contempt"*. Maximum penalty for this contempt was six months, bond could be posted, no one expected the defendants to wait in jail for the appeal. Maxey went to the issue of mistrial. Boldt refused to hear it. Maxey tried again. Boldt reminded *"I have already denied your request"*. The give and take so carefully couched in etiquette and proprieties, all too Golden polite and deadly for me, I held my resolve and went outside, giving my pass to a girl from the Tacoma Defense Collective, taking her place behind the white line. Shivering, vulnerable in pea-coat and stocking cap, no protection against hard-helmets, batons, guns, gas, and the impending Pigs, none remembering we are their daughters and sons. I soon learned how impending when accidentally bumped over the line, Pigs saw this as a challenge and surged. I backed through the crowd into sharp rhododendron branches, there was not enough side-walk, rain falling relentless, and no one seemed scared but me, totally terrified, sweat bursting, standing on explosives, needing to run away, squeezing behind the bushes, leaning against the building, its solidness a fleeting bolster. A girl, someone I did not know deliberately challenged the line, Pigs swarmed her to the ground, cuffing, carrying her rough to a waiting paddy-wagon, cheers answering her every obscenity till the door slammed her silent. Then word came, Boldt would make the defendants serve contempt sentences before a new trial, and there would be no bond granted to free them while on appeal. Five supporters arm-in-arm charged the line screaming at their only convenient target, detonation, signs turned weapons, batons striking shoulders and knees, screaming, and I no longer saw the point, attacking Pigs was not good reason to get my head or knee broken, this would not contribute one coin to winning the jackpot. The five were maced and cuffed and literally dragged to wagons, while Press snapped furiously, the crowd whooping and bawling. I edged along the building, away from men with sanctioned weapons and kids in soft knit caps, away to the corner, and looking back through an aurora of epiphany, this was not for me, not my life and death battle, though some made the courthouse theirs, believing they were ready for the consequences, and others plainly tantalized knowing they would become instant celebs, I did not want this, did not believe it would be enough to sustain me in prison. And yet I knew for sure that I was not a coward, and ran like the wind.

Breathless, sitting on a bus stop bench, rain washing my face of tears, wishing Mom and Dad would somehow just happen to come by and take me home, ten maybe 25 buses passing, no money, my coat heavy wet, I shadowed through streets to the Peoples Coffeehouse. Bear was there, bought me hot cocoa, and with keen journalistic notes read his blow-by-blow of what I missed. Carl Maxey continued to insist on a full hearing with witnesses and jury, holding that Boldt had set himself up as judge jury and prosecutor, while the defendants ripped their contempt citations into confetti, and Chip Marshall, Jeff Dowd, and Mike Abeles unfurled a Nazi flag over Boldt's bench. Boldt seemed frozen, as Dowd railed *"This better symbolizes the court than the American flag which was born in revolution"*. And Ables *"This is more like Nazi Germany. If you think by sending seven people to jail you're going to stop young people from protesting, you're crazy. More people are going to fight to the death to see people like you out of power"*. And Joe Kelly *"I'm glad the charge is contempt, that's how I feel about your flag and all you fuckers, you're all fucked up. The evidence will show I wasn't even at any of the meetings I'm accused of attending, to plan the February 17th demonstration. The case was a set-up and in the end you'll lose"*. Cheering and applause soared with every salvo. Marshall shouted *"You did basically the same thing good Germans did"*. Boldt calmly countered *"There is no German blood in me. My ancestors are Danes"*. Susan Stern scoffed *"Then there's something rotten in Denmark"*. The room went-up, urging Susan on. She obliged with an eloquent speech on racism, the trial, the war, poverty, political protest, refocusing everyone back to the important issues. Boldt threatened contempt if she did not sit down. She continued, unhurried, the room hushed in respect, Boldt affecting disinterest. When she did sit, he sentenced her to six months contempt, Michael Lerner six months, Chip Marshall, Joe Kelly, Mike Abeles, Roger Lippman and Jeff Dowd one year, ordered the courtroom cleared, and left the bench amid shoving matches, deputies, defendants and prosecutors. Two deputies dragged Susan away, Michael Tigar attempted rescue, deputies pinned him against the jury box and sprayed mace in his face. More deputies rushed through the double-doors and hauled away the other defendants, shoving everyone else out, down the hall and onto the sidewalk, where there were too many now to stay behind the white line, batons rained, every one ran, some fell, some were arrested. Bear was worried Ric was among them. But I could see him at the counter ordering coffee. He shushed me with a finger and sidled over. Bear jumped from his chair in pure relief and hugged him off the ground. Ric managed to hang onto the coffee, yes he'd been grabbed, but his leather jacket was so wet, he slipped the grip and got away. Part of me regretted running, missing the high drama, another thankful to be spared the indiscriminate jaws of juggernaut, smelling of warming wet wool, exhausted, all I wanted was to go home.

Afternoon papers told the rest. The courtroom cleared, defendants were brought back in, hands cuffed behind backs to be sentenced. Boldt gave his sermon *"All defendants but Michael Lerner are in contempt for causing riotous conditions in the courtroom. I personally noticed Lerner refraining from joining the fracas. Contempt charges will have to be served before the new trial begins. Similar conduct in the next trial will bring the same result, like a revolving door process with the trial and more contempt hanging over your heads. Disruptive court trials and what to do about them in recent times have become a grave concern to the public and to lawyers and judges, liberal, moderate and conservative, throughout the nation. Many solutions have been suggested, almost all based on the threat of use of contempt penalties as a deterrent of misconduct in the courtroom. But individuals who are determined to disrupt, delay or obstruct proceedings rarely, if ever are deterred by the threat of penalties of contempt. In every disruptive trial in recent times in which defendants were cited for contempt and penalties and jail time for charges, and these were delayed until the end of the trial, disruptive conduct did not stop or even diminish. The particular circumstances in this case, staged by the defendants themselves after numerous warnings, created a situation under which contempt sentences will be served before a new trial in this case begins. Serving those sentences will give the defendants ample opportunity to reflect upon their past misconduct and what it has brought them. I pray it will convince them disruption in the next trial in not worth what it will cost them. If they want a fair trial of the charges against them conducted in a reasonable, orderly and sensible way, that will be available to them. On the other hand, similar conduct in a new trial in all likelihood will bring the same result. I have no doubt my daily prayer for strength and guidance to be calm, understanding and patient in this case and to do that which is fair and just in the sight of the Heavenly Father has been answered. I believe divine providence has given this court guidance to an effective solution to disruptive trials. I pray it may be so"*.

Yikes, Boldt was talking to God. He had the men immediately locked in a courthouse cell on the 3rd floor, to be transferred to the Federal section of the Tacoma jail, Susan Stern held in the defense room in custody of two women deputies, to be taken to the United States Public Health Hospital because of her continuing need for medical attention. Those arrested outside were charged with second degree assault and yelling obscenities in public, the other charges, unlawful assembly, breach of peace and resisting arrest were dropped, bail set at ten-thousand dollars for each charge. Some excused jurors were interviewed. One believed "*The defendants premeditated the disturbances and had an organized plan to stop the trial*". Another "*My best belief is that the defendants never intended for the trial to go on. I think after today's incident, it would have been hard for us not to be prejudice. They were sure guilty of one conspiracy, they conspired to stop the trial*". The perception persisted that we were far more organized that we really were, and it was working against us now. The jurors went home, the defendants to prison.

Gretchen and Leda had gone with Keely and the Littles to Dick's on Capitol HIll for burgers. At the War Table, Ric, Bear, Mark and Arnie were doing shots of Sauza tequila, planning some thing that did not include me. I was stewing in too much reality, caught the bus downtown, another to the Ave, dropping half-a-hit of Sandoz along the way. Raining, I took a seat on the sidewalk under Ness Flowers' awning, back pressed to the solid brick wall, knees hugged-up to my chest, waiting, hats and evening shadows obscuring every face, watching the parade, cold crawling the pavement up my spine, teeth aching with tin foil, sidewalk turned to ice, paranoia my mirror, suddenly every face a menace, maybe Nick, I was never this intimidated on the street and dared not move for fear of being seen vulnerable, set upon, available symbol of the strife, these menacing middle class faces the essential element in any success-full revolution, they had to participate, support the cause or it would not happen, and most were just too damn comfortable at the moment to be moved, the Press effectively poisoning them against us, we were so organized, so strong, and Nixon was telling the gospel truth, and doctors cure all ills, the judicial system is just and protects the innocent, priests save our souls, all singers on TV are not lip-syncing, and we are the real enemy. I felt personally imminently their animosity, and so close to the Event Horizon, being suck into that infinite maze, a willing passive psychic suicide. The pull of weight, an anchor sat down next to me, I rested my head against it. Those green eyes, fine jaw, thick wet blonde hair clinging to his neck, I followed a trickle up to the collar of a fringed buckskin jacket, and was not sure I spoke aloud "Some one really loves you to make such a beautiful coat". Gabriel's lips moved "Woman, you're an incorrigible chauvinistic pig assuming someone made this for me". The word woman roared through my body like hot rum, made me feel respected, so much better than girl or chick or lady or ol'lady "It's not possible for me to be chauvinistic. That comes with men entitled to power. It would mean I have some over you, and in our society I don't". A wicked grin spread slowly across his face "Oh yes you do woman, big time, and you know it". Power to stiffen his dick was not what I meant, I had never felt lust on acid, could follow the line all the way back to our first trip when the redolent promise was made, how inevitable, how irresistibly humiliating, how my body wanted him too, how my head knew better, and where was my heart in this. Gabe stood-up and offered his hands "I heard Nick got busted at Sky River and he's out on bail waiting trial. The day he threatened to break my hands, I moved. You know, there's something wrong with his head. Word is he hears voices". Putting mine in his sealed the deal, he lead me to his place over the ID Bookstore, we hung our clothes above the gas heater, and kissed and fucked and smoked flower-tops and listened to music and drank tea, and when we came down enough, slept.

Just another musician's conquest, even so the sunny morning found me content in human contact, I did not need psychic suicide, we showered and went to the Hasty, agreeing over omelets and coffee, no regrets and no commitment. Gabe asked me to band practice. I knew in my bones it was now-or-never-time for California and without explanation kissed him farewell and went home. I was just living at Hydra, not accomplishing anything significant, the trial on hold, and I knew now or sure Nick was at liberty. Leda was ready too, for different yet similar reasons, too many hounds on her scent. Gretchen ready too. And though Ric hammered relentless on how only a terrible mother would leave her husband and children behind, Keely sat-in on our plans at the War Table. Hitching was illegal in Washington State, we needed a ride to Oregon, Keely knew someone driving to Portland in three days and would make the arrangement. We pressed her to come, we needed her to complete the MotherTruckers, to be safe. Her smile lit the room, hands went into her mouth nibbling those nails, yes she would come, but only for a few weeks.

The papers were full of trial articles and editorials. Boldt adamant "*This court is satisfied there is a high probability that each and all of the defendants sentenced for contempt will take flight, go underground or abroad or otherwise become a fugitive, frustrating a new trial. Recent instances of such flight to avoid prosecution by persons involved in activities similar to those admittedly engaged in by the defendants, and under similar circumstanced have not been uncommon. The court is further satisfied that all of the defendants sentenced for contempt have urged and incited physical violence in their planning and execution of revolutionary activities, and there is evidence that several of the defendants have committed such violence. The violent language and actions of the defendants and the threats of violence openly stated by them in the court-room and in the judge's presence, and the misconduct outside the courtroom, in the opinion of the court, makes it highly probable that potential witnesses, officers and staff members of this court and members of the community in general will be put in danger of their physical safety and lives if the defendants are permitted to be at large on bail"*. Pitkin sent a corroborating memorandum to the court *"There is a substantial risk the defendants may flee, as have some of their fellow revolutionaries, for example Angela Davis and Eldridge Cleaver upon finding themselves in jeopardy"*. Recommending if bail was granted, $25,000 for each contempt charge, claiming there had been threats on Horace L.Parker's life, on his life and others. Carl Maxey would appeal the 9th Circuit Court in California to overturn Boldt's denial of bail. Sadly the defendants would be held behind bars until that decision. I personally heard those threats of violence, they were public posturing in the heat of overwhelming injustice, none of us were killers. In this promised land of the free and home of the brave with truth and justice for all, I did not want to believe persecution could be so blatant and the public such fishs. The whole thing poisoned me, Nixon's popularity at an all time high, my head rolling round in lies, I began talking to my self outloud "Snares. You will not step in the quicksand. Snares. You have been down this road enough times. You know where it leads. Snares. There's nothing more you can do. Snares. Get busy going South. Say your good-byes".

A still December morning, I walked through Volunteer Park, by the Big Stone Ram on my way to Ida Rose. She and Eddie were leaving for the QFC, and warmly invited me along. The thrill of inclusion, solid ground. I pushed the cart down aisles while they filled it. Her long time students Milly and Maynard were driving from Eugene Oregon, Maynard coming to do an audit, and Ida Rose wanted to make them Carbonnade á la Flamande for supper. She explained he carried the Dragon with him like Tom carried the Archangel Gabriel, and it was vital for her work to have that entity's point of view. Having intended to quietly sponge-up the conversation, I worried this was the same Dragon as my own, and found my self spilling a long held shame. Ever since I could remember, monsters came to my bedroom at sun down and stayed till first dawn. I particularly hated dead Winter with its 16 hour nights. The monsters never showed themselves to anyone but me and never appeared outside my room. I could only really see the big one, clearly delighting in flaunting her mouth full of grisly teeth and slamming that thorny tail with such authority, either would have been enough. The smaller one showed himself at the very corner of my sight, mostly those shining black eyes, my imagination left to bloat the menace. I dared not sleep, knowing they would carry me forever into their dark realm the moment my eyes shut. Sleeping became the enemy, fought-off with a 25 watt lamp and radio on till morning light rescued and I could rest. I told my Folks. They said mine was an over-active imagination, just go back to sleep, you are safe, do not worry, they were there for me, never understanding even if what they said was true, it did not matter, I was left to fend alone, wondering what terrible thing I had done that monsters came after me, only me. So I collected soldiers at every turn, sent-in cereal box tops, traded my Brothers for Cracker Jack prizes, begged more for Chanukah and birthdays. When Mom would take us to Kress or Woolworth's, and give each a dollar to get what ever we wanted, I would buy the green rubber soldiers instead of the more expensive painted lead, numbers were important. At dark I would ring the army around my bed, quick hands darting over the side for fear of what was underneath. On especially terrible nights when I could not hold vigilant eyes, I would scramble to the closet, under the bottom shelf where nothing could sneak-up from behind, line my army four and five deep infront, lamp and radio always on. And those nights when I could not keep eyes on all the monsters because they brought friends, I would leap from my bed far as I could, sneak into my Brothers room and crawl under one of their beds, or creep down stairs and slither under my Folks double-bed, careful not to wake them, for they would take me back. The monsters stayed behind, not interested in anyone else, not wanting to be seen, no proof. Sometimes so exhausted on a long Winter night, I would just sink onto a desert of liquid rolling sand, relief, I could see and hear forever, no one could sneak-up, and I would rub my hands together, feel them silken and light and lovely as the sand, but the sand would suddenly turn to shards, and my hands thick and heavy and jagged, and I would panic, extremes making me hysterical, screaming, the sound coming from far away, bringing Mom or Dad, who carried me to the downstairs bathroom sink, and held one hand under cold water, one under hot, somehow calling me back together, mortified this was happening to me. Eddie and Ida Rose were glued to my story. She assured me I knew the Dragon well, that it loved to prey on children, such easy prey, making way into their souls for yet another lifetime, inspiring shame and fear, and control. That this was the mighty battle of the opposites, good and evil, innocent and not, the Dragon using anything to establish its premise that children are plainly not innocent, proven by their shame, and therefore fair game. She praised my intuition, my understanding that Christ symbolically rose with the dawn, that the Dragon could not live in the presence of that shining light. I had always believed the monsters were not just my imagination, and though they faded to shadows in my teens, I was still afraid of the dark, ashamed they were still after me, stalking through Nick and others, proving yes, somewhere inside I must be bad. Ida Rose knew these terrors well and offered sweet consolation, I should not feel responsible for the Dragon's interest, for this was exactly what it wanted to inspire. That I should be proud, honored the Dragon pursued me, it wasn't punishment for some awful flaw but a measure of my worth, for the Dragon only went after those worth getting. Her words were a healing resolve, all I ever wanted was to be worth getting.

As we carried groceries into the house, Eddie sheepishly confessed to monsters in his childhood room. Ida Rose gave him a knowing smile. He kissed her lightly on the cheek and left for an appointment. I loved being in the kitchen with her, she prepared food like the Baba Yaga of my dream brewing her potion. I did dishes as used. And when the beef shanks were floured and set to browning in butter, she made coffee, we took cups to the Mahogany Table, and lingered through the big picture window, hills clothed in red and golden maples, frosted-white Cascade Mountains floating in the Eastern blue sky, Nature's symphony sipped in comfortable silence. I felt so special, so privileged here just me and her, and did not care the Dragon was due. Intermission over, Ida Rose looked to Maynard and Milly's arrival, the shanks needed simmering for hours in beer, guest bathroom and bedroom made-up in fresh linens. I carried my cup to the sink. She did too, and taking the top sheet from a pile of papers on the counter, offered it to me as we walked to the front door "This is an audit I typed-up for my students. I know you'll be glad to have it. Such good news. It came in answer to a question I asked one of my young auditors during a recent audit". I folded the paper and put it in my coat pocket as she opened the door. Words so inadequate, I wanted to hug, touching her arm instead "Thank you Ida Rose. You help me so much I can't even tell you. I'm leaving for California in two days, and came to say good bye". She said my favorite words "Come and see me when you come home".

Wholly restored, the sidewalk soft as rubber, I hiked up Galer and into Volunteer Park. Sitting at the Ram's feet I opened the audit.

Ida Rose: *Who is talking.*

Auditor: *I am the Christ.*

> *And in this New Reign*
> *Nobel intention*
> *Good will*
> *Loyalty to principle*
> *Dedication to human welfare*
> *These things are now free to be exalted*
> *And afforded their rightful place*
> *Which is at the top of the world*
> *Throughout every level of human affairs.*
> *And those who assemble in the name-natures*
> *Of these high ideals*
> *Shall hence forward prosper.*

Ida Rose was right, this was good news. Putting it back in my pocket, thinking of maybe reading this to my Sisters, I bid Ram adieu, and headed down Aloha to my Granny's house on 12th to say goodbye.

She was not home, most likely senior square dancing at the Seattle Center, I kissed her door, walked by my place on Republican where Jeffree, Bonita-Kay and Casey came into my life, and the apartment Katey and I shared, then along Broadway, wrapped in a bitter-sweet nostalgia for simpler days, I could not would not go back, my journey from Golden calling, everything up in the air, and I could be gone a long time, making these old haunts seem so much more dear. Where Broadway splits to East Roy Street and the Quest Bookstore, the De Luxe Bar & Grill's cheer summoned me in. I was hungry, the place made a great spinach salad with mozzarella cheese and warm honey mustard dressing. Waiting for a seat I heard my name called from the bar. Two high school classmates, now seniors at Seattle University, on their way to Ivy League Law Schools, and still jocks-jerks, their Golden superiority carefully studied to seem humble, exactly the contrast I needed to take the charges off Hydra men, who in comparison were progressive saints. Polite hellos and what are you doings, and then came the same ol' "Aw, come on, just one liddle beer, you know you wan' to". I hated being told what I wanted and walked out without a word, stopping by Dick's Drive-in for a large order of fries, the best in the city, they cut their own. Taking a seat at their outdoor bar, eating the thin and crispy on the outside soft and flakey inside salty greasy piping hot and oh so satisfying morsels, dipping one by one in sweet ketchup, I looked-over the just delivered complimentary afternoon Seattle Times. Jeff Dowd and Roger Lippman had been transferred to McNeil Island Federal Penitentiary, Joe Kelly to California's Lompoc Prison near San Luis Obispo, Chip Marshall and Michael Lerner to Terminal Island in Los Angeles Harbor, Mike Abeles still in the Tacoma Jail waiting transfer to Terminal Island, and Susan Stern taken to the Seattle City Jail. Justification for this, Tacoma City Jail officers feared the daily demonstrations protesting the defendants' imprisonment, and other prisoners busting cell windows in sympathy. This was so clearly punitive, making it difficult for the defendants to talk to their attorneys and each other, putting them in with hardcore inmates who were sure to punish them for their pinko-commie-long-hair-faggot ways. The Ninth Circuit Court was said to rule on bail soon, I expected them to delay and delay. And I worried what the FBI had on me, felt my arrest looming, not sure anymore who or what was following me, being as careful as could be, insisting on cash for my handiwork, no bank account or checks, no bills in my name, no income tax, no traffic tickets, no trail, maybe I could get away. And since the trial began, I removed all labels from my clothes, bought new fake ID, stayed away from most public events, hoping I was suffering from an inflated ego, that they did not really care about a little fishela like me, although Nick was certainly real.

Bedroom shades drawn tight all morning, reading Elizabeth, I hardly slept thinking-out what was I doing. Ric and Keely were fighting loud about her going, Leda gone to Mom's for her things, Gretchen too. I took my suitcase from the closet and opened wide, having filled it so many ways in my mind, the first thing in, Ida Rose's book, lingering on the photo of William and Tara used as a bookmark, I decided to call her Folks in Garden Grove California. Her Mom sounded relieved to tell me, Tara broke off with William, moved to San Francisco hoping to join the American Conservatory Theatre, and last she heard was staying at the YWCA until she could afford a place of her own. One more good-bye, bathing in preparation, I caught the bus to Mercer Island, arriving for roast chicken dinner. My Folks instinctively understood I was running away. Dad's uncharacteristically restrained manner puzzled me, he always said he worried twice as much about me as my Brothers, for he knew only too well what guys thought and what they wanted from a girl, though truth be told, my curiosity alone was twice my Brothers, much more to worry about even if I had been a boy. Mom's avoiding eyes said she assumed I was running from her. I put on a gay face, wishing to explain I was running toward something too. Her anguish mostly not about me, more what could happen to her Little Girl out there alone in the big bad world, and how terrible she would feel if I came home damaged or not at all. Haight-Ashbury, Texas, the fact that nothing bad had actually happened to me not included in the equation, her what if might or could happen fears I had no open way to ease, so I spun the lie "Mom, I know you liked Keely. Her and me and two more girlfriends, Gretchen and Leda, we're going to California tomorrow. Gretchen arranged for a ride the whole way. We're staying at her family vacation home in Santa Cruz for as long as we want. Imagine going to the sunshine in December". She vented familiar motherly warnings, and I yearned to take the pain from her heart, listening quietly without defense, eating roast chicken in amends. Soon as dinner was done, I made a lame excuse "We're leaving early, so I better get going". We all stood. Tears filling her big browns, Mom put arms out for me "Oh Shoshy, I'll miss you so much". Realizing she already missed me and I was not gone, feeling like a five-year-old I went to her bosom "Me too Mom". Dad stood quietly waiting, and reaching into his pants pocket for a twice-folded 100 dollar bill, he pressed it into my hand "Just in case you find yourself in a situation you don't like, money will give you a choice". He never carried folded hundreds in his pocket, I smiled at the premeditation. Not done he reached for the sleek little three-inch blue enamel Seiko folding knife ever in that pocket, placed it on the 100, and close my hand over "You should always travel with money and a weapon". I hugged him tight "Thank You Daddy". We held our tears, Dad and I so much alike, often butting heads, I could rely on him to see though my lies, thrilled-to-wings he would send me off with these gifts. They were such a pair, still crazy for each other after 26 years, standing on the porch, arms around, watching me walk to the bus stop, their love my standard for what a man and woman could have together. They could not have known the Sixties would happen, that times would change so much, that the old safe ways could not be mine, that I would have to become my own paradigm. Tears came as I sat on the bus, how fortunate to be loved so much, I would miss then too.

Caressing the lovely blue knife now in my pocket, my Excalibur, Dad's wisdom and protection coming along with me, I would keep it close. A VW bus followed as I hurried three blocks to Hydra, sword opened, testing the razor-sharp two inch blade, slicing my thumb enough to bleed. The house quiet, Gretchen and Leda sleeping sound in their bags on the bedroom floor, Amaru lying in-between, looked-up, sighing as if waiting for me, she closed her green eyes. I liked this big-toothed Amazon coming with us, though Leda refused to leash her, stubbornly insisting it was too much an affront to Amaru's sensitive spirit, leaving me nagging and uneasy about her safety on the road, remembering Nick's Dog. I lit a candle and finished packing, California received me so well last time, and now I knew exactly what to take, the magic teapot, all my embroidery floss, hoops, needles, thread, thimble, scissors, pinking shears, a five-inch cast-iron jewelry anvil, ball-peen hammer, rawhide mallet, hand-drill, awls, wire cutters, needle-nose pliers, all my copper wire and beads, jewelry glue, a small jar of gold-leaf paint, brushes. The suitcase would be heavy and clumsy, but if I expected to stay, I would need all these. Lately my jewelry found its voice, with Nixon's devaluation of money, I'd taken to cutting-up coins, exposing their false pretense, incorporating them into whatever I made, their zinc interiors covered with copper or silver, metaphor for the hidden agenda. And I foraged every street, making whole breast-plates of bottle-caps and pull-tabs, and the new throw-away Bic lighter, as disposable as people might be, I found so many, and would sew them little outfits, and beaded jewelry, painted on a face, and make them into necklaces and earrings. Often I found shoes, cut stars from the grommets, painting with gold leaf, adding to necklaces, earrings. And radio dials, watches, glasses, a pair of dentures, road-trash strung together with beads copper and glue, things that usually were not associated, my creations found a voice. Especially the gowns, current fashion held us hostage in tight gaudy geometric printed mini dresses, girdles, padded under-wire bras, platform shoes. Mine were about moving free, long easy skirts, comfortable sitting, able to run-away if you must, and big usable pockets. Almost as an after-thought I packed my clothes, the velvet gown, tapestry halter-dress I wore to my cousin's Bar Mitzvah, a new frock made from a long-sleeve cotton Mexican wedding-shirt with four rows of embroidered patches added to make an ankle length skirt, naming it my living dress since it continued to evolve as I continued embroidering the patches, often while wearing it. And a green wool V-neck sweater, one pair of bell-bottom jeans, a Lanz flannel nightgown, all my scarves, and black knee-high lace-up English hiking boots. I would wear my jean skirt, maroon sweater, waffle stompers and pea-coat, the cold and rain constant now, I could not know how long we might be standing on the side of a road.

Unable to shut-off the possibilities reeling my head, when our 8AM ride arrived I had been showered and dressed for hours. Gretchen, Leda, Keely put their packs and sleeping bags by the front door. Gretchen wearing a long striped gypsy skirt, her favorite black-satin push-up bra showing through a white-cotton peasant-blouse, cinched tight with a wide leather belt. Leda in a purple suede vest, red glass beads strung on the long fringes, lavender-blue turtleneck sweater and purple corduroy jeans. Keely as always, skin-tight faded bell-bottoms, tight fitting t-shirt. I took the red bandanna from my neck and with Amaru's consent tied it round hers. She looked-up, shining green eyes delighted to be part of the fashion show. Going up-stairs for my suitcase, Arnie coming down, I had given him a very hard-time for being such a jerk, and grown to respect his smart strategies and dedication, he was heading home to Ithaca in a few days and I would even miss him a little "Hey man, give my love to Max when you see him". Surprised by my friendly, head shaking side-to-side he smiled "Such a shame you and me never got together". I smiled too "Ya know, I might even miss your sort of handsome face". Seeing an opening he kissed my mouth, and I kissed him back, no unrequited sparks flying either way, in a twinkle all was forgiven and we laughed a mutual regard. I lugged my suitcase to the door. It was an instant joke, Gretchen warning I would be sorry, she would not help carry that thing. Our driver called himself Fixer, a dealer making his usual run, Vancouver BC, Bellingham, Everett, Lake Stevens, Snohomish, Seattle, Tacoma, a special delivery from Hydra to Castle Rock, then Vancouver Washington, and Portland, we were welcome cover, he would drop us anywhere in Northern Oregon. I had a sinking feeling, fingering Excalibur in my pocket, it was my own damn fault, I should have asked more questions, pulling Keely aside "You didn't tell me he was a dealer. Maybe he knows Nick". She shrugged her shoulders. I pressed "Dealers know each other. I'm scared Nick 'll find out where I'm going". I called Gretchen and Leda over "Look, this guy Fixer could know Nick, he's a dealer. You have to call me Suzanne till we leave him behind". We put hands on each others, and the promise was sealed. Ric went outside for a word with Fixer, giving him money, and glaring at Keely, he stomped upstairs without good-bye. We stowed our gear in the trunk of Fixer's black 1965 4-door Pontiac Bonneville, atop maybe 100 brown plastic wrapped bricks of Marijuana, the Littles crying and clinging, not so much for our going, more they were not. Carolion promised to keep good watch over them, Mark and Bear did too. Tears streaked Keely's face as she scooted in with Leda, Amaru and me. Gretchen took the front seat and turned on the radio, James Taylor's song *Fire and Rain* was playing – *Suzanne the plans they made put an end to you.*

Chapter Thirteen

THE MOTHERTRUCKERS

Me and Mom and Dad and my Brothers were going on vacation to Seaside Oregon, I was always too excited to sleep even after Aurora drove the monsters off, and so my eyes were always heavy from the motion of the car as we passed Tacoma, struggling to keep them alert. Now, passing Tacoma again heavy-eyed, I snuck half a Sandoz onto my tongue from those still at the bottom of my shoulder bag, did not want to miss a minute of this adventure, believing since I was little, if I kept my eyes vigilant, everyone in the car would be safe. Amaru rested her head in my lap and sighed resignation to the cramped indignity of the floor. I stroked the pink insides of her beautiful ears and watched Gretchen cast her spell on Fixer. Such an accomplished siren, I gave-up condemning her behavior, though I thought these seductions earned nothing in the long run, she made it clear the long run did not particularly interest her, she wanted the goodies now. The baled-hay fragrance of mediocre weed pervaded the car, and because I was tired, Sandoz came on faster, tuning me in to the more instinct driven game under the surface, the sport of user using user in the front seat. I was embarrassed, uncomfortable even as a passive player in the cannibalistic despair beneath such seeming playful pretense, and turned my full attention to Amaru, some times all I could stand were animals and kids. Her head heavy, she had fallen into a chase dream and I gladly attended each nostril twitch and muffled huff. Leda and Keely were busy heart-to-hearting their perfect man, how they would fall in-love.

Two hours South, Fixer took the Castle Rock exit to Seaquest State Park and Campgrounds, where those who planned on living at Sky River had built a Tent City after police evicted them for Edwin Tate's farm. This was the first I heard of them, and was interested to see. Parking in the lot, Fixer ordered us stay in the car. Gretchen got out anyway, obstinately determined to claim every humiliating privilege she had earned. Taking five bricks from the trunk, he put them in a canvas bag, and yielding to her prerogative offered his free arm. She took it, they disappeared down the wide dirt road to the campground. Keely's thick hair could hide any thing, she magically pulled a fat joint from behind her ear, wet the paper with spit to make it burn slow, lit with a Bic, sucked a long slow hit, put it to Leda's waiting lips, and then mine. Neither had a clue how high I was already. Amaru watched our every move, breathing in the passive smoke, sneezing, and I realized she was not tame, simply obliging because she liked us, resting her chin in my lap, nudging my hand for pets. I stroked her softly, and as always does on good acid, epiphany dawned, I dream, she dreams, animals dream, I had been reading Carl Jung on dreams, learning the language, they were becoming profound in my waking life, and this dog creature with the white-rabbit fur and me, we had common ground. Then all the animals I had ever eaten appeared in a long procession, deep yet innocent blame walked with me down the line asking each forgiveness, promising the killing would stop with at least me. I had gone Vegetarian for personal selfish reasons, but now, in-respect for a common psychic dream ground it would be for them. And revelation swelled, I heard Bonita-Kay's wisdom, lessons and reason come clean when space and time fall in between, I could clearly see why I had to leave the Liberation Front, how purpose and courage that can capture people's imagination and shift the direction of society was becoming reactive, idealism turning to paranoia, community to defense, heroism to celebrity. A majestic clear crystal castle rose around me, I saw how thoughts were stored in this cosmic-world-mind-bank, and were available for withdrawal to those with enough credits. Ida Rose said thoughts were things, maybe if enough of us thought-it-up and then lived the New Myth it would come true, not user using user, but lover loving lover, giver giving giver, there was enough for all of us to have. Long held principles of Physics were changing, Quantum Mechanics had blown-away the old Newtonian dogma of opposite-and-equal-reaction, sub-atomic particles called Neutrinos had been found with no measurable mass or charge, Heisenberg's Principle of Uncertainty corroborating Ida Rose, that thoughts had substance, that by consciously observing, a person affected the outcome, that the space between us was not empty but filled with an all-pervading infinitely elastic ether, what Ida Rose called *cosmic blood plasma*, what I understood as Tao. No matter how abstract, consciousness was valuable, no matter how isolated my thoughts made me feel, I had consolation knowing Ida Rose, and could hear her admonition, *this is not a summer camp Little One*, and marveled how she could be so simply profound.

Amaru's neck muscles tensed, the crystal castle fell, Gretchen flung open the front passenger door and dove in "Lock all the fucking doors right now". We did. Hands shaking she lit a smoke "I was talking to some Tent People while Fixer did the deal, they really bought into in Sky River's promise of a permanent home and feel they been totally fucked-over. I thought they were mad at the cops evicting them, and boasted I'm from Hydra. They think it's our fault they don't have anywhere to live and no money to go home. I got really scared". Amaru stood with her front paws on my legs looking out the window. An angry gang began circling the car, 9 males, trying the doors, pressing their tongues against the windows, pounding their fists. Amaru jumped in front barking, spitting, showing those lovely teeth. Fixer's key was in the ignition, I sort of oozed over the seat, started the engine, released the emergency brake, laid my body on the horn, left foot hard on the brake pedal, right foot full-throttle gas, engine whining. The crush fell back, my foot slipped-off the brake, we fish-tailed up the dirt road maybe ten yards, horn blaring, foot finding the brake, I was too high to do any more. Fixer seemed to appear from the air, screaming at Gretchen to unlock the passenger door. She was frozen. I leaned across, pulling-up the handle. He grabbed a Remington 12-gauge from under the seat. Amaru leapt over Gretchen, out passed Fixer, snarling a fearless deadly warning, charging the men. Leda panicked, scrambling after, commanding her to stop. Amaru would not, anything could happen, I shifted the transmission into reverse and sped toward them. Fixer sprinting after, demanding "God damn you Bitch, stop". It seemed someone else's heart was pounding in my body, someone else driving, and it seemed way too long till I came to a soft stop, hitting no one. Leda held Amaru by the red bandanna, wagging her finger at her nose, scolding. Amaru stood tall, unabashed, her unflinching eyes fixed on the rabble. I could only smile thinking how silly, for Amaru was not tame and would do as she pleased anyway. Fixer smacked an open hand on the driver's side window "Get the fuck out". For some reason I was not intimidated by this guy, unlocked the door and sat there till he opened it, stepping-out like arriving royalty, waiting for Leda and Amaru to get in back, I turned smiling to the now circumspect Tent People having been joined by some of their females, only one smiled back, I could not hold her gaze, my eyes falling to her feet wearing my stolen shoes.

Fixer slid the shotgun under the seat and drove away from Seaquest Park, no one spoke till on Interstate 5 going South, when he coldly informed us Ric had arranged delivery of the weed, so the Tent People could deal for money to go home. I looked at Fixer with new eyes, Amaru too, and totally wasted, settled quietly in my place, her head again resting on me. The MotherTruckers dynamic had begun to show. Gretchen the Straw Queen, her flamboyant sexuality most evident. Keely was a follower, sometimes running herself right over the cliff before she thought things out, spending many of her years dealing with the consequence. Leda the youngest though somehow the oldest, a compelling mix of reckless curiosity and sincere compassion. Amaru, our magnificent Amazon Warrior and rightful Queen, who knew the Alchemical secret, that the King, or in her case the Queen does not rule but serves. And me, the looker-in looker-ahead, the only one of us humans here who seemed to value her self. Everyone else was over-amped from the ordeal. Keely questioning coming with us, certain she just escaped death, wanting to go home to her Boys. Leda sure Amaru would have killed someone had she not stop her. Gretchen resumed her seduction, if she had been scared it no longer showed. Fixer saw us as silly girls, plainly his swaggering shotgun machismo saved the day. I stroked Amaru's noble head, thinking how naive my preparations for this summer camp, yet compared to my Sistas I was more equipped, for none had begun the long journey inward, I knew some serious introspection was necessary to hear that still small voice, the one that tips me off, that makes at least some things action instead of reaction, and I needed to consider how being the more responsible one cast me Mother-Hen, and how we might just possess enough individual strengths that in the mixing we could compensated each others weakness, that together we were safe, safer.

Fixer made no attempt to disguise his glad-to-be-rid-of-us in down-town Portland, rewarding Gretchen for her exuberant ego-stroking with a fat lid of flower-tops from his personal stash. As we stood blocking the view, she sat on my suitcase and rolled a joint, and every one took their turn. Hunger now the primal concern, another chance to eat might not come for awhile, somewhere Amaru would be welcome to also dine. We paraded to a family-style restaurant. The hostess seated us as if Amaru was just one of our number. And the waitress brought her a soup bowl of water along with our glasses. She lapped it dry not spilling a drop. I was happy to put the suitcase down, hoping to discuss some basic ground-rules for the trip. Omelets, bacon, extra bacon, hash browns, toast, more toast and jam, coffee, house special pecan pie, an extra plate for Amaru were all con-suming. I drank my tea quietly and ordered two large fries, extra packets of ketchup, and two slices of pecan pie to go, never caring to eat on acid though I was coming down. Gretchen questioned my appetite. I confessed taking Sandoz to stay awake. Leda showed me the stash in her back-pack, Yellow Jackets she scored in early summer, when hitching with Amaru to Topanga Canyon, two were enough to be totally awake the whole trip. She had stayed with friends, met and moved-in with Gene Clark of the Byrds, not a month and the relationship soured, and two Yellow Jackets were enough to get her home. Gretchen had only traveled with guys till hitching with me from Seattle to Sky River. Keely thumbed small rides round town. So, I suggested we stay together no matter what, that every one had to feel right about a ride or none would take it. We piled hands in solemn agreement, together we were strong. Attention went to my suit-case. Gretchen took off her cinched leather belt and looped it though the handle "I'll help carry this beast if I get to sit on it". Leda "Yeah, dump the damn hammer and anvil and I will too". I balked "Come on, without tools how can I make a living". Gretchen boasted "Don't worry little Sista, we'll be fine. I get my welfare checks again soon as Ava's back from her Dad". Keely put a nibble hand out to Leda "Gimme two Yellow Jackets please". Gretchen too. Leda downed one with the last of her coffee, hand-ing me two for good measure. I dropped them in my bag. As we waited by the cash register to pay, a man struck-up conversation with Leda about

Amaru, and offered us a ride to Salem Oregon. Amaru's mouth opened, she was smiling, breathing ha ha ha, fanning that long tail, we looked at her and each other and went with him to his white Ford Van.

Going home, having given the keynote speech on marsupials to a Veterinarian's conference in Vancouver BC, the Vet raised kangaroos, bandicoots, wombats, koala bears, jumbucks and emu on his ranch East of Salem, and gently admonished Leda "Please listen to me. Leash your friend for her own good, or you will drink a bitter cup". He spoke so well, I was grateful someone else recognized the risk, but Leda could not hear passed her own pride "Amaru would never wander off. She loves me". Grimacing of heard-this-before, Vet tried again "A leash might just save her life. It will not humiliate or break her spirit". Believing loyalty and love were enough to stake Amaru's life on Leda bristled "Yes it will". He let hers be the last word, having made the point clear to all of us. I liked this man and felt at ease, my Sistas had not spoken my real name around Fixer, and this ride wiped all tracks clean, Amaru and I curled-up together on the rear seat, and listened to the speed-spawned talking-frenzy, enjoying Vet enjoying three beautiful women's fizzing attention. Nearly down, my eyes drooped as we made Salem. Vet offered over-night accommodations, but the mild clear evening beckoned, and he left us at the main Salem on-ramp to I-5. Leda took his number, promising to bring California eucalyptus leaves for the koalas when she came back North. Vet admonishing one more time "Leash her".

We waited optimistic, lots of cars were leaving Salem this time of night, and not one slowed for us. An hour, and bummed we quit the ramp for a small clearing. Gretchen pulled the baggie of flower-tops from her coat pocket and grinning waved her short-run gain in my face. There was nothing I wanted more than to get stoned, offering her a seat on my suitcase. Sticking two papers together she rolled a fat joint. Deep inhaling, holding, and aaaaah the solace and cohesion, we were of one mind, the night became enchanted, stars so big they seemed reachable, a warm Southern breeze promising what's to come, being on the road again flushed me with excitement. Unwrapping the fries and pie we dined, lots of ketchup, taking turns sitting on the suitcase, singing, smoking Marlboros, telling our stories. Keely no longer thought she ought to go home, wondering aloud was this Salem named for the Witch-burning one. Gretchen and Leda freaked at the thought. I tried pushing back the Darkness, telling my favorite joke, what do you call an alligator in a vest, an investigator. But the specter of burning witches had their imaginations, Gretchen hoisted her pack, she was going into town to call Vet to come get us even if she had to go alone. Keely put her backpack on too. Leda began to cry, we promised to stay together and she was more afraid of the town than out here. Gretchen set-out. Keely too. I begged please stop, Leda was right, small towns were far more dangerous than where we were. Closer to instinctive wisdom, and with bigger teeth, Amaru went after them, barking her supreme authority, herding the naughty lambs, and only when they rejoined Leda and me and relinquished their packs would she stand down. I felt all along some thing trying to divide and conquer, now it had shown itself, we needed an antidote, a witch's ritual, and every one was game. We gathered a pile of dry maple leaves, sat in a tight circle, each lighting a leaf, symbolically burning-up the Darkness, repeating this five times for five MotherTruckers, making a pyre of the rest, smoke ascending in long graceful arms, opening our rite of passage, Luna's light anointing us in renewed optimism and strength, I rose as if lifted and began to dance, slow at first, circling, taking Leda's hand, she knew the dance, and Gretchen's hand, and Keely and Amaru, gamboling in moon shining consent, virgin wildlings, Children of the Flower, the latest in a long line of joy-full power-full Sistas, reaching to the sky, taking their hands too.

Head-lights turned the tule-fog on, a yellow school bus, too early and too late for school crept-toward the on-ramp till we could see a peace sign painted on the side, stopping, opening its door, we filed in as if spellbound boarding a space craft. The driver's seat had been replaced with an easy chair, a long-hair rugged handsome man smoking a Missouri Meerschaum smiled offering it to me. Head shaking no I carried my suitcase to the last of three couches, all the customary seats had been removed. Gretchen of course arranged herself closest to the driver. Leda and Keely on the middle couch. Making sure we all were there, Amaru padded-in like a wolf, gave the driver a decidedly unfriendly snort, and climbed-up with me, flaring her nostrils, that nose knew better. The bus was loaded with baskets of leather goods, I sat quiet, breathing, catching a hint of rotting cedar and old books under the leather, this ride was not a good choice, maybe not even a choice, hopefully not a terribly regrettable one.

Salem's lights fading behind, Griffin introduce him self, and offered only Gretchen the Meerschaum. Pocket full of flower-tops and still she went to work, cooing her thank you, adjusting her body. Griffin cooed back "I could hardly b'lieve my eyes, you chicks just dancing in the moon-light". Gretchen preened and giggled. I caught the under-tone, to him our sacred dance a titillating revel of whores. Griffin was a member of The Family of the Mystic Arts, a commune near Oregon's Southern border, he made leather goods and peddled them to head-shops, calling on Salem's one-and-only "The owner's really beautiful people. I got ripped with him and stayed longer than I thought, but it all works out now doesn' it". To establish every one had not fallen for his charm, I dress my remark in plain disdain "I'm so relieved you're not the only freak around". He turned, giving me an eye-to-eye long enough to make me wish his were back on the road "Yeah. It's pretty conservative here 'bouts. But there's pockets of us. Plenty to support a head-shop here and there. Let me caution you though little girl, stay on main roads an outa towns". Amaru burned her eyes into the back of his neck. Me too, here was one of the Monsters of the Dark, thinking I did not recognize the danger because he wore a human body and spoke English. The Girls were captivated, but I knew him and would keep them safe by staying wide-awake. The conversation grew increasingly provocative. And it crossed my mind, he was their Monster god-damn-it, not mine, maybe they deserved him, earned him, why should I care if he devours them, they don't, then it hit me, he had already infected my head, irresponsible was exactly what he wanted from me, I re-glued my eyes to him. Leda offered him a Yellow Jacket, soon everyone was rushing but me, speed something I never wanted to use again, vigilant Mom, the warm bus conspiring to close my eyes, I slid open a window, night air in my face, fingering the Sandoz, Gabriel's caution loud in my ears - take too much and you'll lose your spiritual connection. I had to wonder if I already had, sleep was on me so hard, I laid half a white tablet on my tongue and swore it would be the last.

Griffin exited at the Wolf Creek Café, stopping for food and zuzus, those delectable homemade cinnamon rolls to bring home to the Family.

The hostess refused Amaru entrance even with Leda claiming blindness, that she was her seeing eye dog. Amaru gave me a resigned look, and I stroked her beautiful head as Leda went in to get her a cup of water, and they went back to the bus. I remembered this Café from my trip with Casey Marlon Kitty and Euphoria, even at 4AM it was full of truckers. Sipping tea I considered how could the Girls and Griffin down these enormous zuzus with such gusto on speed, maybe eating something would keep me from getting too high, I ordered the oatmeal and toast, took a bite, could not get my throat to swallow it, thinking better of dropping the acid, how utterly irresponse-able, I had not yet tasted the tin foil, and went to find the bathroom, to throw it up. The night had turned so dark and thick I had to push against it, my whole head suddenly warped in tin foil as I felt my way round the outside of the building to a filthy restroom. I hated throwing-up, took a few deep breaths standing over the toilet, stuck two fingers down and wiggled, dry heaving, convulsing, nothing came up, so I tried again, but the ride had already begun, splashing water on my face I looked in the dirty mirror, under my right eye the missing piece that always showed on acid, it was not missing, a good sign, I pulled up my sox, finger-combed my hair back and put Blistex on parched lips, hoping the boney loneliness showing under my face was just a trick of the harsh bare bulb, anxious to rejoin the safety of my Sistas, the door handle turning easily but it would not open, panic seized, I pushed hard with my shoulder, urine, disinfectant burning my nose and mouth, foul dark corners threatening, I had to get off the floor, away from mercenary insects sent by Monsters who used them for stalking when they can not be there in person, sitting on the sink, not so solid in the wall, feet off the carnivorous crawling floor, what a waste dying here like this when I had not really lived, hearing paws on the door, Amaru pushing it open, I had pushed when I should have pulled, laughing a high wild sound, in one leap I was out-side in the open air, death driven-off but not the portend, I hugged her neck, she snorted and licked my face, I followed to the bus, the door wide open and empty, she glided-in and took the driver's chair, telling me she was in control, wide awake, response-able, pure majesty.

I went back to the Café, which had been invaded by some of Griffin's clan on a zuzu run, mountain men like him, they were all over us. I forced down mouth-fulls of cold oatmeal, hoping Leda or Gretchen or Keely would recognize what Amaru and I did, noting from their mischievous and yet mostly innocent, or was it ignorant faces, the danger was mainly mine. They wanted to see the commune. Three Family men joined us on the bus, one girl for each of them. I fed Amaru my toast and searched her face. She ate with such calm restraint, I took her lead. Griffin drove slowly by the Wolf Creek gas station which along with the Café was the whole town, through the even smaller town of Sunny Valley, along Cemetery Road and up a long loose gravel road to the compound. The Family of the Mystic Arts owned the whole mountain, each man had built a cabin surrounding the central community lodge where we got out. Modeled on an Iroquois Longhouse, all the lodge doors were open, a blazing flagstone hearth fire greeted us, and beautifully made wooden picnic tables and work stations, lots of benches, a community bathtub, and though it was still dark and very early morning, three young women in calico pioneer dress, busy in the kitchen, waiting for zuzus. Thinking communes would be like collectives, on seeing the pentagrams on the floor, I was again in the lair of that ardent force that kept laying itself in my way, tempting, tricking, terrorizing, playing to my attraction for the dark side, for Nick, hoping I still craved it to be whole, hoping to distract me on this narrow high-wire crossing that frees a stained soul, hoping I would falter in building enough character to make it across. I felt I wore horse-blinders, determined not to be distracted to the left or right, looking only straight ahead or lose my self in a blink of an eye, a fragile balance. The Family gathered for zuzus, cider, tea and home-grown weed, nine young women in long calico dresses, none too happy to see us, eighteen men, some young some older, one-year-or-more grown hair beards and mustaches, amusing themselves with a favorite parlor game, attempting Astral projection. Ida Rose warned about this manner of travel, that bodies were extremely valuable vehicles to disembodied Astral entities, leaving yours unprotected automatically lit the neon vacancy sign, and once having taken possession of it, an Astral entity was not likely to leave upon your return. And the round-up began, fortunately enough oatmeal in my belly reining-in the Sandoz, my feet felt ground, mind present, nine single men wanting us, Gretchen and Leda flattered and fully engaged. Heeding Persephone's mistake, abstaining from any proposals, I discreetly asked round for some one going back down the loose gravel road. One let slip of a late morning delivery, I requested, coerced, demanded a ride, and he had no choice but to relent. Hours remained, The Family withdrawing to cabins, Leda and Gretchen took their packs and went with Griffin, the Chief. I had playing cards in my suitcase and challenged Keely to penny-a-point Gin Rummy. Though paranoid and a follower, she was also anxious to leave.

I was down $1.06 when our ride appeared, he was going in twenty-minutes with or without us. We took our stuff with him to a white Chevy Van. Gretchen and Leda's voices lead us to Griffin's, them chanting Lure Lure Lure, swaying their hypnotic Hula-Fandango for him and another blade, who caught in who's spell. I saw Amaru through the window stretched-out by the fire. She raised her head looking at me. I tried the handle, pulled the heavy door open, and taking a small step over the threshold, kept my voice low and calm "We got a ride down the hill right now, come on". Keely made her vote known "Yeah, come on Gretchen, Leda right now". Amaru on her feet ready. Griffin took hold of the bandanna round her neck and turned to Leda "Leave 'er here, then I'll know my angels're coming back to me". Amaru looked-up at him showing her teeth. Leda sighed "It's up to Amaru". I stomped my foot hard on the wooden floor "No. You let her go right now, she's one of us and we stick together". The spell broken, Griffin opened his hand. Amaru walked to the door and sat where it could not be closed, waiting as Leda and Gretchen gathered their things and silently filed-out, and she had our backs behind Keely to the Van. Griffin and the other hound followed. All aboard for Yreka. My sense of foreboding, of never escaping the spider's web, becoming living-dead began to ease descending the mountain.

A short ride over the border to Yreka's Frosty Freeze, solemn pledges of return, impassioned good-byes, The Family let us go. Frosty's manager welcomed Amaru upon promise to leave if anyone complained. I picked a local paper from the counter, front-page headline boasting record-breaking heat, and scooted in the booth close to Leda. She was flaunting the Ankh necklace Griffin gave her. Gretchen's face peeved at coming away empty-handed. The tireless weightless Sandoz had worn-off surprisingly fast, leaving a leaden gravity, taking so much certainly built a tolerance and shortened the trip, or else I was so saturated it was not that far up or down anymore. I ordered coffee, a double-cheese-burger, the insides for Amaru, and three large fries to go. Sistas ate burgers, finishing their milk-shakes with another Yellow Jacket. And there was nothing to do but continue the journey, we walked to the I-5 on-ramp, suitcase five-thousand pounds, my mind sailing-out into a cloudless powder-blue morning sky, I was in California again, the land of milk and honey, and after living through an infernal night, all was still intact. We arranged ourselves in a line, Gretchen Fetchin-Fine infront, thumbs out. Cars stopped in rapid succession, none would take us all but a Chevy Corvair, two not so clean-cut, very willing fellows going to Oakland, an empty roof rack for our gear, bucket front seats, we all squeezed in back, me on Gretchen's lap, Keely on Leda, Amaru cross our feet, and yes uncomfortable and the day heating, but these guys were no danger, the call to be vigilant quieting, I nodded-off.

No motion woke me, our driver had stopped for gas on Shasta's high plateau. Clothes damp, muscles aching, five sardines unpacked to stretch and breathe, finding a welcome breeze from heat and humidity on this high-land. I stood awed as the first time by the pristine panorama, sweeping in every shade of blues and grays across the plateau, swelling into mounds of bare foothills, cattle crazing between shadowy folds, Little Shasta a freshly dumped pyramid of black sand and sharp rocks, its symmetry marred only by a few malformed pines holding-on dearly, and Big Shasta, the blue titan crowned in vanilla ice cream, and such unearthly silence, the enormity of standing so near the sky seemed impossible and overwhelmingly sacred. Gretchen followed Driver and his more vulgar Pal into the gas-station-grocery-store. We too the Deers room not the Bucks, clean, sparkling clean, Amaru first, water from our cupped-hands, we washed faces and under-arms, brushed teeth and each others hair, and discussed another ride, agreeing we would wait here for a bigger car. Gretchen pranced in, hands-full of paper bags, Driver bought smokes, Fig Newtons, beef jerky, potato chips and orange juice, enough for all, he was switching–off driving with Pal, she would ride up-front on his lap, there would be more room. Keely explained our plan. Gretchen insisted, Shasta was a one-gas-station-town, we could be stranded forever, or find plenty of rides in Oakland. Recognizing her real need for this seduction to redeem a bruised ego, and since none of us minded her being Queen, we were persuaded, and packed back into the Corvair.

Leda gave the boys each a Yellow Jacket, they called them Bumblebees, an inane conversation that required amphetamines to participate began to whirl at a blistering speed, even with all windows down I was too hot, and yes there was more room for us to settle, however Pal's eyes were too often fixed on Gretchen not the road, as Driver groped and petted her, and she giggled and cooed, and made us uncomfortable voyeurs. Restless, I stroked Amaru's head and let the scenery suck me out the window, Castle Crags towering in the sky was a gothic impenetrable mountain fortress with gray stone sentinels and jagged flying buttresses, we sped high bridges over Lake Shasta's thick turquoise water rimmed in brick-red earth, Ponderosa pines standing tight guard along the edge, their plush green in stark contrast to the burlap landscape and clusters of brilliant orange poppies, then down, steep down, hotter and hotter, every direction mountains, over the Sacramento River and just passed Red Bluff the land changed, I saw a palm tree. It was ninety-plus degrees, speeding the endless wide central Sacramento Valley, hot as Texas and so dry the farm tractors threw-up tall waltzing dust funnels, brown-skin women and men in big straw hats bending-over in fields, cloudless relentless sun beating, clusters of gray silos and occasional Cypress spires, I looked down the straight rows whizzing-by like a flickering old movie reel, walnuts, almonds, persimmons, lemon trees fruiting and flowering all year round because of the heat. Amaru crept lightly into my lap and rested her chin on the window sill, wild yellow mustard flowers framed roads and fields, the only color vivid enough to penetrate the dusty wash, Vacaville lay wasted, uninhabited but for herds of cattle and sheep. Amaru's lovely nostrils flaring the first to notice a salty breeze in the air nearing Vallejo, mercifully cooling us to the high 70's, terrain changing to hills from an old Hollywood western, sculpted smooth in brown billiard-table felt, munched to the nubs by grazing sheep, medieval oaks sprinkled in the dells. We crossed Benica's toll-bridge spanning Carquinez Strait, where the Sacramento and San Joaquin Rivers and Suisun Bay meet San Pablo and San Francisco Bay, graveyard to rows and rows of once mighty blue-gray Navy ships, docile carbon hulks rusting to dust. Both my trips to California, a child on Family vacation to Disneyland, and with Casey, took the coast-road, this way was faster yet seemed so much longer because of the monotonous sweltering Sacramento Valley.

Coming in from the East, through Lafayette and Orinda, going down MacArthur Boulevard in Oakland, Driver invited us to his apartment. I was surprised Gretchen turned him down, a decision none of us contradicted. Pal pulled immediately to the curb, where MacArthur crosses Grand Avenue at the Lake Merritt Embarcadero. I happily hopped-out and began untying our gear from the roof rack, thinking Driver had gotten out to help. But aroused and unsatisfied he backed Gretchen against the car and began humping "Come on Baby, you know you wan' it". Amaru was quick, at his back, growling, her front paws went to his shoulders, full weight. Driver froze. Leda ordered "Get down". Amaru obeyed her own heart and did not, making this poor horny schmuck certain who was who. A very long seconds, she stood down, and he darted into the car and locked the door. We barely salvaged our stuff when they sped away. Over-wired on Yellows, the Girls applauded Amaru, crackling high manic laughter. I tried to underscore how guys never seem to believe what we say, my mouth clogged with a parched swolen tongue. We marched cross MacArthur to the Flying A gas station. Amaru and I first to the drinking fountain, water warm, smelling, tasting like sewer, spitting-out the first swig, I ran the faucet hoping for better. Amaru did not mind, and drank deep. Giddy, exhausted, I did not know how much longer to Santa Cruz, and sure I could not make it, place a hit of Sandoz on my tongue, slurping only enough swill to wash it down, and I had to wonder was I strung-out, I never heard of anyone addicted to acid, promising my self again no more for a while, this was the last one, shit here I was, of course I had another good excuse, addicts always have a good excuse. Thankfully Gretchen knew where she was and hada sorta plan, we would hitch over the Bay Bridge to San Francisco and catch a ride down Highway One to Santa Cruz. The restroom was so clean, the evening promising low 70's, we changed our clothes, me into my tapestry halter dress, Keely her short cut-offs and a tight yellow tank-top, Leda shed the purple-suede fringed-vest and turtleneck for a purple tube-top, Gretchen slid the neck of her peasant blouse off her shoulders leaving black-satin bra straps in plain sight and tied a red scarf round her waist. We brushed and lip-sticked and splashed Jean Naté, paraded across the street, lined-up and stuck out our thumbs, Gretchen infront.

Not one breath and a black Plymouth Fury stopped, dark-tinted passenger window opening automatically, Gretchen poked her face in, was he going to San Francisco. He nodded yes and popped-opened the trunk for our things. Gretchen took the front, Amaru too, laying her head contently on his thigh. We slid into the delightful roomy air-conditioned back-seat, and though Driver turned on the radio as we left the curb, I knew he was deaf. On the 580 West ramp, he lit a fat joint and passed it to Gretchen. She drew a tight-lipped hit, turning completely round, passing to me, brow furrowed deep, worried eyes motioning in Driver's direction. Ms.Fetchen-Fine wasn't so good at picking-up on some subtle or for that matter not so subtle signs, Amaru conspicuously liked this man, I realized Gretchen did not know he was deaf, and why her cooing not working, she likely thought we had taken a ride with a real weirdo. Smiling innocent I took the joint, having skipped the tin foil and gone-up though not too high, I could see Driver's aura, clear yellow edged in soft pink, according to Annie Besant's Thought Forms, this means high intellect softened by unselfish affection, I was not worried and decided to have a bit of fun watching Gretchen squirm. Over the Bay Bridge she giggled at me "You Witch, you knew didn't you". I echoed her giggle "No way". She swore "You did too. Just wait my pretty, I'll get you back when you least expect".

San Francisco coming in from the East, a view so common in movies and on TV, seeing it for real for the first time made me feel glamorous, important, I was clear and calm without any hallucinations. My Sistas jangled and rustling, marijuana a weedy counterbalance to the Yellows. Our Driver took us on the scenic tour along Market Street, the Haight, by Kezar Stadium, West on Lincoln Way, coming to the curb at Sunset Boulevard on the Southern perimeter of Golden Gate Park he unloaded the trunk, gave us each a kiss and was gone. Seeing dear old haunts made me feel solid, not much had changed, we could stand right here and easily hitch Highway One to Santa Cruz, but I thought we should walk back to the Haight and rent a cheap room for the night. There was no way,

Gretchen, Leda, Keely inisited we must go on, and I felt it too, pulsing the thrill of our strength together, indomitable, buoyant, adventure, never mind manic Yellow delirium that electrified and inflated their confidence. Eucalyptus dancing on a mild Pacific breeze tossed our skirts and hair, we stood on the parking-strip curb, Gretchen infront, thumbs out, waiting in the glorious early December late afternoon sunshine, anticipation, something unknown yet seemingly planned, something promised by the Sweet Sisters Fate. Gretchen lifted her skirt flaunting those legs, car after car skidded to stop, none would take us all. Morale dented, I launched into *Zippity Do Da*, everyone joining, every word remembered from childhood, we even had good harmony. And Keely sang *The Wayward Wind* with such genuine yearning we could only listen. Rumbling to our curb, a gleaming-new black Boss 351 Ford Mustang, joy-riding in his 16th birthday present, a Driver eager to take us all the way to Santa Cruz, springing-out to stow our packs and bags and suitcase in the trunk. Amaru glided approvingly infront, Gretchen also, Amaru unwieldy in-between the too young and tender prey, crowding Gretchen against the door. We went West maybe 10 short blocks to the ocean, that new car smell and Great Blue Water going South on Highway One, passing Daly City, I had never seen anything like Daly City, house on house, mirror images but for minor pastel color shifts in pinks and blues, the setting-sun washing sandbox yards and concrete patios pastel too. Keely noted not one tree survived the developer's homogenized version of heaven, that we were looking at an Orwellian seed of suburban nightmare, that mark-her-words would spread like a disease through the country in the name of progress. Awed speechless by such free-spirited older women, Driver found his voice, proudly reporting Daly City had a nickname, Ticky Tack, from an old Folk song *Little Boxes* by Malvina Reynolds.

Feeling his Mustang manhood and the Yellow coming on strong, Driver flew by less homogenized Edgemar, Pacific Manor, Rockaway Beach, Leda and me and Keely, heads back looking-up through the rear window, movie screen sky, Venus already shining, Keely sighed "I wana fall madly, passionately in love with someone". Leda resonating "Yeah". These wishes from the heart always set things in-motion, and always seem to come true, one had to be care-full what you wish for, I said nothing. Keely's life was a conspicuous lesson for me, she had not done much of the deciding, more let it decide it self, too her credit she did her honest best, having married a man she loves no more, bearing four Littles under eight she dearly does, wanting the liberty she had far too much conscience to take. Her life had consequences that made me see how critical it was to know there could be choices, conscious choices, to be the driver not the passenger. Past Linda Mar Driver pull onto a high cliff with beach access, sun-set pinking the waves, and all trailed after Amaru down to water's edge but me. No matter how many times I saw the Pacific, thrill never failed, it scared me too a little at night, boundless undulating muscle, unpredictably predictable, physics its master though I was sure it could break the rule at will, that it might have a will, this Great Dark Deep, fathomless, swallowing, amplified on LSD. Reading Carl Jung, what I was able to digest anyway, had opened my mind as much as any acid trip. He did not intend to write over my head, but what he was trying to say was not linear or even rational, and he had to devise a lexicon for his new ideas, to borrow, even create words to describe the unconscious, what by its very nature can not be objective, because our mind is in us, and therefore always subjective. Just the three letter word ego, the what-I-am what-I-think what-I-want center of me, I had not been able to grasp enough of yet to think of my own. And now I had archetypes, anima, animus, individuation, transformation, self, shadow, synchronicity, all subjective structures of the psyche that have no solid body like a tree or a rock or a hand, they are too fluid to hold still, like trying to sew water, and too far beyond the conscious mind to behold entirely or get a good look at, like a black hole whose presence is known only indirectly by how it influences its surroundings. These structures that I could only see in projection onto the objective world, fleeting, apprehended at the corner of an eye, can be recognized using the mirrors Bonita-Kay taught me, detecting the face of my own unconscious projected onto the Other, for that is what the unconscious does hoping to be recognized, to communicate over the threshold, and in withdrawing that projection is where Jung said knowledge begins. For me synchronicity was the most enlightening expansion of all, maybe because I sort of understood, when something inside and something outside connect, something thought manifests in the material world, without intention, with out seeming connection, when they happen at the same time, most will brush this off as coincidence, and coincidence is stirring, but synchronicity is charged with a wonderment, a marvel at how a thing inside your head can manifest unexpectedly and unmistakably meaning-full on the outside, the only time I know for sure without a doubt that I am where I should be in the Universe at the exact moment I should be there, going in the right direction for now, and that I am okay. I first really recognized synchronicity driving to an anti-war rally with Keely, we had fears of walking into a police riot. Her way was to stuff her feeling, chattering about last night's dinner, all fears and anger focused on the high price of mushrooms, on and on. I just listened. She found a parking spot, we stepped-out, our eyes going to a large clump of mushrooms growing on the parking strip. I started laughing, knowing instinctively I was exactly where I should be and things would be okay. Keely accused me of picking the spot to park, that I knew the mushrooms were there and was playing a trick on her, refusing or unable to imagine order so liquid and without apparent cause, blind to the gift slipping in from the larger quantum, that temporary moment of solid ground, surety there is solid ground, forgetting it was her that brought-up mushrooms, her picking the parking spot, one persons synchronicity, another's coincidence, a trick. Jung called this feeling of connection numinous, supernatural, a knowing, defining synchronicity as an acausal orderedness, unpremeditated, an underlying order to the no-order of seeming random events, independent of space and time, with no way to predict in advance, one's psyche manifesting in the material, a magical meeting. Only lately did I feel headed in generally the right direction, I was no longer so frantically searching, wasting so much time going down the wrong mental avenues, though I did not exactly think I had gone the wrong roads, every thing so far taught me where the righter ones were, and maybe I still wasn't on the precise path but then Ida Rose would say *right for what*. For I had begun to find out who am I, it was like peeling onion skins one thin layer and another, so much to learn and read, always hungry for the next bone, in my head I saw my self a black short-haired mongrel about the size of Amaru, roaming the land looking for morsels of significance, and when I found one, I was just so hungry, gobbling it quick as I could, immediately looking for the next, I could not read fast enough and wondered if there would come a time when I would not feel so anxious to catch-up that I could savor the morsel, dine at the table, come to some summit and enjoy the view, sneak a quick look behind the veil, I suspected if I could it would be so fundamental, that the secret language was numbers and life was as simple as one, a person had to do it for themselves. I tried sharing with Ric, Keely, Gretchen, they did not want it, Leda showed some real interest, but so wild and careless, as if she had nothing inside worth keeping safe, she seemed to think we all lived like her, never questioning behavior, it was inevitable, and it drove her so she could not really concentrate on anything in the whirling drama of her life, though her spirituality was more evident than Gretchen or Keely, she spent her self with more abandon, I hoped she could catch-up with herself before hitting a wall so hard it knocked her silly. Sitting on the front fender watching my friends play at water's edge, Sandoz suddenly came on, I felt light as the breezes, at this exact moment no one really knew me or cared what I did, I had no responsibilities, no politics, no cops, no bills, no kids, no parents, almost no worldly possessions, no Nick, nobody to answer too, I could float-out into the universe and no one would ever know what became of me, dispersing on the rusting threads of sunset.

Brushing sand from shoes and paws, their physical mass pulling me in, no it was the stink, not from 36 hours on the road but speeding flesh burning too fast too long, they were skirting the same psychotic hole I fell-into on that dime-bag of Crystal Nick scored, if I had Thorazine I would give them some. Next best, Gretchen rolled a fat joint of flower tops. Driver got stoned too, and being prudent enough not to drive so fucked-up, tossed me the keys. Cool veneer miss-taken for inner composure, they were all farther gone, I probably was best taking us to Santa Cruz, my palms itching to reign the Mustang. Gretchen and Leda sandwiched Driver in back. Keely, Amaru rode with me, her discerning green eyes still on Gretchen's behavior toward the whelp. I sank into the agreeable leather saddle, a heady young stallion that once up-to-speed turned into my own private jet airliner, instrument panel a dazzling display, I soared the hills to how many thousands as the tachometer, swooped winding curves, everyone enjoying my smooth command on the edge of the world, moonlit Cabrillo Highway newly blacktopped, rolling silent, and now the airliner was a metal pinball, smooth effortless gliding through fresh-painted white lines, electric green median reflectors, golden head-lights, red tails, yellow flashing exits to somewhere, totally in the groove, all-time high points, me, the silken master of the game.

Slowing sliding into downtown Santa Cruz after 10PM, a car full of magpies, Gretchen directing me, Laurel Street, San Lorenzo Boulevard, East Cliff Drive, left on 4th Avenue, a small dirt cul-de-sac. Not entirely stopped when she hopped-out, I inhaled salty ocean through the open door. Taking the three-stair porch in one she knocked. I held my breath. Andrew opened no delay, the greeting enthusiastic and surprised. She trotted back proud, announcing we were welcome. Driver unloaded the trunk, in a hurry to collect a waiting Gretchen's full-body smooch, he rode-off in the warm night. Andrew offered to carry my suitcase. Not much bigger than me, I let him, grinning at his chivalry, such an elfin innocent, I trailed into the tiny living room, of the little house, with a longish-narrow teeny kitchen and eating nook, wooden stairs leading to a loft big-as-a-pool-table, and underneath that a one-person bathroom and shower. Andrew's roommate Luke, diesel mechanic day-job, One Hand Clapping Roady by night, did not come to Sky River, or Seattle for the New Years gig, commonly handsome, conspicuously strong, tight jeans, bare to the waist, wearing too much cologne, something so phallic about the way he held his hairless torso, the texture of his skin, on acid a big stiff dick. Keely could not keep her eyes off him.

Feeling terribly uncomfortable, as if Erik or Joey were here, I stowed my gear under the coffee-table, waited-out polite introductions, and slipped-away to sit on the porch and breathe. Amaru came along. And soon Andrew, White Owl Panatelas in his dress-shirt pocket, Golden Delicious apple in one hand, horse-size Milk-Bone dog biscuit the other. The way her fur lay soft I could see Amaru liked him, she knew the biscuit was hers, sitting patiently almost face to face, and when he offered, taking it with restraint, settling-down to dine. Still too high to eat, I accepted the apple, stashing it in my bag for later. Andrew handed me a cigar too. I held it in my lips. He lit mine and his. Finding taste and companions pleasurable, we puffed and watched the sky in quiet company. Amaru's ears went up, leaping from the porch to greet a large creature emerging from the dark, her tail's easy sway signaling no alarm. This was Andrew's fair-haired Great Dane Fordo, black wavy cartoon lips and nose, ultra-intense eyes, Groucho Marx eyebrows, Andrew said he had eaten three hits of purple Owsley off the coffee-table three weeks ago and was no longer a dog. For Amaru and Frodo it was love at first-smell, she liked us well enough, but humans were merely surrogates. Smiling ear-to-ear we attended their love tango, testifying to the older knowledge of Isis not Eve, that species lay with species, like with like, dog with dog, god with god, cat with cat. I felt Andrew's gentle sweet soul, no games, happy to begin a friendship. Cigars to ash, he went inside to the laughter and mischief. And my mind rambled out into the friendly night, tempted on fragrant eucalyptus and jasmine, shameless salty ocean fingers teasing my bare shoulders.

Frodo and Amaru came to sit infront of me. I untied the bandanna from her neck, tore it in-two, tied one round her and one him. Snorting, Frodo pranced some yards off and looked back come-hither. Amaru sniffed a ready yes sauntering to him. Waiting on me, we crossed East Cliff Drive, and the meadow of scents, down a narrow path through the ice plant to Frodo's beach, crests of waves shimmering neon mother-of-pearl, hovering moon enormous benevolent witness. Though afraid of the night Deeps, I felt safe in Frodo's world, sharing a connectedness these hounds took for granted, their natural participation with nature as we skirted water's reach, playing tag with phosphorous waves left fleeting on the sand, chasing little night birds running the shoreline, completely un-ruffled, knowing full well we never intended on catching them even if we could, under the sparkling sapphire dome, often howling to moon. When Luna blushed at Sun's coming, I came down softly and nibbled my apple, the most delicious ever tasted, Eve must have felt this too offering hers to Adam, it was not the apple but self-awareness she hoped to share, eating the first communion, I wished on the dawn for my Adam true-love to find me in time, offering pieces to Amaru and Frodo. They each took only to be polite, chewing chewing, maybe it would leak-out the corners before having to swallow. Morning exceeding the phosphorous waves, exposing a sweep of white diamond sand and turquoise water at near high tide, so unlike the black sand of Washington and Northern Oregon beaches that were populated with shells rocks driftwood and tide pools and bordered in forbidding cliffs, the blue-grey water would be storming white and frigid this time of year, while Frodo's beach was sculpt-velvet, gracious, California's seduction living–up to itself. I stood planted in the sand, taking in the curve of sea as it kissed the pink sky. Strolling home I thanked my Dears for allowing me a fearless night by the Deep, for sharing their honey-moon.

Leda was sitting on the bottom porch step, waiting red-eyes, anxious, ashtray full of butts, still speeding to fast to sleep, absolutely frantic where was Amaru. I presented Frodo, explaining how he took us to his beach for the phosphorous waves. Her emotions ragged and bouncing, I quietly looked at the ground as she reproached me taking Amaru without asking, though she figured we were together and that was okay. As if anyone could take Amaru anywhere, still I appreciated Leda's need for friends who always included her, did not defend in my apology, and only when her fire was spent, asked what was going on inside. Luke had Gretchen upstairs in bed, Andrew sleeping on his hide-a-bed in the front room, Keely in her bag on the floor, Leda had taken an extra Yellow along the way, could not sit still, and decided to go see the phosphorous, though I told her it was no more. After sharing his porch water bowl with Amaru, who went with Leda, Frodo gladly lead the way as I slowly opened the door and crept in, breathing rhythm with the sleepers, unrolled my bag next to Keely, folding a pea-coat pillow, surrendering to gravity, physically exhausted, though I could not stop my head-movie, staring at the ceiling, listening to collective breathing, impressed at how much living could fit in two days, time expanding and contracting on circumstance, hours could disappear in a blink of rushing uncanny momentum, flush with incident and intrigue, timeless, I was far from Nick and the distance had substance, feeling now, realizing how numb I had become to his menace, I wanted to stay here forever, possibilities reflecting down the mirrored hall of mind, so pleased I brought my tools. When Leda unrolled her bag, with Amaru taking all the rest of the space of the tiny living room floor, my eyes gratefully closed.

Chapter Fourteen

SANTA CRUISE

Jealous faceless girls ripping at my dress, Sun's light bridging the threshold of my dream, and waking, still weary, to a brilliant December day summoning I could only oblige. Leda and Keely, tranquil sleeping faces so sweet and innocent as I stepped over them, yawning my way to the kitchen. At the breakfast nook writing in his journal Andrew smiled shy and pointed to the coffee pot. All I wanted was a shower. He invited please make your self at home. Years of paranoia and fear ran down the drain on soapy water, I donned my living dress, feeling new-born, invincible, emancipated. A cup of coffee waited for me, I sat across from Andrew. If Tolkien had not yet penned Bilbo Baggins, he would have modeled Andrew, a slender devout vagabond in not-so-white t-shirt, not-so-new khaki trousers, tire-tread-sole huaraches, unkempt nails all around, his long flaxen hair beard and mustache thinning, pensive blue-gray eyes, and oh yes, his canine Fordo. I sipped contently looking-out the window, having forgotten how nourishing, intoxicating the California Winter, I must hunt the thrift shops for light fabrics and clothes. Coffee loosened our tongues. Andrew wondering why I carried cinder blocks in my suitcase. I told of my plans to stay, for making a living, if he knew any good thrift shops, and places to sell my jewelry and clothes. He offered to take me to the Santa Cruz Import Shop, the Yellowbird, and his favorite thrift shop in Capitola. My stomach rumbled a long lament, I was starving. Andrew proposed we walk to a near-by restaurant. Full-length on the porch, nose-to-nose Amaru and Frodo barely looked-up, Frodo did not come along.

We crossed the cul-de-sac and turned up 4th, I could see in Andrew's posture the unexpected turn of his friend's loyalty had genuinely injured him, and suspected Frodo was the only living creature he let inside his world. Andrew stopped to light a stogie, offering me one. We stood facing, he struck a match and asked if I made my dress. I nodded yes. He stepped back for a longer look, smiling, calling it inspired and beautiful, if this was an example of my work the shops would certainly buy from me. I was most proud of this particular piece, explaining the idea of a living dress, the bodice could be any favorite, this one a Mexican wedding shirt, the skirt an ankle-length patch-work of fabrics, feather-stitched together, attached to the top just below the waist, and because I continued adding symbols and words to mark milestones in my life, it lived as I lived, an embroidered peace symbol, one mushroom, hexagrams from the I Ching, a pink starburst with a rose in the center, Jack-in-the-Box head, Boeing 727, and soon the moon smoking a cigar. Andrew was surprised such complex thought lay behind sewing and design, that it didn't seem to matter what kind of art one did, the process was the same. He took-up playing the jug on his first acid trip, finding its simplicity as complex as the slide trombone he played since childhood. I asked about his first acid trip. Taking a puff, he blew a long thin white stream, giving his mind a moment, confessing to working for the enemy, on the fast-track at Standard Oil, promoted at 26 to district manager, driving formula race-cars for them on week-ends, and then came the summer of '68 and the Haight, he took another puff and read a passage from his ever present journal "Shoshannah's a strange quiet bird, intense while soft. I liked her when we met at Sky River. I like her still". Painfully embarrassed by our loneliness exposed, relieved on reaching the Harvest Inn.

Sitting at an out-door table, Gretchen and Luke waved us over. The way they leaned into each other, again I felt my fortunate lot not being her, so casually giving her self away, believing her body the one thing she had to spend, needing to flaunt her recompense, I had nothing so tangible to show, dignity, friendship of no apparent value in her tally, and those rude insults to her body, crabs, bladder infections, yeast infections, the clap, and her callous contempt for women by sleeping with their men, how could she be a friend when she could be trusted to disrespect. And even with all the men, she counted none a friend, her riposte always the same, a fetching smile and quick friendly arm round Keely, Leda, me. I realized as I took the bench opposite her, Gretchen Fetchin-Fine was mostly an extrovert, her self-worth pinned on material objects and possessions, proof need be visible, and I an introvert, accounting my worth by how it felt inside, we were engaged in a classic polemic, our friendship balancing on a thin edge and would likely fall over some one we both wanted. For sure I had to admit some envy, I often wanted to do it her way, but her life, like Keely's was a lesson laid-out, a gift for my teaching, and perhaps she did not have the same things to lose as me. Nonetheless, I saw her and the others as Virgins-in-Spirit, and I was bent on rescuing the word from a purely physical male identification. To me Virgin was a state of mind not body, a Virgin was dominated by no one, sufficient unto her self, doing what she does because it is true for her, and not some dictionary definition based on Christian myth that woman is tainted, sullied, impure whether willing or not, and so being born of woman made every child originally sinned, the story had Jesus born of a virgin so he was not tainted, but how could anyone believe in a virgin birth, maybe psychologically, metaphorically. like Athena born in full battle gear from her father Zeus's head, but come on, not literally, it seemed to me that Yahweh committed the original sin, then as criminals do, blamed it on some one else, condemning Eve and her progeny to bear children in pain. I was so sick and tired of being despised because of Yahweh's immature jealous insecurity and need to retaliate on Eve for becoming self-aware, shaming her for nakedness because even in Eden God was clothed, right. And as for Mary, as the story goes, the Holy Spirit was sent to do God's dirty work, because he was repulsed by his own taint of woman, but if Joseph didn't get her pregnant, then Mary was raped. I was grateful I did not feel this taint, this Christian hatred of woman, that it had not been programmed into me from birth, and though our dominant Christian society tried to make it stick on every girl, so far I was still a Virgin in my eyes. Alfred North Whitehead said God was deficient, I heartily agreed.

Andrew's voice ordering a vegan nut-burger dispelled the reverie. There were no restaurants in Seattle like the Harvest Inn, Morningtown the closest with its vegetarian pizza, I ordered a nut-burger too, made of soy bean curd, bulgur, rolled oats, ground almonds and walnuts, sunflower and sesame seeds, minced onion, celery, tamari soy sauce, coriander cumin and turmeric and potato starch, flame-broiled, with organic alfalfa sprouts, sweet pickles, tomato slices, and eggless mayonaise on a whole wheat bun, with a side of crispy sweet potato chips. I ate slow, quiet, savoring, watching Andrew, executive gone to seed, the latent ghost of corporate days still evident in his quick wit and casual command, lending elegant composure in the shadow on Luke's machismo. Luke was careful not to reveal anything personal, reminding me of Ida Rose's caution to always look for the hidden factor, what wasn't said often more important than what was, leading me to wonder what he had to hide. They ordered beer, intending to idle the afternoon drinking in the sun. I finished my meal, sat back and finished my stogie, and excused myself. To the house, to crash fully dressed, Leda and Keely still snoring.

Voices delivered me from a vivid familiar nightmare, faceless girls tearing at my clothes, a dream repeating, straining to pass my threshold of consciousness with a message, I tried to linger, grasp the meaning but it withdrew into the labyrinth. It was Joey's voice from the breakfast nook, muscling with Luke for Gretchen's favor, the band was playing at the High Street Local tonight, Luke would be leaving soon to set-up equipment and sounded worried Joey came to horn-in. The testosterone stink nauseated me, I crept from my bag, over Leda and Keely and out the door where the noon sun struck me blind, where Andrew and One Hand Clapping's manager stood talking. Stoney had not come to Sky River or Seattle, Andrew politely introduced us. Stoney was heading to the club to smooth the way, bashfully hesitantly inviting me along for a beer, his tar-brown close-set timid eyes veiled in near-sighted horn-rim coke-bottle glasses. I appreciated the opportunity to avoid Joey, and went in quickly for my bag. Brushing my hair in the car, we shared a joint, and I felt no need to ease the self-conscious silence, Stoney was not a smooth lady-killer with all the right moves, I found him refreshing.

He took the scenic route by the boardwalk and pier into downtown Santa Cruz, an arty beach community infested with Hippies, I noted the Yellowbird and Santa Cruz Import Shop on Pacific Avenue. Parking on High Street infront of the club, Stoney offered his arm as we neared the door. Normally I would not, but this seemed a magnanimous gesture not chauvinism, and I knew it would thrill his shy soul wearing me as decoration. We took stools at the end of the bar. Feeling expose, lighting a smoke, more defense than pleasure, I was pleased Stoney made no move to light it for me, maybe he really could care less, no matter, I dearly appreciated his assumption I was not a helpless female that could not manage to light my own cigarette. When the bartender came, Stoney introduced me as one of the MotherTruckers, ordered beers and asked for the owner. Bartender wanted to shake my hand, seeming way too thrilled to meet one of the MotherTruckers, my amazement only just contained, this was glamorous groovy Santa Cruz where the ultra-hip from the Haight immigrated, I could not imagine our arrival being even a ripple in these laidback waters, then again, One Hand Clapping's success at Sky River made the Festival and Hydra legendary, and the MotherTruckers were the mystique personified, we were a sensation, yikes, people wanted to meet me. This ignited my paranoia, though politics and Nick were far away, I gave my first name only, and ambiguous answers, always turning the spotlight around, where were they from originally, and depending on the answer, following with how they came to live in Santa Cruz or how lovely it is to be a citizen of paradise, could they recommend the little known wonders only a native would know, inciting them on and on about themselves, away from me. I learned this from the three French revolutionaries, Jean-Pierre, Patrick and Ophélie, sent by their benefactor to the United States to learn about American grassroots organizing, starting with the Ithaca collective that Arnie and Max came from, onto Los Angeles, San Francisco and finally to Hydra. Since I took French in high school and they spoke little English, I was their natural escort, taking them to the War Tables of Mother Jones and the Country Doctor, to demonstrations, spirited political discussion at the Last Exit on Brooklyn and the Hasty Tasty, drinking and dancing the Rainbow and District taverns, and the week thoroughly consumed, to Sea-Tac Airport for their flight home to Paris. As we waited for their boarding, Jean-Pierre spoke some English and offered his observation, how all across the country he found Americans talk to them selves, pausing only long enough for some assurance their listener is listening, a head nod, an uh-huh, while the listener being reminded of some experience of their own is not really listening, far too busy thinking of what they want to say when the speaker gives them an opening. Jill takes Jack aside to reveal a bad acid trip, Jack instead of being engaged, co-opts the topic by launching into a story of his own bad acid trip, and Jill feeling slighted does not listen either, thinking how selfish Jack is for not listening, for having no compassion, after all she brought-up the matter, and hoped, needed to be heard, and neither having listened, neither had been heard. I liked people's stories, and they loved talking about them selves, and from that day on I became an interviewer, not waiting for my chance to talk, asking questions, never ceasing to be amazed how much some one would tell a stranger that listened, finding this permitted me almost complete anonymity, and the real advantage of knowing something about those around me.

Stoney was not a bit timid when it came to business, negotiating the owner to 100 percentage of the door for the band. Luke arrived with the equipment, Stoney went to help unload and set-up, leaving me to the hounds. My spine instantly stiffened, head high, do-not-approach under penalty of ego death, this always gave me a powerful headache, I lit one smoke on the next to the last, sorry I came. Then Delroy Bogave walked through the door, coming directly over to me, the first thing off his lips "Gretchen with you". I pouted "Glad to see you too". A practiced charmer, he took my hand, kissed the back and smiled "You know I am. I heard you Girls were in town. Is Miss Fine with you". Delroy was the biggest dog in town, his attention granted me royalty and I appreciated it, just the stock to bay the hounds "No. We're staying with Andrew. I think she's still sleeping. You got a smoke". A flick of his wrist and up-popped one unfiltered Camel from a nearly full pack "Will you tell 'er I'll be here tonight". I took the smoke "Thank you. I will". Fans, devoted, wanting to be near celebrity hemmed me out.

Set-up and sound check done, Stoney offered his arm. I took it. He hailed Delroy, who hailed back, and we left the dark club into sunshine so hearty I had to catch my breath. Talk came easier on the ride home. Stoney grew-up in Santa Cruz, a surfer and rabid music lover with little talent for playing or singing, but a good business head, when One Hand Clapping asked him to be their manager he gladly took the job. Turning into the cul-de-sac he asked tentative "Ah, you need a ride to the gig tonight". I had not thought of going "Don't know really. I'm still so tired". He waited till I stepped from the car "Well anyway, I'll be by later if you wana go". He sped off. Andrew had gone shopping for a new shirt. Sistas and Dogs were heading for the beach to celebrate sun set, offering to wait for me. I would catch-up, and sat down in the middle of the living room floor, empty house pure luxury, opening and closing my knife, thinking how my skin crawled when ever I saw a naked blade, how I could feel the cold sharp edge so easily slicing my flesh, how I always had this terrible fear of knives though unable to recall every being cut. I was the right age to have been in the camps my last life, perhaps a demonstration of how to flay a Jew while keeping her skin in one piece, for use later maybe as a lampshade. But this was the knife Dad gave me, Excalibur, and it felt good in hand as I cut the legs off my jeans, fashioned a halter top from a large scarf, pulled my hair into a high ponytail, and dashed across East Cliff and through the meadow of scents. Amaru, Frodo came running, shepherding me to the giggling porcelain goddesses lying naked in the sand, daring me disrobe, Dogs would not allow anyone near. I sat down, hugging knees to bosom, toes digging into the warm white sand, thinking somehow I had managed to grow-up over-night, the invisible hand seemed to have let me go, taking a full breath I looked-out on the curved horizon, sun and sea meeting soon, and relayed Delroy's message to Gretchen. She wiggled excitement, insisting we all must go, no refusal or excuse. Never able to sit still long, especially at the beach, though I did not really need one, I offered to take the first shower. Gretchen begged to wear my velvet gown, caterwauling till I reached the meadow of scents and the ocean drowned her out.

The equipment van was parked by the porch, front door ajar, Luke calling down from the loft as I came in "Hey Baby-doll, come-on up". My skin crawled "It's Shoshanah. Is it all right if I take a shower". He sounded disappointed "Yeah, sure go ahead". Maybe it wasn't a good idea to take a shower, I turned on the hot water and hung the velvet gown over the shower-curtain rod, steam would loosen the creases, I would not get-in, only change clothes, slipping them off. Without a sound Luke unlocked the door and barged in fully-cocked, wearing only an expectant grin. I was too startled to be frightened, frozen for endless seconds while his eyes feasted, I took a towel for cover and calmly balked "You made a mistake Luke, Gretchen's at the beach". Still smiling he snatched the towel

"No mistake Doll". I could not believe this was happening, could hardly breathe, instinctively knowing if I flinched, if I covered my self with hands as I desperately wanted, I would lose this, my heart beating wild, knees weakening, I glared indignant into his eyes "This is how you treat a guest". Cologne assaulting my nose, his erection failing, exasperated he sneered "You're a Dyke right". Now I was terrified, facing a jerk with a weak ego blaming me for his aggression, I tried not to sound scared "Look, us Girls made a solemn pact. No messing with each others boy-friends". He seemed to understand this kind of loyalty "You're not a groupie". I could only suspect what Gretchen promised so we could stay, some atavistic corner of my psyche was powerfully attracted to his impressive body, nipples standing at attention as I tried to be sincere "I'm a big fan of the band since they came up for Hydra's New Years party. Look. I'll be happy to pay some of the water bill when it comes". Suddenly embarrassed he left the doorway. I did not bother locking the door, pulled on my gown, letting the shower run, sitting on the toilet shaking, sick to my stomach, waiting for my Sistas, I would never be alone with him again.

The incident fell on unwilling ears, showering and dressing, Leda, Keely would not believe my story, finding it easier to think I misread or enticed Luke. Gretchen's brows knitted, she looked away when I cautioned being alone with him, and I knew she knew and despised her for keeping silent. Why were girls at fault for what boys did to them, I wanted to jump-off the planet, fishing at the bottom of my bag for a Sandoz, a booming voice in my head warning, you might never come back. I let the tablet fall from my fingers, considered calling Ida Rose, dialing my Folks instead, collect, time to allay worry that knew no distance. Tired from the day's work, relieved to hear their Little Girl's voice, they got on both phones. As always I found my voice higher than normal, girlish innocent, chatty, perky, never a hint of distress, yes the trip went perfectly smooth, Gretchen's family vacation home right across the street from the ocean, we all went afternoon sunning, being somewhere warm enough to go to the beach in December so incredible, I gushed all the California hype, glad to talk to them as they to me, aching to tell, ask advise, but it would only worry them more, and there was really nothing they could do to help. After high school, parents who could afford it sent their kids to a kibbutz for the summer, Gentiles sent theirs to Western European countries of ethnic origin, hopefully to gain a wider life perspective before going to college, choosing a career, I wanted to go somewhere too before school, anywhere, there was no money. I don't know what they expected me to do but get a dead-end job and get married, fortunately Revolution raged in the streets, the Haight, Texas, Hydra, Ida Rose, I had my education. Dad could always read between-the-lines, Mom accepted the half-truths, I promised to call again soon, we said our I love yous, this truth spoken and it was enough.

Andrew came home from the Capitola thrift shop with a beautiful navy and tan western shirt trimmed in rust piping, over an hour till Erik picked him up for the gig, he snapped it on over his t-shirt, carefully placing the jug in its bowling ball bag by the door, he asked "There anything you want at the store, I'm going for a walk". Luke bulling around, Sistas primping, I went along, Frodo, Amaru too, a sultry big evening, Luna not yet risen, far enough from city lights to see the Milky Way. I was too quiet. Andrew sought to engage me "You look like a precious jewel in your velvets. Did you make that one too". I did not feel precious, did not want to cause trouble for Luke "Yes thank you. Sorry I'm so down. I must still be tired". Thankfully it was fine to be down around Andrew, he did not feel it his god-given obligation to put a smile on my face, or insist that I am smiling, instead revealing his passion to study the 5000 year old language Cuneiform at UCSC, what ancient secrets he hoped to discover, he was writing a grant. I thought being taken by such an obscure interest, he must be an old soul, must've had something to do with Cuneiform long ago, and then there was playing the jug, such a primary way of making music. Dogs waited outside the store without being asked. Collecting oatmeal, almonds, bananas, milk, whole wheat flour and corn meal for chapatis, peanut butter and honey to dress them, Jasmine tea, dog biscuits, I would cook in exchange for my little space on the floor. Andrew bought bread, cans of tuna fish, mayo, lettuce, beer and Panatelas, offering one as we lugged our fodder home.

The Band gathering before the gig, Erik, Joey, Moby Grape's drummer Stanley Malville sitting-in for the night, come to see the MotherTruckers. And we were worth seeing, flashing again on what a magnificent force we were together, arcane substances, water wind earth fire, North South

East and West, a formidable whole, I did not speak to anyone and took the groceries into the kitchen. Andrew set his on the counter and went to the front room, asking over his shoulder "Could you put mine away too please". I smiled "Yes Dear". Erik insisted his musicians ride together to a gig. Andrew poked in to say good-bye, took his bowling bag and left. Luke ordered us into the equipment van if we wanted a ride. Watching from the kitchen window, Keely scooted in next to him, Gretchen and nearly 20 year old Leda who probably would not get past the ID check climbed in back, I hurried out to lend her my id. She pushed my hand away "No way, you promised remember, we stick together". I looked tenderly into her electric blue eyes and whispered "I know, but I will not ride with him". Luke growled "Get in or get out". Leda closed the door, Gretchen flipped me the bird for staying behind, and they left. My stomach fell forsaken, Dogs followed me in for a biscuit. I did not hear Stoney drive into the cul-de-sac to be my ride.

The backs of our hands stamped, get-in-free on the manager's arm, Stoney took his place at the sound board with Luke and a robust red-head, introducing me to Ted. The High Street Local simmered for One Hand Clapping to show, not a strait person in the crowd, Sistas no where to be seen, I recognized Erik's wife Colleen at the Band Table alone and went to say hi. She gave me a blank-eye stare of hey stupid, you know Groupies are not welcome at the Band Table so get lost, and turned away. Hit so hard I nearly lost my balance, taking an empty chair behind her at a neighboring table, room swimming I lit a smoke, telling my self she must not remember. When collected I leaned near to refreshed her memory "Colleen, you were so much nicer with tea and Sandoz at Sky River". No reaction, I drew away, plainly a threatening unattached female. Joey's ol'lady Cherry joined her, huddling, whispering. I was legitimately with the band too, and not with some one already spoken for behind some one's back, considered just boldly taking a seat at the table, Andrew or Stoney would certainly claim me, but that would be a new confrontation, and with far too many today, I conceded the standing accorded long suffering ol'ladies and wives, even if they used it indiscriminately as a weapon, went to the bar and ordered Tequila.

One Hand Clapping took the stage to wild applause, the mating-dance commenced, being there alone presumed my willing participation, I scanned the room, saw none I cared to tango, a few tunes and I went outside, walking round the building, finding a shadow to hole-up, lighting the stogie Andrew gave me, leaning against the cedar siding. Delroy came out the back door, ostrich skin Tony Lamas, grey Stetson. I stepped into the light "Hey cowboy, find Gretchen". He smiled that charming face "Yep. She's hanging in the band room with the Girls". Making conversation I asked "So where you going". Again the winning smile "I have this killer gooz. How about we get ripped". Delroy was such a rascal and yet I felt safe with him, we walked to the equipment van, rear door unlocked, we got in, roosted on two blown Marshall speakers, he put most of the fat joint in his mouth, wetting it to burn slow and even, struck a match, took a long slow drag and passed to me. I did the same. The door swung open, Stanley got in and sat on an amp. I passed to him trying to stifle coughing my lungs out "Harsh". Delroy billowed a cloud "Yeah. Dipped in something called hash oil. Little brown vial from a friend a mine in Oregon". Oh shit, little brown vials from Oregon, suddenly Nick was near, and I was not prepared for more than a puff of good weed. Inhaling most of the rest Stanley passed to me. So high my ears were ringing, I shook my head "No way". Ever the gentleman Delroy asked "Hey girl, you know Stan the Man". My voice came from far away "Yeah, I saw you earlier at Andrew's". Delroy introduced "Shoshannah, this is Stan, my drummer. He's from up North like you and me". Stan flashed a ready grin "I hear you're one of those Womens Libbers. Come on, do some of that Libber shit on me". I was furious at Delroy for not telling me about the hash oil, and now totally ripped, about to have another unavoidable confrontation, this time with a shit-head I viscerally loathed, pushing my palms flat on the rough speaker skin, lifting my body slightly off the surface, a trick to lower my voice to ring with authority "What do you mean Stanley". He salivated "You know, that ball-breaking stuff you Libbers do". I smiled toothy and insincere "No thank you Stan, I have no interest in your balls". In one smooth motion I slid-off the speaker and out the open door. Delroy burst-out laughing, catching-up, putting a hand my shoulder "Don't worry about Stanley. He's really a pussy cat". I snapped "You jerk. He's just a fool, it's you I'm mad at. You should a told me about the hash oil before I smoked that joint. You should have given me a choice, that's what us Libbers want". Ever honeyed, he cajoled "Oh now sweet girl, did I play too rough". Suddenly vertigo staggered me, I leaned into him as we walked through the back door, wanting to go home, lay down, not knowing where home was anymore or how to get to Andrew's.

And there were my Sistas sitting at the bar, even Leda, no ID needed in-through the band room, glad to see me as me them, my balance restored. I noticed Gretchen and Delroy exchanging mouth twitches, keeping discrete distance, his Wife had her spies. Luke joined us. I braced for trouble. He nodded to me like nothing ever happened, grabbed Keely up off the stool and French-kissed her, tongue so far down her throat he seemed to eat her face. People went from one to an other, consuming, disposable as Bic lighters, anonymous, instinctive, physical, I wanted someone too, but not like this. Gretchen disappeared on the first note of the first song of the second set. Delroy soon after. Keely in Luke's lap at the sound board. Leda and I danced, nursed beers, fending all comers, finding but one person of interest, a girl dancing alone, head down, jigging like her shoes were on fire.

Last call, not everyone paired-up, those desperately looking round for eye contact as the lights flicked on. Leda was drunk "I hear Delroy's got a wife named Catlin, and Stanley's married to Pam. Those pigs, cheating their wives. Fuck em. Pigs. Fucking pigs". I took her with and sought asylum in the band room, perching on the arm of a dirty couch. She curled-up close to me closing her eyes "Pigs. Just fucking pigs". I agreed, it was all about getting girls, and I hated being caught in-between, knowing The Wife, who comes to a gig, and puts on a proud front if The Girlfriend is there too, and Girlfriend knows the rules and stays out-of-peripheral-sight, while Wife maintains high-profile at the Band table as if she doesn't notice, like Colleen and Cherry tonight, while some Roady claims Groupie Girlfriend as his chick, and everyone knows, everyone plays, everyone follows the rules, that work just fine for the Boys, humiliating Wives Groupies and women in general, pitting one against another, tainting the word Wife, always prefaced by The, always whispered, oh The Wife's here better watch-out, no wonder Colleen would not recognize me. It was simple to see why guys wanted to be musicians, but I could not understand why a girl would want one, she could probably never trust him, so casually cheating on their promises, Groupies so plentiful, and like Gretchen often willing to be treated like shit to get what she wants, how could a musician respect any woman with that kind of proposition in his face all the time, why would he. It was a sick game, I swore to Leda "I'll never fall for another musician". She was snoring.

Last to go, Leda and I rode with Andrew and Stoney. Keely and Luke already upstairs fucking so enthusiastic Stoney was too embarrassed to stay. Andrew stacked some records on the player, turned-up the volume and opened his dope box, apologizing for the lowly homegrown as he packed his pipe. In some circles weed had become a competition of who knew what dealer with the best and most expensive and how ripped-out-of-you-mind-into-you-own-private-world one hit could take you, I thought this corrupted MaryJane's gentle nature as a doorway into another consciousness that fostered common ground and cooperation not narcissism. We shared the bowl, and stretched-out on the floor listening to Simon and Garfunkle's *Bridge Over Troubled Water.* When dry mouth and the munchies called, I brewed Jasmine tea and made peanut butter and banana sandwiches, while Leda rubbed Tiger Balm on Andrew's temples and announced she was hitching to Topanga Canyon in the morning, to Christmas with friends, inviting me please come along. I had enough travel for now.

Leda, Amaru left early not waking us. Frodo's melancholy farewell did. Andrew and I rose at noon to another perfect California day. He took me into Santa Cruz, 605 Front Street, for omelets at The Broken Egg. We walked them off along Front and Pacific Avenue, and like he supposed, the Santa Cruz Import Shop and Yellowbird were good for my stuff. Looking over their wares, I would make jewelry, gowns, bikinis, done without my Singer.

Christmas always made me feel an outsider, just about everyone assuming every one was wrapped in Yuletide, and if not, humbug what is wrong with you. I squirmed in elementary school, required to sing the hymns and carols, and when I refused, was cast Christ Killer, pretty heavy load for a little girl. And then there was the having to represent all Jews, expected to be an expert on Judaism, obliged to clarify, no Chanukah is not the Jewish Christmas, Jews celebrate the Festival of Lights for 8 days, always beginning on the 25th day of Kislev, to commemorate the bloody military victory of the Maccabees in 165 BC, that's before Christ, over the Seleucids, and the retaking, cleansing and rededication of the Temple in Jerusalem, and the miracle of one-days holy-oil burning for eight. Such arrogant Christian sensibility to history other than their own, Chanukah thought of as a mere jealous reaction to Christmas, they were plain ignorant of the Jewish calendar, yes it was 1970 years since Jesus, but Jews were living in the year 5731. Twas always the season to lay-low publicly, the constant Merry Christmas To You feeling more like an assault, I wondered what it would be like to be in Israel, be the majority, and realized how lonesome I was for my Mom and Dad. Gretchen's Mom had sent her a bus ticket, she would be in San Diego with her daughter Ava. Colleen, Erik, Cherry, Joey shared a house, inviting Andrew, Stoney, Ted for eve-dinner, and again to open presents in the morning. Luke and Keely never got out of bed.

So, Christmas eve I spread my tools on the floor and began to conceive. Fragrant eucalyptus nuts, beach bird feathers and bleached bones, sparkle from the Santa Cruz Bead Store, thrift shop fabrics and other treasures, people had not discovered thrift stores were the final resting place for Grandma's exquisite handwork. I found my execution had progressed with experience, and watching with these new eyes of mine that were somewhat more objective, I was delighted as the pieces came together. Absorbed completely I hardly slept, Christmas slid by, crocheted pot holders became string bikinis and small pouches lined in silk, scrolled brass wire grew into ornate earrings with feathers, and copper wire breast-plates of crystals, beads, bones and eucalyptus nuts, long gowns of pot-holder bodices and cap-sleeves, embroidered table-cloth shirts and silk-tie skirts, magically every thing fit together, all essential aspects of the same plan. Andrew's respect for a fellow artist grew as he watched my process, like an album of songs, he suggested I take it as a whole to the Santa Cruz Import Shop.

My timing was flawless, shelves were thin from Christmas, and there still were tourists coming. The Owner, a nice guy in gold-rimmed pince-nez did not poker-face me. Arranging the collection on the counter I stood back. He inspected each piece carefully, admiring the innovation, praising my skill and talent "How much for all of it". I was thrilled "What do you think its worth". His voice turned worn and flat "Look, if you don't know what your work is worth, I don't want it". He went into a small back office and quietly shut the door. Mortified, stunned, loser glowing neon on my forehead, I shoved all into the bags and fled, sinking onto a bench outside the shop, how could I have been such an unprofessional wide-open fool, going in a tender artist instead of saurian-skinned agent, unprepared for being whacked so hard, I could not think, and the sun was too hot, I must get away from this store. My legs bearing me down Pacific, shops streaming by as if on a conveyer belt, clean little Golden Ghetto movie-set head-shop, music store, clubs, so many banks, quaint post office, hotels, cafes, hardware store, plants and flowers, natural food market spilling in granola, fresh milled flour, raw milk and spiced tea, near every one impeccably dressed designer Flower-Children.

I turned into the Catalyst, a friendly open place, hung with paintings and Boston ferns, fans spinning the high pitched ceiling, well-worn wooden dance floor and large stage, the deli bragging of fresh-squeezed orange juice, sandwiches and soup, oak tables and nice high back chairs, wicker couches beckoning relax and hang-out a while. Though it seemed laid-back, everyone, everyone watched as I dropped my bags on an empty table and stepped-up to the long marble bar, thankful the bartender did not put me through stand-and-wait unnoticed new-gal-in-town initiation. I ordered two bottles of Coors, took them to the table and slid down in the chair, my money was almost gone, if I couldn't make a living with my hands I would have to get a strait job, what a god-damn fucking stupid fool, the guy was right, I should have thought this out, priced my stuff, even if I had nothing to compare too. One bottle gone, sipping the other I just barely heard "You mind if I sit". Looking-up at a six-foot handsome Irish, I nodded "Okay". He turned around the chair and straddled, lush burnt-umber hair, gentle liquid brown eyes that looked dark against his ivory skin, freckles sprinkling his fine nose, cheek bones, and onto the backs of his hands, he said "Thank you. I'm Steven. The paintings are mine. Today's my opening, and I know every one here but you". The lovely indulgence of talking to a stranger "Well no worry, I'm not a critic". He laughed easily "Never thought this would happen to me, opening day jitters. I'd rather be almost anywhere else". I warmed to the synchronicity of being exactly where I should "Yeah, I can definitely relate". He prompted

"You an artist". I quickly summed the last hour. He eyed my bags wanting to see. And I wanted too but said "No way. It's your time not mine". He was resolute. And so, piece by piece I spread the collection across the table. His friends gathering, and on hearing the tale, priced every thing for me, higher that I had courage, some offering to buy. Steven said "No. This is a body-of-work and should go as a whole". These avenging angels were a core group of artists living in Santa Cruz, here celebrating Steven's first showing, and they agreed, I should march back to the shop with every thing priced, thank Owner for teaching me a valuable lesson, and ask him to buy all or none. Steven offered to go with me. My head shook "No. I must do this my self".

Owner totally appreciated my tenacity, did not quibble, bought every thing as priced, three gowns $40 each, five pouches $8 each, seven necklaces and seven earrings $10 each, inviting me to bring all I made to him first. Off-the-ground, I could make it here on my terms, floating away with under-the-table cash in-hand, to the Catalyst, to buy a victory round. If I could only remember before getting so upset, Carl Jung says you have to *let things develop*, let the Sweet Sisters Fate take me to people and places better than my own will, people who gave me a triumphant standing ovation on successful return. The Renaissance had relegated woman's art to the craft heap, sewing, needle-work, weaving, cooking, to be done out of sight, taken for granted, mostly unpaid, uncelebrated. But here were women and men, weavers, jewelers, potters, cooks, basket makers, woodworkers, sculptors, painters, all making seen art, eaten, worn, used, touched. Steven took me to each of his paintings, abstract, psychedelic, many details only noticed close-up, a different meaning depending on where you stood, and they were good, and did not speak to me or elicit much emotion, which was my unschooled criteria for great art. I was restless, not wanting to be rude, and made the lame excuse of having to go find a Seattle newspaper. Steven knew where, happy to show me. And I felt caught as we walked over a little bridge to the Avenue of Diamonds, crushed-glass mixed into new black-top, glittering in the sun. The news-stand man greeted him by name, and yes he stocked the daily Seattle Times. Front-page headline below the fold *"Judge Boldt refuses to act on Seattle Seven bail plea"*. I did not want Steven or anyone knowing my politics, and tucked the paper under my arm.

The Santa Cruz Sentinel sent staff reporter Jay Shore to cover Steven's opening. While he interviewed, I settled in a corner wicker chair to read *"United States District Court Judge George H. Boldt refused today to take any action on bail for the seven defendants in the Seattle conspiracy trial. In addition, Boldt expressed displeasure with the Circuit Court of Appeals' ruling on bail last Wednesday. The Appeals Court in San Francisco said the seven should be allowed bail pending an appeal of the contempt sentences. Boldt denied bail to the defendants December 5th, saying if his order was overturned, bail would be set at "not less than $25,000". Boldt said the Appeals Court had not seen the trial transcript nor a video tape of the courtroom disturbances December 4th which were an important part of his no-bail order when it ruled bail should be allowed. "Despite that" Boldt said "The panel made the decision without waiting for the vital material. I can't understand how it could act without giving at least lip service to the transcript or audio visual material". Defense attorney Jeffrey Steinborn argued this morning that the Appeals Court ruling required the judge to set bail. Charles Billinghurst, Assistant United States Attorney working for the prosecution, said the government had filed a motion to have the bail order reconsidered because the Appeals Court did not have a complete trial record. Judge Boldt again affirmed his conviction that the seven defendants were likely to flee or pose a threat to the community. The seven have been confined since December 5th when Boldt sentenced them to contempt. Judge Boldt called Steinborn on the carpet over attempts by him and other defense attorneys to contact him at his home during Christmas. Steinborn said it was a misunderstanding. The Appeals Court ruling would have allowed defendants to post ten percent of the $25,000 bail figure. Steinborn said before going into court that he had funds for five of the seven defendants bail."*

Poor little Boldt didn't like being bothered over Christmas, didn't like being disturbed at home, no more than we did by the FBI, and he would not abide the higher court ruling to grant bail because he didn't think they made the right call, we didn't think he made the right call, pompous potentate with power to decide lives, I was spitting-mad, the savor of selling my stuff gone sour, I closed the door that had been easing open, locked it tight, every one I did not know long and well was again suspect. The Catalyst filling-up, Steven the soul of attention, his opening about to formally begin, time was ripe for a clean get-away, I folded the paper unto my shoulder bag, stood with the crush waiting for a moment to thank him for being a friend, to congratulate, and to split. He would not let me go without a phone number. I shivered as if cold hands touched my back "I'm staying with One Hand Clapping. I don't know the number". The look on his face said he felt the dodge and did not understand, the attraction was so strong "How about I give you a lift home". I did not want him or anyone "No, you can't leave. It's your big day". He would not be put-off "Then meet me here tomorrow at four and we'll have sup-per". Flattered and caught I promised "Okay, tomorrow". Wending Front Street, melding in with the tourists, along the Boardwalk and onto the beach, easy to see if anyone was following, I knew I was nuts, too little a fish to be followed, still I needed to be certain, sitting on the wet dark sand, thinking I should go back to Seattle, maybe find some way to help the Seven's defense, if a newspaper article could make me this crazy, this paranoid, then maybe not, but I felt like a deserter, AWOL from responsi-bility, and marveled at what a presumptuous ego I had, that I would make a difference, at the same time believing I could, and then there was Nick. I walked to Andrews.

Keely barely glanced at the newspaper, only interested in fucking Luke. And I cringed at what she would do with a Husband and Littles. Gretch-en, Leda, Amaru still gone, I sat on the porch with Frodo, head-to-tail slow-pets not enough to soothe his pining. When Andrew came home from Band practice, we walked to the beach. Tail hanging, Frodo came along, the seagulls were safe today. Cigars well lit, I crowed half-hearted on selling my collection. Andrew as proud as a parent, wisely over-looking my less than genuine zeal. I thanked him for his gracious hospitality, and having decided yes to going North for a while, asked would it be all right to come back. He guaranteed my little space on the floor, suggesting I should stay through New Years Eve, the Band had a big gig at the Zyante Club that could be the party of the year. Three more days, and how to travel to Seattle, I would have to let things develop.

Four PM, standing by the entrance to the Catalyst, Steven walked up to me with newspapers folded under his arm, the Whitefish Register, Santa Cruz Sentinel, Seattle Times, a thought-full gesture or maybe slick ploy, either fueled my paranoia, still I took the Times with smiling thank you and we walked a block to the Broken Egg. When seated Steven pardoned to the boys-room. I scanned the paper, page three headline *"Court stays action on contempt bail"*. My heart racing, I did not read the story, folding the paper neatly on top of the table, it was just to coincidental, some how Steven must know, I waited till he settled across from me and ordered coffee, patting the paper, offering credible ruse "The paper was so thought full. Thank you. I get home-sick, a little news makes me feel better". So lame, transparent, yet he seemed not to notice, shining a commiserate grin "Me too. I'm from Whitefish Montana. Get the Register everyday". The part of me that knows said this man was not a threat, that I should relax. The Broken Egg served eggs, only in California would a restaurant be so specialized, I ordered an omelet stuffed with fire-roasted green chilies, tomato, corn, black beans, jalapeno and cilantro salsa all over, polenta on the side. Steven a steak omelet rare, little rivers of bloody juice running with each bite, as he bubbled over the opening, four of the 12 paintings sold, he thought I must be his good luck charm, reading aloud Jay Shore's glowing Sentinel review. Ah yes, a review, credible reason to buy the paper, I hated being one of those self-absorbed Americans Jean-Pierre spoke of, waiting to say my piece, but nothing seemed to lighten my paranoia, and I waited, deaf, giving polite uh huh's and nods, till Steven exhausted his enthusiasm, and I could turn the conversation however clumsy to his politics "So do you think a country that eats meat without a thought for the animals ever thinks it's doing the same to what else it dominates, like Vietnam, and minorities, even the environment". He took what seemed a deliberately large bloody bite "I don't really see the connection". What I said was so blurry maybe no one could have made the connection, I hoped it was honest on his part, for he was intelligent, and I was so purely physically, so awfully attracted to him, unabashedly flirty, letting slip One Hand Clapping's New Years gig at the Zyante. He knew, confessing if I had not come today he would have gone looking for me there. Mentally slapping my cheek hard, I knew I should keep this person at stiff-arm, a very nice guy I would get-to-the-bottom-of too fast, people were not food, I didn't want to simply eat him and spit out the bones, resolving to stop leading him to think we should be more than friends, though I would go home with him this instant if he asked. The waiter filled our coffee cups a third time, and I asked for the check. Steven automatically reached for it. I insisted buying my own. This was new for him, he took it in good humor. And we strolled to the Boardwalk, out on the Municipal Pier, I was so enthralled with the Santa Cruz ambiance, warm December winds, white sand beaches, lingering orange sunsets, the casual pace, nothing heavy seemed to happen, fashion ten years ahead of Seattle, my work well received, yet I found no real juice here, every one looking forward to the coming Age of Aquarius, asking your astrological sign, talking all kinds of metaphysical magic, sounding so enlightened, so liberated, but it was a thin surface, wearing peace symbols and spouting end the war rhetoric as fashion and abstraction, no one did a thing about it but talk and talk, no one spoke of racism or Women's Lib or god, and that was the charm for me, being so far away from the action, though I missed high-times at Hydra's War Table, those days were gone and the brave and foolish soldiers who stuck their heads out-too-far were prisoners of conscience. Steven was more than just surface, but I was too distracted, needing to be alone, and staying long enough to leave, made another transparent excuse, how late it was, I should get back to my work. He offered to drive me, when I declined, he was a good boy and did not persevere. I hurried along Riverside Avenue, across the San Lorenzo Bridge, down East Cliff Drive, to a bus-stop bench beneath a bright street light where I opened the Times to page three.

"The Ninth Circuit Court of Appeals in San Francisco yesterday stayed its order granting bail to the seven Seattle conspiracy defendants. It gave United States District Attorney Stan Pitkin until noon Monday to present further evidence supporting a government motion that the Appellate Court reconsider the bail order. Also yesterday the 9th Circuit Court set an early hearing date of February 11th in San Francisco on the defense motion appealing the contempt sentences. The government had moved for expediting the appeal, which normally would take six months to a year. Judge Boldt declared a mistrial, contending disruption by the defendants had prejudiced the case with the jury. Defense attorneys have contended there were no grounds for a mistrial. In sentencing the defendants for contempt, Boldt denied bail. He said that if the Appellate Court found him in error he would set bail at no less that $25,000

cash or corporate surety. The 9th Circuit Court ruled last Wednesday that bail should be allowed and defendants should be able to post ten-percent of the total bail with the court for their freedom. Judge Boldt refused to act on the Appellate Court's bail order. Defense attorney Jeffrey Steinborn said "Boldt has no authority to defy the order". Steinborn said he received word that some male defendants in federal prison were forced to have their long hair cut. Lisa Johnson — a University of Washington law student and member of the Seattle Conspiracy-Defense Collective said "It is the judge that is the stumbling block. We're now concerned with one man's opinion - one man's power".

Bail, no bail, it felt like witnessing a whipping, each blow on me too. Boldt was playing god in the worst way, I could just picture his delight hearing of the hair cuts, symbolic Samson castration. I had money in my pocket to fly home, thinking I should go and see maybe what I could contribute. The salty night air caressed my skin as I walked the last blocks, taking pleasure from it felt some how a betrayal. The house dark and quiet, I sat on the porch, Luna rising with Orion Calisto and Cygnus, I stood with my arms reaching up to greet them till they could no longer stay, tip-toed passed Andrew and Frodo snoring softly, beneath Keely and Luke in the loft, into the kitchen to brew some tea, the 15 watt bulb above the nook still on, and there was Gretchen. She giggled and gave me a bear hug. I giggled too, surprised how satisfying her touch felt. She sounded depressed "I only had two days with Ava and Mom. My ex showed-up, made it so fucking impossible, you know, like Nick does. So I called Delroy, and met him in Berkeley. We stayed with Brian". I laid the Seattle Times on the table "Who's Brian". She didn't look up from the paper "Oh, a friend. Turns out he's Delroy's dealer. Guess he's everyone's dealer". I waited till she looked at me "I'm going to Seattle for a while". She hushed a giggle "Well isn't that lovely how things work. Leda's going North with Brian in a few days too. He's making a run up the coast, we can catch a ride". Having heard nothing from Leda had truly worried me "You seen her". Gretchen would not look at me, lit a Marlboro, smoke curling into her eyes, wiping with her hand "She's at Brian's a couple days now". I sat down across from her "How's she know Brian". Gretchen took a long drag and blew smoke slowly at the ceiling, still not meeting my eyes "Okay, here goes. She lost Amaru in Topanga Canyon. Hasn't slept in days". The impact brought

Grampa's death fresh with it, my chest sunk in pain welcoming his ghost "Shit". Gretchen cleared her throat "She's out of her mind nuts from it. Dropped a bunch a Yellows and some acid, combed the streets, beaches, every door, ending-up at a Boz Scaggs concert in LA, and went home with him to Berkeley. Brian's his dealer too, and he brought her over the next day when he went to score. I was so glad I was there and made her stay. He seemed really happy to be rid of her". Ever since meeting Josh in the Huston Airport, I was beyond awe at the unmistakable order back of seeming fickle circumstances "Why didn't she come with you". Gretchen eyed me "They're going North New Years day. Leda finally put a collar and ID tag on Amaru, with her Mom's address. Maybe she'll hear something if she goes. Her Mom's such a witch, I couldn't stay there again, so I came back here with Delroy. But I'll go if we can stay at Hydra". I pressed "Call her now okay". She did "They're leaving the 2nd. There's room for us". I pushed "Get Leda on the phone". Gretchen asked, then hung-up "She's been smoking opium and's finally asleep".

We stayed-up talking, commiserating, crying. Gretchen brewed coffee and woke the house before dawn. Andrew and Frodo first, and Luke, and Keely who after hugging Gretchen demanded why were our eyes so puffed and red. Gretchen looked at me then broke the news. Frodo's ears went-up with Amaru's name, then down, clearly understanding the tone of Gretchen's voice and Keely's reaction, he went to the front door, standing motionless, nose on the knob. Andrew let him out and followed. I went too, and we stood in silent vigil as he paced round-and-round the cul-de-sac, whimpering, snorting, ears down, making smaller and smaller circles, shaking his head side-to-side, lips loose, at length sagging down on his haunches, bawling a low dirge that rose to peak range, calling her name Aaa-Ruu Aaa-Ruu Aaa-Ruu, each chorus ending with teeth bared, each round cutting deeper. We waited witness, till his voice was spent and he crumbled at our feet, rusting eyes closed to find her in his dreams. Frodo knew Amaru would not be coming back to him. And I knew in my heart this would happen and there was nothing more I could have done about it, at least Leda put ID on her, Scarlet O'Hara's words running though my head, *I can't think about that right now. If I do, I'll go crazy. I'll think about that tomorrow,* I resonated to the wisdom. Gretchen came out to bum a smoke. Sun beginning to light the sky, I gave her ten for cigarettes and beer if she would go to the store, and got busy making chapatis with peanut butter and honey. Luke ate most of them. The rest of us had little appetite but for beer. We talked of going North. Keely was not ready to face Ric. The admiration I had for her as a mother faded each day she did not call her Littles and explain her absence even with lies.

The house all went back to sleep till well after noon. Frodo had not budged from his collapse. Andrew and I coaxed him for a cigar walk to the beach. Then each of us used the tiny shower, getting ready for New Years Eve. Gretchen wangling to wear the velvet gown, reminding how I promised, we sparred all afternoon, warding-off the terrible loss, she was hoping to see Delroy, if he could slide away from The Wife. I hoped to see Steven, keeping it to my self, resisting till she was already dressed to hand her the velvet. I wore my living dress, too blue for glad-rags anyway. Keely left at 7PM with Luke to set-up. Erik and Joey came by for Andrew. Stoney for me and Gretchen. We wound the Santa Cruz mountains on Zyante Road almost to Lompico, climbed zigzag flights of stairs, crossing the patio, passed a steaming swimming pool into the dining room, it was just after 8PM and mostly empty but for the Band and entourage. I saw Colleen sitting alone at a table and decided to try once more. Gretchen wanted to come with but could not, having slept with Delroy, according to the rules she forfeit public rights when The Wife or Ol'lady was round. Keely waved from the bar. Miss Fine joined her, and I took a seat at Colleen's table. She smiled with her eyes "Your dress is wonderful". I tried not to show surprise "Thank you. I made it". Smiling with her whole face now she nodded "I know. Andrew took me by the Santa Cruz Import Shop to show me your collection". It was generous of her to let me know, and so sweet of Andrew to tinker between the lines, even so things were stiff, my stomach cooperated by growling "So, what's good on the menu". She warmed "The eggplant sandwich. Grilled French bread, melted Gouda and lots of mayo". I caught a waiter's attention, ordering the sandwich, a pitcher of beer and two glasses. Colleen smiled again and nodded. We sat in awkward silence till beer loosened our tongues. She told how the band needed a keyboard player and permanent drummer to make it big, and as luck would have it, the right ones had recently come to town. And I told of Frodo losing Amaru, and going North with Brian. She knew him, and confided finding out today she was pregnant.

The Zyante's massive raw-log building, two vaulting rooms, one for eating, one music and dancing, an high archway between, the music piped-out to the patio and pool. Cherry appeared, plopped on the other side of Colleen, skinny as Olive Oil, she ignored me. I did not like her either and politely excused my self to Colleen, leaving an untouched sandwich and pitcher. Wishing I had not come, Gretchen, Keely no where insight, I went out to the pool, found a secluded little café-table, losing Amaru had knocked the wind out of me, as if someone was sitting on my chest. The pool began filling with naked bodies, I grudgingly compared mine to these uninhibited water nymph. And the band launched their first set. And I broke a Sandoz in-half, maybe 30 still left in the bottom of my bag, the last of the Lysergic Acid Diethylamide manufactured by an American pharmaceutical company before it was illegal, the last dependable acid trip, I laughed aloud at government funding my imminent escape. As if she could smell it, Gretchen stood at my side, smiling, her big shameless greedy hand-out "Gimme, gimme". Feeling grateful and generous to this Swan Queen, so resplendent in the velvet, I decided to give her the gown, but not now, it was acid she wanted and I placed both halves of the broken tab on her waiting tongue. She giggled and sat down. Together afforded us aegis, watching the pool party, music stirring our bodies, and we went into the Ball.

Girl-girl dancing always seriously rattled weak-ego jackasses, Gretchen and I could do without them. Occasionally one would make it their sacred duty to avenge this behavior, and tonight's persecutor was Raul, rudely handsome member of the Santa Cruz Hell's Angels. The Angels had adopted One Hand Clapping as their club band, deemed themselves security when ever the band played, unfortunately Raul was smitten with Gretchen, and she wanted nothing of him. His beautiful long-legged The Wife sat ring-side drilling him with her eyes, he much too drunk for her to be any kind of civilizing influence, nabbed Gretchen from behind and began humping. She sat down on the dance floor and screamed above the music "Don't touch me". Raul lost his balance and sat down too, gesturing vulgar "What's a madder cunt. Only hole tight enough fer fuckin's yer ass. Fuck you. Fuck you cunt". She sprang to her feet in full acid bloom, flipping him the bird with both hands "Not on your best day creep". This goon would kill her, and though everyone looked on, no one would stop him. I wanted to dissolve into the floor, thank-full he was not fixed on me, and found my self reaching in my pocket for Excalibur, surreptitiously opening the blade easily with one hand, stepping-up to Gretchen's side. It was a fool's game tangling with a sot, but in her native way Gretchen Fetchin-Fine equaled the task, and I admired her headlong nerve. Raul continued his tirade, the Band never missed a beat, she took my arm, turned her back on him and led me to the center of the floor, the crowd closed-in around us, and we resumed the dance. My take on the little three-letter word ego, it was the container of individual consciousness, and no matter how big, if full it was not fragile. I had built some confidence in what I could do, what I could be, what I could not, a female with an ego was threatening to both unliberated men and women, but my container could take a blow without breaking into destructive defensive behavior I would hate my self for later. Raul suffered from a bulging empty container, the slightest bump even unintentional caused a tidal wave of over-reaction, he sustained his harangue to save face, then yanked his Wife onto the dance floor, mauling her, the way a man colonizing a woman's body takes his liberty. One girl sacrificed for another.

It was over for now, Gretchen went to the bar, in-close to Keely. I ordered two shots of tequila, and feeling the claustrophobic anticipation of desperate fresh starts that dog every New Years Eve, went pool-side, the undulating naked bodies a relief. Waitress brought my shots, and everyone seemed to turn and watch, tequila being a man's drink, I guess to see could I handle it. Having worn my living dress to be a more subtle-bird, it made no matter now, salting the back of my hand, licking the white crystals, pressing them to the roof of my mouth, dissolving, I saluted the pigs and fishes with the glass and downed in it one swift motion, sips would have been preferred but public pressure ruled, men drink like their manhood depends on it, I bit the lime in-time to beat the bite, turned the glass down on the table, took the next and did it again. Two too many, the Bacchanalia hideously exaggerated, good tequila much like mescaline, suddenly a naked wet man scooped me from my chair to toss in the pool,

I bit his wrist, landed on the ground, and Steve just appear from nowhere, offering me a hand up. One Hand Clapping in a frenzied winding jam, their congregation in ardent pulse, alcohol and music too much to speak, we danced, and kissed in the New Year, a kiss I had been avoiding, feelings I did not want to have. A marijuana-cloud hanging low to the dance floor, beer and champagne slick, I wanted to go. Steven too, he would take me to Malio's on the Pier for a drink. Gretchen stubbornly waiting for Delroy, Keely a drunken bitch-in-heat stuck to Luke, I felt guilty, liable, leaving these muddle-heads behind, and felt a bust lurking.

Careening down the mountain we passed no police. The Santa Cruz Municipal Pier spawned a block over the water, Malio's Italian Restaurant more than half-way out, was still full with a private party, so we took an empty bench at the on-ramp to a moon-shine silver highway shimmering across the water, and touched and kissed, and Steven wished "Come home with me". I did not want to lead him on, and still desire won. His bunga-low three blocks, thick with his paintings, barely room for a new mattress on the floor, we unwrapped each other, eager precious presents, amorous fingers, breathless kisses, ready skin, I rustled "Let's be safe". He inhaled "Aren't you on the pill". Instant resentment, so it was only my responsi-bility "No, aren't you". He sounded disappointed and a tiny bit dismissive "Ahhhh, a girl with a sense of humor". I pushed him off me "Girls don't get pregnant by themselves". Rolling onto his back, withering, he sighed "But you're the one who gets pregnant, so I thought it was your job". I sat-up, savoring his long lean beautiful body, smiling "No protection, no sex". He sat-up too, stroking a hot palm along my thigh, tickling my foot "Okay, then I'll feed you". We smoked a joint while the potatoes fried, ate with hot sauce and fingers, and slept into the afternoon.

Showered, hair still wet we proceeded to the Colonial Inn on Ocean Street. Steven ordered New York Steak rare. Watching the blood run, I had no taste for my Eggplant Parmesan, or his talk of buying a box of Tro-jans and using them all by midnight. Tequila had swayed the evening, now my mind was heading North, anxious to see Leda, in reluctant fairness I told Steven. He leaned in his seat as if struck "Tomorrow. When're you coming back". I regretted disingenuous "Don't know exactly. Soon maybe. Do you mind taking me to Andrew's after we eat". But for directions we rode silent. I took-in the ocean with every breath, hoping to keep some, hoping it was not my last time. Steven drove too fast, skidding to a stop in the dirt inches from the porch, he broke the ice "Can I have your Seattle number". I did not like poisoning him with more deceit and did "I would but, I don't know where I'm staying yet". He jammed on the emergency brake and reached to the side of my face with his big hand "You're just so beautiful. Promise me you'll keep in touch". I lied "I will". He held on tight with those liquid brown eyes "You know I'm falling in love with you". Oh shit, looking at my lap, refusing the heartfelt "Steven if you knew me, you wouldn't". I opened the door. He put that big hand on my shoulder, not enough to impede "I would". This was so way too fast, we never talked, about god or Ida Rose or politics or anything, I took my bag, slid-away, walking around the car. His door flung open, falling-out on his knees, he stood-up, and giving no choice really, wrapping me in his arms, kissing long and hard. I did not open my mouth or return the embrace, I did not like most men much these days, how they wanted what they wanted and took it, I did not want another ride on the emotional roller coaster everyone else seemed so eager for, never again Nick's consuming effacing jealous love, I wanted some one who would not be intimidated by me thinking all the time, having opinions different from theirs, opinions I would fight for, some one with a filled-in ego, I would not have to play dumb round him or his friends, some one who would respect me, want an equal, a partner not just a cocotte cook house-cleaner, that would happily cook, and keep house for, even be some one's whore, but that was not enough, I believed deep-down I would know him on sight, and if he ate meat it would be well-done. Steven understood my body language, lightly kissed my nose and let me go. We said no more. His tires spun just a little in the dirt as I climbed the three porch stairs, wishing he would fall in love with someone else.

Andrew and Gretchen waiting, worried, for I was usually the responsible one, had vanished from the Zyante, and she did not remember my asking her to go with. Our trip was on, she had spoken to Brian, just postponed a few days, he would not say why over the phone, but Leda wanted us to come right away. All I needed, we would leave in the morning. Gretchen besieged Andrew, get-up early and take us to the highway so we could catch a commuter. He let her beg and plead, at last revealing Stoney was driving to Berkeley to check-out a possible gig at the New Orleans House, he was thrilled for company, would come for us before noon. Now to a farewell dinner. I browned several sliced yellow onions and pineapple, brewed a thick peanut-butter-curry sauce with honey and pineapple juice, spooned it over steaming jasmine rice, with Major Grey Chutney and crisp-sliced Bosc pears on the side. Luke and Keely got out of bed to join the feast, she wanted my pledge not to say anything to Ric about Luke. Feeling sorry for her, so blindly consumed by a wish-come-true, I forewarned please call him, he would push me why she stayed be-hind, and I would have to say something. Gretchen's easy promise not to breathe a word sowed a prickly seed between us, but they had been siding with each other more and more. As the sun began its setting, Andrew and I coaxed Frodo to the beach, smoking our Panatelas. And every one sleep-ing early, I folded ten-dollars for the water bill in a note thanking Luke for his generous hospitality, and left it on the coffee table.

Chapter Fifteen

NO KILLING TONIGHT

Approaching a curve, unable to see around it, questioning my life going in the right direction, I woke to a quiet house, pulled on my jean skirt and sweater against a foggy morn and walked the meadow of scents to the beach. Bitter-sweet, maybe I would not return to paradise, finding a skinned log rolled-in on the tide, settling, watching sea-gulls and busy lit-tle birds running water's edge, wondering how I could know I was making right decisions, what was right anyway, did it matter, I needed to grieve Amaru with Leda, to go home for reasons of conscience, and I had this haunting feeling in the gossamer threads of my intuition there was some-thing here in Santa Cruz, and that going away could afford me the long view or sever Ariadne's thread. Frodo sat down, sniffing the air, allowing me to stroke his head till I understood he came to fetch me. We dawdled as the sun burned through.

Fingers tucked into her arm-pits, dark and scowling Keely leaned against the door jamb. Andrew already had my suitcase in the trunk, he took my hand and kissed it "Been a genuine pleasure Shoshannah. Come back and smoke another stogie with me". I kissed his cheek "Thank you. I'll miss our walks". Gretchen appeared, ghostly, breathing heavy, lugging her stuff, crawled in back and laid down whimpering "God, I feel like shit". Assuming a hang-over I closed the door and got infront with Stoney. He started the engine, Keely stepped onto the porch, eyes glittering tears. I rolled down the window. She sobbed "Kiss 'em for me. Tell 'em how much I love 'em". Nodding I will, we were gone. Gretchen slept in fits. Stoney and I shared a joint, he talking the Band, all he talked. This was my first day-light Highway One trip, I was taken at every turn by unexpected sweeping spectacle, and could not give him much sustained attention. By Half Moon Bay he fell silent. Highway One merged into San Francisco, over the Bay Bridge, North into Berkeley, on Shattuck Avenue he managed a shy "If you want, we could drop Gretchen and you come with me to the New Orleans House". I knew better than to accept "You heard about Amaru right. I need to see Leda". Eyes never looking at me he resigned "Sure, I understand". I turned to wake Gretchen. He snapped "No need, I know the way". Silence again, I took-in the distinctive old English of Berkeley, thinking maybe I could find a collective here, amused at the thought, they must be under attack too, every bit paranoid as the Seattle Liberation Front, I would not be welcome.

Parking on Euclid Avenue under some ancient oaks, I hopped-out, opened the back and roused Gretchen. Clammy, fevered, putting my arm round her waist, we bumped along the narrow concrete walkway, up three-stairs, into the ground-floor flat's darkened front room, Leda curled-fetal at the far end of a long velvet couch, I laid Gretchen at the other. Leda opened her puffed eyes, forcing a twisted grin. I bent over, kissing her forehead, quietly asking had she heard any thing. Shaking no she pulled me down, face in my bosom, sobbing soundless. I hugged, rocking gentle. She pushed me away and curled-up. I knew it was all she could do and covered her with a crocheted shawl fallen on the floor. Stoney brought our things, introducing me to Brian, who was not uptight at my being there while they did a dope deal. Stoney left. Me trailing to the car "I'm really worried about Gretchen". Abruptly in a hurry he directed "Take her to County emergency. It's free. Brian knows where it is". I did not blame him for not wanting to be involved and put out my hand "Thanks for the ride. Good luck at the New Orleans". He took it, looking quickly in my eyes then to the ground "You coming back". I smiled "Yeah I am, one way or another". He shook hard and let go "Until then".

Expecting buyers, business first, Brian would not drive to the hospital, I was welcome to take his car, maps in the glove compartment, he offered the key just as every Golden Girl's ideal walked into the room. So blonde she was see-through, natural honey-streaked long platinum hair, thick and slept-on, milk skin, cherub's mouth, faultless nose, slight on her frame, pained ice-blue eyes, a fresh cast on her right arm, Brian introduced his wife. April could not drive, but knew the way, been there days ago. We were instant friends, bundled Gretchen into the car and set-out for Oakland.

Emergency admitted her immediately. April and I took a corner in the lobby, smoking cigarettes, skipping the small-talk, she said Leda was loaded on codeine, had been mostly sleeping, and believed Amaru was still alive, being held by who ever found her. I did not feel her life extinguished either, just the ache of never looking into the fierce and patient wisdom of those shining green eyes, tears rolled my face, who would ever give her up. Chain-smoking Kool menthols, gritting perfect white teeth, shifting the cast, April offered me a tissue from the blood-stained wad in her sweater pocket, and smartly changed subject. Leda had talked of my conviction for the Women's Movement, and April agreed with all-her-heart that women could be friends and allies, on the matter of men she mirrored Gretchen, having one made her feel whole, safe, Brian took high-style care of her and their three-year-old son, who was staying with her Folks till the arm was better. How it got broken remained unsaid.

Two hours, smokes ash, Gretchen appeared, color slightly improved, diagnosis, virulent Gonorrhea plus urinary tract infection, they shot her full of penicillin, more to take in pills for 10 days, gallons of water, complete rest. Listening, I realized the only one healthy here was me, we were killing ourselves, the public heard about the famous ones, but so many were invisibles, over-dosing, minds blown permanently, strung-out, broken, and sterile from untreated venereal disease, going to jail for political and social beliefs, for thought crimes, and if they could not get us on those, then for small drug busts, some murdered by Pigs in the street-wars here and friendly fire over there, disillusioned, molested, raped, coerced, having babies too young to be grown enough to raise them well. I dodged my share with Nick, Josh, Gabriel, but my luck was naïve, I would see someone soon about the pill. Having read-up on it, a double-edged proposition, high doses of hormones so unnatural they had to be unhealthy, side-effects of elevated blood pressure, possible stroke, acne, weight gain especially the thighs, after the Thalidomide catastrophe, there had to be more things they did not know yet that would show in time, and then there were those men, like Steven assuming me totally responsible for protection, if I took the pill, in my mind it somehow made their case, yet it was 94% more effective than nothing. Sex had not been casual for me, and now there was little dialogue about consequences, men simply took for granted we were on the pill, did not even bother to ask, yet all they had do was look around, so many had babies or were pregnant, Keely four, Gretchen one, April one, Colleen one coming, with Amaru gone Leda probably would not be long. I drove us back to Euclid, and put Gretchen to bed in the guest bedroom.

Brian had the heavy velvet window curtains drawn, all candles lit, sitting on a matching velvet couch across from Leda, leaning over the coffee-table and large silver Rococo mirror, chopping cocaine crystals into fine powder with a pearl-handled straight-razor. Coke dealers had such beautiful mirrors, I wondered on them alone could I deduce was a person a dealer or just using. April and I sat on either side of him. He cut the powder into four lines, offering me firsts. Turning down drugs causes a dealer homicidal paranoia, no matter this was my host, I politely declined. If ruffled, Brian did not let-on, re-cutting lines into three, snorting the fat one, half in each nose. April took the rolled one-hundred-dollar-bill in her awkward left hand, offered Leda, and when she did not respond, promptly snorted both lines. Brian growled low and mean what a strung-out Bitch. Shrinking into the couch, fumbling for the tissue in her sweater pocket, dabbing a red-trickle from her perfect nose, she blamed him for making her test each new score. Here was the dark secret and I did not want to know, excusing my self to the hall, looking-in on Gretchen sleeping hard, I unpacked my magic teapot, went to the kitchen, put it on to boil and sat down at the table. A Bay area phone-book lay open, I thumbed for Tara's name, found it and dialed. Far more excited than I could have imagined, she insisted I come to the evening performance of Alice in Wonderland at the A.C.T. Theatre, it was closing night, she was the lead, and would pick me up in one hour no excuse accepted. There was a PG&E bill on the table, I read her the address. April and Brian into the silent treatment, I asked to bathe. Brian showed the way, one of those long high-ceiling wooden-floor Berkeley flats with kitchen and bathroom at the rear, he turned-on the water, a graceful claw-foot tub, lit the pot-belly stove and candles. And he took the liberty of bringing my forgotten cup of tea after I slipped into the water. I did not mind much, men who took the amount of drugs he did were eunuchs.

Gretchen, Leda out-cold, April goof-balled on codeine and cocaine, puking her inners out, Brian edgy, waiting for buyers, I was glad for some where to go, curious what Tara had come to on her own. My long-sleeve living dress badly needed washing, it would have to be the tapestry halter gown, I borrowed a shawl from the many draping furniture, and waited on the porch, heavenly late afternoon eucalyptus-breeze drying my hair. Tara unfurled from her Karmann Ghia and I remembered, one of those females, detached, competitive, superior, something about the way she held her neck and jaw gave it away, though we had been physically close, we were never tight. There were two hours to be at the theatre, she was dying-curious to meet my friends. Brian's sarcastic I'm so honored to meet a star taken sincerely, Tara went on about her self and playing Alice, shining, coquetting, indifferently turning-down the line he cut for her. So typical of a dealer to offer first hits free, so insidious to fuck her up before a performance. April graced us, seeing the line sat close to Tara. Who gasped "Oh my God, I have to show you to my agent". April had to know she was a stunner, but coming from a bona-fide actress seemed to flatter, her eyes fixed on the line, shaking her head "No thanks, I don't have any talent". Tara laughed "Oh honey, looks are talent". She turned to Brian "Pictures, high quality, that's all she needs. She's got that one thing you can't fake. They'll see it. You either have it or you don't…". Poised, knees together, back arched, extravagant deliberate gesticulation, Tara enunciated vowels and letters as if practicing her lines, smiling with too many teeth. I had been jealous of her schooled polish, she had ripened artificial, calculated, beautifully unoriginal. April's body stiffening as Tara ignored her, occupying Brian. He preened to it. April picked a perfectly rolled joint from the coffee-table, malicious stalking horse, eyes gleaming she lit the ultra potent flower-tops and passed to Tara. I warned "Weed makes you forget things, like lines". Tara took my counsel as a challenge "Oh Hon, I can still handle a little grass". An insolent hit, joint paper sticking to her bottom-lip, burning-ash falling on her pink linen pants, swatting it, coughing the harsh smoke, her studied composure crumbed. April was delighted and used the subterfuge to snort that line. Brian called her a fucking Bitch, storming from the room. April after him.

I gathered my bag and Tara "Come on, we better go". She floated along to the car, and sighing handed me the key "Here. Please. I'm way too zonked to drive okay". Suddenly more trouble than worth, I did not want to go anywhere with her "No. You should take a cab". She chummed an arm round my shoulder "Thanks for trying to warn me Shoshy, you know I can be such a moron. But you, you were always the smart one, you can do this. I give good directions". Her charm did not sway me, I did not feel responsible for her predicament, however I did make the phone call "Yeah, okay. But you have to let me know where to go way before we get there. I'm a little freaked driving in such big traffic". She was a first-rate co-pilot, smoothly injecting "Take a right onto West MacArthur. Look for 580. Thank God I didn't marry William, he doesn't have any ambition. My Folks said he would never amount to anything. I don't think I would either if we stayed together. There's the 580 exit coming up. He's working at the Mark Hopkins as a doorman. Honey, imagine, a doorman. Lives on Pine, just a few blocks from the theatre. I run into him sometimes". Thinking of Nick I asked "Is he stalking you". She pointed "Just stay in this lane, 80's right up there. No, but I get the feeling it isn't always by chance. You know he changed his name to Will". I understood how names can affect "That's a great choice. I have a friend who changed hers from Margo Strange to Marigold Hill". Tara was not listening "I had to get away from him. Live my own life. And I'm finally getting a break, playing a rape victim in this new TV pilot". She sounded bitter "You know, it's a savage business. If you want to make it, you compromise more than you ever wanted". Tara had this knack of making her life seem a fairy-tale come true and she the pampered princess, I realized what a good actress she was, and for the first time felt sorry for her.

One hour before curtain, some composure returning, Tara hurried backstage to costume and make-up, towing me along. I needed to get away from her, saying I'm hungry, crossing Geary Street to David's Jewish Deli, a stool at the long busy counter, cold beet borscht and sour cream, soaking-in the atmosphere, I was thrilled to be in San Francisco again. Ten to eight, Tara had a ticket in my name at the box office, 7th row center aisle. The theatre filled, and from opening lines I sat motionless, in awe. As if born to the role, Tara was Alice, an innocent taking necessary descent into the Underworld to redeem her dark side, tossed on unavoidable circumstance, without the wisdom of experience, pulled by whim and curiosity, too young to recognize the patterns, and just enough helping good hands from the Sweet Sisters Fate and all the critters to be borne again to surface light, whole. My cheeks ached from grinning, two exuberant curtain calls, the theatre emptied, I wend back-stage, down flights of metal stairs, narrow noisy hallways to a flurry of unpinning wigs, unbuttoning costumes and cold cream, the cast crying, laughing, satisfied with their finalé. I found Tara still in full make-up and hugged her "You were wonder-full, magical, possessed. I forgot it was you". She clutched me whispering "I was so stoned, Alice took on a whole new meaning. Look, you're the only one, these creatures don't know my history. Promise you won't say a word". Not waiting for response, she hastily introduced Cheshire Cat and Madd Hatter, announcing to the others "We have to fly now. You can all meet my Shoshannah at the party". Taking my hand, whisking to the parking garage, she was wound-up and beaming "I'm the only one with a place big enough, so they volunteered me for the cast farewell party".

Tara rented a 2nd floor one-bedroom near the corner of Chestnut and Franklin, not far from the theatre, parking blocks away to find a space late on a week-night. The halls smelled of pot roast and garlic, inside she lit incense and candles and swung open the frig to a bounty "Honey, would you mind getting these out, I'll be right back". She disappeared into the bathroom. I had platters of sliced meats, cheeses, crispies and dips unwrapped when she re-appeared, shiny-clean face, hair in simple ponytail, wearing the halter-dress I made her three years now, her freshness even more dazzling. She waltzed around the room, holding the long skirt above her knees, swinging the ponytail, confessing "I think of you whenever I put this on, the delicious pleasure of something custom-made for my body. You're a real genius you know". She seemed to be courting me, I was flattered and a bit ambushed "Maybe I'll make you another sometime". Sashaying close she spoke in a secret hush "None of the cast are my friends like you. No matter what it looks like, you must be careful or they'll eat your sugar right up". Spinning away on her toes "Because you're still sweet, living in the moment, not standing back thinking how can I use every experience for my own fucking benefit, for my art". I did not want to lead her on "You sound bitter. Aren't you suppose to use life to make your acting authentic". Chuckling wry she marched to the brick-and-board book-shelf, bringing her audition portfolio, giving it to me like a disease "Yes, but you get so premeditated, so opportunistic, you don't actually live in the moment, more watch it from outside your body". The pictures were provocative and beautiful and humiliating, I felt a little sick, and hoping these first few pages proved her point, closed the collection. She insisted "No. You have to look at them, all of them. You're the only one on earth who knows me even a little. I need to know what you think". Relenting to the couch I began again. Putting-out napkins, silverware, plates, uncorking wine, she justified "I need those to get work". Closing the portfolio I said nothing. She defended "This is a rough business. I need to land some commercials to pay the rent". I did not worry offending, she had already bargained a pair of tits with enough reason to gainsay any degradation, and if I was not strait with her I would be just another toad "These mostly disgust me". She threw her head back in a raunchy laugh "See Sweetie, you're a breath of fresh air, a piece of candy. They'll eat you right up". It was easy to read between-the-lines, Tara was beginning to rot, Alice might be the top of her career, the one pure thing, and from now the game begins, to stay-in she would take offers, not for what made her extraordinary, and forfeit the struggle where an artist is won or lost.

The cast poured through the door all at once, strangest beautiful poised human beings I ever met, self-absorbed passed the point of incest, facial features boney, protruding, their heads were just too big, Jiminy Cricket on acid. They pressed me for dirt on Tara, I chain-smoked in defense, keeping her secrets, feeling cornered, feeling like food, they fancied the sweet little FlowerChild, dining on every response along with rare beef and cherry tomatoes, I had to get away before I could not, hitch to Brian's screaming in my head. I thought no further than what excuse, standing waiting for a breather in the exchange between Tara and the tall heavy-boned woman "I had my first proposition today, this man stopped, asking did I wanted a ride". Tara frowned "Tell me you didn't get in the car". "Well he was nice looking, you know, well groomed". "Honey so was Jack the Ripper". "Well, I looked him over and decided to get in. He asked me for my number". "Tell me you didn't. He could find where you live". "Well, don't worry, I'm unlisted. Anyway, I told him I'd give mine if he gave me his. Then I said you know I'm transsexual. Well, he said he knew, that's why he stopped. That he couldn't give me his number because he was married. Well, I thought he was being so honest, I gave mine". "Honey, I thought you didn't like men". "Funny isn't it. Since the operation, the estrogen makes them look better and better". "You have to be careful. Promise. Meet him somewhere safe, and don't let him know where you live". "Well, I'm no fool. You know I'm technically a virgin. I feel like a teenager again, you know, about dating, but I want some romance first". "Good for you girl. Men are all romance up front to get you in the sack". "Yeah. I remember my first time as a man, it was really awful". "Honey, if you want romance, don't be easy". "Well, I'm not looking for a relationship right now, just a little romantic fling. Take the new equipment for a spin. I been doing my exercises and everything works. I want to see what it feels like to be a woman". "Look, I don't mean this to hurt your feeling, so take it right okay. You're wearing the breasts of a teenager. At 50 your nips should be pointing more South. Those are up too high, they look fake". "Well, you know with the cost of the operation, all the debt, they're all I can afford right now". "With the estrogen, will yours get big enough so you can toss those". "Well, I don't know. Have to wait and see". "Honey, just wear them a little lower and they're fine". Tara turned to include me

"Us girls have to watch out for each other right". I smiled "Indeed we do. Ah, look Tara, I'm going to hitch home now. I'm taking some medication and forgot to bring it with me". She was not even a little fooled "Can't wait to get out of here huh. Honey, you're nuts to hitch this time of night, wait and I'll take you". I stood firm "You're probably right. But I don't think it's any more nuts than here". She laughed at my candor. Thanking her for an interesting evening I fled.

As if bursting to the surface, I took a whole breath, outside, wrapped the shawl around me and walked Franklin to Lombard looking for a pay-phone to call a cab, my only company two street cats. Leaving Brian's I did not note the address, so I would take a taxi to Euclid and have the driver cruise till I recognized the flat. Cats scattering, a black Ford Torino slowed, did I want a ride. Two blades, hair too short, too clean shaven, too strait for my taste Berkeley graduate students, Euclid was on their way home. I thought they were being honest and took the back seat. Conversation flowed polite to mid-span Bay Bridge, then taking an all-to-familiar turn, an invite to their place for a little party, I thanked but no-thanked, they moved to you owe us for the ride, pretty little Hippie-Chick like you, free love and all, isn't that why you got in. My mind did not forsake me, heart-racing, breathe, breathe, you have time, be real to these Neanderthals instead of a wet-dream, say your name, be a person, some one they would not want to hurt, say your name. The irony of today deciding to take the pill was not lost on me, too bad I didn't grasp the warning from that part of me who sees danger ahead. Wrapping my hand round Excalibur, opening to blade's edge, holding voice calm and low I became Scheherazade, weaving, spinning tales of living with the Seattle Liberation Front, opening Hydra's door every morning to feed any kids who wanted breakfast, understanding empty stomachs get in the way of full heads. I let the weight of truth pull them, telling of Sky River and the Seattle Conspiracy Trial, these young predators go to the most radical of colleges, they must surely care. And they were captivated as I transmuted Hippie-Chick who probably doesn't wear underpants to socially conscious, Shoshannah Leibofsky, political force for change, and they did not care. No where near Euclid the Torino stopped for a red light on the way up to Claremont. Having already eased-down the door-handle, adrenaline firing I sprang from the car, ran into a yard, over a fence, across Ashby Avenue, up onto a large covered porch and laid face-down, listening to them drive around, looking, heart beating so loud I could barely hear, the porch thick with dust. I stayed motionless till fingers lit the sky, monsters run from the light, this morning was no exception.

Stinking of fight-or-flight, chilled in dew, neck back arms legs jaw tongue stiff, wanting to ring the doorbell, Mom and Dad would welcome me in, love me, take care of me, I better get-off this posh Tudor porch before someone notices and calls-in their law. Not registering the heel had come-off my shoe, loosing balance going down stairs, skinning my palms on the concrete walk, I sat there wondering, okay, what else. Every house in this pricey neighborhood suddenly looked forbidding, gaining my feet, gathering bag and shawl, licking my hands, I limped the sidewalk, no people, no cars, turning North on Telegraph Avenue, a warm light from a little bakery on Russell Street drew me, open 5AM to 3PM flashing neon. I pushed the door inhaling fresh-baked, instantly better, my shaky voice queried the woman carrying an enormous silver tray of éclairs "Excuse me Ma'am. Could I use your phone". Her shriek brought the Baker running to rescue "We don't feed beggars in the morning. Come back after three". He pointed to the door. I could not take another blow, standing ground "These two guys kidnapped me. I got away and hid on someone's porch all night. Please. Do you have a phone so I can call a cab. I have money". Ma'am hurried around the display case, cupping my elbow in her gentle hand, steering me to the nearest booth "Oh jeez, I'm sorry, sit, sit here, you're safe now. We have a phone. Do you want me to call the police". I sank on the seat, knees weak "No. I just wana go home". Baker set a mug of hot cocoa infront of me. Kindness an elixir, I inhale the spicy steam and sighed "Would you have a restroom I can use". Baker pointed "Around there. And when you're ready I'll drive you home". Smudged face arms and hands, dirty frock, scrambled hair, visage in the mirror some one I never wanted to see again, cleaning, combing best I could, soap stinging my palms, I resumed the cocoa. Ma'am looked-up from stocking the display case and smiled warm. I sipped the merciful tonic, as if from a great distance watching my hands tremble bringing the cup to lips, tell-tale revelation of stupidity and good luck. This was the second time I took the wrong ride with two brutes, I should have learned the first, should have called a cab, exactly why Dad gave me the one-hundred. I believed that once I chose to fight my Dragon, it was a foregone conclusion that I would win, just making the choice to fight, even knowing I had a choice, and taking it on made me an instant winner, how long and bloody the battle would depend on how well, how quickly I could learn. And I could not afford to be naïve, for this Dragon was mine, came along with me, and plainly intended on winning even if it meant my demise, but I did not require the same, I intended to tame the damn thing, consecrate its power, add the formidable shrewd calculating terrible to my own, I needed its dark side.

Baker patiently drove Euclid Avenue, I spotted the ancient oaks right away, noting Cedar as the cross street. Finding my way around using landmarks, I swore from now on to look at street signs, the ubiquitous markings Boys are taught to see from early age, and Girls are not. Thanking Baker, I offered five for gas. Having done a gallant deed, his face so awfully offended, he sped away to my I'm sorry, thank you, thank you. The door should not have been unlocked, no one up, I shed shoes and padded down the hall, drew a hot bath, lit potbelly and candles, and slipped under water, holding my breath as long as I could, watching bubbles rise, allowing my face to float to the surface, fourteen hours ago I was right here, it seemed a life-time. Too-hot water sapped my remnants, towel wrapped, hair dripping a trail, I crawled-in the other guest-room bed.

The Beatles Abbey Road on the record player called me from slumber, night here again, I fumbled for the bedside lamp, finding my living dress, tapestry gown and the shawl spread-over the blanket, clean, smelling of sunshine. Leda poked-in "There you are". Carrying a tumbler of orange juice she sat on the bed "Here, for you". Sitting-up I drank the whole thing like a good girl. She smiled lovingly "Yep, it was me, I washed your things in the tub and hung 'em on the line. Could tell something happened. All I could do to make it better". We reached for the others embrace. Leda's reckless ego governed mostly by impulse, she was compassionate and generous, able to effect more than lip-service, able to make me feel snug as a goose, unassailable, I did not mention the night, content in her custody. Grief's burden evident in her electric blood-shot eyes, she forced another smile "I'm glad you're okay. Gretchen's better too. We're going to some health food restaurant she knows. You feel like coming". I nodded "Sure, I'm starving".

Gretchen had magical powers of regeneration, her pace near a race, I had to bleat "Miss Fine, could you please slow down for your entourage". She would not be bridled, giggling, parading down Cedar to Shattuck, gossip-mongering "Brian's doing his best to appease April. Took her to Jack London Square, the Grotto for wine and dine. We won't have to wait long to find out, he's expecting buyers tonight. Should be home by nine". I was glad one of us had her energy and mischief back "The real bummer of dealing must be you never know who's a friend and who's just coming to score. Why's Brian need to appease April". Leda spilled "He's the one who broke 'er arm. Scored a bunch of cocaine, stashed it in the safe. He's been trying to cut her off, but she's so strung-out, waited just till he was gone to help herself. Then she cut it with powdered sugar so he wouldn't notice". Gretchen took it "Brian uses her as a shill. April's just so beautiful, he sits her next to him for deals, they both taste. Come on, course she strung-out. When the guy came to score and the coke tasted sweet, he accused Brian of ripping him off. A dealer's reputation's all he's got, April knows the safe combination, so he wrenched her arm behind her back till she told what she did, and it broke. The guy really believed him. Reputation safe". I burned indignant "What a jerk. It's his fault she's strung-out". Gretchen harmonized "That's why the wining and dining". I caught-up with her "You sure it was an accident". She scowled "I've known them a year now. He's never been physically violent. But I can't say for sure, he's totally strung-out too". Another woman with a child in a bad relationship, so entangled she thought it was all good. I felt for her, the magnetics of a Soul Mate, mistaking intensity of the fray for true love, feeling addictive necessity to work-it-out instead of walk away. How long I languished with Nick, I could not fault April for staying, especially with a little one, if only I had some magic words for her, though none could have said any thing to make me leave till it was time. All I could do was be a whisper in her ear like Ida Rose had been for me.

Very good polenta and beans, and a carefree mood escorted our stroll home, another fragrant California Winter evening. Two men were seated on one couch in the shadowy front room, April on the other, supernal in a long silver-blue silk dressing gown with belled sleeves to blur the cast, stalwart beside her man. Chopping a snowy pile on the mirror, Brian presented us as if we were his personal harem, charging us join-in for a line. Servile eager noses, Gretchen, Leda pulled hassocks to the coffee-table. I understood the summons was meant to pre-empt any buyer's paranoia, feeling used, erased, I was not willing to assume the position. Brian cast me a daggers-glance. I considered April's arm, and took demurely to an uncomfortable chair at the edge of candle light. The older man leaned-in for a line, resembling my Dad, making me miss him, resembling Ken Kesey even more. Samples snorted, all sat back for the rush but April, sniffing the crumbs, dabbing at her nostril with a clean tissue. Conversation intensified to predictable maddness, every one leaning-in, revving. The younger man, bewitched by Gretchen Fetchin-Fine's ever-seething juju made his pitch, how rubbing cocaine on his cock would give him an erection for hours. Gretchen giggled unimpressed "Yeah, I know". Money changed hands, and the Older left a curious old emerald green bottle on the table. When I questioned Brian was that who I thought it was, he would only smile.

Deliveries needed making. Soon as Brian was gone, April announced brownie baking time, she had two full cups of finely sifted Acapulco Gold ready, and could not manage on her own. Leda and I went along. Gretchen waylaid "Shoshy, can you wait". We moved to the couch, she gathered-up her legs, facing me square and serious "I'm falling in love with Delroy, and I think he's falling for me. You know him. Do you think I have a chance". The way she took-and-gave, her robust abandon, it never occurred to me she would fall, become open, fragile, I could not reprove "He's always been a real gentleman to me. May be you have a chance. You know he's married". She scoffed "But he's so into me, he can't be so in love with her". I knew she only wanted an ear and granted the appropriate nods. She hankered "I need someone to take care of me, us, so I can raise Ava the right way. He's famous. He's got to have money. We could travel all over the world, and I'll keep him so fucking satisfied he won't have a drop left for anyone else". Tears welling, she unfolded full-length on the couch. I quietly rubbed her back till she closed eyes and settled, checking-out the emerald bottle on the coffee-table, Pernod Fils Absinthe, then walked down the hall to April and Leda and brownies. Brian came home with bottles of Liebfraumilch, we rounded the small kitchen-table, them feasting on fresh-baked, smoking stuff dipped in hash oil, drinking. There were cartons of little brown vials stacked against the wall, Brian claiming oil was the next big thing, it would make him a rich man. I thought Acapulco Gold brownies and hash oil smokes insane-overkill, sipping a small flute of Liebfraumilch, relishing the Woodruff after-taste was enough for me. Bottles empty, Brian went for the emerald bottle and Gretchen, boasting Absinthe was illegal, smuggled in from China, slightly psychedelic, rumored to melt your brain to tar. Gretchen filled a small brass strainer with sugar cubes and held it over a crystal pitcher as if she had many times. Brian poured the liquor slowly through, dissolving the cubes. Melting brain to tar not my idea of an endorsement, yet ever curious I took a jigger of the sweet brew, and when lines were chopped on the table, excused my self, outside for a walk, away from the ravening, anxious to be going North, Absinthe enough to enchant a coatless Winter evening.

Brian cutting more lines, April's nose waiting, Delroy, his Moon-Goose drummer and bass player sitting comfortable in the living room, Gretchen, Leda perched on the hassocks, undulating in unison, hypnotic hula-hands incantation "Lure. Lure. Lure". The spell reeking, invoking the darkness, the Dragon, I backed-out and ran many blocks, needing distance, no juice left for another battle, and breathless on Spruce Street and Hearst, having lost the fight anyway by losing my head and my way, I took haven on a bus bench. Hearst Avenue crawling in college kids on Winter break, rude-drunk-boys hanging from car windows - Hey wana party - What's a matter cat got your tongue - Aw come on baby - You know you want it. Did they actually think this would work, I wondered if it ever worked for them, or if they had been turned-down so much they just turned awful. I loathed them all right now, except for my Dad, his class and solid self-esteem, he never disrespected Mom or me, so I knew it was possible, thought it was ordinary growing-up, glad I knew it was possible now, and so dismal finding-out how rare. A mellow friendly voice behind me "I saw that look on your face, and figured I better follow, find out what". It was Delroy, relief swam-over me. He sat, did not crowd me.

And I revealed more than I would have "Leda, Gretchen's lure lure spell, it's just too much for me. I can't be there when they do it". He smelled too ripe "You know they're good girls. And believe me, those games are harmless compared to most". To me those were not harmless, but I realized it was me, I was scared, confused, losing trust, making bad choices, projecting them on my Sistas "You're right. I'll stick with them where I'm safe". We took our time, small talking, strolling back, Delroy prying "Do you think Miss Fine's really into me". I knew she would not want me to tell "Yeah. Falling in love. She thinks you're a real catch". His face lit "You know, she could be the best thing ever happened to me".

Delroy took his place on the couch. Gretchen gave me a worried look, wondering did I tell him about the gonorrhea. Leda floating at forty-thousand feet barely noticed. April too. Brian, Drummer and Bass doing lines. I picked-up William Blake from the table, did not bother with good-nights, only a thank you nod to Delroy. Closing the guest room door I laid down and opened the book.

TYGER! TYGER! BURNING BRIGHT
IN THE FOREST OF THE NIGHT,
WHAT IMMORTAL HAND OR EYE
COULD FRAME THY FEARFUL SYMMETRY?
IN WHAT DISTANT DEEPS OR SKIES
BURNT THE FIRE OF THINE EYES?
ON WHAT WINGS DARE HE ASPIRE?
WHAT THE HAND, DARE SEIZE THE FIRE?
AND WHAT SHOULDER, AND WHAT ART,
COULD TWIST THE SINEWS OF THY HEART?
AND WHEN THY HEART BEGAN TO BEAT,
WHAT DREAD HAND? AND WHAT DREAD FEET?
WHAT THE HAMMER? WHAT THE CHAIN?
IN WHAT FURNACE WAS THY BRAIN?
WHAT THE ANVIL? WHAT DREAD GRASP
DARE ITS DEADLY TERRORS CLASP?
WHEN THE STARS THREW DOWN THEIR SPEARS,
AND WATER'D HEAVEN WITH THEIR TEARS,

DID HE SMILE HIS WORK TO SEE?
DID HE WHO MADE THE LAMB MAKE THEE?
TYGER! TYGER! BURNING BRIGHT
IN THE FOREST OF THE NIGHT
WHAT IMMORTAL HAND OR EYE
DARE FRAME THY FEARFUL SYMMETRY?"

Oh my, where was this Tyger, big enough for me, inviolable, no need to fear I have an ego too, no need to disrespect me, I read the poem again, imagining, aching for some one this big. The soiree still high-spirited, I closed my eyes.

Bass player, Drummer, Delroy gone, all else in stupor-slumber. I made coffee and took my journal out on the porch, to bathe in mid-morning sunshine, my dreams so strange, evanescent, leaving vivid embrace, a tone I let into words.

NO KILLING TONIGHT
THE DANCE OF THE COBRAS
HYPNOTIC STARE
LOCKED FAST IN THE MOMENT
YOU DARE - I DARE
MY BITE CAN BE DEADLY
IF YOU MAKE THE WRONG MOVE
LIKE THUNDER AND WIND
WE DANCE IN THE GROOVE
KISSING WITH POISON
TONGUES FLASH IN THE NIGHT
EYES GLISTENING DIAMONDS
LOCKED FAST IN THE FIGHT
SO INTENSE AND SO HUNGRY
THERE'S NO WRONG - THERE'S NO RIGHT
WE SWAY IN THE MOMENT
THERE'S NO KILLING TONIGHT
HOW LONG CAN THIS LAST
CAN I QUENCH MY DEEP THIRST

IT'S BEEN WITH ME ALWAYS
THIS VAMPIRE CURSE

I LOVE YOU - I HATE YOU
YOU'RE MY PAIN MY DELIGHT
WITHOUT YOU THE MORNING
BEGINS WITHOUT LIGHT
MY BITE CAN BE DEADLY
IF YOU MAKE THE WRONG MOVE
LIKE LIGHTNING AND THUNDER
WE DANCE IN THE GROOVE
SO INTENSE AND SO HUNGRY
THERE'S NO WRONG - THERE'S NO RIGHT
WE SWAY IN THE MOMENT
THERE'S NO KILLING TONIGHT
NO KILLING TONIGHT

Writing teased the whispers across dream's threshold, releasing forgotten subterranean inspirations. I could not recall in which one of Carl Jung's books, reading the case study of a woman who dreamed of two cobras, one larger, their bodies entwined, Hermes' Caduceus, facing each other, striking back and forth with deadly intent. Profoundly disturbed at what this might mean the woman sought-out Jung, who helped interpret. Snakes being the avatar of female power, these two creatures were the contrasting qualities of her nature, conflicted amid Victorian tight-laced passive female virtues and the more emancipated post-Victorian age, one foot in the old, one the new. Jung understood that behind the dream's frightening symbols, she was engaged in an essential struggle, for character is built or lost in conflict. Here was the deadly dance, the Dragon fight, an inside battle of wits, that had to be fought and won as Ida Rose said, with discriminating choices, honorable choices, or you build nothing but a relentless and escalating bloody battle. A car door closed, familiar face I could not quite place walking toward me. He smiled, and sat too close on the top step "Anyone else up yet. Brian's expecting me". I leaned away, poking my chin how dare you. He hopped-off the porch, contrite at my feet "Let me start over okay. My friends call me Limey. Brian and I're old friends. I know you're Shoshannah, but we've never been introduced". Paranoid recognition gripped me, silver-tongue devil, he was the one who sold Hydra all the weed to finance Sky River, the dealer in the green Nash Rambler station-wagon who bought Nick's cocaine, oh shit he knows Nick, I forced a smile "No one's up yet. So why're you here". He seemed comfortable with my suspicion "Brian and I're taking a business trip North, taking Leda home. I was suppose to be here a few days ago but delays happen". So we had been waiting on him, I prodded "You do any deals lately with Nick". He held my eyes "Not with that Wop. Glad to see you got away. He's crazy, poison, got busted after Sky River. He's out on bail waiting trial. I won't ever go near him again. Hey you want to get some breakfast at Mel's". He did not seem to know Gretchen and I were coming along, still I felt my body calm "Only if it's Dutch". Smiling, offering an arm "Only if you insist". I did not take it "I insist". A rabid fan of One Hand Clapping, Limey knew every one, and Delroy, and Ric, Mark, Arnie, and me wearing a beautiful velvet dress the night Dellinger came to the District Tavern fund-raising for the Seattle Seven. Limey was a shadow, seen but not, married eleven years to Grace, two kids, a nice guy depending on which side you're on, who did not hit-on me even in suggestion, was probably Brian's supplier, scrupulously vague and surprisingly candid. I did not give my self away either, knowing he could be a slick under-cover narc, dealer is such a great cover, it struck me funny that I try so hard to stay away from speed, not wanting to end-up permanently paranoid like every speed-freak, and here I was anyway. Mel's so typical California, we ate in the station wagon, brought to us by a busty roller-skating leggy blond in black satin short-shorts.

Muddy-eyes, wondering where I had gone, all in the kitchen, Gretchen scrambling eggs and canned corned beef hash, Leda making toast, Brian coffee. The men embraced dearly. April too. Limey did not notice her cast. The squeezing he gave Gretchen, I knew they were lovers. We would leave after breakfast. April to remain, her Folks bringing the boy home later in the day. We would over-night at Limey's farm in Oregon, an easy ride to Seattle the next day. Gretchen would go back to Berkeley with them, and Limey would go home. So, the MotherTruckers were over, melancholy swallowed me, Keely was left behind, Leda would stay with her Mom, waiting for news of Amaru, I could not see what for me, and Gretchen was joy-riding, if she expected custody of Ava, she would have to establish her self soon.

Chapter Sixteen

THE LEGEND

Gretchen Leda and I assembled, while Limey and Brian went to rent an invisible Blue Ford Galaxy. Straight through the now not-so-hot Sacramento Valley, we stopped in Redding for gas, and at Gretchen's behest the Wolf Creek Café for zuzus to go. I bought three stuffed Smokey-the-Bears for Robby Lance and Scottie. Griffin and two more Family of the Mystic Arts came-in as we went out, too coincidental, my skin crawled. Gretchen and Leda were delighted pawing and kissing then. Before leaving the parking lot, Limey packed a soap-stone chillum with Maui Wowie and stoked it. Passing to me, and here was my disappeared green pipe, Nick must have gifted it to Limey or he surely would not take it out infront of me. I kept mum, he didn't seem a thief to me, and I did not want to raise Nick's ghost. Smoking weed like tobacco, Limey, Brian trading the wheel, ten hours on I-5 to that Salem Oregon exit The MotherTruckers stood on going South, we crossed the Willamette River in the dark, the Yamhill River, Chehalem Creek, and South of Newberg climbed Limey's blocks-long gravel driveway, conveniently close to a small air strip.

The house smelled delicious. Wife Grace had roasted chicken, baked potatoes and home-grown string-beans waiting. Hungry and grateful I ate all she dished on my plate, even considered licking it clean. Grace showed me to a fresh empty room. I rolled my bag onto clean thick carpet, undressed and slithered in, weary from all-day riding, too wired to sleep, eavesdropping the thin walls on Brian and Gretchen, and on Grace simmering to Limey, how could he let them bed together here, April was her friend, demanding to know did he sleep with Gretchen too, did April know, quietly suffering his repudiation, how unfounded her distrust, how cruel. I did not care who slept with who, all blame-worthy of one thing or another, April and Grace maybe less so, though I imagined they knew in their hearts what their men were like, maybe closing eyes for all the money. And Gretchen, still contagious and she knew it, cold-blooded, inexcusable, giving it right now to Brian, who would certainly give it to April.

I woke to cold and dark, remembering January in the Northwest, rain near freezing, morning-light after 8AM, coffee tickling my nose, I joined Grace in a toasty kitchen. She poured a generous cup and brought the cream, this elegant Jean Simmons brunette, white-silk skin, hazel eyes, urbane, deteriorating in rural boredom. We talked like old friends till the gang woke hungry and she lovingly accommodated their needs. The downpour moved North by 10AM, and Limey Brian Gretchen and me overtook it passing Portland, now a thick soup, cars air-planing the road, truck tires throwing monsoons at frantic car wipers, and yet Brian out-drove his visibility, fool-headedly passing most cars, even more considering how stoned, considering what he had in the trunk. I was the one strait enough to drive safe, and no-way allowed to take the wheel, three jaw-clenching hours and he swerved off the Federal Way exit to Leda Mom's. A hollow-eyed good-bye smile, Leda promised to pass on any news of Amaru. Limey knew the way to Hydra, they went in, and I took things up-stairs to my empty room. Finding all adults around The War Table, the green soap stone chillum passing from Ric to Mark, obligatory sampling, some deal had been struck, and ready, Limey needed to get on to the next. Gretchen pulled me into the kitchen, apologizing, she was going with them. Not surprised, Miss Fine could be counted-on to go with the something-in-it-for-her, I thought, so this is it, over, the MotherTruckers are totally over, and wrapped her in my arms "I'll miss your brave heart pretty girl". She giggled that music of hers "Ditto. But we're not done yet little Sista, so no sad good-bye, you'll see".

Soon as they were gone, Ric started Keely grilling. I sat patient, listening, sympathetic, giving him only the phone number to reach her. The Littles trooped in from somewhere, and began Mom grilling. I said they must ask their Father about their Mother, but I could tell them she was fine and missed them terrible. Feeling confounded they pushed where they could, what did I bring them, what did I bring them, bustling me up-stair to get the presents. Being among their still mostly unspoiled natures gave mine freedom to be, too bad they would get older and learn all the polite and not so games. Smokey Bears in precious greedy mitts, their interest in me gone, these wonder-full fearless brothers ran-off in bear wars. Mark, Ric, Littles had Hydra all theirs, Carolion moved-in with a law clerk she met at the Trial, Bear hitched East to Ithica, to visit and maybe stay with Arnie and Max, pursuing a dream to be a reporter for the New York Times, his Trial work a first offering. Solitude and space welcomed, needing some to look-inside, I had joined the revolution believing I could help make the world a better place, feeling the unlimited idealistic kinetic power of my youth, willing to break the law, sacrifice for the cause, inciting, abetting, aiding, we will win because we are right. I was no longer any of those fine young things. Living in the Golden Ghetto, I never imagined the hand of Authority coming-down hard on anyone I knew, certainly not me, now we were foes, and I was scared of losing my freedom, for doing what I believe is right. Nixon, Agnew, J.Edgar declared war on us in our own homes, the Movement became defensive and aggressive in response to the violent actions of the police. I took pride and consolation in our success, more than ever demonstrations over-ran and closed-down college-campus after campus, hundreds-of-thousands were in the streets all-over the world, current occupants of the White House were barricaded-in against their own people, John Lennon was singing *All we are saying is give peace a chance*, Americans raged over the once secret invasion of Cambodia, and still after ordering the National Guard onto the Ohio Kent State campus, to crush a peaceful demonstration against this illegal invasion, killing four students, wounding nine, Nixon had not learned, and was again calling us bums and thugs. Ultimately these public murders, not of Black Panthers, not in Watts or Berkeley, but White kids on middle American soil, in Ohio, at the hands of their own government, this is what it finally took to knock the white middle-class off their fences, to openly question this undeclared war's daily body-bag count. And the near nightly coverage of the Chicago and Seattle Conspiracy Trials, they were getting a chance to see us speak, not just being attacked by police, and hear what we were really about, get used to us, public opinion had begun swaying to us. None of this lifted my despair, I had given away my time to the cause, no other plan, no time for higher education, no relevant job skills, no one to talk too about what really mattered to me, and I was far too paranoid to try any one new. A defiant optimistic FlowerChild grown despondent, growing cynical, once upon a time every thing seemed possible.

Ric phoned Keely in the morning. The volatile indignation after the call, he was intolerable, Mark quickly disappeared, leaving me and the Littles convenient targets. I wanted to be Ric's friend, wanted to run interference for the Littles, was too busted to bear the weight of his verbal resentment. Bundling against probable snow, I walked to Safeway for a Seattle Times, folded it into my pocket, and caught the bus to Volunteer Park. Standing at the Stone Ram's big feet, staring at the curled horns and stoic face, my first acid trip four years now, so very long ago, I needed to find some wonder, some hope-full, some of my old mojo. Big Ram never looked at me, nothing but snow melting on my pea-coat, laughing out-loud, realizing I had not come here for the Ram but Ida Rose, her place only blocks away, I walked the steep grass parking-strips down East Galer and East Crescent. She answered my knock right away, warmly inviting "Oh my Lamby, you're out here in this weather. Come in, come in". Seeing her face, being welcome over this threshold gave me a feather lightness. I hung coat hat scarf and gloves above the hallway heater, put my shoes under it and followed into the dining room. She sat me on the hearth by the fire and brought two steaming mugs "I'm delighted to see you Little One. And your timing couldn't be better, I was just going to sit down with some hot cider". Everything came into my head at once and began to spill "I'm so glad you have time for me Ida Rose. Even if I wanted to I couldn't stay in California any longer. I loved it, Winter in paradise and all. And I have a real feeling there's something important there for me, and I got away from Nick, from the constant fear, but it's like I was pulled back here". She twinkled "You're very perceptive. California is a lodestone for inane spiritualities, and completely covered over by Astral fluvia, dross so thick nothing significant can penetrate. I'm sure I could not conduct a legitimate audit there. You must be sensitive to the deprivation and came home to recharge your batteries". I felt my heart beating normal again, blood coarsing though my veins, coming to life, I was not alone, she knew what I was talking about "I know that's exactly true". She smiled "That half you had to leave behind took most of your spiritual protection. I believe you will be given a substantial reward for all the hard work you've done on your self, well more a gift. Maybe it's there for you in California". The hairs on my nape rustled "Somewhere in me knows that too. I just couldn't stay any longer. I feel this commitment to the Seattle Seven, at least till they get out of jail". She nodded "That's integrity speaking. You being true to your principles". I smelled roast turkey and savored the nostalgic aroma "One of my friends is genuinely interested in meeting you. Her name's Leda. She's the only one I can talk to about you. Ric won't let me even mention your name. Would it be okay if I brought her sometime". "Certainly, yes. I'll be interested to meet your friend. Bring her anytime". Ida Rose excused herself to the kitchen "Three long-time students are driving up from Eugene, today in this weather, Maynard, Mildred and their dog Tweedy, I could not dissuade them. Maynard carries The Dragon on his spirit. I need the perspective of his audits. Would you like to join us for dinner, I'm baking a turkey". Dinner with The Dragon, I was just learning how to deal with mine, and she was cooking this one a feast "Only if you let me fix your hair, if you have time". Delighted with the pact "Thank you Lamby, I do. I'll baste the bird and run upstairs to wash my hair".

Head wrapped in a plush white towel, cheeks flushed, arms full of rollers and hairdryer, Ida Rose took a seat at the big mahogany table. And I combed and separated and rolled, and told of finding her aura in Annie Besant's book Thought Forms, and my frustration reading Jung "Sometimes I drown in the big meaning words, like ego, anima, shadow, self. The unconscious is so illusive, I can't seem to pin any thing down. All my internal voices sound so nearly the same. It's like they have fuzzy edges that over-lap". She assured "It's not you. I don't believe it's possible to pin down the unconscious, and I don't think Jung wants to. Your ego is always subject to your unconscious, and visa versa. You can not step outside yourself. It's not possible for either to get an objective look at the other. But your effort, taking your brain and working it over with your mind, stretching it, making room for the new, and consciously reflecting on what you've learned, gives you a good idea of both. If you persist, your view becomes less ambiguous, gives you greater critical agility. As Korzybski said, *it becomes geometric*". I wondered if LSD had given me a real outside perspective, somehow it mattered little right now, for I did not feel paranoid or broken-hearted or sour or confused around Ida Rose "If I'm anything, it's persistent, dogged. I read and read, sometimes the same paragraph, the same sentence over and over. Then I have to go back and read again after I sleep on it to even begin to understand. Sometimes I'm sure I'm too thick-headed to ever get it at all". As I covered her head with the dryer hood, she put her hand on mine "Your far from thick headed Lamby".

Looking in the hand-mirror, Ida Rose sang praise "My hair is so wiry, even the best have trouble. You used twice as many rollers, took the time to wind each perfectly smooth. Thank you, now I will look presentable for my guests". A twenty-two pound turkey, tin-foil tent covering, roasting on a rack breast-side down so the juices flow over the white meat, continually self-basting, although this did not make for a lovely crisp brown breast skin or beautiful appearance, the white meat would be succulent. She said any turkey under 14 pounds didn't have enough flavor to bother with, and began to make gravy. Thickened gravy something my Mom never did, none of the women in my enormous family thickened the natural juices, it just was not done. Ida Rose drew pan drippings with a turkey baster into a large cast-iron fry pan, when bubbling she whisked-in Wondera flour, sprinkling one tablespoon at a time, whisking smooth till all the fat was absorbed to a rich brown roux, only then whisking-in clear-strained broth from simmering extra gizzards and necks with unpeeled onions, parsley, rosemary, mushrooms, carrots and celery, half-cup at first, whisking, adding, whisking to a velvet-cream texture, bringing back to full boil, covering, setting aside. She explained, when the turkey was done, it would cool on a platter for 30 minutes covered in a clean dish-towel, this lets the juices coagulate in the bird, making the white meat less likely to fall apart when carved, and for those minutes it was essential to bake the gravy at 350 degrees, or the flour would be too raw and cause indigestion, never something a cook wanted to serve her guests.

Ida Rose worried, Maynard and Mildred driving in such weather. They arrived safe, with Tweedy, a black and white Boston Bull Terrier who was not any more a dog than Frodo or Amaru. Bending to stroke his head, Ida Rose explained "Tweedy and I are old friends. I was Bufano for Barnum and Bailey in my last life, the clown with the tear-drop painted under his eye, and Tweedy was my dog. Certain dogs run away to join the circus you know, they want to perform. I've been terribly murdered in so many of my lives, the circus was a much needed respite, whimsy being one of my rays. I was a splendid clown, wasn't I Tweedy". She poured Maynard a jigger of Wild Turkey, Mildred a mug of hot cider, Tweedy a saucer of cool turkey broth, and we settled around the fire. I could hardly wait through formal introductions to ask "Ida Rose, who else have you been". Her face was serious "I've always been a light bringer, and have been both male and female, such as Queen Elizabeth who brought the Renaissance". Grinning ear-to-ear I stepped-on her words "She's one of my very only heroes. Being near you feels like being near her". She spoke in a proud voice that was not the least bit arrogant "My Great Great Grandfather was George Mason, the American Statesman from Virginia and member of the first Continental Congress. His criticism during the Constitutional Convention was directly responsible for the drafting of the Bill of Rights. I descend from the Hohenstaufens and Hohenzollerns, and Nicolai Aleksandrovich the last Czar of Russia". Knowing she had not revealed lineage to impress I was puzzled "If you can come a man or woman, why did you come as a woman this time when men have all the power. Wouldn't your work be taken more serious if you were a man". She smiled with a mother's pride, and seemed to be talking for Maynard and Mildred's benefit too "That's such an intelligent question Little One, and quite apropos. It's high time on a large scale for the feminine principle to assume her rightful place. I chose to come as a woman again to help this come to fruition". I was beyond excited "It's working Ida Rose, for me anyway, cause you're real. My role models are all mostly dead or characters from Ayn Rand books, and the comic strip reporter Brenda Starr and Katherine Hepburn. The only other one, Bonita-Kay lives down in Texas. I'm struggling for my place too. I always wanted more than was expected of me, but it's so hard, men are so stubborn and blind to things that need changing. Even the so-called enlightened ones. I'm beginning to hate them all a little". She shook her head "Our audits tell us the Feminine Principle withdrew eons ago to protect her children the Rays-of-Potential from being misused by the Masculine Principle, leaving it to develop out on a limb so to speak. That solitary growth skewed the Masculine Principle and it became arrogant". She warned gently "You must not blame men in general for what some do, then you would be suffering from Allness. Lumping all into one is not good critical thinking. The Brigands and Fallen Gods are to blame. It's never been Hu-man that is deficient, but the soil they were planted in". I did not understand, though somehow I did.

Turkey placed on a platter and covered, all the precious browned bits scraped and juices from the pan, whisked into the gravy and put in to bake. I set the big mahogany table with Limoges. Maynard and Mildred carried their bags to one of the upstairs guest rooms. And we gathered to feast, roast turkey watering my mouth, white-meat juicy and firm as Maynard carved, I sat quiet, feeling I had taken enough asking questions, passing my plate for a slice, and stuffing, and gravy over, and cranberries and string beans. I liked Mildred instantly, and stole glances at Maynard, having a time reconciling this middle-age mild-mannered man carrying The Dragon. I'd pass him on the street without a second look, and would never again reckon someone's stature on the way they did not look. Maynard planned to take Ida Rose downtown after-dinner, for brandy at the Cloud Room, the Camlin Hotel's penthouse lounge, their favorite group the Gil Conte Trio was playing. Ida Rose seemed disappointed the audit would have to wait till morning, agreeing to go only if streets were bare. Maynard went out and came back grinning, rain was falling, the streets were bare. I offered to do dishes. Mildred said she would in the morning. So it was time for my glad-to-have-met-yous. Ida Rose and Tweedy walked me to the door. I thanked her for the cooking lesson. She nodded "You see the beautiful way my life works. How could you or I know that I would be going out on the town tonight, and you would fix my hair. Thank you precious Lamb". Precious, she called me precious Lamb, I had no words sitting down on the floor to pull on my shoes. She smiled "Before you go, let me get a mimeo-graph copy of The Legend. I will include it in my next book. I'm revising the Original and New Testaments". She returned, three folded-pages in hand "My new book is drawn from more than 30 years of research, auditing students' past lives to learn the truth of that death in Palestine, using the words of those who were there. The Original Testament I call The Comedy because of Yahweh's antics. Yahweh will be saved, and go on into the new age, because he gave his people a philosophy of integrity, personal responsibility, and justice. The New Testament I call the Tragedy, because it tells the story of the death of Love". She offered me the pages saying my favorite words "I'm sorry we must rush off. Please come back anytime". I pushed them in my pocket with the newspaper and without thinking hugged her good-bye. Letting me, she patted lightly on my back. The night clearing and drying as I hiked home, feeling taller, light on my feet and in my heart. Ric was gone, Littles on the couch, sleeping on each other, Mark presiding over, watching the Flip Wilson Show, I said hello and went up to my room.

The Legend

Once there was a man, prominent in his community, called Nicodemus. He sought out a great sage who lived amongst them, looking for relief from his human dilemmas. Being an honored and highly placed citizen, he discretely crept out in the night for his rendezvous, for respectable citizens must be careful of their reputation, after all, sages can be odd and unusual people. Approaching the sage reverently nevertheless, Nicodemus spoke: Master, I have observed your miracles and am sure no man could do these things except God were with him.

The sage answered: Nicodemus, unless a man be born again he cannot find the Kingdom of Heaven on earth.

Amazed Nicodemus exclaimed: How can a man be born again when he is old? Who has ever crept back again in to his mother's body to be born again a second time?

The sage answered with some surprise: But Nicodemus, except a man be born again from above and from the inner spirit he cannot find understanding or peace. That which is born of flesh is flesh, but that which is born of spirit is spirit. It is the immortal inner spirit which carries the patterns of life, not the temporary flesh which is only a shadow playing out a role. So marvel not that I said you must be born again. Man is deluded into following false aims when he does not know the quality or design of the inner evolving self. Life can be painful and sad if there is nothing in control but ambition. And so men become skeptical and doubting towards the mention of spirit. But why should they Nicodemus? They hear the wind blow and it pleases. They hear the lilting whisper of the breeze and then the destruction of the tempest. But who can say from whence it came and where it will go? So, likewise, men's acts vary from calm to fury. Their only hope is to find the mainspring which set in motion the action and then, perhaps, unravel the tangled skein of life.

Strickened by these words Nicodemus whispered to himself:

How can this be.

Surprised by this the sage exclaimed: You are a Master of Israel, Nicodemus, and you know not these things?

On another occasion the sage was approached by some doubting skeptics who asked when the Kingdom of Heaven might come.

The sage answered saying: The Kingdom of God comes not with observation, it is not something one sees. It is something which happens, an inward change in process. So no one can say, lo here or lo there! For the Kingdom of Heaven is within man himself. It must be developed and become apparent in the life itself. It is the Pearl of Great Price which may be found and will flourish with proper integrity and justice. Then a look of stern sadness passed over the gentle face and the sage added: The values which lie back of a life are subtle and unsuspected. When the Books of Life come to be balanced many will say: Lord, Lord have not we prophesied in your name? And in your name cast out devils? And in your name done wonderful things? The answer will be: I never knew you. Depart and go on your ways.

The world has puzzled over these words for almost two-thousand years. But it has improved very little in certainty or in overcoming the old and familiar negatives of sin, sickness, and death. What one might call the race-mind. And no man can assume that his own individuality is understood. It may be that most or nearly all of human disorders, illnesses, forms of neurosis and psychosis, annoying personality defects, and just plain "hang-ups" stem from some inner source: an inner compulsion based on a particular delusion acquired under painful stress and strain, toil and trouble, even despair. The conditions around the time, even an item of food, can be over-emphasized and fastened onto the soul-self. There to remain, to be brought out time after time in later years where it maintains distortions of conduct, sustains weaknesses in personality, and wreaks lives. It might even be said that they put one out of harmony with the life-principle itself. In which case we are witnessing a panorama of sought-out, self-inflicted annihilation. So our motive here must be to uncover the event which brought about the irresistible, repeated, and irrational impulse or pattern which has crippled the life. This is what the sage called being born again. Returning to the catastrophe and revealing its lethal hold on the self.

History has recorded and marked out these casualties amongst mankind and we see about us every day citizens searching out group-therapy techniques, psychiatric and psychological diagnoses, yoga-type disciplines, prayer, astrology, retreat into Zen-like practices, and extreme Pentecostal emotional deluges. All searching for liberty and some peace of mind.

Then you may ask, where may this be found. I do not know about the rest of the world, but in my research I have been able to achieve results, while always keeping in mind the admonition that under the basic law of free will and freedom, the final decision rests with the entity. I use the word advisedly for there is more than one level of consciousness to be dealt with in most of us, all entitled to some respect and consideration, even if not approval.

This made me giddy, the unconscious had to be the monster of all adventures, and though I could not swim to the depths of what I read, it made a power-full impression on a little Jewish tribe-girl. Plainly Jesus was this sage, and I did not feel traitor to my heritage taking an open-minded look, whether he was God or not, whether I was called Christ-killer, did not change the message. And no wonder the Brigands had to get rid of him, to hold onto their power, concocting a tale to define that murder, conveniently blaming the Jews. I could not help think if he had lived how much more would have been, had those dark forces who aim to keep us ignorant, to feed-off our misery-energy, had they not buried this wisdom with him and re-written the story. And then Ida Rose dis-covered auditing, bringing this message again to light, gleaned from the mouths of those who had been there, allowing ordinary people like me the chance to wise-up, to see my programming, my engrams, and with the tools of General Semantics to disconnect the bad wring, to rewire, take ahold of my own reigns. Heart-broken Hippies and FlowerChildren were going religious Born-Again, and it was so exclusive, you must join-up, belong to the elite, be separate. Whereas Jesus' message was so inclusive, *I came that they may have life, and have it abundantly.* To me, being born-again was not a one-time event but commencement, apprehending the convictions of my life, the sacred things assumed inevitable, rethinking how I have always thought, being born again and again. And this wrestling should not be a spectacle, for it is too personal, precious, tender. The Born-Again movement's public drama, the TV evangelists, speaking in tongues, the flailing and falling backwards, looked more like possession, like business than a saving-grace. And then giving all credit to some outside force, absolved of any personal responsibility stealing away your chance to reflect, handing your reigns over to most likely the same power mad Brigands behind the scene of what-ever church or deacon, such good little ignorant sheep, someone else will take care of it for you, someone else died for your sins, no way. Some I knew felt deeply the same lost I did, many were frantically searching, sincerely, willing to sail oceans, take drugs, join communes, and revolutions, and were still looking for what they could stand-firm on, even when she turned into a skeleton right infront of their eyes. Ida Rose did not require I dedicate my life to her, my soul, time, money, or that I fill my head with a dogma, she had this direct-line too I was not sure what or who, yet no matter how fantastic, every word rang true. The responsibility for my life was mine, not Gods, and I wanted it, wanted to explore it, see it with new-eyes, passed my narrow customs and indoctrinations, maybe the terrible indignity I felt wasn't what I thought, now that I know more, maybe I could lay down my anger or lust-for-retribution for something better. I took a deep breath, and a patient inner-voice waiting for an opening spoke - You're looking-on people with too cold an eye Shoshy, lighten-up, and give your self a break too.

The music of Littles padding the hall woke me. Stretching, I took the newspaper from my coat pocket.

Bail Ordered for Seven in conspiracy Case

Freedom on bail was allowed by the 9ᵗʰ Circuit Court of Appeals in San Francisco to the seven Seattle-conspiracy case defendants, who have been in jail or prison for contempt of court. The three judges ruled: "The government has failed to establish that the appearance bond will not adequately assure the appellants presence or that the appellants would pose a danger to others if released on bail".

Jeffrey Steinborn spoke for the defendants, they would be free in two-three days, the 9th Circuit Court ruled they could post ten-percent of bail, all the money had been raised. I hoped Judge Boldt was choking on his prayers. The 9th would not let him get away with his legal tantrum even after seeing the video and reviewing the transcript. I felt release too, from honor's obligation.

The morning sunny cold and hungry, I tucked Ida Rose's book in my coat pocket and caught the bus to the Ave, drawn into Arabesque by a small wooden pipe in the window, finely-carved winged-dragons along each side, thinking how Ida Rose said change was one of the universal truths I could count on, and she was right, things had changed. I was content to be on familiar turf, heading to Morningtown for a pizza breakfast, a good place to read again about my two brains, the conscious cortex and unconscious thalamus, how in-coming stimuli travel the nervous system to the thalamus first, which is a library of old tapes and learned reactions. If I could remember to use delayed reaction, allowing the incoming a count-of-ten, giving it ample-time to go from thalamus to cortex, where I can at least have a chance to choose to act instead of re-act. I wrote delayed reaction on my palm in red ink, a little prompting never offended my ego. Ida Rose said if I worked hard, General Semantics would begin to geometrically progress instead of arithmetically, like after learning to drive or swim, practice and it just works. She called the process digging canals, canalization, an innate skill in all life, without which we would have to learn to tie our shoes or walk or talk all-over-again each morning, never getting anywhere, never building anything. Many of these canals were already dug when we were born, and the rest were dug for us by cultural canons, accepted family community and trusted national beliefs, programmed without our choosing or even conscious knowledge, too young to know, too young to think, beliefs and behaviors that were usually left unexamined, and deepen, like racism, anti-Semitism, obligations, impulses, currents so strong, carrying us where we do not intend to go, often against our most earnest will, canals so worn, so swift, even if we no longer want to, the undertow is tenacious, overwhelming, easy to give-in, easier to rationalize, an old friend. Ida Rose said it took dogged diligent conscious persistence to dig and deepen new pathways, and like change, she considered canalization another universal truth to count on, another underlying structure, allowing plants to know when to bloom and lose their leaves, genes to make an eye ear or a hand, baby birds to peck their way out of the egg, the unthinking thinking process that can become a pathological rut. When auditing, she would often take a person back to the scene of the crime, sometimes lifetimes ago, she said this was not essential because the same affect in varied form is evident life after life, however, going back gives them a look at where it began, affording a chance to liberate bound-up energy from the unconscious, born-again to now, making it available to build anew, she said the rest was up to the person, to learn GS, use its tools to build the canals, and bridges over old ruts. Getting this even a little made me feel bright, full of my self, I took a bite of cold pizza and turned the page to Allness, which she called a disease, *mind cut asunder,* a mental dichotomy, like science and philosophy, yang & yin, mercy and justice, neither sane nor balanced without the other, and if you choose one, believed only one side to be all, you suffer the narrow-mind of Allness. I decided to call it know-it-Allness, make it easier to remember. The chapter concluded:

If we survive at all, our civilization will need to stop swinging with the pendulum from one extreme to another——the fanatical rock crushers on the one hand, and the apathy or even savagery of the followers of instinct-control on the other hand. It is doubtful if simplicity can live in our world now. For, with dialectical materialism came a new phase, with a sharper tool for manipulating people. For that matter, we must acknowledge the "few" have ruled the "many" too long. For the few know what they want. And now in our twentieth century they have another slick tool, another device——that of educating the hands while they indoctrinate the mind. This way lies madness, too.

To live together at all, both children of the materialists and of the idealists, the children of the initiators and of the imitators, will have to become disciplined from infancy in using bridging devices – (thoughts and actions that bridge the chasm which has lain in our thinking, between the world that is in us and the world that is outside us, for it is all made of the same substance) – such as the disciplines of Allness and Delayed Reaction offered in General Semantics. For neither extreme can be said to be "whole", as it is, we are like giants—maimed and suffering, screaming across a chasm at one another, each thinking he is "right", each dividing himself into pieces and forcing dichotomies onto his environment as though they were real.

School taught me to multiply and divide, to memorize, not how to use my mind, how to evaluate information, organize thoughts to make sound decisions. No one taught my Folks either, they did their best passing-on what they knew. Now I had some means for making better choices instead of just choices, making life work for me instead of just work, there was more to choose from than either/or, for it might be both and it might be neither.

Asking the waiter for tin foil, I wrapped pizza for the Littles. Walking to the bus, the clouds opened, I took refuge in a phone booth and called Leda "Hi honey". Her voice taut "Hi". I tried to ready for the blow "You hear anything". She signed "No, nothing. I'm going to my Grandparents farm for a week, up near Port Townsend on the Olympic Peninsula. I have such good memories there". She changed the subject "Look, watch out, Keely called from the San Jose airport. She's coming to get the Boys, take them back to Santa Cruz. Probably already in at Sea-Tac". I could not help admire Keely's gumption "Wow, thanks. I'll stay away till the fireworks 're over. When you come back call me at Hydra, maybe we can go back South together". She sounded disconnected "I thought you were going to stay and work with the Conspiracy Collective". I could tell she did not care, was just being polite "They got bail. Everyone will be out in a few days". Her voice faded "Yeah, well, I'll call you". She hung-up before I could say good-bye. Rain still beating, I dashed into the Rainbow Tavern, ordered coffee, reread the seven-pages on Allness, took every refill offered, and reluctantly went home.

Front door ajar, flower-pots spilled, kids clothes strewn along the way-in, I found Ric at The War Table, offered him pizza. He shook his head angry "Keely took the Boys. They wanted to go. No discussion, nothing. She refused to even talk to me". He held my eyes "Did you know". I did not blink "Yeah. Leda told me on the phone a couple hours ago". He slid-down the chair onto his tailbone "Shit. Just fucking shit. What did I do".

I wanted none of this conversation "It's not you Ric, it's Keely. Hey, let's go to the Blue Moon and get wasted, it's on me". He lit a smoke "Limey 'll be here soon. We got a little more business. How 'bout later". I pulled the dragon pipe from my bag and handed to him "Okay, then let's get stoned". He sat-up, stuffed the bowl with a bud from his stash-pouch, in-haled the entire contents, coughing bad, coughing "I can't believe they're gone". Tears welling, he shook them off "I'm goin' to pay-off Sky River's debt, thirty-grand. Hydra's falling apart, and I want to leave it with a good name". Ric's integrity was his best suit, and made people want to follow him, I asked "What can I do to help". He leaned close in a we're-probably-still-bugged-hush-hush "I'm planning a one time coke deal. Fly to Costa Rica, make a buy with Limey's money, fly home, he'll take it from there". I could not imagine a drug deal being so easy, and tried whispering reason "You know the FBI's probably still watching us. Go for a day or two and come right back, they'll know what you're up to. You'll get busted for sure". Ric was in no mood to listen or care "You got a better idea". I spoke my mind anyway "It's a suicide mission. If it's so easy, why doesn't Brian or Limey go themselves". Knocking on the door ended it. When Limey sat down I asked "Where's Gretchen". He did not look at me "She flew to Berkeley with Brian". I told Ric to come to the Moon when he was done, and left.

Pitcher of beer brought to my booth as they scooted-in. Limey ordered two more glasses. One sip and Ric turned to me "You serious about want-ing to help". I nodded "Yeah. The debt's totally bogus, but I agree paying it off is the right thing to do for Hydra". He smiled "So hitch to Costa Rica with me. If they're watching, it'll seem more normal. My Uncle's the Minister of Justice there, we'll be welcome, treated like royalty". I had promised my self to do no thing ever again that would jeopardize my freedom, thinking, drinking my beer, staring at the smudged words writ-ten in red ink, delayed reaction, counting to ten "I'll do it". Ric seemed surprised, putting his arm around my shoulder, squeezing "You have the heart of Ulysses. We'll get our shots and passports tomorrow".

Chapter Seventeen

THE INVISIBLE SUIT

I could hardly sleep for thinking, an adventure so unexpected, so satisfying. In Junior High, Rachel and I dreamed-of, planned-on signing-up for a new government program called the Peace Corps, going somewhere to help people less fortunate. We never did, so the Seattle Liberation Front became my Peace Corps. Still hungry to experience other cultures and political systems, Texas, California showed me North America's far right and left, the bit of Mexico with Casey only whet my appetite for more experience outside such a White run country. However, anticipation also felt like fear, for even a petty drug bust carried extreme penalty in Central America, and the cholera, diphtheria, dysentery, malaria, typhoid, tetanus.

Rousing me at morning light, certain we would have trouble with passports, Ric wanted to get going. The process only took forty-minutes each, neither ever arrested, no record, never a traffic ticket, we could not be denied. Then to Harborview County Hospital for shots. So much disease eradicated in North America, I wanted to understand why unnecessary invisible death stalked other countries. Ric said it was all political. Limey took us for dinner, to Vitos, authentic Italian, dark-lit, tufted red leather high-back booths, low-key glamorous, just the place to take your mistress, everyone looked like gangsters, Ric and Limey fit-in, I wondered did I. Over bottles of Brovia Barolo, antipasto, Veal Parmigiano for Ric, Fettuccine Alfredo Limey, Eggplant Parmesane me, Tiramisu for dessert and Ruby Bishop at the piano, they planned the trip. Limey would take us to Portland and then disappear, we'd hitch the coast, into Mexico from San Diego, down Baja to La Paz, across the Gulf of California to Mazatlan, through Guatemala, Honduras, Nicaragua, and sail the Caribbean Sea to Panama, coming into Costa Rica from the much less suspicious South, do our business and fly home. Leaving in two days, I decided not to call my Folks, so I would not have to lie.

January 10, 1971, Limey drove to Portland, leaving us at Denny's just before 1PM. I bought a Seattle Times on the way in. Buddy Miles had his memorial for Jimi Hendrix at the Seattle Eagles Hall. And Michael Lerner, Chip Marshall, Mike Abeles and Joe Kelly were released. Jeff Dowd, Roger Lippman, Susan Stern would be tomorrow. Susan was quoted *"No amount of jail time can change the basic foundation for people like us. As a group we'll continue to build a counter-culture and a revolution to fight war, poverty, racism and oppression"*. She had a strength and commitment I envied, the Chicago Seven were far more famous, but we had Susan, one woman's voice heard among all the men, evidence one white woman took part in the revolution, proof we were threat enough to also be arrested. I kept thoughts to my self, Ric suffered a bad case of Allness, boiling mad at Keely, at all females, spilling onto me, there was no safe ground anyway, since taking him to Ida Rose, we never spoke of anything beyond politics. He spent weeks rationalizing her turning into a skeleton, a fault in his rock-solid foundation, he was a scientist, it was some thing he could easily embrace on acid, but, seeing it strait was inconceivable, psychotic, he settled-on Ida Rose played a trick on him, using some kind of light, image manipulation, projector, she was a charlatan in-league with the Devil, thoughts I had managed to go beyond. I wanted to ask him - and so she did this to what end, instead taking two Excedrin for a cruel headache creeping down my neck. From behind newspapers we ate our eggs and toast, and did not linger. The best thing about Denny's, proximity to freeway on-ramps, it had been agreed all up-front expenses were on Limey, Ric paid the meal, shouldered his backpack and headed for the ramp, he carried all the money of course. I shouldered my very light one-shoulder knapsack too, and with that one-hundred dollar-bill safely in my shoe, I could not keep-pace, coughing, my chest too tight, legs of lead, throat burning acid, I'd made a mistake eating eggs and Excedrin instead of oatmeal. Ric goaded, you're a light-weight, wimp. Nevertheless, the day would be too miserable without Tums, reminding him of my coming at his request, I insisted on side-tracking to a drugstore. Half the roll eaten, little relief, I shed my pack and roosted on the guard-rail post at the bottom of the ramp, eating the rest. Ric turned-down every ride, till an unmarked Chevy van, owners of the head-shop in Salem, on their way home. I laid myself across the rear seat. While Ric got them stoned and rapped politics. Four PM we took the off-ramp to Salem, Driver kindly offering a place to crash the night. I felt worse and posed we should. Ric's quick-tongue made clear the matter was not up for discussion, we would continue.

And here we stood, the inevitable on-ramp where Mr. Veterinarian left the MotherTruckers a month ago, sun disappearing into dark purple, temperature waning with the last of my intensity, few cars, none stopping. I leaned-back against the sign-post, contemplating this runty man in black motorcycle boots, black leather jacket and pants, short-blade Kabar sheathed at the belt, black Gaucho hat, black hair growing-long again, mustache and beard an homage to Ché, he was a prince of outlaws, often dictatorial, worthy leader, but we had no Goddess dance, no songs, no howling to Luna, I understood why Keely had to leave, he was all business. An hour surely less, no conversation, night's boney fingers shivering my whole body, I grumbled "We could have been warm". Ric growled "You Girls are just too much trouble. It's not even close to cold, buck-up, try being a good soldier". I did not want to be some macho soldier and sorely regretted coming along, insensitive-fucking-pig almost rolling-off my tongue, a gleaming-white two-door hard-top brand new Lincoln Continental rumbling to a stop, dark-tinted windows, the heavy passenger door swung open like a hungry maw. Ric gave a look-in and whispered me warning "The guy thinks were both girls". Sure, he might think so in the dark, why did it mattered, I hitched with my Sistas, and certainly appreciated someone driving a brand-new luxury car was from another realm, still I knew guys made different dicisions than girls because their being in the world was so different, and I knew this on-ramp, very reluctantly threw my sack over the seat and slid across the white leather. Ric did too. One whiff of Mr.Continental told me Ric's hesitation had grounds. Big as both of us, ripe in a whipped-cream polyester leisure-suit, shirt unbuttoned, hairy chest, gold shark's tooth, surrogate dick nesting from a chain around his neck, open quart of Dewar's between his legs, he slammed down the gas pedal, snarling disappointment on seeing Ric's facial-hair. Speedometer to ninety, he pointed at the Scotch "Go 'head sweed thing, have yer self a liddle drinky poo". Skimming the top of my head, he flopped his arm on the back of the seat behind me. Inching to Ric, knowing he carried a stash, I prayed for a cop anyway, and tried being polite "No thank you sir, I only drink beer". He did not offer Ric, who stiffened as I leaned on him for a little camaraderie. Walking my hand into my pocket for Excalibur, I could not seem to catch a whole breath. Mr.C took a long swig that leaked out a corner of his mouth, racing the dark highway he laughed "Then sweed thing, we're goin' ta Tom's, hic, an I'll buy ya a beer". His hand slithered onto my breast. Almost petrified at this speed, I automatically slapped it hard. Bobbling the wheel he swerved. Ric pinched my arm, whispering through a tight-jaw "Just play along". I could not breathe, a gruesome movie reeling in my head, Mr.C rapes us both before-and-after killing, mutilating, dumping us in a ditch on a dirt side-road. Maybe he cared about his new car, I whimpered "Oh god please stop, I'm gona barf". Laughing again he pointed a fat thumb to the back seat "Stop so ya cun run. Go 'head, puke yer preddy liddle brains out back thur sweed thing". Pointing that fat thumb between his legs "Here's some mother's milk 'll soothe yer fever". Slowing into the Albany exit, going West not-a-mile on the two-lane, skidding, stopping in Tom's Roadhouse Bar & Grill crowded parking lot, jangled, unharmed. We all got out, and I was ready to run. Ric grabbed my hand and squeezed too hard "No. Leave the door unlocked".

Prize live-stock herded though Tom's, I struggled to ape Ric's loose-joint-ed cool as he bellied to the bar. Mr.C ordered "Hey Cal. Beer fer my Hib-bies here, an me too". The place bristling with Redneck, every eye on us as Cal set the foaming mugs infront "What you got here Eldon. They boys er girls". Mr.C roared with laughter and chugged his beer. Ric turned to me "Follow my lead". He addressed Mr.C in low direct command "Thank you for the ride Eldon. You're a true gentleman. We won't impose on your generosity any longer". Mr.C just stared as Ric strode to the door. He somehow had charmed the cobra, and I fell in-love, and followed in his tail-wind. Someone yawped at our crossing the threshold "Hey, th're gettin' away". Queasy, dizzy I fought an overwhelming need to barf and lay down, eyes lashed to Ric, heart in my ears, I kept-up. We made the

Continental, the door opened, Ric smiled at me, calmly retrieved our packs, helping mine on. And we did not run, through the lot or down the sidewalk, passed the Grange and gas-station-grocery-store, and East toward I-5 on the narrow dirt shoulder that fell-off six or seven feet, I found every speck of stuffing I had, encouraged by the distant freeway lights. Pick-up trucks, two, gun-racks mounted in rear windows, slowed to our pace. I opened Excalibur. Ric's naked blade gleamed in the head-lights, and he walked. Too scared to think, my legs did too, one foot appearing, the other, again, again, I began to count them. The beer cans flying by our heads seemed in slow-motion, slurring men howling in glee "Let's gut 'em. See if commie blood's red 'r yeller". I could not suck enough air into my lungs, not so scared really, just sorry I had not gone to see Dad and Mom one last time. And Ric kept-on, not speaking or turning to see was I still there. No matter, I could not utter a word to save my life, my count slower and slower, beseeching to that God I no longer believed-in, if He would just help me now, I would be good forever, what ever that meant. A third truck joined the hunt, driver hollering how he would mount our heads on the hood. Tunnel-vision had me, I did not see the black & white Chevy hardtop stop infront of Ric, barring the way. He slid down the shoulder, and not looking back took-off across the fallow field. Legs solid concrete, I could only wait my fate.

The Chevy rolled down his window and called to Ric "Hey buddy, I'll take you to Eugene". The hunters split like cockroaches. Ric ran back, slipping swearing falling twice on the loose dirt scrambling-up the shoulder. Chevy "Come on, get in. I'll take your guys to Eugene, it's safe there". I did not blame Ric leaving me behind, but could not look him in the eyes, croaking with the breath I had "You make the decision". He laughed sarcastic. Chevy prompting "Hey, it's okay buddy, I'm a Nam vet. I think the war stinks too. Come on, get in". Slowly walking around, Assessing the driver, Ric opened the passenger door, pulling the seat forward for me. I crawled in and gratefully laid down, certain Chevy saved our lives, not my prayer.

Discharged three weeks, living with his Folks till he got feet on the ground, Chevy took us to a friend's place, in the liberal college town of Eugene. Four students avoiding the draft by staying in school, they welcomed us on his say-so, we could crash on the couch. Chevy was heading back to Eugene from his Fiancée's in Corvallis when he saw our predicament, now he needed to go home, sleep, be up at 5AM, working his Father's gas station. I kissed his cheek, pressed two hits of acid in his hand and whispered "Sandoz". He winked and tucked them in his wallet. Ric offered a twenty. Chevy shook his head slowly "No man. The ones with conscience and conviction, they're in Nam and right here in the streets. Good soldiers putting their lives on the line. I consider you guys vets too". He saluted "It's my duty and honor to be there for you. We never leave anyone behind".

This trip was way too dark, too rough, something in me capitulated, gave-in, before closing my eyes I told Ric "You make the decisions from now on. I won't challenge". Raising his head from the other end of the couch he sighed "Uh huh". I needed to talk, exorcise the remnants, make some sense of the night. He feigned sleep, an ordeal that should have bound us, had not. I gave into Morpheus bearing disjointed apparitions, wolves, vultures with bloody heads, the earth from far away undulating in giant black worms, a half-buried naked woman, someone looking sort-of like me squeezing through a partly-open doorway, worried would I have time to squeeze back before I grew too big. And in what seemed minutes, the smell of coffee and voices delivered me. Our hosts sounding thrilled to have a real Revolutionary in their midst, his life the stuff of myth and legend, Ric was basking in the veneration. I listened, breathing shallow, still too heavy to move. They had all gone to Sky River, a major turning-point in their lives. I smiled to my self how work never goes for naught, that the government's levied price and penalty could not arrest the spirit of Sky River taking root, thriving in the imaginations of these four University of Oregon students. Sky River lived.

Small but significant vindication, enough succor, I joined the table for coffee. And they begged us stay a while. I deferred to Ric, taking a thin breath hearing him consent to a day's respite. We were served breakfast like visiting royalty, sliced Red Delicious apples and Bosc pears, Malt-o-Meal with brown sugar and milk, raisin toast and butter. I sat across from Jamie, and found my self drawn into his soft chocolate eyes, olive skin, flowing dark brown hair, beard and mustache, the Christian image of Jesus himself. After the fare, he asked would I like to go to the noon showing at the Planetarium. Terribly weary, I was eager to get away from Ric's condescending for a while. As we walked, I fished a well-chaffed Sandoz from the bottom of my bag and split it with him. The hint of tin foil between my teeth heralded a mild trip, as we lay in the dark on the Museum of History's thick-carpet floor, the curator taking us through the stars, we were the only ones attending. Our eighty-seven year old guide did not seem the least intimidated by long-hairs, ushering to the door after. Sandoz did exactly what I hoped, masking my fatigue, making me feel weightless, no hallucinations. Jamie hadn't dropped since Sky River, and was eager to show me Eugene from Spencer Butte not far from the planetarium. An easy climb on acid, maybe 600 feet on a well-traveled not too steep trail, onto a flat grassy plain that seemed to be floating in the sky, sun warming, we ambled the edge hand-in-hand, looking-over Eugene, the Cascades, and Willamette River snaking-off in the distance, spending the rest of the trip sitting in the bend of a graceful old White Oak branch, facing South, solving the questions of existence. Jamie's dream was to see California, meeting me gave him a destination. I did not mention Costa Rica. We came down with the 4PM sun set.

Ashtrays full, beer bottles empty, Jack-in-the-Box taco wrappers littering the kitchen table, everyone still sitting round the kitchen table listening to Ric. Folding arms over his chest he glared at me. I could not think why "You mad at me for something". Tapping his boot "Why would I be mad". Hip to his way of answering with a question, intended to put me on the defense, I was not an opponent and approached with open hands "Okay then, have I missed something". He pushed the local underground paper across the table, ride sharing ads circled in blue ink "We split tomorrow early for the Bay area". Fatigue won "Okay Boss, bright and early". Smiling, pleased with my continued capitulation, he was paternal, controversial, charismatic, luxuriating in the eye of interest, dismissing me, resuming his political tutorial. I just wanted to lay down before gravity took me to the floor. Jamie showed me his room, graciously closing the door on leaving.

Dawn's light woke me somewhat rested with an irritating deep cough and Jamie snoring in a sleeping bag on the floor. I tiptoed, showered, and finding him in the bed, slid close and shut my eyes. Till Ric's authoritarian voice outside the door "Our ride will be here in twenty minutes. Ged up". If he didn't lighten-up soon, stop treating me a naughty child, humiliating me infront of people, I could not tolerate paying all women's supposed wrongs to him, even to leave Hydra with a good name. The ride showed at 9AM, three budding FlowerChildren and a Volkswagen bus taking their baptismal trip to the Haight. Our hosts offered their place to crash anytime we came through Eugene. Jamie handed me a pencil and his journal, where could he find me in California. I wrote Andrew's address and phone number, cautioning I may not be there, making him promise to call before coming. At the curb he kissed me, purring softly in my ear "See you soon". An electrifying first kiss, and I knew he was not the one.

I took the empty stern. Once on I-5 the first bowl was passed. One small toke and I coughed my lungs out. Ric seemed sincere asking was I all-right. I forced a smile, nodding yes, relieved at his lightening-up, including me. When munchies possessed, I suggested zuzus from the Wolf Creek Cafe. We walked-in, Griffin walked-out, winking at me. Such bad-timing on my part, I shuddered and turned away. Again taking the rear, arms too heavy to raise for a bite, I settled my cheek against the cool window, lull of the tires rolling over the land a soothing waltz, again going South, to the warmth, the promised land, looking-out I slowly realized there was snow on the ground and the warmth was a fever, oh shit, I couldn't get sick now, my adventure, just as things had begun to smooth. Ric offered the pipe. Frowning I shook my head no. Climbing over the seat he sat close, and softly and too matter-of-fact said "So look, I'm falling in love with you, and figured you felt it too when you agreed to come along. Then you hooked-up with Jamie and I sort of flipped-out. So I want to apologize for being such a jerk". Contrite from Ric was rare and sweet, I felt certain his falling for me was just trying to soothe a wounded heart, and did not want to add injury or grounds for further animosity, I had to say something true "And I love your cool under fire. Apology accepted". He held my eyes. I held his speaking soft "Ric, you know my rule, never mess with girlfriend's boyfriend, or husband". He looked down knowing this. I could not stand the weight of the moment "Could you put your hand on my forehead, see if I have a temp". A cold palm felt good, he pulled-away "Wow, you're burning up. I had no idea". Content to be ill and not weak with fear and paranoia, relieved the focus shifted, I sighed "So I'll just lay-down here for a while". He climbed the seats. I dozed though the Sacramento Valley. Paying for gas in Vacaville, he took a-turn at the wheel driving us to Brian's.

Dragging my knapsack to the spare room, I crumpled on the bed. Gretchen seemed a whispering dream. The lamp switch snapped-on, it was April stroking my head, her cast slung in a chrysanthemum-flowered silk scarf tied round her neck, eyes blood-shot "Sorry waking you. Gretchen's gone to Santa Cruz". She signed heavy "My Folks're coming. I'm taking my child away from all the cocaine". She crawled in with me, sobbing silent, breaking my heart. I gently rubbed her back, whispering words I would have wanted to hear "It's hard I know, but you're doing the right thing. You're made of good stuff, and it matters what you do. You're the only one who knows when you had enough, when it's time to go. I had to do it too, had to go back again and again till I could finally stay away. I won't lie, it's really hard, but you can do it". Horn honking outside, persisting, April kissed my cheek, leaving without good-bye. I sank into fevered oblivion.

Morning seemed a thick nightmare, Ric wagging my shoulder too hard, concerned I was breathing so shallow, he and Brian holding my elbows to the car, driving to County, verdict, acute walking pneumonia, white-coat shooting me with a silver needle, another prescribing pills and complete rest. Ric held his tirade for the ride home "I can't wait around for you to get better. God damn it, now I have to make new plans. You Girls can't be trusted, bitching on the rag, too fucking delicate to bear-up. Fuck you and your pneumonia". I closed my eyes and made no response, sure of one thing, there were too many users and takers coming through a dealer's home-base, I could not recuperate at Brian's. Yep, a Buyer waiting on the porch, Brian all smiles, ushered him into the living room. I coasted to the kitchen and phoned Andrew. Glad to hear my voice again, he invited "Absolutely, come on. I'll take care of you, good as your own mama". His voice made me feel better, I washed my face, combed my hair and joined the men. Buyer spent 5000 dollars and was gone, cash in neat piles on the coffee-table, Brian and Ric celebrating with lines. It made no matter, Ric was bent on taking every whit of me "Well if it isn't little miss cop-out. You look like shit". I sat down and looked at him, keeping my face completely relaxed, no emotion, I could afford him none, no use anyway, nothing I said or did moved him, and suddenly it struck me funny how the Sweet Sisters provided such a fortunate, legitimate pardon, I sank into the couch. Brian cut another line, and they snorted and spun a new plot. Ric would fly to Costa Rica, stay with his Uncle long enough to score, call me at Andrew's with details, fly home to Los Angeles, I would pick him up in a rental car, drive to San Francisco's Fisherman's Grotto for the drop, then we go North to Redding, leaving the rental there, no trail. This was an order not a request, no response needed. Ric tried on Brian's suits, they were close to the same size and height, picking a understated brown & gray pin-stripe, white dress-shirt, grey tie, brown wing-tips, brown leather brief-case, dark-brown short-haired wig, a semi-convincing businessman if he shaved. Brian would take him to the LA airport tomorrow, leaving me with Andrew on the way. They went for Chinese food, Brian invited me. Hungry, I was too weak to go. Some time in the night he left a take-out-box by my bed, Egg Foo Yung, Shrimp Fried Rice, Coconut Prawns, Sweet & Sour Sauce.

I got out of bed only for the necessary till we left. Dozing in the car, gleaning from the conversation, my transport less a compassion, more an opportune ego-saving pretext for Ric to see Keely. She was not there. Andrew explained, Gretchen again had custody of her little girl Ava, Keely hocked her wedding ring, they pooled money and rented a house. Ric was all business, handing me an envelope "Here, for a plane ticket to LA and car rental deposit. There's a license too. I'll call you here with flight and arrival time, maybe five six days. Wait outside baggage for me. Got it". The envelope held three-hundred dollars and a drivers license with my photo in the name of Martha Jane Burke, born July 4, 1945, making me 26, I smiled, Martha Jane was Calamity Jane's real name "Yeah, got it. And thanks for my new identity". He set a too-stuffed-to-shut valise infront of me, hat, boots, leather pants, jacket and Kabar "Sure Martha, no need anyone knowing who we are. Bring this when you come get me". Ric and Brian were off. And I was grateful to find Luke gone to see Keely. Andrew and Frodo put me to bed in the loft, brought me juice and pills on the six hours, tea and toast when I could eat, reading aloud even while I slept. In their maternal custody, day four I felt human once more, showered and hitched to the MotherTruckers new house. A sparkling January afternoon, I caught a ride to Fairmount Avenue just off Highway-One with Lorenzo, who asked for my number and did not press when I said no. Littles playing in the big yard, ran me down full-speed, tugging, pleading would I take them to a near-by burger-stand. Gretchen and Keely sun-bathing, hugging, kissing, begging me to move in, even four kids did not bring enough welfare to live on, all of us sharing expenses, Leda too, we could keep the place. A small two-bedroom rambler, already three adults and four kids, Gretchen please-pleasing in her seductive disarming way, I needed to not be where Luke lived, and still I said maybe, for he was here some of the time, still I felt safe and full in the company of these beings again, like organs of me growing outside my body, living lives fortuitously not mine.

Keely heard Ric had been looking for her and needed to know what was he saying. I looked round, Littles not in ear-shot "He's just so mad at you, hardly says anything at all. My ride was just an excuse to come see you and the Boys". She scowled "He's always taken me for granted. I tried at first. Gave up after having Robby. Ric's just as satisfied with a hot dog as a five course meal, and no more appreciative". I knew the more of it "Yeah, he communicates with strangers better than me, and the power trips, he's a brave insensitive self-centered jerk that doesn't know how to respect women at all". Keely snorted "I'm glad someone else knows what's under the hood". I let her in "He flew to Costa Rica. Doing a deal to pay-off Sky River's debt, leave Hydra with a good name. I'll pick him up in LA soon". Her eyes blazed, shooting to feet, stomping in a small circle "That idiot. He's the Father of four, if he gets busted, it could be life in jail. If he makes it, bring him here okay. I need to talk about divorce". I was alarmed "Aren't you moving awful fast. You that sure about Luke". She stopped circling "It's not fast. I been thinking about it a long time. Ever since I fell for Justin, Ric's best friend. We never did anything, he's got kids too. God, I haven't seen him in over three years, since we started Hydra. He's still married". Already considering divorce she had one more kid with Ric, I could only wonder why.

When Ma Bell pulled his truck into the driveway, the Littles all over him, wanting to carry equipment, help install the phone. Keely made tuna sandwiches on Wonder Bread. Gretchen rustled Ava from a nap. When the phone was in, children were driven-out to blankets on the lawn for lunch, there was no table in the kitchen. Gretchen left the door open, climbed onto the counter for a Folgers coffee-can atop the cabinet, half-full of weed, she rolled a fat joint. And we sipped tea in the living room, and puffed, catching-up conversation leading to Leda and Amaru. Gretchen twinkling mischief, picked-up the new phone and dialed. Leda just home from her Grandparents, no word of Amaru. Gretchen incited house-sharing, leaving-out how many people and bedrooms. Desperately needing our company, Leda promised soon. Then Luke swaggered in the front door, quart of Southern Comfort in-hand. Every one else was delighted, I made a pneumonia apology, having spent too much vital already, and headed to Andrew's.

First ride letting me off on the Avenue of Diamonds, I bought a Seattle Times at the news-stand, and walked to Riverside Avenue before catching another. Andrew, Frodo gone, I settled on the porch, letting the sun minister warm fingers, and read about the Seattle Seven. Chip Marshall and Michael Lerner were in San Francisco with attorney Michael Tigar, arguing the validity of the contempt charges in front of three Ninth Circuit Court Judges. Chip told the court *"I'd be less than honest if I didn't say I had skepticism, and the result of our trial has reaffirmed that skepticism"*. He claimed *"Boldt was prejudiced against us and acted as jury, prosecutor and judge. I don't think we were going to get a revolutionary judge to hear our case and we are revolutionaries. Perhaps some of the things we did were not in the proper mode. But the judicial system has to be aware that justice and obedience are not the same thing. If obedience and order come ahead of justice, the whole power of contempt has been overdone. We may have used strong language, but we were not intent on disrupting the trial"*. Three hours of presentation, the Judges decided to accept the case. And until they rendered a decision the defendants would remain free. I was beginning to understand, resolving a thing too soon would put the judicial system out-of-business, their contempt appeal would go on and on. I had physically and mentally moved-away from the drama, cynical and too spent to be more than interested spectator, the only thing anyway was contributing cash for the defense. I had $49.17 plus the hundred in my shoe, and could not think of what but to wait and see, obstinate limbo, the only tangible of my almost adventure, a tender arm-full of unnecessary disease shots. I climbed the loft to sleep.

Gretchen's signature patchouli-jasmine perfume-oil and palm on my brow brought me round. According to her Highness I was all well, no temperature, she took my hand down to the shower, ushered me in and closed the door. Keely and Luke were home with Kids, she had his car, we were going to the High Street Local to hear the Doobie Brothers, $1.25 cover-charge, she had money. Her beguiling infected me, the world rose-colored with her in it, as she towel-dried my hair, I luxuriated in her friendship "You need me". She feigned exasperation "You're so way off little Sista. You know I'm a mercenary and don't give a shit about you. It's the velvet dress I came for". Knowing this so I laughed "Left it behind. Didn't think I needed velvet in Costa Rica". She swatted my bare bottom "Damn you, go get dressed". The phone rang as we left. Ric would flying into LAX in two days, dictating flight number, arrival time, wait outside baggage, bring his leathers, he hung-up. My depression evaporated, it seemed to have worked-out best, me going along would have been wretched, futile.

Gretchen coming for me was more than a dress, she and Delroy had their first fight, he would be at the High Street, she wanted to show, and not alone. We took a table yards from his, thick in fawning fans, she ordered a pitcher, turned her high-beam lure-lure on him, and he came trotting over like a good boy. Full of antibiotics I passed on beer, and shrank from this dark spell, Gretchen Fetchin-Fine sometimes had no scruples, Delroy was not better, but her avaricious libertine sexuality had repercussions his did not, and I wanted little implication. She cooed to him "No one's home at Andrew's. We can use the bed". Turning to me an after-thought "If you think it's okay". Already her shill, the impudence still flattened me "It's not mine to offer". She giggled me off, pulling Delroy from his chair and out the door. My cheeks burned neon, all eyes seemed on me, alone, I took a stool at the bar, ordered 7UP, chain-smoked till lungs would no longer, trying to relax, enjoy the Doobie's music, wolves sniffing my scent, asking a dance, buy me a beer, join their table, why didn't I have that obligatory benign smile on my face, disinterest taken as flirty ploy, unaccompanied female, I simply had to be looking for a man, what value was I on my own. Boiling at Gretchen, I could not go home, they were fucking in my bed, she didn't want to come here alone yet so easily left me, forced into Stuck-up Golden-Bitch, meeting each incursion with "Thanks for asking but we haven't been properly introduced". Though not a rejection, they always walked away, some calling me Bitch under breath, others insisting, then calling me Bitch, few were ever bright enough to take my proposal. One more 7UP, over my shoulder a smooth voice offering to buy it for me, or anything my little heart desired, the clever rascal meeting criterion with "Then please Mademoiselle, allow me to introduce myself, my friends call me Santa". Momentarily surprised, my hand extending automatically, I was fascinated how it transformed when placed into anothers, watching him lightly kiss the back, well well, someone with a working brain, and style, and a really stupid name, I did not smile "What do your enemies call you". He smiled clean-shaven, five-ten, sandy-brown hair, veiled blue eyes, claiming the next stool, and we leaned our heads and small-talked over the enormous amps, how the Doobies were sure to make it big, how lovely warm the weather, affable nothings that happily kept the other wolves at-bay. Nosing between, cigarette in her generous mouth, chipped front-tooth, explosion of honey-brown Medusa hair, spare frame, her voice brandishing "Got a match for me Santa". I appreciated this woman's chutzpah. Santa had that silky charm, indistinguishable face, of course, a dealer, he presented Cyrene. She shook my hand, resolute grip, then Santa's, palming a five, Kool menthol now at the corner of her mouth, she rolled it to the center, and insisted "So, you got a match for me now". He poked the money in his vest pocket, pulled a small cardboard matchbox from the other, and struck a wooden-match on the black strip. Kool to the flame, she took the box, and saying she hoped to see me again, melted into the crowd. I thought I recognized her from somewhere. This dance continued, people hovering, interested only in a five-dollar sifted Diamond matchbox of MaryJane, just fine with me. The club a hemp fog, everyone contact-high, end of the second set, I could not stop yawning. Business satisfied, Santa offered me a ride home, he knew the way.

Delroy, Gretchen sat across from Andrew in the breakfast nook, smoking cigars. They knew Santa and were delighted to see him, dealers have the best dope. We smoked his personal stash sprinkled over home-grown,

464

so deliciously pungent I took but a small hit, remembering sinsemilla's intense psychedelic. The night peeked-in beckoning electric and warm, and we could only follow it to the beach. Inspiration held Andrew to stay and write. Santa pulled two satin quilts from the back seat of his car, handing one to Delroy. I was not happy paring-off as we crossed the meadow of scents, Frodo leading the way. Near the lip of high tide the satins were spread. Delroy undressed Gretchen. Santa looking at me. Sex seeming a sacrilege so high, I shook my head "We just been introduced". He snatched the quilt and bristled-off dragging it behind. Again surprised by this person, his expectations were not my fault, so why did I feel I'd done something wrong, maybe it wasn't so easy for him infront of the great Delroy Bogave, maybe I wasn't raised to be smitten with Santa. Any way I went after, catching him in the meadow, Frodo at my knees, keeping wary eyes. Reconciliation snubbed with not a look or word. I continued after, Santa threw the quilt on his car, it slid to-the-ground as he swung the screen door wide going in the house, letting it slam hard. I quietly passed through and up the stairs. Andrew "Good night sweet bird". Taking the spoiled sheets from the bed, Gretchen, Delroy had no manners, I rolled them in a ball, drew the spread over and laid down to think. Should I stay, move-in with the MotherTruckers, waiting for what, or go with Ric to Seattle, be close to Ida Rose and her work, I needed a long count of ten, eyes shutting to Andrew and Santa's drone.

Stoney came in the afternoon, business with Andrew. He just so happened to be going to Berkeley tomorrow, meeting with Kitty Griffin, proprietor of the New Orleans House, well-known launching pad for bands, setting-up a gig for One Hand Clapping, and would be only too glad to drop me at Oakland International Airport.

I bought a one-way, still uncomfortable flying, my life in someone else's karma, white-knuckling into Los Angeles International. Walking through to Hertz Car Rental, I thought of Josh people-watching Houston Airport, how he would love this one. Martha Jane Burke had no problem renting a dark-green Chevy Impala, the most common-place car Hertz had available. Parking outside baggage, waiting, waiting, waiting too long I locked the doors and went in to check flights. Ric landed over an hour, paranoia chilled through me, he's been busted, they're looking for me, save your self

Shoshy, run. I fired the engine, and there he was, clean-shaven, banker's haircut, invisible suit, and still he did not blend-in, looking like someone more than no one. I stood on the door-jamb. He saw, taking his time, head down, lugging a hard-shell suitcase to the trunk, commanding "Give me the key". When I sat behind the wheel, he ordered "Move over". Ric drove only the speed limit, so frosty unfriendly, I decided it was a good time to deliver his Wife's message "Keely wants to talk". One tense eye in the rear-view mirror, he snarled "We're going to Frisco. Take this shit to DiMaggio's, drive to Redding, leave the car and go home. She'll have to wait". I had nothing more and turned-on the radio, not wanting to think of what was in that hard-shell suitcase.

Grown-up in LA, Ric knew the way, West to Santa Monica, North on Pacific Coast Highway toward Malibu, passed Pepperdine turning East up a narrow winding canyon road, parking on a ridge to watch were we followed. I remembered his leathers. Taking the valise from the back seat, he stepped-out and pulled them on, relenting just a little "You chose the right car. Good job". Getting out too, I did not trust this "You know, I can't be in the middle of you and Keely". Pain betrayed his contempt "That's just fine with me". Unlocking the trunk he snapped-open the hard-shell "You wana see thirty-grand". I peered over his shoulder at the brown plastic wrapped bundles, three cigars tucked in-between. Collecting them, he folded and laid the suit on the bundles, slide a cigar in the breast-pocket and locked the case, telling me Brian would be waiting at DiMaggio's. I did not react outwardly to the contents, cocaine seemed such a mocking pay-off for Hydra's debt, I hated being party to this. One twenty-minute rock-et-ride explodes your entire store-house of natural brain opiates, a body needs two weeks to replenish enough just to quench it's everyday needs, leaving nerves naked to the mildest pressure, slightest wind, god-forbid a hurricane, and you soon discover the insidious hoax, if you stop, you feel like shit for weeks, and if you don't, you need more and more, and if you don't know coke shoots your whole wad the first time, and every time, you think it's only the drug that's getting you off, and then comes the final insult, it's never as good the second time, that's why dealers give you the first hit free. Ric handed me one of the cigars in celebration. Sniffing its length slowly I made the compulsory congratulation, thinking it foolishly premature, we still had a way to go. He lit our cheroots, we climbed the guard-rail, leaning against, looking West to the Pacific. When Ric felt sure no one had followed us, he drove-on, connecting to the Ventura Freeway East, the San Diego Freeway, North to I-5, keeping the speed-limit to the Wharf. He went in DiMaggio's Restaurant with the hard-shell, I waited, never seeing Brian, then we crossed the Bay Bridge, through Oakland and Sacramento, North at Vacaville to I-5. It was not hot, I relished a long silent meditation through the Sacramento Valley, making Redding after dark. We checked into the Imperial 400 Motel, twin beds, and starving, catty-cornered to a Chinese restaurant, mine Vegetable Chow Yuk, his grizzly Sweet & Sour Spare-Ribs with pink-puffed mystery chips and pineapple. Ric decided to take the bus to Santa Cruz and confront Keely. Still no clarity of focus, I would go along. We slept till 9AM, dropped off the Impala and took a taxi to the Greyhound station.

Chapter Eighteen

EVIL SPIRITS TRAVEL IN STRAIGHT LINES

The Silver Dog pulled into San Francisco's Mission Street Station, we got off to stretch. Ric pressed three one-hundred dollar bills into my hand "I planned on spending much more than I did. You came through like a champ, and I don't want to leave you on a limb". Surprised by his generosity, and how thing develop, my direction came clear, Ric had given me the means, I wanted to find William, maybe he was why I was in California "Thanks. Look, I hope you don't mind but I'm going to stay here and look for an old friend. Good Luck with Keely. And could you tell her I'll be down in a few days". Head already in Santa Cruz, he boarded without a word. Shouldering my pack, walking to a phone booth on Market Street, I remembered Tara said William worked the Mark Hopkins Hotel as a doorman, and lived just blocks from the theatre.

W.Paten listed near Geary Street, seven blocks up Larkin, I dialed, ringing ringing, no answer. Windy and warm, I felt taller in San Francisco, negotiating the steep hill, to talented forbidden William. The apartment building between Polk and Larkin, three flights to the security door, recognizing his handwriting, buzzing number 106, no answer. I settled on the stoop at the foot of the stairs, watching colorful denizens of this consummate city pass by, till hunger drove me to find a small grocery on Van Ness. Clerk could not take anything bigger than a twenty, directing me to a bank near by. I had not been inside one since cashing my last Boeing check, felt outlaw in red neon blinking off my forehead, trying to ease through the lobby slow and calm, this was drug money, could be counterfeit, surely bad karma, and still I laid a hundred on the marble counter and asked for change. The young Teller looked at me hard, holding the money up to the light, locking eyes onto mine, keeping the bill, ordering me wait while he calls the manager, who held it twice to the light, and authorized. Fresh-out of obstacles, Teller counted in slow motion, four twenties, one ten, one five, five ones, counting again and a third. I focused on breathing, hands open, letting gratuitous hostility pass through me, humming Three Dog Night's *how can people be so heartless, how can people be so cruel,* watching the game, realizing this had little to do with me personally, that people treat you like they feel. This was Ric's game too, misery projected onto a convenient screen, and I did not have to be so convenient, so according, and if I chose to, did not automatically have to fire back in kind, for a good alchemist is full of the unexpected, when given shit, she can spin gold. Fishing a hit of acid from the bottom of my bag, I placed it on the counter Sandoz up and smiled "Here, for you, enjoy your self". Totally disarmed, Teller smiled so big it brightened the whole bank. I folded the money into my bag, flashed him a peace sign and sailed through the revolving door, down the block to the grocery, for bananas, Fig Newtons, Benson & Hedges, and back to William's stoop.

Ten Newtons, one banana, five cigarettes, my name spoken in tender amaze. William stood before me, so handsome he took my breath away, long hair tied back, gray uniform piped in red. I stood too "Well, look at you". His greedy embrace lifted me off the ground and set me down at arms-length for inspection "Well, look at you. God I'm glad to see you. What are you doing here. How did you find me". I could feel high color on my cheeks "Your number's in the phone book". Smiling those broad perfect teeth he took my pack "I'm really glad to see you. Come on up". Weary standing Doorman on the sidewalk most of the day, he fell back into the soft couch "Mi casa es su casa". We giggled nervous at broken taboos. I took the other end. He closed his eyes "I have a gig tonight at John Barleycorn, and you're coming with, no excuses. It's really important to me. I've been too excited to sleep. Oh, you know Tara's here in San Francisco". I lingered on his achingly beautiful face "Yeah I know. I went to see her the last night of Alice. She was amazing". William opened those sad eyes "I didn't want to crowd her". Then he grinned "It's taken me five months to set up this gig. Important agents are coming, all my stuff is written for Tara, and just look at what Lady Luck brought me, a good luck charm. I'll sing to you". I was not thrilled to be Tara's proxy. He yawned "With you here, I think I can close my eyes for a while. Go use what ever you like". Jasmine shampoo, lavender rinse, naked so near him, the shower drumming my body, a vivid disturbing flash of Leda and Gretchen popped in my head, and out. I put on the tapestry halter gown, wishing I had the velvet, and gently nudged William "Bathroom's all yours". He took a deep breath and stretched his whole body "Wasn't sleeping". I asked "Can I use the phone to make a long distance call. I can pay for it". He took me in with his eyes "You look really wonderful. Sure, go ahead. And don't worry about money, I made some fat tips today". He closed the bathroom door. I dialed. Life had filled Leda's voice again "Wow, I just hung up on Gretch. She's flying up here with Ric tonight. He got in Keel's face, an Luke knocked him down right in front of the kids". I was not surprised "Is he hurt". She ignored me "I'm moving in. Gretchen's coming to get me so we can go together. Be there in a couple days. She said you're moving in too". I owed her the whole truth "I haven't exactly decided yet. It's a small place, one bedroom for the kids, and only one more. When Keely and Luke aren't using it, I know Gretchen will be. All that's left for us is the couch". Leda jumped on my words "I don't care where I sleep. You guys are the first real friends I ever had. I just want to be there". This was her whole truth, I withdrew "So, you hitching or flying". She sounded confident "Hitching. We're gona drop acid and catch a ride". I did not ask after Amaru "Be careful okay, we're not all together". She laughed me off "Don't worry about the mighty MotherTruckers".

William was anxious to show me off, feelings kindled he thought were dead. Remembering how Gabriel made me feel after leaving Nick, I thought most of the anxious was gig anticipation. Guitar case in-hand, he took mine too, unusually warm evening breeze just enough to dry my hair and dance my skirt, we walked to Enrico's Café, sipping coffee and posing like movie stars at a sidewalk table-for-two. William could have been, broad shoulders, narrow waist, white poet's shirt tucked into chocolate-brown wide-wale corduroy bell-bottoms, cherry-red braided-leather belt, chestnut mane loose to his shoulders, Paul Newman looks so deliciously clean-shaven. Java properly sipped, we strolled Broadway arm-in-arm, he seemed to know everyone's name. Then it was down Larkin, though the Backdoor Pizzeria into John Barleycorn, acoustic Folk Club, heavy in dark wood and church pews. William seated me in a white rattan peacock chair at the end of the bar, facing his wooden chair on no stage, just a space infront of the cobblestone fireplace. Carefully lifting the Gibson Hummingbird 12 string from its case, he fine-tuned, and filled the place with intelligent woven lyrics of love and promise, a choir-boy gone bad, beguiling a room full, and me, and the usually reserved agents, all making offers after the first set. I was flattered and embarrassed and used, a pretense, for like Tara, William was groomed young, voice lessons, music, class president senior year high school, he was always on, something rigid in him, living his expectations and those expected of him, and though the sleight appeared ideal, it was second-order. He did not sell-out like Tara, but the artifice made it seem he was trying to fit the guitar into a violin case. He was not who I came South for, I could consume him is a week. And I did not want to be a cannibal.

We trudged the flights to his place, 3AM, sprawling on the couch, sharing a bowl of good Mexican weed, left-over pizza, Fig Newtons, bananas, as he weighed and measured the evening's overtures, a demo record, bookings, meeting the right people, possible album and tour, all with a melancholy in his voice I could not interpret, till hearing this meant moving to LA, away from Tara. When I mentioned leaving for Santa Cruz in the morning. His face fell "No no no no no, I was hoping you'd stay a while, let me show you my town". He looked at me "Get to know each other". His loneliness so bare I did not have heart, Gretchen, Leda would have to wait "Well, it's not like I'm on a schedule or anything". Still wired from the night's excitement he sat-up "Hey, let me play you some new tunes. You'll be the first to hear". I closed my eyes as he played and sang. Bus ride, long night, too much food, I woke to his gentle prodding "Shoshy, Shoshy. You can have the bed. I'll sleep on the couch". I would rather have just gone back to sleep, but did as told. Sometime in the late morning he slipped in, we held each other, and kissed, and giggled, no sparks, no more wondering, no more pressure, we were friends.

Beaming in satisfaction having made San Francisco his town, a breezy warmish afternoon with nothing to do but walk, we poked our heads in clubs, most I was too young for when living on the Haight. The Condor Club featuring Carol Doda lowered from the ceiling on a grand piano, strip-teasing, her gigantic tits enough for three women, what choice but to become a pair. The Peppermint Tree's marquee boasting the George Freeman Trio. Big Al's had Murl Saunders and Troy Dodds. The Black Hawk George Shearing. Pierre's the Beau Brummels. The Black Sheep Earl "Fatha" Hines and the All Stars, Rich Dean playing intermission. We climbed stairs to the Carousel Ballroom on Van Ness and Mission for coffee. Then Chinatown, walking through Dragon's Gate at Bush and Grant, flanked in stone lions and shiny green tiles, I felt transported. People living above shops, laundry hanging from balcony clothes lines, women playing Mah Jongg, herb doctors in the back of shops, wearing white coats, listening to complaints, examining eyes, tongues, skin, hands, pulse, prescribing bark, roots, seeds, dried bugs, preparing packages to be boiled and taken as tincture, envelopes of raisins included to chase the foul taste. Yellow, red, green predominant, when I asked a shop-keep while William bought Gunpowder Tea, she explained, green was nature and progress, red brought happiness, yellow prosperity, instructing us to offer and accept a cup of tea with both hands as it signified mutual respect, walking us out the door, she pointed to a pagoda "Chinese believe evil spirits travel in straight lines, we curve our roofs to ward them off". So many temples, Joss Houses, blending Buddhism, Taoism and Confucian ethics, each dedicated to a patron Joss, Kuan Gung, God of War, Tianhou, Goddess of Seafarers. The crowded streets, narrow alley-ways, bustling in the grace of a normal daily dance, squeezing by, sideways, selling, Chinese brush paintings, silks, delicately embroidered linens, kimonos, carved jade, toys, paper lanterns, kites, fans, flags, dragons, they knew dragons, and exotic vegetables, Buddha's hands, wood ear mushrooms, foot-long string beans, and sea cucumbers, urchins, eels, live octopi, giant crabs, oysters, every color and imagination of fish, shark fins for soup, one-hundred dollars a pound, and thousand-year-old eggs, really one month, preserved in salt and ash they turn black, and roasted ducks hung by the neck, dripping fat, roast pork, barbeque pork, pork ribs, pigs ears, and all kinds of prepared vegetable dishes. We ate at William's usual, a three-seat out-door food-bar, hot-and-sour soup, swamp spinach stir-fried with bean curd and oyster sauce over steamed rice, Chinese beer, and a large order of deep-fried bean curd and plum sauce to take home. This day was a gift, a real friendship blooming, moving a past so pain-full and secretly personal behind, one we both spent too much courting the sickness. William made tea in the only thing he had of Tara's, offering it with both hands, he would go to Los Angeles, become a star, and come see me in Santa Cruz. I accepted with both hands, promising to introduce him to the fabulous MotherTruckers.

In the morning we lingered over breakfast tea, deep-fried bean-curd and plum sauce. I would hitch South. William carried my pack through the Haight, West on Lincoln to 19th and Golden Gate Park, waiting till I picked a ride with a girl who worked at the new Santa Cruz Jack-in-the-Box, leaving me wanting a good-bye kiss, and like Josh, sorry he was not the one. Smitten by his handsome, my ride chattered of little else. I was glad to get-out on Riverside Avenue in Santa Cruz and walk the bridge and beaches to Andrew's, turning over thoughts of living with the MotherTruckers, all the guys that would be coming and going, no where to set-up shop, fortunately Andrew enjoyed my company and did not assume friendship was more than friendship. But Luke.

Frodo sat on the corner of 4th and East Cliff, eyes straining passed me down the road, he reluctantly followed into the cul-de-sac. Andrew was standing on the porch smoking a plastic-tipped panatela, delighted to see me, he carried my pack upstairs. After welcomes, Gretchen and Leda heavy in-mind, I shared my apprehension. Andrew would drive me to the MotherTruckers. I called, no answer. Keely, Ava and the Boys walking home from the burger stand as we pulled into the driveway. Keely bawled me out for Ric's visit. I did not bother defending, went in and phoned Leda. Her Mom remembered Gretchen arrived just after my last call, and their early departure next morning. I could not shake a bad feeling. Keely, still in full-heat with Luke could not hear over the carnal rush, scoffing at my fears, guessing they caught a string of short rides or met some cute guys and would soon show. So it was up to me, I fell quiet, introspective on the ride home. Dear sweet sensitive Andrew held intuition in high regard, suggesting a cigar walk to the beach. Hesitant to leave his vigil on East Cliff, Frodo trailed along. Andrew lit our stogies, and tried to flesh-out my premonition. The tide coming in high, silent waves crossing the sand to our feet brought the specter of Griffin's face at the Wolf Creek Café "I know where they are. The Family of the Mystic Arts". Andrew was fascinated with the growing lore of the Family "You think they're Druids". "No. They're vampires, and the Girls are in danger. I have to go get 'em". He harmonized "I hardly know Leda, but Gretchen's head is easily turned. Ted's going up to his Folk's cabin on the Rogue River. I could call him". I wondered "Do I know him". "Yeah, he's our sometimes Roady for the band, and a good friend. I introduced you at the High Street gig. He's barrel-chested with curly red hair. A real class guy. You'll be safe with him". Frodo howling over the water took our attention. Andrew called him as we headed for the meadow of scents. Frodo did not come. Andrew worried "He's not eating or sleeping. I took him in. The vet said there's nothing wrong. I don't know what to do". I said the stupidest of all possibles "Maybe you should go to the pound and get him another girlfriend". Andrew shot me a terribly disappointment. What a jerk I could be "Oh shit, I didn't mean that. I just felt so bad I thought I should say something. Please let me take it back. Please". He gave me a shy smile "Okay. Let's go call Ted".

Up for an adventure Ted would come for me in the late morning. I called Keely asking her along. Resentment sharpened her voice "Geez, I can't just go anywhere I please. If you had kids you'd know that. The Girls are probably having big fun and I wish I was there". Luke shouting at the kids in the background clued me, I pressed "Can't you see our protection went away with Amaru. I know what I feel, and even if you don't believe me, they're still not here, and we haven't heard from them. I'm leaving in the morning. If you change your mind call me, and if they show-up let me know right away, okay". She said sure and hung-up.

I remembered meeting this rich white prince, humbled by LSD, experiencing his existence as part of the whole, Ted loved music so, he cooked his ear-drums spending too much time too close to big speakers and was becoming hard of hearing. We smoked cigarettes and swapped Golden Ghetto stories most of the trip. Finding Cemetery Road, his jeep easily took the steep mountain road. A thick black velvet night, the Family already retired to their cabins, playing instruments together in perfect rapport as we walked into the longhouse. The power-full mojo impressed Ted "Wow, I never imagined a band playing together from their own separate homes". I pulled him to me and warned "Be careful, stay awake, the bargain is struck here almost without your knowing, and the price is terrible". Longhouse empty but for Leda curled infront of a blazing fireplace, naked. When she would not wake, Ted wrapped her in his coat and carried to the jeep. Boiling mad I gathered her clothes and pack, some one in the far dark corner cleared their throat to make known. Courage born of anger I approached, demanding "What happened here". A lithe slow moving woman leaned into the fire-light, monotone long beige hair and skin, long limbs, long nails, coal black eyes, voice a vindictive hiss "What always happens to whores". A woman who hates women, I knew them well "So where's the other whore". This took her by surprise, eye brows raising as she leaned back into the dark "With Griffin". I had the sickening impression countless girls and boys came through here and were devour, this creature was hungry, I ran to the jeep, remembering Griffin asking Leda to leave Amaru with him, wishing she had. Setting Leda's things down by the jeep, I charged Ted "Get her dressed, I know where Gretchen is". Griffin's door opened at my knocked. He seemed bigger, holding a bamboo flute like a weapon. I could see Gretchen sitting on the floor by the fire, also naked. She made no sign of recognition. Heart pounding so hard, shaking me in fear, I planted my feet and turned to stone "I came for her". Griffin stepped back, allowing me in. A neat one-room raw-log cabin, blazing in candles, animal skins on the floor and handmade furniture, bleached skulls, jawbones, antlers, hunting knives, a crossbow hung the walls, suffocating Frankincense could not mask the tang of unwashed

474

fucking. I crossed to Gretchen. She looked up, pupils fully dilated, staring right through me. Griffin stepped between us "She's mine". This Grand Wizard struck the same awful chord as the Monsters in my room, Taliesin, Nick, I dared not flinch, completely astounding my self by pointing a steady sharp index finger in his face and walking around him. Eyes glued to my finger, he let me. I took Gretchen's hand "Come with me right now". She did not return my grip. Remembering Ric handling Mr.Continental at Tom's Roadhouse, I pulled her to feet, smiled in Griffin's face and declared "Thanks for your hospitality". He smiled too and sprang like a flea to the door, kicking it shut, eyes gleaming with the game "But Little Red Riding Hood, there's big bad wolves out there". I squeezed Gretchen's hand hard and stuck-out my chin "This is a free country and we can go anywhere we want". It was the lamest thing I could have said, an unmistakable flinch, I had to do something now. Gretchen's heavy hand fell from mine, I grabbed it and pulled "Come on". Defiantly holding Griffins eyes, leaving her clothes and pack, I walked passed him, opened the door, and plunged into the dark thickness, towing Gretchen like I knew where I was going, falling three times before my pupils adjusted, I found the jeep, Griffin did not follow, or if he did, saw Ted. Leda was dressed and in the back seat. I pushed Gretchen in with her. And we sped headlong, haste more important than safety. The Girls must have taken the same drug, they seemed catatonic yet in total communication, I hoped they had not more likely been given so much they could not find their way back.

We rode in near silence to Ted's Family cabin, after putting the Girls to bed, he built a fire and set a bottle of Dewars on the table. We drank ourselves out where we sat. By noon Gretchen and Leda were able to walk to the jeep on their own. Ted and I traded driving, everyone quietly exhausted from the ordeal. Leaving them with Keely, she apologized for being such a Bitch, a large bruise just above her elbow that looked like a hand-print. Far as I was concerned, Ted's willingness saved Leda and Gretchen's lives, at least their souls, I thanked him as he turned off East Cliff onto 4th. Leda and Gretchen never clearly remembered what happened or wanted to, the incident drifting away like so many unlearned lessons never spoken of again.

Chapter Nineteen

STILL POINT

I felt at odds with my Sistas. Andrew was glad for me to stay with him. Sewing string-bikinis, selling bundles of ten to the Santa Cruz Import Shop, I wrote in my journal, did the cooking, read, took daily cigar walks to the beach with Andrew, and sometime Frodo, whose nose always smelling the breeze, blood-shot eyes ever watching for Amaru. I was content working, no night-life, no drugs but the occasional skinny joint, on February 7, 1971, walking to the beach alone, screaming to the sky because 66% of Swiss men voted to allow women the right to vote. This shook me hard, I had assumed peaceful neutral Switzerland so Democratic, so civilized, liberated, but this meant 34% of men voted no, I wondered how many were like that here. Two days later, an early morning earthquake near Los Angeles, 6.6 magnitude, with 64 deaths I worried about William, went in to Santa Cruz, to the newsstand for an LA Times, Seattle and New York Times. There were no names of those who died, and nothing about the Seattle Seven or Seattle Liberation Front, though Keely heard Ric paid Sky River's debt off and had contributed $5000 to the Seattle Conspiracy Defense Collective from Hydra. We no longer existed, but had our good name. Other than the Country Doctor who got their federal grant and were opening a free Open Door Clinic, the other collectives, Sundance, the Grodes, Mother Jones, the Rebels, the Fortress had gone the way of Hydra, the SLF no longer formally existed. Still, the papers were full of sit-ins and anti-war demonstrations on college campuses and in the streets of the world, and I felt real satisfaction having been one insignificant soldiers, and as time passed, a little less guilty having quit the battle before won.

Valentine's Day, late morning there was Steven at the Catalyst. When

I saw his fine face, it made me feel good, and I knew I had come looking for him "Hi. Is it alright if I sit here". Just a touch squinty-eyed he nodded yes "You been back long". Without thinking I said "Not too long". His face pinched "Didn't you promised New Years to call me when you got back". I did not want to mislead him "Steven, I had some heavy things to do that wrung me out. As my friend you have to understand". A filmy shade rolled over his eyes "Well you couldn't a found me anyway. I moved in with friends. We're caretaking the Lighthouse Avenue Mansion. The owner died and the will's tied-up in probate court. Whole family's fighting over who gets what. I hear it's a really nasty fight, money always is. So the house is full of stuff, and they don't want it sitting empty. We can live there free until the matter settles. Could be a year. There's plenty of room if you need a place". I gave no answer, and we drank too much coffee, and like any form of speed the conversation turned inane, and all I wanted to do was go home and work. Of late, human interaction felt more like an interruption. I'd come to a still point, what some called the dance, and caught a fleeting glimpse of my own conscious immortality, an unlimited consciousness, almost not personal, full of fierce qualities, courage, integrity, compassion, kindness, things that could fit through the eye of the needle and depended for their life on every choice I made. Against the lives and choices of those around me, I was able to measure a bit of my own character, and it seemed right now, only in working, writing, reading, in being alone could I see more, get an idea of what was worth doing and not, every thing else seemed irritating, frustrating, trivial, not the dance. I made the case to Steven. He said as a painter he understood the need to work, wrote his new address and phone on my hand, reiterating as I stood "There's room if you need a place. Call me".

Sitting cross-legged on the floor sewing, listening to Andrew laying on his bed reading the Rubáiyát of Omar Khayyám aloud, he was the only person I could stand to be near. But Santa showed-up, a month since the satin quilt, I did not have the juice for any confrontation, put my work down and set to leave. His smile was so open, genuine, as if we had no history, and he brought pollen to smoke. I got too high, beyond light-speed straight-up to the realization that drugs transcended by a road too cheaply won, and that Santa was too well-mannered, too sure of himself, too moody. Frodo came in and sat beside me. I stroked his head, and passed on seconds and thirds. Santa took us into confidence, he owned a cabin in Santa Clara County, a friend crashed there last night and called saying it had been broken into, he was heading there now for a quick look-see, and invited us along for the ride. Andrew sounded truly disappointed, saying it was a beautiful ride, but he had band practice. I had been wanting to see more of California, figuring if Andrew wanted to go it must be okay.

North on Highway 17, East to Coyote, then off the main road for miles, the countryside color-full as Washington in July. Santa's cabin was trashed but not by thieves, unmistakably a crash-pad that no one bothered tending, every surface sticky with fast-food wrappers, returnable beer bottles, over-flowing ashtrays. He built a fire in the red brick place, took a baggie of pills from his pocket, plopped down in a mangy over-stuffed easy-chair, put his feet close to the fire and ordered me "Get comfortable". My spine tensed, inviting Andrew overwhelmed the warning siren in my head, I felt for Excalibur's blade "No thank you". He opened the baggie, pawing through, not looking at me "Aw, come on Angel, sit a while, get comfortable, take some time". I told my self stay cool, relax, he was not Nick, could not know how freaked I was, standing full-length, invisibly shifting weight foot-to-foot, I protested "No god damn it. You said we came for a quick look-see. I have a ton of work to do and don't want to take some time". Laughing high and wild Santa raised his eyebrows "God's got nothing to do with it Angel". I could not quite wrap my mind around this or think of anything more to say, hurrying out the door to find a ride home. Night had fallen so dark, Milky Way diamond sky, I would have craned my neck for hours so it ached in the morning, instead straining for cabins or lights or a car, hoping it was just familiar old paranoia mugging my brain, that Santa was not a Monster. Freezing cold nothing, coyotes howling, inhaling several deep times to ease the vise-grip crushing my chest, I walked back-in "Wow, you should see the Milky Way, it's incredible". Giving me a sidelong look he refused, "Looking out in space makes me lose myself. I don't like thinking about infinity". Only Devils fear the horror of infinity flashed though my head, I sat down in the other mangy easy-chair. Santa offered the bag of pills "Here, take what you like". I shook my head "No thanks". He offered a pipe full of pollen. I

478

shook my head no, staring into the fire, stone still. Leaning toward me he whispered "They're telling me to tell you. Now. Confess. I'm in love with you. We'll get married soon as possible". I caught my breath, yikes, voices only he heard, turning him from Jekyll to Hyde, be very care-full Shoshy, sincere, I smiled not too big and lied "You flatter me Santa. I'll think about it". Hyde mocked "You'll think about it, right. For me, I need to trust. How can I do that when you lie". He leaned more "You see, I don't care if you love me back. I'll give you all the money you could ever want, all the drugs, you can go anywhere, be with anyone as long as you don't embarrass me". Sinking back he stared into the fire and dismissed me. This moment only truth would forestall, I tried to relax my voice "There's nothing you have I can't get for my self. I'm not interested in a bargain. I'd eat you alive in three days and spit-out your teeth". He laughed in delight "Don't tell me you don't love money. All you thoroughbreds love to shop". Hoping to engage Jekyll I tried to keep it light "Horses don't shop". Hyde was not amused, seeming to read my intent he lit a smoke "Well, I'm in no hurry. You'll change your mind". I smelled the same psycho-poker game Nick used to play "I will not change my mind. Anyway Andrew knows where we I am, so why don't you just take me home". A slow long drag on his Marlboro, he blew three perfect smoke rings "No matter, he doesn't know where this place is". I shot to my feet, crossing the room, into a filthy bathroom, closed the door, broken lock, and discovered my period. Never cramping, I always had to count, it was simply as a matter of course, but standing over a scummy toilet, stained undies and jeans at my ankles, this was the final insult, my neck could no longer hold up my head. And it dawned, the Sweet Sister were with me, men fear the bleeding, I would risk, pulled-up my pants, and took a seat on the hearth by Santa feet, blood-stain impossible to ignore. His eyes un-able to look-away. I let a few tears leak. Ambushed, Hyde turned Jekyll, and I whimpered "I just want to go home". Bleeding without wound, without death, sacred Women's Mysteries, old magic still potent, Santa bowed to Her power-full presence and took me home. I had no easy breath the whole way, sprang from the car not completely stopped, ran inside, bolted the door and leaned against it till the car engine faded. Andrew was not home. I soaked my pant in cold water, and showered-off as much as soap and hot water would, mentally slapping my face, wake-up girl, you were just plain lucky, but this is the last time you go alone anywhere with any guy your not already friends with, no more guys, no matter what they offer, they're all jerks, from now on listen to your gut.

One Hand Clapping sometimes-drummer Stanley and his wife Pam had adopted a baby and were celebrating her long awaited arrival at their home in Boulder Creek. Andrew invited me along. I preferred not, but Luke bulled-in the door angry and I would not be alone with him. Among those gathered around the bar-b-que, Eric and Colleen, Joey and Cherry, MoonGoose Drummer and Bass and their beautiful wives, perfect family weekend, playing perfect husbands. I'd seen every one with other women, and swore on my dignity, never get married, never be that dirty-word Wife, whispered from stiff mouth-corners when she showed-up at gigs unannounced, routinely deceived, how could she not know, and if so, how could she take it and take it. Colleen smiled at me on first-sight, then as if mistaken, did not know me. Pam seemed a strong woman, a possible Sista, tending the burgers, hovering her precious Little Girl, she avoided my eyes, likely assuming Andrew brought a Groupie, how dare I defile her home, though these guys would never breach the unspoken bargain and bring a Groupie to a Family function. In this hypocritical melodrama I was the pariah, other circumstances I might have tried to humanize my self, but this was Pam's party, her Baby's big day, her prerogative, and out of respect I left the assumptions to entertain. Delroy arrived, always the gentleman he greeted me as kissing-kin, graciously introducing his Wife, who gave a reluctant nod. Stoney and Ted came together, actively court-ing my favor, still I was handy target for Joey, Erik and Stanley, openly disdaining me, somehow a counter-balance to the humiliation they cause their wives, curled-lips, stabbing glares pecking my tender hide. Finding no reason to endure punishment for their misdemeanors, I told Andrew I had an important appointment. Knowing this was not so, his face betrayed genuine relief. And I did not slink-away down the long driveway, standing in plain sight, thumb-out, taking a ride with a woman on a noisy Vespa. To the MotherTruckers house, to be among my Sistas, who were not stainless, yet had over-come some of the deep-seated hatred that society and religion heap on girls, to destroy our bonding, demolish our self-confidence.

In her big bare feet, hand-tilling a small fenced plot behind the house for a vegetable garden, the sun pinking her neck, shoulders, apple cheeks, Leda never looked more beauty-full as she showed me seed-packs and where their beds would be. Desperate for unconditional love, she had saved a white Bunny from the pound. Exquisite long ears, shrewd ruby eyes, observing me from the corner of the shed, he hopped-out presenting him self. Leda introduced me to Merlin, we laughed at her turning magician into a rabbit. Though modest surrogate for mighty Amaru, Merlin was a worthy diversion for Leda's grieving heart, his hot pink ears the color of Ida Rose's aura. I told her they shared a passion for growing things, that I asked Ida Rose could I bring her over sometime, and she said yes without hesitation. Squealing, Leda gamboled the cultivated dirt, pledging to hitch North anytime I wanted. Merlin hopping maddly along. If I had not already deduced Keely and Luke's situation, her swollen purpling cheekbone screamed the tale, nevertheless, she was delighted to see me, waving a letter from Ric's best friend Justin, the one she had been in-love with so long, bearing news of his pending divorce. She was sailing on candy-cotton clouds, anticipating her next perfect love. Keely and Leda believed a man, the object instead of the subject would solve their I-just-want-to-be-happy riddle. Gretchen was not so ingénue, demanding every detail and impression of Delroy's wife, and wanting, needing a kitchen table she could not afford. Investigating the shed, stocked with hammers, nails, saws, two-by-fours and old wooden doors, we built a ledge on the kitchen wall under the high cabinets, a frame and two legs, and fastened one of the doors on top. No one could contain their imaginations, a door for a table, the green glass knob inspiring endless knock-knock jokes. Although too small, the MotherTrucker's house was an oasis, they believed I was the only missing element. I stayed the night, and we slept in the queen-bed, wishing, hoping, planning, dreaming, giggling.

I stayed a week, and needing to work, began a eucalyptus nut curtain to hang in the doorway between the kitchen and front room. For one dollar each, Lance and Robby picked-clean the floor of a nearby grove. I softened the nuts in boiling water, strung them on white cotton twine, tied the six-foot strands to a broken shovel handle, and fastened the pungent chocolate waterfall above the door. Leda, Gretchen, Keely started haunting the clubs, every night, taking advantage of my misconstrued penchant for staying home. After tucking the Littles in, I would light candles, incense, take a long shower, drink tea, admit to my journal thoughts too strange to share, and lay on the velvet couch and read. After last-call, they would sweep-in, often with impassioned suitors. Taking a sleeping bag to the back hall I would bed down by the Littles door. When they brought one home for me, handsome, drunk, presumptuous, and probably would not remember if we fucked, I considered anonymous human contact, instead taking him by the hand to the kitchen, made tea, and made certain he knew this was all he was getting. Sobering, explaining Gretchen's promise, apologizing and apologizing, he turned-out to be good company. We played Gin Rummy, smoked unfiltered Camels, tittered at the rhythm of eager copulation, and made coffee and toast and jam on sunrise. These comings quickly turned oasis into bordello. One late morning while everyone still slept, I left a note, gone to Andrew's for a while, and hitched to 4th Avenue.

A frantic pale shadow of himself, Andrew had not slept, Frodo was missing. We made posters and taped them to every possible surface, walked roads and beach over and over, looking in every ditch. Andrew could not be comforted, would not rest. The ache inside me for Amaru made this unbearably heavy, I had to lay down. Finding Luke home, I sat on Andrew's bed, hardly pulling-off my boots, I could have slept though an earthquake, offering no resistance to Luke's bitter Keely diatribe, and me by association. Tiring of a one-sided battering he went outside. I laid-down, drew the quilt up over my face, Luke was such an angry jerk, but not much more than others, people's lives were so overly dramatic, roller-coastering all around me, and I had to share the karma staying with them, it was clear, I needed to make more money and get my own place if I wanted to remain, and then why was it that I wanted to remain. Luke's buzz-saw snoring in the loft woke me, it was morning, Andrew still not home. I gathered every thing finished, bikinis, necklaces, earring, some Frodo posters, and hitched to the Santa Cruz Import Shop. Owner laid $200 cash on the counter "Keep these coming. I'll buy everything you can make". I had means, walking Pacific, putting Frodo posters in windows that would allow, buying a Santa Cruz Sentinel to look for rentals, I took it to the Broken Egg, and was not surprised to find Steven. We ate together, again he offered the Lighthouse Avenue Mansion, promising I would have my own room, no pressure. I could not mistake the Sweet Sisters sure hand here, Steven being in the right place right now, we finished eating, and he drove me to 4th Avenue for my belongings. Lying on his bed, Andrew did not move when I came in. I sat on the edge and stroked his woolly head. Tears ran from the corners of his closed eyes "Frodo's dead". The pain electrocuted me, I could not speak. He opened those swollen broken-hearted eyes "I went to the pound. They kept him five days, without a tag, and then just put him to sleep. I should have gone sooner". Pain all that remained of his partner, I knew he needed to be alone with it, kissing his wet cheek "I loved him too".

Chapter Twenty

NOT REALLY SNAKES BUT DREADLOCKS

Three-stories, nineteen rooms, seven with beds, four baths, I was gracefully embraced by the old Lighthouse Avenue Mansion. Mine was the sewing room, perfect, just off the living room, oak floor running twenty-four feet by twelve, South-facing windows the length, rising almost to the ten-foot ceiling, best light for seeing true colors, hand-sewing details. Under them were window-seat cupboards two-feet high, two-deep, covered in beautifully-tailored grass-green leather cushions, the only furniture a fine old wooden chair and massive mahogany armoire against the far wall. Dizzy-sick on Frodo, I could not meet the others, Steven gave me a key, I closed and locked the sewing room door, my eyes unable to look away from the perfect floor, long enough to lay-out a most demanding piece of material, wide enough to walk around so it might tell me what to do with it, smooth enough the fabric would all but floated, and the soft leather cushions, my couch off-the-floor. This room had a euphoric feeling, like a good drug I never experienced, gentle, hope-full, electric, as if I slipped through a shift into golden-sunshine welcome. I took what seemed my place cross-legged on the middle cushion, cat-bird seat over the Mansion's park like back-yard, shaggy hedgerow borders, once loved rose gardens, brilliant bougainvillea arbors invoking Southern charm, romantic walk-ways by now fishless ponds, little waterfalls, lemon, orange, avocado, almond trees, feeling their hospitality, greeting, I could unclench my jaw here, approach my work, tomorrow I would hunt thrift shops, bead and fabric stores, begin a collection. The mourning was physical, five-hundred pounds, I laid down on the butter-soft cushions, but the cupboards were calling my name. Number one, boxes of buttons, sixteen little sterling-silver tulips strung together through their loops with slender silk ribbon, locket buttons, violin buttons, clefs, musical notes, carved shells, ivory, onyx, crystal buttons, and pin cushions sprouting every curve and size needle, glass-head pins, tailors chalk, crochet hooks, graduated embroidery hoops, thimbles, snaps, frogs, scissors, oh what lovely scissors. Number two, hand-made tatting and lace, rolls of bias tape, hem tape, whale-bone stays, cotton and silk thread, crochet, embroidery floss, linings, sheers, tape measures, rulers, bees-wax. Number three, yards of silks, satins, rayons. Four, ribbon, velvets, linen. Five, wools and challis. Six, hand-made patterns. Seven, design sketch books, and photo albums. Eight, one ribbon-bound bundle of letters in a tooled-leather sewing box. I laid down with each sketch book and album. And the letters, love letters, Monique, seamstress of this room, died in 1964 at 81, 55 year never legal Wife of Loretta, the Mansion's owner and respected concert violinist, who preformed only in Monique's custom black silk tuxedo tail-jackets of crow feathers. I opened the armoire doors wide, full-length mirrors on the inside, fold-down ironing board, Singer sewing machine, and in the drawers, irons, pressing hams and cloths, more carefully folded original patterns, matching the sketches and photos, an unfinished tux jacket wrapped in white silk, each crow feather sewn precisely on the last so no one was individually noticeable, shining as if still in flight. I was thrilled how things could so unexpectedly develop, somehow I had my hearts content in the midst of being broken again, finally falling asleep on the soft cushions.

In the morning, I took Steven to the Catalyst for a thank-you breakfast. Home again, some phantom nudging me to the basement, I spent the day opening cedar-lined storage wardrobes, hanging thick and neat in Monique's work, trousers, blouses, jackets, coats, slips, night-gowns cut on-the-bias, pajamas bottoms, tap panties with tiny shell button side-closings, matching camisoles, even the simplest with shirred bodice, matching bed-jackets, silk-ribbon ties at the collars, some embroidered in flowers of same color floss, and shawls, capes, scarves, hats, parasols, handbags, maybe fifty silk bags of custom-made shoes, all lined in kidskin, with real pearl buttons, suede soles unmarked, imagining Loretta's feet never touching the ground. I was intoxicated, turning each garment inside-out to consider, admire the construction, every stitch a perfect balanced rhythm, everything, even the shoes exactly my size, as if waiting for me. I took to wearing nightgowns and slips as dresses, bed jackets, camisoles as tops. And I heard the Old Women approving me bringing them back to life. No one else in the house cared a whit for these things, the relatives' interest only in selling for as much money as possible, the old clothes would be a donation tax-write-off to the Salvation Army when the estate closed. Keeping his word, Steven painted, and left me to work. Five days, Monique always near my hands, I made three gowns, one with a cape, simple and elegant, my best work ever, I needed a bath. And a cigar walk, inviting Steven, first to the Smoke Shop on Front Street, then we shed our shoes, following water's edge, puffing the harsh cigars, sitting on logs, talking. His not quite radical enough politics and corny sense of humor were fun, brother-fun, I was care-full to encourage only friendship, no flirting, no suggestion or touch to be miss-taken.

Again in the basement, delaying the sale of my collection, I found Loretta's sterling silver music-stand folded into a brown leather quiver, and knew no one alive would appreciate it more than Andrew, good reason to visit. First to the Smoke Shop, this time asking the keeper to recommend, two expensive Cohiba cigars. I rambled Riverside, enjoying my body walking, the temperature, salty air, over the San Lorenzo River, down East Cliff, still expecting to see Frodo at the corner of 4th. Andrew took my gifts and set them aside, there were no words, we held hands, his letting mine know it was glad for the company. Soon he laid down and closed his eyes. I put my hand on his heart, and went home.

Sometimes the Old Women sat on the cushions, knees touching, shoulders, elbows, hands, while I worked. I was the inheritor, my work blooming, still I felt lost, and wrote to Ida Rose - All I do is work. I have no social life, because nothing else interests me. She wrote right back, counseling – *The value is in doing the work from beginning to end, the best you can. Working in process is the law of the cosmos. If you do this, you will make your way. And try not to be too impatient.* This amazing woman took the time to write me, communicating, no delay, I did not feel so solitary. The wardrobe drawers were troves of embroidered handkerchiefs. I laid them out on the sewing room floor, five rows of 40, sewn into a patchwork, into a floor-length skirt that gathered tightly into a wide waist-band, kerchief halter-top pleating into that, sash of forty tying into a long lazy bow at the back, a feather-light floating fairy garden, I had to keep it, there were enough for three more. Things grew from silk neckties, crocheted pot holders, fine-cotton napkins and table-cloths so richly embroidered, I cut them as little as possible, my style a fusion of American Hippie and Japanese. And my reputation spread, the Yellowbird sought me out, making offers. Flattered, I could see no point competing with my self in a small town. And, as I worked from vapour to material finish, burning hot, Ida Rose was right, beginning to end with passion and patients built solid gold bricks of feeling-good, accomplishment, the physical process enabling mental, and selling, another kind of wealth, I had no qualms getting paid for my work, even asking a little more to remain exclusive.

The house-party in constant-swing, I went to visit my Sistas only once. Otherwise, musing new ideas, I would sit in the Mansion's back garden with a book from it's library, volumes on the Civil War, one with Mathew Brady photographs, one of their family history, handwritten by Loretta's Grandfather, a Georgian plantation owner, who's slaves worth more than his land, he still freed them and fled the War with Family to California in 1863, settled in Santa Cruz, building the Mansion. Steven shared some of my interests, the others never missed a chance to stick their right-leaning politics in my face, they drank every night, and on Sunday went to Jesus Freak Church. I tried to be where ever they were not, this was taken as rude, and I compensated being overly sweet, polite, cheer-full, showing the wolves no whiff of weakness. They took to calling me Princess, making certain with tone I knew it was not a compliment, that I was a phony, far too full of my self being a known artist in town, far too stuck-up for their dear Steven. In part I was grateful, this afforded me some distance from him. And they were right, I was a phony to them, and understandably proud seeing my things on strangers, wanting to run-up and touch their arm, hey wait, did you know you're wearing my dress, necklace, I made that, feeling the rush a song-writer must hearing her work on the radio. And, there was their patronizing attitude that I am not baptized, not Born-Again, I was not saved.

One Mansion tenant was very pregnant, with no money the happy couple decided to have Baby at home, no mid-wife, no one with real experience, just a trapeze hung low from the ceiling of their bedroom, over a blue plastic children's swimming pool in the shape of Shamu. When labor began, Shamu was filled with warm water, and Mother held onto the trapeze, squatting, struggling, swearing, panting, pushing, Husband swabbing her enormous belly and breasts with big wet sponges, others keeping Shamu's water warm, Mom grunting, moaning, hands white-knuckling the trapeze bar, seeming endless hours, hanging, gravity as mid-wife, stress enough to make my head burst, I felt voyeur, terrified they would certainly die of complications, terribly relieved when tearing and bleeding, Baby crowned, and with one more exhausted push gushed into the water, everyone laughing, cheering, Dad's hands tying the cord and snip, Mom's sister taking and tenderly cleaning the bawling Boy. Wholly ecstatic Mom after-birthed, Dad taking it to the kitchen sink, washing, placing it in a large soup pot to simmer, for Mom to eat in the next days, getting those essential nutrients into her breast milk. I had new respect for this Mother, eating placenta stew, and it grossed me out, I had to get away, giving birth was definitely compelling, and way too intense, I did not consider it a life-affirming beautiful experience, even Lizabeth's ever so civilized delivery had not waxed me wanting one as it had William and Tara. They were just lucky it did not happen for them. Maybe some thing was wrong with me, or not, no matter, witnessing this again made me ever more certain one would never issue from me. I did not own courage enough to suffer this birth-curse, Yahweh's quarrel with Eve, regardless that all societies count female worth by her children, are suspicious of childless, pity barren, I did not feel any less woman not wanting babies. I would be care-full.

Steven caught-up with me on the Boardwalk, a cool March weekend afternoon, not many people, we bought merry-go-round tickets. I took the white stallion, flaring nostrils and powder-blue tack. Steven the Palomino to my left, initiating conversation I hoped he never would "I know I promised no pressure, and I meant it, but I have to ask you". He took a deep breath as the go-round began, loud above the music "Shoshannah Leibofsky will you marry me. Let's run away". Friendship killing, I shut my eyes and shook my head "No Steven. I would only make you miserable". He waited till they were open "I wouldn't mind being miserable with you. I'm miserable without you. No pressure, honest. Just think about it okay. You'd make me the happiest man in the world". I wanted to scream, I have thought about it you fool, but his heart beat on his sleeve, and I could not bear to see it bleeding "Okay, but my answer will still be no".

Knowing Steven's routine, I side-stepped him. When the Catalyst bought two of his painting for their own walls, everyone wanted to go celebrate, I stayed home with Baby, granting Mom and Dad an unexpected few hours out together. Twice checking, Baby sleeping sound in his upstairs crib, I settled within ear-shot, infront of the dining room TV, the finale of Gregory Peck in *Moby Dick*. Required reading in high school, I never noticed how Ishmael's fate was bound to Ahab's dragon fight, with Ahab's ego represented by the whale, that Ishmael must share Ahab's karma, whose life is ultimately extinguished by the wounded leviathan, lashed to its side by his own weapon, beckoning even in death to Pequod's crew, all aspects of his ego, all drowned in the struggle but Ishmael, the outcast, clinging to Queequeg's wooden coffin, life borne on death, I faintly registered the living room brighten, my eyes glued to Ishmael's promising flicker of consciousness bobbing on the surface of the Great Water, the Sweet Sisters his only salvation from a watery grave, smelling smoke, oh shit there was fire in the living room. I rushed to the kitchen sink, filled the soup pot, and threw it on a basket of kindling and newspapers burning next to the fireplace, quenching a small portion, flames zipping across the rug, this was my first fire, I could not think of anything but water, running for more, dropping the pot mid-way, adrenaline-super-charge elongating time, I flew the flaming rug, took the stairs in threes, gently plucked sleeping Boy so not to frighten, gliding down smooth, and next door into willing arms, a neighbor who already called the fire department and had come to see what was burning. I darted back, Steven was there using a throw rug, beating flames heading for the bookcase. I took another and did the same.

We sat coughing, triumphant on the porch when a fire engine in full siren and the Others came. My bare-feet had tiny burns I was too exhilarated to feel. Steven's hair singed-off the right forearm, the side of his baby finger burned when the rug fringe ignited. Two firemen hurried inside, another checked us, offering oxygen. We gladly took the masks. Against advice we did not go to the hospital, burns minor to us and the house, we had kept the flames to the living room, Steven and me, I felt good and mighty and safe. The kindling basket and rugs we beat the fire with were charred, living room Persian carpet badly scorched, smoke mottled the stucco walls and ceiling, but damage to precious books, valuable paintings and furniture almost insignificant. The firemen made sure every ember was out, applauding our cool-heads, saying there would have been much spoiled if they had to use the hoses, pin-pointing the source to a lit cigarette thrown into the fireplace that rolled-out, lighting newspapers in the kindling basket. Every one in the house smoked, and none could remember tossing theirs on the way out. When the truck left, I put ice-cubes in a bowl, took Steven to my room, opened the windows, we cooled each-other's wounds till the heat was quiet. I felt close to, could have easily fallen for his modest courage, but would not fool my self or him, carefully keeping my emotional distance, letting the moment go, sending him un-willing to his own bed.

Early morning, Loretta's children and lawyers came to see, taking-out their rancor for each other on us, we must be out by tomorrow night or police would be called. Baby's Folks pleaded newborn with no place to go, Others an accident that could have been much worse, all falling on lawyer's ears. Eviction made perfect sense to me, we were suppose to be care-taking not burning down, I phoned my Sistas. Leda had gone North for her Mother's 50th birthday, Keely and Gretchen were anxious to have my help with the rent. I locked the sewing room door and laid down on soft cushions, my beautiful room, long wooden floor and good light, looking-over the garden with Monique and Loretta. Early evening, blisters scabbing, Steven and I took a stroll along the Boardwalk. Wanting to return his kindness, I offered a place to stay "I'm moving in to the MotherTruckers. You're welcome to land there too, for as long as you need". He smiled sadly "I'm leaving for my Folks place in Montana. There's nothing here for me anymore". Another page turning, emptiness inside, I missed Steven already and wondered would I ever get used to people coming into my life, and going.

With Monique and Loretta's blessing, I filled pillow-cases with bed jackets, nightgowns, slips, camisoles, shoes, buttons, fabric, slipped Monique's initialed sterling silver thimble in my pocket, thanked them for their loving tutelage, and quietly closed the sewing room door, leaving the Singer behind, and them still sitting side-by-side on the green cushions. Steven and I packed his car, walked to the newsstand for papers, read them over omelets at the Broken Egg, and said our good-byes as he drove me to Fairmount Avenue. I felt the same ambivalence with Josh, maybe Steven was one of the good ones, my heart knew he was not big enough, I would go through him, consume him, we would both be sorry.

The Littles' jubilation on my arrival sweetened losses as they took my things into their room and began planning my day around theirs. Gretchen and Keely were glad too, they bought a car for $100 and had only half the rent paid this month, even with government surplus food, there was shampoo, tampons, deodorant, growing kids clothes, shoes, phone bill, electricity, gasoline, laundromat, laundry soap, welfare did not stretch this far. In the morning I readied my collection for sale. Gretchen pleaded to wear them first, oh please just a few days delay, getting far too mad when I said no. Three long silk dresses, one with a matching cape so light it fluttered like birds wings with the slightest movement, two handkerchief dresses, one gourd-shaped long skirt and vest of silk neckties, six crocheted pot-holder string bikinis, two table-cloth halter-dresses. Owner gave his usual approbation "My customers eat your stuff up. These are really beautiful, the best ever. Keep 'em coming". A very good payday, $225 under-the-table, yet I felt torn and bleeding, for he was right, these were the best ever, and money could not compensate for never seeing my one-of-a-kind darlings again, strangers bought them, a few I caught sight of on the street, and they were gone, soon the money too, so what did I actually have, doing what I do best, working for my self, paying my own way. And paying more than my share of the rent, gave me legitimate access to the house, I needed room to work, the shed the only. Everyone helped clear and clean and decorate, doors made fine work-tables, I quickly settled into a groove, hunting thrift shops and yard sales for material, working day-light hours and playing with the Littles, who had become a symbiotic singular creature. And I waited.

Another well-paid collection, walking the Avenue of Diamonds for the Seattle Times and San Francisco Chronicle, I took them to the Catalyst over lunch. Opening the Chronicle Women's Section, Tara smiled from a full-page ad for Salem cigarettes, cavorting a street, fixed in mid-flight, smiling so Mary Tyler Moore, in a sleeveless white ribbed turtleneck sweater, A-line plaid mini-skirt, Salem in one hand, the other swinging a small white quilted-leather shoulder bag from its long gold chain, blonde hair tossed in the air. I was struck with the thought she did this just for me to see, and suddenly there was a golden brick road ahead of me and I knew my path. Smiling at Tara smiling, she did not smoke cigarettes, what an impressive fake, I thanked her for showing me the way must be genuine. Putting the paper down to eat my grilled-cheese, Cyrene had slipped into the chair across the table, grin overflowing her face, beaming, waiting to be asked. I loved her confident attitude, and feeling flush offered "I can buy you lunch". She was impatient "Thanks, maybe a beer". I bit "Okay, so who you fallen inlove with". Her giggle filled the room "Is it that obvious". Moving to the chair beside me she leaned close "Promise you won't tell". I nodded. She hushed "His name's Stanley Malville". My neck stiffened, oh shit, Gretchen heard from Delroy that Stan's wife caught him in their bed with a groupie named Goldie, threw him out, and soon as she could would be taking the new Baby to live in Washington, and that Stan moved-in with Goldie waiting for Pam to go, this was not some one to fall inlove with "I hate to be a bummer. Do you know he's married". Her eyes veiled, this was not welcome "Yeah, I know, and he's living with Goldie. I don't care about her or his wife, he loves me now". I barely knew Cyrene, and did not want to be a finger-wagger "Well, then good luck". The waiter came to our table, and she ordered smoked salmon, the most expensive thing on the menu. I knew she had a five-year-old Son, this should make her sympathetic to busting-up a family, and that she just broke-off with a drummer named Spider from the band Swifty Too Loose, some girls had a thing for guys who played particular instruments, making me think they were inlove with the instrument not the musician, Cyrene seemed smarter. We ate and drank a pitcher of Coors, speaking of every thing else till tongues untied and she revealed her subtext. What I had miss-taken for self-respect, on closer ear was thick-skinned will-full bravado, raped by an alcoholic Father who had abandoned her Mother when she was born, and sometimes came back unwanted into their lives, she dropped-out of high school senior year, and now on welfare, carrying the stigma and shame of raising an illegitimate, Stanley comes along with all the goodies guys have to offer, power, access, rock-star standing, the possibility of big money made him seem shining knight to her woes, she teetered on the edge of desperate, her bluster masking a cheap self-esteem, a bottomless sucking hollow that craved even vicarious worth, though it would be hers only by proxy and easily taken-away, she did not think she would ever amount to much, what man would want a girl who bore to her own brother, Stanley might be as close to the flame as she would ever come. Looking at her watch, Cyrene jumped to her feet "Oh damn, kindergarten's out. If you want, I'll give you a ride, it's on the way". I was surprised she knew where we lived, inviting her in to meet Gretchen, they were so alike, perhaps kindred-souls could succor each other. Next time though, she was late.

Solo, aching, maybe the only one of my kind, contemplating does life imitate art or art life. I leaned toward life imitating art, for mine seemed to happen as if predestine once I finished a collection, and my volition definitely counted in doing the work, and then coincidences coming close together, too close for coincidence, making the artist god, an imperative for good art or you were creating a nightmare. But mostly while working I wondered why some people were turned-on and others settled for less, why some came in lit from the inside no matter their circumstances and others were dim bulbs. I could not believe it was all nurture, the core of a person had to continue with them life-after-life or what would be the point of building character. My Little Brother was pig-headed and controlling but had some compassion. Big Brother inlove with his own face, every thing relevant only to his fragile ego, caring about no one but him self, never making solid human connections, and since I had become what he disparagingly referred to as one of those Women's Libbers, he did not know whether to sock me on the arm in a guy-thing or say you're pretty, neither generating good effect from me, he turned increasingly aggressive. And I had to conclude nurture could not influence a nature that was not willing, for my Brothers were raised by the same Parents, they must have come-in with programs already operating.

The Fairmount Avenue house was cheap rent, directly across Highway One from a mushroom growing factory, any Easterly carried manure-stink though the shed slats, so acrid my tongue could taste it, I would take my work to the kitchen and close the doors and windows. Keely nor Gretchen had any concept of creative concentration, disrupting mine without thought, wanting to recount even the humiliating details of their nightly escapades, wanting to borrow money for just one beer, confident some one would buy the rest, wanting my promise to stay home again with the Kids, forgetting I never went out, wanting to try on every thing I made. I loved watching them swan in my gowns and jewelry, Cinderellas, pushing to wear them to the Ball, oh please oh please, my no-can-do, they would accuse me of being mean, no fun anymore, and maybe they were right, maybe I was the grown-up, but these were my living, and they were far too care-less, prowling, bringing home indiscriminate lovers. often I heard them using my words in their ears, amusing me, for I was not using them right now.

Delroy regularly came to fuck Gretchen in the afternoon, he heard Andrew was slowly surfacing, that Erik was urging him to play jug and trombone again with One Hand Clapping. I wondered was Erik so wise and generous as to know how healing that would be for Andrew, or simply a selfish ploy to revive his own languishing dream, I wanted to believe both. Another solid payday, I walked by Colleen's, and on to Andrew's. Sitting on the porch stroking a hound he just rescued from the same pound that murdered Frodo. A full grown, 80 pounds, short-haired mutt, mostly white with well-place velvet-brown puddles, long lazy swaying tail and winsome grateful blue eyes, Jennifer was poetic justice, greeting me with a welcoming look, happily accompanying us through the Meadow of Scents to the beach. Shy warm smile, Andrew offered me a Cohiba, the small but steady twinkle deep in his eyes filled me up, life was budding in my friend once more. He had band practice. Walking home I stopped for a tall jar of green olives stuffed with pimento, two Cup-of-Gold candy bars, Hostess chocolate cupcakes, two bottles of Coke, and took a look going by Colleen's again. She and Erik, Joey and Cherry rented a two-story on Liberty Street, I stood infront a while, making sure she was the only one home before knocking. Pregnancy precarious, ordered off-her-feet much as possible, she was more than glad for company, and treats, we nibbled and sipped, almost a tea party, chatting in the shallows. Erik, Joey blew in before practice, before I could escape. Colleen said nothing to their brutal indignity at me being in their house. My hide never tough enough, I hoped it never would be, I had begun to think their vitriol more an homage to my influence, for I posed a terrible threat to the patriarchal canon governing their Ol'ladies behavior, because it did not contain me anymore, and here I was in their house, yes I was something for sure, but more kin to the Gorgon Sisters, Stheno, Euryale and Medusa with their dreadful visages and snaking locks, maligned and cursed likely for the same reason, hair not really snakes but dreadlocks, and I summoned their fearful specter, tall and proud and took my leave. Rumor began to circulate, I knew from who, that I was the dangerous ring leader of the local Women's Lib Movement, who hated men and was out to destroy the Band. I was the entropy that tears through an organized status quo, Ida Rose would say – *dangerous for who.*

By far the sweetest of diversions, every Wednesday afternoon I would take Lance, Robby, Scottie, and Ava who maintained she absolutely hated me, to lunch at the burger stand two blocks down. We would prepare, folding newspaper hats, painting faces in bright tempera, making wildflower necklaces and bracelets, and parade the street an eager extravaganza, ordering more burgers fries and shakes than could possibly be eaten, feasting at the outdoor tables till we could no more, packing the considerable left-overs home for Moms. These children were insight-full beyond their years and knew to leave me alone in the embrace of creative concentration, this pack of wild Otters, long as I did not wield age or rank, would not turn on me.

Ric was kind enough before closing-up Hydra House to send my tools, magic teapot, clothes, arriving April Fools Day with Leda, who was wracked from time with her Mother. We were all invited to Raul's annual April Fools party, the Girls excited to go. His behavior New Years at the Zyante ugly in mind, I would not be anywhere near him on purpose, reminding Gretchen's convenient memory loss. She shrugged me off, Delroy might be there, and seeing the velvet gown unpacked began her importune, after all I had promised she could wear it. I cared little for the dress anymore, and had my fun taking hours to honor the promise. Leda begged my tapestry gown. I said yes. Living in emotional limbo, content in worn bell-bottoms and tight t-shirts, Keely just wanted to party. I stayed with the Otters. We played tap-the-finger in the dark, and when exhaustion they willingly went to bed, and I put my teapot on to boil, lit candled and incense, stacked Crosby Stills Nash & Young, Dylan, the Moody Blues on the record player, and spread my jeweler's findings on the kitchen door-table, thinking how jeweler started with Jew, how Diaspora Jews were outsiders with constraints, often not allowed to use the banks, having to keep their wealth with them, making precious metal and stones into common objects, plates, cups, adornment. I felt awe and comfort looking back on 5531 years of unbroken history, seeing my self another jeweler in a long line, wondering if Christians had any notion of the civilized culture preceding their Messiah by 3560 years or so, if they even realized Jesus was a Jew.

One magnificent breast-plate complete when Keely drove in after 2AM, puking over the toilet she went straight to bed. Gretchen and Leda not home after four, I knew I should go get them, woke Keely for shambled directions, slipped Excalibur in my pocket, and lead-footed the cantankerous 1952 Plymouth Concord Sedan up Highway 9 to Boulder Creek. Spotting Joey's car on Bear Creek Road, long driveway full, loud stereo, I walked though Raul's gaping front-door not surprised to find Leda curled on a couch amid other catatonics. I shook her eyes open "Hey, where's Gretchen". She pointed to the bathroom and tried to get-up. Pushing the door open with my foot I stopped breathing, Gretchen looked dead, splayed face-down on the white-tile floor, arms trussed over-head in a leather belt, bruises burgeoning her porcelain bottom. Rolling her over, red lipstick smeared her mouth, leaning my ear close, yes she was breathing, undoing her arms, I took wrists and began towing her to the car. Unsteady, Leda took ankles, whimpering how stoned she got on opium, she couldn't do anything when Raul tied Gretchen and Luke held her, taking turns. She dropped Gretchen's legs in the dirt. Such grave weight I dropped her too, railing at Leda "Get yourself together right now or I swear I'll leave you both here". We stuffed Gretchen in the back-seat, Leda with her, and sped away. When Gretchen surfaced, I wanted to take her to County Hospital. She insisted going to her own bed and went back under. Burning mad I took her home, wholly disgusted picking these Maenads off dirty floors, warning Leda "You have to find something valuable inside your self and pay attention to it. Don't you see you're living down to the worst of your self. I love you way too much to watch you destroy your self. Gretchen 'll do it anyway, but you're made of better stuff. You need to start living-up to it or you'll be dead before I can take you to meet Ida Rose". She sounded broken "I know you're right, but I can't help it. You guys are the first real friends I ever had. I waited my whole life an still can't believe you like me. I just want to be where the fun is". I thought what fun is she talking about, this does not look like fun. Leda helped me put Gretchen to bed, and crawled in. I stood there in the dark-morning looking on these three beauty-full fallen angels who fly too low, folly, desperation leading to ruin, I could only hope it was provisional.

Too tired, to angry to sleep, I took the velvet gown into the kitchen for repair, never again could I wear it without seeing the lipstick smear. Just as the sun licked morning I heard glass break in the Little's room. Lance came running to me, keeping a brave face "Some guys broke the window". Too furious to be scared I picked the Louisville Slugger off the hallway floor, and finding Otters big-eyed in the farthest corner, collateral victims of their Mothers' karma, I assured soft and even "Don't worry Little Piggies, I can handle the Big Bad Wolf. Go on now, into the kitch-en". No time to marvel at their compliance, mist carrying a strong smell of shit and alcohol, Joey and Raul's snickering through the busted glass, these fucking narcissistic assholes coming here for more, assuming there would be no consequences, no repercussions, I slammed the Louisville on the sill, cracking both, missing Raul's hands not on purpose, frightening my self, thundering "God damn you fucking Dogs, get out of here or I'll fucking kill you". Raul fell back laughing and scrambled away, Joey too. I waited, car pealing, gravel flying. The Littles swarmed in, clapping,

496

cheering, dancing wild-eyed around me, broken bat pieces raised high, their new talisman of power. I did not want to frighten them again, but hyperventilating, heart banging, I fainted where I stood.

For a time I did not know where I was, Raggedy Andy under my head, Lance plying a sour wash-cloth to my face, Robby, Ava fanning with color books, Scottie lying on the floor holding my foot. These dear Littles, more grown-up than their opium-dreaming Moms, exalted me, Lance recounting me chasing the bad-men from Hydra with a steak knife, they offered me the pick of their beds in respect. And I considered taking the position, knowing full-well how they would delight in deposing me later, they were done-in too, I tucked them, taking tribute in kisses and hugs. Mayhem did not wake the Girls. An intense thirst for sweet, I drank the last bottle of Green River in the frig, and crashed onto the couch, headache splitting, arms heavy as stone, shoulder burning where I fell, considering how sanity was a matter of degree, how going this far beyond my self was dangerous, I walked through the insidiously sweet-smelling door of the Labyrinth once before when Nick had me down slapping my face, only blind-luck found me exit. I was stirring from California's implicit sunny promise, it was not enough when things like tonight happened, baby-sitting everyone did not feed what I craved, living a dangerous roller-coaster soap-opera not my idea of living. I needed to re-claim my own direction, go see Ida Rose, bring Leda if possible, no one here cared for interests but their own, maybe me too. And there was Erik's latest tittle-tattle, Shoshannah lives with three women, doesn't sleep around, she must be a Dyke, and we hate Dykes because they do not need men. And the weekly job driving one of the Girls to County for an anti-crud shot, the cost for what they called freedom way to high, way too pain-full to continue witnessing, free-love as revolution or liberation was a fraud they swallowed without ever considering the price, even Keely who knew better. Perhaps the tired old darkest hour comes just before dawn was true, but that did not matter now, I was giving-up on something being here for me. Tara's picture in the Chronicle resolved my path, this terrible night set the schedule, if fucking and drugs were enough I would stay, but when this collection was done, I would use the money, pay a months rent, or two, and go home.

Chapter Twenty One

TYGER TYGER

Two notable San Francisco musician's had settled in Santa Cruz after a three-month gig at the Shutters Restaurant in Carmel, Delroy was playing a one-night collaboration, the show sold-out, Gretchen flirted Stoney into taking her along. He was running their sound board, and came by after sound-check, just as I presented her with the mended velvet gown. Delighted by my generosity, she stripped infront of us, put it on and twirled the front room "Is this just for tonight. Oh please, can I keep it". So resilient, showing no obvious damage from Raul's, I had to marvel at her acting skill, her hungry optimism "It's yours sweet heart, to keep". She rushed for an all-is-forgiven-forever embrace, taking us to the floor. Giggling I realized she could wear the dress without pang, no thought of the lipstick smear, she had not seen her own face, maybe doesn't even remember. Enjoying the show Stoney offered "Shoshy, come to the Gate of Horn with us". My ears went-up, acid-trip flash-back to the great Buddha Diabutsu at Kamakura bidding me seek the Gate of Horn elsewhere. I had planned on sewing, finishing, telling the Girls I would be going home to Seattle soon "Thanks, I'd love to". Gretchen took me to the bathroom, painted my face, pull my hair into a high ponytail, and pulled my living dress over my head.

The marquee read - Grand Opening - The King and I - formerly the Gate of Horn - tonight only - Delroy Bogave on guitar - Lorenzo Biancalana drums - Corbett Hawkins keyboards. If Gretchen hadn't flirted him-up, if Stoney used the club's new name instead, I would not have come. If, if if, augur of long anticipation, I hesitated taking Sweet Sister Clotho's hand, realizing Gretchen, Leda, Keely were my Sweet Sisters Fate incarnate, and maybe Lachesis Atropos and Clotho were flawed as their human counterparts, and maybe it was all coming from me. Stopped at the door, Stoney explained to skeptical toll-master we-three really were with the band, our hands reluctantly stamped. The room rowdy sardines, smoke-curls of weed floating, dance floor empty as we crossed to waiting chairs behind the mixing board, Santa at the bar. All the little fishies flapping and squealing as the band took the long high stage. My eyes saw only the keyboard player, taking his position behind a Spinet piano on the right-hand, Hammond B-3 the left, foot-peddle bass, his beautiful face shining, a welcome inundation, I knew I would know, this one was definitely big enough for me, and oh shit a musician, over-blown fragile ego, handled in alcohol and drugs, the headache and heartache of falling for a boy who never grows-up, getting more so with age, his life always prime, and the sloppy clandestine trysts, complication, exasperation, humiliation, this man was not these. Elastic-time lingered abundant, space disappeared, his eyes found me looking quickly down to my bag for a cigarette, those only eyes, a blaze of blue-intellect, golden-brown eyebrows, splendid English nose, grown-out haircut, freckled Irish skin, thick mustache and long side-burns framing a clean-shaven chin, and best of all, green stay-press pants, starched blue-and-white pin-striped dress-shirt, button-down collar, and green boat shoes, he did not need to be cool. Time, space gave way, another layer showing through, I saw him in silk top-hat and tails, the Ring-Master opening with the *Tennessee Waltz*, just piano, so brave, so beyond cool in this ultra-hip club, so totally out of context for this crowd shocked to silence, the Waltz becoming the *Wabash Cannonball*, metal-wheels from burning drums, tracks a screaming guitar, every one jumped aboard the speeding train, I leaned close to Gretchen's ear "Wow, the keyboard player, I would take him home with me". Concentrating her lure lure on Delroy, she turned to look at Corbett and licked her lips "Me too". The little Lamia, what I wanted she wanted, I sat back, sorry I confided, personal rules forbid me competing for a man, and even if I wanted to, I could not with the likes of Miss Fetchin-Fine, she had no rules, allowing her things I would not do. Her men, other than Delroy, lasted maybe two weeks, if she could beguile Corbett, I thought let her, get it out of the way, she could have him as long as it lasted, and if it lasted, he was not who I thought he was. Leaning again I pushed-back "This mean you're done with Delroy so I can have him". Her face went dark confusion "But he's married". I taunted "And you were planning to fuck him till he didn't want any one else. Why can't I". Shooting me daggers she resumed her thrall on Corbett. I closed my eyes, taking his genius version of *Chantilly Lace* into my heart.

Delroy closed the set with a solo frying everyone to the walls. He and Corbett came to the mixing board table. I wanted to run and could not move. Delroy took the chair by me, putting his arm round my shoulder in friendly squeeze. The game was on, Gretchen bristled, turning her eyes to Corbett who sat the other side of Stoney, arching her back ever so obviously, lips pouting, nipples too, looking down at them, then up with her eyes, curling hair around her finger, lure lure. Corbett seemed oblivious, talking sound with Stoney. My heart swelled at the reedy low timbre of his voice, I could do nothing more than ask Delroy for a smoke and wait for a light. He grinned, seeming to enjoy the game, struck the match and whispered "Hawk's a great guy. He doesn't have a girlfriend". Delroy knew this was important to me, but was I that obvious, red neon, more alive than in so long, and terribly vulnerable, I did not dare look at Corbett for fear naked lonely showed in my eyes, maybe too raw, too needy, I held them on my hands, wanting to run, scream, tear my clothes off, unable to move. The more he overlooked Miss Fine, the more her back bowed, lips like a fish, while ardent fans approached Delroy one-by-one, with albums, arms, clothing to autograph. Waitress brought Corbett a tall beer. He gulped it fast as drummer Lorenzo put a hand on his shoulder "Break's over Champ, come on, let's go get 'em". He stood six-foot-two, I caught my breath, our eyes touching for the first time, and I knew him to his core, a shy grin spreading across his wonder-full face. Delroy smiled "Corbett Hawkins, this is Shoshannah. You know, I don't know you last name". I looked-up at Corbett, hardly enough breath to say "Leibofsky". He reached for my hand. I gave it to him. His soft and big "It's my pleasure meeting you Shoshannah Leibofsky". We looked down at the same time, unable to stand the intensity, the exposure. I murmured *"What immortal hand or eye dare frame thy fearful symmetry"*. Bending his knees, facing-to-face "I couldn't hear you". I took deep breath of him, the sweetest ever "My pleasure too Corbett Hawkins". Delroy stood and winked at me "Come on

Hawk. Let's do this". Hands lingering letting go the other, I watched him take the stage, settle behind his instruments, and I was scared to death, wanting to cry and scream and laugh and pee and throw-up all at the same time. The set opened with *Honky Tonk*. I could not sit, burning in red hot neon, some guy asked me to dance, I never did with strangers, took my bag, followed him to the dance floor and went on out the door. Glorious Luna clear and golden, I took a full breath, gathered my self while she walked me home.

Slipping in bed with Leda and Keely, still to excited to sleep, their even-breathing, soft warm bodies my tether. How could I know someone so completely in one look, how unexpectedly thrilling, how absolutely witless to flee without a word, leaving Gretchen with her high-beams on him. She was not home when morning lit. I showered, and feeling new-born, weightless, purposed, took all my finished work, and the bus into town. Owner paid what I asked, all my things already sold, he wanted more. Then to the Smoke Shop for Cohibas, bakery for half-dozen maple bars, and then by Colleen's. She was sitting in a rocker on the porch, waved me come, groaning, shifting in her easy chair, ankles bloated, blotchy rash checkering her arms and neck, looking far more pregnant than she should. I opened the donut box and placed one in her hand. Laughing like a naughty child she took a huge bite, uumming, ooing, breathing hard though her nostrils, switching hands to lick maple from her fingers. I told her of meeting Corbett, how I could not sleep. She knew him only by reputation, Erik and Joey had nothing but good to say, and were trying to get him and Lorenzo to join One Hand Clapping, she thought I made an excellent choice. I knew it was mostly the Sweet Sisters not me. We finished every gooey glob of thick icing stuck to the box, two for her, two for me, two for the Baby. Struggling to her feet, asking me in for peppermint tea, Erik drove-up, and she sat down heavy, taking a resigned long inhale, exhaling all the way, she just looked at me and shrugged her shoulders. I wanted to scream, god damn it your silence makes you complicit, bit my lip, didn't look at Erik passing on the stairs, he could not restrain hissing "Bitch".

Taking Riverside over the bridge, I saw a little dirt trail down to the San Lorenzo River, followed the bank to the beach, fuming, men never thought about swelling-up like Colleen, and our Mothers waxed romance and ecstasy over giving birth, conveniently, maybe deliberately, maybe naively leaving-out the agony, they bought into getting married, having babies as the best of all possibles, the end-all be-all of our lives, as if we were primarily wombs. Sitting on a driftwood log, gleaming white sand beach to my self, I lit a smoke and counted my earnings, 260 dollars, hoping this would exorcize the looping, what I should have said to Erik's poison, two-hundred-and-sixty-dollars, proof I could do something people wanted to pay for, fuck him and his fucking problems, making me the excuse. I closed my eyes and let the sun shine my face, enjoying ebb-tides thundering hush, what should I do about Corbett, run flashing bright in my brain, go home a while, talk to Ida Rose, he's a musician, I promised never again, my heart singing above reason and promise, feeling something boundless, maybe his boundless, maybe that's how big enough feels. I was scared of losing my self in happily-ever-after if I did not run, some distance, Bonita-Kay taught me things look different with distance.

Walking East Cliff, wishing to see Frodo, into the cul-de-sac, onto the porch, in such a whirling daydream I smiled and said hi to Luke busting by out the door, catching him so off-guard he smiled saying hi too. Andrew was up for a cigar walk. I did not mention Corbett, just grinned and offered a Cohiba. Jennifer lead us through the Meadow of Scents, we followed her gently swaying body down the shore, small-talking music and art. An hour, and again we followed Jenn though the Meadow, my ping-pong head resolving, go, stay, no go, no stay, go, stay, go, if this connection was so unsubstantial that taking time to think would dispatch it, then as Doris Day sang - *what will be will be.* Using Andrew's phone to call my Folks, they had closed a deal to purchase Chicken Valley, a retail fresh poultry store at the Pike Place Market in downtown Seattle, were beyond happy, their chance had come to be employers not employees. Dad asked me to come home, give them a needed hand getting things off-the-ground. I had to say yes, it was settled. And as though designed by some extended part of me that blazes the trail ahead, while we sat on the porch drinking cold beer, Andrew gave me the way home. Jamie from Eugene had come by for me, he sent him over to the MotherTrucker's house, asking in earnest "He sure looks like Jesus. You think he could be". Laughing I kissed his cheek "No, I promise he's not Jesus".

Hurrying home, content to find Jamie under Leda's electric-blue spell. He hugged me tight. Noting Leda wilt, I whispered in his ear "I met someone". He whispered "I think I just did too". I giggled "So what do you think of the fabulous MotherTruckers". Leda perked-up and I caught her eyes "Jamie and me are just friends". Her face lit a million watts. Keely came-in the front door, Littles trailing with bags of welfare food. Lance put his on the floor, pulled a chair to the frig, climbing, opening the freezer for popsicles, stopping when he saw Jamie, leaving the door open, leaping off, eyes glued to Jamie's face, sidling, looking in wonder "You're just like the Jesus lamp on my Gramma's mantle". Leda laughed at the truth of it. I could tell Lance was not kidding. Keely's face darkened as she handed-out popsicles to the Otters. I knew her fear of God's omniscient omnipotence every time I spoke of Him in what she called dangerous irreverence, and could not help my self "Well then Jesus, how about turning popsicles into wine". Squirming, she sneered at me. And I asked Jamie "Your timing couldn't be better. I'm not trying to hurry things, but when're you going North". Leda looked down at his replied "Tomorrow. Spring break's over, and I've got classes in three days". It sounded like a final tumbler clicking in place "You mind if I come along". Jamie smiled "No. Sure". Keely's voice had a sharp edge "You're leaving. You just paid most of the rent". I decided to keep Corbett all to my self "Yeah, I know. I have to go home a while. My Folks bought this business and I'm going to help 'em open it". Lance protested "But you can't go. We need Wednesday burgers". I sat on my heels, eyes-to-eyes "Yeah, I know. I promise to come back in a month". His face hardened "Cross your heart and hope to die, stick a needle in your eye". Not waiting for my oath he screamed "I hate you. Who's gona buy burgers". My worth to him so refreshingly simple "Me sweetheart. I'll leave some money with your Mom". Stomping his feet, roaring frustration "No. She'll just spend it. I hate you. It's not fair. I hate you". He bolted outside so I could not witness the tears.

Jamie and Leda took the bedroom early, singing springs telling tale. Gretchen still not home, again I could not sleep for thinking, somewhat reconciled knowing this time I would come back, packing light, I folded my sewing shed into boxes, sealed a five-dollar-bill in 5 envelopes, dated them consecutive Wednesdays, and while Lance slept, stuck them under his pearl-handled Colt 45 cap-shooter atop the dresser, he was right, Mom would just spend it. Gretchen not home in the morning. Keely, the Littles angry at my going refused good-bye. Leda drove us to Ocean Street, where Highway 17 meets Highway 9 out of Santa Cruz. Jamie promising to come back on Summer break, and she to Eugene. The ride was seamless, delivering an air-conditioned Cadillac Eldorado to a dealership in Eugene, a short-haired Freak took us all the way, we smoked his dope, sang to the FM stereo, traded driving, hit the Wolf Creek Café for zuzus without incident, a good sign. And as we took our packs from the trunk in Jamie's driveway, Mr.Freak queried "I know this sounds nuts, but are you Jesus". Jamie smiled "No man, I'm not. Thanks for the ride". I stayed the night, sleeping on-and-off, incessant mind, skeptical, was running the thing to do, maybe I should go back. Come morning, I boarded the Silver Dog to Seattle. Dad came for me.

Her Little Girl apparently healthy and thank God not pregnant, we sat around the dinner table, Mom waiving her usual inquisition, filling me on meatloaf, baked carrots and potatoes, and my Brothers' shiksa girlfriends, and Granny's Seventh Day Adventist boyfriend, a square-dancer who believes Jesus second-coming and the destruction of the world are near. Dad, talking expectations and concerns for their new business. Reluctant to speak of a love-life since Nick, I could not help let Corbett Hawkins escape my lips, immediately wishing I had not. They exchanged those looks, and their worries and deep-seated prejudice spilled out, life was hard enough, especially when you have kids, why make it harder on them with a mixed marriage, I would always be an outsider to his Family, they will eventually call me a dirty Jew, look for my horns, and came the mantra fathers give daughters, why buy the cow when the milk is free. I wanted to scream what's wrong with you people, can't you see I am not a cow, I have a brain and I'm never going to marry, never have kids. And I understood, like Rachel, my Folk's were first generation, their fears closer to the Holocaust, they surrounded themselves almost entirely with their own, while I had pushed-out, made friends with White people, and knew instantly because of the crap-o-meter in my gut that went ding ding ding ding ding, who hates my kind, Judenhaas, and who doesn't. I protested, Jews of all people should know better than to practice prejudice, and speaking to their unspoken concern, I had learned my lesson well, Corbett was not Nick, and they were already making conclusions when I did not know he was the one, that I would respect their wisdom only after they met him, and bet when they did, that they would approve, heartily, shaygetz or not. We all backed-off and ate slices of Mom's sugar-free lemon-drizzle poppy-seed cake, the bitter under-taste of saccharin impossible to cover completely. With a long exaggerated yawn, I excused to my room. This cozy childhood haven, I stood looking at my self in the long plate-glass mirror back of the door, thinking nothing but fashion changes in the Golden Ghetto, dogmas are too uncompromising, society too closed, genteel camouflage, above suspicion, the very air anathema to intuition, originality, here I was again, the players walking and talking as if I am exactly the same as I used to be, and though I learned something about my self always remains the same, this Humpty Dumpty had fallen off the wall *and all the king's horses and all the king's men couldn't put* me *back together again*. I had discovered the way was not all an ego choice, that I had to trust the Sweet Sisters, trust my karma, try not to build any more bad. And I learned some of what I would fight for and would not, and maybe just maybe I met some one. The last time I slept in this room I could not have imagined friends I would make along the way, and the really awful people. My way was going okay except for this running away thing, leaving Gretchen Fetchin-Fine free to enchant Corbett, I stretched-out on my extra-firm queen-size mattress like a corpse, waiting for morning, this room frozen in time, wishing Mom and Dad would turn it into a business office and let me grow-up.

Mom reluctantly lent me her car for the day to go visit Ida Rose. Driving Crescent Avenue, there she was kneeling in the dirt, and I was again struck by this woman's modest nature. Her face lit on seeing me, saying I was the answer to her prayers, they told her someone would come help finish planting boxes of tulip bulbs finally arrived from Holland, that must be in the ground at once if they were to bloom this year. I was happy to help her do anything. The soil rich and well-worked, we were done in half-an-hour. Tools put away, washing our hands in the kitchen sink, Ida Rose asked "Lamby, I see you have a car, would you have time to take me up the hill to the QFC. Some new students are coming for dinner and I would love to make the lamb-chop recipe in this months Gourmet magazine.

You're welcome to stay too if you like". The heady privilege being in her company and more brought tears of pure joy, I did not want to load the moment with them and bent to tie my shoe "Sure I will, I have time. And yes, I'd love to stay for dinner. You know I try not to eat animals". Nearly always taken by carnivores as a personal rebuke, they turn defensive, but Ida Rose had an exquisite lack of intellectual prejudice "Well then Little One, I'll make you potatoes mushrooms and peas, and fresh fruit for dessert. How's that". Oh shit, what a presumption on her menu, I ate Mom's meatloaf and should have just kept my big mouth shut "I'm really sorry Ida Rose, I don't want to be a bother". She placed her hand lightly on my cheek, looking in my face "You're no bother at all Sweet Child. Quite the opposite. I want you to remember, insufficient protein will drive the soul from the body. Be sure you learn how to combine your food to get all the necessary amino acids. Mushrooms and potatoes together make up a complete protein". She hurried upstairs for her billfold.

On the way up to QFC I thanked her for answering my letter. She said her work had been tremendously rich since last we spoke, that she had written a letter, a compendium of the latest audits to her student Wyatt, and would be happy to give me a copy. She explained "Through these audits I have come to understand my cold rayed students. The cold rays being *aspects of personality, latent frequencies of thought and action based in the plasma of life and light which are innately intelligent, threads of God's mind reflecting his very facilities, that endure because they are genuine. These cold rays comprise the very fabric of intelligent life, they lie hidden, latent and undeveloped until minds with freedom to do so make use of them. And those moved by these cold frequencies, harmony, rhythm, brilliance, persistence, precision, perception, ingenuity, spontaneity, bloom, justice, compassion, adaptability, faith, hope, charity, radiance, joy, temperance, agility, integrity, understanding, service, patience, determination, perseverance, courage, faithfulness, diligence, mercy, endurance, sincerity, ethics or ethos, benignity, and whimsy,* they are the future. They have demonstrated more ability to understand the new information and act in new ways, while those on hot rays, *love - to care protect and nourish, truth - to tell, beauty - to attract, power - to do with a capitol D, and wisdom - the organizer and learner that formulates the resources,* have been corrupted by the dynamics and exclusivity of those rays, *selfish beauty, arrogant power, insolent wisdom,* these contaminated the hot ray spirits. Beauty became the overt sexuality of a Marilyn Monroe, truth and wisdom the emphasis of conquerors whether military, economic or religious, love for possessions, and life and light - creation was by light, and everyone participates in life and light, these two hot rays are common to all living things. Life and light are the very plasma of the cosmos, and though not available exclusively to individuals like the other five hot rays, are terribly exploited by science, medicine and business. The hot rays depend on negative power, Machiavellian might, Mafia-type power that rules for its own personal interest instead of serves. And because of the misuse, nearly all hot-ray spirits have been lulled into a decadent sleep, grown unable to absorb the consciousness of General Semantics, strayed-off the path so far, and become lost. Where as cold ray spirits stayed true, learning to think for themselves and discriminate, eating General Semantics up. As for your rays, I have never known anyone on the charity ray to succeed in saving it from turning negative. Charity is too easily seduced, giving itself away for any reason, often casting its pearls before swine. It's simple to think charity should be right and good in any situation, but without discrimination, it fails again and again. If it doesn't learn when to give and when to withhold, it turns negative. Charity for charity's sake is a fool's game. As for your other rays, faith and hope, they are not tough enough allies in the battle. Courage and perception would have been more helpful". She explained *"This solar system was a school, a cosmic school for Galactics to learn to cope with substance. For they were just emerging from the Hydrogen Era, a cohesive but outmoded system, a vehicle too introverted and subjective to handle evolving life. For with all its faults as seen in the world, this Carbon Era of heavier form could help build intelligence in its people. So Galactics might have traveled 'down' the Cabalistic path from Saturn to Earth. At Saturn they might have learned to know denser form, then to Jupiter on the path of mercy to learn about law and order, then back to the path of severity to Mars to learn about strength or even force, then to Venus to learn about the artistic and esoteric, back to Mercury to learn to build mind, and through Yesod - the Astral, to Earth - Malkuth, to live in bodies. But they were not to be of flesh and blood like Earth's Adam-man, but of a more gossamer fabric, and the chemistry of any one place would affect them but little. Nor did they need to experience death. This Earth environment as it is, had to be subtly adjusted to the particular needs of Adam-man. Then souls had to be given so that man's experience could be recorded on something that would not die, but carry the impressions and facilities and talents from life to life. Another system of evolution, actually. A system within a system. The recurrent theme of many philosophies including that of Plato and the New Testament is that man is compounded of a lower perishable organism and a higher indestructible vesture of spirit, with an intermediate principle of soul linking them togeth-er.* And so the Christ Conscious gave out souls. And the White Brotherhood, who reveled in mischief and misery, handed-out rays for those souls in combinations that were intentionally incompatible, intrinsically polarized, that could not support each other. They vicariously enjoyed the struggle that more often than not defeated the soul". I desperately wanted to say something smart, who was this White Brotherhood and Christ Conscious, and why, who gave them the right to hand-out souls and rays and play such an insane game. I knew she was right about giving charity without withhold, feeling the depth of repeated disappointment fully for the first time, the defeat of a ray that always goes negative "I don't care how weak charity is. It's mine and I'm going to learn to use it positive". Ida Rose's smile warmed me down through my toes "I know you work hard Little One. With determination and courage and perception, I think you might just be the one to save that charity ray. It would be nice to take it into the New Age with us".

Walking the grocery store aisles, she continued "Christ is *the living presence of the cosmic intent,* and through consciousness Jesus became the first fruit. The first capable of walking in grace. What the Cabala calls the middle path of the Redeemer. Where as only the paths of mercy and sever-ity had been available, he set us a new middle path to go home. The gray between the black and white". She laughed "He looked God in the eye and God blinked. Allowing us to withdraw the projection, become con-scious. Jesus graduating opened the Books of Life for all to read. You kids, you young students on cold rays, you are the proof". This was way beyond what I could absorb "What are the Books of Life". She looked pleased "You see Lamby, when Yahweh breathed life into his creation, he installed his own private telephone line, the unconscious, so he could speak to us without our knowing. Humans are influenced and manipulated by this vast unconscious drama being played out under the surface in each of us. A drama until recently only hinted at in fairytale, mythology, religion, poetry, science, alchemy. Hidden knowledge, the ability to discover our unconscious patterning, consciously reflect on it, affect our own behavior, inaccessible until the game was exposed by Freud, Jung, Neumann, Whitehead, Korzybski. And through my auditing, tapping the unconscious consciously, discovering the truth of that tragedy at Palestine. For Jesus came to give us a message of transformation, and General Semantics is part of the road map, a schematic for understanding the influence of the unconscious, how to initiate discriminating behavior, walk the path of the Redeemer. Through auditing, knowledge of the earth experiment, its purpose, you see we were up against fallen Gods, the Christ Conscious and White Brotherhood, all with rampant free will and no responsibility or consequence. Understanding what makes us tick, well enough to make our own map instead of automatically following Yahweh's, or any God, ultimately allows those who will do the work, an opportunity to study the Books of Life, the human map, their own map, and follow Jesus in transforming a circular closed-system into a spiral that ultimately leads home. Have you noticed the subtitle of *The Pink Elephant* is *A Challenge to Confusion - There is a Way Out*". She said firmly "This has never been a battle of physical strength or fitness as Machiavelli and Darwin believed, but a battle of wits. And Jesus is the way out, the first to wire-tap Yahweh's private phone line. It's been my experience that cold ray spirits are more free, more willing and capable of doing the work, and the hot-rays want others, slaves if need be, to do it for them. Some of my older students wanted me to start a church, like Hubbard, so they could stop thinking and follow a dogma, where as the cold rays understand no one can do the work for them". All hairs were standing on my arms, for one glorious moment I held the whole cosmic panorama in mind "I'm getting good wits". My eyes welled "That's what levels the playing field, right, learning how to think. I can't hold onto this whole thing for long, it's way too big. But I know for sure what you already passed on helps me make better decisions, makes my life better. And the more I get, the more I want". Her face shown on me like the sun "You're a brave soldier Shoshannah. You are proof to me the larger cosmos has gotten it, heard our pleas, stopped turning a blind-ear. You're not one of my old crowd who have hung around life after life and become complacent, but part of the baby born in travail, the Lords of Humanity. Rightful heirs to the New Age".

A sweet quiet accompanied us taking in groceries. We began preparing dinner. I told her of falling at first-sight for Corbett. She wanted to know what he looked like. And I gladly painted his wonderful face, shy intelligent eyes, freckled Irish skin, golden-brown hair, mustache and sideburns more red, his Clint Eastwood shoulders, grace-full gait, and those gifted hands, like giant tarantulas on the keys, and the underlying reality showing-through, a robust king dressed in silk top-hat and tails, his charisma shining. How familiar he seemed, how Gretchen wanted him too, how I ran. Ida Rose listened with real interest "He must be a gift to you for all your hard work. Recompense. A king would indicate spiritual protection from that dark half you left behind. Love is serious business Lamby. Running away only temporary. You need time to consider, and so does Corbett". This struck me right and true, dinner preparation done for now, and two hours till guests, I offered to clean-up while she washed her hair. Smiling, nodding she vanished upstairs. I felt normal here, seen, and though I could not always say what I thought, Ida Rose understood what I meant.

Winding brush rollers into spun-silver hair, bobby-pinning the first at her forehead, I pushed the pink plastic pokers into previous rollers not her head. And Ida Rose read me a letter from the Institute of General Semantics. She sent the Pink Elephant for review, and seemed to have expected this reaction, explaining the Institute had their darling, S.I. Hayakawa, however his book *Language and Thought in Action* had the Structural Differential, one of the main teachings of General Semantics upside-down. It was a glyph Korzybski created for the purpose of visualizing the many levels of abstraction, helping students learn to stop *pinning finite prejudice on infinite process.* She set that and other fallacies back on their feet in her book, the Institute did not appreciate the embarrassment and responded with censure and suppression of her work. I was puzzled how people who call themselves the Institute of General Semantics could act so contrary to their principles. Ida Rose smiled at me "Just because someone reads GS, are members of the Institute, doesn't mean they get it".

Hair combed-out to her delight, I laid the big mahogany table in linens, Lenox and sterling. She put the potatoes in to bake and set the lamb chops ready to broil. When the doorbell rang, I opened to a smart-dressed man in navy-blue suit and tie holding the hand of a woman in long brown velvet, my brain stopped at how much they looked like Howard and Lizabeth. Howard's familiar laugh suspended my disbelief, he glided over the threshold with an eager hug "Monty finally introduced us to Ida Rose". Lizabeth hugged us both "Wow, it's been what, three years. What a nice surprise". They looked so strait, but as with William in San Francisco, I felt a resonant reclaiming of some part of my longer self on seeing them again. Slipping her arm though mine Lizabeth whispered along the hallway "Nick went to trial in March. I heard he got six months for the bust, and five years probation. They sent him to McNeil Island Federal Penn". I insisted "Don't tell anyone you saw me, promise". She squeezed my arm "Promise. We don't see him anyway". My eyebrows knit on Howard. Putting hand over heart he pledged "Tell that jerk about you, no way". I helped Ida Rose bring the food. And it was delicious, as Lizabeth spoke of playing cello again with the symphony, and what a bright three year old their daughter they had. Howard was wholehearted on the proposed Twenty-Sixth Amendment, that if passed would lower the national voting age to 18, just how important that was for someone old enough to be drafted and die for his country, to be able to vote for or against the man sending him to die, and of his Father, who considered a Psychology Degree useless, and yet was still paying his way through the University of Washington. Ida Rose talked tulips. I briefly of William and Tara, wondering why we were having such chitchat, no talk of audits or General Semantics, feeling a selfish delicious satisfaction that Ida Rose did not endear them Lamby or Little One. We chased dinner with Coors beer, traded best jokes, and when Ida Rose began to yawn, she gave us mimeograph copies of the Wyatt letter, and we left. Standing outside, not knowing did they experience the same giddy elation that had now turn to indifference, I did not offer address or phone number. They did not either. Driving home, I was certain they would talk and Nick would find me.

Walking in my garden, suns and moons growing on trees, animals talking with each other, and me shining pure gold. I woke and turned-on the radio, 500-thousand people in Washington DC, 125-thousand in San Francisco marching against the War, Charles Manson sentenced to death, the Doobie Brothers album, and Boz Scaggs. Brunch-time I joined Mom and Dad around the table, hung-over and thank-full for Sunday. Nearing twenty-three years old, Mom thought I was fourteen and start-ed-in, why did I have to go get drunk, and with who. Leaving Lizabeth and Howard's names out, I told of dinner, and jokes, and the seventy-four year old woman they absolutely had to meet. Shaking her head like I was spinning-a-story, like I actually would hang-out all day with a 74 year old woman, more likely I went to see Nick or my dangerous revolutionary friends, Mom pointed her finger "I'll think twice before lending you my car again Shohannah". This made me sad, how could I possibly tell them about Ida Rose, I said no more. Chicken Valley was tomorrow morning, the grand opening put-off some weeks while we learned what and how much. Dad decided to keep the woman who had been there two-years, give her a raise, and she would teach us to cut the birds and rabbits, but the place had not been kept clean enough, business had gone bad, and we would have to work hard to win trust and stomachs, he was confident with the help of his children, Chicken Valley would be a success. I was thrilled for them, this was a big deal, and promised to stay a month, sitting long as I could before headache took me to bed with aspirin, a large glass of orange juice and some of the Sunday Seattle Times. Looking for news of the Seattle Seven, there was none, but pages of lingerie ads, slim women in girdles, most now wore the panty-kind, daily, Mom too, only bad-girls jiggle and wiggle any part of their body in public. I put down the paper and unfolded Ida Rose's letter, the process of audits still beyond me, how some one could conduit information coming from I could not say where, and that information could ring so true.

Dear Wyatt,

Thank you for the beautiful bouquet you sent for Christmas. It was gorgeous, and lasted for days and days giving a wonderful scent throughout the house.

There is a cogent, consistent and complete picture of the Cosmos which I have gradually experienced but only one Beauty Spirit has been able to stand the story. Lamont *and his wife* Patsy *fell by the wayside years ago and she was once the best auditor of all. Only Curtis as an auditor was totally reliable because he had not axes to grind. But he ran audits exclusively for the Christ Conscious and hence was partly mistaken, for the Holy Spirit/Christ Conscious pretended to be on Jesus' side but was really a cheat and eventually left us all high and dry.*

The story is too intricate to relay in a singular audience. It would take several days and I am not coming back to Eugene ever again. I ran the Dragon down in his lair (to wit – Maynard, the arch enemy whom you must not think of as Maynard, but as Aristotle, Beethoven, Leonardo da Vinci) who had great stature but no integrity. He has always said he should have been the Messiah, as Jesus was "too naïve"!!!

And remember, he was St. Luke who aided and abetted Paul in killing off the early Christians, getting his information from the infamous Mary, mother of Jesus, who always called her "that woman".

Of all my early students, you were the most difficult and the most ill. I have been pulling your back from the jaws of death since your mother came to me with your first serious operation. What were you 16? You wanted beauty to be the center of your Cosmos and that automatically made you an adversary of the supreme ray of Jesus — love – which holds the rays life and light together as the basic plasma of the Cosmos. We were never out to cure people, not at any time. We were out to disclose what their warped thesis might be and show them up for the Greater Cosmos to understand. For the Cosmos itself was against us, and I am the only remaining one of my group who came to help after the Arch Angels failed. I alone wanted to halt the foolish cosmos with its ever-going expansion. A false thesis. As Carl Sagan said it could only end in black holes, super novas, and exploding stars with all the moisture on the earth at boiling point. That was the absolute truth too!

We only convinced the Holy Angels at Christmas of our terrible suffering which included quite a few of us for Maynard's spirit boasted to people that he had been up to Seattle "pestering Ida Rose" and he literally pulled my leg out of its joint, put scabs all over my back and face, the same scars left over from tortures inflicted upon me in incidents such as the life of Job. When I saw that play of Job in New York, I fainted dead away and went into hysterics and had to be taken out of the theatre so the play could go on. I have been tortured in almost every life on earth. When I was 30 and doctors had to take out most of my stomach, I ran a whole series of these tortures, one in India where they made me drink acid and burned my stomach out. I starved to death with a river-flood in China, died crawling around on my hands and knees trying to find a carrot in my garden.

Only with my cornering Maynard as the Dragon of Revelations who stood by all those centuries waiting to destroy the Books of Life which the unborn Baby would be able to read, and I am that woman in travail and the Baby was every one of you and each particular thesis. Jesus himself spoke to my inner self and told me what we were up against. Of course Maynard has always threatened me, to kill me, through the years he would say "My spirit is telling me to kill you while I can". Remember the second name of General Semantics is the Non-Aristotelian System. Lucifer also; incidentally, he came to an audit recently in Seattle and told me that he was an angel of light compared to Aristotle. And Lucifer did almost kill me one day, pulling on the silver cord which usually causes massive brain hemorrhages and I vomited for nine hours and suffered such pains in my head I became delirious and kept asking who I was!!! This suffering has extended to everyone who has ever known Maynard. Perhaps even yourself. For the last three months especially. He has most recently struck at a valve in my furnace so I had no heat for ten days. In his human career he is primarily a valve engineer for the Eugene Water and Electric Board, that is his specialty.

Remember I am only saving two of the disciples. The others all came and were dismissed in no uncertain words by their own audits. I am saving Thomas, because he was Benjamin Franklin who saved Jesus' experiment – America! Even your wife as Marie Antoinette, sold her diamond necklace to buy John Paul Jones a ship to fight the embargo and the British Navy so Washington had the arms and medicine for war. And I am saving Judas Iscariot, of all people, because he paid his karma down to the last farthing and remembered every word he was ever told and has acted on them. Legend has it that Jesus preferred him and he has been with me or around me in many lives.

Only the last three months have the Angels of Heaven joined my lonely spirit to turn back the expanding Cosmos, heal the breach which lay between the Great Father and his Cosmos. I told everyone as Omar: Pray not to the inverted bowl we call the sky for it rolls on just as impotently as you and I.

The whole Cosmos hung in the balance. Many brilliant people have kept coming to me though the Seattle years and they stay as long as I will let them, usually three or four hours and they get the message loud and clear. But any thesis diametrically opposed to love has no chance of even hearing it right, none at all. They will have to pick it up when they are taken somewhere and cleaned up. I am the last of the Doppelganger, the "Ghostly Double", the killer, one of many but the only one who stayed alive and active. The only one who could take the terrible punishment where even Angels and Fallen Gods were up against us. Some of my deaths were so terrible they had to put sides on my bed for several days after my stomach operation, sodium pentothal brought back the whole digestive-stomach chain of deaths and sever pain so terrible I blocked them out again, gone!!

Wyatt, Lamont ran a whole series of his lives with such agony and such suffering he fainted, then said he had never been to my house. His wife Patsy who had watched him, and other persons described these episodes and we allowed him to read the audits and he asked how anyone could do this, and now he has wiped them all out again, says they never happened. He has high blood pressure of course of which he may die at any time. If you think you have seen insanity, you should have watched from my station. Your audits were honest enough but you could only see them though your thesis. True of everyone, that is why the stories were so conflicting. But I did not stay around Maynard to help him, but to uncover the steps he has taken to confuse our work so the Baby could not be born who would read the Books of Life. The main students you have never seen. They are here and around the world, People like Dr.Zygmunt and his wife Dr.Margaret Zygmunt of Cornell who came here for a short time to my house. And Marietta Chicorel, top library publisher in the world, who did over the Library of Congress. Those on "cold" rays ran the only true audits. The "hot" rays will be gone forever from the Cosmos. No one will ever, in the Democracy of the New Age, be certified exclusively on these hot rays and especially beauty, which has to be sustained by a power structure of wisdom, power and truth. That is why you were with your father and his evil rays. He represented the background structure of negative power wisdom and truth and was telling you he had no intention of being a background for your beauty ray so you began the long trek of paying karma which has lasted for about fifty years. I know how agonizing this is for an organism. I, too have paid endlessly for my spirit's thesis, in torture in almost every life. But my thesis was positive towards love.

I appreciate your loyalty, Wyatt, *but it took far more than that, which has been given by many persons here who are available to me in droves. These are all young, freed to act and on clean cold rays such as precision, perception, integrity, faith, ethics, ingenuity, etc, etc,*

The only power spirit I saved was my husband Doctor Barber and he only tentatively and over some long periods of time and evolution. I'll save no wisdom or truth unless it might be Edison who is a brilliant young student whom we have watched since before his birth. He is a genius now also.

I remember all those trips to you in Eugene and those audits some of which were wise and to the point and others obviously true in a philosophic sense and from a well-intentioned source, one who wanted a decent Cosmos and was a fine entity. But the work had been done here in Seattle through cold ray entities and it is correct most of the time, no human knowledge is correct, we look though the glass darkly with only a small slit of light and sensation.

Another aspect which I have never had a chance to share with you was my own inner guidance which never let me down but cannot be used to maneuver the students or as a clairvoyant. That would never do, but when it deals with my family the information is infallible. Maynard began his final machinations last Spring saying I must die, reinforced by four other people. <u>That had to be</u>. It took me two months to put my yard, house, papers, estate in order and pass it on to my daughter. I read family papers going back three generations for ten whole days and destroyed three garbage cans full.

That spirit Maynard carries knew I would run him to the ground and so he thought he could fool me into dying, so he could live. He will never live to go on with me, I would not accept him. But he insists he has to see that I run the New Age properly, that only he is smart enough to know. It is unbelievable! But the Dragon had to be indentified and run to the ground, deleted or the work is not finished. That spirit will either die or be exhibited to eternity with the scars inflicted on Jesus, Job, etc., anything he caused. I suppose he was the wily Devil who got Lord Jehovah, Yahweh, a fallen Jewish race-God, to torture

Job in the first place. Remember that little organism of Maynard's suffered as much as anybody with his injuries from football with an ambitious spirit in a 147 pound organism pitted against 250 pound football players to appease his ambitions to be top dog.

Many wise people were kept from being religious by the story of Job — Carl Jung and Robert Frost etc. They said they could not accept a universe with that God and Job together. Job was better than his creator.

My message is not for the world, I am never going to be allowed to tell it, and even Jesus will have as his church but a few thousands, <u>words do not save</u>. The world would have lionized me and the Cosmos would have been lost, for the whole thing was at stake and we only recently have built a tunnel (my spirit with many Holy Angels) across the chasm around the Great Father, made because Maynard opened the doors of Chaos and filled the world with incomplete devils and threatened the throne itself. He wanted perfection for his Cosmos, a ray from Hell because it would have stopped all growth and evolution for the future. I want no recognition. With such points of view I do not respect mankind that much, they are nearly all too narrow to keep pace with the actual job which was done. It was beyond anything of worldly considerations whatsoever. It allowed Jesus to graduate, without which no one could have returned home. It was in recognition of truths we researched, remember, this work has never ceased and it involved scores of people playing for high stakes — their cosmic future always hanging in the balance.

No person whom you knew from the Portland era of my work was "saved". Walter was Caiaphas the high priest who crucified Jesus and burned his body. Neil the Centurion who actually burned the body. Wally foisted a false religion on the world as Swedenborg. Iris tried to defeat the whole early American experiment and get the Louisiana Purchase away from us for England. A rabid anglophile during the revolution. The list goes on and on. These people were all on "hot" rays, were called to suffer — Iris a bed-ridden addict for 30 years! They are centered in control of power, the antithesis of Democracy. The era of free will can never be anything but a Democracy.

Matthew 10:34 "I came not to bring peace but a sword. For I have come to set man against his father, a daughter against her mother — a man's foes will be those of his own household. He who loved father or mother more than me is not worthy of me. He who finds his life shall lose it, and he who loses his life for my sake shall gain it." Jesus was fighting to save the Cosmos itself not the world. These words make no sense for the world, nor for himself as a person. It was the "cause" and this is all I've ever followed or believed and why I had to die so terribly. The world is finally populated by cosmic brigands and pirates, even the animals are cursed, over half of them are poisonous to life.

Incidentally, I was not in the world at the time of Palestine. Tom as Gabriel representing the Arch Angels, and I representing my group stayed to watch over Jesus' soul when he passed else it would have been destroyed. Billy Graham knows this: I've heard him say that was the biggest concourse of Angels ever to gather in the Cosmos and the most significant occasion, a matter of life and death for the system. But then I know the metaphysical person in California who writes his sermons!

My daughter always insisted that Maynard was a phony. But who else did I have besides old Lucifer in Gordon? Your audits gave me no insight into the defects of the higher Cosmos. And finally my devotion to the cause won even the demon in old Aristotle to come over to my side, who while trying to kill me personally, audited the true picture of the Cosmos. You would have to be a Semanticist to see good doing evil and evil doing good, <u>that</u> insight the "hot" rays totally lacked because of their dichotomies, needing to see death in order to see life. And remember all this came through Maynard's later day audits, he has only run significance the past three years when the net began closing around him.

I am not able to "run" the time tracks of the cold ray spirits, Eddie and Curtis have to do that for me. Did you know Curtis gave up a fine career as a professor of language at the University of British Columbia to move here and work with me. That is dedication, the only hope I had for several years. No one whom you knew amongst the Portland students were even eligible to run significance for me, they were all on the "wrong" team, all off chasing rainbows of some fancy church where salvation would be delivered to them on a silver platter in spite of their cosmic defections. I think most of them are in Chaos. I know Iris and Margaret are, and they appeared to be two valuable and competent citizens! You should have heard what was said about them through their own lips (while they were running their past lives), not mine, I do not interfere. All

518

these people are children, too shallow to play the cosmic game. My new book - The Comedy and The Tragedy - is a re-telling of the bible and it says frankly that it is a detective story chasing down a terrible murder. Jesus died because of defects in the Cosmos itself, it should never have produced brigands, it was too immature to test its own intelligence. As Whitehead said it was "actually deficient" and it is redeemed only now because their flaws were identified for it to see, very reluctantly and only by the skin of our teeth the last three years.

The only religion the Cosmos has to offer is General Semantics as we are told. And not by Maynard, he cannot read it, neither can Lamont. *Where as these young cold rayed students can recite it page after page, it is their bible. That is my contribution to the world, open up your copy of A Challenge to Confusion.*

Love to you, Ida Rose.

I could only hold on while reading, the territory outer-space-big, and yet I understood, the Sweet Sisters Fate took me down the rabbit hole to Ida Rose's house, finding the big story back of the smaller, I was a cold ray soldier who got a peek behind the veil and met the war, bigger but so like the underground anti-war movement, and I had become part of this something beyond my previous imagination. The grandiose wonder of it all, I was in the game, this girl of little promise was in the game, and I felt so very far behind, though Ida Rose seemed to have confidence in me. I understood why Nick had to dismiss her as a mad-woman, if he accepted her story, he would have to pay *his karma down to the last farthing and* remember *every word he was ever told and act on them.* To have the Books of Life opened and not be able to read them would be the essential worst, living in the time and place and miss the moment, terrible. Ida Rose was absolutely right, I took her book with me, and when there was no one to talk too, would open and find a way into my self, her voice reading aloud in my ear, it was my bible. When I called on Yahweh's house after Grampa died, he was not there. And my believing a Father God would be there, come to my real need, the understood promise of religion collapsed, bottomless, and I fell away, wandering, disconnected, hoping for some true ringing, looking for something to believe. Dressing God in human qualities, creating Him outside no longer made sense to me, I had this new budding something to look-up to, aspire to, what I was looking for was not outside, and I was almost afraid to think it, I had become god, shining pure gold inside. When I was little, Yahweh had me by fear, and I tried desperately to believe He cared while monsters lurked in my room. He never showed Himself. I knew I had not created my self, did not believe I came from monkeys, and preferred being Jewish, beloved and despised people with such a true understanding of social justice, but I never honestly bought into the religious autocracy, my Dad was my Father not Yahweh, he was there for me, my Mom there for me, not Yahweh. I always suspected those Monsters must have known my bent, tried to break me, frighten me into survival soap-opera mode, too occupied in high-drama to think, and like the Christ Conscious and White Brotherhood, I always suspected the Monsters got-off on my anguish. Some kind of untouchable sturdy had come into life with me, unwreckable, and my Folks were so good to me, I never had to fight for my life with them. People often thought me arrogant, and I did too till I found-out near everyone was broken growing-up, no one had been true and good to them. I was more whole, which I finally understood seemed to the broken as arrogant, when it was actually confidence, I guess they thought it arrogant to have confidence. Maybe that's why I seemed to have time to think, while my Sistas made such dreadful choices. I had always been a soldier, always worth getting, and now the Monsters no longer lived or breathed in this room, Nick no longer ruled my life. I turned off the light and radio and did not sleep on top of the covers.

Chicken Valley, ten hour days, six days a week, constantly propositioned by pimps with wads of food stamps, buying only the most expensive, capon, rabbit, goose, duck, chicken breasts. I became a butcher for the Family business, chopping bird bodies, vital yellow fat and blood staining my starched white-cotton butchers-coat. First sharpen the blade, then separate the wing right there where its little shoulder bone attaches to body, leaving as much on the breast as possible, then pull the whole leg away from the body at the hip joint, detach it at the thigh, careful to take the oyster from the back, thighs weight more that way, disjoint it from the leg, slice the back away from the breast, and chop through the rib bones with a cleaver to complete dismembering. And then there was the river of people, gorging on broasted chicken livers, gizzards, hearts, parts, endless carnage crossing our sparkling clean counters, all done with a smile. We made the place gleam, smell good, the new improved Chicken Valley, serving up Seattle's very first taste of broasted chicken proved to be a smash hit. Mom invented our own over-night marinade and breading. Dad installed a fan to waft the mouth-watering aroma out into the market. And jostling, salivating, clamoring bird-eaters lined-up every day waiting for succulent body parts to come out of the broasters, buying fast as we could cook, before any made it under the warming lights in the showcase, the phone ringing ringing with orders we had to say no, Mom and Dad flying high on the adrenaline of success. Nightly I curbed an aching desire to phone the MotherTruckers, find out about Corbett and Gretchen, telling my self I would rather not know. Three Sundays in, Leda called from her Mom's, having flown in for her brother's Chiropractic School graduation, she would stay two night, all she could stand of her Mother, and wanted me to take her to meet Ida Rose. I phoned to find a house-sitter, Ida Rose was in Alaska for the weekend, her Granddaughter's wedding. Leda came to my house. And I restrained, while she told me everything, getting to Gretchen and Corbett, they'd gone on a date, Gretchen thought she found her ticket to the good life. Relieved to hear it was mercenary greed and not love, my heart slowly sank, for he might not recognize Circe, fall under her spell, become a pig. I told Leda I would be going back to Santa Cruz in a week, resolving no matter how my Folks wanted me to stay-on, needed me, I had promised one month, and they would have to forgive me for needing to live my own life.

One more long week, business had smoothed into comfortable routine, and Dad hired a young man. Excusing my self from Sunday Family gathering, Mom lent me her car without question, and I went to see to Ida Rose. She had a house full too and still invited me in. I shook my head "No thank you Ida Rose, I don't want to intrude. I can't stay anyway". She stepped onto the porch "Why of course Little One". I did not feel any hurry in her "I just wanted to come an say good-bye. I'm going to Santa Cruz tomorrow to see if Corbett's the one. And if not, I'm coming back here for good. Probably work for my Folks new business. There's no reason to be away if there's nothing for me in California but good weather". She smiled "Exogamy can be very liberating for a soul. You bring Corbett to see me when you come back. I know you'll be just fine". I didn't know exogamy and did not ask "You're always so generous with you time. I can't even find words to say how much you mean to me. Oh, and mazel tov on your granddaughter's wedding". Her face crinkled lovingly "Thank you". Before I could think I was hugging her. She stiffened only a little.

Though disappointed Mom nor Dad tried guilt-tripping me into staying. Dad understood it was their chance not mine. Mom had a good month to look me over, seemed content even if she did not approve-of or understand what I was doing with my life. Monday morning on their way to work, they dropped me on 8th and Stewart downtown. I boarded the Silver Dog with $1200 in wages, dozed through most of Washington, Oregon and the Sacramento Valley. Stepping-off the bus in Santa Cruz late Tuesday morning, I headed for the Boardwalk, shoes off, the waves heated on their long slide over hot sand welcoming my feet, sun glittering the robin's egg water, same color as the sky, eucalyptus on the breeze, I did have reason to return to paradise, it made me feel good. Stopping at the cotton-candy concession, I bought four wrapped in different colors cellophane, and hitched to the Fairmount Avenue house. Leda saw me though the kitchen window and shrieked, alerting the symbiotic cohesive singular creature that was the Littles, and they came flying-out the back door "Wednesday burgers is here. Candy cotton's here". Ava tried to be first by placing a strategic kick at the back or Lance's knee, missing she fell hard instead. Lance laughed wildly at her "Karma kickback, karma kickback". Robby, Scottie mimicking, wagging. I marveled at such a grown-up concept from Lance's young mind. Desperately glad to see me, Leda tried to stop candy cotton given into greedy grimy hands, grabbing me, marching into the kitchen to witness the bread massacre, complaining bitterly she had been left to baby-sit these monsters. I could see she made the fatal error, assuming she had authority and power simply because of she had years, where these whelps did not respect age for age sake, and took every possible opportunity and advantage. She had baked bread, setting loaves on the counter to cool, and while she showered, the kids tore open all three, eating the soft centers, leaving husks behind, and were stead-fastly maintaining a crazy man crawled in their bedroom window and did it. In so many ways these little Otters were already smarter than me, I had learned not to tell them what to do, for they would co-operate only because they loved and trusted and even admired and not because you had years. Leda was angry beyond any reason, seduced by the irresistible frictionless slide into unconscious high-drama, insidious because initially it feel so familiar, so easy, even pleasant, and so righteous, and then it's too late, you've already been sucked-over the Event Horizon into the land where youngers can also be elders and easily out-wit you, for unconscious wits are irrational and have more to do with instinct than brains and age, and in this land where Titans battle to the death, she was no match for a Firstling like Lance and his loyal band. I listened quietly and cleaned-up the massacre, so much anger in this house made me sad, a nasty battle waging between Leda and the Littles, she stormed on them, threatening big trouble soon as the Moms came home, sounding more her Mother than her self. Littles fled outside with their candy cotton. And I took the fat joint I stashed under shelf paper in the cupboard above the refrigerator and lit it. Sweet MaryJane induced mellowing, Leda settled on making more bread, and even bid us bon voyage as we trooped away for day-before Wednesday burgers.

Ava, necessarily precocious, frighteningly perceptive, began as soon as we left the yard, she liked Hawk just fine if he wasn't her Mom's boyfriend, but why should she like him if he was going to go away like all the others. It made her want to barf how her Mom hung all over him like she was his Little Girl. They went out two times, and her Mom had it all planned, talking about Hawk behind his back like he was a job she could get rich on or get fired. Lance raged how they were always left behind for some guy like his Mom wished he was never born, and how many spankings he got since I was gone. I just listened, their need to spill the anger on some one, relieve their little bodies of the unbearable pressure. And they made me cross my heart and hope to die stick a needle in my eye that I would not tell or Mom would kill them. I felt relieved too, for other reasons. As always we ordered way too much food. I so enjoyed their put-on manners, the who can take the biggest bite, stuff the most French fries in their mouth, and the care-full wrapping of remains to bring home, knowing their Moms' flaws they also knew their perfections.

Gretchen, Keely came home with bags of welfare food just as we did, fussing over me while devouring every ketchup-soaked French fry, partly eaten burger, fishwich, and melting shake. Leda's bread rising, she pleaded, please don't slam the doors. Gretchen lost no time boasting how Hawk was coming to pick her up soon, taking her to a wedding, she would wear the velvet dress. My heart swelled at the thought of seeing him. Ava foamed "You never stay home with me. I hate you". Running-out she let the screen door slam. How dare the child of her womb sass, Gretchen threatened a soapy mouth-wash, and resumed her dreamy reverie, how she had Hawk wrapped round her little finger. I knew she wanted under my skin bad, for this was the one time she had something I wanted, and she was just dying to see would I keep my vow of girlfriend's boyfriend, and if not, her behavior would become entirely vindicated, she could then accuse me of fraud, ethical compromise. I would miss her friendship, but if I had to choose, it would be Corbett in good conscience, and if we were meant to be I would not have to take him from her, it would be his choice. Such subterranean hostility, I did not want to play, fake-smiling, excusing my self outside. Gretchen to the bedroom, trussing in the velvet, belling round the house and yard, fantasizing loud about Hawk's eight-bedroom Tudor in Berkeley like it was already hers, how they would travel Europe, him playing the clubs, becoming rich and famous, how he would take care of her. Never mentioning love, character or personality, she thought of him only in terms of herself, the same old Gretchen-Fetchin Fine, any guy could be the one long as he rescued her, she would seduce him, keep him with hot sex, and he would blithely go out and make money for her. I believed with all my heart in love, believed the person mattered, that what he was made-of and not things counted most, and if Corbett was mine, no way would he settle for a user's alliance. Still Gretchen dug-under, and I gave-way "So's Ava going to Europe with you". Face clenching, she ignored me. I pushed "When're you all leaving". Swaning to the bathroom, she tossed over her shoulder "Soon, real soon".

Having trouble catching my breath, I realized how excited I was to see Corbett. While Gretchen primped, I looked-up exogamy in Webster - *The custom of marrying outside one's own tribe, family, clan or other social unit.* Ida Rose said this was liberating for the soul. I changed into my living dress, combed my hair, fetched the bead basket from the shed, located my self on the brown velvet couch facing the front door, where Corbett would see me first thing, and began a necklace. Gretchen swaggered by into the bedroom and slammed the door.

Chapter Twenty Two

SOME ONE TO TALK TOO

Three PM, Corbett James Hawkins walked-in, blue eyes turning shy on seeing me, gazing down at those big feet, clearing his throat "Hi". I could not help smiling "Hi". Glancing-up, clearing his throat again "I've been looking all over for you. Where you been". Blushing neon, I held that glance "In Seattle, helping my Folks open their new store". Compelled beyond self-conscious we clung to the others eyes. I wanted to raise my voice to the top, it's you, it's you that I love, your beauty-full shining face, only you, always you. As if hearing, his eyebrows went up "Would you go with me to a friends wedding reception in Berkeley". My heart thrilling oh thank you thank you, you love me too, some how my voice seemed composed "What about Gretchen". Corbett closed his eyes "I guess she'll just have to understand". He was right, she would just have to understand "I guess she will". I nodded toward the bedroom "She's probably got an ear on the door". He hesitated, took three long strides and knocked "Hey Gretchen, can I please talk to you". Her voice lilting "Is that my darling Hawk". I could feel him wince as the game began, his tone slightly impatient "It's Hawk". She oozed sultry "Come on in". He turned the knob and let the door fall open of its own weight, squaring his shoulders, standing feet apart in the jamb "Look Gretchen, you know how I've been asking after Shoshannah. Well, she's here now, so I hope you understand, I'm taking…". Running-over his words Gretchen snarled "Understand. Hey man I hope you understand, I got a date with Delroy and you've been canceled". Corbett cooperated "Well then you're not mad". She pushed by him, flung me a fuck-you-face and high-tailed through the eucalyptus curtain. Corbett sighed, offering his arm and a smile "Shall we go". I smiled too, feeling sorry for Gretchen but not one bit guilty, for she drew the same closed-circle over and over, if it wasn't Corbett, it would be the next good prospect.

Bus fatigue should have owned me, riding in the soft leather bucket-seat of his yellow Austin Healey convertible, every drop of my body fizzing from our first moment alone, talking and listening, there were no gaps, wanting too know, too be known. He was raised ultra Roman Catholic, church first thing most days, hoping to meet something higher, admittedly with questionable results. This to me was an earnest spiritual quest, I did not care he had taken the conventional route. When he spoke of God the Father, I was excited he dared talk God, and decided to risk "You know the Father probably has a Father". Corbett went quiet. I did not breathe, waiting for crash-and-burn or borne on wings. He laid shining eyes on me "That could be the most profound thing I have ever heard. It's like thinking of your self thinking". Updraft, he saw me and did not turn-away, our union would be incorruptible, I could breathe "Wow, that's really profound too. Doesn't it feel good to have this conversation outloud with a real-live flesh-and-blood human being". He was near blindingly radiant "Yes, it does". This man was a stray-starveling like me, with all the dignity and restraint each could muster, we sipped words and ideas, delicious erotic mind-fucking.

Our elastic-time snapped, ending on Gravatt Drive in the Berkeley Hills. Corbett's college chums Mike and Marsha holding court, their wedding reception lovingly given by her Folks, an extravaganza affair, the bride bare-foot and gorgeous in strapless Chanel, an orchid and gardenia coronal containing her abundant black hair, and still I could not help seeing another virgin gone to slaughter. We joined them in the gazebo-bar, everyone well under-the-influence, and generous in their approval of me. I took a flute of champagne. Corbett three in hasty succession, though they did not seem to faze him. We could stay through toasts and cake and bouquet throwing, for he and Lorenzo had joined-up with One Hand Clapping, and Erik had called for a late night band practice, getting ready for their debut gig tomorrow. Some how this made perfect sense, Corbett and Erik in the same band, oh shit. We took the scenic route passed Corbett's parents eight-bedroom five-bath Tudor on Ashby Avenue in Berkeley, and I did not kill them off so it belonged to him, through San Francisco, South on Highway One, Luna smiling her Cheshire light on the only people in the whole wide world. Turning into the MotherTrucker's driveway, it seemed an impossible illegitimate sacrilege we should part, I wanted to howl to the moon oh no no no no noooo, we have only found each other. Corbett held my whole face in his gaze "I had the best time with you". Aching for those arms around me, to feel his heart beat, I put my hand on the door handle "Me too". In his throaty baritone "I'll see you soon". My heart leapt "Yes, soon". I stood in the dark, listening to the Healy's engine going away. The house was quiet, taking a chaise lounge and sleeping bag to the shed, fatigue owned me, still dressed, I was asleep before my head felt pillow.

Standing in a circle of smooth black stones, inside a circle of larger stones, I am alone on a vast high plateau just after sunset, my face shining pure gold, a trousseau carefully laid on the ground inside the bigger circle, and hats bags scarves jewelry gowns, every thing I ever made. Gretchen and Keely appear and stalk the perimeter, ineligible to enter either circle, stretching long rubber arms, grabbing what they can reach, clamoring "Why should you have these. You don't need all of them. Those should be mine". Their long red nails pecking at my living dress hem, hungry entitled baby seagulls, red nails coming for my face, I'm awake, my neck, my hair wet, a hot wind bringing morning and mushroom factory stink through the slats. Giving-up, going into the house, I hear Gretchen bitter-complaining to Keely, how she never would have lost Hawk if she didn't have Ava. How Ava was a mistake she wished never happened. And Keely's commiseration "Yeah, I know. Guys don't want your kids unless they have some of their own and need a live-in sitter". They hushed on seeing me. I tried small-talking and made coffee. They gave me only the silent treatment. Leda did not show herself. I withdrew to the shed, thinking of my own Folks, forgiving them every real or perceived wrong, how lucky I was never having to fight for my life as a child, allowed to become strong and confident, no matter Mom and Dad did not know me, they unconditionally loved me, their faces lit-up on me, I could see this was the reason I did not step-over the event horizon as easily as these.

As if a personal kindness, the wind shifted sweet and cool through the slats. Leda at the door, cups of steaming coffee in-hand. I never smelled any thing so good, never loved her more. Hopeful, she proposed "I think they're jealous. You and I seem so free, and the Kids tie them down. You know cramp their style. It's not right, but I think our friendship's strong and they'll come around". Not realizing how hurt and mad I was till it came out my mouth "When I walked in this morning, Gretchen was wishing Ava had never been born, blaming her for losing Corbett. And Keely agreed. It's the cruelest thing they ever could say about their Kids. Even if they think it, they should never let it pass their lips. Kids have the biggest ears, and I feel so sorry that their Folk's eyes don't light up when they come in the room. We all make our choices, it's fine to do what you want on your own, but I got no respect for such selfish irresponsible shit when someone else's life is in your hands. They're always swearing how they'd give their lives for their kids, but they're the ones who put them in danger. And I don't like them taking it out on me either. I haven't given them one reason to be such selfish jerks. You know how many nights I stayed with the kids so your guys could go out, and I paid the last months rent, and I wasn't even here. They wear my clothes, they even say my words. It's always bummed Gretchen I'm so particular about who I go out with. I know she wanted Corbett mostly because I did. And I knew he wouldn't want her for long. Anyway she couldn't keep him even if I didn't come back. I know I'm a fucking hypocrite for messing with a girlfriend's boyfriend, but Corbett could just as well been anyone to her. Not to me". Leda's head hanging, her slumped shoulders stayed my rant, electric-blue eyes looking-up in tears "You guys're the best friends I ever had. Please, I don't want us to fight. Is there anything I can do to fix this". Private battles spilling-over, collateral damaging the innocent, her loss of Amaru still too fresh, and now her friends, I knew what I had to do "Oh Honey Pie, none of this is your fault. You don't have to choose between us". I hugged her "We'll always be friends. You'll see, Gretchen will come around. And Keely always follows her. We just all need some time to work this out".

Corbett phoned late afternoon, inviting me to the Catalyst, frustrated, apologizing he could not come get, Erik was crazy nervous, insisting on practicing up to the gig, demanding the Band all go together, but he would put my name on the guest list at the door. I thrilled to his voice saying my name, and promised to come. Hardly able to wait, I showered, pulled my hair into a high ponytail, did not tell anyone and slipped away. Taken by a balmy fragrant night, resplendent out-house moon, and release from the Darkness that had always gripped me, I enjoyed the bus ride and walked. Corbett's Hammond building the bridge of *Light My Fire* summoning me down Front Street, the doorman finding my name, stamping my hand, the room packed, Ted gave me his chair next to Stoney at the mixing board and went to the bar. Corbett sang *Chantilly Lace*, for me, clandestine salutation. I decided to write him a note on a coaster, I'm yours tonight, asking Stoney to please put it on Corbett's piano. He looked quizzical, mouthing "Okay". And I watched him walk to Steven and give it to him. He must have misunderstand over the music, maybe he did not know who Corbett was, maybe he only knew him as Hawk, he must have assumed I meant Steven, I had not even seen Steven, he should be in Montana, or maybe this was some treacherous sabotage to keep me away from their new keyboard player screamed in my head, helpless I braced for repercussions. Following Stoney, holding the winning ticket high in the air, Steven smiling puppy-dog-eyes. I sat-up starched, calling-out over the music "Hey, you're back from Montana". He held the coaster high "Is this true". Nothing but the truth would do here, I let him in enough not to shout "No. It was for the keyboard player. Stoney made a mistake". Crest-fallen he went for the door. I went after, onto Front Street, pleading "Steven. Come on, wait. Please, wait. I never meant for this to happen, and I don't know how to make it right". He kept his pace "I know you didn't, but it did". Stopping, he faced me "The only thing now is leave me alone, just leave me alone". I came up-close, he reached, and I let him fold me in his arms and body and kiss me good-bye. I kissed him too, loved him too, just not enough. Pushing me away, his long legs took him quickly around the corner. Corbett would have to understand, I was too upset to go back in, bussing, walking home, talking out-loud, what is this love thing, it felt like standing on the edge of the known world and I could not help going further, or was it farther. Ida Rose taught me expect a price on either side of a choice, I had not reckoned-on love costing others so dear.

Corbett phoned on the noon hour, and though Gretchen grudgingly called me in from the shed, I was content she had spoken to me. One Hand Clapping was suddenly the next big thing, playing a double-bill with the Doobie Brothers at the High Street Local, he had practice and again could not pick me up, if I could come, my name would be at the door, his guest. Not one possessive word about why or where I had gone last night, I was so smitten with this unassuming man, saying quietly, eagerly "Yes, I'll be there". Feeling the heat of taking sides, Leda borrowed Keely's drivers license for ID and came with. We walked, and hitched, and she let me in-on the blah-blah behind my back. I was a radical man-eating Women's Libber and Hawk a religious fanatic chauvinistic pig, both far too extreme to ever make it together. I knew this came from Gretchen, and cautioned her swallowing the poison, to hold judgment, that Corbett was the most innately liberated man I'd ever known. She said she would, sheepishly admitting never having met or spoken to him. The line at the door moved fast, lights were up, jukebox loud as the doorman looked over the guest list for me. I paid for Leda, and swept the room for Corbett, eye-contacting Colleen. Showing big, she reigned the band-table, attended by Cherry and two other women. I could go sit with them, but not Leda. Colleen motioned me over. I chose not to see, took Leda's arm to the bar and ordered glasses and a pitcher. Selectively benevolent Queen Bee, Colleen pushed-out of her chair, wearing a beautifully embroidered Moroccan Kaftan and sunny earth-mother smile, graciously waddling over, inviting only me to the royal table. Leda shifted on her stool, painfully unwelcome. I winked at her, and politely begged-off. Colleen endeavored, how Cherry changed her attitude now that I was seeing Hawk, and the others, Lorenzo's wife Marion and her brother's girlfriend Amber wanted to meet me. Other than Delroy, Colleen was the only one happy for me, still I knew she invited me because the band wanted to keep Corbett and sort of had to embrace me. Smiling affectionately, not wanting to make her stand longer, I nodded gracious as presented, and quickly returned to Leda.

The lights went down, my heart banging for him, stage door opened, the small army of One Hand Clapping took it, and Corbett stealing a look at me began with *Chantilly Lace*. Soon his monster tarantula hands filled Erik's original songs with unexpected and compelling melodies, singing falsetto to Lorenzo's rich playful voice, that if trained could have been opera. Smiling ear-to-ear, cheeks aching, I had not taken one sip of beer when the set ended on Erik's song - *Everybody Needs Someone to Love*, a very good song, the whole room singing the refrain – *everybody - everybody goda have somebody – everybody needs someone to love*. Unrestrained ovation, they disappeared into the private shadows of backstage, lights-up, dogs sniffing, roadies re-positioning the stage for the Doobie Brothers. My eyes fixed-on the stage door. Corbett emerged sooner, and came right to me, shining everything I needed to know. I introduced Leda. Pleased to meet a friend of mine, he shook her hand and invited us to the yellow school bus for treats. Surprised, enchanted he spoke to her with such respect, she declined to be anywhere near Erik or Joey, urging me go. I slid-off the high bar stool, ready, for Colleen had tipped me off, they wanted, needed Corbett, and must be nice to me. I knew this sort well, like many of the boys I went to high school with, like my Big Brother, scared-to-death to be found with a fragile ego, protecting, using intimidation, muscle, rumor, they were a poor lot, Ida Rose said a person should not feel bad about picking the best of a poor lot, if that was all there was. I did not mind one bit Erik's paranoia of pushing Corbett into choosing me or the band, but that was all on him for I had no such intention, the addition of Corbett and Lorenzo made for a really great band. Corbett held onto my hand as we took the bus steps, and introduced me to Lorenzo. Up-close I knew why he seemed so familiar, the same one who gave me a lift hitching to the Fairmont House, who asked for my number. He recognized me too, and exposed launched an insistence, Hawk was his best friend, they played 5 years around the Bay Area, Monterey, Carmel, and recently settled into a house on Cabrillo College Drive, Marion's brother Frank's friend Jimmy Mesa's place, Marion was pregnant, they needed a place to settle with plenty of room for a baby, and of course Hawk. It was easy to gauge how much he thought me a threat on volume alone, or maybe he was going deaf from playing the hi-hat, I said only that I was happy to meet a friend of Corbett.

Limey climbed-in with a briefcase, apparently expected, he took the drivers seat, and spread his glistening snow on that ornate mirror. Andrew, Stoney, Luke, Ted, Erik, Joey, Lorenzo, put their eager nostrils to the glittering lines. Delighted Corbett did not present his lovely nose, I did not either. Limey took a golden-ball of hash from his briefcase along with my green soap-stone chillum and a lighter, tendering Corbett. He took a small hit and offered me. I thought better stay strait in this environment, took the smoke into my mouth only and fake coughed. Corbett coughed too, his blue eyes amused, inciting, he stood. Me too. Darting the center aisle we escaped into night's cloak. Finding my willing hand, he led me round the corner of the club, his sweet breath my breath, our lips finding the others for a heart-beat, we flew apart as if electrocuted. Corbett crossed his arms over his chest "Wow, you're such a rush". I inhaled and exhaled "You too". He inhaled and exhaled "Sorry I couldn't come get you. Erik's become a drill sergeant. He wants the band to practice day and night. We have an audition for Fantasy Records and he wants to be ready". He paused to engage my eyes "I missed you last night". Clasping my hands behind my back I explained Steven without justification. Smiling satisfaction that my absence was not because of him and definitely not bothered by me having a life before him, Corbett playfully lamented "I wish I got that note". Feeling safe I teased "Oh you'll get notes".

Erik's voice pierced our wrap "Hawk. Hey man, come on, in the dressing room for a powwow right now". Corbett put his arm around my waist and signed "I can't take you home. I don't have a car". On my toes, I surrendered, tongues meeting for the first time, delicious rich promise. Erik cleared his impatient throat. My hand in Corbett's, we trailed him into the club, the Doobie Brothers making pandemonium, yet all eyes seemed to see our tongues had met, and I could not stand something so private so public. Corbett squeezed my fingers softly and let go "See you after the next set". I could not stay "No, I really need to go home". Unexpected privation knit his brow "Okay. But I'll call you tomorrow". He went through the stage door with Erik. Leda was perched high and stiff on the bar stool, her scent drawing the hungry hounds. Remembering my first bewildering venture out to the Red Robin, Nick-sickness still fresh, attracting those perfectly trimmed beards and mustaches, I could see Leda did not have an idea these were bad dogs, and telling would reach her ears as a shame-full reproach. I waited till One Hand Clapping had the stage again and Corbett caught fire, his big engine racing with one foot on the brakes, crowd begging him let go, he did, the room blew into outer-space, they owned him, and I took Leda's arm and pulled her out the door.

Walking Front Street toward the Boardwalk, Northerners, still not complacent to the warm May night, Leda admitted her approval of Hawk, and of growing bored with the party, same guy different face every night, she wanted to go home to Seattle and begged me go too, we could get a place together, I could take her to meet Ida Rose. Drunk and self-absorbed, she did not have a clue how serious my feeling was for Corbett, that I had absolutely no intention of leaving, and it would do nothing to tell her now. Mourning the MotherTruckers disintegration, she spilled how Gretchen and Keely were planning to kick me out soon as they could afford it, so I might as well go North. I regretted her being in the middle.

Whetting a groove for the New Orleans House audition, One Hand Clapping played the Zyante Club, the White Buffalo, the Catalyst again, the Chateau, the Crow's Nest, and practiced constantly. Ralph Gleason had agreed to come to the audition, he was the music critic for the San Francisco Chronicle and Beat Magazine, co-founder of Rolling Stone, Artist and Repertoire agent for Fantasy Records, and actively scouting bands. As the date bore down, a cabal grew between Erik, Joey, and sometimes Lorenzo to keep Corbett from me. When I came to a gig, they were sticking the ever present Groupies in his face, look what a rock star can have, why would you want one when there's a willing menu. This flashed me back to Nick's womanizing and I refused to engage, trusting Corbett instead, befriending the Groupies, for if he wanted the menu he could have it, but not me too. And of course the rhetoric of hype geometrically grew as Erik intensified, this was his big chance, maybe his only one to make a living playing music, become more than a killer Green Beret, and everyone better conform to the cause, or when the Band got famous he would not know your name. The rub of this kind of hyperbole, it's somewhere out there in the future, and if might and could game, never where the heart beats, an if he was not care-full being totally absorbed in the big possibilities of his greatness, he might miss the point entirely and discount those right infront of him, those creating the very environment for his success, family, friends, fans, the people he needed, and though some were desperate for the patina of vicarious self-worth and would gladly accept abuse just to be near the flame, others would withdraw, and if he continued to cannibalize his following in the name of, a following that might seem unlimited depending on how big he got, he could unwittingly lose the ones he loves and reap the cold infidelity of indifference. A wall of exclusivity went-up around Band practice, protecting the illusion, imminent stardom creating its own morality, no girls allowed in except Groupies who don't suck-off the Band's vital energy while they adore, no emotional commitments, just pieces of ass, like fighters believing some girls devour their potency before a fight, especially my kind of girl. Stoney, Ted, even Andrew went compliant, their big chance to be somebody. But Erik was wrong about me, in an upside-down backwards world I would have admired, even liked him, and honestly wanted the Band to succeed, because at their heart they were great. Focusing my time on sewing, Corbett and I had no where to be alone, when practice was late we would meet before in the Compass Room at the Dream Inn for coffee, which he chased with a shot of tequila. If practice ran early, we went to dinner after, if it was all day and night, we met on the phone, never a lull in our conversation, looking forward to the long ride together to the New Orleans House. Corbett resented Erik's manipulation, and his hostility toward me, and wanted to warn him it would only serve to drive him away. Explaining Erik's behavior toward me far preceded us, I suggested he wait till the audition was over, that as long as he understood what was going on, I was okay with it, for now. The irony of Erik fearing me taking Corbett had become real by Erik's own instigation and it amused me, unlike the wish-maidens hanging-round the Band waiting to be used, I did not want my life consumed, did not want to consume, and did not need a man to have a soul.

Corbett called the morning of New Orleans "Erik's insisting I caravan with the boys. You know his deal, no girls allowed. I think it's time for an ultimatum". I knew he was excited, probably wanted to go with the Boys anyway and prescribed "No, don't. No use making him crazier. Stay tight with the Band, it's a big deal. Erik's just excited and scared and gets the two mixed up. You know, closing ranks to feel safe. I think he's still partly in Vietnam. Anyway, I'm a resource-full independent Women's Libber and can get there on my own". Corbett sighed "Yes you are. But the hypes so out a control. I know Ralph Gleason. He lives just a few houses down from my Folks. I used to mow his lawn when I was in Jr. High. He's one of the few music business people who really loves music. His whole house was stacked with records people sent from all over the world. And I know the club owner's daughter. It's a great launching pad for us, but hype's just fool's gold. Erik wants us to act like some band we aren't. Play songs he thinks Gleason will like. Wants us to wear clothes we feel stupid in. Our rawness and unpredictability make us good, not some contrived plan and a suit". I could hear Lorenzo pushing in the background "Come on Hawk. We got to go". I deferred "You go". Corbett's voice hushed, "I'm sorry. Erik called practice before we go, and Renzo's on my back to leave. He's pretty spun out too". I hushed "Where's the club". He laughed "Oh yeah, on San Pablo in Berkeley. Take a cab and I'll pay for it. I'll leave your name at the door. I'll leave all the MotherTrucker's names at the door. Bring anyone you want. See you there Sweetheart". I was his Sweetheart.

Scoffing the invitation, Gretchen and Keely were going to a big party at a farmhouse on Trout Gulch Road, and Leda had promised to baby-sit. I called Yellow Cab, the ride would be at least one-hundred dollars, too much. Uneasy hitching so far alone, nothing could stop me, I put on my living dress and black English hiking boots, hair in a high pony-tail tied with a beaded leather-thong, slipped Excalibur in my pocket, Leda drove me to where Highway 17 goes North to San Jose. Abundant with Friday-night commuters, I paid attention to my intuition, turning down four before accepting the white Corvette. Businessmen regularly assume Hippie means whore, Mr.Corvette was harmless, the type who did not take his suit off even when sleeping for fear of waking and not knowing who he was, his car a surrogate penis, all the testosterone he had. Curious about the counter-culture, he flirted, predictably offering dinner and a hotel as we drove-off the freeway into San Jose. When I laughed him off, he laughed too and pulled to the curb, assuring me 10th was a good street to catch my next ride. North 10th was coming-home residential not leaving, maybe convenient for Mr.Corvette not me, I began walking, thumb-out, people peeking through their curtains, no car dare be seen stopping here for Hippie-harlot invading their upper-middle-class neighborhood. Till a titanium white Cadillac Eldorado glided to the curb as street lights lit. I approached the dark-tinted passenger window silently rolling down, and looked-in at a handsome man maybe thirty, big-tooth smile, sympathetic eyes, who just happened to have business in Berkeley and would gladly chauffeur me to the New Orleans House front door. I could almost hear his appraisal, his under-estimation, a run-away alone on the street after dark, scared and naive with no where to go. Zoe was not bigger than me, conspicuously a pimp, nevertheless I felt no bad vibes or fear and boarded his land-yacht without hesitation. By the time I was eight years old, my family still living in the Mount Baker district of Seattle, I had learned about being underestimated and how it could give me an advantage. Leland Brown bought the house directly across the street from us, he rode a Harley, and Dad said he was a greaser and forbid us going over there. While he was at work, Big Brother went anyway and I had taken to following him everywhere. Well, Big wanted to show-off how strong he was for this biker, and asked me to hit him hard as I could in the stomach. I could not believe my ears, this person who knew I was terrified of the Dark and way too often enjoyed scaring me, who when I was six coaxed me into a wooden barrel and rolled me down a steep street promising I would not feel a thing, and when I crashed against a parked car, and could not stand, and threw-up on my pants and shoes, and Mom wanted to know what happened, he insisted I begged him to do it, and threatened to beat me up if I said otherwise, this person who pulled me up into the big-kids tree-house, then took the rope and left me over-night and swore I made him do it, who told me there was a giant hand that only attacked girls living in the vacant lot where I loved to play, where I then played no more, who made sure when I followed him I would somehow hurt my self, on a tree branch that he oops let snapped back on me, or a ditch that was too wide for me to successfully jump, and then threatened me with worse if I kept following, to which I would defend with, "It's a free country. I can go anywhere I want, and you can't stop me. You're not my Dad". This person already understood he had the power and temperament to lie and be believed and that I did not, this person who always got away with it had just invited me to hit him hard as I could, I tried not to smile, while he instructed "Don't hold back because you're my liddle sister". He pointed to his stomach. I clinched my right fist like Dad taught me, thumb tucked tightly over my knuckles, and swinging with my whole body, delivering a side-arm blow just below his breast-bone.

Big's knees buckled, he crumbled to the parking strip surprised and gasping for air, and could not legitimately be mad at me because he asked me to do it. Leland laughed out-loud. I did not dare, trying to help him up, and it suddenly occurred, this was to this day still the problem between us, in one humiliating realization Big Brother knew he could not trust his own judgment, that some one he under-estimated, a little girl could knock him down, and he must be worried I might do it again, he would have to be on the offense to protect his fragile ego, and he became even more dangerous. Zoe did not believe my story of hitching to see Corbett, saying he heard the same from lots a runaways, but he know the place, would take me there anyway, and then if I needed somewhere to stay and a job, he was The Man. Such a sly engaging pervert, I was momentarily flattered, intrigued how pimp-seduction worked, designed to beguile you unknowingly over the Threshold, still I recognized the Wolf and wrapped my fingers round Excalibur to remind my self to stay totally vigilant. I could have easily gotten out when he stopped at a gas-station-grocery-store on San Pablo to fill-up, returning with a bottle of Liebfraumilch, the scoundrel picked my favorite wine. He opened it, the woodruff tempting, knowing Persephone's err I politely declined. He plied smack, speed, weed, clothes, jewelry, love. I said no thanks. When we arrived at the New Orleans House, so totally charmed by my refusals, he parked and came with to see was my story true.

Corbett's keyboards welcomed us walking toward the club, my heart pounding anticipation, I offered to buy Zoe a drink if he came in. He was amazed my name was on the guest list, paid his $5.00 cover and escorted me in. On my trip now, in my power, I was relieved to be out of his, and enjoyed being with the only Black person in the place, unfortunately a stereo-type flamboyant pimp in a well-tailored banana-yellow shark-skin suit, lapels wide as the belled-bottoms, his neck spindly-contrast to a massive afro and over-sized collar of his pink polka-dot black silk shirt, black patent leather platform boots making him five-inches taller than me. The band into the first set, all playing Kazoos in harmony, except for Corbett on Hammond, piano and foot-peddle bass, singing *Ooshka Mooshka Looshka*, a song he'd written about an Eskimo riding his dog sled from Nome to Seattle to find his sweetheart. When he saw me, he forgot the words, looking quick away, regaining his composure. A fog of marijuana hung the room, the club near full, we found seats at the bar, I ordered Zoe a Mai Tai. He looked small and nervous and drank too fast, I would too had I been the only White. Lighting a smoke I blew the first puff in his face to get his attention, to vent "You know, what you do is totally disgusting". With a charming smile he spoke in rhythm to the music "No no sweed thing. Me, I'm helping my girls. Fillin' a need. It's the oldest profession you see, and my girls, they dig the work. They dig me". I mirrored his smile "Well isn't that so very philanthropic of you. Slavery was probably defended the same way". He was no longer smiling "What else could those cunts do. Junkies with babies to feed. Gots ta feed the babies. Who else'll take care of 'em but me". I grudgingly acknowledged "There aren't a lot of opportunities fer single women with babies, but I don't believe any girl really likes being a cunt or a pair of tits". His eyes were cold fire "Mosta you er dumb cunts. And the ones 'at leave me are just one less fucking hole". I really wanted to knock the wind out of him, clinching my right fist and tightly tucking my thumb over my knuckles "So you hate women". Offended, he protested puffy sincerity "Me. No I love women to death. Adore women. Women 're my bes' friends". Customary response of guys who have mistaken misogyny for love, who think they treasure us but do not trust us, who put us in cages and tell us they're pedestals, protect us from life by doing our thinking for us, and of course sleep with every one of their 'best friends'. I thought any guy who believed he needed to protect me really believed I could never be more than a child, emotionally unable to handle my own life. And since escaping the Golden Ghetto, my attitude usually pissed these 'women lovers' off, like Erik, Joey, Luke, Stanley, Big Brother, Arnie, Nick, a confused Princes' Society prepared to do all my thinking for me, who did not understand my resentment when they did. To me their chivalry was chauvinism, kindness control, their ego building at the expense of mine, well I had claimed my royal birth-right too, and in claiming the benefits I had to pay the price. But Zoe was a depraved low-life, far from Erik and the rest, making his living off girl's backs, insuperable karma, and having shown him best I could that all girls were not what he thought, I dismissed him with a curt "Well, I guess we ain't never gona be best friends". Stretching a cardboard smile across his

538

beautiful big teeth "Yeah baby, that's what they all say up front. So I got bidness ta do. This joint ain't my bag". He took a card from his breast pocket and left it on the bar "Ever need some scratch, call me. I'll take you back". He strolled slowly out the door. I ordered a Coors, staring at the business card's simple black printing – ZOE 444-6969, thinking how funny even pimps have business cards.

A graying-hair man maybe fifty, mustache, roundish glasses, wearing a dark-gray shirt, brown tie and jacket, dark-gray slacks and brown penny-loafers asked if the stool was taken. Looking round, the club full, I smiled and invited him to sit. He looked comfortable in his clothes though they did not fit the crowd, and we exchanged about the band, till Corbett took his foot off the brake and fried everyone to the walls with a Jerry Lee Lewis medley, size-twelve green boat-shoes tap-dancing the foot-peddle bass, singing lead and falsetto, monster magician masquerading as musician, hiding in plain sight, sheer talent affording him cover, only every time or eyes met he forgot words, fumbled notes, shrugging his broad shoulders we knew he could look no more. Colleen and Cherry had not shown-up, I guessed it was not their choice. Stoney and Ted hovered the sound board anticipating every need. Limey came with an oozing buxom blonde reeking money, he walked passed me without recognition. A fat joint made its way down the bar, I took a taste and offered Grayhair. He passed it on without partaking, and I went instantly paranoid, he must be a narc. And there was Erik, sweltering under the stage-lights in a three-piece blue-and-brown striped wool suit, rusty curls stuck to his face, for some reason glowering daggers at me, freaking me even more. I told my self he was always scowling at me, that like Howard he had been a Green Beret and came back to The States a killer, and once home Uncle Sam provided no help to ease the trip from killer to civilian, that Erik played music with the same fervor he soldiered, seeking a path more conducive to life and growth, I admired his effort, but he was mentally still in the jungle, and he had made me the enemy. The story went, every morning his Dad, a military lifer would check his room for dust with a white glove. I heard the same from Howard, and could only hope having a baby with Colleen would ground Erik like Lizabeth's had done for Howard. That is if he didn't lose her in the deadly dance, selfish deception on one side, humiliation and subtle retaliation on the other, all in the name of love. Except for books and movies and my Mom and Dad, I'd seen little evidence in real life of any kinder dance, been called crazy for wanting something more, generally despised for refusing to take my turn, but I would not dance that dance again. My Folks always told me never to settle for second best, that I was more valuable than that. Well, I wanted what they had, Dad still called Mom his girlfriend, bragged they broke the mold when they made her, like Tristan and Isolde, I wanted that kind of love, sacred love, respect, not a compromise, a business deal, I wanted co-operation, something Gretchen did not believe-in, and for that matter nearly every one I met along the way. As kids do, I grew-up assuming all moms and dads were like mine. Bitter-sweet realization found them the exception not the rule, sweet for their unconditional love, and bitter that my Friends never had the same advantage and paid relentless consequences. I believed most of a person came in with them, but a good dose of young self-confidence helped a lot, and that came from parents. I knew something of Corbett's Folks, and somehow, probably because he came in a King, he had managed to separate his masculinity from their version of Catholic patriarchy, he seemed to know my kind of dance, yet all the others and situations could easily poison us apart. Tonight I would be as vulnerable as I felt, tell him I love him, see how good a dancer he could be.

Grayhair asked too many questions, I felt certain he was a narc. The band took their break, stepping-off stage they all came toward me. Corbett put his hand gentle on my shoulder and began talking to Grayhair "Hi Mr.Gleason. Glad you made it. You still live by my Folks". They shook hands and Gleason smiled sentimental "I do Corbett. Please call me Ralph. You always did the best job on my lawn, and you did the same tonight. It's good to see you again". Corbett's hand still on my shoulder, Erik, Stoney crowding-in for introductions, I excused my self, to the ladies-room. On coming-out, Erik caught my arm with vise-grip and growled "God damn you talking to Gleason". He scared me and I wanted to scream, knowing in my bones he did not want to hurt me, I kept a calm voice "He got really high on the music and wanted to talk. I thought he was a narc. Now let me go". He did, putting an arm round my shoulder. I laughed nervously and tried to spin away. Holding tight, he hustled me to the bar, Stoney and Gleason fast in conversation, let loose and took my bar stool. From behind Corbett placed his hand lightly on my shoulder. I flinched. He whispered in my ear "Come on, let's get some fresh air".

Walking half-a-block before speaking, he went first "How come you call me Corbett when my Friend call me Hawk". I looked-up at him "Exactly cause those Friend call you Hawk". He grinned "That's so totally cool, I love it". He added casually "So who's the banana split you came in with". I felt no need to explain "Just a ride from San Jose". His faced pinched "You hitched, alone". I hated his concern and loved how we leaned in–and-out in graceful sway "Yes I did, Leda couldn't come". His troubled voice swelled "I knew I should've picked you up". Joey interrupted from behind "Hawk, hey man, shit, Gleason fucking loves us. He's bringing Saul Zaentz to hear us next week. The fucking president of Fantasy Records". Joey knew I saw through his well-born looks and spoke to me like a dog "Why don't you just git. This is none of your business". Corbett stood his full six-foot-two "Watch your mouth Joe". Joey walked away, toward the club. We did too, unhurried, Corbett offering an arm and vain reason "Don't let Joe bother you. They're all being jerks tonight". I was indignant "Don't defend them. They're always jerks". Lorenzo came toward us "Hawk, come on man, powwow in the dressing room". As we went in the door I let go of Corbett's arm "Go on. I'll see you later" He smiled grateful and went.

Stoney had taken my stool, still talking to Gleason. I spotted Andrew leaning against the far wall smoking a panatela, and leaned-up next to him. He handed me one and mused "This whole scene's just too funny. I play jug, carry it around in a bowling bag for Christ-sake". He winked at me "And put my music on a sterling silver music stand. I just can't see how this will make me a rock star". He chuckled "Erik's really pissed we wouldn't wear the suits he got us. They're fine suits, but I promised myself never again". I was so glad Andrew had come back to life "Shouldn't you join the Boys for the powwow". He struck a stick-match with his thumbnail, lit my cigar and smiled "Naa, I'd rather stand here with you".

The club at capacity, more, my stool at the bar taken soon as Stoney went to the mixing board, Andrew carried a chair there for me, though I was not entirely welcomed by Stoney and Ted. The Clap lived-up to themselves. Lorenzo's voice powerful, Corbett's liquid mercury fingers giving bold wings to even the most mediocre guitar riffs, the room completely in their control, this Band of disparate contradictory elements that under no other circumstance would hold together, a compelling demonstration of their magic. Again I saw the King beneath the man, Corbett was part peacock, and stalwart royal who understood the King serves, someone big enough to love with all my heart, some one I could not consume. And when the rocket-ship landed, Gleason gave Erik an encouraging smile and thrums-up, saluted Corbett and left. The band swarmed into the dressing room, with Stoney, Ted, Luke, Limey, and the Oozing Blonde. Bartender announced last call and turned the lights-on. I sat in my chair, avoiding eye-contact with the remaining dogs, chain-smoking, grateful when Ted and Luke returned. Their almost frantic exuberance in breaking down drums, unplugging, winding cords, moving amps, keyboards and speakers, betrayed the lines they snorted. The room finally empty but them and the bartender, I waited for Corbett, beginning to feel an awkward foolish self-consciousness creeping-in, scolding my self for not being more prepared, at least bringing Brian and April's phone number along. Stoney came out of the dressing room near 2PM. I asked for a lift to Santa Cruz in the equipment van. He smiled "We're all going to Joey's Folks place in Orinda to celebrate. You can come, and I'll take you home in the morning". Heart sinking to my heels, I did not like the sound of this, but I had already been out here this late once before, alone, hitching a ride did not sound good "Thanks. Please don't leave without me, promise". He nodded "Promise". I went by the dressing room to the ladies. The door was wide-open on return, the room empty, I hurried outside in-time to see Corbett rounding the corner in the passenger seat of a red Corvette convertible, top down, Oozing Blonde at the wheel. Sick, I stood by the van talking to my self "Shit. I sure can't compete with that". Stoney answered with un-mistakable satisfaction "Yeah. That's Elvin Bishop's ex-Ol'lady. Something ain't she". I sat down on the curb, if Corbett could be so easily seduced, I would finish my new collection, sell it and go back to Seattle with Leda. Having grown uncomfortably familiar with lonely, and not yet used to some one to talk too, I reconciled, at least I would not be intellectually alone near Ida Rose.

Chapter Twenty Three

WEDDING GHOSTS

Loading the equipment took another half-hour. I rode with Stoney, following Ted and Luke South and East through the Caldecott Tunnel. We were last to arrive at the party, no Wives or Ol'ladies, just the familiar predatory Groupies, something nasty about their loose-lipped mouths, like they had been stretched too far too often. When I did not see Corbett, every wall I ever built flew-up with my game face, I hunkered on the couch next to Andrew waiting the morning. Drugs abundant party favors, Stoney sat by me, and leaning over the coke pile on the glass-top coffee-table, picked-up the razor blade and began chopping lines. I remarked "Wow, Joey's Parents're really liberal". Andrew burst-out laughing "They're gone for a week, golfing Indian Wells". Stoney rolled a fin into a tight tube and snorted a line up each nostril. Kneeling down across the table, Erik glared at me and repeated the ritual. Limey came in from the bright kitchen and placed a bowl of hash oil dipped joints on the table, seeming not to recognize me. I told my self his eyes were not adjusted to the dark. Stoney took one, lit it with his Zippo, sucked in a slow drag, and filled with cocaine-confidence turned square to me "So look, I been in love with you since we met, an, shit I'll just say it, would you consider being with me". Not entirely ambushed, I cleared my throat to mask a laugh slipping-out, not for his sweet proposal but what it said of how little he knew me, for I had been care-full not to give him one wrong signal, and was so plainly inlove with Corbett. Counting ten, avoiding his eyes I whispered soft "Stoney, I'm flattered, but you know we're jus' friends". He face fell "Yeah. But I had to try. Maybe you'd say yes now the Band's making it and I have something to offer". Something to offer, he was what to offer, so he sees me as merchandise available at the right price, I was no longer flattered, no matter how I tried, except for Andrew, Boys mistook my friendship. I did not know what to say but "I'm sorry Stoney. You have to excuse me, I need something to drink". Walking into the kitchen, there was Corbett sitting at the table with Oozing Blonde and Brian, our eyes met, my mind raced, okay, stay cool, he's with her, don't act a fool, the floor suddenly uneven under my feet, I willed them to cross the room, take a beer from the sink full of ice and go back to the dark living room. Corbett came right after "Hi. Hii". I sat in the first empty chair and opened the can. The room hushed as he stood infront shifting foot to foot "I'm so glad. Don't be mad, I brought my car up here before the gig and we all went in Joey's Lincoln". Raising my eyes and brows I did not speak. He did "When I came out of the dressing room and didn't see you, I thought you'd gone, so I took a ride". I knew he had been set-up, but did not think him quite as naive and innocent as he wanted "I must have been in the ladies room". Even so, I was a goner, he leaned close, inviting in John Wayne's voice "So you wana get outa here Missy". Being called Missy by anyone else would have infuriated me, smiling, setting the can on a now flat floor, our hands finding the other, I snatched my bag from the couch, and we escaped through the front door.

Corbett took Fish Ranch Road off Highway 24 to Grizzly Peak Boulevard, parking on the high bluff in Tilden Park. We stepped over the guardrail close to the lip, San Francisco Bay to the lighthouse on Alcatraz Island spread at our feet, eucalyptus groves waving their scent hello. Corbett put his arm tightly around my shoulder, pointing-out the Oakland Bay Bridge, the Golden Gate, and the Richmond San Rafael, noting "Wind's coming from the East, that's why it's so clear and warm". I slipped my arm round his waist, we swayed to our own music, standing above this incredible glittering panorama I had seen only in the movies, and here I was in my own, wishing we had somewhere to go. A couple intruded on the bluff, soon arguing about their new credit card. As if hearing me, Corbett suggested "We can stay at my Folk's house tonight, they're camping in Yosemite".

I could see why Gretchen so wanted this four-story off-white Tudor, with dark brown beams, and covered porch on two-sides. Inside, teak paneling halfway-up stucco walls, Sarouk rugs much like Ida Rose's blanketing the hardwoods, I felt we were trespassing. Corbett said no it was okay. We went to the large kitchen, he scrambled six eggs with sliced green olives, Velvetta cheese and Trappey's Mexi-Pep hot sauce, toasted English muffins, poured apple juice. His eggs so light and moist and fluffy, making me think there had not been many cooking for him since he left home. And he was such a mimic, anything I said, he answered as James Cagney, Elvis, Dean Martin, Donald Duck, Mickey Mouse. I laughed and laughed an did not feel one bit self-conscious really alone together for the first time. Heaping most of the food on his plate, exonerating himself as Peter Lorre "I'm so greedy, I can't believe how much I want to eat. I'm always so hungry after my music performance". He placed the rest infront of me and sat across the table. Oozing Blonde suddenly on my mind, I took a chance "I always knew you were a scoundrel. I saw you leave the club in Blondie's Corvette". Making me wait, taking a mouth-full, chewing slow, eyes twinkling in fun Corbett use his own voice "So you did. She a great package don't you think. For that matter so's Miss Fetchin-Fine. The thing is, all they have is great package. Not that you aren't great package too, but you're more than package. You have content". I was completely slain, we were introverts taking our worth from character not things, kindred in essential foundations, I flirted back "I like your package too". Leaving dishes on the table, I followed upstairs to his Folk's room, they slept in separate beds. Fully dressed, yawning, he laid down on one. I the other, disappointed and relieved we did not use his room, his single bed, this was so important, I was not ready. Listening to his breathing even into slumber, sure I could never fall asleep with him so near.

Corbett woke me with a kiss on the nose "Good morning sleeping beauty". I did not open my eyes, thinking how wonder-full waking to this person. Sitting on the bed he stroked my hair "You awake". I hummed "Uh huh". His spent voice was solemn and eager "Good, cause I had this dream, maybe more like a vision". He laughed nervously "I left my contacts in last night, and woke up with them stuck to my eyeballs. You know I'm actually legally blind without them. Anyway, after taking them out, I laid down again, watching the ceiling, listening to you breathe, and this host of forms began to gather, filling the ceiling, like hovering ghosts, their eyes the only really solid part. They were celebrating, talking to each other though I couldn't make out what. And I wasn't the least bit freaked out. They let me know, I guess telepathically, they were our relatives and ancestors, Catholic, Jewish, assembling in honor of our finding each other. They came to celebrate us". He laid down next to me and fixed his eyes on the ceiling "You think I'm flipped out". I looked when he looked "Wow, no, not by a mile. I think they're right to celebrate. I think you been given a gift, and should trust your eyes and ears. I've seen things that are hard to believe, that challenge ever thing I ever knew. Things that were gifts only for me, and I chose to trust my mind and eyes and never regretted it". He turned toward me "I hope this isn't too soon Shoshannah Leibofsky. I love you". I caught my breath "It's not Corbett Hawkins cause I love you".

All evidence of us in the bedroom and kitchen smoothed away, we left, trading secrets on the ride to Santa Cruz. Corbett conceded my feeling of trespass true, he'd come to a bitter impasse with his Folks and their rigid insistence Catholicism was the only way to heaven. Listening to him talk, I realized that me living outside the American socio-economic structure, and believing it made me safe and smart was immature on my part, for he lived almost entirely within the system, had a checking account, Diners Club card, a car loan and student loan, owed the music store for his Spinet, paid income tax, and was paying down a house-full of furniture he put on his Sears and JC Penney accounts, a wedding present to his sister Maggie and her new husband Diego, that he was the one who looked to the system like one of their very own darlings, never suspect as long as he made the payments, that he was the one who was truly invisible. We lunched at the Catalyst, bagels, cream cheese, beer, and I told how I saw him a King. He smiled "Funny thing, I knew you too, the instant you walked into the Gate of Horn, I mean King and I. It was like honor and courage were headlights shining through your eyes. I could listen to you talk for the rest of my life. So much of what you say's in my head too, though I never told anyone, no one's interested, they all want to talk music, fame, rock star shit". He paused "So, why did you run away from me". I squirmed "You mean up to Seattle". He nodded "Yeah, the real reason. I didn't know if I would ever see you again". My eyes glassed "Me too". I took a deep breath "Okay, here goes. Well first when I saw you, it scared me down to my bones. I told Gretchen I wanted to take you home with me. Thought she was stuck on Delroy or I wouldn't of said anything. She instantly wanted what I wanted, and I completely refuse to compete. Anyway, she and I don't play by the same rules cause she doesn't have any. I knew there was no stopping her, so I left, figuring if you were who I thought, when I came back, you would of found her out". This was more than expected, Corbett hesitated, shifting in his chair "I did. You were gone and suddenly she was everywhere, staring at me, and she wouldn't tell me anything about you except you went home. I like her, but that's all. She wants someone to take care of her in the way she would like to become accustom, and that someone could be anyone. I don't really matter to her. I'm not interested in being just anyone". Knowing Gretchen, they slept together, knowing Corbett's upbringing maybe not, I smiled "Me too. I guess I'm jealous she had some of your time. It's fine you have a past, so do I. So I won't bring her up again". Giving him a wide toothy grin "Or Corvette Babe".

Erik had imposed a strict plan for the band, practice every day till the audition for Saul Zaentz. Corbett reluctantly drove me home, grumbling "Erik's totally going to blow it, trying to cater to what he thinks Gleason and Zaentz want. Gleason already likes us, because we're unpolished, un-inhibited, unpredictable, we need to just go and be our funky selves. Erik can't see that, he won't listen". Concurring "I know you're right. Trying to be someone else, you just get found out, and they get rid of you anyway. It's only for a week". Stopped in the driveway, he leaned shyly toward me "How'd the voice of wisdom come to reside in such an unexpected package". This rare mortal understood the way to my heart was through my head, I seized a handful of his shirt and pulled, kissing him, letting go "I can't believe I said only a week. I didn't mean it. When the drill Sargent's not looking, come see me soldier. Now go on, practice, I have dresses to make".

From the kitchen window Gretchen's eyes burned a hole in my back as I stood watching Corbett drive away. I did not want anything robbing my mood, went to the shed, closed the door wishing it had a lock, and stretched-out on the chaise lounge, Corbett swirling all around me, loving some one made it plain how lonely I had always been, now I felt fastened, deeply touched on an intensely profound level. When Ida Rose explained sacred and profane love, she said all sacred marriages were metaphorically made in heaven, as spiritual as they were physical. At the time this had little real meaning for me, her words came full now, I closed my eyes and began to float over sleep's welcome threshold. Gretchen's cold voice near my face jerked me back "So when're you and Hawk leaving for Europe". I did not want this conversation and kept eyes shut. She snarled "You never could a stolen him from me if I didn't let you". My eyes opened "You had your chance, I left town for a month. And Corbett made his choice". Her body went rigid, fists clinching at her sides "You're a lying bitch. Always pushing your nice girl rules on me, and now look at you, a fucking hypocrite. Well you and Hawk're nothing to me". I still loved the best of this naughty succubus and bit my tongue, letting her ego keep some dignity. Crimson face, she stood tall "I got a real date tonight and wana wear your living dress". Sitting-up I remembered the dream, her and Keely grabbing with blood-red nails "No way I'm taking this off. I gave you the velvet. That's it. You sold-out for what you can get quick, lost your self in an empty game. You can't be me to make up the difference. I need me now, and you have to stop saying my words and wearing my clothes. There's some one I my life that matters. I need to be me now. This is the real thing Gretch, you just have to understand". Dumbfounded she stuck her tongue out and left.

Corbett's loud voice coming from the front room woke me "Knock it off Gretchen, I came to see Shoshannah". I found him pulling her arms from his neck, lipstick on his face. She smirked at me over her shoulder, clearly relishing Corbett's exasperation. I crossed the room in an instant, took hold of her shoulders and said too sweetly "Where are your manners Princess". She went flat-footed, Corbett let go of her wrists, she ran into the bedroom and slammed the door. Corbett sat down on the couch. I did too, facing him "You all right". He grimaced "Wow, I didn't know she was like that". Raising a finger to my lips "Shhhh". He grasped my meaning and filled the room with his husky voice "Practice got over at six. I went home for a shower and nap". He smiled and reached in his coat pocket "Give me your hand". I turned-up my left palm. He placed two half-inch square pieces of red construction paper on it "Limey gave us all some blotter acid". Raising his eyebrows "You interested in a little trip". I wondered "Is it pure". Corbett put his right hand over his heart swearing

"Limey guaranteed 100 percent, absolutely uncut, made by some chemist friend of his". I put the red squared back in his hand "Ah, but we know Dealers lie. I have this habit of never taking acid unless I know someone who's taken the same before me. Blotter's usually good, but I just happen to have some pharmaceutically pure Sandoz". Corbett's eyes lit, Clark Gable came out "Quite frankly my dear, I've always wanted to give Sandoz a damn try. They're right impossible to come by, how did you ever get those". I nearly finished explaining the FBI supplying Hydra with it for Sky River, when Gretchen flung open the bedroom door, a wet-dream incarnate, strutting across the room in black satin push-up bra, black lace garter belt, no panties, black fishnet stockings, wearing my size-six black velvet and rhinestone spike-heel mules on her pretty size-eight feet, she slithered though the eucalyptus curtain. Corbett and I just looked at each other. He took a deep breath, exhaling slow "Maybe we better go". I shook my head "No way she's making me leave my own house". His eyebrows knit "Okay, but I don't think this is over". Folding my arms "I know, but she has a way of making everything about her and I won't have it". I took a deep breathe too, unfolded my arms "So how was practice". He leaned back into the couch "What little we got in was really good. Joey, Erik and Stoney big talked most of it. The hype's gotten where they believe we're already rock stars". Half-way into my scathing exposition on hype Gretchen reappeared, pouty lipstick, powdered Little Girl coming to seduce Daddy as he must have methodically taught her to do. I flashed on my friend Penny whose Daddy came into her room, her constant warning how all men only want one thing, and realized Gretchen had been trying to tell me about Daddies and their Sons all along. And Carolion's Daddy taught her, and Cyrene's, and my heart broke and bled-out on the floor, for Gretchen had been trying her best to warn me too, watch out for Daddy, trying to show me, prove to me though really to her self that Daddy did bad things, then bought her silence with token recompense, that all men were Daddy and I should forget looking for a good one, should take control, use sex as power, get from Daddy what I could. And I had been trying to show her how to be one-in-herself, how to be a Virgin Daughter of the Moon, that sex was not the only thing between a man and woman, there were other ways to be a woman and other kinds of men, and I wanted to throw my arms around her and make it all right, tell her it wasn't her fault, promise she would never have to be Daddy's again, this delicately painted curled and perfumed kitten who thought she was forever stained, and might never claim her demons or let feelings reach her heart, this insolent Bitch sashayed into the room and plopped on Corbett's lap. I went immediately into the kitchen, began to fill my magic teapot from the tap, maybe Corbett could deal with her Daddy's legacy, for she would not hear me anymore, it wasn't even me she was battling, but the haunting specter of Daddy's perversion. I heard Corbett "Come on now Gretchen get off me. I'm standing up now". There was a soft thud on the floor, the bedroom door slammed and Corbett came through the eucalyptus curtain "It sounded worse than it was". I poured tea as Gretchen's date arrived. We invited him into the kitchen for a cup while she made him wait. And when her new Daddy had been properly subjugated, Venus Rising presented herself in the lavender and peach silk gown stolen from my new collection. I did not flinch, just wanting them gone. Daddy punished her for making him wait, smacking her bottom hard as they left the kitchen. She giggled softly calling him such a naughty boy.

Another unusually warm night, wanting Corbett all to my self, not knowing where Leda Keely and the Littles were, I proposed taking the Sandoz to the beach. Corbett had a sleeping bag in his trunk. We drove to Andrew's and parked, Jennifer laying guard on the porch, waving her tail, did not bark and did not follow. Hand-in-hand crossing the Meadow of Scents onto the sand, a weathered log close to high tide's lip, we unzipped the sleeping bag, satin side up. Sitting cross-legged, knees-to-knees, I placed a white tablet on his tongue and kissed his mouth. Swallowing he remarked "Better than communion wafers, but the priest almost never kisses you. I was an altar boy you know". He chanted in Latin, made the sign of the cross, ceremoniously placed a tab on my tongue and kissed my mouth. We settled close, against the log, waiting, Luna extending her sparkling silver bridge across the water to our feet. And when the tin foil did not set my teeth on edge, I knew we were in for a mellow trip. Hoping Corbett might understand a still potent paranoia, I recounted some Hydra FBI stuff, which lead to Buckminster Fuller's geodesic domes "Every one needs a place to live. Domes are way more sturdy than box houses, about a third less to build, and cause they're round, two-thirds less to heat or cool. And I think living in a round open space has to be more spiritual". Corbett's voice was tight "Domes 're a Communist plot to rob everyone of their individuality". We both laughed at the same time. He explained "You have to understand, I'm raised by Dan Smoot Republicans. To my Folks Commies are the Devil incarnate, blamed for every evil in the world". I giggled "Well my Dear, the Devil's sitting right next to their precious Sonny Boy. And my Grampa Joe was born in Moscow. And I'm hatching a Commie plot with Buckminster Fuller to help more people live in dignity. People who can't afford homes will be able to have one. So they better lock me up now, I'm the worst kind of criminal". Corbett put his arm around my shoulder, and the Big Bopper sang *"Oh baby that's what I like"*. I laid my head on his chest, listening to the thump thump thumping, Sandoz was not going to take us into outer space, we would not disappear or see god, only solve some of the problems of the world, for eight months at the bottom of my bag must have sapped some juice. I sat-up to finish my thought "Just the word Communism scares Americans. But we shouldn't be afraid a words. I think Nixon and his Goons wan' it that way, some big bad Communist bogeyman to blame for all the wrongs. Something to preoccupy our thoughts so we don't focus on the real big bad, them. Just like yer Folks do with guilt and religion. Communism's idealistic as well as political, Democracy too. You have to admit our Democracy isn't working real well right now. It's suppose to mean equal representation". I looked in his eyes "Bet you can't name one American woman or Black person with any real political power in this country that isn't dead". Corbett grinned delight "I love you're so passionate. I wish I was too, but I'm just a musician. And I'm ashamed to say you're right, I can't name one". I kissed him "Don't get me wrong. I wouldn't want to live in Stalin's Communism, wouldn't want to live any where but here. I just want it to be better, a Socialistic Democracy, free education, healthcare, food, housing, unquestioned inalienable rights just for being alive. There's enough for all of us to have. All the misery is political, everywhere. That's all I want". Corbett applauded "Your world would be a great place to live. I hope it comes true". He seemed to apologize "But I'm not political. I don't march in the streets, I just play piano". The claim of not political amused me

"Yeah right, just playing rock'n roll makes you a political poster boy for the movement. Rock'n roll screams freedom. An you know it's the music of the Devil, right. I mean, we don't march to Roger Williams, we march to Buffalo Springfield. So, sorry, but you're political every note you play. I read something this Women's Libber Carol Hanisch wrote – *The personal is political*. What we do every day in our lives, how we act, how we live is political, and playing rock'n roll is definitely political". Corbett's face was solemn "Wow, I never thought of it that way".

Alone together, deep in the other's head a sustained satisfying mind-fuck. Corbett summoned his younger days "When I was almost sixteen, I had a hit record, *Daydreams*. My Band was The Panics, Eddie Castillo on drums, Martin Carillo and Richard King on guitar, Richard's older brother Al played bass, and me on keys. *Daydreams* was this instrumental I wrote, and I don't know if it hit beyond California, but KYA radio in San Francisco got behind it big-time, played it every hour every day for weeks. And this station KEWB in Oakland did too, especially these two Disc Jockeys, Gary Owens and Frank Bell. The Band was totally blown-away when the record started selling like crazy in Bay Area record stores. We opened shows for Little Eva, Richard Berry and Bobby Rydell, the Righteous Brothers. Everyone wanted us to play their school dances. My Folks said using my talent for anything but serving God was a sacrilege, they turned on me. So did the Christian Brothers at Saint Mary's. I can't remember not playing the piano. My Mom says I started at two, and by five began composing and putting on living room shows. Learned everything by ear. I'd hear a record or a song on the radio or tv and go right to the piano and play it. Only realized when I got older that I had perfect pitch. My grammar school Band at Saint Augustine's was called the Loafers. Let's see, Herb Peterson played banjo and steel guitar, Butch Waller guitar, Mike Holly on trumpet, and Martin Carillo drums. We played school assemblies and dances". He paused "Wow, I'm going on an on about me me me. You must think I'm totally self-centered". Cradled in the rich timbre of his voice, the way he expressed him self, I loved that he trusted me with secrets "No way. I wana know every thing about you". He looked thrilled "About me". Clearing his throat "Well, hum, let's see. I'm the eldest child. My Folk's say they expected me. And groomed me to be a priest, to use my gift for the glory of the Lord. Imagine the respect they would get with a priest in the family, or a nun. My Little Sister Maggie could sing, went to Holy Names, and onto Holy Names College. Get this, she took the name Sister Mary Martin, but left the convent before her final vows. I'm not sure why, she never said. And my Little Brother Paul went to Saint John's Seminary, studied for the priesthood. He left after falling in love with Angela. We'll have to go up to Mountain View so you can meet them. They're living together. My Folks don't know. I think she might be a real angel, rescuing him from a life my Folks wanted but he never did. And me, I was the rebel, never bought into my Folk's religious fervor. Always said what was on my mind. And boy when my record hit, I was in way over my head. No one at home or school would talk to me about what I should do. This agent would send his Cadillac around to pick me up for shows. I'd ride in the back alone, feeling confused, guilty just for being alive, thinking I should be happy, why do I feel like such a piece of shit. And we never saw one cent from the record, agents and promoters took it all, easy pickings from fifteen year old kids. My Folks used this as proof rock'n roll was evil. I'd come home after school and there was no plate at the dinner table for me". I put arms around him tight, hating these selfish pigs for breaking the parental covenant to be on their kids side no matter what, for undermining his future "My Folks, you'll love 'em. They don't know who I am anymore, but they love me anyway, unconditionally".

We settled into the unsaid, and each other, feeling the Earth turning, wishing on shooting stars, morning poking fingers into the dark sky, we had come full circle, supplicants in some ancient ritual renewing itself through us. Corbett asked me to trust him, took me to the Santa Cruz bowling alley for the over-eighty tournament, our table over-looking the alleys. I adored his quaint sense of place, and that he was not a vegetarian and still never ate animals in my company. We ordered waffles and maple syrup, and near oblivious to the balls crashing into pins and gutters, watched every bite into the others mouth, Sandoz leaving us a mellow after-glow. And he took me home, and we kissed good-bye, whispering I love you, and kissed good-bye and kissed, and everything seemed right with the world.

The house sound asleep, I took the phone into the closet and called collect "Hi Mom. I wanted to catch you before you left for work. Guess what. Corbett loves me too". She guilted "Shoshannah, it's been weeks since we heard from you. You know we worry". Already regretting, I took a breath "Yeah Mom I know. I'm sorry". She relented "So when're we going to meet your prince charming". I cringed "Don't know Mom. I just wanted to thank you and Dad for loving each other so much. You made it easy for me to recognize the real thing when I found it". She persisted "We only hope you learned a lesson from that Nick". The last thing I wanted was thinking of Nick "Mom, I never loved Nick. Anyway, you'll absolutely adore Corbett. He's a good boy. And the best piano player in the world. And so funny. We laugh all the time". Her voice wagged like a finger "Don't I remember you swearing never to get mixed-up with another musician". I wanted to hang-up "Mom, sometimes a person ends up doing what they say they won't and it's exactly the right thing". Her voice softened "Well, I can't argue with you there. Say Honey, if we buy you a plane ticket, round trip of course, would you come for a week and manage the business. You know how. We could really use a rest". My answer surprised me, it was not how about your sons, they live in Seattle, but "How can I say no. But I have to go now. I'll call later and make arrangements. I love you. Tell Dad I love him too". I stood in the closet contemplating how she said we, speaking for Dad, in a way doing his thinking for him, and promised my self I would never do that to Corbett. The bedroom door ajar, Gretchen and Keely snoring softly, I crawled in with them. And slept till the Littles came screaming in, they found Leda's bunny dead in the yard. We all followed outside. Merlin looked so small and still, yet there was no sign of death but a little pool of grass vomit. Keely remembered hearing pet rabbits would eat themselves to death if given a chance. The Littles could not be consoled, and when Leda had not come home by mid-afternoon, I dug a hole in her fallow garden, they picked wildflowers, lining the grave with them, swaddling Merlin in Scottie's treasured blue flannel blankey, they bore Bunny's little body to the hole in Ava's dolly carriage, crying, promising to see him in heaven, each placing a precious possession in the hole. Lance a full box of caps, Robby his Santa Claus Pez dispenser, Scottie chocolate Fizzies, Ava her only intact Barbie, and they took turns shoveling dirt, and covered the barrow with stones.

Corbett called at 4PM "Hi. I hope you had as sweet a dreams as me. I just got to practice, and Erik volunteered us to play a party tonight. Some buddy of his rented the Presbyterian Church in Aptos. It's on Trout Gulch Road. You can't miss it. Anyway, no big surprise, we're going directly from practice and I can't come get you, but I can take you home. Why don't you invite the MotherTruckers and come". I loved this man giving me reason to talk to Gretchen "Leda's bunny died this morning. We don't know how. And she hasn't come home yet and doesn't know. Maybe having somewhere to go will soften the blow". I could hear Erik "Damn it Hawk, come on, you think we could have some of your precious attention for a while". Corbett's voice lowered almost inaudible "Sorry, I got to go".

Gretchen and Keely were fixing food for the Littles, and fell silent when I walked though the eucalyptus curtain "So I was thinking, I know we're not talking and all that, but maybe for Leda's sake we could just cancel the war". A co-operative Yeaaaa came from the Littles. I realized this was for them too. Gretchen's eyes narrowed "I though you hated me". It was her who said she hated me "No I don't. Hating you would be like hating my self". Ava's little voice pleaded "Mooooom, come on Mooooom, pleeee-ase". Gretchen went flat "Well, it's fine with me". I looked to Keely "And you". She hesitated "Yeah, course, you know I'm against war". We laughed. As the Littles marched around the kitchen chanting "No more war. No more war". They sat down for bologna and mayo on Wonderbread and Campbell's tomato soup. Lance raised his sandwich to me "Wana bite". Though it was dead cow and pig and chicken and who knows who's parts, such an innocent peace offering could not be denied "Okay, one bite. I don't usually eat animals". Awkward unwelcome silence, sorry I said it, fortunately Corbett had given me ready antidote "Hey, there's a party to-night and the MotherTruckers are invited. Let's go". Gretchen had only one question "Sure, if I can wear the silk dress". An impudent exploitive test of new-born peace, I wanted us to be like old times, Sistas even if short-lived "Oh, you mean the one you wore yesterday. Well, just because I love you, you can have it". She shrieked, and kissed me on the mouth "Wow, cool. What time's the party". I realized Corbett didn't say "Prob-ably eight". I looked to Keely, the friend who took me in to Hydra "Hey you. I know you're a jeans and t-shirt kinda woman, but I have a gown for you too". She smiled her crooked-tooth grin "Who's party". I sniffed sarcastic "Oh your faves. The Band's playing the Presbyterian Church in Aptos. Some buddy of Erik. Luke and Joey will be there for sure, so I understand if you don't want to go". Gretchen put her hand on her hip and stuck-out that fine-cut chin "Those fucking assholes don't determine where we go". The we again, still I loved the best of these audacious women and they loved mine.

Painting, primping, Keely trying on all nine finished gowns, picking the high-neck new-grass-green silk ankle-length sleeveless, slit up the front to above-the-knee, a plunging-V down the back, burgundy and petal-pink braided silk belt wrapped twice round her daffodil stem waist, tying in the back, the knotted ends hanging to the hem, it fit her in all the right ways. And we waited for Leda. She and Keely had taken the Littles to Capitola's Carnival and Sandcastle Building Contest yesterday. Lance made the finals with two other Boys, and started a broil with one for copying his moat. Leda and the other Boy's Mom Cyrene found me in common. Lance won the twenty-five-dollar second prize, and being himself, spent it on rides and candy cotton for the Gang. Cyrene invited everyone home for a bar-b-que chicken dinner. She and Leda were taking magic mushrooms when Keely and the Littles left. Leda called from Cyrene's just before 7PM. Stanley had invited them to a party at the Presbyterian Church and asked her to extend welcome to us. Gretchen did not have heart to tell of Merlin on the phone. Keely hired the fourteen-year-old neighbor girl to baby-sit. Lance went furious, indignant, insisting he was grown enough to get paid the money. I think Keely asked her mostly to placate me, for she and Gretchen often left the Littles alone. I'd come home more than once to Ava Scottie and Robby huddled in their bedroom closet. When I voiced outrage, Lance was quick to protest, he was a Big Boy, and those Babies were just playing hide-and-go-seek. I pitied the sitter, if she tried to rule, we would find her gagged and bound in that closet. Corbett called before leaving practice to see was I coming. I told him the MotherTruckers would be making maybe a final a appearance in all our glory. Like a great band, we were a volatile and divine mix of Valkyries, Medusa and the Muses, in silk and feathers, patchouli and glitter, we stepped into the Plymouth Concord, it started on the first try, Littles chasing us down Fairmount Avenue.

Trout Gulch Road took us to Church, both sides lined with cars, the parking lot was jammed, our trusty Plymouth barely making it up the long dirt driveway of the farmhouse across the street, someone Gretchen knew. It was after 9PM and still light, *Get on Board*, Erik's best tune beckoning us come be one of the happy crowd, the in-crowd. Electricity prickled the air as we marched arm-in-arm down the driveway, meeting Leda and Cyrene in the lot. Every head turned as we made entrance. For me there was none but Corbett, his eyes holding me tender for not a second, hands soaring an organ solo that stood everyone on sacred ground, and then seamlessly into *Chantilly Lace*, just for me. The modern glass and exposed beam Church looked more like a tropical fish tank, teeming, feasting on long folding tables of sliced meats, smoked salmon, Boston baked beans, macaroni and potato salads, corn-on-the-cob, cornbread, French bread, green Jell-o molds, orange Jell-o molds, watermelon, cantaloupe, cold beer, wine, an enormous punch bowl, and a full-sheet-cake saying Happy Anniversary Genie and Ronnie. I knew better than to eat a thing. My Sistas did not share Persephone's concern, eagerly joining the Bacchanalia. I took a bottle of Coors, made sure it hissed inviolable as the cap came-off, and tucked myself under a shadowed balcony, leaning against the wall, watching Corbett. One Hand Clapping was easily ready for audition, taking the congregation into outer-space, yet they did not appease the electric-shudder in my bones, testifying to what could not be seen, Nick was not here but I felt the Dark Brotherhood. The Band landed with *Sentimental Journey* for a break. Corbett scanning the room for me, snatched a beer and went out the main door. Staying still, watching through the glass as he walked into the parking lot, I darted-out the back door to meet him, and found Gretchen, mascara streaking her pale face, she clung to me like a terrified cat, stoned on bad acid, swearing she had not taken any. I flashed on the red confetti floating in the punch bowl "Gretch, listen to me. The punch has blotter acid in it, did you drink any". She pushed me away "Joey's got a knife". Covering her tits with her hand she pleaded "Says I'm teasing him from the dance floor". Leda came running "Oh God, oh God, Joey. This is such a bummer. I wana go home".

They began gabbling a private language, the sound of scared easily understood, the acid so brawny and possessive I could feel it unsettling the air. And they became pastel feathered birds, gibbering louder, faster, flying out onto the lawn, settling in slow-motion. I did not go with them, speaking deliberate "Okay, listen to me, listen. There's acid in the punch, bad acid judging how freaky things are. We need to find Keely and Cyrene and go home". Eyes wide, glittering at me as if watching some hilarious puppet show, they began clapping in delight, spawning rounds of *Pease porridge hot*. My mind went to Corbett, I must warn him, touch him, one more try "Gretchen, Leda, come on, please". Oblivious, spaced-out children chanting abracadabras to ward-off the Monsters, Corbett's *Light My Fire* overture filling the air, interrupting acid's reign, popping-off the ground they trotted blithely into Church.

Joey Angel-Face stood on stage blowing his harp. I remembered Lucifer being called the brightest and most beautiful, and wend the crowd to Corbett. Blue eyes shining a comforting embrace, he mouthed "You okay". I nodded "Are you". He nodded, and went to work. His talent, his command giving him sway over circumstance, everyone on the same bad trip, and the local chapter of Hell's Angels had arrived, drunk and high on every things, and as usual under the guise of doing security, assumed control. Raul walked-up to Keely and grabbed her proud little tits. Rage shook her face, in a blink of super-adrenaline she knocked his hands away, seized the front of his black leather vest and threw him to the floor. Backs tensed in anticipation of the Dark Brotherhood's automatic code, ego preservation irregardless. Corbett had his wits, turning the Hammond into a circus calliope, capriccio snaring every one, and sensing they were his, he announced round two at Madison Square Garden and unleashed an intrepid rendition of the Gillette Cavalcade of Sports theme song, somehow so right-on, imminent hostility bowing respectfully in the face of Court Jester and King, collective sigh exhaled, still too close to the raw edge, threatening to escalate at any thing. Word circulated the acid had been cut with strychnine to boost heart-rate, enhance the high. The Angels gathered round the punch bowl and drank it dry. The Band played one more song, Corbett stepped-off stage and took my hand. I could feel the Event Horizon, music had been the anchor, the building about to be sucked-in, if we did not go now we would have to take the ride. Threading fingers though his I pulled him toward the door. Corbett did not want to leave his equipment behind, it wasn't even paid for yet. And I did not want to leave my Sistas, but it was too late, like Sky River, the congregation had decomposed into a writhing heap of earth worms. We made for the Healey.

Taking the Sandoz and not Limey's Confetti, we had been spared last night and tonight. Corbett drove into Santa Cruz, there was no where for us to go but the Dream Inn. Leaning across the small booth, we sipped Mai Tais and whispered till the place closed, then walked the Boardwalk onto the pier, kissing under every lamp, content in each other's company, we talked little important details, stories, not noticing dawn expose our communion, another morning, aching and no where to be alone, the pier coming alive with bushy-tailed fishermen and bakery trucks delivering fresh to Malios. Corbett took me to a bar he knew, open 6AM, the door knotted with Solitaries, we all stood anticipating our respective fixes, and when it swung opened, were swept-in. Bartender came to us first. Corbett ordered beers and pickled eggs. The Tender smiled "Sure thing Hawk, on the house as usual". Corbett turned to me "I'll play some tunes. Do you mind". I was delighted "No, not at all". Every red-rimmed eye lovingly escorted him to the cigarette-burned, well-tuned Baldwin upright against the wall. *Take Five, Green Dolphin Street, Green Onions, Take Me Out to the Ball Game*, I marveled at his repertoire, his empathy for these walking wounded, transforming isolation into morning sing-along. I fell inlove with him again, and simmered pure hate for his Parents wounding him like these Solitaries. Corbett introduced me to everyone by name. And beer exhausting the last of us, he drove me home, still no where to go, we needed some sleep. I was happy to see the Plymouth parked in the driveway, all home, still tripping, heads pounding, joints aching. Leda sat on the floor in a puddle of tears over Merlin. Gretchen's upper arm had a bruise the size of a big hand. Keely's gown dirty, torn. As long as they were safe, I kissed Leda on top of her head, and went to bed.

After noon, Girls still sound-asleep, I made coffee and took it outside. Littles, building a massive fort in the front yard, kitchen chairs, sawhorses, shovels, rakes, sheets, blankets, towels, they were starving. I gave Lance five-dollars for burgers, then showered, folded eight gowns, tried to start the Plymouth, and hitched to the Santa Cruz Import Shop. Owner balked at my higher price, fifty-dollars each. I could have argued they're silk, but did not have it in me, folded 320 dollars into my pocket, headed to the news-stand for a Seattle Times, and on way to the Catalyst stopped to phone Corbett. Lorenzo's wife Marion answered, acting as if I was a complete stranger, she said he was not home. I left no message, frustrated, weary bearing-up to such ill-will. Settling into a chair, I ordered cream-of-broccoli-soup, two whole wheat rolls with butter and jam, coffee, and spread the paper on the table. Front page – *The Pentagon Papers* – Daniel Ellsberg, a defense analyst for the Pentagon and former Vietnam counter-insurgency advisor, and Anthony Rosso, who interviewed Vietcong prisoners and conducted studies on the chemical spraying of rice crops in Vietnam and Cambodia. They had copied and stolen from the Rand Corporation in Santa Monica a classified history of United States Policies in Vietnam through the summer of 1968, including secret memos, and released them to the New York Times, stating *that the anti-war movement had moved their conscience to act.* These documents confirmed what the Movement claimed, that Lyndon Johnson was planning military action as early as 1964 while publicly pledging - *No wider war.* That the United States was in Vietnam mainly to preserve an image of strength, and knowingly violated the Geneva Accords. I was out-of-my-skin, vindicated, angry and sad so many had died, and been arrested, and grateful, indebted to Ellsberg and Russo for being response-able. My insides filled with the warm nearly forgotten feeling of hope, the playing-field had suddenly tilted our-way, it was no longer our word against Nixon and his brigands, two of their own found conscience and gave us proof the government lied and conspired, and protected their egos with the lives of other people's kids. Now maybe the middle-class would stir and join us to stop to the war.

Cyrene came in the door, I waved her join me. She ordered a Budweiser, and had no interest in my exhilaration "Please, lay off that save the world stuff. My head's got a freight train running through it. Every joint in my body's on fire". I fished a tin of aspirin from the bottom of my bag "What happened last night. I left early". She took three "Thanks. Guess I was lucky. I drank just a few sips of the punch. Everyone else got totally wasted. Thank God Stanley took me home. I heard the police came after we left, busted the people that threw the party, but couldn't do much more, there were too many out of their mind to take 'em all in". A grin lit her face "Stan invited me to a party tonight. A house on Granite Creek Road. Moby Grape's gona record an album there". Her grin grew "He invited meee. So I came in town to find a dress. Hey, we should go together. You know how awful it is to be around those mighty bitches when you're an outsider. Hawk'll be there". I was surprised "Corbett didn't say anything. How do you know he'll be there". She was so pleased "Stan told me. One Hand Clapping's gona play for an hour at the party". I did not want to be the voice of reason but couldn't help my self "You know Stan's still living with Goldie". Her eyes flashed "I don't care. He invited meee, not her". If Corbett wasn't there I saw no reason to go "Maybe you should ask Gretchen, since Delroy will be there". She shook her head vehemently "No way. His Wife'll be there. If I'm with Gretchen, it'll just make my life miserable". Excusing my self to the bathroom, I called Corbett instead. This time he answered, having just phoned the MotherTruckers for the third time to reach me. Erik had arranged for the Band to play. Record execs would be there, he could pick me up at 6PM. I explained going with Cyrene would make it easier on her, and I would have some one to hang with while he played. He cautioned she was not as true as she might seem. I returned to the table thinking, does it really matter if I'm being used, my old friend Rachel used me most of our friendship, and I her. On first realizing this, I was repulsed, feeling exploited we did not have an ideal completely altruistic friendship, but came to understand some Friends are necessary convenient allies in a mostly hostile callous world, there for a time and gone, a little platonic love affair, and knowing this instead of expecting perfection was one way, a forgiving way of being friends. Cyrene thanked me over and over, guzzled her beer, and rushed me to finish the soup, she would take me home and go get ready. I obliged. Driving a bit giddy and giggling, she shoved a Santa Cruz Import Shop bag across the seat for me to check-out her one-hundred-and-twenty-five-dollar dress, excited for Stanley to see her in it, confident she would be utterly irresistible. I ooed and awed, silent about just selling this gown, wondering how she had money to buy so expensive on welfare. Dropping me at 5PM, she would return in an hour.

Crossing kitchen's threshold, Keely and Gretchen summoned me from the living room. Sour-faced, spread on the couch, leaving me no where but standing, our truce plainly over. Leda came from the bedroom, puffy face, clothes rumpled, and stood near me. I wanted to hug her but stayed my ground "You okay Sweet-Pie". Looking at me without expression she shook her head no. Gretchen dispatched "Keely and I want you to move out as soon as possible". I took-in a slow breath and let it huff out my mouth "So, I guess the question is how come". Gretchen would not look at me "You been hitting the Kids and it has to stop". Staggered, I counted to ten, flattening my feet, glaring at Keely, she was still so needy, I wanted to buy her twelve place-settings of deluxe 24-carat gold-rim Lenox dish-es, cups, saucers, teapot, sugar, creamer, serving bowls, platters, and let her smash them one-by-one on a stone floor, maybe it might begin to pacify her relentless lack of self-worth "Are you in this too". Looking at her nails bitten-to-the-quick she said nothing. The house seemed holding its breath. I slowly inhaled to contain a rising fury "Okay, um, I don't know how to respond to this crap. But you know it's not true. I am not the one who hits the Kids. You've mistaken power tripping for love, for caring, and want me gone before they know the difference. I have to tell you, it's too late, they know. I guess you don't remember your childhood. Kids are smart, they see everything, they have big ears. It hurts me how much they want your love. So, I guess the question is, who paid the rent, and who should move out". No one made a sound. I was trembling from confrontation, slipped though the eucalyptus curtain to disappear, and found the Littles gathered in a tight ball eavesdropping. Lance took my hand "Pleeeeease don't go". I kept my voice deferential "Would you come in the living room with me". Willingly, bravely he pulled me though the curtain to face Mom. Ava, Robby, Scottie following. I spoke soft and even "Have I ever laid a hand on any of you". Lance stood tall "No way Jose. My Mom hits us, and Gretchen, not you an Leda". Arms straight at her sides, fists clenched tight Leda hissed "This just stinks. I will not be part of it". She faced Gretchen and Keely "If you want Shoshy to go, I'm going too". Her resolve was contagious, I had chosen better that the best of a poor lot in her "She's right. This stinks. You're jealous of my freedom. I made choices in my life, an you did too, an you hate me for mine and somehow think it's okay. Well it's not". I waited, not one sound "Well, I guess if you won't talk to me, there's no more to say". Leda withdrew to the bedroom and quietly shut the door. Littles ran though the curtain. Heart thumping in my ears, I took the phone from the floor and called Andrew. He welcomed me stay, Luke had gone home for his Father's funeral. Leda was welcome too. And though they heard every word, I announced "I'm leaving". Gretchen was not moved. Keely made timid eye-contact "You don't have to go". I laid the Seattle Times on her lap "Oh yes I do. Here's some good news. I hope it makes you happy".

I went after the Littles. They were throwing toys round their room starting a fight. I stood at the door "Thank you for the truth Pussycats. Can I come in". Robby screamed "No. Who's gona buy us burgers". Smiling inside how open, how unashamed these mercenaries, I knew they would be all right without me. Lance threw his baseball mitt at me "I hate you". I let it hit my thigh "It's okay Mr.Man. You can hate me cause I love you". Ava and Scottie took up the chant "Hate you. Hate you. Hate you. Hate you". Lance fought tears and strode-up to me "I'll go talk to my Mom". This one was far too good at mediating, having done it too often "Thanks Mr.Man, but no". I took five from my pocket and gave it to him "Here's for burgers". Leda warned me a storm was brewing so I was not completely ambushed, but I could not have imagined such a heinous lie, and breezed through the living room, ignoring, into the bedroom where Leda was packing her things "Thank you. I'll never forget how you stood with me. Andrew offered us a place to stay. Luke's gone". She had resolve "I'm hitching to San Jose and flying home. I'm done here". Her tears came fast "This is the end of the best friends I ever had". I took a step "We're still friends Honey. And I'll probably be in Seattle next week. Take you to meet Ida Rose". We hugged dear and tight knowing it was not the end. Gretchen and Keely stayed on the couch waiting me out. I went to the shed, packed my tools, fabric and notions in a few cardboard boxes, pulled on my living dress, stuffed everything else in the back-pack, set them outside the kitchen door, and strolled-out into the golden evening sunshine for a smoke. Leda found me for good-bye. I worried her starting so late, alone, it wasn't smart. She would not stay in this house one more minute. Leaning against the door jamb, I lit another Marlboro, watching her steady gate down Fairmount Avenue, envying those big feet planting so flat on the earth, mentally dressing her in all the protection I had even after gone from sight.

Cyrene drove into the driveway. I raised a just-a-minute finger. The house echoing my foot-falls, spreading the eucalyptus curtain I did not walk through, Gretchen and Keely rooted to the couch. Leda had not said good-bye and maybe I shouldn't, but I wanted, needed a last word "Miss Fine, I hate that our friendship has to end over a man. I still love you, and wish you well". Her head stayed in the newspaper. "Keel, I know you always go along with Gretchen, but you were there for me when I started my new life, and I want you to know I will always love you". Leaning forward, she stood, right hand extending an envelope, voice a tired effort "Here, it came for you today, from your friend Ida Rose". Cyrene honked. I murmured "Thanks". Swinging the curtain together hard, the clatter-ing last word no satisfaction. I had never seen Cyrene in anything but faded jeans and t-shirt, she stepped from the car in peach and carnelian silk clinging to all the right places, natural curls cascading over shoulder blades, and unlocked the trunk. Littles had collected by the boxes, insist-ing on carrying, loading them, and scurrying-inside hoping Moms had not noticed their high treason. My head whirling as we drove North to Granite Creek Road, I thought a last word would ease losing the Littles in the fray, it did not, they were not mine no matter how much I loved them, well fuck you Gretchen, fuck you Keely, just fuck you, fuck you, fuuuuck you, John Lennon's *Imagine* on the radio not enough to stem the rolling poison. I'd learned it's the rolling that marks emotional-poison, round-and-round faster faster swallowing every other thought, I needed to short-circuit the spinning, and told Cyrene. She stiffened "Look, think about it tomorrow okay. There's a party". Scarlett O'Hara, my Granny would say the same, and maybe they were right, why let Gretchen and Keely reach beyond their grasp. And somehow, consciously considering instead of letting it consider me ended the whirl.

A charming old ranch house, long driveway lined with trees and cars including Corbett's Healey, we parked next to it, the yard spreading gently to Granite Creek, a newly build low wooden stage set-up with equipment.

People glutted the covered front porch, taking their turn at a gas-mask attached to a large silver-metal container with Nitrous Oxide stamped in red on the side. Cyrene wanted. I waited with her, looking for Corbett. The few times I'd taken laughing gas sent me out of my body, made me care less what happened to it, a true relief when teeth are being drilled, but I liked being inside now, and other than Maryjane had sworn-off all drugs, having been spared the red confetti, clear warning every trip held the risk of losing my self, going so far into the unknown I might never find the way home again, I did not want to risk this now there was Corbett. Erik had some built-in wire that caused him unbearable pain when ever I was near, way beyond our little battles in Seattle he suddenly burst through the screen door onto the porch glowering at me, and I realized every rejection, every perceived offense he ever suffered at the hands of a female, every emasculation to his ego, he projected on me, treating me accordingly, which on the bright-side probably saved Colleen a ton of grief. I wondered why she married him, specially some one like her, for of all the Girls involved with the Band she was the one who liked her self a little, who liked females in general, the Others had the same disdain for themselves as Erik for me. As he took the gas-mask from Cyrene's hands his eyes burned my face "Shit, what're you doing here". Ignoring him I pulled her though the same door, and there was Corbett's beauty-full face seeing me from a long couch, Andrew and Lorenzo close on either side. Erik pushed by us "Let's go Hawk, Renzo, Jugman, it's time we do it". Looking easily over Erik's head as he stood, Corbett smiled "Hi Sweetheart". We were left with Raul and his Angels gathered round the glass coffee-table lined in coke, Colleen swelling on a wicker love-seat, proudly displaying her belly, Cherry jealously tending, her eyes so forbidding I dare not approach, and Moby Grape fans, albums in-hand waiting for autographs. I was glad Cyrene and I came together, clinging arm-in-arm we pushed on to the kitchen. Stanley and Goldie there, facing, circling. Cyrene froze. I pulled her through another screen door onto another covered porch. She wanted to charge back in and rip Goldie's throat out. Holding-firm I asked why so mad at Goldie and not Stan. This she did not want to consider, resigning into an old rocker. This porch had the best view of the stage and began to fill, I took the corner of the top step, eyes on Corbett as he found just the place on his organ bench, all the equipment had made it safely home. The Band opened with *Highway One*, Erik on guitar, Joey harmonica, Lorenzo drums, Andrew jug and trombone, none quite in sync with Corbett, no matter how he danced the foot-peddle bass laying a groove, they were just ahead or behind, likely still stung from strychnine. Goldie and Stan were shouting obscenities at each other, the screen door slammed open, he marched onto the porch, stood over Cyrene, ordering her to leave with him immediately. Glancing me a side-ways I'm sorry, she went with. Exasperated at the desertion, I would never trust her again, so desperately wanting this man, me a convenient sacrifice, another girl devalued by another girl for a guy, another collateral cost of what they miss-took for love, I over-grinned in fake-polite, and followed.

April had moved in with Cyrene. Brian was Cyrene's boyfriend Spider's dealer so they knew each other, Spider had moved-out over another girl, Cyrene needed someone to share rent, and April having split with Brian for being violent again, needed to leave her Folks place, they were threatening to take her Son away. Helping my things from the trunk into Corbett's Healey, Cyrene whispered apology. I did not respond, her eyes only for Stan, willing to suffer any humiliation. The porches and house a salad of friends, fans, record people, I did not go in. Uncomfortably considering my own humiliation, walking the yard, trying to relax my shoulders, I took the long wooden-seat of a rope swing hung from the presiding Grande Dame Gothic Oak, feeling some protection beneath her muscled limbs, in clear sight of the stage. The Band did not sound like One Hand Clapping, Corbett the only one cooking an authentic potion, having execs who could sign them, he was a champion, living-up to the Band's cult-status, while the rest had become who they thought the signers wanted them to be, acting accordingly, not their risky intense fuck-you street-selves, making them boring two-dimensional cardboard-cut-outs of themselves, not the People's Band with a message, just another good band. A wave of excitement telegraphed Delroy's arrival, seeing me alone he came over, ever the perfect gentleman "Hey there beauty. Is Gretchen with you". Grateful he shed his grace on me in such a public way, I smiled at his predictability "Don't know where she is. Don't live there anymore". He knew "Aw, she's just pissed. You know, always the one ending things, and you went an spoiled her perfect record". I shook my head "I'm not giving Corbett up for her perfect record". Delroy was amused "I wouldn't give him up either. A great keyboard player's better than a piece of ass any day". We both laughed at Gretchen's expense. Mine was counterfeit, I felt terribly sad, Delroy surely cared for, loved her in his way, and she him above all even knowing he would never be hers alone, but I did not think she thought herself a piece-of-ass to him. Delroy was the Man, the Stud, Mr.Rock-God, definitely enjoying the advantages of his standing, and scared as he professed to be of us Women's Libbers wising-up the rest of the Girls, I think he wanted to believe a boy and a girl could be friends. The moment always fleet with him, Delroy had more to charm, giving the swing a gentle push sideways he moved-on. The moment enough to make my ease, I held the ropes and swung slowly, eyes on Corbett. The Band never made it into the groove, Erik's face a pinched concern as he called the final tune.

I could feel my cheeks heat at Corbett's approach, sliding over on the wooden seat, arranging my dress. He sat close, we laced fingers, comfortably leaning against the other, burnt-orange and purple sky fading through twilight, every thing right with the world. Though tired, we made an appearance in the house. Corbett introduced me to Patty Allen, a gorgeous singer from Seattle who Stanley promised to make a star. Walking the hallway, an ultra-hip record exec hyping plans for the Grape's *20 Granite Creek* album and tour, Erik and Joey posturing a kind-of courting dance, Ted, Stoney, Lorenzo standing like big dogs drooling over the high-class Groupies that come with the ultra-hip. We moved on, Colleen still sitting in the front room, handed Corbett a joint. He passed it to another ultra-hip. Who point it at Corbett "Man, you're the best fucking keyboard player. Fucking genius. I would sign you right now if you ditch the Band". Corbett knit his brows and shook his head "No thanks man, I wouldn't". Limey came in with more cocaine, lining it on the glass coffee-table as we left.

Corbett was delighted at my things in his car, at managing to fit them in the trunk. I felt so unconditionally safe with him, and driving into Santa Cruz, I explained. Listening in earnest, he was sorry circumstances had gone bad, convinced the clash was unavoidable, that Gretchen knew she could only have a piece of Delroy and needed some likely prospect to support her and Ava, some one so enthralled he would happily turn a blind-eye when she went to Delroy, and that could never have been him, whether I came along or not. We went to Jack in the Box, bean tacos three for a dollar, eating slowly, speaking softly, mostly with our eyes. Food began to close them, Corbett took me to Andrews, protesting "Don't you think this is kind of ridiculous, leaving you at another guy's place when I'll just come back tomorrow". He suggested coyly "You already have your stuff in my car, maybe you should move in with me". My head screaming yes yes, oh yes, smiling 10,000 watts I held still "Yikes, I'll have to think about that. Probably won't think of anything else". He reluctantly helped my things to the porch. Jennifer waving her tail, I stood on top step, him on the next, nearly face-to-face, finding our mouths, and said good night. Andrew was not home, I laid my sleeping bag on Luke's bed, Jenn climbed up with me, and before closing my eyes, read the letter from Ida Rose.

> *THE MIND CAN BE CORRUPTED*
> BUT THE HEART ONLY BROKEN
> ITS INTEGRITY ALWAYS REMAINS INTACT.
> THE HEART IS THE REAL CAPTAIN OF THE SHIP
> AND IF THERE IS MUTINY
> THE SHIP FLOUNDERS.
> YOU CANNOT WILL THE HEART
> IT IS TRUE ONLY ONTO ITSELF.
> THE HEART PLAYS ITS ROLE
> *AND I AM HELPLESS TO STOP IT.*

Waking early, somewhere deep in the night having decided yes to moving in with Corbett, helpless to stop my heart. Fresh coffee roused Andrew. I poured him a cup and spilled my joy. He smiled "You two're like John Lennon and Yoko". I laughed "You're right. They blame Yoko for breaking-up the band. And Erik treats me like the Dragon Lady". Early sun sparkling in that unused way, we decided to walk with Jenn to the beach. Andrew had two #4 Partagas he'd been saving. As we walked water's edge, he confessed to a dreadful anxiety for tomorrow night's audition "Erik's attitude is so fuck-up. He's making everyone goose step. Playing's no fun. If we aren't having fun, the audience doesn't get off. You saw it, even Hawk's gargantuan talent couldn't lift us off yesterday". I ventured "It's life or death for Erik". Andrew laughed out loud "Yeah his life maybe, not mine". We walked on in silence, enjoying each other's company, Jennifer in between, pudgy torso swaying to her tail, a kindred spirit like Amaru, and when cigars were stubs, we went home. Andrew's strychnine hang-over still ahold of him, I rubbed his neck and shoulders, and he went back to bed. Jennifer and I to the porch, she put her head on my thigh, while I wrote in my journal.

> I REMEMBER THE LONELY BEFORE YOU
> OH HOW MY BODY ACHED
> WAITING TO FIND YOUR LOVE
> NOW THAT YOU'RE HERE
> WHAT I WANT TO DO TO YOU
> IT MAKES ME SHIVER
> WHAT I WANT TO DO
> I KNEW YOU WHEN I SAW YOU
> DON'T ASK ME HOW I KNEW
> THE FRENCH CALL IT DÉJÀ VU
> IT'S SO EASY TO LOVE YOU
> I NEVER REALLY HAVE TO TRY

Do not go near the audition boomed in my head as if Yahweh himself had issued an edict. I put my pen down, some part of me was laying down the law. I could no longer allow being treated like shit or accept excuses for Joey and Erik's behavior. Stoney, Ted, even Andrew's silence had made them complicit, and from the sound of the Band yesterday, I did not want to be there for what was sure to happen, Erik would find a way to make it my fault. I phoned Mom at work. She called back in ten minutes, there would be a ticket waiting for me at United Airlines leaving San Jose tomorrow night at 9:30PM, Dad would be waiting infront of baggage claim at midnight. Like Bonita-Kay taught me, seeing thing more clearly needed some distance between me and the drama. Corbett joining One Hand Clapping made it certain Erik and Joey would me in-my-face. I was not likely to bear well more abuse, meaning I would have to stay away from practice, gigs, away from Corbett, meaning Erik would wield some control over my life, which he seemed to instinctive understand I could not tolerate, and he would certainly continue to make my life wretched, maybe Corbett and I would fight, maybe I would give-up to save my sanity, and they could have him all to themselves. I had learned well this deadly win-lose dance from Nick, given a choice I would pick win-win, Erik and Joey only knew how to play win-lose, so they must lose.

The phone rang just after noon, Andrew snoring though. It was Corbett "Hi Sweetheart. I'm on the way to practice. But I needed to hear your voice first. Can I pick you up for dinner after". His voice was food to me "Yes please. Ah, I have something to tell you, I'm flying to Seattle tomorrow night". Silent for a long breath "Okay, well, I a, I guess I understand". "No, it's not about you, it's about me. I woke up knowing without a doubt I would move in with you, but first I have a lot of thinking to do, you know like Joey and Erik being in my life". I could hear Lorenzo and Marion arguing in the background. Corbett's voice hushed "How long you plan on being gone up there". Suddenly realizing I would not see him every day choked me up. I cleared my throat "Ahh, I'm not sure, maybe two weeks. My Folks're exhausted. They need a break, and I said yes". He cleared his throat too "What time's your flight". "Nine-thirty from San Jose". His voice smoothing "Good. I can drive you on the way to the gig, okay". I smiled at this willing accommodation "I was hoping you would". He sighed "I've got to go. See you after practice". Andrew and Jennifer snoring in duet. I was restless, nothing to do but wait, and went walking, to Cyrene's. Stepping onto the porch, I could hear Brian and April in high-pitch though the open door and shrank away, stopping by the grocery for peaches, some smokes, the first issue of a new local paper called the Santa Cruz Times that the reporter from the Santa Cruz Sentinal Jay Shore has started, and rambled back into the cul-de-sac thinking how I was going to miss Corbett. My heart leapt into my throat seeing his long frame leaning against the Healey. AWOL from practice, he came to take me walking in the forest of Nicene Marks, 10,000 acres of one-hundred-year-old second-growth.

Flora and her Darlings enveloped us on the wide earthen boulevard that led into this woodland. Once well-traveled by horse and buggy, the dirt ground to fine-powder from hooves and metal wheels, I took my sandals off, the silken earth squishing though my toes. Corbett did too, his long beautiful feet reminded me of Merlin's bunny hoppers. A primeval canopy high above us, statuesque trees, some fallen and turned lush moss couches for Elves and their Consorts, huge thick-stemmed mushrooms convenient landing-pads for Fairies disguised as butter and dragon flies, a winding stream, seeming by chance to dam at the bend, making a clear pool for Dryads and Naiads to bathe, all too shy to let us see more than ambiguous shadows. And the vain and boast-full Feathered Tribe, their lives and conversation not the least disturbed by two mere mortals. Three-leaf clovers big as my hand edging our way, I bent and picked one, offering it to Corbett "I wish this was a four-leaf clover and all your wishes would come true". His whole face turned-up as he took it "From you a three leaf clover is just as good". He leaned down for a kiss. And I could no longer lie to my self, I was running away, and this time I would for sure come back. Standing on my toes I put arms round his neck "You know I'm scared of you. You're the only one ever big enough for me. I'm scared I'll lose my self in you". He hugged me off the ground "It's not so lonely knowing you're in the world". I wanted him so I could only giggle. Hands held, walking our sylvan mansion, children of the slow lane, regarded with not quite wholesome interest by the Elementals and other furtive Creatures, content to let the verdant solitude insulate us for a time, long dusty rays of gold shining though the canopy.

We drove into Santa Cruz, a meal at the Colonial Inn on Ocean Street. And I owned-up to running away, to not being sure I could suffer Erik and Joey regularly. I knew I was asking Corbett to choose "You know it's not just what they say, that's the easy part. It's all the machinations behind the scene. They set you up, and I'm left bleeding". He leaned across the table "I'll never be silent again, even on the subtleties". I felt him sincere "You know those Guys bond over talking about girls' body parts and what they're going to do to them. If you don't participate, they'll turn on you". His smile lit the dining room "I kind of have an ace in the hole, they need me. If they turn on me, so be it. My life doesn't depend on this Band making it. I'm not in music for the glory or the girls. It's the only part of me my Folks couldn't touch. My own place where no one can tell me what to do or how to do it. I guess music saved my life. I've had so many wonderful opportunities because of it. I was hoping the same for Erik, he got wrecked in the army. But I'm not about to sacrifice you for him. My talent won't save him, he's got to do that for him self. We all do". I luxuriated in his torchy voice, his big presence and fearless honesty, flashing-back through the truth of my own life, leaving Casey, Joshua, Nick "It's the same for me sewing. I'm not better than anyone else for it. It just feels good having something that's my own, something I'm good at". I smiled "Funny how we both make a living with our fingers".

Corbett promised to be at practice by 7PM. We left the Colonial, cruised the Boardwalk, Riverside Avenue, East Cliff Drive. Andrew was waiting to catch a ride. Jenn and I sat on the porch till after sun set, never tiring of its resplendent nightly extravaganza, two silly girls missing our men, needing something to fill the void. A can of Alpo beef stew, she gulped in three bites, I ate peaches, showered, and laid down on Andrew's hide-a-bed to read the Santa Cruz Times, Jenn close by, our eyes closing easily to slumber. I found my self in a vast airplane hangar with high gleaming golden roof, huge rolls of paper feeding into huge metal printing presses, becoming a fearsome whining paper snake roaring at terrific speed, that tamed into neatly folded newspapers on black conveyor belts, moving and stacking them in neat bundles, all run by little lizard-people. Feeling too big just standing there, I tried reading the headline, everything was moving so fast, all I could make-out was the logo, a triangle inside a circle inside a square. One of the Saurians, larger than the rest, wearing a white jump-suit and white go-go boots, hurried to tell me "Wait right there, I'll get some tissue paper so you can wrap it". He rushed-off, and suddenly I was overwhelmed with no time to spare, a giant German beer-stein to my left, lifting the ornate silver lid, I scooped a handfull of the gooey-oatmeal gray matter, shoved it in my pocket, some sticking to my fingers, incriminating evidence I am a thief. Everyone, even the presses and conveyor belts went silent as I ran for the only door. Mr.Go-Go Boots clamoring after, waving the tissue paper "Wait, here, use this. No need for a mess. No need to run, it's yours anyway, five times more precious than platinum". I did not slow though the hangar, extremely upset with my self, the door never getting closer, no one else seemed to care I was a thief. Then I was outside, surrounded by four tee-pees, each painted in triangles inside circles inside squares, and two blazing bonfires, one bigger than the other. The Tribal Chiefs were here for a summit, wearing different colored velvet leisure suits with all their traditional beaded symbols and rank sewn on. I was the one dressed in buckskins, face painted red across the eyes, indicating my life-blood flows through my intellect, seven eagle feathers fastened in my long braids, I stood, solitary, content, watching in wonder as The Elder came through the larger fire, unscathed, walking in slow measured steps, long white hair unbraided and floating, face proudly lined, he addressed me with kind yet piercing faded-blue eyes "Dear Princess of the Golden Roof". He laid one hand on his heart, soft fingers of the other barely touching me just below the eyebrows "You will see with your heart". And he took my hands and gently stretched my arms out infront, turning the palms up, my heart pounding anticipation, this was a rite of transformation, I widened my stance to the ready, and a cold cylinder was laid in my arms, elbows bending under the weight. The Shaman had given me The Sacred Calumet, unlike any I ever imagined, five-inch diameter copper pipe, twenty-inches long, engraved in a winged-snake biting its tail, a double-headed eagle, an eight petal rose inside a circle, rubbed to gleaming, and fitted with a carved bone bowl and mouthpiece, a finely braided rawhide carrying strap hanging down with seven eagle feathers attached. The incongruity of what I expected a peace-pipe to be and what I had been given made me burst out laughing. Laughter woke me.

I knew I had been given magical gifts. But what to do with a huge copper pipe and sticky oatmeal five-times more precious than platinum. A forgotten dream came up in Technicolor of a cloaked mystagogue giving me five new magic colors. When I said I could not see them, his voice assured me "Don't worry, you will". I had come to see them as inner bounty, inner wealth, and these gifts of copper and cookie dough, mundane stuff like my self, a girl of little promise, with help from the Sweet Sisters Fate and remarkable teachers I had actually managed to learn to think. And now there was Corbett, the grim specter of loneliness banished, in this alchemy, this Chymical Marriage, my straw had spun into platinum, I'd become the Princess of the Golden Roof, and I loved how it felt. Ida Rose was right, I had been given a gift for my hard work. Jennifer heard the Healey first, we hurried to the porch. Andrew went in without a word, Jenn too, her love-struck brown eyes fixed only on him. Corbett and I sat on the top step, arms, shoulders leaning, sweet melancholy, tomorrow heavy in the fragrant night air. Practice had gone bad, Limey brought cocaine, Erik and Joey too needy-greedy. I listened, not caring much about Erik and Joey, Corbett was here, and his voice was a comfort-ray that soothed my whole being. He reached arms around me, I wanted to take us to the loft, our love so private, it could not conscience Andrew and Jenn's big ears and a bed Luke fucked Gretchen and Keely's brains out. So we kissed and held, and no where to go Corbett stood stretching his hands to the sky "I guess I'll go home for a while so I can come back. You want to go for lunch". I stood too "Yes, I want to go anywhere with you". He kissed me and walked reluctantly backwards to the Healey, singing *Goodnight Sweetheart.* My head streaming with every thing I wanted to say to him, and dear Leda's sparkling loyalty, Merlin's death, and those rolling poison words with Gretchen and Keely, I tried reading them quiet and could not concentrate.

After 10AM, waking, deciding not to pack a thing, proving my return, I showered, made coffee, and waited. Corbett came before noon, we drove the beaches to the Boardwalk, walked water's edge, picking-up white-banded wishing rocks, throwing them over our shoulders, wishs into the waves, Corbett mimicking Mickey Mouse, Donald Duck, Porky Pig, Daffy Duck, Sylvester, Tweedy-Bird, Gladstone Gander, making me laugh, writing our names in the sand, singing Pat Boone's version of *April Love, Red Sails in the Sunset, Love Letters in the Sand.* And to the Broken Egg, omelets and coffee, time ticking ticking, revealing our selves in small ways. And over the mountains to the San Jose Airport. A long good-bye never suited me, and happily not him. Leaving me at check-in, giving me his sweater incase I got cold, he would call me 9AM with news of the audition. I watch his car till it was long gone, how many time I watched him drive away.

Chapter Twenty Four

THE COSMIC PARADOX

Early June nights were often still cold in Seattle, coming though baggage claim I wrapped Corbett's sweater round my shoulders, Dad honked, Mom waving madly. Everything so familiar felt good, I rode quietly in the back-seat, looking-out the window, over the Floating Bridge to Mercer Island, diamond ruby emerald lights rimming Lake Washington, not much had changed but me. Mom and Dad were ragged from working six-a-week twelve-hour days, thankful tomorrow was Sunday. I asked to save our catching-up for breakfast, they were happy to, we hugged and went to our bedrooms. Standing infront of the full-length mirror on the back of my door, I took off my clothes, wanting to see did love show. Yes, I had drawn my quills in a bit, ever so slightly smoother. Ida Rose was right about Corbett being my spiritual protector, no longer alone, his vigilant blue eyes had my back. I slid open the closet, pulling-on some of my high school clothes, molted skins of who I used-to-be, and yet I was still that same girl.

Sleeping only in Corbett's sweater. I dressed and waited by the phone before nine. On-the-minute, he voice sung-out, whispering pure and hollow in that low reedy timber "Hi Sweetheart. I haven't been to bed yet". It felt so deep down good to hear his voice "I miss you. Can you feel the distance". His voiced smiled "Yes, I miss you too. How was your flight". I whispered "For the first time ever I wasn't scared. Soooo, tell me about the audition". He sighed "Ah, where to start. Since I didn't ride with the troops, Erik was spitting nails when I got there. Limey had lines set-up in the dressing room. I knew better. So did Andrew. But everyone else indulged big time. Those fools, they got so wired, you know, cocaine music only sounds great if you're jacked-up too. Ted forgot to plug in the mics. We had no opening vocals, and when he did, the feedback fried everyone's ears. Erik had this frozen grin on his face, and wore the red wool suit. He looked like Santa on acid, sweating right through it, itching like a chimp. And Renzo". He chuckled "Renzo thought he was Mario Lanza instead of a good drummer from Novato with a great set of pipes. We never made it into the groove, he kept speeding ahead, playing his kit like a machine gun. Erik too, and Joey. It sounded like an assault, like we just started playing together. We never got near any magic, never really got the crowd off. Saul Zaentz and his wife did come, and left after three songs. Gleason got a hold of me after the first set. He was really pissed the Band embarrassed him infront of his Boss. But you know, I thought the whole thing was kind of Keystone Cops. We weren't One Hand Clapping, but some slapstick version of what a band should be when they're about to make it. We deserved what Gleason said, that we *weren't ready to stand naked and honest and take an audience somewhere they'd never been.* No one gets off on self-indulgent children showing off". Mom came into the kitchen, hugged me from behind, kissing my neck just at the shoulder like she had since I could remember, and started the percolator. I could hear people on Corbett's end too. A muzzled pause echoing the distance between us, we let the silence breathe. Corbett sounded formal "I'll call you later". I understood "Okay". He waited for me to hang-up, and I waited for him.

Dad booked a room at Harrah's, they would leave tomorrow morning sun-rise, drive through Washington and Oregon, maybe to Yreka, spend the night, and take Highway 89 through Lassen Volcanic National Park to Lake Tahoe. Over brunch he wrote-out a daily schedule for running Chicken Valley, what to order, when, who to call, when to pay suppliers, employees, how to do bank deposits. I knew it already, my mind on Corbett, determined to keep feelings for him private, postpone the inevitable sermon on his religion till they met him. Mom asked who called, and I did my best to contain the gushing. Dad was all caution, from his experience even the best Catholic would call you a dirty Jew at their worst, meaning Christ killer, and he didn't want his Little Girl's heart broken like that. I argued all Catholics were not the same anymore than all Jews. Dad couldn't help beaming, he knew how tough it was too stand-up to him and was always proud of me whenever I did. And I knew nothing I could say would reconcile his fears. Mom and Dad had given their Children such a stable loving upbringing, I'd been spared fearing the dreaded knock on the door. They were liberal Democrats, always voted, though Dad believed government mostly served itself and the wealthy, he would often grumble at the end of a complaint – go fight city hall. And they stayed mainly within the Jewish community, didn't have gentile friends that came over to the house. And I did not blame them, having been called dirty Jew plenty they remembered every ugly face, nonetheless I knew in my heart Corbett was not. After noon I borrowed the car to go see Granny. Driving 23rd Avenue South by Hydra and the Country Doctor, demolished to make room for the I-90 expansion and Judkin's Park, all traces of us gone, only time would say if we made a real difference. I went by the Charles Street house, Maya's, and up to the Ave, Hippies, panhandlers, FlowerChildren sitting on the street smoking dope, they looked strange, sadness pinched my heart, that part of my life had passed. Granny, Mom's Mom, I loved her dearly, for unlike Mom she never expect me to be like her. The sweet beauty of grandparents, once-removed from the tangles and issues of parent and child. At fifteen she went from her Father's home to Grampa, who at 27 was a father-figure. Since his death, she had grown drunk on liberty to make all her own decisions, and still quite beautiful, became more vain, focused on flirting, pleasing the male ego, all power to her sexuality. Grampa left her well-off, no need to placate for survival, and yet she did, maybe a necessary diversion to losing her husband so young, maybe she had played the less-than-grown-up arrangement so long it was automatic, maybe she forgot it was a posture, maybe it was all she knew. Since meeting Ida Rose, at seventy-five so wide-awake, ambitious, going full-speed, she took away my fear of growing old, frivolous, waiting to die, if I stayed awake I could continue the adventure. Granny looked years younger than her age, had great legs, and in a kind of competitive desperation, wore fur mini-skirts and flaming red hair. I felt distant and sorry, telling her some about Corbett, while she dressed for an afternoon dance. All she wanted to know, did he have money, was he stingy. I drove her to the Seattle Center for the Sunday Senior Dance. And then by Ida Rose's. No one home.

Mom, Dad were off, and I to the market. It went very well, the man

Dad hired to replace me knew everything I did not, and was so smooth I knew better than to trust him. Corbett and I talked mornings before work, setting up times during the day to do things together, have coffee at ten, a smoke at noon, go outside at 8PM for a cigarette, him facing North, me South, take a bath at 8:30, play solitaire, sympathetic magic making distance not so unbearable. And we planned our living together, our love so young and self-conscious, it was easier saying it on the phone, in letters. I spent nights writing, drawing elaborate borders of bugs and flowers in colored inks, going by the post office first thing. Corbett wrote too, and we began to know each other, our flame given time to steady, not burning quite so hot without the physical distraction, it did not consume us and burn-out. Running away had been the right thing to do.

DEAREST SHOSHANNAH,
HELLO! I MISS YOU...
WHERE ARE YOU RIGHT NOW? I'M PLAYING A LOT OF SOLITAIRE, BUT THAT'S WHERE I PRETEND YOU'RE HERE TOO. IT'S LIKE MEETING A GIRL, FALLING IN LOVE AT A SUMMER RESORT, GOING BACK HOME AND RELIVING ALL THE GOOD FEELINGS. I CAN'T WAIT TILL NEXT SUMMER. IT'S ONLY A FEW WEEKS AWAY.
HELLO AGAIN! I LOVE YOU...
COULD YOU HEAR ME ON THE WIND LAST NIGHT WHEN I SANG CHANTILLY LACE AND CALLED YOUR NAME? I COULD SEE YOU IN MY MIND'S EYE, BUT I'D RATHER LOOK INTO YOUR EYES AND WRAP YOU IN MY ARMS.
LOVE, CORBETT

One Hand Clapping, Erik fell apart after the audition. Renzo, Corbett and Delroy took a five-night gig at the Colonial Inn. So many flocked to Santa Cruz summers there were no rentals available, but I should not worry, he had been to every real estate office, put his name on every list, left the required deposit, and we could stay with Renzo and Marion till then, he swore it was just fine with them. I knew Lorenzo was afraid of losing Corbett to me, that Marion barely hid the same behind her diplomatic smile, and I did not care where as long as we were together, pure happy

Erik and Joey would no longer be in my life.

SHOSHANNAH MY LOVE,

I WANTED TO SAY (AND SEE IF YOU AGREE) LOVE IS SOMETHING YOU NEVER COULD EXPERIENCE UNTIL YOU HAVE IT. WORDS DON'T DESCRIBE IT. ALL YOU'RE SURE OF IS EVERYTHING IS ALL RIGHT AND THAT'S A LOT OF THINGS TO BE ALL RIGHT. IT HOLDS FAST LIKE AN OLD OVERCOAT THAT FITS A LITTLE TOO TIGHT, AND I CAN'T TAKE IT OFF UNTIL YOU COME BACK.

YOU KNOW MARION'S CAT HAD KITTENS. ONE HAS ADOPTED ME. BUGGS-THE-CAT-EYED-BUGGER IS SITTING ON MY SHOULDER AS I WRITE THIS. I'VE TOLD HIM ABOUT YOU AND HE MISSES YOU TOO. WE BOTH HANG AROUND REMEMBERING THE GOOD TIMES. BUGGS SAYS, CORBETT YOU'RE OKAY, BUT NOT HALF AS MUCH FUN AS SHOSHANNAH AND CORBETT. TELL HER TO COME HOME AND MAKE ME SOMETHING TO EAT. I'M TIRED OF YOUR MISERABLE ENDEAVORS TO SATIATE MY APPETITE. I WANT GOOD GRITS. DO YOU UNDERSTAND, PEOPLE GRITS!!

I JUST NUDGED HIM OFF MY SHOULDER. HE'S GETTING A LITTLE PUSHY FOR A CAT WOULDN'T YOU SAY! HIS LAST MEAL WAS SIRLOIN STEAK, FAT JUICE, SPRINKLED WITH CRAB MEAT, MARINATED IN SANTA CRUZ WATER AND MIXED WITH PURINA CAT CHOW. HE SAID IT WAS OKAY BUT NEXT TIME HE WANTS A MENU!

SMALL GRIPE SECTION: RENZO AND MARION SPEND 95% OF THEIR TIME HASSLING WITH ANIMALS. I HOPE IT CHANGES WHEN THE BABY COMES. I GUESS THEY LIKE ALL THE MESS AND CONFUSION, ALL THE ANIMALS BREEDING ALL THE TIME. I DON'T.

RENZO JUST CHASED DOWN A BLACK MONGREL THAT'S BEEN BOTHERING THEIR DOG ANNA (SHE'S IN HEAT). HE FELL DOWN AND RIPPED HIS PANTS. ANNA ALREADY LOOKS PREGNANT ANYWAY. THEY COULD

WRITE A BOOK "THE ZOO KEEPERS OF APTOS: HOW TO REPRESS THE SEX LIFE OF ANIMALS UNSUCCESSFULLY". THEY SEEM TO ENJOY IT THOUGH. I THINK THEY'RE DESTINE FOR AFRICA. BUGGS IS ENOUGH FOR ME, AND THAT'S ENOUGH GRIPING FOR TODAY. ANYWAY IT'S A GOOD THING TO CARE FOR ANIMALS.

LAST NIGHT BUGGS CAME THROUGH MY WINDOW. A LARGE SHEEP DOG THOUGHT IT CONVENIENT AND TRIED TO GET THROUGH TOO. HE GOT STUCK IN THE MIDDLE. MEANWHILE I WOKE OUT OF A LOVELY DREAM WITH YOU TO FIND THIS BEAST HOWLING AND FLAIL-ING IN DESPERATION, WILLING TO GO EITHER WAY. I HELPED HIM OUT THE WINDOW AND DOWN THE SIDE OF THE HOUSE. BUGGS THOUGHT IT ALL VERY FUNNY. IT TOOK ME TEN GAMES OF SOLITAIRE TO FINALLY GET BACK TO YOU AND SLEEP. SUCH IS LIFE AT RENZO AND MARION'S MENAGERIE.

PLEASE COME BACK AND SAVE ME. YOU'RE EVERY FLOWER, EVERY THOUGHT, EVERY HAPPINESS, EVERY SADNESS, EVERY EVERY.

I LOVE YOU, CORBETT

Phone wires, letters, meeting in the air, I ached for his arms, his energy, sleeping wrapped in his sweater.

MY DEAREST CORBETT
IT WAS WONDER-FULL
TO WAKE UP WITH YOU ON MY MIND

AND DREAM OVER COFFEE
AND REREAD YOU LETTERS

IT FEELS GOOD TO BE ALIVE
KNOWING YOU'RE ALIVE

YOU MAKE MY INSIDES FEEL GOOD
MY OUTSIDE FEEL GOOD
MY HEART BEAT FASTER
MY EYES LEAK HAPPY TEARS

MY NOSE WRINKLE AND RUN

WHEN I'M ALONE I'M NO LONGER ALONE
YOU SEND ME SHIVERS

I KNOW I'M ALIVE
I KNOW YOU'RE ALIVE
I LOVE YOU
SHOSHANNAH

Time began to weigh, lifting thirty-pound boxes of iced bird carcasses, chopping their plump little bodies into parts. But mostly, tending a public that said the same thing over and over and over "Is that a good chicken". My sense of humor mostly brought vacant stares "Oh that one, why yes sir, she's a recent Vassar graduate". And their implyed price gouging "I can buy those thighs cheaper in the grocery store". I wanted to tell them, then go do that and leave me alone, or maybe attempt to educate, those cheap grocery store thighs are from Arkansas, land of the lowest standards for growing poultry, and these beauties are grown here, Washington has the highest standards for growing poultry in the country, the exact reason these thighs cost more. They usually bought anyway, and I put my finger on the scale of the mean ones, and said nothing by thank you. Pike Place Market was a main tourist destination, every sort walked by Chicken Valley, and I found my self too tender to deal with the public in such an arbitrary and unprotected way, most especially with tourists, for they were transients, this was not their home, the eyes of their community were not on them, they were free to be their worst, likely to say and do anything. Just the smell of the Market began to make me sick, I began to think of it as the arm pit of humanity.

Mom and Dad came home tired from driving, and refreshed and ready, and winners, 700 dollars ahead. Having taken as much public abuse as my mettle could bear, I had done a booming business, and Dad offered me salary and a car to stay. I loved their selfishness, and owed them the truth "I'm going back to Santa Cruz to live with Corbett". Dad would not look at me "Are you getting married". I folded my arms "No Dad, I don't believe in it, what does a bondage contract have to do with love". Mom was hurt "Is that what you think of our marriage". Unfolding the defenses "No Mom, I'm sorry, you know I don't mean you and Dad. But getting married is legal ownership, I would be owned, can you imagine me owned. Times are different now, women are more liberated, I could never sign my name to something like that." Dad stroked his chin "I never thought of it that way. Your Mother and I wanted children, the right thing to do was get married". I took a deep breath "I know, and you did the right thing. But you got married in 1943, and this is 1971". I hesitated knowing they would not, could not understand "And I don't want any children". They looked so hurt I was sorry I said it "You already paid a big price for me Mom. I heard your Brother and his Wife accused you guys of being bad parents, not keeping your thumb on me. I love you so much standing up for me. They shouldn't be pointing thumbs, I saw their son more than once on the Ave smoking dope. He lies right to their faces. They're the fools, not you. I'm asking you to understand. Wouldn't you rather I tell you the truth". Mom had tears of vindication in her eyes "You saw him smoking marijuana. Are you sure". I nodded "Yeah Mom, I'm sure". Dad's eyes smile at me through a gruff voice "Well, I want to meet this Corbett, as soon as possible". I smiled back "Me too Daddy, cause I know you'll love him".

Booking United Airlines for July 3rd, to land in San Francisco at 11:30AM, I called Corbett. He would count the half-seconds and breaths till picking me up. And I phoned Leda, hoping to take her to Ida Rose. Her Mom wasn't sure but thought she hitched North to Vancouver a few days ago with some friends. It was not her time to cross the threshold, hoping it was mine, I drove to Crescent Avenue. A warm welcome banished any doubt "Oh how lovely. Please come in Lamby. They told me someone would come and help me today. I couldn't be more delighted it's you. Clarence will be here about 5PM. He's driving up from Eugene to run and audit. One of my long time students. I don't think you've met". I shook my head "No, but I heard about him in the audit Eddie did for me when I first came here. He's the one with terrible arthritis". She had a magazine in hand "You have an excellent memory. I've been pouring over this latest issue of Gourmet and want to make the scallops in cream sauce for dinner. Will you stay and eat with us". Not only was I welcome to spend the day, I had to fight wrapping my arms around her, touching her hand lightly instead, my words sounding so inadequate "Thank you. I'd love to". Down the hallway to the dining room I took a seat at the big mahogany table. She brought a cup, poured my coffee from an insulated carafe, and sat infront of her half-full cup "Now tell me, why haven't you brought your Corbett". Exactly what I was aching for, I told of running away to Seattle, writing letters, feeling more able to make clear decisions at a distance, and my Folks' fears. She leaned back as if to get a longer look "Your parents' fears are quite understandable. And well founded. They want you to be safe, and what you're choosing puts you beyond the pale of a Jewish community that would gladly protect you. Every choice has a price. To me Catholic and Jewish together are an influential symbol of healing the cosmic dichotomy. I think you and Corbett must be representatives from your respective cosmic groups. And if your coming together flourishes, you will set an irrefutable example for all the Cosmos that the split can be healed". I recounted the night at Corbett's Folks when he saw wedding ghosts. Leaning-in at corroboration of what could only be supposed, she wanted to hear more. And I felt such relief telling what I could not to my Folks, how in his heart Corbett had fallen-away from Catholicism, yet for lack of a better way continued the rituals, still going to church, and that the more we talked, we understood Christian and Jew were the same. Ida Rose nodded smiling "You right Lamby. Jesus was a Jew. However, there are substantial differences between Catholicism and the original Christians. Jesus' message was of love. But love has not turned out to be strong enough by itself. It needs justice and integrity, something the Jews truly understand. I don't think you and Corbett have been together on this earth plane before, though I'm sure you have been through several days and nights of Brahma together. Your coming together has such potential for conscious reflection, for breaking the old patterns of opposites locked in perpetual conflict". This woman made me feel completely sane.

We finished coffee, and went to the QFC. I pushed the shopping cart, she carefully selecting fresh scallops, shallots, asparagus and fruit, and I hung on her words, too quick for others I brought, but to me the sparkling violins of Glinka's Ruslan and Lyudmila Overture. "You see Lamby, *my spirit has been on this earth 100 million years, and finally my work is culminating, because of new cold-rayed students like yourself. You are the necessary element. The Baby of Revelations, born in travail, the third incarnation after Adam and Jesus, you are the Lords of Humanity, able to read and understand the Books of Life that were opened with Jesus graduation.* What Corbett was raised to believe would save him, *vicarious atonement, well, it's the single most insidious hoax ever perpetrated on humankind, the Great Whore of Revelations, a most difficult indoctrination to get passed once taught. One cannot forgive St. Paul's shattering the real efficacy of the Christian thesis with his classification of Jesus as the Scapegoat of Judah, ushering in vicarious atonement. The idea that someone else can do the work for you, and all you have to do is believe will never do. Though it will be difficult for* Corbett, *or any Catholic to depose the ritual of the Eucharist, he's quite right to reject it. Humans have to do the work for themselves. And do it here on earth. This Carbon Age is the densest stage of the evolutionary experiment so far, giving what we do consequences, and those who would a chance to build character. Working in process in such dense material, not just playing with high order abstractions, has made all the difference. You cold-rayed children are learning to be responsible by becoming conscious. In the Age before our Carbon Era, which was hydrogen in essence, and characterized by group-consciousness, where there was no free will, the mind-activity was of a dream nature. Objects might be imagined, in fact were, for short periods of time, but the gaseous substance had no structure for holding form, with one significant aspect as Whitehead assumed, there were no negative prehensions, no sin, no sickness or death, a world of innocence such as one finds in our Bible, in the somewhat naïve and oversimplified story of the "Fall", where the moment you stopped thinking of something it disappeared, there were no apparent consequences. But with the dawn of the "Big Bang Carbon Era", of a more gross substance, it became possible to handle substance. Whether it was inevitable or even over due is left to conjecture, but some stalwart entities ventured away from the ritualized hydrogen chemical-mental, restricting but orderly system and began experimenting with thought and process. Some materialized as the Fallen Angels, but many so fragmented themselves they were practically morons. They had fragmented themselves into oblivion, for they were cut off from primordial energies, and the Bible says, driven down into creation to work the mayhem described in the Book of Enoch. The earth and its life forms are not the direct creation of a universal God. It is as though the whole Cosmos were but one living organism carrying the basic potential for all that happened, and is ultimately self-purifying. The trouble lay in those two words good and evil. For some reason the Fallen Angels chose to know life through death, good through evil, male through female, spirit through form, and the great dichotomy entered the thought process, carrying with it the inevitable or at least consequential battles of mind and body. What did emerge into use at that point was what Whitehead called God's conceptual experience. This emerges as being plural. In our audits we found at least 50 aspects so far, extracted from the inner memories of actual people whom had two or more, qualities of mind dealing with process overshadowed by motivation. I call them rays, designations, frequencies with which mind can work, and they are in part; life and light, the basic plasma in which all others work, then power, truth as an on-going cosmic factor of dynamic creativity and evolution, beauty, wisdom, love, and the cold rays; precision, perception, brilliance, clarity, charity, harmony, integrity, faith, courage, justice, diligence, ingenuity, service, hope, endurance, ethics or ethos, and the frosting on the cake whimsy. It seems there was no humor in the Older Cosmos, deficient according to Whitehead. If humor is derived from the juxtaposition of the incongruous and they had no negative prehensions, how could they laugh. Anyway, when the plea went up to heaven, according to Enoch, the Arch Angels were sent down. This was not altogether effective if we are to judge by the earth being destroyed in the deluge of Noah. Then another plea went up and another group came and established the Cabalistic structure in our planetary system, with three staffs, one of spirit or male, one of form or female, yang or yin, mercy or severity, with the center path of moderation being the path of the redeemer, which Korzybski enunciated in his disciplines of General Semantics. The ancients of the older Cabala had no method for walking the middle path of moderation excepting by astral travel, another regressive trap. They went to Venus to learn love, Mars to learn force, Mercury to learn mind, even the moon was a stage in the cabalistic development and once supported life. We need only look at how the Fallen Gods playing with abstractions eventually destroyed those world, to see where earth was heading too if we hadn't graduated Jesus. If the brigands had won, we'd be dead pock-marked worlds all. Then a plea went up once more and Jesus was sent down. Someone had to graduate from the world to complete the circle, the snake swallowing its tail as in the ancient Cabala. No wonder Jesus is spoken of as the trail blazer, the first fruits of the spirit. It had to be someone, an entity capable of walking in grace which he certainly was, and yet having the human-carbon experience. Someone, who while being divine, had known suffering in a fully conscious body. We must deduce that some music, art, writing and poetry are derived from the intuitive form of the Hydrogen Era process, such as the writings of Virginia Woolf, and by her own admission, Taylor Caldwell, not to mention the music of Mozart, who had to dart from his carriage and hasten into a building in order to write down the music being played for him in his brain-mind before it got away from him, in contrast to Beethoven who toiled away four years on one symphony, working with calculations or whatever mechanism musical genius uses when creating the hard way. I think also, one needs to mention the efforts of a whole civilization such as Tibet to graduate their Dalai Lama, free him from the wheel of rebirth, while he comes back time after time, they claim. As Jesus said, "By their fruits ye shall know them". Isn't the sad plight of India, with some 50 millions spending their lives sleeping on the streets in rags and dirt, some indication of being held in remission to some previous state of thinking rather than moving on into positive consciousness. This older system is the roots of the new growth, toward finer and finer perception, to a true democracy, and the essence of humanity at its best and most thoughtful will comprise this new age. In fact, we are told in the audits that America was a divinely inspired experiment making possible Jesus' promise of life more abundant, which was not realized in his time, excepting in idea, where the "river of life would flow more abundantly and whosoever would, might drink of it freely". When I once asked Korzybski why he developed General Semantics, he said; "I hoped to make thought competent enough to overcome egocentricity and impulse". Some physicists are suggesting that all brain functions, ESP, direct-brain perception, clairvoyance, distant viewing, psycho kinesis, out-of-body experiences, telepathy, and cosmic consciousness or enlightenment are aspects of one phenomenon, a subatomic and universal intelligence system that receives, integrates, and transmits information at a level much deeper than the sensory appearances of what we call space/time and separateness. And this intelligence system, although outside space/time as we know it, manifests within space/time as electrons, atoms, molecules, cells, complicated creatures such as man, planets, stars and whole galaxies. In our cos-*

mology we describe this as an underlying structure of consciousness, pro-grammed by some kind of cosmic DNA factor, emergent from the basic cosmic-plasma called light, life, and love, the cosmic cement, all innately beau-tiful and intelligent, but rather blatantly misused in the creative efforts of the Fallen Angels. Hu-man has come a long way, and we are given to understand that any cosmic process and evolvement from now on will carry as a spear-head the essence of that marvelous product achieved by hu-man, the development of a brain-vehicle which has more possible interconnections than all the protons and electrons in the known universe, and that this "mind", this consciousness will be the flower of the Tree of Life beyond any reasonable expectations ever conceived or dreamed of in the older Cosmos. General Semantics can help us to read the Books of Life with more accurate tools for judging truth, if it's ever allowed to get out to the public. And I doubt that will happen except in small frames of reference. There are powerful deadly forces opposing me, but it only take a few to hold up the whole world". I could not have repeated this to save my life, but I got it, wanted her to know, and fumbled for something to say "Ida Rose, can even the Devil hear the truth". She smiled big *"Yes, at some level every entity recognizes the truth".* The fuzz on my arms stood "Good, I'm glad no one escapes. Look, my hair's standing up". Smiling bigger her eyes twinkled "Now isn't that just a perfect example of how the unconscious recognizes truth".

Back in the kitchen, I washed breakfast dishes, and Ida Rose peeled the fat stalks of asparagus so no grit could hide, floured the scallops, and inquired of my Folks "They must be extraordinary people, you've turned out so well". "They are. I didn't have to fight for my life growing up. I told them about you, and they had a hard time believing I hang-out with a 75 year old woman. If you're ever down at the Market, stop by Chicken Valley and say hello". Ida Rose had a hearty laugh. And I offered "If you want, I'll do your hair". She took me upstairs, Clarence would be staying the night, if I put fresh sheets on the spare room bed, she would have time to wash her hair.

Rolling each curl carefully. While she sat under the dryer, I vacuumed the front room, hall and dining room. Her hair combed-out just right, she made her famous spaetzle, steamed the asparagus, sliced the kiwi and strawberries and lychee nuts onto a platter, drizzled them with honey and fresh lime, and prepared the cream sauce. I went into the back yard, cut some pink roses, arranged a centerpiece, and set the table with starched linen, sterling and Limoges. We were a smooth team, dinner rested in a warm oven, scallops waiting the last minute to be quick-fried in butter and garlic. And we sat down in the living room to sip peach brandy with our pinkies in the air.

I took an instant visceral dislike to Clarence, felt it was mutual, and remained politely quiet though dinner, listening to them talk of old friends. After the fruit platter, we went into the living room. Clarence took off his shoes and laid down on Roosevelt's green brocade couch. Sitting up straight on the Louis the 15th chaise longue, hands folded in my lap, I stared at his striped-silk sock. Ida Rose situated in the winged chair near his head, took her yellow legal pad and pencil from the side table, dated the page and asked Clarence "Are you ready". He said "Yes".

Ida Rose petitioned: *"Please take Clarence into whatever valence, stream of consciousness, point on the time track necessary for what you may wish to say to us. When I count from five to one you'll be there. 5-4-3-2-1."*

Clarence began to speak in a way that was not entirely his: *"I see this entity who we identify as Jesus silhouetted against a golden, orange-golden light. As though with a wave of his hand, he lays before us the panorama of those whom you label as the "Fallen Angels" or Gods. But you must know their role was legitimate, some were motivated by the meanest of motives and some by the noblest. Some seeking self-aggrandizement, some playing the role of sacrifice. They are neither good nor evil. They are players of the cosmic game, striving with desperate intensity to make the thesis that they impressed upon the Cosmos a viable one.*

Ida Rose, I see you and three of your friends playing pinochle, and you are apologizing for the intensity with which you play the game. But with intensity is the only way to play the game. It has no substance, no permanence, but it does have the essence that forms character, builds substance, provokes growth, breeds attitudes, emotions. These are the realities of the game, all intangible, non-physical, but they have their permanent ever-lasting effect.

Now we take the cosmic view, extend the parallel of the pinochle game and view the desperate, intense reasons behind this tremendous cosmic drama. It's a paradox in that what we see has no substantial reality, yet, we live with the effects, the changes it promotes, the growth it stimulates. Heaven and earth can pass away, but the effects of this cosmic drama live on forever.

There is nothing so small or insignificant as to be unnecessary in that the smallest of these things that exist are part of or have their effect on the cosmos. Nothing is unnecessary — from the least significant item to the greatest entities; there can be no separation or divorcement.

I refer again to the pinochle game: the player makes a bid and exercises every means at her disposal to make that bid viable, to see if by any means with the cards at hand, she can meet the bid. It's not good. It's not evil. It's simply playing the game.

Before the game could be played, an environment had to be created and the implements of the game created. Just as to play the pinochle game, there must be cards, the game, a table, house, language, etc. All these had to be created before the game could be played. In a sense, this creation is the greatest, yet it is a transient creation because it is only supportive of the contest — the conflict of theses that is to take place. When its purpose has been served, the cards, game, table, house can vanish forever. But the theses that were tested, the growths that were made, the communications that took place, the sheer intensity of living will forever exist.

This entity, this Christ, truly the Son of God, the incomprehensible God, charged with the responsibility for the feeding and upbringing of the people of earth — I see him, almost facetiously as the janitor of the earth, cleaning up the debris of the battles, seeing that the garbage is dumped off the earth. Seems to be his big task at the moment. This was a brawl, worse than a 'western' saloon fight. The job being done is tremendous, Christ is not pushing a broom but directing the clean-up. He has many friends and servants who are actually doing the job.

But the important thing is that the brawl is ended. The dust has settled and order can be restored. It would have been foolish to call a saloon a chapel while the 'western' bully, typified as in 'western' movies, the tough guy in the black hat, was saying, "This is my town. We do it my way. We do not want law and order".

The villain had the right to be there. And had not the righteous had the te-

merity to meet this challenge to dirty their hands, the work of Christ could not have been done.

Referring again to the cosmic paradox. The Great God, before whose light Christ is but a silhouette, created the universe with the potential for everything to happen which has happened. One cannot play pinochle without cards and without rules. One cannot play pinochle just staring into space. The Cosmos was created with all the potential for challenge.

But a thesis being pursued by a lesser god which is flawed, be the flaw ever so subtle, such a thesis will be destroyed by this flaw – it is self destructive. And the only thing which can persist forever becomes, therefore, only that which is truth. And, thereby, the Cosmos adds substance to itself because all that is destroyed by this flaw is the untruth, the anti-truth. Similar to a crucible, the dross is separated from the gold. It's a valid underlying principle.

We view the Cosmos with such a small eye, having not the capacity to appreciate all that's going on, the thesis being tested. We only see a small segment at a time and are only concerned with that small segment. And only a few people know that there was a fight going on at all. The rest have just been dealing with bric-a-brac, thinking it's the reality when it's not.

In this brawl, this mess that was of such importance to the world, there were a lot of innocent bystanders who were hurt, but they were here by their own choice and in that sense, not innocent bystanders. Some came to do their little bit. Some came to see the big guys square off. Some came just to observe, but all came of their own choice.

The most important phase of His work is ending. I feel a strange thing – that the world will not be saved, not in a total sense. But His disciples, those lovers of truth, those handmaidens of love shall be saved. It's as though I see Him turn from the world, followed by a multitude of His disciples, many, many thousands, and it is as though He is turning His back on the world and moves toward this vast light, and His disciples follow Him. They get clear of the earth's influence. He turns to face the multitude and says, "Beloved, thy Father", and He points toward the light. With Him they move into realms we cannot describe, work, learning, a living that is so intense in its beauties and purpose that those of us here would perish in the intensities of the thing.

I seem to have come to the end of this though it is not the end, there being no end. The cosmic paradox apparently has no end. The cosmic purpose has no end – always growth – always greater substance."

Clarence fell silent and Ida Rose asked: *"What's next. Is it cleaned up now so it can generate some decency?"*

Clarence: *"There will be continuity. Great things are expected, but there again, the cosmic paradox – there is no certainty and yet, there is certainty. God does not create without purpose. Only an insane person would create just for his own amusement. Nor does the Grand Creator abandon those element which are part of His creation. No one will be abandoned by God, but no one will know God without being introduced by Christ. The important thing is the brawl is over. Those issues have been settled."*

Clarence went silent again. Ida Rose prompted: *"In relation to the twelve disciples, can you see how many I've saved."*

Clarence hesitated: *"I can't answer because it's not like a line that you step over. We don't view time correctly."*

Ida Rose rested her pencil, leaned in slightly and said softly: *"Please ask the Master to heal Clarence so he can sleep."*

Clarence sighed: *"I see rays coming from Him. I seem to get a very tender answer toward you Ida Rose. "Yes" as though I'm incidental."*

Ida Rose waited a moment but Clarence said no more: *"Thank you Master. Please bring Clarence to present time. 1-2-3-4-5 present time."*

Clarence's arthritis was visible in his knurled hands as he sat-up, put on his shoes, and excused himself to the spare bedroom to lie down. Ida Rose and I went into the dining room and cleared the table. She poured more brandy and we finished the strawberries and lychees. I was confused "How come auditors tell different stories, conflicting". She nodded "You're quite right. I listen for where the information crosses over, that's where the truth is. Each auditor has their own motivation, their own point of view that colors their audits. Some are Angels of the Christ Conscious and their symbolism of course is very Christian. Some have been here a long time, like Clarence. And some are new. But all points of view are necessary to sift out the truth". I wasn't sure if I should and did anyway "Ida Rose, I don't like Clarence, he thinks he's the only one who knows anything". She smiled "I am not surprised, considering he was Mary, mother of Jesus, and as such deliberately broke that beautiful little pot you made for her after the crucifixion". I caught my breath "Wow, you mean those feeling can travel across centuries, across lives". She nodded "Oh yes. Engrams can be laid down on the soul at any time, and if unresolved travel with it life to life. You can see poor Clarence is paying a terrible price for his spiritual thesis". I looked down at my hands "Ida Rose, I don't mean to be insensitive to his pain, but his audit bothers me. It was so, you know, exclusive. Only Jesus Christ can get you to God, like Christians know everything and the individual doesn't count. I think every person's important, and I don't trust some god deciding my fate, none of them know me". Her eyes glittered like diamonds in the sun "*Through auditing I had to find the truth of that momentous death in Palestine, imbedded in the regressed memories and experiences of real people, alive in the twentieth century, many of whom went screaming through their agonies of awakening consciousness and awareness. But it's you new cold-rayed students that have made all the difference. You Lords of Humanity who dare to challenge God, dare to ask questions. Jesus' favorite was doubting Thomas.* Now too your question. *Graduating Jesus has been the heart of my work precisely because he was human. His humanity put the individual at the top of the world. He said "If I be lifted up", and you have done that. You've struggled to consciousness, slipped from the grip of the unconscious directing your every move. Jesus' graduation is symbolic of that consciousness. His graduation has made it possible for humans to have a say in their individual destinies, to access the information they need from the Books of Life, which can only be read consciously. And now that the truth of the story has been told, you can by observation read the Book of your own Life for yourself. Unravel your tangled skein and build conscious immortality. The work had to be done here, in carbon, where thought doesn't just disappear, where you could build a foundation by working in process, affording humans the structure and order to build character in lasting, consequential ways. The earth environment has given Hu-man the opportunity to grow in ways no other world could, to become greater than their creator".* We were a little drunk and Ida Rose yawned. I knew it was time to go and kissed her good-bye on a rosy cheek "I don't know when I'll be back, but I'll write". She walked me to the door "That will be fine Lamby. I'll send any significant audits along to your return address. Thank you for all your help today. I couldn't have done it without you. And please bring Corbett with you when you come back".

I sat in the car watching the lights go out, her thanking me for coming made me feel solid, valuable. Mom was up folding laundry, with a message from Corbett. He couldn't pick me up at the airport, I was to go to his Folk's house instead, stay the night, and he would be there in the morning. She was tickled having talked to my mystery man, thought he had such a nice voice, such good manners, and felt a measure of peace knowing I would be meeting his Parents. I was shaken at the last minute change, suddenly feeling unsure, betrayed, forfeit, and took the phone into my room. Corbett answered whispering "Hello". Hearing his voice, any breach vanished "Hi". He did not ask where I had been "Hi you. Everyone's asleep here. Marion's having a really hard time being pregnant. Guess you got my message". I hushed too "Yeah, but how can I just show up at your Folks. You told me you weren't on the best terms". Corbett sounded stressed and miserable "I'm so sorry Sweetheart, the Colonial's having their grand re-opening. We start playing at noon, and go all day until closing. I'd hop in the Healey after and come get you, but it'd be 4:30 or five when I got there and my Folks would be really mad. Carvel, the owner, he's got all his money in the Colonial and freaked when I said I'd get a replacement. It's really a great gig, five nights, permanent. Renzo needs the money with a baby coming. We could use it too, for our own place. So I thought maybe you could change your flight one day, or stay at my Folks". Calling every airline flying to San Francisco, Oakland and San Jose, it was 4th of July holiday, not one open seat. I tried car rentals, thinking drive to Santa Cruz, and found why Ric made Martha Jane Burke 26 years old, no one would rent to under 25 no matter how large a deposit. I call Corbett again "Hi. Every seat's full. I can't even rent a car, you have to be 25 years old". He tried to sound up-beat "Don't worry Shoshy, I promise my Folks'll be nice to you, they're very careful to make a good impression. I'll call and arrange it". I would trust him "Okay I guess. But come as early as you can". He lit a smoke, took a puff and blew it slowly into the mouthpiece, "They're always up for coffee by 8AM, I'll be there with bells on my toes".

I lit a smoke too "Okay. I can hardly wait to see you". He sighed "Me too". Not wanting to end the wire connection we finished our smokes.

Working two more weeks. I tried to reach Leda three times, and worried her Mom had not heard from her. And I read all the papers looking for news of the Seattle Seven, there was none. Evenings I hand-sewed a blouse from a fine-linen tablecloth lavishly embroidered in Calla lilies and bachelor buttons, that I found for $2.00 in a thrift-shop downstairs at the Market, something special for Corbett to see me. The eve of leaving, Mom arranged farewell dinner at my favorite restaurant, Tai Tung, on South King Street in Chinatown. A slender jet-haired woman in tailored jade green Mandarin silk showed us quickly to a table for six, our waiter interpreted the hand-written in Chinese menu. I was relieved Big Brother could not make it, Little drove three hours from College. Barbeque pork and egg rolls came to the table with Granny and a man she met dancing. Dad took pictures with his new Konica. This always seemed annoying imposition growing-up, every holiday, every party, every date, every dance, every every, and not just one, but three snaps, four. Now I smiled easily, wise enough to appreciate how his diligent photo chronicle allowed me a look back like no other, at my own face, to contemplate who I used to be and who I still am. I'd run from my Family, searching for freedom to make choices, to find where my edge was by going over it, deal with the consequences on my own terms, take all the credit or debit. Right now sitting around the table eating with chopsticks like we had so many times before, I embraced the sweet belonging of Sister-Daughter-Granddaughter.

Morning. Mom made me promise to bring Corbett to meet them, Dad palmed me an extra hundred, and Little Brother drove me to the airport on his way back to school. I bought a cool pair of shades and the Post-Intelligencer before boarding, took my window seat and opened the paper. Front page, Jim Morrison dead from an over-dose at 27 years, another star burning too bright, another bard who dared speak for us and paid the ultimate price, another tragic casualty of a pernicious culture war. Below the fold, the Godfather of Seattle, Frank Colacurcio had been convicted of conspiracy to promote illegal gambling. Conspiracy could be wielded to put real criminals in jail. And the voting age had been lowered from 21 to eighteen, boys drafted could vote for or against those sending them to die. It was a good and bad brilliant clear day as the plane flew over snow-capped Rainier, Mount Saint Helens and Mount Hood, and I imagined the dead bard in the air with me, on a journey though his next door. Smooth touch down, amazingly no fear of flying this time, 11:30AM, few things thrilled me more than being alone in a big city and knowing my way. I postponed the Hawkins, took a cab to Geary Street, went into David's and sat at the marble-counter people-watching behind my new shades, eating cold beet borscht with sour cream and chopped chives. Crossing Geary to the A.C.T. Theatre, Tara's name was not on the marquee for The Fantastics. I felt physical relief not having to share my day with the past, nearly 800 dollars in my pocket, two-hundred in my shoes, following Geary to Grant, I walked between the stone lions into this Chinatown. And bought three-yards of soft-pink silk to make Corbett a French-cuffed shirt, ordered swamp spinach stir-fried with bean curd and black mushrooms at the out-door restaurant Will and I ate, browsed the narrow bustling red green and gold street, and the precious gewgaws in shops, smiling, feeling so grown-up, and for the first time so comfortable, somehow being inlove, having someone to lose made me unafraid.

Clocks chimed 4PM in the jewelry store as I paid for a pair of antiqued brass cuff-links set with seven pink jade stones that matched the silk perfectly, seven to symbolize the seven hot rays, life light truth beauty power wisdom and love, potent talisman for such a wizard as my Corbett. I loved having Him on my mind, and knew I would be unforgivably inconsiderate if I did not head for Berkeley. Walking Grant Avenue I side-tracked into a headshop-bookstore, bought four packs of Blanco Negro rolling papers, a small oblong tin box painted with frogs inside and out, just right for a few joints, two boxes of Sherman's queen-size Cigarettellos, Nag Champa incense, a journal of hand-made paper, and finally unable to sanction any more delay, marched resolutely to the Market Street bus station and caught the 5:48 to the Claremont Hotel via Ashby Avenue. Staying on the bus two-blocks passed the Hawkins, where Ashby crosses Domingo and becomes Tunnel Road, the Driver made a left into the Claremont parking lot, announcing she would remain for 35 minutes before returning to San Francisco, everyone must get off. The hotel beckoned, I went into the lobby and sat on one of the many couches to think, why had I agreed to go to Corbett's Folks, I wanted to make a good impression but it was hardly in me to just walk-up to their door, I could take the bus back to the station and catch another to Santa Cruz, walk into the Colonial before Corbett's gig ended and totally blow his mind, now that was me. But he'd called them and they were waiting. Ambivalent inertia stuck me to the couch, till the house cop plainly not happy with a FlowerChild lolling his lobby, stalked over, stiff-legged, arms folded, menacing elbows jutting, inquiring would I be checking-in soon. I understood his insult and left without a word.

Reluctantly walking down Ashby, imagining my feet where Corbett's had been when young, I stood infront of the Hawkins house, and it hit me, this was the porch I hid-on all night after Tara's party. I stole onto it, quietly staring at the white intercom button, plenty of money to stay at the Claremont, Lily Tomlin performing in the lounge, yet I felt bound by the Sweet Sister Fate to push the button. Looking my self over, hair tossed but tolerable, jean skirt and English riding boots presentable, blouse wrinkled but could be seen as the charm of linen, I shook back my shoulders, took a deep breath and buzzed. A man's voice gruffed "Who is it". Sure Corbett forgot to call I wanted to just run but had already stepped over the event horizon "Mr.Hawkins, my name's Shoshannah Leibofsky. I hope Corbett called you. He told me to come here". The voice softened "Oh yes, Shahona, there's been kids ringing the buzzer all day. Wait right there". Wishing to evaporate, my heart pounding, I told my self to breathe. A handsome man maybe 60 with a full-head of thick gray hair opened the door and ordered "Come in, come in. I'm Corby's Father". He messed my name, I felt it was intentional and did not correct him, smiling bright, taking my best Golden manners across the threshold "It's nice to meet you Mr.Hawkins". A woman stepped from behind him as if to bar my way "I'm Corby's Mom. We've been waiting for you all day". Though it seemed warm concern, I could feel the freeze "Thank you Mrs.Hawkins. You're so kind to let me stay".

Last chance to run, I followed their backs to the kitchen, mind-full not to let on I'd been here. Mrs.Hawkins pointed to the chair I took when Corbett cooked my breakfast "Sit down and I'll cut you a big slice of German chocolate cake". I did not want to eat with them "Please, no thank you. I ate in Chinatown and couldn't possibly eat any more". She shook her head "How anyone can turn down German chocolate cake is beyond me. It must be how you keep your lovely figure". This was definitely not a compliment, she placed a fat slice infront of Mr.Hawkins. He shook his head tisk tisk "I've never been able to turn down German chocolate cake". Taking a mouth full, he swallowed, licked his lip and turned cold eyes my way "Don't tell me a nice girl like you went to Chinatown by yourself". Stomach falling with insinuation, I played the game as if I did not understand "Yes Mr.Hawkins. You see I haven't traveled much, and there's no place like San Francisco's Chinatown. The one in Seattle, it's just a few blocks. But here makes me feel like I'm actually in China". The questions, how was my flight, did I have any problem finding the house, innocuous at first quickly moved to full-blown inquisition, how was my last name spelled, what did my Father do for a living, how did I support myself, where had I gone to college, how long had I known their Son. The interrogation reminded me of Keely and Dancing Bear's paranoia when I first showed at Hydra, I kept hands soft in my lap, did not rush a reply, tried not to seem defensive, smiled while being vague as possible, lying sweetly, never answering with a question, yawning often, and so awfully tempted to call them by their first names, yes Halls I am a Jew, no Arlene I did not personally kill Christ. These were the Goyim Dad warned of. My hopes for another Mom and Dad to love me unconditionally as their own putrefying before my eyes, still I kept cool, unwilling to get on my knees to be acceptable. Arlene could no longer comfortably ignore my yawns, and took me upstairs. Passing her room I tried seeing where we slept but the door was closed. Maggie's room at the end of the hall, every thing mauve, frilly, organdy-curtains, and stale, Arlene said good-night and shut me in. Waiting for her steps down the stairs, I lock the door and laid atop the small bed, too tired to sleep, mind running in tight poison circles, listening to the cuckoo clocks all over the house crowing out-of-time every 15 minutes, and Halls and Arlene finally going into their room, voices too soft to make out. They were the whitest people I had ever met, that bright clean white goodness and humility meant to obscure a petty selfishness and malicious cynicism for anything that is not them, so unmistakably righteous, so tolerant, and so hard to finger in the blinding glare of their whiteness. The night humid, I took off my clothes, opened the window and lit a stick of incense to banish the long waiting bogeys, chain-smoked Shermans, rolled my stash into joints and put them in the frog box, trimmed split-ends one-by-one, wrote in my new journal, read *A Challenge to Confusion*, and dozed. Six-AM sun brought enough light in to reveal years of untouched dust, this was such a big house, Arlene could not possibly keep it all clean. And once gone Corbett's little Sister stayed gone, I respectfully looked though her closet and drawers to see who she left behind.

Slipper feet scuffing the hall, Arlene rapped on the door, saccharine voice amid the cuckoos "Eight AM. Rise and shine Shahona. Come down for breakfast". I answered a sleepy croak "Thank you Mrs.Hawkins". Waiting on them to get-up so I could bathe brand-new for Corbett, I hung my blouse by the shower, letting steam relax the wrinkles, cleaned-up the room as if I had never been there, put everything in my shoulder bag, and hair damp went down, leaving my bag on the banister by the door. Feeling the ice crack under me as I sat in the same chair, the smell of food making my mouth water, Arlene offered, and I dared not eat with them "Thanks Mrs.Hawkins, it smells really good, but I never eat breakfast. Only coffee please, watching my figure you know". I reached for the hot-pot on the table. She reached infront of me, eyes closing to slits, doling me a stingy cup "Corby called from a San Jose gas station while you were in the shower. He should be here soon". Never raising his eyes, Halls dug into five strips of bacon, three eggs, three pieces of toast. I sipped my coffee "You must be looking forward to seeing him as much as me". Arlene sat down with her plate and stretched a taut grin across false teeth "Of course, he's my Son". I felt the rivalry, and thought maybe this wasn't about me, Corbett had not actually seen them face-to-face in more than two years, maybe it was about them "You make a good cup Mrs.Hawkins, can I please have some more". She filled to the very rim, I could not help spill, this was an all too familiar deadly dance, just as Nick knew every nuance, so did Arlene and I did not want to tango. Mind racing for exit, I put a napkin under my cup, Bibliomania flashing in my head, the bookstore I'd seen on Telegraph Avenue when April and I took Miss Fine to County Hospital "There's a book I been wanting. So I think I'll walk down to Bibliomania". Halls put down his fork and looked at me for the first time "They're not open today, it's the 4th of July". He poured-on the stare "You really should eat breakfast. Didn't your Mother teach you any manners". Well, I was wrong, this absolutely was about me, and my Family, I wasn't getting off the dance floor so easy, and need a weapon, some thing to back him off "Why, yes Sir, my Mom and my Dad taught me every kind of manner. You see Sir, I was being polite, I'm a Vegetarian". Wincing at the Sir, snorting contempt "God gave man dominion over the animals". I was so not into this kill or be killed, did not want to, but leaned forward fending "Yes Sir, but where does it say dominion means consumption". He canted back. Arlene caught her breath, inhaling a bit of toast, coughing, coughing. Halls sprang to his feet, clapping hard on her back, too hard, accusing me "Look what you've done". I sat very still, unsure he might hit me too. She gave-up the toast. He sat down and took his fork, resuming, calm. My heart banging, when it settled I would dart for the sidewalk. Thankfully amid cuckoos crowing 8:30, I heard the front door open.

Corbett strode gracefully into the kitchen, kissing my up-turned mouth. I was so happy to see him, the real thing way better than imagination, but choosing me over Mother sank the final nail in my coffin. No one moved till Halls commanded "Sit down Son. We have reservations for dinner tonight at Jack London Square. You'll join us". My head screaming no, oh no, oh please oh please say no. Corbett sat, smiling at his Father "Thanks Dad, we'd love to, but I have a gig tonight". Relief too obvious, excusing myself to the bathroom, I stopped half-way up-stairs to listen. Corbett's voice was growing sharp "Mom, her name's Shoshannah not Shahona". Arlene pitched higher "What kind of a name is that anyway. How can you do this to me Corby. Living together is a sin, you'll go straight to Hell". I marched back in and stood next to Corbett "Let's go Babe". He rose and took my hand "I don't want to argue with you Mom, we better go". I pulled a taut grin across my real teeth "Thank you for your hospitality Ma'am. You too Sir". And took my bag and their son away from them.

Still in his Folks clutches, Corbett burned rubber driving away. I said softly "Don't look back, you'll turn to salt". He did not look back. Stopping for the light on Domingo Avenue, we looked at each other and burst-out laughing. He leaned over the gear shift to kiss me "You're so cool".

Eagerly meeting his lips "Thanks. I never been so happy to see anyone". The car behind honking, Corbett stepped light on the gas "I don't really have a gig tonight. Can you believe I lied to my Dad's face and didn't even blink. And my Mother, god she knows how to push my buttons. Thanks for taking me out of there". I stroked his cheek with my hand "Stick with me Babe and you'll never have to worry, cause they won't ever want to see me again". He covered my hand in his and held for a long moment "Sorry I asked you to stay there. I should've come right after the gig". He paused, and rushed-on "Other than my Sister and Brother, you're the only one who's ever seen the real Halls and Arlene. They're so careful. People think they're so good and holy and kind and humble, shining pillars of the community, you know, always giving old ladies rides to church. You should see my Dad at mass, head down thumping his chest, so into it. He's a convert. And my Mom making sure to tell the relatives how I drink and smoke and play in bars, that I never come see them. But the part that really burns, everyone seems to believe her. Now she'll add living in sin, and how you're not Catholic. Ever since I can remember they told me my habits are so disgusting no one would ever love me. I guess I just wanted them to see you, see you love me, prove them wrong". My heart broke-open, his Folks never took loving care of one so tender and promising. He had to fight for his life, while they did everything to undermine his confidence, make sure he failed at anything that was not theirs, and still he wanted to show them, prove to them he was loveable, when it was apparent they were not capable. I wanted to go back and strangle their lily-white necks with my bare hands "It's fine Babe, I'm glad I saw them so I know. They're lethal. I couldn't a survived what you did, any slight move and you're dead. Well fuck them, they don't see you and never will. They don't matter anyway, we matter. I see you, I saw their cruel game, and I've seen it before, it's not smart or original. Their Folks probly taught them going back twenty-five generations, an their teaching you, passing it on, how not to leave any marks on the body, no proof. Your gona love my Folks. They're a little freaked-out your Catholic, but they'll mellow right away when they meet you. I promise". He took me in with those beauty-full clear-blue legally blind eyes, that with contact lenses could see almost 20-20. And I wondered aloud "How come your Parents don't wear glasses too. Do they wear contacts". His brow rippled "No, neither, but my Brother and Sister are blind as me". I flashed hard "It must be some kind of a curse, keeping you blind so nothing can break their hold. You know, symbolic". A shiver ran my spine "Maybe they're energy vampires, feeding off your juice instead of your blood cause they have none of their own. Saying you're never good enough keeps you always wanting their approval, their love, keeps you coming around so they can feed". Corbett marveled "Wow, you're right, they are vampires".

Leaving vampires behind, we deliberated our near future, via Oakland, the San Mateo Bridge, Highway 35 South to Saratoga, Hiway 9 though Boulder Creek, Ben Lomond, Felton, and into Santa Cruz, the Healey fluently negotiating curly mountain turns, bucket-seats holding us apart, welcome as we were both achingly shy. Lunching at the King and I, taking the same table we sat three months past, our passion jealously guarded from profane eyes, so naked we avoided lingering too long in each others. Corbett was so handsome in-person, a gentle edge to his masculinity, I loved looking at him when not looking at me, how my name sounded coming from his lips, we flirted, knowing each other so much better now from letters and calls, lightly bushing knees under the table. After 2PM, hand-in-hand we strolled the Boardwalk, swarming with 4th of July tourists, yet we were alone. Then to Lorenzo and Marion's, who went sailing for the day on her Folk's yacht off Monterey. We were alone with the dogs and cats and birds, and Buggs-the-cat-eyed-bugger, pure-black juvenile with manic golden-yellow eyes and a smudge of white frosting his nose. We happily sat on the weary couch in a sun-filled living room, doors and windows open, talking, playing with Buggs in our self-consciousness, treating our beginning with the delicate respect it deserved, believing we won our independence together, that the Fourth of July was auspicious, significant, tonight the country would be lighting fireworks in our honor.

Corbett had tried bribing the real estate agents to put his name on-top of their list for a house or apartment. Bigger bribes were ahead of him, the only prospect so far, Marion's Brother Frank and Girlfriend Amber had already rented a bigger house that was not available to occupy for two months yet, and we could possibly have their little cottage on the rim of Seacliff Beach in Aptos if the landlord approved, till then we would have to make the best of living with the Biancalana's. Who came home earlier than expected. Marion went to bed without a word. Lorenzo grabbed two beers from the frig, sat down in the gray-corduroy recliner facing us and explained, Marion usually a seasoned sailor, never seasick, she had a spell of pregnant nausea and couldn't stand being on the waves. This was his living room, he was used to uninterrupted bandy with Corbett, now there was me, I felt the freeze, he made no effort to ease. A telling juncture, Corbett had promised not to act like he didn't see these things. Listening polite, asking was there something he could do to help, and getting a no, he took my hand and excused us. We drove by Andrew's for my things, then into Santa Cruz for sunset, and fireworks off the pier.

Delroy, Lorenzo, Corbett played Tuesday through Saturday at the Colonial Inn, the house was always full. I bought a $39.95 plus tax Sears zig-zag sewing machine, set it on the floor in the living room, good light coming through the window, and began a collection of swim-suits and casual dresses. No one here knew anything about sewing, I did not need to hide taking measurements from Corbett's shirts, designing, constructing the pink silk right under-his-nose, presenting it with the cuff-links the morning of our one week anniversary. And I might have been wrong, for he acted surprised but it seemed not quite true, and I was delighted I could not do some thing so palpable without his noticing. A fine fit, he looked exquisitely wrapped, said he'd never felt so special, and took me with to work, bragging to anyone who remarked, my Sweetheart made this for me.

Marion's gynecologist ordered her complete bed rest, she was spotting. I thought I could help with cooking and cleaning. The kind who wears her pedigree in her eyes, blue-blood patriarchal Protestant lineage, genes back to the Mayflower, she treated me an interloper no matter what I did, that same old Golden Ghetto prejudice, if you aren't born to it, no matter when you come, you're second-class, a Johnny-come-lately. It was near impossible to imagine such sustained hardened disdain in the face of kindness, I could only reason it had to be more than a difficult pregnancy, more than pedigree, and one evening, the men gone to work, it surfaced. She lay on the couch watching TV, in terrible burping indigestion. I offered a steaming cup of fennel tea on the coffeetable in easy reach

"Maybe this'll help your tummy". She eyed the cup and me "I didn't ask for anything. You're just too damn good to be true. I'd love to get you drunk and see what you're really like". I would not be baited "You'll just be disappointed, I'm pretty much the same. Maybe a little more talkative, but that's all". She smiled, a touch green-eyed "You know when I first met Hawk and Renzo, I had my pick". I was pure innocence "Then I'm sure you're happy Corbett found someone too". She turned her head to the TV, never touching the tea. Telling Corbett later, he hugged me tight "Don't let 'er bother you. She's had Renzo and me all to herself until you came. She'll just have to get used to it. So will Renzo. They have to".

We took all the time away we could, out to breakfast, lunch, walking beaches, afternoon drives into the mountains, and I was happy, Marion, Lorenzo's jealousy glancing-off our love-bubble. Every work-night Corbett invited me to come with. I did one-two times a week. Carvel Ellsworthy the Colonial's owner, so grateful to the Band for night-after-night filling the seats, many coming to eat first, he extended their on-the-house bar and restaurant tab to me. Other nights, working till Corbett came home, I tried and tried calling Leda, leaving this number with her Mother, and heard nothing. I did not go see Keely, or the Littles though aching for their pure faces. Or Gretchen. Delroy never mentioned her, I was Hawk's Ol'lady now, relegated to The Wife category, treated in-kind. And when Corbett and Lorenzo began playing Sunday nights with One Hand Clapping at the Zyante Club, and practicing Monday afternoons at Jimmy Mesa's barn, for Ralph Gleason advised Erik that awful night, the Band should not give up, and if they ever got it together again, please get in-touch with him, it was all Erik needed to carry on the hype. Colleen visited Marion on those Sunday nights, they were both first-time pregnant and having difficulties, and though she was my friend too, I was mostly left-out. Mondays I would drive Corbett to practice, and take the Healey treasure-hunting thrift shops, and for slow rides, passed the Fairmount house, along to Cyrene's street, stopping in one day. She told me everything, Gretchen was still seeing Delroy, Keely and the kids were healthy, April and her son moved-in again with Brian, just hours and she was strung-out, Stanley got away from Goldie, rented a studio apartment, he came over every day, and was completely in love with her Son. Feeling my usual penchant to risk someone's anger, be the voice of conscience, I resisted for I did not love her enough, instead wishing nothing but good luck, no need mention the beautiful Baby Girl Stan and Pam had adopted not five months ago, she already heard my dubious warning.

Marion became increasingly unfriendly, and I by nature not a convincing suck-up, but, Lorenzo was scarcely around, she was a beached whale, and I felt genuine concern for her condition, somehow needing to care for even one so unwilling. I shopped her grocery list, cooked her wishes, fried chicken, breaded pork chops, hamburgers. And I went out for her cravings, did the laundry, vacuumed to manage the animal hair, and even self-imposed second-speak hoping by not talking to her Husband she might feel safer, all these only seemed to aggravate her. One weeknight, clearing dinner dishes to the sink, watching in awe the news of Betty Friedan, Gloria Steinem and the National Organization for Women leading thousands though the streets of New York City, demanding 51% of everything because females are 51% of the population, there they were, in legions, seeing them with my own eyes, I was overoyed, I was definitely not the only one. Marion stopped to look in her clean neat full refrigerator on her way to the bathroom, and let loose "God, will you just get out of my kitchen. I'm so sick of you trying to make me look like a slob". I was not surprised, she had without fail miss-taken consideration for competition, the kitchen after-all was her power center, why should I expect her to be more liberated than Josh's Mom, and I knew she felt unwieldy, unattractive, still the blow hurt and I made no effort to hide it "Ouch". I turned-off the water, wiped hands on my jeans and withdrew, and from then became politely invisible. Corbett and I dined nightly at the Colonial, and having moved my sewing machine into our bedroom, I would take the Healey home, work, and go for him after 1AM. It did not end with Marion. Corbett told me how Erik and Renzo took him aside, so deeply concerned, warning I was an evil witch who had him under my spell, and how he laughed at them, and I should too since Erik could not think beyond his coke habit, the Band and the coming Baby, and ditto for Renzo. I said I would try, my head screaming disappointment, witch, bitch, what's the difference, how could he excuse them when he promised. Yes they needed him, for the Band, and for selfish reasons, some well-founded, some not so, still didn't he understand their pardon was my punishment.

Yet, all the machinations brought us closer. When it came clear Corbett would not help burn me at the stake, Lorenzo and Marion confronted him with ultimatum, get rid of the witch or leave with her. To their surprise, he took it as an opportunity not an insult, calling his Sister, arranging for us to stay there. Maggie had fallen for Diego, marrying in the traditional Catholic way. They were renting a two-bedroom house in Concord, we were absolutely welcome, for along with a house full of furniture wedding gift, Corbett had taken over monthly payments on their orange VW bug, repossession would have ruined their credit, they were thrilled to be on the giving end. The phone rang just as he hung-up, his name was-up on this real estate agent's list, if we could come right away to see an upstairs du-plex, one block from New Brighton Beach, available in ten days. Landlady met us there too, pasty-white aristocrat who let us know first thing her standing in Who's Who of American Women, that she had final approval, and there were five other couples courting her favor. Taking instant fancy to Corbett, for the life of her she could not remember my name, I was sure she would have remembered Marions. We so wanted this tasteless box, Corbett pandered, and I encouraged his offer to come over some time soon to her home and play the grand Steinway she just happened to mention no one touched in years. Smitten, she granted month-to-month approval, he wrote the check, we were the lucky winners of our own box. And I knew just how to celebrate, Marion suffered insatiable cravings for Canadian bacon pineapple pizza, we stopped at Malio's for one, a medium pepperoni for Lorenzo, mushroom and black olive for us. Magically all hard feeling were gone, Corbett and Lorenzo went to work, I packed-up my fabrics and sewing gear.

Sunday morning crept in the window, my eyes resting on Corbett's wonderful yummy innocent face till he woke. We took only what we needed. Marion had her territory back, nothing but smiles, Lorenzo and Buggs standing on the porch among the dogs and cats, waving bittersweet farewell. My thorny armor fell-away as I slid into the bucket seat and we drove off.

Looking so like Corbett, I would have liked her irregardless. Maggie was also five-months pregnant, and just laid-off her receptionist job for show-ing, waiting to collect unemployment. Diego worked twelve-hours over-night four-days-a-week, physical therapy at John Muir Medical Center, and with First-Child coming, responsibility lay-heavy on his mind. They were nice to me as my own Family, I had forgotten how warm humans could be, and life was suddenly unwound, save the in-land California heat as humid and unholy as Texas without the air-conditioning. Even the thirty-inch fans full-blasting, daytime was too hot to sew, to unmercifully sticky to think, I sat infront of the whirling blades nearly all day reading, hypnotized by the whirr, making any excuse to go the grocery shopping for the smallest thing and loiter in the frozen food section. Maggie and Diego were okay with the heat, Corbett took it well, I was sure my brain was poaching. We'd sleep till noon, at 2:30 Diego left for work, Corbett 7:00 for his long commute. While we played Gin Rummy, Maggie spilled about him, and the Family, and her self as we strolled the neighborhood in slightly cooler evening air. Having graduated Holy Names College with a Liberal Arts degree, she went to the convent, became disillusioned when a priest talked her into kissing him, saying it was just like kissing Jesus, when he stuck his tongue down her throat she left a few weeks later, Halls and Arlene could not find it in them to believe or forgive her. And she welcomed me into her kitchen, cooking at night, Diego, Corbett both home around 4AM, we had Citronella tiki-torches lit in the backyard to scare-off mosquitoes, and dined at the picnic table. There were two apricot trees in the yard, ripe fruit on the ground, I felt compelled to salvage every one, making upside-down cake, jam, chutney, cream pie, every crumb disappearing eagerly into Maggie's cravings, Diego's frustrated working for the establishment for too little money to survive, and Corbett's content to eat whatever his Woman cooked. And then Halls called, and Maggie let slip we were there, and he browbeat her, warning not to leave Diego and me alone, Cubans and Jews were unable to control their sexual urges, and then Arlene took the phone, demanding Maggie kick us out immediately, before our iniquity corrupted the new life growing inside her, ruined their marriage, maybe even their going to heaven. Maggie tried to laugh it off as she mimicked the conversation over dinner, but all her buttons had been pushed and all her vitality stolen, she broke down sobbing and went

606

to bed. Our love seemed a trigger, forces so disproportionately intent on destroying us, unmistakable indication our coming together must really be significant. Ida Rose saw Corbett and me as a testament to the Cosmos that opposites could solve their differences. And though I felt awful being cause of even one moment suffering for Maggie and Diego, I did not feel guilty, for we were but a small drop of their trouble. Corbett revealed that Halls and Arlene were helping them with rent and food, and though this was blackmail, there was a Baby coming. I left it up to him. He thought it best we go, there were five days till the box was ours, he would call Brother Paul in Mountain View, if we could not stay, a motel was just fine. He phoned in the morning, Paul invited us please come and stay.

Mountain View would nip Corbett's commute to Santa Cruz by half. Paul met us after work at his place, looking so like Corbett I would have liked him irregardless. Angela came minutes later. Living together for months in his apartment, hiding the arrangement from disapproving Moms and Dads, she kept a studio one floor up for appearances, and when Folks or anyone who might tell came by, they pretended. We were welcome to say in hers. As we talked, Arlene called, on-the-scent, maligning Corbett, praising Paul for having such good character to wait, Angela was such a nice Catholic girl, warning for the sake of his immortal soul, turn us away if we come to his door. Taking Mother better than Maggie, he was still unsettled, lighting another cigarette with one already burning in the ashtray, walking in circles, smoking, apologizing for letting Big Brother take his measure of the lash. Corbett laughed easily, persuasively, maybe she would ask him to turn Jesus away too, disposing of the matter by taking us to dinner. I kept my mouth shut, having lied so much to my Folks, sure they could not take the truth, realizing now it was pure-selfish, having little to do with saving their feelings and everything to do with saving mine, making me liar to the People I love. Paul and Angela could do with their Folks as they saw fit, but the truth here was Corbett taking all the blame so Paul could remain in good graces, and I could see from Corbett's forgiving response it was not the first time. And I loved him more for having those broad shoulders, vowing to try and be of the same noble character, telling my Folks the truth about us no matter the consequences.

The 106 unit air-conditioned apartment-complex bordered El Camino
Real Boulevard, an endless bustling four-lane with every imaginable business. Corbett would sleep till noon, while I rummaged the many thrift
shops, so full of treasure, evidently no one cared for the exquisite crochet and embroidery, fine table-cloths and napkins, handmade lace and
handkerchiefs decaying on the shelves. We would go to one of countless
restaurants for a long supper, 8:00PM he'd leave for work. Sewing till
3:00, savoring the alone but not lonely time, I would walked down to the
parking lot, this early mornings nearly silent, a cool fragrant breeze as I sat
on the curb under fruiting olive trees listening for the Healey, filled with
wonder at the little green fruit, till now seen only in small glass-jars stuffed
with pimento, growing right above my head. Being always busy was how
Angela tried hiding cool feelings for me, I was not bothered much by
another Catholic misreading life-without-fear-of-purgatory for arrogance,
and liked her in-spite of the inherited prejudice. She looked like a Christmas card cherub, softly round body and face, china blue eyes, button nose,
apple cheeks, long heavy golden curls she pulled to a tight-bun at the back
of her head before leaving at 6AM sharp in her meter maid uniform. I
understood the need for a severe work-do, but she never took it down
except to wash. Having begun to learn how to move-on from large and
small adversity no matter whose fault, by not blaming others or what-ever
was convenient, by accepting responsibility sometimes even for just being
there at the wrong time, I'd taken some power to affect my life into my
own hands, becoming kinder, and co-author to a degree of my own destiny. And the Sweet Sisters, weavers of character, spinners, measurers and
cutters of the Golden Thread of Life, made sure every grain of sand was
in place, for if one was not, if I had tried to completely will my life, one
grain off could have turned me another way on this impossibly convoluted
journey, and I might never have walked into the Gate of Horn and Corbett. He left for the commute, Paul working late, manager of a furniture
store, preparing for a big weekend sale, I went down stairs and offered to
cut Angela's hair, claiming as credentials a steady-stream of satisfied high
school girls who would come home with me after school for one of my
famous dos. As Fate would have it, she was seriously contemplating a cut
for weeks, my timing so perfect she said yes. Trimming to just above the

shoulders, I layered fat curls to dance round her face. And she confided, how Mom set her and Older Sister against each other, Angela the Smart One, straight-haired thinner Sister the Pretty One. And we laughed and smoked a joint and baked Tollhouse cookies, and for a while I did not seem so arrogant.

Chapter Twenty Five

SATSOP RIVER FAIR AND TIN CUP RACES

Moving in, our upstairs Aptos box, all we owned piled in the Healey, Corbett's extensive record collection and state-of-the-art Fisher stereo receiver radio record player, four pioneer speakers, Ampex reel-to-reel tape recorder, nineteen-inch JC Penney color TV, all begrudgingly let-go by Renzo and Marion. And my sewing machine and materials, two sleeping bags, pillows, clothes, candles, and our privacy. The sand-color carpet shampooed, walls freshly painted the same, acrid smells lingering, instant chemical headaches, we left every window open to the ocean breeze. What looked like an authentic 18th century master-carved English Mahogany Highboy the lone furnishing, we put our clothes in it, hooked-up the sound system, stacked on Ray Charles, the Byrds, Crosby Stills and Nash, Simon and Garfunkel, zipped sleeping bags together, lit candles and locked the door.

I went thrift shopping for furnishings, finding vintage copper pots and pans by Revere, a half-set of Denmark Blue dishes by Furnival Limited England, six place-settings Holmes & Edwards American Beauty Rose silver-plate flatware, good linens and towels, a wooden folding card-table and chair for my sewing machine, and a thirty-two-inch diameter wooden round coffeetable not ten-inches high with fat ball-legs and tooled-leather top, our own little War Table, all this discarded treasure for just over fifty-bucks. And Corbett resumed Sunday nights at the Zyante Club with One Hand Clapping, and Monday practice, and I began to cook for My

Man, feeling uncomfortably domestic. He liked to grocery shop, could not resist a bargain, bringing home the large-economy-size, something acquired from Dad, who did all shopping as Mom was not allowed to spend money. I would pull the packages of eight pork-chops, ten lamb-chops, a five pound chuck roast, chicken-and-a-half from the bags. Food was complicated, habitual, tied fast to emotions, and we were so new I did not want to begin with a struggle. My choosing vegetarian had been a consciousness expansion, I knew in my heart Corbett would get there in his own time, but quietly made the vegetables delicious and the animal offerings never quite done right. We didn't need much, content to sleep on the floor, and leisure far into the morning in each others arms. Our cocoon did not remain, Corbett bragging-on my abundant cooking to Andrew, he began to just showed-up at dinner-time with Jennifer. It was fun entertaining our very first guests, there was always too much food anyway, we would gather cross-legged at the War Table, Corbett lighting candles, saying grace, Jennifer sitting beside Andrew with her own plate, making the evening feel balanced.

Lorenzo, Delroy, Corbett's trio had been enthusiastically embraced by the local music critics, especially Jay Shore and his new rag the Santa Cruz Times which had become wildly popular. He often came by the Colonial.

Of the many establishments in town that provide entertainment, the live-liest, loudest and loosest is the Colonial Inn on Ocean Street which features Lorenzo Biancalana on drums, Delroy Bogave *on guitar, and* Corbett Haw-kins *on piano and organ. Tuesday thru Saturday.*

Everyone dances, and not because they play so loud that you can't talk. You dance because they're bound to play something you can dance to — standards, boogie, blues, ragtime, Latin music and the popular stuff of all ages. And they play originals.

The talents, who have played together for a while, show it. Not only with their sound, but with a gifted style and intelligent wit — both musical and verbal.

Simply put — they are tops. Jay Shore

An uninterrupted place to sew, off the floor, freed my imagination, using Monique and Loretta's rayons and silks I made 10 halter-top, tight-waist-ed, full skirt, floaty ball-gowns and wanted to keep them all, to wear for Corbett. The Santa Cruz Import Shop's new Owner was not interested at my price, bought 'dirt cheap' from Guatemala, Colombia, Nicaragua, and would give only half what I asked. It never occurred to me the store would change hands, my mind scrambled to grasp this unexpectedness, I had planned on selling, and he would not budge, what choice did I have but take the offer. Precisely the question to trigger the truth of the moment, in a flash I saw how fortunate to be not-so-fraught as the labor he exploited, I did have a choice, scooped my goods from the counter and flew away. Having coffee when I came home, Corbett waited till all 10 dresses were hung on the curtain rods and cupboard handles to invite me for a walk to the beach, and talk. I was lost what to do, salving my ego insisting I wanted to keep them all for myself anyway. Holding his counsel still and listening close to every defensive rationalization, every bitter word for that awful new Owner, and a long rant on the exploitation of other countries workers, he recommended "I would take some time, until you can see down the road. Anyway, you don't have to work if you don't want to. I'm making enough for both of us". Sweet, generous, innocent sounding, it was so easy to slip into the old roles, a well-meaning intention that lulls you so pleasantly sleeping in the familiar, and if you ever chance to wake-up again, you find your self years down a road you never wanted to take, lonelier than alone "Thanks Babe. I'll take your good advice. My friend Bonita-Kay would say the same, and Ida Rose's would say Delayed Reaction, but I will not take your offer. I can take just fine care a my self, and I'm glad to do it. If I didn't, you would come to resent me, and me you. I have Chicken Valley money, so I will take some time". Corbett looked hurt and confused. I explained how I wanted to want him, not need him to take care of me, and I wanted him to want me and not need me to take care of him, that we could so easily get lost in some old idea of how men and women should be. Saying he understood. I did not think so entirely.

Coasting felt like bee stings and made me flinch, so I worked for fun, sewing tufted fringed burgundy velvet floor cushions for the War Table, sleeveless cotton summer-dresses for me using embroidered linen dish-towels and lace, patchwork quilts for Maggie Marion and Colleen's coming Babies, tie-dyed long sleeve t-shirts and pants for Corbett. And I went to the Colonial often, in my gowns, loving listening to Corbett play with this gifted trio, flirting with him, he loved it. Lorenzo and even

Marion slowly warmed to me witnessing his happy. Erik would not set one toe in our box, like if he did, it would bestow some kind of blessing or contaminate him to Hell. And, he was bluntly disgusted and angry with Renzo, Corbett, even the great Delroy, for they were prostituting their talent in of all places the notorious Colonial Inn lounge, where they-should-be-ashamed-of-themselves played mostly popular songs, other peoples songs, where business-men who didn't have a yacht or secret beach get-away brought their mistresses. He and Joey fancied themselves bar-flies, too working-class to be comfortable in a hard-liquor lounge, and yet they came slumming almost every weekend, these progeny of patrician families were just flat-out jealous they didn't have the job, mostly living-off Cherry's book-keepers wage, they would sit in a dark corner booth, brooding, having no business disparaging any one making a living playing music anywhere. And they were the only ones still openly hardened toward me, and this dogged contempt had come to be seen as cruel to all but them, happily re-casting me from witch to sympathetic underdog. Having the upper-hand, I savored my own form of torment, sending tequila shots not beer to their table on my house-tab with compliments. Tossing them down, never acknowledging my existence, shouting volumes to the Regulars who had adopted me as one of their own, they were becoming the outcast. The painful thorn in my paw now, the couple in the down-stairs box, always fighting and belittling their three-year-old tow-head twins Troy and Tiffany, bullying them, never hitting that I knew of. We were forced to passively participate, and I often thought just go take those Kids away, neither Adult seemed to have the upper-hand, maybe without Kids as diffusion, maybe they would fight each other to death.

Frank and Amber's bigger house came ready a month early, not telling their Landlord, they moved. And now smiling and smiling that our Landlady had wanted us so beholding she would only rent month to month, we gladly left behind the thin floors and half-month's rent and assumed their identity. Off Seacliff Drive, Court Way a dead-end over-looking Seacliff Beach, our $50 a month flat-roof cottage, towering eucalyptus grove to the South, fragrant blooming yellow acacia shrouding the East, orange and purple Bird-of-Paradise proudly standing the driveway and gaggling round the broken-screen front door, the 1950's one-bedroom came complete with worn-out carpet, shabby striped-wool couch, abused pine coffee-table and end tables, shabbier matching recliner-rockers, lamps, coffe cup stained Duncan Phyfe mahogany dining-room table and five chairs, every cupboard and drawer rife in chipped dishes, bent forks, blackened pots and pans, graying towels, grayinger linens, and a funky stinky bathroom, though everything worked. It also had a 20 foot long living-room-dining-room with East and West large picture windows, a floor-to-ceiling red brick fireplace and hearth, tiny sunny kitchen, our first gas stove, nice double-bed off the floor that took-up the whole bedroom, and from the back deck, a priceless view of horseshoe coastline from Santa Cruz to the Monterey Peninsula. We were finally really alone. I set the sewing machine on the Duncan Phyfe, my back to the West picture window, such lovely light, Corbett wired the sound system, War Table and cushions went infront of the fireplace, our own linens on the bed, and towels, and dishes, and forks, and pots and pans, and starving for lunch we found a trail close on the high-lip of the cliff over looking the beach, three-blocks to the Tampico. A modest Mexican restaurant in the Rio Del Mar Shopping Center, much of the menu happily vegetarian. After, we explored the shops, Yosef's Bakery and Deli, a somber pet store, organic herbs store, vitamins, expensive wines, cheeses, handmade paper and greeting cards, a pharmacy, independent grocery store, and a help wanted sign in the window of an upscale boutique called The Wearhouse. Exactly what I promised never do again, I took the sign from the window, asked for the Owner and was shown to his office in the back. Hired on a hand-shake, I think my sewing skills and experience at Neiman Marcus and Nordstrom, but most likely because we were both Jewish. Starting pay $1.75 an hour plus 7% commission on every thing I sold, and if I did well, he would raise me to $2.00 an hour and 10% commission in two-months, I should report for work 9AM in the morning.

Walking the trail home, Corbett was quiet. I felt surprising relief being able to land a strait job, a sense of security that my future was not closed-off because of my past, even if Nixon's brigands won I could still make a living. We found beach stairs, took them down, leaving shoes on the last one, squishing across the wide warm sand. I felt master of the wind and sky, lifting hands high at water's edge, and draping them around Corbett's neck, leaning against him "You been awful quiet Babe. What's on your big mind". Hugging tight, lift-off, twirling me twice, setting me down soft he took a long step back, pouting "You'll be gone when I wake-up in the morning. This wasn't in my plan. You'll hate having to smile all day for ten bucks after taxes. I make plenty, you don't have to work a shit job. How about I pay you ten bucks a day to stay home with me". I loved him for wanting to take care of me and hated him for wanting to take care of me "You don't even get up till noon, so come take me to lunch, and I'll be home 4 hours later. Anyway, I'll get more like twenty-five a day with commission, and a raise in two months. Did you hear my conversation with Mr. Warehouse". Corbett nodded "Yeah I did. But don't be so flattered he hired you, I don't trust him". I shifted automatically to then I'll show you mode "Well, maybe your right, but you don't go around thinking you don't have to take care of your self. It makes you feel good you can, right". Corbett nodded again. I smiled "Well then you understand, I need to take care of my self too, I want to take care of my self, that's who I am, that's who you love".

Snoring like a big cat, I kissed him and left for work without slipping Excalibur in my pocket, at last feeling safe, walking the cliff trail, high on the edge of the world, a new morning sky and salty breeze rising-off the water, low-tide beach-combers and sea-birds busy feeding, feeling somehow I had won the game. Corbett showed exactly at noon for lunch. Walking hand-in-hand by the pet store to Yosef's Deli, a gawky black pup with a black Lone Ranger mask on his little white face and four white paws, put his black wet nose against the window, making direct eye-contact. I held those milk-chocolate kindred eyes, Amaru's and Frodo's had the same feeling, and fell instantly inlove, telling Corbett I have to have that dog. In perfect harmony, he had so wanted to take Buggs with us, Lorenzo and Marion said no, only to give him away weeks later never asking Corbett first. We skipped lunch, the little hound watching us standing, started barking, yipping, wiggling, wagging like mad, hey, yikes, oh god oh god, me me, you came for me, oh thank you thank you. I never paid money for a living creature, all my childhood pets given by someone who could no longer keep them, and it suddenly seemed criminal how living things were sold and bought. I laid twenty-five dollars on the counter, collar and leash were free. We sat on one of the wrought iron benches lining Rio Del Mar's well-kept serpentine walkway, a grateful and surprisingly calm nine-week Cockapoo tasting our faces and hands. Corbett was saving news for the right moment, he would not look at me "One Hand Clapping's been invited to play Sky River again". He waited and when I said nothing "Erik and Renzo came by after your left and convinced me to do it. It's Labor Day weekend in Washington, Friday Saturday Sunday and Monday, some place called Satsop, fifteen miles East of Olympia. It's suppose to be protesting a nuclear power plant under construction there". He looked at me "I told them I'd only go if you would". I loved he did that, and loved being some one he did not expect "Well then, I'd love to go". Corbett's blue eyes went wide "Wow, cool". I put the Furhead in his arms "I know you set this up to get me fired on my first day at work. Take this little beast home so I can go ask for time off".

Waiting till closing, having sold $452.40 merchandise, $31.67 commission plus $14.00 salary, the store's biggest day ever, after well-dones, I asked Mr. Warehouse for time off to go home, an important Family gathering Labor Day Weekend. Grumbling, reluctant, calling his pregnant Wife, who I had replaced so she could stay home, but since it was for Family, a Jewish Family, she agreed to come-in those two days they were open. First thing I called Leda, thinking we could meet at The Festival. Her Mom gave me her room number at Swedish Hospital, resentful, complaining Leda had an ectopic pregnancy and almost died, that she was such a little whore, what was a Mother to do, and where was I when she needed a friend. I phoned her room. She had people there, laughing, things were not as Mother said, she would be out tomorrow, and glad for somewhere to go, promised to meet me at the festival, stage-left, Sunday at noon. Mom and Dad were next, I told them we would be staying at the Evergreen Hotel in Olympia. Anxious to meet Corbett, Dad was quick "Great, perfect, the whole Market's closed for remodeling. We'll meet you Saturday at noon in the main dining room. Lunch's on me". Mom sweetened "And I'll bring you a care-package, some of your shoes and clothes. You know Shoshannah, I've been wanting to say, these times are different, and if I was your age, who knows maybe your Father and I would be doing the same thing you are. I want you to know, though I don't feel comfortable you living with Corbett, I understand". Hanging-up I had tears in my eye, Mom was the best, she would not give us a hard time. Dad was another story, he would take Corbett's measure first, shake his hand too hard, question his intentions, hold his gaze too long to see would he look away, and then look deep in my eyes to see would I.

We named our beautiful new Boy Argus, after Ulysses faithful Hound, who waited 20 long years for his Master's return, and the only one to recognize him, waving a loving hello with his tail, duty done he closed his weary eyes forever. Argus was a quick-study, and soooo cute, and soon ran our lives, demanding unconditional love, lavish pets, long walks to the beach, barking contests, wrestling matches, tugs of war, things to chew, plates and bowls to lick, our laps for daytime repose, the bed at night, and in return he used the yard, rarely faltering, could hear a cloud go by, alerting us of any thing coming near the house, and unabashedly sanctioned or mostly not all visitors. Erik called for daily Band practice. Limey began hyping a tour of the Northwest and Canada after the festival, to capitalize on the bands fervent Sky River popularity. He would finance this and an album selling hash oil, managing the Band was good cover for a dealer, good reason to travel the coast. I did not like the plan, protesting to Corbett "Limey could get busted easy. Us too. I wouldn't want to lose my freedom for such a selfish cause, would you". He did not seem bothered "Of course not, but it's just hype for now and probably won't even happen. Let it lay, and if it actually happens, we can decide then". Moby Grape was invited to Sky River too, their Manager would not let them play using their name, somehow he had taken ownership of it and they could no longer use it without permission, which he refused to give, some dark and vicious battle was going on. Delroy's other band MoonGoose was not invited this time, so he and Drummer and Bass Player, and the Grape's other great guitar player Peter Lewis would gladly fill-in for Lorenzo and Corbett at the Colonial. Colleen too big, uncomfortable and close due to come along. Cherry afraid to fly. Marion's condition too delicate, she offered to keep Jennifer and Argus. We took him for a trial-run, and he had such a hoot romping with Anna and her puppies, we knew right then he needed more than us humans to be content and would keep eyes-out for one of his own kind.

Sky River would have a grand piano on stage, Hammond B-3, Leslie speakers, foot-peddle bass, drum kits, amps, mics, speakers. Erik, Joey, Luke, Ted road with Limey, Stoney came for us late Friday morning with Lorenzo and Andrew, and we caravanned to San Jose. Walking taller though the airport in new Tony Lama ostrich skin cowboy boots, new black leather guitar case in-hand, Erik's private temperament transformed by public scrutiny, he was quite nice to me. I wore one of my gowns. Corbett his tie-dyes. Andrew his usual khaki pants and not-so graying white t-shirt, carrying the bowling bag with his precious stoneware jug inside. Limey's hand clasp tight to an alligator briefcase likely full of drugs. Everyone seemed to be watching us, wondering who are they, we all walked taller, it was fun traveling with a band. Even the stewardesses were fascinated, attentive, we ordered too many drinks, Stoney put it on his new Master Charge card. Landing smooth at Seatac in light rain, uniformed limo-driver with a One Hand Clapping sign waiting, whisking us 46 miles South to the Evergreen Hotel. It was swarming with freaks, reminding me of the Camas Inn to the tenth-power, hundreds of rooms, indoor swimming pool, sauna, high-tone restaurant, the Gil Conte Trio playing in the lounge, gift shops, clothing, candy, a beauty salon, and heliport set-up on the lawn with two copters shuttling performers to-and-from the site, Eric Clapton infront of us checking-in. One Hand Clapping scheduled to play around 6PM Sunday, it was 5PM Friday night, with keys to our room, we ordered room service, Crab Louis, French bread and butter, a cheese veggie and cracker platter, strawberries and a bottle of Liebfraumilch, anything we wanted Stoney arranged to put on his Master Charge. The food came, we hung do-not-disturb on the door.

Far more excited than I imagined to see my Mom and Dad, looking and looking at the clock-radio, half-hour, another half-hour, another, I was showered and dressed by 10AM, coaxing Corbett pleeease get-up, lunch with my Folks at noon. I thought he was playing with me, dawdling in the shower, shaving, combing, re-tying shoes, looking through his wallet, ready in time, I opened the door, and he sat down on the bed, sure my Parents were monsters like his, he did not want to go. Loosing my cool, I was close to a foolish ultimatum when Lorenzo appeared in the doorway, announcing 3PM practice in Erik's room, he had been-up all-night, rubbing shoulders, jamming with this Big Name and he was starving, did Hawk want to go eat. Corbett explained my Folks. Lorenzo insisted on tagging along, wanting to meet anyone's Folks who would come to a rock festival. I did not want him, keeping silent, grateful he warmed Corbett's ice-cold feet. We hurried downstairs, entering through the hotel as Mom and Dad came-in the restaurant door. I could not help running ahead. Corbett and Lorenzo caught-up, Dad took Lorenzo for Corbett, shook his hand too hard and fixed his eyes, for Dad would happily knock you cold with a look if that's all it took. That's all it took, ripped on hash oil, Lorenzo excused himself, falling over his own feet on the get-away. We all laughed, and Corbett's shoulders relax. Although I made reservations, we had to wait, giving time for proper introductions. Dad seemed pleased with the actual Corbett, still I knew what was about to happen, admonishing "Daddy, Corbett needs his hands". Dad winked at me, clenching Corbett's hand not too tight, staring deep into his eyes. Four-inches taller Corbett held a steady gaze, and knowing who ever blinks first loses, graciously ceded "I know I have your daughter Mr.Leibofsky, but I love her and promise to take as good a care of her as she'll let me". Dad put his free hand on top of the clench and smiled "You certainly know her my Boy, she's always had a mind of her own". Smiling too Corbett added his hand to the pile, they were instant friends. Mom was next, taking both of Corbett's hands, looking-up at this tall lean Shaygets, pulling him down to her eye level "Remember, she's my daughter too". Our table was ready.

We ate, talking best we could among the menagerie of stoned Freaks on food trips and business men. Mom chain-smoking and jumpy, I loved her for bearing-up. If Dad was bothered, nothing showed, talking easily to Corbett, never interrogating. I could see from the way Corbett leaned-in to him, confiding, he was happy his feet had warmed "My Folks never come to see my play. They certainly would never come here". Dad gave him a knowing look "We'd go anywhere to see our Daughter". He turned to me "You know you always have a job at Chicken Valley". What a rascal he was, I could tell by this playful provocation Dad recognized Corbett as substantial, some thing he had never seen in others I brought home, he was a bit jealous, and a whole lot proud that owning his own business gave him the opportunity to offer his favorite Daughter a good paying job. The waitress brought the check, Dad insisted on paying, his rather sweet way of power-tripping. Corbett wisely let him own the moment. Mom eager to depart the zoo, we followed her hasting to the car. She directed Corbett take my care-package from the back-seat. I peeked inside the cardboard box, clothes, shoes, apple glycerin soap, Yuban coffee, dried apricots, smoked almonds, lavender-scented candles. Mom hugged and kissed me. While Dad had last-words with Corbett "Young man, you'll have me to deal with if I hear anything from my Daughter. Remember I'll go anywhere". A punk-kid from 2685 Creston Avenue the Bronx, Dad had belonged to the Jewish Gang and had the knife scars to show. Jews had to fight their way down every block, so did Irish Catholics, Puerto Ricans, Blacks, Italians, Asians, Mexicans, needing their Gang just to survive walking to school. He'd been a champion Golden Gloves boxer, and still a formidable threat at 56, could back-up his words if need be. Corbett was not threatened "You don't have to worry Mr.Leibofsky, you'll never hear a word you won't like. I only wish my Dad loved me like you love Shoshy". Dad gave him the smile reserved only for his Children, put his arms round me for a good-bye hug, and slipped something in my hand. As they drove away, I looked down through tears at a neatly folded $100 bill and burst-out laughing.

Erik's room decorated in nubile Groupies, he plainly assumed Corbett would show alone and boiled at my witness, calling me Yoko just incase I might have misinterpreted his body-language. Corbett pressed him to ease off. I knew Erik could not, and unwilling to sacrifice even one joule of lunch's sunny aura, pulled Corbett into the hallway "Look, don't hassle with him. I'll meet you later in the room, okay". He began apologizing for Erik "He's so high-strung, I think he takes it out on you because he sees a worthy opponent". Stopping him there "Don't make excuses fer him. I don' care what 'e thinks a me or why. I don't wan' the confrontation. I'll be fine. Anyway I want to explore this place. Just you keep those Groupies off you". He smiled and lightly kissed my lips "I will, I promise". The Evergreen oozed drugs, predatory Groupies ravening famous and not-yet musicians, publicly, privately consuming each other, testimony to a generation squandering its momentum, its potential, its power, getting really stoned but not high. I bought a Seattle Times and sat behind it in the lobby, watching the parade, hoping to see some one from the Seattle Liberation Front. I could have sold all my gown here, some Groupies asking to buy mine right-off-me. And when the relentless sniffing took more defensive energy than I could spare, retreated to our room, ordering bagels and cream cheese, I lit the candles from my care-package, got under the covers, turned-on the Jerry Lewis Muscular Dystrophy Telethon and waited. Two AM, Corbett way passed drunk when he crawled in.

Stoney knocked at 9AM, we must be in the Lobby by ten. Corbett had a wicked hangover, ordering two glasses of milk delivered, they helped a little, standing under a long hot shower that helped a little, buying some Rolaids from the gift shop, and taking two Canadian pain pills from Joey. I could hardly stand still, nervous, excited for the helicopter ride. They were no longer flying, and the disappointment hit me so hard I would have gone back to the room to sleep but-for my promise to meet Leda. We boarded a shuttle bus to the site, everyone seriously hung-over. Day three-of-four, rumored 150 thousand attending, One Hand Clapping would go-on at 6PM, after the Youngbloods and Billy Preston, we entered the seventy-seven acre valley, passing-by another shuttle turned on it's side, and were let-out at the backstage gate. Corbett told the Gatekeeper I was part of the Band. Erik rolled his eyes and kept silent. Our hands appropriately stamped, I was amazed by the high probably fifteen-foot stage, three-times the surface area of last years, the massive wall of speakers stacked on both sides, maybe 60 of them, and the uniformed cops with guns, this Sky River had real money behind it. Only performing Bands, Dealers and Groupies were allowed on stage, Delaney and Bonnie jamming with Eric Clapton, we were all so thrilled to be in this company. I stayed with Corbett, holding hands, till he struck-up a conversation with Jesse Colin Young, who looked at me in vague recognition. I walked to the edge of the stage, searching over the crowd for Leda, thinking I said stage left, but was that looking at the stage or looking from it, slowly realizing the tall blonde standing next to and grinning at me was Mark from Hydra. He was not involved with this festival, no one from last year was, telling me Satsop had been selected the site, to protest and publicize a nuclear power plant being built here, this was the full extent of Promoters politics, that it was a faint effigy to lure the faithful, they were in it only for the money.

And Mark had no qualms admitting the same, he decided to try stand-up comedy, scored 100 grams of coke to finance a trip to LA, and came here to deal. We'd been through a lot together, he was always kind to me, we had little common ground anymore, so I bought a gram for 20 bucks to be polite and asked what he knew about the Conspiracy Defendants. Last he heard they were waiting for a ruling on contempt charges. I thanked him with a hug and headed back for Corbett. Mark came along, inquiring after Leda, grinning bashful on hearing we would meet at noon.

Corbett rapt in conversation with Billy Preston, consummate keyboard players, I went out the gate with Mark to find Leda. Youngbloods opening their set, thousands crowding forward, we had to circle around, making it to looking at the stage left after noon, no Leda. Things had changed so dramatically for me, no more Seattle Liberation Front, and what was left of the Movement seemed co-opted by political gangsters, funny how stepping-away from it, how the romance had worn-off, how different it looked, the once great and noble Sky River now a greedy diversion, without grand purpose to inspire the vacant-eyed revelers, all stoned, psyche-deliced, cocained, smacked, I could no longer relate, for I did no drugs now save a little weed, no longer had any explicit plans to overthrow the government or rip-off the man for the cause, I had for god sake a strait job and a dog, and even with a clear-plastic packet of coke in my hand and no knife in my pocket, the chilling grip of my old friend paranoia was not at my throat, this realization alone made the trip worth while. Still I was glad for Mark's camaraderie, we waited by the watermelon wagon half-an-hour, Leda never showed. A cop becoming too interested, Mark faded into the multitude, and I felt the press of crass extremes bumping into each other, and retreated backstage.

Gatekeeper had a little brown vial in his hand as he pulled mine under the black-light to check the stamp and offer me a hit off his joint. I no-thank-youed four times before he let me go. Little brown vials in every ones hands. One Hand Clapping sat in a circle of lawn chairs under a large blue tarpaulin at the back of the stage smoking hash oil dipped Marlboros, drinking Coors. Erik's red-rimmed eyes looked like they would burst as I claimed Corbett's lap, his arms wrapping around me. I smiled at Erik, engaging his eyes, opened my palm-up, offering the clear plastic packet, he thought he knew me, I relished showing he did not. He snatched it quick-ly and stuck it in his pocket. And it began to rain, and no one seemed to know why the long long time between bands. Erik's anxiety swelled in direct proportion, happily he drew Stoney and Luke's blood instead of mine. It was passed 5PM when Billy Preston and his band took the stage, Erik marshaled the troupes to stand ready. Billy recorded with the Beatles, and had just flown in from New York, performing with George Harrison and Ravi Shankar at the Concert for Bangladesh in Madison Square Gar-den, to raise money for that newly won nation, the Beatles aura clinging to him like royal robes, all stood to hear him play, screaming over the Hammond's first bars. Forty-five minutes into a great set, sudden deafen-ing silence, then hooting, screaming, a gun shot pierced our ears, all the electricity was out. Grabbing Corbett's hand I pulled him toward the stairs "Come on Babe, this is bad news, let's go for the bus". He resisted "Maybe they'll go back on". I knew better and I knew he didn't, "No, trust me, it's over, come on". The stage lights blinked on, an indignant voice reverber-ating over the sound system "The fucking electric company turned off the fucking generators". He laughed like a loon "And I turned them back on". The crowd went wild, chanting "Turned on turned on turned on turned on…". His microphone died, and the lights. I locked my arm through Corbett's, towing him passed Gatekeeper and into a packed bus stair-well. He did not like leaving Lorenzo behind. I had been in crazy crowds, holding his tight, the door banged shut behind us, we grabbed onto cold metal poles and each other, lurching, swerving the muddy dimness, iso-lated snapshots of frightened eyes, cops with raised truncheons, a heap of split-open watermelons, the right color blue VW bus with a stove-pipe chimney. Clattering onto the black-top connecting the site to Highway 12, Driver hit something, a sickening thud, the whole bus in loud rebuke could not stop him, we jostled in grim silence, Corbett's arm around me, mine around him. When Driver stopped infront of the Evergreen, open-ing the bus door, we all hurried to the nose, finding blood and fur.

Too spent to order and eat anything, we left our clothes on the floor. I could not shake my head out of seeing Nick's bus, and ours with the blood on it, maybe it wasn't really, but lately I felt him hanging around the edges, maybe because I was so happy now and sincerely wished he would find

622

true love too. I did not imagine my well-wishing would open anything till I saw the blue bus and felt the chill. I knew this door and could clearly see it in mind, Middle Ages old, massive thick timbers, ornate hammered brass bolt and hinges, and yes it was ajar. Pushing it closed I slid the big metal bar all the way into its socket. I intended Nick no ill, only too break forever our connection, this door had been my way out of that maze I'd walked into nearly four-year ago. I locked it shut tight and threw the key into a fire so hot it melted.

Rapping hard on our door Lorenzo woke us "Hawkman, hey say something, you in there". Corbett sat up "Yeah I'm here". Opening the door naked he hurried back to me. Lorenzo filled the doorway, arms folded across his chest "Shit, man, everyone got on the shuttle but you. I was totally freaked. What happened". Corbett put his hand on my thigh "Sorry man, but I knew you could take care of yourself. Shoshy got us on the first bus out. Everyone else okay". Nodding to some kind of shared understanding of women-and-children first, old familiar put-down, the weaker sex needs be taken care of, for they are but children too, Lorenzo snorted "Yeah. But what a mess. The Festival's canceled. Shit, we're not gona play here. Anyway, Stoney ordered a limo in the morning, 7:30, so be in the lobby". Corbett asked "You got a bed somewhere". Lorenzo smiled "Me, sure man, waitin' for me right now". It was 11PM, the few hours sleep were rejuvenating, Corbett ordered filet mignon, baked potato, New York cheesecake, me spinach mushroom omelet, steak fries, tartar sauce, a bottle of Weibel Green Hungarian wine. I lit the candles, and over toasts, made an earnest confession "I been in way worse situations with the Seattle Liberation Front than today, but I had no one to lose but me. I have you now, and a future I want, our life's important to me, and it scares me caring so much about it". Corbett took my hand, placing it over his heart "Me too". Full bellies, sleep took us before dessert.

Room service knocking with coffee, Stoney's 6AM compliments. Eating cheesecake and ketchup-soaked fries, we showered together, stopped at the front desk for strapping-tape to bind my care-package, found the Boys in the lobby, and sat down by Andrew, bowling bag in his lap, waiting while Stoney settled the bill. Erik was glowing surly depression, coming this close, not getting to play, and the new boots gave him blisters, I thought his Sisters Fate plainly were trying to teach him something. Limey was brooding this could jeopardize the Northwest tour. Lorenzo over-heard a rumor the promoters were broke, bands, lights, sound, water, no one got paid. Luke, Ted Joey were zombies. Even a limo ride could not lift the gloom. When Stoney came clean to charging rooms, food, limo, plane tickets, everything on stolen credit cards, I thought I would burst all over the car, again made complicit in crime without my consent, this time it was my fault for being stupid. But for the Fredrick & Nelson black hat I paid cash for anyway, every one of my crimes had been of conscience, not personal gain or pleasure. I kept the outrage to my self, for it made me look ignorant, how could I not suspect, where did I think the money was coming from, it would certainly amuse Joey and Erik.

Fortunately not seated with the rest, the plane was full and we were ushered to a small two-seat lounge at the rear of the plane, facing each other across a table, we looked-out a larger than standard window, over Mount Rainier, Helens, Hood, and played Gin Rummy. The Others did tequila shots and propositioned stewardesses. Troubled by all the excesses, assuming the money came from Limey's hash oil, I never thought stolen credit cards. When asking Corbett did he know, he said he did and tossed-it-off to "You know, boys will be boys". Knowing, and not telling troubled me more than stolen cards, I stood and leaned over the table, close to his face as I could "Yeah, that's always the excuse when Boys do bad things. Like when they can't help cheating on their Ol'ladies, or when they hit someone. Like it's handed down Father to Son in a solid stainless steel chain that can never rust or be broken. What a terrible curse. It means you'll be just like your Father. I can't believe you really think that way". Corbett looked abashed, knitting his brow "I guess I didn't tell you, Stoney fully intended on paying the cards off when the Band got paid". Sarcastic disappointment owned my face "Oh well then doesn't that makes it all right. I guess I don't know you Corbett Hawkins. I thought you were a good Catholic Alter Boy who wanted to go to heaven". Corbett shut-down, staring out the window into the thick clouds. I did the same. When food came he whispered "I'm sorry Sweetheart. I guess I thought you knew. I guess I didn't think". I whispered "Me too. But then you did my thinking for me". He looked surprised "Jeez, I did didn't I". I was so

624

relieved he understood this "Yeah". His face went dark "I don't want to be like my Father. He's so angry and careful to keep it covered, his little innocent Boy Scout face". I smiled "Good, cause I couldn't live with your Father". We landed in San Jose, Argus was in my arms by 4:30PM, once home we walked the cliff path to the Tampico for take-out burritos and beer, ate them in bed, and slept till the alarm rang me for work.

Chapter Twenty Six

THE MAGIC VITAMIN

Each week my sales topped the last, bringing home more money than Corbett, he was impressed, proud, delighted, not a whiff intimidated. Sunday's we'd brunch at the Broken Egg, take Argus for a long stroll on the Boardwalk, buy candy cotton to please Corbett's sweet-tooth, and go by the newsstand for a San Francisco Chronicle and Seattle Times. But for a small article about Nixon paying-off Judge Boldt's loyalty with a fat salary by naming him to chair the new Federal Pay Board, and Colleen having a healthy Baby Boy, September, October were voluble and abundant, Corbett and I discovering the other's rhythm and rhyme, beginning to weave a solid resonant harmony. Ten week of work, Friday closing I went into the office for my check, always waiting for me on right corner of the desk. Looking inside the envelope, I was incredulous, these weeks were the best the shop had ever known, my praise had been deafening, yet the stub read $1.75 per hour, 7% commission, $288.40 gross, $248.02 net, Mr. Warehouse had forgotten his promise. Writing in his ledger, I slipped the check under his nose "Remember, it's time for the raise you promised. This is about 20 bucks short". He did not look up "I never promised. I said if you did well". I was not sure what was happening and began to plead my case "We shook hands, you said if I worked hard, after two months you'd raise me 25-cents an hour an 10% commission". He did not give me the consideration of eye contact "There's plenty a girls I can replace you with.

Why should I give you more". I was speechless, confused, and fled into the empty store, all I could think was to run away from this Bad Man, away from the confrontation, I hated confrontation, but Dad would not be proud of me, this man was no where near his standing, I could brave him, should brave him, and I heard Ida Rose's counsel whisper in my ear - Delayed Reaction Lamby, count to ten, give yourself time to think, then date and index who you are right now. I took three long deep breaths, counting ten slowly aloud, I am not a scared Little Girl, I'm a grown Woman who questions authority, I can do this. Taking my best Golden Ghetto bearing, the indignation of righteousness, and Sister Medusa and her fearsome hair-of-snakes by the hand, I marched back into the office determined to have integrity, to not be like him "Would you prefer two weeks notice. I'll be glad to put that in writing. Or I can quit this minute and never come back. I leave it for you Sir to do the right thing". His nose remaining in the ledger, he spat "Forget any letter. Forget coming back. Just go". My thigh muscles twitching, I mimicked his tone "That's fine with me Sir". He picked-up the check and waved it in the air over his head like come-and-get-it doggie. My heart pounding so loud I was sure it shook my cheeks, I flattened my feet to the floor "Don't think I'm such a fool to take your check Sir. I want cash". He was plainly stung by the Sir, putting pencil down, tearing the check in pieces, he opened the cash drawer, counted $248.02 onto the desk, and looked me chin to shoes. I wanted to spit in his face and yell fuck you asshole, just fuck you fuck you, eat shit and die, you think you're smart taking advantage of me, you're not. His bloodless pallor and dim eyes saying he might be sick and had nothing left to go another round, and I had amazingly held my composure, yep Dad would be proud of me. Taking only the paper money, pushing it into my pocket, I knew this was the moment to speak or walk away with regrets "You taught me a lesson in trust Sir, in how to take advantage. Corbett warned me he didn't trust you. I'll be sure to get the word of an honorable man nex' time. Your years put me at a real disadvantage, but there's no wisdom or respect in your win here Sir. And now one more sucker's been wised-up". Turning on the balls of my feet I glided out, Sister Medusa still holding my hand. He pursued with heavy-feet "You don't understand Little Miss Know-it-all. I'm one of the good guys. This is just business". I could not believe this blood-stained excuse, safely out the front door I turned to face him "Just business, just following orders, isn't that what the good German soldiers said". He fell back silence. And I walked tall as I could, showing him my back without fear, this was one of those singular times I had been able to say what I meant, counting to ten worked, I had time to think.

Sailing the cliff path, a hot southern-wind at my back, singing the bridge of a Jackie Lomax song I heard so often on the radio - *Get out of sour milk sea, you don't belong there. Get back to where you should be, and find out what's going on there.* I wanted to prove to my self and Corbett I could hold a strait job, his intuition about Mr. Warehouse had been right-on, and nothing had changed since I worked Nordstrom or Neiman Marcus, retail demanding you dress like you're rich and be terminally perkier than any human being should have to for minimum wage. I would probably employ my self from now on. Mr. Warehouse had played the if-might-and-could game on me, if I do this, he might do that and this could happen. Now I understood why Ida Rose pointed-out to her students, that Jesus said *if I be lifted up*, he never said when, there was never a promise in it, and a whole religion, millions of people teetered on that if, still waiting.

Corbett and Argus were wag-happy to have me home. I found my groove right away, waking early, head full of ideas, a copper turquoise and peach sky in a dream, colors I never thought to put together, or scalloping a hem, I would begin working, forgetting to comb my hair or dress. Intensely curious, Argus woke with me, wanting to poke his nose in ever thing I put my hands too. We had a running conversation, and depending on what he insinuated him self into, I gave him another name, Mr. Fur Pajamas when I found him under the covers with us in the morning, Mr. Poke when he was nosey, Mr. Pig-Pie for the gusto-way he ate, Pokey Pig when he would nose my hand for pets, Someone-From-Somewhere-Going-Someplace-Sometime when I looked into those milk-chocolate eyes and wonder what old soul had taken residence in those lovely fur pajamas.

Maggie was due the end of November, she invited us to a Sunday lunch baby shower. Corbett bought a big brown teddy bear, Argus a rattle, and I could finally give her the quilt, not one for sleeping under, but washable satin, something to spread on the ground for the Little One to lay on. She was thrilled to tears. When it came time to eat, Corbett wondered where were the other guests. Maggie giggled handing him the signed title and keys to their orange Volkswagen. Halls and Arlene had no idea Corbett wrote a monthly check for their car loan, and had surprised them with a new Ford Galaxy 500 Country Sedan station wagon, a Family car, one of those gifts that came with taut emotional strings. Maggie chafed at having no choice in the selection, making her feel like a child instead of mother-to-be. Diego galled too, at driving a station wagon, symbolizing the passing of his youth, he hated the car and their demeaning implication he could not take care of his own. Still, it was free and clear and they had and would swallow hard for this Baby. I was delighted to have a car of my own and told Corbett I would find a way to make the payments, for I owned no money to anyone, and he owed everyone, monthly, for the Spinet and Hammond, student loans, JCPenneys and Sears credit accounts, the Healey, whose driver's seat would not move far enough forward for me to comfortably reach the peddles. The Bug whose peddles I could easily reach, only had 34,257 miles on it and 36 payments of 39 dollars. When a friend of Andrew's offered to buy the Healey two weeks later, Corbett and I decided one less payment was a good thing and sold it without reservations.

I flourished in the long reaches of uninterrupted time into my work, and found the Santa Cruz Import Shop's only competition the Yellowbird a ready, willing outlet. Corbett set the alarm to wake early on Tuesdays, and would walk to the little Catholic Church across from the Shopping Center for mass and communion, and a group discussion after with the priest and five other Regulars, and he went Sundays too for the same. I felt the isolation of a door closed to me and wanted to know more about the Catholic secrets, but he never asked me along, this was one of those private doors, surely bolted from the inside, and certainly not against me, one I knew would open only in his own time. Other mornings he would sleep till I roused him with brewed coffee and toast, and we would leash Argus and descend the steps to the beach. Work-nights Corbett always asked me along, I went most weekends, and once or twice a week depending what I was working on and how near to finish. Every Saturday night we dined at the Colonial. And Lorenzo began working on Corbett to practice Mondays again with One Hand Clapping, echoing Erik's latest hype of moving the band North, finding a big house, living together, recording an album, touring, calling Ralph Gleason for that second try, Limey would bank-roll the whole thing with hash oil money, Lorenzo believed the Band could make it big and didn't want to miss-out. I wanted Corbett to decide without my influence. And I was not so enamored with Santa Cruz anymore. The Elysium weather and beaches would forever hold the romance of our beginning, however, speculators and vultures had discovered the under-priced property, gobbling every shack and bargain, converting them to weekly vacation rentals, three of the five cottages on our little street Court Way had sold, invariably occupied by transients who thought nothing of trashing a neighborhood they had little investment in. And regular rents were soaring, driving many locals into Northern California, and Oregon where the penalty for marijuana possession had been lowered to a misdemeanor. Though I shrank at the thought of every day contact with Erik and Joey, I would seriously consider moving North if Corbett wanted to go.

The plan was out there some time in the future, there were people to convince, money to raise, scouting trips to take, another Baby to be born, vehicles to repair, and I was home-sick for the woody smells, yellowing maples and Autumn chill of the Northwest. Eager to see where I grew-up, know my Folks better, and hopefully to meet Ida Rose, Corbett phoned Bob Mosley, lead singer for Moby Grape, who said yes to coming down from his hide-out in Boulder Creek and covering a week at the Colonial with Lorenzo and his buddy Delroy. Before leaving, I kept a long procrastinated promise to my self, and made an appointment with a gynecologist, to have the latest birth control inserted-in my body, a contraceptive intrauterine device called the Dalkon Shield. There were so many shadow side-effects whispered about the Pill, I worried too much to take it, pulmonary embolism, cervical cancer, breast cancer, weight gain, the Dalkon was said to be safer, no side-effects, no hassle to remember, and Corbett and I had been just plain lucky with condoms and foam. Insertion hurt something beyond terrible, supposedly because I had never had a baby to stretch the cervix muscle. And the after-cramping, I had to pull-over twice driving home, wishing I had not been so brave, wishing I asked Corbett to come with.

No airline would allow Argus to ride in the cabin with us, he absolutely had to come, we would drive. Five Am Friday, November 19, Corbett phoned the National Weather Service for conditions up I-5, the mountain passes were bare and dry. Taking the Bug's wheel, stopping for gas, the Wolf Creek Café for Corbett's first zuzu, and every other rest-stop for Argus, I drove straight through, 18 hours, high on endurance, finding it reassuring Mercer Island was not so far that I could drive home on thirty-bucks gas if I had a mind too. Waiting at the big front window Mom hurried-out, and Dad with such a big smile it half-closed his eyes. We settled at the kitchen table for homemade split pea soup and buttered challah. Mom gave some ham and the bone to Argus, who set upon it in grateful abandon, and she hovered Corbett, graciously sparing him any question of her favor, even as he transparently sought to win it, his lyrical easy laugh, enjoying his welcome. Dad, never anything but contentious with males I brought home, gave his warm approval too. I was so happy I could melt, but for those little looks Mom and Dad flew between them, speaking volumes, a secret language unless you caught the subtle widening and narrowing of their eyes, worrying, wondering what measure of joy or sorrow accompanied this Lange Loksch. I could not remember an adult Gentile every staying the night, and loved them for being progressive broad-minded practical Liberals not just in-word but indeed. And still this almost irresistible compunction to act chaste ingénue of Corbett's casual acquaintance conflicted my conscience, how plausibly rational, like Angela and Paul, to yield to the deception, temporarily returning their Little Girl with the promise of a virgin wedding to come, a coward's self-serving lie I would resist suffering them for my ease. Happily food unwound us, Mom, Dad needed to be up early for work, there were days to talk. Mom took Corbett's arm and showed him to Brothers' room. I could not believe it, she wanted the deception "Come on Mom, you know we're living together. It's just ridiculous to pretend". Facing me, she was firm "Shoshannah, you'll obey our rules under our roof". She looked-up at Corbett "Right". Not about to argue he nodded, giving me the oh well shrug. I sniffed at him. Mom went on "And another thing, I want the both of you to keep your living together quiet. Your Grandmother and I are telling everyone you have an apartment with two other girls. You know how people talk". Such onerous unexpected affront to our proud love, I wanted to bawl her out, don't you see we've been honest with you, if I knew you would be so pre-historic we would have stayed in a motel. I wanted to take Corbett's hand and flee into the night, counting ten instead, not one word, picking-up Mr.Fur Pajamas I went to my room.

Following Argus up a trail on the bank of a rushing river, knee-deep in falling snow, the trees looked like stoop-shoulder monks cloaked in snowy silent robes, almost everything was bright blue-white, even the boiling foam of the water, and I noticed the river was running up-hill. Suddenly Argus jumped-in. I panicked he would be taken, but he leapt out with ease and raced to the peak of the trail, the top of the world, disappearing through a massive ice door into a glittering crystalline palace. Calling his name, I ran after, Gus, Gus, wait for me. Landing on the roof-peak above the door, and eagle folded mighty wings, cocked his snow-white head and looked inside. I did too, seeing Gus, now a big black short-haired mongrel standing upright, he pushed open the door, a smile half-closing his eyes and bid me come in. His wet nose and hot breath on my face, Argus woke me insisting he must go outside, he had business to do and did not want to embarrass himself. Aurora bringing a cold pink dawn, I waited at the back door considering a river running up-hill, crystal palace at the top of the world, power-full symbols from my inner life. Finding Corbett had fundamentally changed me, appeased my soul of Nick, I no longer felt restless, the rogue black mongrel must be me, reaching the top of the world, standing tall, inviting me in.

Wide-awake, feeling whole, reconciled, I switched on the electric percolator Mom had ready, and browsed the house. Stopping to inspect the bird lamp, remembering how I accidentally knocked it over so often as a child, and Dad never mad, patiently gluing it back together, he'd done a very good job. A photo from our 1957 Family vacation to Disneyland, me and Brothers, over-excited little faces in Tomorrowland waiting to board the Rocket ship ride to the Moon. And the blue ceramic whiskey bottle shaped like the Space Needle, bought to remember our many excursions to the 1962 Century 21 Seattle World's Fair. Each held such sweet childhood recall. I poured a cup, found Friday's paper on the fireplace hearth, took them to the couch. Above the fold tens-of-thousands in the streets protesting the war, below the fold, the shockingly aged faces of Susan Stern and Joe Kelly.

Contempt-Case Reversal---Ruling Surprises Defendants.

Four of the seven Seattle conspiracy-case defendants agreed today they were surprised by the Ninth Circuit Court of Appeals ruling in their favor on one contempt charge, but did not consider it a victory.

But the Ninth Circuit court declined to review an appeal of the second contempt charge against the Seven on a technicality, that details presented in the contempt citation were insufficient, that judge Boldt had not been specific enough in citing and describing what he considered contempt of court, and that the citations of contempt were faulty because some of the conduct cited was not witnessed by Boldt himself. A three-judge panel made the ruling.

United States Attorney Stan Pitkin said he would seek a rehearing of argu-ments on the first charge before a full Ninth Circuit Court.

Defendants Susan Stern, Mike Abeles, Joe Kelly and Jeff Dowd said at a press conference today, they expect the government to carry the case all the way to the Supreme Court if necessary.

Jeff Dowd said: "We feel very tired over things that shouldn't have hap-pened. The fact that we were tried is an attack on free speech."

Joe Kelly said of Pitkin's decision to seek a full rehearing: "The reason he's pursuing this is to make an example of us to people."

Their crucible had boiled the life out of them, evident in the grainy photo. Just looking at their careworn faces, knowing the Government would continue the persecution made me cringe how my life was so good while they still took the whipping, for us, for me. But I also felt a tragic optimism, for the body bag accounting on the nightly news had finally become enough to stir the slumbering Middle Class from their dinner tables and easy chairs and into the streets in such undeniable numbers Nixon had to listen if he was to keep the illusion of Democracy intact, if he was to keep his job.

Coffee's lure brought Corbett, the sight of his face my reprieve, we giggle over our sleeping arrangement and decided to stay four days instead of seven, it was long enough to be treated like naughty children. Mom and Dad woke with their alarm. Dad took his insulin shot at the table, and over breakfast related the story of an older woman walking through the market last month, how the crowd parted for her like the Red Sea as she came up to the counter, her face a shining golden light, she knew him by name, bought three deboned chicken breasts, and introduced herself. I said in delight, that was Ida Rose. Nodding, Dad smiled that approval I sought and valued so much.

They went to work. Corbett went soon after to investigate St.Monica's Church just around the block. His way of connecting spiritually was troubling me, I could not sit, pacing, feeling left-out of something he found so necessary, wondering what was in the big brick building he could not just as well find somewhere else, I had not found Yahweh to be in his promised house, and I worried religion really did matter and the Church would come between us. He was back in-the-hour, frustrated, unsettled, St.Monica practiced the Latin Mass, one his Folks would love, one he had fallen to far away from to find meaningful, it gave him no relief from his feeling inadequate and anxious staying in my Folks house, relegated to Brothers' room, he was use to people knowing him playing music, judging on his talent, while Mom and Dad saw him as their daughter's Boyfriend and were interested only in his character. I knew well the vertigo that comes with letting go of long held belief, the often blind uncertainty that necessarily accompanies it, and wanted to dare Corbett to find God somewhere beside the big brick building, maybe in a sunset, a bird's song, the music of laughter, I wanted him to pray at ocean's edge, or naked in the shower if he needed to, I wanted him, I wanted to assure him his character was enough to put him in good stead with my Folks, and kept my mouth shut, he needed listening to not words. Tomorrow I would phone Ida Rose.

Today, Autumn's majesty called, a sparking blue morning, I would take him on the scenic tour to find god. First driving 24 miles East on I-90 into the foothills of the Cascade Mountains, to Salish Lodge over-looking Snoqualmie Falls, for their famed seven course brunch. It rained hard overnight, the Falls boiling foam so like my dream river. We saved the bacon and sausage for Gus. Then back on 90 to North 405 through Bellevue, West on 520 over the new Lake Washington Evergreen Point Floating Bridge, North on I-5 passed the University of Washington, and the country's first covered-shopping-mall at Northgate, we held our breath through the saw-mill stench of Everett and Marysville, and 70 miles South of the Canadian Border, Mount Baker's pure white rising in almost perfect symmetry, I followed the Stanwood exit West to Camano Island State Park on the Straits of Juan De Fuca, the jagged Olympic Mountains rising purple-and-white from the Olympic Peninsula. Gus chased every seagull landing on the beach, barking at Canadian geese honking their Southern migration, and each clam squirt from under the wet sand. A cold North wind drove us back to the car, and East through Sylvana's lush stands of blazing maples, poplars, alders and birch proudly flaunting their fiery Fall plumage high in the air, then South again on 5, Seattle's bold new sky-scrapers hailing from a distance, boasting some maturation, promising growth so cosmopolitan I would not need seek enlightened culture elsewhere, and South of the City Mt.Rainier's eminent blueberry ice-cream sundae backdrop, I took the West Seattle Bridge exiting passed the Rainier Brewery, and then Harbor Avenue ushering us to sunset on Alki Beach, burnt-orange-pink-purple clouds framing those snowy Olympics, and Vashon, Blake, Bainbridge Islands. The lighted ferry-boats looking like giant harmonicas skimming the silver-blue Puget Sound, and rain threatening to fall, Argus walked us along the concrete promenade till dark. It was dark by 5PM, we headed up to Admiral Way for the city's night-lit panorama across Elliot Bay, and over the Old Floating Bridge to Mercer Island, near-full moon enough to light the Cascades Mountains hovering the Eastern skyline.

One of those robust Autumn days that inspires a person vivid and alive, it seduced Cobbett completely "We absolutely have to move here, I love it". I smiled wry "You don't know how dark it is all Winter, the days only six-hours and gray. Seattle's got the highest suicide rate in the country". Undaunted, putting his arms around, pulling me close "I wouldn't mind hibernating the Winter with you. It's so clean here, the air smells so fresh, the rain washes everything, and there's hardly any people. If the Band moves North, I wouldn't mind, would you". I could feel his heartbeat quicken and realized he's spent his life in California, and how exciting, what an adventure it would be to move here "No Babe, I wouldn't mind.

634

I didn't know till today how much I miss it here. And if the Band doesn't work out, it's still okay. I'll miss the beach, and having the towels dry overnight without putting them in the dryer, and the people are way more liberal in California, and you'll be homesick for sure, but my Family's here, and Ida Rose". Corbett kissed me "So when do I get to meet her". "I'll call tomorrow, after my Folks go to work".

Dad, Mom came home with reservations for dinner at Tai Tung. Granny, her just announced fiancé, and my Brothers would meet us in Chinatown. I'd come to a defiant resolve with Big Brother disowning me, and would rather not endure his self-righteous chauvinism, his con's knack for making me appear perpetrator to his innocent victim. I was a trusted friend growing-up, covering for him, keeping his secrets, he was my Big Brother, until I found-out from one of his creepy Pals that he took my diary and read the intimate details to his Buddies for laughs, a fifth-grader getting her period, the humiliation of changing sanitary napkins in the doorless bathroom stalls of elementary school, the bulging pads, often bleeding over the sides onto my clothes, the debilitating cramps. I found out in high school because one of these creepy Pals was the Big Brother of a Friend who I just by amazing chance happened to be visiting when he called home, and she asked me to please get the phone. He thought since it was so long ago he could tell me and I would not care, that I would find it funny as he did that my privates were just another dirty titillation. I was devastated Big could so casually betray me for a snigger, telling me every thing I needed to know about him then, I swore never trust him again, and began to understand there was something wrong with him. Dad knew too. But Little Brother still looked-up to his handsome Big and actively sought approval. And then there was Mom's blind love for her children, so easily manipulated, deceived. She held the firm notion a Good Mother treated her Children indiscriminately the same, and was determined to be that Good Mother, indulgently ignoring any of our crimes. I would not tangle again with Big, who like Gretchen took advantage of not playing by the rules, knowing I would. If I sank to his level he won, if I didn't he won, for me it was a lose lose game. I wanted to tell Mom I would not go anywhere he was, but that would only cast me mean-spirited to his smug vindication. I felt hurt and betrayed by her steadfast belief no matter how egregious the act, that blood must be forgiven and forgotten, that a Mother's job was to keep her Family together, and somehow by sheer force of will we would return to the loving siblings she remembered. And she showed no sign of ever seeing my point of view, responding to every one of my balks with – Shoshannah can't you just get along with your Brother. No matter he did not get along with me, she had long ago swallowed whole the tales that bore males license to prescribe to females, not by my Dad's persuasion, but Granny's edicts, like she must make her Little Brother's bed every morning along with her own, it still enraged her. And she had stuffed it, complaining but never questioning, and unless she did, unless she dared understand her Mother's naively passed-on debasements, she would see my defiance of male authority over my life simply an aberration, a mistake that only causes me tsuris, and her. She would remain one of those who accepted the lie that men were more important, more grown-ups, that they had the right to do our thinking for us, and that we should forgive them all, for boys will be boys, their needs inevitably came first, and therefore easier to skirt with feminine wiles than contest outright, just like her Mother, although I did not believe she totally believed it because she married Dad. Still she would unwaveringly hope a man, maybe Corbett would ultimately straighten me out, settle me down with children and a more traditional life, one she could relate to.

Corbett had quietly disappeared into Brothers room. While Mom and Dad changed their work clothes, I went in. He had a queasy stomach and did not want to go. I knew he had been born with his nervous-net on the outside of his body, every pore a possible way in, essential equipment for an artist to absorb his environment and reveal it back, leaving him open for vampires and parasites to suck-off his shining light. Barricaded behind the Hammond and piano was some protection, out-in-the-open sometimes shook him. I loved his sensitivity, compassion, empathy, and would not pressure him or presume "You don't have to go Babe". He looked surprised "I don't". I knew he was nervous about meeting the rest of my Family "Nope. I don't mind answering all the suspicious innuendos about your absence". His face lit-up "You little devil. Now I want to go". I kept my voice low "If I could find a kind way-out, I wouldn't go either. You haven't met my Big Brother. He's a major creep. I'd rather never see him again. So, we'll take our car incase we need to escape. I'll say that leaving Argus in the house alone was a mistake, just asking for trouble. They won't completely believe me, but I know they'll go along". Corbett hated the complication of lying, he was so bad at it "Why can't we just". I interrupted "Cause it's protection and that's kosher". He smiled and nodded "Okay. Gus is the the signal you want to leave, and visa versa". I kissed him "It's a plan. Don't worry Babe, besides Big Brother, you'll love my Family, and they'll love you". I could tell from the little glances exchanged, Mom and Dad saw through my reason for taking our car. I loved them letting it go without more than a look.

The jet-haired hostess in tailored Mandarin silk ushered us to our table. Corbett ordered a Mai Tai. His daily drink was concerning me, but I did not know what to do or say. Everyone arrived with his Mai Tai, which he downed in quick gulps and seemed to relax. We ate for two hours, Dad enjoying ordering too much food, insuring plenty of take-home. And I enjoyed an unexpected reprieve, for Big Brother brought his girlfriend Marlee to rule, and they cooed of engagement, taking the focus off Corbett and me. Being Jewish had been an albatross round Big's wanting-character, ferociously concealed, complicating his desperate scramble up Golden Gentile Heights. Marlee, his lily-skin Protestant Teutonic Bar-bie Doll was the ideal business partner, perfect camouflage for the climb. I was sure she would not convert, that Mom and Dad would lean on me for Jewish grand-children. Marlee and I were convenient friends working at Boeing, otherwise she was frosty to me. And she willingly, was even flattered to surrender her ego, molding it buttress to Big's in the name of consecrating her femininity, of getting ahead. My unnecessity with Cor-bett cast a threatening shadow. In stark contrast, there was Little Brother, unwilling, unable to allow the Golden Ghet's pervasive Christian con-tumelies to shame him into hiding any part of himself, and he'd finally come into his own, the Girl next door at school was his steady, though she had not ridden down with him from Bellingham, for which he fended some suspicious innuendo, still his new self-confidence resonated their love. Wisely, he waited for Big to inhale nearly all the air before modestly declaring his intention to ask Girlfriend for her hand. And then there was Granny, fluttering and fussing over her suave fiancé, the best dancer at the weekly senior square dance. She confided to me on the way to the bathroom "I would never go with a Goyisher infront of the Family if you didn't already". An old-fashioned kind-a-gal, she knew how to have a good time, kept her figure eating anything but only a scheemer, unashamedly catered to her Man's ego, and like Big, this Man ate it up. Two of these relationships smacked of teenage romance, fragile shallows, insidious insecurities, frissoning highs, wanting of any depth and therefore possibility. Watching Granny made me squirm most, even with plenty to take care on her own, she demeaned her self as if life still depended on a man worth. She pushed at me "You need some color. Here put on some lipstick, pinch your cheeks. If you want to catch that man, you have to be more like me, more like that pretty girl with your brother. Act soft, make him feel like a man, then he'll ask you to marry him too". I bit down on my tongue, knowing she meant well, giving me her best guidance, and I looked forward, hoped a time would come when I could tell her how Women's lives had changed, how we no longer had to sacrifice our ego for a man to take care of us, how we had choices now she never did, to have children or not, to get an education, a pretty good paying job, go out in the world, choices that were now hers too if she wanted them, and I knew she would only hear this as insult. With all the undercurrents, we had a wonderful evening. Corbett charmed everyone, impersonating Tiny Tim, Al Jolson, Elvis, Mickey Mouse, introducing his keen wit at just the unexpected moment. And I exhaled, snug in the arms of my Family, content watching them fall for him. Mom had us all together, and Dad savored his business success, being able to, making a little show of paying for the feast.

Riding home Corbett began to itch, welt-up, and panic. He wanted to go straight to bed, hide, shiver it out, but Mom had a nose for need, intercepting him, insisting on mothering, and I knew to let her have her way. Taking his temperature, checking his racing pulse, she diagnosed hives, which instantly calmed the panic. And she gave him some prescription diphenhydramine that happened to be in the medicine cabinet, and drew a bath with Epson Salts. Corbett's Mother never missed an opportunity to contaminate the slightest infirmity with accusation of some secret sin and God's retribution. My Mom was not a soul-sucker, and to Corbett's wonderment and redemption, she lifted the curse, his fear that every illness no matter how mild was certainly fatal. His tender nervous system and welts quieted with the bath, Mom went to bed happily having made him one of her very own Dear Children. Our dinner party had raised the specter of toxic Hawkins Family gatherings, Corbett forgot to remember shellfish gave him hives, and in a kind of self-sabotage, set-into-motion a familiar program that would certainly turn-out bad, he ordered the abalone steak, and drank too much. I took him to my room, and Argus who had already eaten every last morsel of leftover Barbcued Pork, Mongolian Beef, boneless Peking Style Spareribs and Kung Poa Chicken. And I set the alarm minutes before Dad's, a teenage fantasy come true, sneaking my lover into my bed.

Just ahead of the alarm, Argus wiggled in-between us nuzzling our faces, impatient to go out. We decided to fix my Folk's breakfast. I set a table of orange juice, toast and coffee. Corbett scrambled his light-fluffy eggs with grated cheddar and hot sauce. Mom rustling at the intrusion into her domain, we all sat down to the meal, laughing, laughing, laughing as Corbett impersonated Jimmy Durante, Rod Serling, Gomer Pyle, Jack Nicholson, Peter Lorre. Mom and Dad delighted in the fun, and went to work smiling. I absolutely adored Corbett's playfulness, how he could make everyone feel so good, me too, and understood in the translucence of epiphany, he was always on except alone with me, and sometimes even then. Court Jester had been his chosen position in the Family dynamic, organ-grinder and when necessary monkey, defusing the intensity, the threat, the danger, using his talent in comic relief to afford respite where no one dare speak of what was really there.

Phone ringing as we cleaned-up, Dad often took home calls for specialty items and large orders from restaurants, making arrangements with his suppliers before leaving for work. I answered "Good morning, Chicken Valley". Someone breathing through his nose said nothing. The hair on my neck prickling, I wanted to suppose who ever it was simply did not recognize Dad's familiar voice "This is Chicken Valley, can I help you". Nick's menace crossed the limits of my supposition, that old compelling, I quickly hung-up. Corbett asked "Who was it". I felt ambushed, angry, and for some reason embarrassed "They didn't say anything. Maybe a wrong number. Anyway, I'll call Ida Rose an see if we can come over".

Corbett shrugged his shoulders and grinned "I hope I'm ready for this". His voice dissolved Nick's shadow, I so loved this man, and teased "Yeah, we'll see how brave you are without a piano to hide behind. I think I'll call Leda first though, I promised to take her to Ida Rose, and our timing's always been off". Her Mom answered, taking the opportunity to rail "I do everything for my daughter, I would die for her and she acts like an ungrateful little whore. You and those damn other ones, don't you know she'll follow you anywhere. Where were you when she came home from the hospital with complications. I had to miss work and take care of her, and then two days ago she up and went right back to Santa Cruz with her thumb in the air, running to be with you God damn little whores, stupid little bitches in heat, you deserved everything you …". Hearing the venom Leda ran from made me ever grateful I would not have to forgive my Mom calling these names, be murdered with that permanent ache, wishing now I had phoned when Leda did not show at Satsop, appreciating unequivocally her escape to Keely and Gretchen, for I knew in my heart despite our sour predicament they would be there for her, and me too. I could picture them soothing, smoothing her now, and knew I would show-up at the Fairmount Avenue house one day soon.

Shaking-off Leda's Mom, and Nick, I phoned Ida Rose. She answered on the first ring "Hello". I was thrilled to hear her compact dancing voice "Hi Ida Rose, this is Shoshannah Leibofsky". She chirped "Oh lovely, they told me some one would be calling. I'm so glad it's you Shoshannah. Tom's coming to audit this afternoon, and I've been pouring over the latest issue of Gourmet magazine. I'll make Carbonnades á la Flamande for us if you can come drive me up to the QFC". I did not mention trying to be vegetarian "I can, I'd love to, but I'm not alone. Corbett's here, we're visiting my Folks". She sounded pleased "Wonderful, bring him along". I hesitated "Ida Rose, you can say no and I won't mind, would it be okay if our little Cockapoo Argus comes too, he very well mannered". She did not hesitate "Why yes Lamby. Be as close to noon as you can. I'm looking forward to meeting Corbett, and Argus". "Thank you Ida Rose. And if there's time, I can do your hair". There was a smile in her voice "I'll make time". Hanging-up it hit me, Corbett would soon be initiated, auditing was the other side, the metaphysical plane of General Semantics, and like LSD, once exposed you are forever changed, and I could not prepare him any more than already. He'd been reading the Pink Elephant, embracing the disciplines, read all the audit Ida Rose gave me, we talked-long on those I witnessed in-person, still the actual experience was so stunning, the whole world tilts 90 degrees, and you must consider, have I lost my mind or not, is this woman crazy or not, is she evil, how else could she do this, and oh shit I'm sliding-off the ground of every thing I have ever believed. Corbett showed no remnant of hives or panic, his frangibility mostly to his Family, nevertheless to watch Ida Rose conduct an audit, be in that presence, to think about what standing she must hold to do this asks a lot, of which I thought him capable. But what if he deems her evil, if he wants no part of her, an impossible breach would come between us, for I was irrevocably on her team. He sat cross-legged on the floor brushing Argus. I kissed the back of his neck "Ida Rose invited us to dinner. She's making Carbonnades". Argus looked so small as Corbett turned him over with those giant tarantula hands to brush his white belly "Great. What's Carbonnades". "Belgian beer stew, you should like it". He caught my drift "Yum. What time we going". "She's expecting us at noon. Her main auditor Tom's coming to do an audit. You're in for a real experience Babe. I hope you're ready for it". Corbett looked-up and smiled "Can we bring Argus". I nodded "Yep, he's been officially invited". Corbett addressed him "Okay then you hairy little beast, I'll give you a bath and cream rinse. You'll be so soft, no one will be able to resist petting that silky hide". Gus wiggled from Corbett's hands, raced through the house, round and round, their favorite game, person lying on the floor, dog swooping in.

Tom had come early, and opened the front door of the white brick house on Crescent Avenue, all but filling the jamb. I had forgotten what a Big Man he was, not just biceps and rough blue-collar good-looks, but in substance, a suitable Guardian at this threshold. I introduced Corbett. He put Argus down to shake hands. Gus looked all the way up Tom, respectfully sniffed his black Converse tennis shoes and scampered inside. I could smell coffee as we followed him to the kitchen, refrigerator door open, Ida Rose stooped, pouring a few licks of cream into a saucer. Argus waited politely till she did, we all stood watching him lap it clean, and satisfied he sat back on his haunches and looked at us. I fought a near irresistible inclination to wrap my arms around her slender frame and hold her close to my heart. She greeted a warm "Hello Lamby Dear. I'm just delighted to see your beautiful face again. And your precious little Dog, so adorably urbane. I have always appreciated the pure uncalculating nature of animals". She turned to Corbett "So this must be your Corbett". I settled for touching her arm "Dr.Ida Rose Barber, may I present Corbett Hawkins. His friends call him Hawk, but I call him Corbett". His relaxed stance signaled relief at finding her made of blood and bone, making coffee, her white hair in need of me, he put out his hand "I'm very glad to meet you Dr.Barber. Shoshy talks about you all the time. Reads me the audits. I'm reading your book right now. Re-reading it actually". She took his hand, looked into his face and smiled that blazing fire "Corbett, please call me Ida Rose. Your splendid blue eyes remind me of my late husband Dr.Barber. Now come into the dining room Children and we'll have coffee". Tom and Corbett eyed each other as we sat around one end of the big mahogany table looking-out to Lake Union at the coming black rain clouds, talking of California sunshine and Catholicism, Argus sitting on my feet. When our cups were empty for the second time, she asked Corbett "Would you mind going to the QFC for me. If I don't start the Carbonnades soon, there will be no dinner". He stood "Shoshy, you know where it is". Ida Rose patted Tom's hand "Go with him Tom, Shoshannah has generously offered to fix my hair. I'll give you a list and some money". Tom's apparently affable acceptance of Corbett had a cooler edge, the result I guessed of a small crush on me. Ida Rose wisely sent them together, and giving me a knowing wink disappeared upstairs to shampoo her hair.

I cleared the table and washed the cups in selfish anticipation, doing her hair justified me touching her, I somehow needed to touch her, and give back something I could do, something she wanted, needed. Combing, rolling her damp silver mane brought a kind of equipoise, and spawned intimate uninterrupted conversation. She asked after Leda. I summarized her Mom, and the mess with Gretchen and Keely. She recommended "Go see your friends now that some time has passed. Good old time always has its affect. Sometimes not so healing as one might hope, still it changes people and situations. Leaving your friends hurting, no matter who committed the crime, will haunt your mind and hold you hostage. Revisiting the scene after time has had its hand at conversion, looking with fresh eyes you can find where there is the possibility of another outcome. And sometimes not". Ida Rose was so cool, I'd done many heads and she was the one who never complained at the necessary pulling of hair and pushing of bobby pins "I will. I'll go see them when I get back. Ida Rose, Nick called over at my Folks' house this morning. He didn't speak, but I'm sure it was him. It freaks me out he knows where I am. And I don't know why, but I felt guilty, or maybe ashamed, and didn't tell Corbett". She was not surprised "You've worked hard to free your self from him Little One. However you're still his other half, and he's lost without you. I can understand your feeling of guilt, like leaving a frightened child behind in the dark. But you've done every thing you can short of losing your life, and he did not learn anything from you. He couldn't. It's your right, you obligation to save your own life, be free of him. And you need not fear, Corbett is more than enough man to shoo Nick away. Men respect each other that way. You two make such a beautiful couple. There's something about him, a Ray, likely Compassion or Empathy, quite a rare and valuable asset for any artist, an open door into people's emotions". I loved how she moved me passed Nick "You're right. He's got this vibe that radiates like sunshine, it comforts people". She nodded "Yes, I felt it right away. He's probably a sensitive, able to feel others feelings, use his music as a vehicle to heal them". I told her about the hives. She nodded again "Yes yes, hives are quite common in true artists". Suddenly I remembered what was coming "Ida Rose, what if Corbett thinks auditing is evil. Thinks you're evil. I wasn't sure my first time here. It took me a whole year to come back". She smiled "I know. My message isn't for everyone. It may shake his Christian sensibilities at first, but he has such an intelligent face, I'm sure he'll be fine. And you Little One, you look so beautifully healthy". She was right "I am. Since Corbett, I feel strong and solid. I'm growing-up. This might sound funny, but I realized I have to grow-up to stay young. That's what makes someone become ridiculous, trying to stay young like my Granny does. She's such a painful example for me, acting like she's 16, wearing her skirts way too short, giving up her ego to men like it's still necessary. And I don't understand, cause Gramp left her enough. Maybe she thinks it's feminine. I mean she's not the only one, it's the norm really, but it's like she doesn't know things have changed, and I want to tell her, and I know she'll just think I'm putting her down". Ida Rose was nodding "Don't be too hard on her Little One. Most women of my generation had to subjugate their lives to survive. And for women all over the world things have not changed. I think all you can do is show her by example. Speaking of your family, I had the pleasure of meeting your Father last month. Tom took me to the market. You tell him for me, he sells the best chicken I have ever tasted. And what a lovely man, you're fortunate to have him". "I know. He said when you walked through the market, people parted like the Red Sea". She laughed quietly "He's very perceptive". I was smiling "Yes, he is. You know, the more I see other people's Folks, Corbett's, Leda's Mom, and their treacherous games, they don't seem to have any love in them, only meanness and calculation. And they look so good and white and clean on the outside, and they utterly despise me". Ida Rose turned her head to look in my eyes "It sounds like Corbett's parents aren't human. Probably small time Lords of Form. Real humans have love and compassion in their hearts for their children". I had been waiting for the time to ask "What's a Lord of Form". She seemed pleased I asked "They're a category of celestial, near gods who take human form. There are Lords of Mind too, some lawyers and philosophers for example, and Lords of Flame like the Arch Angels and their helpers, and now the new cold ray Lords of Humanity, born of the earth experience, who will bring up the Baby. Lords of Form understand the basic structure of the world. If they turn bad, and so far every one I've ever met has, they use their primordial understanding, and very often their hot rays of negative power, negative truth and negative wisdom, to manipulate for personal gain and pleasure, without conscience, without regard for who they exploit or hurt. It sounds like Corbett's parents employ the form of the Catholic Church to control their children for their own aggrandizement. Bigger Lords of Form run the world's banking systems, stock markets and large institutions. They shape the economies of the world, families like the Kennedys, Rothschilds, Carnegies, Rockefellers". I didn't want to interrupt and could not stop my self "Wow, it run in families". Ida Rose chuckled "That's very bright of you. Yes. John D.Rockefeller senior understood reincarnation quite well, how a soul comes back in different permutations of the same family over and over. He arranges his fortune so he can be born into it again and again". I was frustrated "But that's not fair. Reincarnation needs to be changed. And why would Corbett or anyone come to such mean parents if we can choose". Ida Rose pondered "With his talent, it's likely he's been seduced by the Lords of Form and their benefits many times before, but this time he came in on the wrong side of those benefits to have a good look at the cruelty, so he would never fall for or be used by them again. You can not build positive essence as a negative Lord of Form. That old system is being replaced because of Jesus' graduation, by you cold ray youngsters becoming conscious. Your moral rectitude, your apotheosis is the foundation and immortality of the New Reign. Corbett has plainly learned his lesson, and is building essence in a positive way despite and because of his Parents' treacherous machinations". We were on the same wave-length, I told of his Folks perfect eyesight, while the children were all legally blind. How I thought it was symbolic of an effort to blind them to the difference between real Catholicism and their own agenda of control by fear and shame in the name of. She was incredulous "My God they're all legally blind. Yes, it must be deliberate. It's not unusual for Lords of Form to hide behind the Church. And I'm not surprised at their feelings for you Little One. Being Jewish is enough contrast to help him question his parents motives, see though that pseudo-Catholic sham. Their animus for you is a blessing. If you were Catholic, if you had his parents' approval, he may have just gone along with their insidious indoctrination, supposing it was the only way to God". I frowned "But Ida Rose, he goes to church anyway". She touched my arm "Don't let that bother you. I don't think it has much to do with Catholicism. He's plainly a spiritual man, and the Catholic rituals are a comfortable and deeply moving way for him to access that spirituality". I wanted this to be true.

Combing-out Ida Rose's hair, Corbett and Tom returned fast Friends. They took Argus for a walk. And we went to the kitchen. Me crisping bacon in a cast iron fry pan, flouring the cubed sirloin steak, browning it in the fat. While Ida Rose sliced garlic and onions, sautéd, and made a brew of dark beer, brown sugar, red wine vinegar, nutmeg, thyme, dill, parsley, 2 bay leaves, tomato paste, Dijon mustard, salt and fresh cracked black pepper, scrubbed the Idaho potatoes for baking, sliced a fruit platter and placed it in the frig to chill. When the cubes were browned to her liking, she drained the pan of excess fat, returned them, and the bacon and onions to the pan, poured in the brew, brought it to boil, lowered the heat and covered tightly. Carbonnades safely simmering, she took Corbett on the tour, the paintings, the pharaoh's brother's burial plate, Taj Mahal mosaics, Louis XV furniture, Tiffany glass, Napoleon's black lacquer cabinets, and the Steinway Grand. Corbett smiled, seating himself on the bench, at home the moment his big hands touched the keys. I never heard him compose so freely, weaving a seamless ribbon ride that took us along, and gently landed on falling Autumn Leaves. Ida Rose applauded in delight "Absolutely divine. Thank you. You are the best ever to play my piano. And so intuitive, Autumn Leaves is my favorite song. Now please excuse me while I check the Carbonnades and put potatoes in the oven".

Returning, Ida Rose inquired of Tom "May we begin the audit". Already seated on Roosevelt's green brocade couch he grinned shyly "Sure Big Mo. I'm ready". Slipping off shoes, revealing new-white sox, he put a pillow behind his head and laid down, arms soft at his sides. Ida Rose's eyes glittered "Please make yourselves comfortable children". She sat in the winged chair next to the couch, put on her glasses, and took a waiting yellow legal pad and pencil from the lacquered cabinet. Threading fingers through Corbett's, I pulled him to the satin striped divan, sitting close, Argus all-ears at our feet, the hairs on my arms raising testimony as the audit began.

Ida Rose: *"Please take Tom into whatever valence, stream of consciousness, point on the time track necessary for what you may wish to say to us. When I count from five to one you'll be there. 5-4-3-2-1."*

Tom's eyes closed, he spoke in his own voice though not his words: *"There's a torrent of impressions, a welter of ideas. Just single sentence statements, an outline more or less, to refer to later on, or follow."*

"It involves how few, how very very few people wanted justice. The masses cry for justice, plead for justice, but silently seek to avoid justice. The masses seek magic, the masses seek profit without labor."

"Such a huge topic. What it leads up to is: Because the masses seek for ways to avoid the equation - An honest day's work for an honest day's pay, and

substitute - A day's pay for as little effort as possible, they prostitute their own intelligence: avoid what they recognize to be their responsibility, permit self destruction for the quick fix, the magic vitamin. They would be gods without the effort of becoming gods. They seek for more than they deserve. They ignore the prompting of the "still small voice" which cries for truth and justice and seek to quiet this voice by smothering it with illusion, with lies, with false gain."

"So universal is the desire to become great without effort, to become great by any means whatsoever, that the world of the masses was a prime breeding ground for the persuasions of the near gods who would impress their own influence upon creation. (Dope peddlers, reprehensible though they may be, can only sell their wares to another who seeks to avoid effort, responsibility, truth and justice). The earth, like a giant Petri dish, became the prime breeding ground for the errant gods of the cosmos wherein to seed their poisonous promisings on the masses."

"So the errant gods prospered as they peddled their delusions amongst the populace. And the populace, becoming more and more confused, disoriented and lost, grasp more and more desperately for anything that promised them godhood."

"The common man, from within the deep recesses of his being, kept hearing small whisperings of his true self — "the small voice" — and would say to his peddler of the magic vitamin, "I am tormented. Give me surcease. Give me comfort". And the universal small voice answered, "I can give you truth, I can give you justice. I can give you straightness. I can give you that manhood which you have honestly accrued". But the errant gods would shout in their loud, persuasive voice, "Here's more magic, more vitamins, stronger and stronger doses of magic vitamin. I give you nationalism: I give you religion: I give you cultism. Take these and quiet those inner urgings that torment you"."

"Hallucinations, psychedelics, ceremony, delirium, violence, explosion, near death, weakened, disoriented, lost, the man of the masses stirs himself, sits up and looks about at the carnage which surrounds him, bewildered, and now becoming aware of an anger, of his outrage that this world of fantasy has collapsed."

"Only one small thing rings the bell of familiarity, one small thing links him to eternity — that "still small voice" which whispers, "I can give you truth. I can

give you justice". Two plus two equals four, no matter how glib the oratory or propaganda to the contrary."

"What happened to the errant gods, those peddlers of dope, abusers of humanity? Understand free will. Prayers are answered. Whatsoever a man desireth, it shall come to pass. Whatsoever a man desireth hath its price. This price is justice. If he seeks to attain his godhood falsely, with falseness shall he be rewarded. Whatsoever a man desireth to do, he can do, but justice demands responsibility."

"The right hand of free will is responsibility. When one stalwart voice cries continually for justice and truth, his prayers shall be answered. No god, no matter how apparently powerful, no matter how skillfully woven his web of entrapment, can defend himself forever from this single small voice that cries for truth and justice and is willing to accept them. His prayer shall be answered. The house of cards so skillfully and elaborately constructed by the errant god who would impose his system upon the masses will crumble. Would you question that one consistent voice crying for justice can obliterate a skillfully woven web of illusion? Know ye that a single electron unaccounted for or a single packet of energy changed to absolute nothing is sufficient to bring about the unraveling of the entire physical universe."

"Man's direct link to eternity and to God has always been with him, and has always been the same — namely truth. No matter how it is attacked, no matter how many gods would proclaim otherwise, truth persists forever without change, without modification. Illusion can be for the instant: hallucination can be momentarily real, but only truth can persist."

"There is a golden coin, on one side is minted "truth", on the other side "justice". But truth and justice are the mechanical aspects of creation. Truth and justice are the skeleton of the cosmos. Love, beauty, wisdom give it purpose and justification. Justice might be linked to a giant computer in the house of the cosmos, spitting out endless irrevocable truths, but only an individual whose flesh and bone are love can react to these immutable truths with ecstasy or outrage."

"It is said that the environment changes — that justice will prevail. Justice has already prevailed. Those gossamer webs spun by errant gods encasing the structure of justice are now being dissolved because of the persistent prayer of a handful of persons who prayed that it would be done."

"The striking change in your environment will be the visibility and accessibility and the eternal reality of justice. Would you question the validity of the strange theses of the near gods proclaiming themselves as gods and entrapping mankind with illusion and lies to support their posturings? Why question? The libraries are filled with books telling of the rise and fall of Hitler's Germany. A thousand times similar dramas have been played before the eyes of mankind and a thousand times man has chosen to ignore the truths revealed. So the visibility, accessibility and reality of justice will still only be apparent to those who desire it."

Tom fell silent. Ida Rose: *"Thank you, that was beautiful. I'll have to type it up for my students, they need this message. Master we have* Corbett Hawkins *here. What can you tell us of him?"*

Tom: "Corbett *comes from far away. He entered the scene through the brilliant star Arcturus. Like* Shoshannah, *his spirit is old, three days and nights of Brahma, while young in earth years and experience. And like* Shoshannah, *he came to witness the birth of Jesus. His rays are as sweet as ripe fruit. They attract and comfort."*

Tom silent again. Ida Rose asked: *"Is that all master."*

Tom: *"Yes, that's all we have."*

Ida Rose: *"Thank you master. Tom when I count from one to five you will be in present time. 1-2-3-4-5 present time."*

I was riveted to Tom's face. Slowly opening his eyes, looking to Ida Rose he asked quietly "Was it okay Big Mo". Writing in high-speed shorthand she glanced from the yellow legal pad "Yes dear it was just beautiful. Thank you". He slipped on his shoes and began the tying. I turned to Corbett. Witnessing an audit live before his eyes, he was still as stone, eyes on Gus. Ida Rose set pad and pencil on the cabinet and came to him, a tender smile on her face, right hand extended. He took it and stood. Slipping her arm through his she ushered him to the dining room "You must be hungry. I know I am". Tom, Gus and I following.

Seating Corbett at the head of the big mahogany table, Ida Rose asked Tom to pour the Bordeaux, and me to help dish the meal. I was amazed watching her grace-full old frame bend to a low cupboard for a serving platter, how her whole being was so youthful, transformed when caught-up in her work. And her unlikely hierophant Tom, who must have swallowed as many drugs as me, had been a drummer for a rock band, and audited the Arch Angel Gabriel. And my hopefully temporarily overwhelmed Music Man with rays as sweet as ripe fruit, someone one big enough I could run full-speed my whole life and never come to the end. And then me, Golden Ghetto émigré, delinquent Seafair Queen contestant, dormant radical revolutionary, seamstress, girl of little promise, wonder-struck by the improbable confluence of such seemingly disparate elements gathered round this Table, paralleling in many ways Hydra's War Table. The hearty stew suited the conversation. Ida Rose proudly shared news of Eddie, now two years into using the *Pink Elephant* to rehabilitate first-time non-violent teenage felons at Echo Glen, the non-recidivism rate had come in at 84-percent, unheard of anywhere else. General Semantics had proven itself, we toasted Eddie's success. Finishing his second glass of wine, Corbett finally spoke "Tom, do you know what's going on when you're auditing. I mean, are you still here". Tom nodded "Yeah man, I remember every word. I'm totally here, in an elevated alpha state. Ida Rose has the spiritual authority to ask me to go there and then protect me. I just try to stay out of the way. You know, resist editing. We all have nervous systems that want to interpret the information". Ida Rose added "Tom is the most scrupulous of all my auditors. I conduct them by tapping the unconscious consciously. That way the auditor isn't used as a mere conduit, but is an irreducible constituent of the process. They are there, first hand, not just channeling some errant entity with a megalomaniacal agenda, who's never taken human form, has no idea what it's like to live the consequences of flesh and blood, and who wants to play God. Some of the auditors will not admit they have agendas too, their own. That's why I have several. Hearing different sides of the story, mistakes can be realized, become conscious, time binding life's episodes". Corbett looked as if he was facing a hurricane, reached for the Bordeaux and filled his glass. Ida Rose asked Tom to please open another bottle, and I ate around the meat, feeding on the comfortable banter of their inextricably linked lives working for the emancipation of the human spirit. Their lineage was unflagging, uninterrupted from before history, through Palestine, Charlemagne, the first Elizabeth and Sir Francis Drake, George Washington and John Paul Jones, into this life and her discovery of auditing, the ultimate weapon, enabling her to expose the truth, to track the brigands to their lairs, disclosing their tyrannies often from their very own mouths. Ida Rose had a particular distaste for the White Brotherhood and Christ Conscious, calling them celestial Elks Clubs, feeding on human misery by handing out Rays in combinations that could not possibly thrive. She shined her smile on me "You know how difficult it is to embody Charity in a positive manner, with Faith and Hope as companions, almost certainly dooming sweet Charity to give without reflection. By its virtue you would naturally assume Charity could be freely given without harmful repercussions. You have begun to understand that's not true, and are doing a splendid job saving that ray. If not for your efforts to become conscious and bring perception and wisdom to bear, enabling Charity to be used with discrimination, it might have turned cynical and sour and been lost to the Cosmos forever. That White Brotherhood and Christ Conscious, playboys all of them, they delight in human suffering because they don't have feelings, only humans have feelings. They'll give out Faith and Hope with Charity when it should be Perception and maybe Ingenuity, just to watch you fail. It's plain to me suffering is what they want, they haven't learned a thing and must finally be deleted". She took the napkin for her lap "Excuse me Darlings while I fetch dessert". Smiling wide Tom stacked the silverware and dishes "She's an ordained minister in Oregon too. Can you imagine one of her sermons". He followed her into the kitchen. Corbett had been polite and withdrawn though dinner and I knew it would not just wish away, putting my hand gently on his arm, I sought to bridge the distance "You okay Babe". Eyes stubbornly fixed out the picture window, chin tense and wrinkled, he took a labored breath, answering on the exhale "I have an awful headache Shoshy". Ida Rose brought the fruit platter. Tom frosted mugs and two quart bottles of ice cold Miller beer, which he poured, and then launched a string of bawdy jokes gathered from customers of the gas station he managed. Corbett laughed along with us, and when his glass was empty, a pinch took his face, demanding notice, that deep mute Hawkin's Family undertow, don't you dare voice your feelings, they're all bad, wrong, sinful, you shouldn't even have feelings, you don't deserve them, and this woman, you are doomed to hell. I was so sorry for him, there was no need for defensive here, and his stance seemed automatic, like he wanted to put down his fists, and the very second he caught himself loosen they went up again, every thing an attack of some kind, and the wine, the beer did not help for long. As one-of-two, his posture and attendant inertia pushed the response-ability on me to act "I guess it's time to go home". Ida Rose smiled knowingly "Yes Little One. It is". Everyone stood at once. Corbett scooped Argus in his arms, courteously, even sincerely thanking Tom and Ida Rose as they walked us to the door. Not knowing when I would see her again, I could not help lightly kissing her rubicund cheek. She let me, smiling empyrean fire from behind those blue/gold eyes "Come again soon Lamby. I'm always delighted to see your beautiful face". She called after Corbett "You come too Corbett, when you're ready".

Facing the side window, Gus snug in his lap, Corbett began to lather "I couldn't stand listening to her, not one more word. She talks so fast, like she's trying to put something over on you. And who's this all powerful master anyway, and near gods. I like Tom well enough, but come on, the Arch Angel Gabriel is working at a gas station". I understood how big the story was, how it felt like standing in mid-air, every thing ever taught of God not quite true anymore, and some inside-part of you knowing this is truth with immediate conviction, solid enough to hold you from falling. And then there was Ida Rose, who just might be the Devil incarnate, she was impressive enough. I wanted to say yes I understand, I felt all these things too, but this was not about me.

Corbett hurried though the family room, good-nighting Mom and Dad to his bedroom. I wanted to do the same, but Mom's antenna was up "Is Corbett all right". Avoiding her eyes I labored a lying smile "Yes Mom, he's still a little queasy from the hives and probably embarrassed". She drilled me with her x-ray vision and mercifully let go. Dad did not "So how's your friend Ida Rose". I didn't have the energy, and really could not explain "Oh she's fine. I told her about you seeing the crowd part at the market. She got a real kick out of it, said you must be quite a perceptive man". Dad smiled and patted the couch "Come sit a while Shoshy".

Assuming the pat meant him Gus leapt, pushing his nose under Dad's obliging hand for pets, climbing into his lap. My Folks wanted to talk to me alone. And I complied into the couch "Daddy, I know you like Corbett, I can tell by the way your treat him, and I promise he's exactly what he seems. I love him like I never loved anyone before. You know, like you an Mom". Turning my face to her "But don't start making plans on us cause I'm not getting married". Dad's eyes narrowed "Oh, you're not going to marry. Then it's nothing like your Mother and I. So tell me, what happens when you have children. They're the innocent ones in this. Is it fair for them to pay the price of being illegitimate just because you feel like breaking the rules. And what about religion. Jewish law makes them Jews at birth. Will Corbett want to bring them up Catholic". I squirmed. So here it was, the other presupposed and mostly unspoken assumption for their Golden Daughter, producing Jewish Grand-Children for them. I had never been one of those precocious little girls who by 6th grade had her children already named, who dreamily went on about her wedding day, the kind of flowers in her bouquet and had picked out the color of her bridesmaids gowns, and yet, inherent in Dad's mini-inquisition I also heard a sincere challenge to stand-up to him for what I believe-in with my head high and feet planted squarely on the ground of my conviction. No matter how right he thought he was, he would not want me to agree unless I truly did. And then there was Mom, silently yearning for confirmation of her life through mine. She wanted me to see her, to mirror, validate how she had done it right by doing the same, saying by doing that she was a good mother. My choice to be me not her had become a shadow-condemnation. My liberation only seemed to make the tradition binding her tighter. Instead of taking more freedom for her self, she tried not to resent mine, compete with, subtly undermine. And at her worst, there was no possible discussion without her angry denial. Daring to question her life simply by living my own was too pain-full, too much an affront, and indictment, too much stirring seemingly impossible desires. I knew her anger was misplace, a world that only valued men the real problem, that fostered Girls to turn their anger and fear on themselves, and there was no satisfying her unless I lowered my head and submitted to the only power she really had, Mother, and that meant Grand-Children. I wanted to go to bed, but faced Dad "How can you say any child's illegitimate. A kid of mine would have my name, a woman's name, your name. Isn't Leibofsky just as legitimate as Hawkins". Dad beamed at my backbone "You're right, there's no such thing as an illegitimate child. Unfortunately, society doesn't agree with you, and will penalize your children for your sins whether you think they're wrong or not". Mom edged in "I want to know how Corbett feels about children". I understood her implication that it wasn't only my choice, that maybe she never thought about not having kids "We haven't talked about it Mom. We've only been together four-months. And it doesn't matter, I'm the one who has them, and I don't want any. If he does, he's with the wrong Girl. Anyway you don't have to worry, your Sons 'll give you Gran-Kids". Dad lit his pipe "From the looks of it they won't be Jewish". He was right, no Jewish mother, no Jewish children, my Brother's Girls were Shiksas. I contended "Daddy, I know you. No matter how you get Gran-Kids, you'll love 'em. That's who you are. I break the rules and you still love me". Dad puffed his pipe, eyes solemn "This world's hard enough on children. Why knowingly make it harder on them". This was a true mirror moment, by their earnest reactions I could see how abiding Corbett's and my romance appeared. They'd never spoken directly to me about having children, I had not fully understood how they had their Little Girl's future all planned, and how devastated their expectations must be, how Humpty Dumpty would never be put-back-together-again, it was a pain-full loss for them, an impasse unresolvable, unavoidable, I said tenderly "Do you guys know how much I love you. My friends, even Corbett wishes for other parents. I never have once. Can't you just be happy for me. Give me some slack. I'm inlove with a really wonderful guy, and he loves me back". Mom said softly "I do like him Shoshy". Dad nodded agreement. I saw the opening and stood "I'm going to bed now". Gus jumped from the couch and followed me.

Thoughts too loud to sleep, I stood before the bedroom door mirror considering my 23 year-old naked body, pushing out my stomach, contemplating pregnant. I knew we were supposed to be driven by instinct to propagate and perpetuate the species, especially Jews since the latest Holocaust, but why did I have to personally help. There was adventure in my heart, and from the looks of it, kids, even if you are a completely self-absorbed mother, change everything. I didn't care how loud the praises of motherhood were sung, or what a complete woman having a baby would make me. And I did not buy the Aristotelian drivel that a woman's body was made to produce children and therefore should. As far as I was concerned, I was made for other things too. And how come our Mothers kept so quiet about the morning sickness, their back and feet killing them, bodies bulging to burst, growing ripe melons on their chest, complete strangers taking the liberty of putting hands on their belly, and the splitting and tearing of birth, and stretch marks, and leaking milk, and soar nipples, were they afraid to confess, even to themselves, I mean how dare any one say motherhood has a downside. I'd been there for two births and thought it was the bravest thing a human being could do. I was not that brave. And then there was Cyrene, Gretchen, Keely, even Katey parading though my mind, not a Dad in sight. I had zero desire to reproduce my self or be any ones Mother, and I happily was the first generation to have a legal and safe choice. Sliding open my closet door, I tried on a few dresses, each harboring lonely memories. I had been alone ever since I could remember, learned to turn lonely into a friend, and even preferred it to losing my self. Till Corbett no one knew me, knew my true heart and let me be. I laid my near-empty suitcase on the bed and neatly packed scarves, panties, slips, sox, a pink wool cable-knit cardigan Mom made me, the rest belonged here in this room with that lonely girl. Then I stole in on Corbett, to promise he was not alone either. He seemed deep in sleep, I knew better, for he snored softly when really. Even Gus's nails on the hardwood floor did not rouse him. Whispering in his ear "I love you Babe". I left him to think.

Mom and Dad up for work, I joined them for coffee, telling tomorrow morning we would be going. They exchanged those knowing glances, though I knew they did not know. Dad was so resilient, offering to take us out to eat tonight. I proposed let me cook them dinner, something I had never done. He smiled, nodding approval. Mom's eyes involuntarily squinted "What a lovely idea". I could not tell was she grimacing at the thought of me leaving, or bothered by some one messing in her kitchen. They were in the car, backing-down the driveway when the phone rang. I picked-up "Good morning Chicken Valley, can I help you". Someone breathing through their nose hung-up. No more freaked, now I was mad, Nick could get to me here at will, maybe moving North was not a good idea. But then he would be in control of my life, and Corbett's. I knew thought knows no distance, and it travels both ways, that despite our connate link, I must live my life as I saw fit or he won. I had to let-go right here, refuse him any more head-time, go where I want, when I want, maybe find his number and hang-up call, yeah right, then he would have me exactly where he wanted, thinking of him, our minds conjoined, retaliation keeping me in the game, his game his way his power. I had Corbett on my side, and with Folks gone he showed himself, simply being there dispelleing the intrigue, his presence in my life potent protection. Going straight for the coffee pot, he owned-up "I was awake last night when you came in. I just couldn't talk". His eyes fastened on mine "Did we eat Carbonnades with the Devil". I wanted to laugh and cry "That's exactly what I thought the first time I met her. I tried to warn you". He went on as if speaking to himself "Everything I've ever been taught about God is crashing in on me. I'm not sure what". He set his cup on the counter and walked toward the front door "I'm going to walk down the road a while. Maybe if I go far enough I can figure this out". Breaking to tears I followed "Corbett. Hey, come on Babe. Can't we talk about this". No response. Putting my hands on his back "I told my Folks we're leaving tomorrow. We could go now if you want. Corbett, come on, talk to me". He turned, confusion, pain owning his face "I don't know anything anymore. I don't know what to think". With his finger tip he gently lifted a tear from my cheek and streaked it down his own "Don't worry Sweetheart, this isn't about you and me, it's about me and God". He went out the door. I caught Gus in my arms so he couldn't follow and stood in the driveway, watching Corbett round the corner, an empty stone in my gut, tears running my face, sweet little Gus licking them, I buried my face in soft fur and suddenly knew what to do. Ida Rose answered on the first ring "Hello". I blurted "Ida Rose, this is Sho. I'm sorry ta bother you so early, but Corbett jus' walked off down the street totally confused and I didn't know what to do but call you". Her voice composed "You're exactly right to call Lamby. I needed a way to contact you. They told me this morning I must come see you right away. I've already called Tom to pick me up.

We should be there within the hour. When he arrives I'll have him call for directions". My tight throat petitioned "But what if Corbett doesn't come back. He looked so freaked out, like his brain was scrambled". She did not try to unruffle me "Yes, in a way his brain has been scrambled. I've often seen this after someone witnesses their first audit. Corbett's world has been temporarily turned on its head and he's trying to right it. It's never easy on a human nervous system to lose some of its long held beliefs. Corbett has a fine mind and brave spirit like yours. Remember when you first came to see me. Oh, Tom's here. Hello Dear, here, talk to Shoshannah". Tom's warm baritone filled my head like a lullaby. I gave him directions, and with Gus still in my arms and a half-pack of Marlboros, made camp on the porch.

Tom's 1966 VW Bug appeared to the right of my vision-field as Corbett showed on the left. I let Gus go meet him at the bottom of the drive-way. Tom sprang from the car, tall as Corbett, maybe 20 pounds more brawn, and bear-hugged him off the ground "Take that my friend". Corbett laughed, mouth wide-opened "I wondered if I could make sense out of this whole thing and here you are". Wagging madly, Gus stood by the car door waiting for Ida Rose to emerge, trailed her into the family room, laying at her black Chanel ballerina flats, whiskers kissing the right shoe, incase of unavoidable dozing, he would know when she moved. I made a fire and coffee, sliced Red Delicious apples, New York sharp cheddar and figs, and listened. Corbett asking the things burning him, foundation questions, ones I had to ask, who was the master, these near gods, and how did she get Tom to give her this information. Soon running in that deep groove, purring a give-and-take that distinguishes core times, when Friends and words forge enduring, talk of General Semantics, Jesus, Catholicism, Parents, each as far as the day would yield. By 2PM, Ida Rose had to go home, to get ready, it was Eddie's birthday, he was taking her to Canlis for dinner.

We stood on the porch waving, listening for the roar of Tom's aging muffler become lost to our ears. I sighed "I'll miss her". Corbett wrapped me in his arms and kissed the top of my head "Me too. She's another good reason to move North". Exhausted he curled on the couch for a nap. Gus tucked in with him. And I drove to the grocery store, never having cooked in Mom's kitchen but for salad dressing and the very occasional chocolate cake. According to her, Dad's diabetes made our meals a matter of life and death, and she was his vigilant collaborator, sworn to keep a low-sugar kitchen. And I was not about to disrespect the sacred grove, deciding on modest fare, a garbonzo and black bean salad with chopped Romaine lettuce, red bell peppers, red onion, cherry tomatoes, steamed green beans and broccoli, with seasoned bread crumbs, toasted sesame seeds, vinegar and oil dressing, whole wheat garlic toast, and a fruit platter like Ida Rose without the honey. I even boned and cooked a chicken breast for Gus, there were plenty in the freezer. Mom was tired from work, and grateful, declaring herself queen-for-a-day. Everything was delicious, we ate it all. Corbett began the dishes. Dad traded work clothes for pajamas and slippers, switched on the Flip Wilson Show and took his place on the couch, that little grin on his face that glows inner satisfaction. After washing her face and changing, Mom cozied in close to him. Dad stoking his pipe. Gus absolutely adored him, seeming even to relish the distinct aroma of his tobacco blend, and stealthily crept onto his lap for pets. The kitchen carefully returned to its order, we laughed at Flip, and talked through All in the Family and Marcus Welby, till Mom could not keep her eye lids up. Not one word of marriage and children.

Morning brought a tear-full farewell, we left before they did. I did not sweeten good-bye by revealing our maybe move North, something could change, they would be unnecessarily disappointed. Even though, insinuation hung in the air, Corbett taking their Little Girl so far away from home, he shook Dad's hand, intuitively conciliating "I'd like to invite you to come visit Santa Cruz. You're welcome to stay with us". I could not help myself "We'll even let you sleep together". Everyone laughed. Dad hugged me tight and slipped a neatly-folded hundred dollar bill into my hand.

Chapter Twenty Seven

THE REGULARS

Driving away from my childhood home, on Island Crest Way there was Nick heading toward us in a white Lincoln Continental, the kind with suicide doors, his eyes seemed too close together. I looked away refusing the paranoia, choosing to believe Penny must be at her Folks place across the street, that he was going to see her, not stalking me. Corbett commented on the cool '66 Lincoln. I did not mention who. The weather Kodachrome-clear for late November, graceful maples standing on the shoulders of the road, holding on to their yellow and red fire, we were in no hurry, the neatly-folded hundred instigating a stay somewhere along the way, we took every other rest-stop for Gus, brunched at the Portland Dennys, miles disappearing into conversation. Meeting Ida Rose, having the time to ask questions, just talk too her, Corbett was experiencing some release from the dogma he'd been bottle-fed, freedom to consider forbidden ideas, those Mom and Dad warned would shake his faith and damn him to purgatory, from doctrine that kept him prisoner to a warped version of Catholic for their own selfish needs. Smiling, eyes gleaming, he decided to start reading the unholyest of unholies according to Mom, the Gnostics and Rosicrucians. The thing was, in their way they were right holding him mental-hostage, for looking around does shake a person's faith. I loved seeing his hungry black dog, kindred to mine, and this seemed time to ask about the regular church going, what did he find there he could not as well somewhere else. He had no simple answer, church was something always done, a habit, no big deal, he liked the feeling of fellowship, the pageantry, the way stained-glass windows made him imagine being a hero, and he invited me to come along anytime. It was a big deal, he just didn't see it, but the invitation was such a straight-forward remedy to a closed door, such a complete surprise, I said yes I would love to, thinking how right Ida Rose had been about this lovely man. Three more hours flew as one, taking the Roseburg Oregon exit, leading almost directly into a Red Lion Motel parking lot, we went in to inquire would they take us with a Hound. Manager had to think on it, I fetched Argus, one look, one more at an empty parking lot, we had the key for an extra-ten, refundable if no doggie-damage. Leashing him, Gus was a stubborn-mule, never seemed to remember this never worked, for he was almost 10 pounds, so Corbett scooped him up, and we ran across the street to the Chinese/American restaurant. I ordered vegetable Egg Foo Yung to go. Asking would I mind so much, Corbett wanted Porterhouse rare, baked potato, butter, sour cream and chives, the enormous steak plenty for Gus too. Who sat on the bed with us, shiny wet nose in over-drive, every muscle at attention, holding on to his manners as we spread the feast. One bite for Corbett, one for Gus, raising ice-cold bottles of Coke from the motel vending machine to my Dad, thank you for the luxury, it was 8PM, having eaten everything, content alone together, we slept.

An old mansion on the cliffs of New Brighton Beach was supposed to be ours for a week, yet I could hear Cyrene and Stanley playing badminton on the lawn. Voracious readers, Corbett and I came here for the library, and could hardly wait to open the mostly sixteenth and seventeenth century authors, Hermes Trismegistus, Maria Prophetissa, Albertus Magnus, Gehard Dorn, Paracelsus, Ostanes, Yogi Vemana, and the titles, Tabula Smaragdina, Agathodaimon, the Book of Enoch. One lay waiting on the kitchen table, Asmodeus and Ahriman, we set our bags down and opened it, wafting a faint and foul odor. Published 1566, pigskin binding gilded in real gold, elegant penned script on right-hand pages, masterfully painted symbols and copper engravings on the left, we had never seen anything like this, and magically could read the ancient text. Accidentally tearing the corner of a brittle page, a far-off high scream entered my bone marrow, I bolted from the table, out the front door, screen slamming hard, no looking back, into the yard where Cyrene and Stanley were still playing badminton. It was one of those sky blue lazy California days and as I watched them, a furry white bat, more like a plump mouse with gothic velum wings fell from the sky, hitting ground at my feet, already dead. My heart thundering, I looked to Cyrene, Stanley for communion, only

660

to see they were using a live bat as a shuttle-cock. Abusing life with such callus disregard, for amusement, I screamed "Stop". They did not seem to hear, and I remember thinking as I ran, how could they, how can this be, I have to get away from here. Running, running, a sea of ivy snarling at my ankles, stumbling, falling, rolling down a steep hill into a ravine, thick in blackberries and ravenous bloated Zombies reeking the same foul odor as the book. I knew any contact would turn me in to one of them, staying in the brambles, quietly moving away, scrambling-up the far-side onto a barren butte, scorched as an August Texas day, my legs torn and bleeding from stickers, I collapsed on the rusty dust. Not seeing till her shadow crossed me, a Little Girl, my own face at ten-years-old, brown hair in a short bob, light-grey polished-cotton shirt-dress, full-skirt, no petticoats, narrow black patent-leather belt, matching Mary Janes. Her pale face leaning over mine blocked the sun, without moving her lips she asked "Can I help you". I saw a church steeple in the distance not there before, where she must be going all dressed-up, and pleaded "Go and pray for me". She smiled, her dark eyes too close together, and skipped-off to worship. Motionless on the soft ground, blood pooling around my legs, sun blistering my arms and face, the Little Girl was again looming over, I looked up. Her face gray as her dress, bloated, ravenous, she smiled hideous portend "I didn't pray for you. I let the demons in". Laughing wild, anticipating, she touched my forehead, and began skipping around, chanting, initiating. From just below the shoulders, my body began twitching and turning in a cork-screw, spinning my face to the dirt, arms jutting-out infront, palms down, elbows locked, my body twisting tighter, tighter till my feet stuck-out at the end heel-to-heel. Little Girl's chant echoing, signaling, I could see them streaming from the church, a column of black patent-leather ants, coming for the blood, to feed. Trying to cry-out, I could not make a sound, knowing one thing only, I must get to Corbett and destroy the book. It was only blood they wanted, I labored my bulk, a wingless May Fly, to the ravine, sliding on my belly into the brambles, dragging through, now of no interest to the Zombies, and up onto the lawn where Cyrene and Stanley were playing badminton. Like the Zombies, they did not notice me, though it was impossible not to see such a thing. I had only enough left to make it to the screen door, fell against it, my mind screaming "Corbett, tear up the book, you must tear up the book". He heard, carrying me in where it still lay open on the table, and ripped-out the torn page. One bat scream pierced the room. Tearing-out another, another, each followed by a scream, louder, closer, my body beginning to unwind, becoming almost human I sat next to him at the table, tearing-out pages too, screams stabbing the room, no longer just bats. And when all were rend from the binding, Corbett took my hand and we walked out into the sunshine, the silence enormous, every Zombie was dead, and Little Girl, the church ants, dead, the yard was littered with furry white bats, Stanley and Cyrene fallen dead on the badminton court. We were the only ones left alive in the whole world, and Corbett and I lived happily ever after.

I woke him to tell my dream. He was certain I had slain a whole category of corrupt creation, some infernal army. I flashed on Griffin and the Family of the Mystic Arts and wanted to get out of Oregon fast. We did, passing-up zuzus at the Wolf Creek Café, weather cooperating, we pulled into the driveway beneath full-blooming acacias, our welcome bungalow, just us and Gus, who was rambunctious from the ride, insisting on a beach walk. The afternoon delicious warm, we were easily persuaded, leaving suitcases and mail, descending the stairs to the beach, Sol setting in goldens and blues, walking the water's edge, we took the flight up to the Tampico. Climbing, it came clear, I had stubbornly held onto Ariadne's spider-silk thread leading me South, believing something more than endless sunshine was here for me. I would sorely miss the blonde movie star beaches and seemingly Liberal lifestyle, but I found what I came for, I could look into Corbett's eyes with all that lay behind mine and not have to blink, and he could look at me without reserve. We supped on the deck of the Tampico, Furheads were allowed, deliberating our move North. Corbett had never lived through a long dark Northwest winter, and he had never played in the snow.

Marion delivered her Baby, a dainty robust Girl. Corbett resumed the Colonial with proud papa Lorenzo, and Delroy, and Sunday nights at the Zyante with One Hand Clapping, and Monday afternoon practice at Jimmy Mesa's barn. I filed for unemployment mainly to piss-off Mr. Wearhouse, since I quit, I was sure I would not get it. The rules said an applicant must take any job in their field registered with the unemployment office. There was only one listed, the Wearhouse, he had not so easily replaced me, instantly satisfying smug fuck-you recompense. After talking with me, and him, the claims investigator concluded I had valid reason to quit, and did not have to take the job. She even took time to write him, confirming my claim had been approved. Knowing he knew, every Tuesday I would dress ready for work, turn-in a claim form, speak briefly with a case-worker, accept my check for $71.06, look-see jobs filed, always only the Wearhouse, gloating never got old, I was free of him, he was not free of my absence. And occasionally I would take Gus strolling though the Rio Del Mar Shopping Center, when he would let me leash him that long, and sashay by the shop making sure to be seen at my leisure.

Colleen, but more Marion was visibly shaken when I presented the baby quilts, especially since I was not invited to the showers. They had been gift-wrapped for a while, and when opened I was kind-of surprised how really beautiful they were, having some distance, getting a bit of an objective look, I did good work. And Maggie had a perfect baby Boy. And the Band made a unanimous decision to move North in late Spring or early Summer. Knowing we would be going made every beach walk precious, bittersweet, often with Andrew and Jennifer who still showed-up for dinners. Gus had been summarily dismissed by Jenn, too completely preoccupied with her savior to notice his ardent little bandit face and stolen glances. Still, he tried to entice, chasing every gull and shore-bird, running around her in circles, finding a dead bird, any thing, yip yip yip, hey, look what I found, want a smell, wana roll in it. He was simply a bother as she swayed her rhythmic elephant walk, eyes fixed on Andrew. Gus lived for the beach, sometimes going out on his business, if we were not vigilant, he would slip away and head down the stairs. Without a human, domesticated animals were illegal on Golden State beaches. We would race after him, but no amount of reason or reprimand could temper his determination, to take right-full autonomy as a living being on the planet, challenging our authority over him, sometimes daring us with those indomitable eyes to use force. We were not hitters, nor interested in breaking his shining spirit, for he was right, it was exactly that daring we loved most, and he should be able to walk on the beach. One morning I could not find him, anywhere. We searched, neighborhoods, ditches, the shopping center, Tampico, cliff trail, beach stairs, everywhere a wayward delinquent might be. And I slowly began to sob inconsolably, hiccupping, returning to same places over and again, calling, begging that impotent God for one small act of kindness, I was sure the sea had taken him, blame sawing me, if only, if only, if only I had been more vigilant, I might, I might have seen him sooner and could, could have saved him, going no where round and round, maybe God could actually be up there, do something, desperation needing some one to take the blame, some thing to believe in, round and round the life-sucking poison that had me all the way back to losing Grampa, had me afraid to love, afraid to extend my self, afraid to lose. I sat down in the sand waiting for his body to wash ashore. Corbett sat next to me and put a heavy arm around my shoulders. The Baton Lady approached, her timid breathy child-like voice "Dog catcher nabbed your little guy". So light we levitated the stairs, ran some stop signs to the pound, bail was 50 bucks, Corbett and I so happy we did not care. And Gus, cowed by jail, was weak-kneed, earnestly contrite. We had escaped what Leda and Andrew must bear.

Possessed by fertile creative passion, my hands worked the last pieces of Monique and Loretta's silks and lace, certain my stuff would not be so well-received in Washington, I would make a final grand collection and take it to the Yellowbird. And Erik began coming by, I think to get away from Mommy and Baby, Lorenzo too, and Joey, Andrew, Stoney, talking business, wishing, hoping, hyping, planning, dreaming, jamming in the afternoons, taking-up my creative space. Gus's was bothered too, he would bring his leash and take me and my journal to the beach.

THE REGULARS

IT'S ALREADY BEEN A LONG DAY
AM GLAD IT'S AWAY
NO MISTAKE - I LOVE WHERE I'M AT
SOME DAYS ARE JUST HARDER
PEOPLE MAKE 'EM THAT WAY

SO I COME TO THE BEACH
WITH MISTER DOG
AND FROM BEHIND DARK GLASSES

WATCH THE REGULARS
AS THEY WATCH ME

THE GRAY OLD LADY WITH HER GREYING DOG
SWEET FACES RECONCILED
CASHMERE SCARF KNOTTED BENEATH HER CHIN
FROWZY WOOL OVERCOAT
EVERY BUTTON DONE

AND DOG HAS HIS TOO
A TARTAN WOOL UPHOLSTRY REMNANT
SECURED WITH A BROWN LEATHER BELT
NO MATTER THE WEATHER - NO MATTER HOW WARM
HE WEARS HIS COAT PROUDLY
IT'S ONE OF A KIND

I IMAGINE HER KNURLED FINGERS DRESSING HIM
LOVING DESPITE THE PAIN
AS SHE SLOWLY WALKS BY
OLD FRIEND AT HER SIDE
NODDING MY WAY

AND SIMPLE SIBYL – THE BATON LADY
SUN-BLEACHED LONG THIN HAIR FLYING THE WIND
SHE HAS A GREAT FIGURE AT SEVENTY-THREE
AND WEARS A TWIRLER'S SHORT SKIRT OVER HER
SWIMSUIT
TASSELS DANCING THE NECKs OF HER SCUFFED
WHITE MAJORETTE BOOTS
SHE PRANCES THE WATER'S EDGE
TWIRLING FIRE-BATONS TO THE PRIVATE MOVIE IN
HER HEAD

AND THE SUN-BAKED OLD MAN HAS A FULL HEAD OF
SNOW
YELLOW LIZARD EYES
HE SITS ON THE BENCH BESIDE THE PUBLIC BATHROOM
VENERABLE – EXCLUSIVE - RECEIVING HIS SUBJECTS
THE REGULARS - IRREGULARS - INQUISITIVES

HE HAS A GOOD FIGURE AT SEVENTY-SOMETHING
SWEAT PANTS ROLLED UP TO HIS KNEES
LONG WHITE BASEBALL SOX RIMMED IN RED
TENNIS SHOES TWO SIZES TOO BIG

MONTHS PASS FOR HIM TO ACKNOWLEDGE ME
PAYING NO HEED TO SHORT-TIMERS - TOURISTS
AND ONCE SURE I WAS NOT
AND USED TO ME BEING SO YOUNG THIS TIME OF DAY
GIVES A NOD IN MY DIRECTION
GRANTING ME REGULAR STANDING

Our first Chanukah-Christmas would have been war if we were our Parents, Christmas Eve on the 3rd night of Chanukah, and as naturally as Spring follows Winter, we wove our symbols together, more out of habit and respect than any religious reason. Dad had given me the brass menorah he carried in his backpack while serving as a Survey and Instrument Man in the Army Field Artillery during WWII, it stood 2 1/2 inches high and used birthday candles and still held the power of that heroic time in his life. Corbett's was a perfectly carved wooden Christmas Tree his favorite Auntie Anne gave him, only tall as the menorah with candles. We set them side-by-side on the fireplace mantle, mixed the few cards we received, and opened presents as they arrived in the mail. Wanting to show me off to the rest of him Family, needing to challenge in-person the bad reputation his Folks slapped him with, Corbett asked would I go to the annual Family Christmas party at his Uncle's house in Lafayette. I did not want to be the only Jew at a Christ Party, but it was so plainly consequential to him, I waived my desire for alone together, and would become his inviolable familiar, his eager trophy. For my debut, I made a seriously form-fitting and still tasteful chestnut-brown panne stretch velvet gown, so Morticia Addams, ankle-length, flared hem, long tight sleeves. And I tie-dyed t-shirts for the Littles, and made Egyptian cotton sun-dresses for Keely, Gretchen and Leda if she was there. Holiday presents giving me cause to stop by the Fairmount Avenue house on the way to the party.

Gretchen opened the front door and threw her arms around me, both-of-us laughing and talking at the same time. Keely waiting a turn. And the past ebbed as Littles ripped open their packages, pulled t-shirts over dirty clothes, and finding five one-dollar bills inside each, disappeared down the street for milk-shakes, leaving me the somber sting of a sudden and maybe final farewell. Corbett and I were so unforeseen, gifts so unexpected, my Sistas were somewhat reluctant to open theirs. I waited for their surprise, genuine delight filled me, the dresses fit perfectly. And after modeling, not to be out-done Gretchen, smooth as if long planned, lifted the house palladium, her prized brass candelabrum from the window sill and presented it to us. This seemed a symbolic surrender, a sincere peace offering, and a malicious reminder of her forever interposing our life, these were the truths of the moment. Ever the partisan advocate, Keely disappeared into the bedroom, and then standing infront of me smiling, ordered "Gimme your hand". I did. She placed one of her few prized possessions, a very small crystal perfume bottle over-laid in silver leaves and flowers with orange coral centers, pressing it into my palm, closing fingers over. Awkward silence held us all, till Gretchen offered "Hey you guys, I'm cooking my very first turkey. Come see". We followed through the eucalyptus curtain into the kitchen, oooing and aaahing at the not yet brown 16-pound hen. I wanted to pass on Ida Rose's turkey and gravy tips and did not. Keely picked a half-full glass of spiked eggnog from the door-table, raising it in salute "Merry Christmas". Bending over to baste the bird, making sure Corbett had an eye-full of her red lace push-up bra and what it held, Gretchen Fetchin-Fine flashed a wicked grin at him "Hey Keel, where's our manners, pour Hawk a drink". Till now Corbett stayed-out-of the mix, his sung-out baritone croaking "Thanks". The thing I did not want was to cede any edge we might need at the Family party to alcohol, and here we were in Gretchen's web, one I walked into willingly, knowingly, and would have to play smart. I slipped my hand though Corbett's arm "Yeah Keel, pour me one too". She put two ice-cubes in a tumbler, nearly filled it with nog, barely splashed rum on top and handed it to me "Merry Christmas". I smiled big at Gretchen, passed the drink to Corbett and waited for another. It was such a canny move, she lifted hers respectfully to me "Here here". I nodded thinking, there could not be a better ending for us, we had such distinct takes on life and love, and in that often harsh-light I had seen my self more clearly, could weigh mine alongside hers, learning I should, could trust my choosings, that my journey was not so much her one dramatic disaster upon another roller-coaster, I did not want or need extremes to feel, I was not that numb, that we could never completely reconcile, and this ending had always been coming. Toasting the season, the MotherTruckers, Amaru, and Leda, who stopped over-night in mid-November on her way to Los Angeles with Mark. They somehow found each other at Satsop, Mark was going to try stand-up at the comedy clubs, and she went along for the ride. As usual Gretchen knew everything, about Babies born, the Band moving North, Argus going to jail, and bragged how she finally met her for-sure one-and-only-true-love on the Boardwalk, a handsome talented poet vacationing in Santa Cruz, who worked as a postman in San Diego, only until he got famous that is, who owned a house on Alabama Street by the zoo, and she and Ava were going to move in with him. Keely had plans too, the one she had always been truly inlove with, Justin was divorcing his Wife and wanted to explore a relationship, she would fly North in January to spend a week with him. And Ric was in LA with his Folks and Sundance, preparing a move to Capetown South Africa, where he would collect rare bugs and smuggle them into the U.S. for big money. When Delroy arrived, an easy way-out opened, Corbett and I had to get to the Family party at a decent hour, it was a long drive. Gretchen nor Keely minded. I kissed them lightly on those beautiful cheeks, inhaling their sweetness, and in my mind's eye opened my hands and let them go, dandelion seeds on the wind. Delroy I would see again, he did not escape my judgment, giving him a hug I whispered "Go home to your Wife and Kid on Christmas Eve". He winked at me and poured himself a drinkypoo.

Lemon trees in fruit and bloom, and a warm breeze coming from the East made Christmas seem staged on a Hollywood set. Corbett's Uncle's place was a sprawling mansion, the long circular driveway trimmed in six-foot candy-canes with red bows at the neck, and jolly plastic snowmen in black top-hats. Life-size Magi lead camels across the immaculate lawn to a life-size Nativity Crèche. Towering before the house, a perfectly proportioned Fraser Fir, flocked-white with a star glowing on top. And Rudolph and the rest were on the roof, Santa unloading presents by the chimney for nice children. This man in the red suit could *see you when you're sleeping* and *know when you're awake*, I had always been glad he was not interested in me, Santa was such a Peeper. The columned porch and big windows dripped in tiny white lights, and holly branches with those lovely red berries, huge pine cones, dried flower wreaths, maybe 200 candles, and a host of wooden elves ushered us through the front doors, and down three stairs to the sunken marble family room.

Thirty-seven heads turned from the sumptuously laid tables, dazzling ice sculptures and two bars, and yet the party was disconnected, like walking into a diner. Maggie and Baby Boy swaddled in my quilt hurried toward us, Coebett closed his fingers around her elbow as she whispered in his ear. Paul smiled in our direction care-full not to make eye contact, Angela too. And Corbett left me standing, alone, as he took the bench at the Steinway Grand, and began rolling-out Christmas tunes, full-filling his Family function. Having grown-up loved just for drawing breath, my heart ached watching him animate the place with his abundant juice, shining that Comfort Ray, the Ringmaster, making the room whirl in magic merry, glasses clinking, voices raised in song, he could do this for them and only him. If it wasn't for Uncle Henry, who looked remarkably like Fred Astaire, and was on the outs with the Family for drinking too much, bringing me a Dewars on-the-rocks and standing making small-talk, joking, chain-smoking, telling me who was who and what was what, I would have quit the battle for the car. Corbett played an endless hour, and one-by-one they all floated by him with good-doggie pats on the back. Returning to my side, rustling his tail-feathers, for a long moment I considered playing-out my agreed-on smiling part. His Family, his Mom and Dad really, felt entitled to, and never showed appreciation for their Children's accomplishments except with stingy jealous tight mouthed thank yous, and his Brother and Sister mostly had to compete with each other and him for that limited affection, and I was murderous mad at the Others so cold to me except for Henry, and was tired of holding my chin up, back straight and face pleasant. Christmas Eve would have been just another dull party without Corbett, every one getting drunk, no wonder there were two bars. I put my arm though Corbett's and whispered "Come on Babe, let's go".

He seemed surprised, did not resist, and I realized he had been completely absorbed in the Family drama, this was his role, one he had not yet questioned. Thanking Uncle Henry for his kindness, I steered Corbett toward the front doors. Halls and Arlene cut-us-off at the stairs, Arlene pandering to a hushed room, bubbling hollow how generous of us to make an appearance, God bless Corby for sharing his heavenly music, what a glamour girl (puss) I was in my skin tight dress, and oh yes merry Christmas and the happiest of New Years. Their flawless surface, their public faces so white and clean, casting us ill-mannered, disrespectful leaving so soon, the same malicious up-side-down blame game my Big Brother use to pull-off so skillfully on me, making victim look perpetrator. A piece of me warned now just-be-nice, but I was still murderous, and if they insisted on playing sweet daggers, I could do that too, for I no longer cared if Corbett's Parents ever liked me. Conjuring the old Golden Ghetto glamour that could make a person seem taller, beckoning Medusa, I merry Christmased and Happy New Yeared, glowing, instructing ever so tolerant, that we Jews are months into the New Year of 5732 incase she were interested, and oh yes happy third night of Chanukah. Corbett's eyes danced to life, following my lead he shook his Dad's hand a bit too vigorously, planted a loud kiss on Mom's cheek, and melodramatically wrapping his arm around my shoulders, pulled me tight to his side, waving a smiling good-bye we made our get-away.

Still, I burned indignant having been sacrificed on the Family alter, and once on the road cautioned "Why didn't you let me know you were gona just leave me standing there. You can't ever do that again. I hate those people for treating you like a trained monkey, an I think I might hate you too for acting like one. There's no way I'm going to ever spend one more minute trying to make your Folks like me, and neither should you. According to their rules we're doomed to hell anyway, right". Delighted, Corbett whole-hearted "Yes, right, you're absolutely 100% right. No more. I'm done trying to win their love. It never works anyway, never lasts because I have to do it all over every time, prove I'm not a Bad Boy. Well, I'm not. Thank you Sweetheart for coming with me, letting me show you off. When I found you, and you could see me, I understood, I knew my Folks would never see me. They're not capable of the kind of love I want from them. Maybe they're not capable of love at all. And now it's their turn to try and win mine, ours". Excited by this man's capacity, resentment vanished "Yeah, do what they do, face 'em with their own ugly puss, see how they like being accused. I do it, imagining I'm holding onto my Sister Medusa's hand, I needed her to be terrible enough. The weird thing is, people who take such a hard-line will often jus' jump on your side if you take theirs. They can't stand it. That's how you know they're full a shit, they don't even care what side they're on or what they believe in. They only know how to play win-lose, and they have to be opposite of you to be the winner. And knowing this, if you don' care about winning your point cause it doesn't matter anymore, and don' care about being right, then you're in control, you can pick what side they'll be on by taking the other, and then they're standing in your shoes, and you don't have to play anymore. I think it's a lose-lose that way which somehow to me is a win-win. Did anyone in your Family every say anything about your treatment growing-up". Corbett was far away "And get my Folks mad at them, you know, so holy and respected in the Church. No way, everyone acted like my Family was perfect". He smiled "Except my Auntie Anne. One day when I was eight, I think it was 4th of July, the whole Family was at our house for a barbeque, and Mom was on my case big time right infront of them, I was in big trouble for wearing out my shoes. Auntie Anne stepped into it, telling her to ease-off on me, that I was a Good Boy. It was a revelation, someone siding with me, someone who knew me since I was born, confirming my good heart. I knew from then on, and I didn't feel so crazy anymore, so completely alone and ashamed, so unlovable. It was the first time someone saw me, some one knew I wasn't bad, the only time until you. Auntie Anne died when I was twelve. I still miss her". I could not imagine being made to feel guilty for wearing-out my shoes "My Family has two shoe stores. Eight year olds wear out their shoes, period. Maybe your Mom thought you should walk on water". Corbett laughed "My little heretic". We drove into Santa Cruz, to the Dream Inn for a drink, and home to Gus.

New Years Eve at the Colonial Inn, Delroy, Lorenzo and Corbett in towering command of their full house. Andrew, Joey, Erik, Stanley taking turns sitting-in. Stoney and Ted brought Girls with fake-IDs. Luke too, letting it be known he was leaving the Band for a job on his new Girlfriend's father's dude ranch in Montana. Delroy's Wife huddled with

Cherry, and Marion and Colleen who left the Babies with a trusted sitter for a few hours. Frank bought a round for the whole room to announce Amber and his engagement. Brian and April drove down with Limey, a tell-tale black-eye shining through her carefully layered make-up. Cyrene wore the dress she bought of mine, and stuck close to me while Stanley took Lorenzo's drums. Though I did not really recall specifically, she said Stan came from Seattle, was in a band that played my high school dances, that he planned on moving home some time in the New Year, and had asked her and her Son to come along. A little too inebriated to hold my tongue, I offered them a place to land if Corbett and I got there first, and was immediately sorry. Groupies came in necklaces earrings and gowns from my Santa Cruz Import Shop and Yellowbird collections. And Gretchen in the velvet and Keely in the tapestry, made only a fleeting appearance on seeing Delroy's Wife, and Luke. I heard said that the mark of a real artist, they are prolific, there's plenty evidence of their work, the array of mine here tonight made me feel real. Corbett shined in his pink shirt and matching cuff-links. And I wore the handkerchief dress and hair in a high pony-tail, *Chantilly Lace* in-the-flesh, doing a few tequila shots, dancing infront of the bandstand for Corbett. All the Regulars were here but Leda, this farewell of sorts, though no one was actually leaving if at all for months, nevertheless the coming migration signaled a closing. Movements move-on or convictions become clichés, passions harden into routine gestures, ideals to pedantic custom, and this movement seemed to be heading North, maybe Seattle was the New Jerusalem, Ida Rose lived there, it made sense. Corbett did not call a break till 11:15, making sure everyone got-off. Taking the stage only ten minutes later, he invited me to come sit on his bench, I was happy to be above the crush, beyond the sniffing hounds. Putting on his signature Gibson L-5 he had named Bulah, Delroy tipped his Stetson to me and smiled. Lorenzo snarled, how dare I step on the pulpit with him. I paid no heed, sharing the Sorcerer's perch as he conjured the sprit of renewal, haunting primordial melodies, unprecedented bridges, teasing Delroy into a soaring eagle, guitar and keys trading powerful leads, seducing Lorenzo's full effortless voice to its height. As midnight came, I could feel the collective anticipation lean toward anxious desperation, hear the plea, will this coming year be the one when my life lives-up to its potential, and the resolutions, and the more immediate desperation, will I go home alone again tonight, all vested on the Band. The countdown, Auld Lang Syne sated them who had some one and somewhere to go, leaving those in-need of one more drink. After midnight, the Band wooing them onto the dance floor with *Maybellene, Johnny B.Goode, Whole Lot-ta Shakin' Goin' On, Kansas City, Route 66,* and the long version of *Land of a Thousand Dances* finally wearing them out, Lorenzo let them down-easy with his signature finalé *Goodnight Sweetheart.* And two-thirty in the morning Corbett and I stood in our driveway kissing in the New Year, a light mist of rain, black clouds sailing the full moon sky, and something amazing, some thing we never imagined, the dusky iridescent-white of second-hand sun light reflecting off the moon, creating a colossal moon-bow arching across the horizon. Standing struck, this singular herald marking a beginning, 1972 promised to be a whopper.

Argus, Corbett and I were just so contented together, making everyone who knew us want to barf. We walked the beach daily, read Carl Jung and Ida Rose aloud to each other, threw the I Ching, only beginning to understand the wisdom of the ancient and current oracles. And we talked and talked, pledging to trust, to believe the other always, no matter how far-out the story. And, Corbett came to vegetarian, at home anyway, for I often smelled Jack-in-the-Box and Jack Daniel's on him after work. I never sought contentment, it sounded so docile, uninspired, yet here I was and happy to be, our love solid, subtle, constant. Corbett found everything I had to say worth his time. I thought this must be what security feels like, not the kind that comes from things you buy or put in the bank. And I began to see how all that happened in my life brought me to here, and I was grateful, even for Nick, again wishing he should find love, be content like me, but keeping that door locked tight.

Our peace together allowed for intense focus and my best work ever. I finished seven gowns and brought them to the Yellowbird. Owner met my price without flinching, seventy-dollars each. Shoving cash deep in my pocket, I walked the Avenue of Diamonds for a paper, taking it to the Catalyst.
Seattle Times
February 23, 1972.

"Seven Plead No Contest"

"Tacoma: The seven Seattle Conspiracy Case defendants whose original charges stemmed from a demonstration at the Seattle Court House, placed themselves at the mercy of the court here yesterday.

All pleaded nolo contender (no contest) to a contempt-of-court charge. The pleas while not an admission of guilt, have the same effect as a guilty plea.

United States Court judge Russel Smith, visiting from Montana, set March 20 as the day to hear "mitigating circumstances" from the defendants, then pronounce sentences.

Charles (Chip) Marshall III, one of the defendants said "We don't feel we did anything wrong, but we don't want to contest the facts. We're out of money. We've been harassed and we just want to get it over with".

The seven were organizers or supporters of the now defunct Seattle Liberation Front, which led the demonstration to protest the war and the contempt of court sentences against the Chicago Conspiracy Case defendants.

Judge Boldt denied bail and the seven spent 40 days in jail before the Ninth Circuit Court of Appeals over turned the bail denial. When they are sentenced, they are expected to get credit for the 40 days.

Later the Ninth Circuit Court over turned one of judge Boldt's contempt citations, remanded the case for further action and recommended that another judge hear the case if conspiracy charges are refilled.

Stan Pitkin, United States Attorney for Western Washington refiled new contempt charges.

Judge Smith told the defendants they had the right to a jury trial to determine if they were in contempt, and by pleading no contest they waived that right.

Judge Smith said he would study the transcripts and Judge Boldt's notes, then hear from the defendants before pronouncing sentences.

Carl Maxey, Spokane attorney asked that the March 20 appearance be in Seattle because "All the defendants live there and are in dire financial conditions". He said the trip to Tacoma was a financial burden.

Pitkin said the government had no objection. The government declined to say whether they will retry the seven on conspiracy charges."

Like mice caught by a big cat, they had been overcome, played with, and would be eaten alive if Nixon and his Pitkin had their way, if like

Boldt this new Judge was bought-off too. I had a good feeling he was not, would remember to buy the March 21st paper. And to ease a still stubborn guilt, I went to the bank for a $100 money-order, and mailed it to Carl Maxey's office with a note.

My Folks surprised us taking Corbett's invitation. Little Brother on Spring break would run Chicken Valley, they were coming to the sunshine, four days, five nights, and Dad had tickets for the Pebble Beach Golf Classic. I offered to come get them at the San Jose airport, they wanted to rent a car. When I insisted they stay with us, yes came easy. I knew they wanted a closer look, and I wanted them to sleep in our bed, implicitly condoning, sanctioning our living together. Corbett and Dad brought in luggage. Mom took me out on the deck, not yet noticing the amazing view, and trying to make it sound like the poison came from friends and relatives who were always whispering just loud enough to be over-heard, she bared her fears, what kind of a mother is she, what kind of a girl lives with a man, a goyisher, is she pregnant, the children will be bastards, such a shame, at least they'll be Jewish. And she grumbled how her Mother was badgering, when are they getting married, when are they getting married, when, as if my choice was her fault, she pushed "So, would it hurt you so much to get married". I hugged her tight, sorry she had to take this for me, and whispered "Yes Mom, because it would be for everyone but me".

We took them to dinner at the Colonial Inn. Carvel seated us, personally bringing a White Bordeaux to our table, and pouring it addressed my Dad "Mr.Leibofsky, this wine is best with lobster, please allow me the honor of ordering and buying your Family dinner". Dad was properly impressed, the Owner himself. And the most expensive items on the menu were brought to our table, fresh oysters on the half-shell with caviar sauce, steamed Maine lobster tail, baked-potatoes, spinach sautéd in butter and garlic for Mom and Dad, Caesar Salad for me minus the anchovies, Corbett never ate much before working, ordering a small dinner salad just to join in with us. We followed him into the lounge, it would be the first time they saw him play. And I just achingly loved watching their faces watching him reveal him self as artists do though their work, their initial delight at how good he is, how he seemed to just know what the audience wanted before they knew, and then generously giving it to them better than they could have thought, how he ruled with those big tarantella hands, they barely noticed Lorenzo and Delroy. The Band took a break, Delroy and Lorenzo politely came with Corbett. Lorenzo's laugh was nervous "You remember me Mr.Leibofsky". He tentatively put out his hand. Dad stood, taking it firm but not too "I do, from Satsop. You shouldn't have run off so fast, I wanted to buy your lunch". Lorenzo's face flushed "Thank you Sir". Backing away, he nodded to Mom "Scuse me Ma'am". Corbett smiled and introduced Delroy. Who was totally relaxed, lit a Camel and offered one to Dad "So you went to the Sky River. My Mom went last year". Dad turned down the smoke with a slight headshake no. Delroy looked to Corbett "Hawkman, you didn't tell me how cool your Ol'lady's people are". He offered his hand to Dad "I'm the one who introduced your daughter to the Hawkman. Really nice to meet you". Delroy couldn't have noticed Dad's slight hesitation, but I knew, even clothed in the saving-grace of his very real talent, the instant Dad laid eyes on Delroy Bogave, he knew a smooth rascal and did not really want to lend his hand, and he did not bother to squeeze "You sure can play that guitar". On some level Delroy knew he'd been seen, and covered himself with that effortless charm "Well thank you. Now I better go make the fans happy". Taking a long drag on his smoke before gliding away, he winked at me "You look beautiful tonight Shoshannah". Dad sat down, beaming at Corbett like a proud parent, directing him "Sit my Boy". Beaming back Corbett did as he was told. The most important men in my life genuinely liked each other, I inhaled the honey of the moment and settled in my chair.

Corbett lit Mom's smoke and one for himself, then leaned close to Dad "My Folks would never come see me play, especially not in a bar". Dad couldn't pass this up "Even Jesus drank wine". Smiling Corbett nodded yes. Dad's eyes blazed as he continued "In younger years I sang. My Little Sister was a guest coloratura soprano at the New York Metropolitan Opera, often singing on the radio, and for countless Jewish fundraisers. I'd walk her to lessons, and sit outside the door listening. Her teacher offered to train me for free, said my voice was promising. But I had to get away from my terrible Father, and joined the Army. Then Roosevelt declared war". He looked at me, and Mom "When I met your mother, that was it. Trying to make a living in music would not have been a good life for

676

children, and that's what we wanted, a Family". Mom smiled at him with such love it took my breath away. I had always known my Dad's wonder-full tenor voice, quietly crooning me a lullaby, accompanying the car radio, or his Mario Lanza records, resounding in his morning shower, but I never dreamed he considered a singing career, or that he could relate to Corbett in this way. Everything Corbett had become was in-spite of his upbringing, and though Dad rarely mentioned his, I had not missed the words terrible Father. He went on "Make no mistake, I'm not saying I had your kind of talent. But I had some, and know an artist's life isn't much easier today. You're always looking for work, there's lots of ups and downs, and no pension or retirement, it can be very hard. You see why I might worry about my Daughter's future". Dad rested both palms on the table "But then you my Boy are the real thing. You may just be one to make it". His mouth slightly agape, Corbett was staring at him. My Dad was so straight-forward, so generous, with no dagger hidden in the folds of his garment, he was the real thing too, I was used to the real thing, and while Corbett was not used to speaking his mind around Family, I has something to say "First of all Daddy, I love you so much. Second, I can take care of my self. And third, most people work jobs they hate for people they hate their whole lives. If Corbett and I do what makes us happy, we'll be fine cause we'll have each other". Dad chuckled affectionately "Shoshy, if I could wish it true for you I would. Young years are always a little naïve, and necessarily so". Corbett found his voice "Mr. Leibofsky, it's a brand new experience for me being part of a Family that talks to each other. Thank you, and I promise to think about what you said". Lightly kissing my cheek he went toward the stage. I could hardly hold myself together knowing this Monster was mine. Taking his place behind the keyboards, the circus began anew, and Corbett seemed to grow taller by a foot, and completely absolute, the Hawkman was on the wing, why the audience came night after night, a willing accomplice, needing their fix.

Dad and Mom left for Pebble Beach early, never before in this part of California, they wanted time to take-in downtown Monterey and Carmel. Stopping on the way back at a roadside-stand in Castroville for deep-fried baby artichokes. We ate them with my homemade polenta, crock-pot pinto beans and mango salsa. Dad golfed whenever he could, and was so thrilled having seen Jack Nicklaus and Bobby Jones in the flesh he positively glowed, Mom marveled at the 75 degree Winter sunshine, and exhausted they excused to our bed soon as Corbett went to work. Next days, breakfast at the Broken Egg, lunch at the Catalyst, we walked Pacific Avenue passed the Yellowbird, one of my gowns on the sole window mannequin, I could see Mom's pride and disbelief. And we strolled the boardwalks of Santa Cruz and Capitola, walked the cliff trail to dine on Tampico's deck, and down the beach stairs nightly for sunsets. I found them fun-loving, energetic, and so definitely another generation, some times just barely tolerating our likes and suggestions. Corbett and I spontaneously toned-it-down, at the same time feeling no need to defend or justify our life. Still, Mom saw vegetarian as a personal affront to her cooking, living together disrespecting their marriage, wanting no children negating their sacrifices, and she hardly missed a subtle or not so opportunity to say so. Four days, five night too many, I was ready for good-bye, soothing a bittersweet farewell by telling of our plan to move North. Mom was so happy she burst into tears. Dad kissed my forehead and slipped a folded hundred into my hand "You're doing the right thing coming home to your Family". He shook Corbett's hand firm but gentle, looking into his eyes "You take care of my Little Girl". Corbett smiled "I'll try Sir, but you know she can take care of herself". Dad still holding his hand "I mean her heart my Boy". Corbett smile "Yes Sir".

The first day of Spring, I took three gowns to the Yellowbird, Owner paid my price, and kept them for her self, then floated down the Avenue of Diamonds for a Seattle Times.

"U.S. Closes Books On "Seattle Seven" Case"

"Five of the seven conspiracy defendants charged with contempt of court for twice disrupting a Tacoma trial 15 months ago were sentenced to 5 months today.

Ordered to Clearwater Forest Camp, near Forks in Clallam County were Charles (Chip) Marshall 3ᴿᴰ, Jeff Dowd, Joseph Kelly, Mike Abeles and Susan Stern.

United States District Court judge Russel Smith, visiting from Montana, also sentenced Roger Lippman to 30 days at the camp.

The defendants were charged with contempt for disruptive actions at the

Tacoma trial on December 14.

Michael Lerner, the seventh defendant in the original conspiracy trial was not charged with contempt in the December 14 incident.

Judge Smith gave Susan Stern credit for 39 days served in prison after being sentenced by judge Boldt.

Marshall, Dowd, Kelly, Abeles and Lippman were sentenced to 50 days confinement for the first disruption but were given credit for time served and the rest of the sentence suspended.

Judge Smith gave Mrs. Stern and Mr. Lippman until tomorrow to surrender to the United States marshals."

The word surrender ran through me, burning my cheeks, like I thought, Judge Smith was not one of the bad guys, still Nixon appointed judges had been used successfully to kill change and civil outcry, and Boldt had prevailed, directly bringing some of us to our knees, indirectly shredding the Seattle Liberation Front, although it was not looking so good for Nixon and his bunch now the Pentagon Papers went public, proving they were liars, cheats, thieves. The Seven's ordeal was not over, and I felt as aggrieve and importuning as ever, with no where to vent. Santa Cruz wasn't exactly a trove of political unrest, there were no coffee-shops filled with clandestine revolutionary discussions, no demonstrations, no Hippies sitting on the Ave smoking dope in public, pushing the envelope, only sun-worshipers, astrologers, tarot readers, musicians, small town gossip and lots of good weed. Erik, the one Vietnam Vet I knew here was well-aware of my political persuasion, and never would allow me conversation. Gretchen's Postman-Poet had come for her and Ava, she was never political anyway except as it served her amusement. Keely and the Littles moved North to live with Justin, her political past now an albatross around her neck, she would not speak of it anymore even if she were here. And Corbett had been so caught-up in fighting his personal demons he had not paid close attention to Martin, Bobby, anti-war, civil rights or Women's rights, and still my darling Corby listened to me with both ears. So, I had Gus who willingly took everything from me, and my reliable fabrics, ever amazed how productive I could be with such fine raw materials, how I could cannibalized the rancor, regret, frustration though my fingers, wrestling, consuming, making them into things for profit, contending with my self, shame-on-you, just feel these feelings, let them be in their uncooked state, anything else is exploitation and wrong. Even so, their transformation was so beautiful, so whole, and transformed me too, building something from my imagination with my hands, extraordinary how anger, pain, guilt became art, and not just for art's sake. Ida Rose wrote in *The Pink Elephant* "*And that might be the highest function of art, to allow the sensitive artist of any time to depict in startling fashion his feelings about the age in which he finds himself, so the less discerning imitator might see his age in caricature and, haply, might awaken to his responsibility as a molder of history and restore some order while there is yet time*". Clothes were considered craft not art, still I thought mine high art, offering females full freedom of movement was an act of revolution against the Patriarchy, a powerful political statement I happened to be good at. And this faced me with the artist's predicament, the price for inspiration = the struggle to tell truth, it was a foregone conclusion just being human on earth I would suffer, and putting my work out there made me more vulnerable. Ida Rose often reminded her students "*This is not a summer camp*". So why not make art the tangible goods of my suffering, the voice, the reward, I wondered was this what Dad meant when he said an artist's life was hard.

Playing five night, Sundays afternoon at the Zyante, and Monday practice at Jimmy Mesa's barn, Corbett was all but taken from me. To keep them honest, I would sometimes show-up at the barn, lines of cocaine on the glass-top coffee-table, Groupies on the couch. The latest hype swirling the Band had drawn an impressive class of them, Gretchen-Fetchin-Fine's all, angelic mercenaries, muses, eager to be close to the flame, and of course Wives and Ol'ladies were expressly forbidden the barn, we might interrupt the serious business of making music, and they obeyed orders. Erik, Joey, Lorenzo shit-their-pants when I would waltz-in and sit down with the Girls, who openly respected my brazen violation of clubhouse rules, and as I hoped, came to know me, like me, and therefore in their book of rules going-after Corbett became bad manners. I knew Erik wanted to punish Corbett for not controlling me, and would if he did not absolutely need his magnitude. With all the playing and practice, One Hand Clapping was again living-up to their potential, *depicting in startling fashion* their *feelings about the age in which* they *finds* themselves, inspiring Limey to make preparations for the move. We would caravan North, stopping a his place in Newberg Oregon over-night, then go-on passed Seattle to the small town of Arlington 35 miles North, to a rented farm, with a big old main house, a barn he would convert into a recording studio, and 20 acres of pines and maples to absorb the music without disturbing neighbors. The Band would record there, tour the Northwest and Canada, then Erik would again approach Ralph Gleason on signing to Fantasy Records, this time with an album already in the can, while Limey financed everything, till the money came rolling-in to pay him back. Corbett and I decided to go along for the ride, no matter my clash with Erik and Joey, it was plain One Hand Clapping had that essential it-thing, the consequential charisma, that impossible to intentionally manufacture quality a Band must have beyond talent to make the music of their time, and if the ingredients weren't so volatile to hold together, the Boys would succeed, and if not, that was okay with us too. Santa Cruz had been discovered by investors who were buying it up, and run-over in week-end Hippies and tourists, more and more always coming. Jay Shore offered me a job, write a weekly gossip column for his paper the Santa Cruz Times, as he put it "Gossip's the currency of a once hip small town gone stale". I thought about it a lot, and said no, believing a person like-it-or-not pours themselves into what they do, and what they do pours into them, telltale was not something I wanted to be, and I knew for sure I would always regret not becoming a newspaper woman like my comic hero Brenda Starr. My gowns hats bikinis and jewelry still fetching best prices, they were now mostly bought by passers-though, takers who belly-up to the local banquet, grab the choice morsels and carry them away. I could see how capricious the Spirit of the Time was, if you were fortunate, the Sweet Sisters would catch your hand and take you along, if not, they would bind the thread of nostalgia around your soul, turning you to living stone. It was time to go.

Cherry left Joey and moved home to Modesto. Colleen and Marion were always together with their Babies. We were very often in the same place, and I quickly learned to keep my thoughts to my self. Any mention of Ida Rose was greeted with fish-eyed suspicion, she must be a cult leader or something worse. Every allusion to Women's Liberation disputed, raising propaganda specters of those dreaded co-ed bathrooms, women being drafted, the protections and privileges of Wife and Motherhood annulled. They believed their second-class status inevitable, and wanted to keep what privilege they had thank you ma'am, while freely and bitterly complaining about their men, more and more bothered I would not join the chorus. Here I was again, excommunicated for not obeying the cultural canon I had no hand in making, it felt like my first Women's Lib Collective meeting only so much longer, embracing liberty, wanting to do something about it cast me out. I guessed they thought I did not suffered enough, maybe it was the other way around, no matter, they could not see my scars, know my battles, my obligation to Bonita-Kay, Marigold, the MotherTruckers, Amaru, Ida Rose, my generous wise remarkable teachers. I carried them in me, owed them to continue, felt sad for Marion and Colleen leaving the wonder-full adventure to me. And there were more than just me, I'd seen them on TV, each of us would accumulate, demand freedoms, benefits the sleeping hounds would also enjoy whether or not they ever woke.

And yet, Colleen, Marion were friendly when we were one-on-one, especially Colleen, who tried to explain her ambivalent behavior to me, confessing a real fear of being labeled Women's Libber, sometimes she sympathized, but any public relationship with a known Libber would bring guilt by association, and the possibility of violence, she feared for her Baby's safety. I cast no blame, she would be baited in public by the likes of Raul and Joey, and would likely be at home too. I could still see Nick treating me like a queen in public, grinding me down in private. Colleen, Marion believed they were inlove with their Men, and maybe were, they had the obligate Babies, settling for doors opened, chairs pulled-out to make them feel cared for, and consequentially feminine, living though husbands and children. I had come to see these deeds as romantic farce, chivalry that at its core said I was not whole, needing rescue when I did not. But they complied, fearing the unspoken decree, take you liberation and you are disenfranchised, you forfeit all that is considered feminine. If my hands were full, I appreciated a door opened, and would do the same, common courtesy called for no less, but permitting men to define me by what I was not allowed to do for my self was insane. Being treated like royalty in public while Females around the world were brutalized, had little or no rights, was just too absurd to continue the pretense, taking the privilege would sully my oh-so-lily-white ethics, it was the same argument I had with Gretchen. Corbett with all his demons had somehow built a tall and sturdy ego, my freedom did not scare but delighted him, he wanted a partner not someone walking behind. Ida Rose taught there was a price to consider on either side of a choice, yes would cost me and so would no, I had to weigh what I was willing to pay for what I was getting or not. Having weak-ego troglodytes flex their muscles and call me names I would unhappily pay. The afternoon Tom and Ida Rose rushed to my Folks' house for Corbett, I asked why she had come as a woman in this life when it was such a man's world. Ida Rose said her message was only for the eligible, and if some discredited it because of her gender, it only made her work easier, because those who weren't eligible eliminate themselves.

Chapter Twenty Eight

KARMA KICKBACK

Packing, I found three ragged hits of Sandoz in the bottom of the bag Casey bought me in Ensenada, an unopened box of Sherman's Queen-size Cigarettellos from the headshop in San Francisco, Excalibur, and my magic teapot, each still vital in their own truth. I welcomed the memories, far from an albatross round my neck, they had been necessary companions, added eyes, ears, arms affording some perspective, to consider the sacred and not-so-sacred foundations of my life, the soundness of my judgment, probabilities of my expectations, and the undisputable nature of my self, the part of me that always remains the same. We celebrated our first anniversary. Delroy's band Moongoose took the gig at the Colonial Inn. And the day-before leaving, Corbett invited me along to his little Catholic chapel. Excited, nervous, though it was a muggy summer morning I dressed in long pant and a high-neck sweater. Amused, Corbett took my hand as we walked the cliff trail "Don't worry Sho, the Father already knows about you. He's the one who suggested I bring you". I felt the bottom of my stomach, no Gentile no matter how well-meant could wholly know the implicit fear Jews have of Christians, the Crusades, the Inquisitions, their complicity with Hitler, slaughtering us in the name of Jesus or just standing-by for nearly 2000 years, in the dark reaches of my secret terrors, I did not feel at ease among them, especially in their holy places. Slipping my hand from his "You know this is a set up, right". He looked puzzled "No way Shoshy, what kind of a set up could it be". I gave him a tight-lipped smile "You'll see". He stopped "You want to go home. I will if you want to". I hated him putting it all on me "No, I'm going to church". We walked the rest in silence. Father's morning prayer lead to reading the Epistle of Paul the Apostle to the Hebrews, Jesus this, Angels that, he he he, no matter where I was I never felt included when it was all he he he. This Jesus did not seem the same one Ida Rose spoke of, and Paul damning the Jews from heaven except by this Lord Jesus, what outrageous hubris, and so transparently chosen for my edification. I felt deliberately set apart, those peopled, terribly self-conscious, and could hardly sit still. If Corbett noticed he did not let-on. And then the reason everyone came, eating Jesus' wafer-body and wine-blood, communion's ritual leading back to Isis and Osiris, so faded and condemned as to be imponderable. Though it was flagrant violation, because I did not confess, I followed Corbett and received the host.

Hurrying home without speaking of it, we shed our dress-ups for beach clothes, leashed Gus and descended the stairs for a long last walk, I counted the 106 steps. Corbett spoke first "So, what'd you think of church". I did not look at him "I thought I might die taking communion. I thought the host would poison me cause I'm not baptized and didn't confess. I wanted to see if your God was for real, you know, baiting him in his own house. When my Grampa died, I thought I needed the Jewish God, and went to synagogue. It was late, maybe midnight, no one there but me. And I knelt down on both knees and said Jesus Jesus Jesus real loud, thinking this will get Yahweh's attention, He'll at least strike me dead with a lightning bolt and before I died I'll at least know there's a God. Nothing happened. So I went up on the pulpit. I'd never seen a woman up there except in the custody of a Holy Man and figured if this doesn't break the rules nothing will. Nothing happened. I really didn't care if I died, I was in so much pain losing Grampa, and so mad at God, so then I took the Torah from the Ark and read from it. Nothing. So I put it back and left. God is not in the houses we build for Him". Corbett was solemnly nodding yes "I went today to say goodbye. Saturday at confession, I told my sins, and the Father said they weren't sins. After, he invited me over to his place for a beer. It was like I was the Father and he was confessing to me. He said when he stood there in front of his congregation, he felt like a fraud, like he was just going through the motions, acting like he knew more about faith and God than they did. He said he could tell I was a spiritual man and wanted to know what I knew. I was flattered, but mostly blown-away his faith was so rocky. All I could do for him was tell about Ida Rose and her work. He freed me though, you know, saying my sins weren't sins". I had rationalized Corbett's exclusive church-going by supposing he felt guilty of what looked to me like a Eucharist addiction, was thrilled the door had finally opened, and I did know what he meant "Yeah Babe I do. You don't have to worry anymore if you're naughty or nice according to their rules". He put his arms around me and kissed my neck. Gus saw an opportunity, jerked the leash from my hand and took-off after a seagull. We followed, pausing to chat with the Regulars, these genuine beach bums, frozen in time, sharing the same attitude, good riddance to the Spirit of the Age, maybe it will take some of the mangy tourists with it, only the ocean mattered, only their daily pilgrimage made them feel good enough to live another day. My last unemployment check came in the afternoon mail. We supped quietly on the deck of the Tampico, gazing down the coast to Monterey, sun sparkling off the water, feeling the bittersweet of impending adventure, of leaving paradise behind. Even Gus seemed to know, instead of the usual straining against the leash, He stubbornly lingered, poking whiskers into every shrub for his scent as we walked the cliff trail home to finish packing. Together a year, all our belongings would fit in the back-seat of the Bug, except Corbett's keyboards. Ted and Stoney had loaded the Hammond, foot-peddle bass and Leslie speaker directly from the Colonial, but the equipment van was full, with no room for the piano. Corbett was not so fond of the Spinet's tone and itched for a Baldwin upright, so when Limey promised one would be waiting in the Arlington barn, and arranged for Tom Luaggi, owner of the Zyante Club, who was looking for a house piano, to pick it up from the Colonial and make the final four payments, Corbett was a happy man.

The usual Northern California morning-sea-fog breezed through open doors as we tramped in-and-out packing the Bug. At the same instant we both realized Gus was gone, and knew where, racing down the stairs, and the beach, he was nowhere. Our telephone already disconnected, Corbett's long legs took the stairs to the Tampico by threes. When I caught-up, he was hanging-up "Gus isn't at the pound". Panic, I ran headlong, down Seacliff Drive, alley-ways, culverts, ditches, sobbing, calling. Corbett too, trying to comfort me "We'll find him, the dog catcher probably didn't get there with him yet. Don't worry Shoshy, we'll find him". Though heartfelt, his words sounded blah blah blah, action mattered, soothing me did not. I wished he understood without having to explain, of course I'm upset, duh, but it makes me sharp, throws me into over-drive, and that's where I need to be, so don't try an soothe or console, I don't want it, I want my Dog "How could some one I love be gone so fast". Stoney, Andrew and Jenn were leaning against the equipment van smoking cigars as we rounded Court Way. Stoney looked bothered "Where you guys been. You know we been waiting at Biancalana's". I mouthed fuck you as I ran into the house and out on the deck. Corbett told them what happened. Jenn, Andrew followed me, understanding there was no comfort or console, he simply said "I'll take Jenn down to the beach. Gus loves the beach". Stoney drove to the Tampico to phone the pound every 10 minutes. Corbett walked the cliff trail again. And I waited for Gus to come home, pacing, out and in, reprimanding aloud that all-seeing-all-knowing Jesus-Yahweh-God-of-the-stone-building, who surely saw me eat the Eucharist "You know he's innocent". I felt such bitter resentment swell, as if my heart would detonate and burn me alive. The equipment van skidded into the driveway, Corbett's voice resounding as he came running "He's at the pound Shoshy, he's at the pound". Unconditional release rushed though me like smack, I sank to the floor, Corbett with me, burying my face in his shirt I wept. Gus yelped impenitent outrage on seeing us, wagging, plying his charms, peeing uncontrollably. I glared hard as we passed his cell to pay the fine, this second offense a whopping one-hundred-twenty-five bucks, and at such a dubious time, when our lives were not in our hands, when we did not know where our next money would come from, I would have paid everything and borrowed more. Gus leapt into my arms when the cage door opened. And I pranced around the parking lot, kissing his face safe in my arms, he would not be trusted again.

Before leaving house keys on the kitchen counter and doors and windows locked, we stood holding hands on the deck looking down the coastline. Never having quite gotten used to the thrill of stepping from my kitchen first-thing in the morning to find this view, or any of California's exuberant natural treasures, I picked a few eucalyptus nuts from the ground, a fragrant cluster from the loyal Acacia, and bid our Seacliff sanctuary good-bye, a big part of me not wanting to go. We cruised Cabrillo College Drive West to Lorenzo's in silence, and took last position in the caravan. Limey lead, with Joey Andrew and Jennifer in the green Nash Rambler station wagon. Erik, Colleen and Baby-Boy in the big yellow school bus. Lorenzo, Marion, Baby-Girl in their two-tone blue and white 68 VW bus. Stoney, Ted in the equipment van. Corbett and me, back seat lade to leave some view out the rear window, the full-length Alaskan Seal coat Granny gave me, something in conscience I could never wear and considered leaving behind, spread over all, Jail-Dog perched on top, collar and leash still fastened secure round his neck. The caravan gassed-up at the Jackpot on Ocean Street, 29-cents a gallon, and passed the Colonial Inn onto Highway 17. The heat was Texan, a suffocating 95 degrees by Vacaville, equal humidity through the Sacramento Valley, we had the wing-windows turned backwards, scooping in an unavailing heat. Argus lay spread-eagle on the fur, tongue hanging the side of his mouth like a dying gooey-duck, barrel-chest panting a fast beat, moaning an unremitting grievance. It seemed we must be heading strait to hell, and I wondered to my self were we going in the right direction, not so much physically, but in the company of such egocentric outlaws and thieves. Since I knew the way to Limey's we lagged further and farther behind, taking every rest stop to drink, and soak a kitchen towel, laying it over Gus. Passing the Yreka exit, Corbett saw the caravan parked at Frosty's Freeze, taking the next we went back. According to the five-foot tall thermometer mounted by the door, it had cooled ten degrees. Plainly stoned, the Gang food-tripping on cheese burgers, fries and shakes, the place a cool air-condicioned 72 degrees. Erik glared as Gus and us pulled chairs up to the table "Something wrong with your Bug you can't keep up with the rest of us". Corbett just laughed "No man, we're just taking the scenic tour".

We ordered cones to go at the counter as everyone left, a small one for Gus, I was content speeding by the Wolf Creek exit. Eleven relentless hours from Santa Cruz we snaked-off that Salem exit, crossed the Willamette and Yamhill Rivers, Chehalam Creek, and outside Newberg passing a small airstrip, turned up Limey's block-long newly black-topped driveway. Grace was out on the porch to greet us, dark-haired, beautiful, in her early thirties, she had a fresh feast from her garden prepared and on the table. I admired how this genteel woman carried her load, would have certainly been her trusted Sister had we the chance. After dinner, and bottles of Liebfraumilch, lines of coke, pipes of sinsemilla, Limey laid bad news on us, the Arlington farm would not be ready for three weeks, we were welcome to stay here till then. Astonishment darkened Grace's face, she slipped from the room. I followed into her Boy's bedroom, we stood looking at the sleeping tow-head, hall light catching her perfect white teeth, smiling pride-full she whispered "He only looks like an angel sleeping". I nodded smiling too. Unexpected she wrapped arms round me "I'm really glad to see you again". Her crushing isolation reached into me, I felt my self falling with her and stiffened involuntarily "Me too". She let go "Come on I'll give you the room with the best rug".

Night too close to sleep, bathroom occupied by Mothers bathing Babies, we lay atop our sleeping bags, too sticky to touch, listening to the house settle, nearly 800 dollars between us, we had not anticipated spending any on a motel, however there was no way I could stay here three weeks, even with our own bedroom. Corbett never did coke, but he was drunk. Argus lay on his side by the open window, scratching fleas in his sleep, wasted from a first encounter with plebeian farm life, two busy-body goats, a gentle-eye sway-back mare, rambunctious chestnut pony with an overbite, three cranky geese, a duck that thought he was a goose and followed them everywhere, maybe two dozen hens, one rooster, and two sweet-tempered German shepherds. I fell asleep to their soft snoring. Gus nuzzled me to take him out around 8AM. Grace had bread rising, was outside gathering eggs. Colleen, Marion up feeding Babies. I sat in the morning sun smoking a Sherman before joining them in the kitchen for coffee. Grace got to frying eggs, pancakes, home-raised pork chops, and wanting for every crumb of appreciation, apologetically turned-down any offers to help. The aroma of fresh-baked bread drew the Boys, all hung-over and hungry. We sat the huge dining-room table, another War Table, set with bone china and silver, glass pitchers of maple syrup, ceramic pots of home-grown raspberry jam and hand-churned butter, while Grace brought platter after platter. Suffering a wicked headache, Corbett ate quietly, relishing two thick chops, pancakes and lots of syrup. I noticed too much alcohol always seemed to call for meat as the balance. Every morsel enthusiastically devoured, the Girls excused to the kitchen, no one spoke waiting for me to go with them. I sat back in my chair and lit a Sherman. Boys Club reticence weighed a long moment before Limey stood at the head of the table, the clicking open of his briefcase directing attention, he took-out seven envelopes bearing hand-written names, and distributed them down the table. Four-hundred for families of three, $300 to Corbett and me, $200 each for Joey Andrew Ted Stoney. The money brought deliberations to swift consensus, we would all meet-up at the Arlington farm in three weeks. And, finally a private moment with Corbett, I all but demanded "Let's get out of here today, now. We can go to Cannon Beach. It's maybe two hours. You'll love it there. We have enough for a few nights. Then we can go to my Folks". Corbett smiled what I saw as obliging "Sure, if you want to". Beyond frustrated with this muddled ghost displacing my beloved Paladin when he drank too much, who resigned all power of decision to me, and consequently all responsibility, and blame, I stopped trying to co-operate, called Mom at Chicken Valley and explained our situation. A warm welcome in her voice "Come any time, you have the key".

No one was going any where but us, they had no where to go, making it awkward for Corbett. I could feel the pulling, them or me, me or them, it was always the same competition, loyalty to the Band or me, and I would have happily made room for both if certain people would stop treating me like shit. They would not, and it was easier for Corbett to blame going on me, they already considered him pussy-whipped. This saving him self from confrontation at my expense left me angry and hurt, for it was my best qualities they wanted rid of, a resilient stubborn aplomb, abundant creative ideas and the single-mindedness to carry them out, and I think most egregious, my total absence of Christian guilt, allowing me a healthy ego to speak my mind. Somehow in this upside-down culture where acceptable female qualities were still relegated almost wholly maternal, soft, childlike, or whore, surprise surprise I was not appreciated, not welcomed, even threatening, though adding them to the stew would surely have made a tastier stew. Grace walked along with us to the Bug. I felt betrayed and alone, could not bring myself to speak to Corbett, and wished she would just get in and go with me, for her world was such a lonely mental vacuum, even a Golden Ghetto offered some urban mediocrities, nevertheless this was her karma, her choice, and I could not come to the rescue, she had to do that for her self. But I could let her know she was seen, and with a hug tendered "If I was your neighbor, we'd be Sistas". She hugged me closer.

I drove, I-5 North to Portland, West on the Sunset Highway though Clatsop and Tillamook State Forests to Highway 101 South. Gus smelled the salt air first, his stubby little tail a whirling propeller, snorting frenetically from his fur perch, licking, nibbling my bare shoulder just enough to make me flinch. Corbett beckoned him to the front. Leaping with such exuberance, he crashed into the dashboard, yelping, sliding down Corbett's legs to the floor. Corbett's big hands took him, gently smoothing his wounded pride, holding tight while he poked his face and then most of his body out the window, mouth open, tongue flapping. I was still simmering, unable to find temperate words beyond civil necessities, wondering if Corbett even remembered the night, I'd heard that drinking could make you blackout. Corbett growing indignant at my chilly distance, for what he clearly perceived as an insignificant isolated incident that he would readily remedy if only given the chance, let Gus car-fly too far out the window for my comfort, surely to make me say something. I knew he would not let him go, and when Gus had his fill and settled into Corbett's lap, he gently admonished "Now remember you little jailbird, your freedom's officially limited to a leash". I recognized speaking first as the unmistakable sound of contrition and decided to give-up the ghost "Yeah, we learned our lesson even if you haven't". I often taught Gus by holding his head gently in my hands, encouraging him to make eye contact, that it was not a confrontation, not an affront to look directly when spoken too or wanting to speak. Head cocked, smiling at me, he sniffed, and resigned his chin to Corbett's thigh.

Five miles to Cannon Beach, Hemlock Street though the town, we stopped for flea soap. One more mile, West on Chinsana to the Major Motel, destination of many Leibofsky Family vacations. The no vacancy sign was lit, I went in remembering the owners often forgot, and good-luck, a four night cancellation, waterfront facing Haystack, the largest monolith on the North American coast, with a small kitchen, adequate bathroom, king-size bed, deck onto the sand, and yes Furhead was allowed, 55 a night, more than we should, I said yes anyway. Corbett brought in what we needed, and I took Gus to the kitchen sink for a flea bath. Us next, showering away a long journey, water liquidating any lingering resentment as it can be counted on to do.

Our hair and fur still wet, feeling brand-new we stepped-off the deck onto warm sand, and turned South from Haystack, so massive it seemed at hand, a tall crisp blue sky, enough breeze to soften the sun, roaring surf overwhelming yesterday and tomorrow, tide -3.6, laying bare Poseidon's treasure. Rocks clothed in gooseneck barnacles large as tulips, enormous high-gloss muscles anchored in black bouquets, some twelve inches and longer. This strand of coast a National Wildlife Refuge, nothing could be disturbed, tide-pools, sea flowers, anemones, purple and orange starfish, surly hermit crabs, gulls sailing the currents, all safe. Sensing freedom ahead, Gus strained at his leash as we passed Tolovana Beach, couples with pants rolled-up walking in the water, kids flying kites, running, digging, the waves sliding in across exposed fields of brown sand, coast-line disappearing into the mist. I imagined we could walk all the way to Santa Cruz, and kept imagining Charlton Heston bare-back on a horse, and the Statue of Liberty jutting up from the sand around the next bend. How I loved these familiar Northwest beaches, strewn in tumbled round smooth rocks, tumbled shells I called sea bones, driftwood, and the water greener than California, sand not so blonde, a sadness I did not realized lifted from me, it would not be so bad leaving plush-velvet Santa Cruz behind. Passing all vacationers, our foot-prints the only ones, we let Gus go, following water's edge to Cape Falcon, till we had gone too far and sat down on a bleached log, part of a driftwood pile resembling a pack of howling wolves, the Great Water's chthonic soul incarnate. No need for words, this humbling face-to-face with proportion, simple harmony of the whole, listening to the hush of changing tide. Heading back, every wave brought more treasure, sand-dollars, jellyfish, razor clam shells, blue muscles with mother-of-pearl insides, limpets, chiton bones, crab and gull skeletons, feathers, sea whips, each wave rearranging. My hands were full of riches when I saw a gleaming ahead. Gus ran with me into the flow, plucking a glittering thing before it was taken away, clear as ice, nearly the size of my fist. I could not believe my eyes, ever since always I had searched these beaches for some thing this grand, finding green glass fishing-net floats, perfect shells, jasper, jade-stone, pale blue chalcedony, petrified wood, but this diamond agate was what I had been looking for, like finding Corbett, my search was over, now I could look up. Dropping all but this wonder, I ran to show him, Gus barking, the sparkling jewel balanced on my open palm, every thing right with the world, I was exactly where I should be, on the exact spot in the Universe, and this was the only way I could possible know. Gus chased every bird, especially those running water's lip, and though he did not have a chance with his half-pint legs, he had such gusto, such heart. The tide began to come in strong and fast, we had to wait for full ebb to round Cape Falcon, and then people again, Gus had to leash. No objection, he finally understood it was not meant to punish.

A mellow evening walk to the Surfcrest Market for supplies, and a six-pack of Coors. I would have preferred no alcohol and gave Corbett a look. He returned such a wide innocent playful grin, I let it go. And we settled into chairs on the deck, witness to Helios driving his sun-chariot into the sea. Instead of one, I drank three. Corbett gave me a look. I knew he presumed five for him one for me, though we had never agreed, except in that unspoken insidious orchestration that goes on without conscious over-sight, that pretends to be so blameless the moment consciousness takes note, but I'd seen enough of the fleeting drama to fathom its core intention, its pattern of presumption, and was no more willing to sleep-walk my role. We needed to resolve this drinking, out-loud, I did not want our life automated, dumbed-down, he had to be willing at least to

692

acknowledge something was up, and that meant exposing him self, or else I would be taken for nagging judgmental. I flashed him the same innocent smile he gave me at the Surfcrest Market. His face did not betray him, still I knew somewhere in his heart he understood exactly what was up in this silent deadly dance around the bottle, that there was something he was not ready to face, some shaming tongue booze hushed, and this time again I conceded its deception. Sundown was plainly their signal, hundreds of gulls made for Haystack to sleep the night. Corbett stood at the edge of the deck and threw a hand-full of Fritos high in the air. One gull swooped down, calling the others, and they came, maybe 50, bold, crowding Corbett's feet, squawking, squabbling, hopping into the air, beaks snapping, he threw more chips, the drab gooney babies larger than their mothers, biggest grabbing the most, so many I held Gus in my arms thinking they would eat him too. He struggled, fearless, after all he was Dog and they mere Bird. When the Machiavellian frenzy dispersed with the last morsel, though a few remained to press the matter, I let him chase those off. Nightfall overwhelming the sky with broad strokes, vivid pinks descending to smoldering umber coals, a snowy foam capping incoming waves, their long slow creeping across the sand, we sat close together on deck's edge, toes wiggling the still warm sand, silent in solemn benediction till the panorama faded. What a complex and wondrous day, one I would never have foreseen at the outset to end in this way, I blessed the Sweet Sisters Fate for attending our journey, and the hallowed Great Water for our sanctification. Corbett built a small bonfire, the smoky redolence taking us to childhoods, we traded camp stories, hulking mutant crabs inching toward us in the night, monstrous squid tentacles prowling the sand, ravenous stinging jellyfish that swelled a thousand fold after dark, and golden-brown toasted marshmallows, talking plans, hopes and dreams.

Our final morning and still no plan but go to my Folks, we needed to be out of the room by 11AM. Taking another walk, tide so high we had to scamper onto the rocks to beat its reach. Gus discovered a seal carcass and had to roll all over it. I bathed him, while Corbett packed the Bug, and we drove to Mo's Surfside Café on Tolovana Beach for brunch. Over one more cup of coffee, watching the waves rushing out, why not call your old roommate Katey lit-up my brain. It had been almost four years and made no sense, all that terrible Nick stuff and her pregnant, still I was learning not to rationalize intuition. Using the Café pay phone, information gave me her Mom's number, who gave me hers. And as if the way had been made by some synchronystic underlying engineer that does not live in our time-frame and negotiates the space between us, Katey had a dream about me last night and was thrilled and amazed how sometimes inside and outside magically link up. Renting a two-bedroom house in Rainier Beach, on two-and-a-half acres sloping to Lake Washington, with her nearly 4 year old Son and Boy-Friend Willy, and she was pregnant with his baby. We were welcome to sleep on the couch, or pitch a tent anywhere on the property. I fancied the tent idea, we could be alone, if we only had one.

I would live in Cannon Beach if it wasn't so religious, so conservative, Corbett could play the hotels and golf clubs, and I could make things for the bunchs of tourist shops. But, we had obligations, and headed North on 101 to Astoria, crossed Youngs Bay's low long bridge where the mighty Columbia River meets the Pacific, and East on Highway 30, stopping at Humps Restaurant in Clatskanie for coffee and lemon-meringue pie, then across the Columbia on the Lewis and Clark Bridge to Longview, Mount St.Helens coming to full view on I-5, three rest stops for Gus, and my Folks driveway on Mercer Island, Mom waiting on the porch, smoking a Benson & Hedges. I let her know first thing we would only stay the night. To my surprise and relief it did not ruffle her, she hugged me "That's fine, my Little Girl is home". Gus absolutely adored Dad and followed him everywhere. We gathered around the table for Mom's stuffed peppers, some made specially without meat, and I was emotionally ambushed how tender and deeply satisfying it felt surrounded by these particular people. Even when Dad brought-up marriage "Your Mother and I have been fending off some pretty mean remarks about you two". Corbett became very interested in his food. Mom took over "I tell them, you wait until your kids grow up before pointing a finger. But what I don't understand, since you're planning to be together anyway, what's wrong with making it legal". No matter what I said before, or now, they were listening only to change my mind, Corbett would not step into this, and I would not either "All I'm going to say is, I'm so sorry you have to take these blows for me. And thank you". They did not push. Helping Mom with dishes, Dad

694

took Corbett into the carport and offered a tent, Coleman camp stove, kerosene lamps, cooking pots, utensils. And no argument was made to us sleeping in my bed.

Katey's boyfriend Willy was easy to read, eyes flickering with the same flirty paranoia as Nick, a smooth-operator, with all the right words and things to move in close and sweet-talk you vulnerable before you realize he means to sacrifice your soul on the alter of his ego. Katey was expecting and maddly inlove, and I kept quiet. She had been chosen to take part in the Women In Need Program, the first of its kind in the nation. W.I.N. hoped to make 100 welfare Moms into responsible taxpayers though education, by paying for tuition and books, housing, utilities, healthcare, childcare, transportation, food stamps, cash for necessities, all while they went to school. In her second-year of practical nursing, Katey had transformed from everyday dope-smoker into an eager straight A student, resolved to become self-sufficient, able to provide for her son and one-on-the-way. Having the Boy had given her focus and reason beyond herself, to live up to the best she could do, taking responsibility for her life and progeny, instead of blaming them for it as I saw Gretchen and Keely do, I greatly respected her for this. She had taken the requisite summer job, nurse's attendant at the Kline Galland Home, leaveing before 8AM to bring her Boy to the sitter, coming home exhausted before 6PM. Willy never got up before 11AM, leaving soon after to where-ever he went, eyes hollow, dark circles, complexion ashy, sleeves long in August shouting junkie, probably dealing to support his habit.

We pitched Dad's tent on the only near level spot some fifty-yards from Lake Washington's Western shore, beside five rows of eight marijuana plants, more like sticky bushy trees, taller than Corbett. Gus loved being Mr.Ferocious, every large bug and small had to endure his enthusiastic scrutiny, every Robin, Stellar's Jay, Red Wing Blackbird, Lake Mallard, Dragonfly or Garter Snake a joyous occasion. This was our humble beginning to life in the Northwest, nonetheless we were alone together, our bio-rhythms tuning naively to rising with the sun and bedding with the set, snug in conjoined sleeping bags at the high end of the tent, finding ourselves at the low on waking. No where is Summer better than Seattle's balmy nights and long warm days. We read aloud to each other, played gin rummy, sang songs, wrote songs, made love, swam in the cold lake, picked wild huckleberries and blackberries, and a few buds from MaryJane, fancying ourselves the only ones left alive in the world, Adam, Eve and Cerberus, two weeks passed in simplicity. My 24th birthday, I set the magic teapot on the Coleman for afternoon brew, Corbett strumming the cheap Yamaha Limey gave him, teaching Gus to sing the *Tennessee Waltz*, when he began growling intense and low. Two cops came barging down the path from the house, their guns drawn. Corbett grabbed Gus, teeth bared, spitting, hissing, rigid, ready to die for his Family. The men stood over us, teapot shrieking its whistle, I took it for the burner, and smiling with all I could muster asked "Are you here for tea". Corbett managed a thin grin. The burly cop looked in our tent and holstered his gun. The leaner one did the same. This appeased Gus, who withdrew his teeth. Burly cleared his throat seeming to suppress a smile "What are you kids doing camped in marijuana". I knew only the truth would work, these old soldiers had heard every possible excuse by now and would be pigs or peace officers mostly depending on us. Censoring all sarcasm I looked Burly in the eyes "This is the only nearly level spot on the property". Charmed he insisted "You know you're camped in marijuana". I nodded respectfully "Yes Sir". He motioned to Leaner, who followed him around the plants. Without moving his lips Corbett whispered "I can't believe you". I smiled "Shhhh". Leaner took the path toward the house. Burly circled the tent, and with thumb and forefingers cupping his chin stood over us again "It's plain you two know, but I don't think you're in on the operation. If you want to pull up stakes now and go, my partner and I will be back soon to confiscate the plants". With this he headed toward the house.

Corbett was blown-away by my composure "You're absolutely amazing. I never thought they'd just walk away. Can you believe they didn't bust us". Jumping to his feet, reaching for my hand "Come on, let's blaze". I did not reach, instead looking into his face, his beauty-full worried face "And go where". He shrugged "Don't know, anywhere but here". I patted the blanket for him. Gus took the spot, panting, tongue hanging, proudly looking from Corbett to me, waiting on pets for his extreme valor, like Amaru he owned the heart of a warrior. Corbett folded his long legs and sank-down facing me, stroking Gus ears to tail, waiting. And I knew what to do, pouring hot water into the cups "Look Babe, I'm scared too, but if they were going to bust us, they would of, so we might as well stay put". He leaned forward, "I can't believe you want to". I leaned-in too "They didn't even take our names". Corbett picked-up the guitar "You know your absolutely nuts, right. And I am too for going along with you". Gus's ears jumped to attention, radar nose twitching, he did not bark. Corbett began strumming, dissonant chords matching the dread-full resignation in his voice "I guess were gona find out right now". He started singing *Folsom Prison Blues* as Burly and Leaner arrived, this time armed with black plastic garbage-can bags and lopper shears. Leaner set to cutting the weeds. Burly strode-up smiling "Great song. I play too. Can't say I'm surprised you're still here". I shook my head slow "We just don't have any-where to go for the next few days". He shook his head too "Okay then". Neither gave us another notice, but for Burly flashing the peace sign as they carried-off the goods.

Corbett popped-up like a spring, again offering a hand "You ready to go now". So totally full of my self, not a hair of my old paranoia had raised its ugly shaft, I knew we should go now, someone was going to get busted, taking that hand "Thank you, I am". Packing, I stepped on the guitar and cracked the neck. We drove to a pay phone, Corbett called Newberg, Grace said Limey would be at the farm in Arlington tomorrow, giving address and directions. We decided to go back and wait for Katey. On hearing, her chin trembled in anger "God damn Willy putting me in this". I could not help think her outrage disingenuous, she had to know about the plants "The cops didn't bust us". She took a deep breath "Yeah, but the house's rented in my name". I tried to assure without making it sound okay "These cops seem to know the difference between good guys and bad, but they might not be the ones coming back". She gathered her self "We'll go to my Folks place right now. And I'll try an find Willy, but I don't know where he is". My hand went to her arm, I needed to touch her "Good idea. We're going to my Folks. Look, incase something goes bad with you and Willy, you're always welcome at our place, when we get one. Call my Mom, she'll have our address". Katey stiffened "Wha' do you mean". Hesitating, deciding I owed her the truth "He reminds me of Nick". She gasped at the truth of it.

Returning camp gear to the carport, we spent the night. Gus was over-joyed seeing Dad and followed him to bed. Morning, they went to work. We put our stuff in the Bug, Corbett drove North on I-405 to Highway 9, filling the gas-tank in Clearview, and another 15 miles, standing in-line at the 7-11 for smokes and Pepsi he wallet was not in his pocket, remembering he had payed for gas and set it atop the car while filling the tank. I had not done this, and yet guilt swallowed me, how stubborn and deep my fetters still ran, most of our money was in his wallet, I had as much to lose, and still had automatically, silently deemed him more reliable, more responsible to keep most of it. We drove back, scouring the road sides, and pure joy, there was a brown leather wallet lying on the shoulder, but this one had forty-dollars inside, and belonged to Jarl Sezby. The station attendant solemnly swore he had not seen Corbett's and promised to call if someone turned it in, I left my Folk's number. No mortal could be so good as to turn-in a wallet with over 700 dollars, we resumed North in crushing silence. Again I had to wonder were we going in the right direction, disaster flashing, even the one-hundred-six dollars I had in my bag barely lightened Corbett's load, even when I handed him half, his face remained etched in stubborn guilt.

The Arlington farm's previous tenants raised illegal fighting cocks, tell-tale downy-feathers floated the breezes, abandon cages stacked five high alongside the barn. Thick pines and alders held the property on three sides, a rutty gravel road lead in from the barn to a dry lake-bed where the savage contests took place, now a lonely trampled ghostly meadow, tall grass bleached in summer sun, wildflowers softening the lingering awfuls, nothing of the debacle could have been seen or heard unless you knew it was here. From the barn a gentle curving dirt road wound to the house, built on a hillock close to the two-lane road. Six adults, two Babies and a dog were already occupying three-bedrooms and one-bath. Last to know, last to arrive, we had no where but the small living-room's gracious carpet, the main artery in-and-out, always someone passing through, rude contrast to the Major Motel and MaryJane garden. Everyone else enjoyed some private space, Erik Colleen and Baby in one bedroom, Lorenzo Marion and Baby another, Andrew Jenn and Joey the third, Stoney and Ted the equipment van, Limey a hotel in Arlington. We kept the lost wallet to ourselves.

Half the barn had been walled-off and sound-proofed, and Limey good for his word, had a blonde Baldwin upright waiting for Corbett. Practice began next day, as usual no Chicks allowed in the studio, every one tacitly going along. I named the studio the womb, it caught on, no one got the mock but Corbett. I believed keeping Chicks out would make for ineffectual, sterile music, yet wrapped in the Sweet Sisters web, I went along, letting things develop, staying out-of-the-way or become scape-goat, Bitch, Witch, there was no difference, the same ones who burned us at the stake were calling us Bitch now, I must be care-full not to be convenient cause for any thing still-born. Corbett's time all but taken, I found Jarl Sezby in the Arlington phone book, called and arranged a meeting at the Turkey House near I-5 to return his wallet. An old, lined, and sophisticated farmer, so blown-away finding his Diner's Club card and money intact, he handed me the forty dollars. I gratefully took the reward and stashed it away, a Girl needs a little knipple. Next, I phoned Ida Rose, hoping for a visit. Tom explained she had gone to Juneau Alaska for two weeks, her Grand-Daughter's wedding. There was nothing for me to do, and no discretionary sanctum to do it, save the moss-infested back-porch, too rickety to be safe, over-hanging a ravine snarling in brambles, and therefore all mine. I spent days with Gus and sometimes Jennifer, making Raggedy Ann and Andy for the Babies, dear play-things with finely embroidered faces, wool yarn hair, denim, silk and lace clothes, beaded moccasins, envisioning them cherished companions, threadbare from years of love. I was still optimistic our common prohibition would eventually bond us, yet Marion, Colleen only grew more cliquish, excluding me from trips to the laundromat, grocery shopping, and cooking, always meat.

August was too hot. Gus and I took daily long walks down the shaded two-lane roads, and found Jim Creek. A lazy tree-covered stream where we sat in the cool water, no one ever but us and the birds, and Gus hunting crayfish and whatever wiggled in the shallows, never actually catching any thing. I spent three-dollars of my reward money on Germaine Greer's book, *The Female Eunuch*. Megaera, Alecto, Tisiphone, the winged Furies with their serpentine hair, who pursue and punish doers of unavenged crimes were born whole in me as I read how every natural function of a Woman's body had been made disgusting repulsive nasty unwholesome and ugly. Hair, smell, libido, shape, size, even pregnant, everything must be hidden, plucked, perfumed, bleached, made smaller or larger, all to fit some impossible male fantasy-ideal, effectively castrating us, making us eunuchs, disconnected from our own bodies. This was about the Golden Girl in me, I read every chapter twice, and then left it on the kitchen counter, maybe Colleen, Marion might get curious. And I finished the Ann and Andy, and then found my self walking in circles, going madd, when Corbett presented me a gift. Limey took the Boys to American Music in Seattle to buy an Ampex reel-to-reel, Koss headphones, Shure mics, and other necessities needed for recording, and gave each a one-hundred dollar bill. Corbett bought me a beautiful blonde Guild D-44 guitar. At first irritated at him spending precious money on some thing we did not need, I soon fell inlove with this instrument's full rich voice, and it called my name when I woke in the morning, every day spent on the back porch practicing till my fingers bled and finally callused over. When I was four-teen, listening to Dylan's raunchy voice on the radio, singing as if directly to me, I saved-up, Mom took me to my Uncle's pawn shop, and he let me buy a 1955 Martin D28 guitar for all my thirty-four dollars, one of those things left behind with Nick. I taught my self from books, playing Dylan tunes for hours after school in my room, discovering I had an ear for mak-ing-up simple melodies, and finding that again in these yawning summer days, more little originals. Corbett was impressed, still no matter what I did was marginalized by the Others, my creativity considered arrogant, presumptuous in the face of the Band, when all should be unselflessly given over to them. The question hanging in the air like summer rain, what's wrong with Shoshannah, why doesn't she just get knocked-up like the other Girls.

Recording commenced. And Limey booked a gig at the Medicine Show Tavern on Capitol Hill in Seattle. I so needed my life back, needed ground to call my own or totally lose my mind, reluctantly concluding if Corbett could not, I would take Gus, go stay with my Folks, find a job maybe at Chicken Valley, rent a place and wait for him to complete his commitment. On hearing, he moved us into the open corner of the barn, far as possible from the womb, and no one said a word, betraying how monumental he was to the Band. Just us three, extricating nights from surreptitious eyes and ears did help some. Nevertheless Corbett's head was so into arranging and engineering, he could not know how tedious, how unavailing my days. I retreated into a MaryJane fog, making doing nothing sufferable, even tolerable, quietly hanging around the Women and Children. Marion, when she would speak to me, took to calling me Ms, not Ms.Shoshannah or Ms.Leibofsky, just nameless Ms with too many zzzzs on the end. I knew she was baiting, and so damn persistent I could not help re-acting as if the insults were really generous concessions on her part, for it exquisitely belied how much Women's Lib scared her more than she probably even knew, and consequently how far I had crept under her skin. We were for the-time-being in a mini-version of the larger struggle, a vicious backlash championed by Pope Paul VI and the Vatican to discredit demoralize disregard and confuse the surging of Women toward equality and justice. Marion adopted the Catholic propaganda, a Women's body was made to bear children, her creativity best expressed in suckling, any advocating for contraception or safe and legal abortion was tantamount to murder, childless Women were unnatural, to be pitied and regarded as a dangerous threat. And she made a show of keeping her Baby away from me, even rejecting my gift, insinuating the doll came with a Vodoo curse. When her brother Frank and Amber arrived for a visit, she turned full attention to the soon-to-be Sister-in-law, and summarily dismissed Colleen. Who turned to me. I was sadly grateful for the crumbs.

Frank went and came with Limey, dealing, always leaving a stash of the best for the house, sinsemilla, cocaine, Seconal, the ever present hash oil, and one five-ounce baggie of Psilocybin mushrooms in the freezer. Corbett and I were only interested in the shrooms, waiting a week for any one who wanted to take firsts. None showed any interest, so I put the entire glob of brown fungi in a pot of boiling water, covered, simmered 20 minutes, and set it aside to steep for an hour. Fighting with Marion, Lorenzo joined us without asking. I was loath to share our trip, knowing Corbett would not, could not say no, finding it would not pass my lips either, I poured three cups of tea. We sat on the top step of the front porch watching the sun turn the sky to fire, sipping the buttery pungent brew, waiting, wondering was it too much or too little, and the familiar overture to shrooms, stepping-off into mid-air, the trick was, do not look down.

All light gone from the sky, we were trifles against an infinite ink that suddenly burst into raining ribbons of green neon, the Aurora Borealis inviting us to cross the nocturnal threshold. We felt the need to move, shrooms intensifying, timid yearlings gliding from the porch, venturing the dirt road to the barn, Gus belly-aching, hey you guys what's going on. Bats, I saw white ones out the corner of my sight, never getting a solid look. And Lorenzo was in my head, finding it frightening big fun, reporting news of rabid bats in the area, and of course then we all saw them fill the sky. Grabbing Corbett's hand I ran for the barn, Lorenzo streaking by, swinging the big door shut behind us in vain attempt to bar the swarm. Whatever we thought, what ever spoken-of spawned, all possible nightmares, the dose way to much, we were in for a steep ride, agreeing to be care-full thinking and saying. I asked how was the Band doing, magically transforming predicament into hype talk and live interviews on Dick Cavett, Ed Sullivan, Johnny Carson, opportunity to play for millions, and big money. The bats that made it inside withdrew to the rafters as we traveled this safer mind-scape, till the hype swelled and the barn shrank, and claustrophobia pulled us into an electric night tide, out of the barn and down the gravel road to the killing floor, where giant maples long fallen lay on cock-feathered silt, their gothic roots flung high in the air, towering petrified Medusa heads coming to life. A warm fruity rain began to weep, turning to deluge, filling the dry lake as we ran, shoes sucked-off in the mud, sacrifice left behind racing for the barn, never feeling the sharp gravel on bare feet, not leaving a mark. No matter how vigilant, none of us had been so far-out, and looking down for bearings, looking at anything only initiated a falling, till Corbett mentioned how much his tooth ached, and when he was a star he would find a Beverly Hills dentist and buy the latest 1972 Hollywood smile. Magically transformed, we suddenly all had gleaming chrome teeth smiles big as the grill on a 1950s Buick, Gus too, and anything spoken, our teeth flashed from big red lips and we roared with laughter, breaking the fall, finally floating, staving-off the fire of Hades, like Ida Rose said, *One drop of love or levity would shake a million tons of evil to its very core.* We held to this line, leaning away from the lurking shadows, grinning away, time did not exist, until just like when I was little, Dawn's fingers touched the worn-out moon, monsters running from the light, we had come down just enough for feet on ground, and to re-alize how bad the over-dose, poisoning every joint, our hearts thundering in our wrists.

Lorenzo had a bedroom. Corbett and I took Gus to Jim Creek and let the water wash over our bodies, humbled having been struck by lightning and lived, grateful poisoned was the sole price for so fierce a trip, con-ception by merely thinking and it springs to life, becoming god, we were overwhelmingly relieve none that we knew of had taken on permanent form, creation without responsibility, transgression of the fallen gods, and only our innocence, and likely Gus's, returned us whole, mentally intact, pardoned this once. Still, considering the perils and potential unholy harvest, Corbett and I knew we would not have foregone this rock-et-ride for the world, our feet too heavy, we made it back to the barn, and slept the day. From then I was a full-fledge human being to Lorenzo, holding my own showed something he could respect, no more an evil Witch holding Corbett under her spell, but a worthy Ol'lady for his Friend. And I was no fool, though I considered his approval to-little to-late, crumbs gagging my throat, I smiled amiably, an ally was an ally was an ally was an ally.

For some reason Carvel replaced MoonGoose at the Colonial Inn, and with hostile manager problems still sabotaging Moby Grape, Delroy and Stan flew into Seattle, Delroy to visit Folks, Stan his wife Pam and their Baby Girl who were living in Lake Stevens, fifteen-miles South of us. I sus-pected they also came to see what One Hand Clapping was doing and was there something in it for them. Limey took the Boys to meet the plane, all but Corbett, who needed a break from them. I had composed a melody, he loved it and thought we should jam, taking advantage of an empty studio, playing my D-44, him on the Hammond and foot-peddle bass, round-and-round, cooking to a whirling smooth groove, Corbett pushed the Ampex record button. We were listening to play-back when the Boys came in. Seeing me, Erik exploded "God damn it Hawk. The studio's no fucking play pen for amateurs". High noon, and everyone knew. Corbett stood, six-inches over Erik "We're working on some really cool stuff here man. Shoshy wrote a sweet little tune. You know she's given plenty for the cause, so what's your problem". Not looking up, Erik shook his head

"I don't have a problem man". Joey, Andrew, Ted, Stoney, Stan, Delroy, Limey, even my now good-bud Lorenzo were all silent, complicit, there was nothing to do but walk. Corbett gently took my hand, we stalked the dirt road, Gus at our toes, climbed into the Bug, drove South on Highway 9 through the Snohomish Valley, stopping at a roadside stand for a gallon jug of fresh local apple cider, so delicious, amending our mood. Corbett's appetite for the Band was nearing gone "I'm not sure I want to play with those assholes anymore". And still he apologized for Erik "You know he doesn't really mean what he says. If he knew you better, you know, like Renzo does". I hated him putting words in Erik's mouth "He knows me just fine. If we had our own place, I wouldn' have ta be around him. He's strung-out, Joey too, and maybe Lorenzo. There's no dealing with them like that". Corbett agreed "Yeah, it's every day now, uppers, downers. You never know when they'll bite, you just know they will. I wish Limey wasn't so generous with the merchandise. He thinks he's helping, but coke and Seconal don't make for good music. You just think it does when you're that fucked-up, and no one wants to hear it. Lately I feel like I'm wasting my time. I'll get paid for the Medicine Show. We can use the money to get a place".

More than a year since I'd seen Leda's face, taking a chance calling her Mom. Leda answered, I invited her to the Medicine Show, Corbett would put her name on the guest list at the door, she promised to come. Limey hired a 4PM limo for the Boys, us Girls could follow later. Amber would stay with the Babies, recently speaking in tongues, going Born-Again, giving her life to the Lord, boozers and bars were not something she could to do anymore. I thought it the perfect place to find and prose-lytize sinners, and wondered if she noticed Frank was dealing. Last in the bathroom, I was lucky to enjoy a luke warm bath. Marion and Colleen left without me. I had assumed we would go together on this big important night, and could not wrap my mind around them being so mean-spirited. Driving the Bug into Seattle, raging at the steering wheel "Chump, Polly-anna fucking chump, just grow up will you. This is the last time you will ever look at those jerks as possible Sistas. Like they're ever going to wake up. This is the last time you will ever reach your hand in their direction. They're too mean, too selfish, too scared, and too small-minded".

The Medicine Show was sold-out, only guest-listers allowed. Waiting in line I found my self staring at the man guarding the door, long wavy chestnut hair, full beard and mustache, leathers, looking remarkably like Jake, my Big Brothers girlfriend Marlee's ex-boyfriend, my ultra-strait neighbor who broke down Katey's and my apartment door to save me from ruining my life on weed. Seeing my face, his beamed, and faster than I could avoid, hugged me off the ground, roaring to the night sky "Haa ha haa. You're the Chick that changed my life". Holding me so tight against his body, whiskey mouth pressing hard over mine, plunging a fat sour tongue down my throat, I thought to bite, kick, playing heavy dead instead till he put me down. God damn fucking pig, long hair just lipstick, here he was taking some god-given-male-right to trespass in my life again without asking. I wanted to knee him in his god-givens, but he had the authority to let me in the club or not, smiling nice I put out my hand for the stamp "Jake, what a surprise seeing you here". He branded a black-ink peace symbol on me "Yeah. Wow, you sure look fine. How do you know the band". Smile stitched to my face "I'm with the keyboard player". He let me pass.

So madd I must have glowed red neon, shaken, self-conscious walking-in alone, the lipstick I rarely wore and so liberally put-on to flirt with Corbett smeared across my face, I went to the ladies room to wash-out my mouth, scanning the crowd, no Colleen, Marion, or Leda. After nine and the Band still in their dressing room, I commended my self for dressing-down in jeans and t-shirt, bar full of hounds, single female negotiating the ever-same melodrama, keeping my eyes low, fresh lipstick invitation enough, I found a dark corner asylum. Leda made an impressive entrance, gleaming shameless in a scanty halter-dress blue-electric as her eyes, peacock feathers in her now long blonde hair, silver-glitter on lips shoulders eyelids, silver-glitter finger and toe polish, silver platform sandals. None of her usual demure, the two of us seeming opposites, and still I felt my Sista's power and protection, it was wonder-full to see her. The Band marched from the dressing room to wild intoxication. Corbett last, finding my eyes as he mounted the stage and settled behind his keyboards. Leda and I took the dance floor to *Chantilly Lace*, Sacred Priestesses of the Bacchanalia, effortless, fending-off incubus and comer, doing tequila shots, toasting the MotherTruckers, Amaru, Ida Rose. One Hand Clapping lived-up to themselves, their street-savvy, political, cohesive, unpredictable live performance exalted them sublime, the multitude calling for more, mission accomplished, they still had it. On leaving Leda made me promise, take her to Ida Rose soon. And Corbett, deaf to Erik's braying accusation of deserting the troops, was happy to ride home with me. The Band shined live tonight, recording was not going so well, he made the right choice, I was his long run, and they likely were not.

Sprawling on the front room couch, looking as if they had been sucking lemons, empty beer bottles lined across the coffee-table, ashtray over-flowing, Marion, Colleen growled as we passed to the kitchen. They took a wrong turn, drove endless unlit country roads, finding Highway 9 sixteen-miles North of Arlington, then an awful clanking, engine grinding, they sputtered home praying the whole the way. I made no attempt to wipe gloat off my face, or disguise relishing the delicious cost of leaving me behind, of discounting the simple truth, I had grown-up here and knew my way. As Lance so wisely said to Ava when she tried to trip him and fell instead, karma kickback.

Hung-over bad and so completely full of themselves, the Boys took the day-off to revel in a load of cocaine. Their voices loose and rich from singing all night, Corbett pushed to lay down some vocal tracks. Andrew too. The Others refused, leaving Corbett and me alone in the barn, a sweet slow summer day, stretched-out on sleeping bags zipped-together, talking in caresses giggles and whispers, day-dreaming if only we had money for our own place. Early evening I drove us to West Seattle, for Spud's famous Alaskan halibut cheeks fish'n chips, spending some of the twenty-bucks Limey paid Corbett for the gig. We carried the feast and fries and extra fish for Gus, drenched in fragrant malt vinegar, wrapped in the Seattle Times, across the street to the bleached wooden picnic tables on Alki Beach, where I had taken the purple Owsley and grown too big to fit in the police car. Gus sat on the table, over-looking an army of pushy gulls and more reserved pigeons wrangling for the greasy tidbits. Every salty morsel eaten, we yielded silent witness to Hyperion's seed Helios doing his celestial duty, driving the Chariot of the Sun and those Stallions over the edge of the world, till all but the deepest blue remained in September sky, and the mosquitoes began to bite. Cruising Harbor Avenue on the way home, I pointed to Rachel's and my old apartment, five years now since we had seen each other's face. I wondered how was my old friend.

Morning mail brought Corbett a letter forwarded though his Folks from the Berkeley Police Department, everyone in the house hanging around for him to opened it. I just loved how no one could rush him, reading to him self, no facial expression, allowing everyone's worst fears to full bloom, handing it to me, waiting till I was done to explain he lost his wallet, the drivers license had his Folks address, so it went to the Berkeley Police. Corbett phoned, asking to please have it sent to the Arlington Station. Four days, officer Davis called, Mr.Hawkin's could come get his wallet. We dressed strait as possible. Walking in the station door I flashed-on Nick and William and me that night late going to do laundry in North Bend, those pick-up truck cowboys hunting us with shotguns, running to the police station, the cop seeming to enjoy our fear, dismissing us, and the Texas farmer who shot at Arthur and me, Arlington was kissin-kin to them, to every small-town dominated by landed Good Ol' Boys and their associates. Corbett was not troubled by police, had never a tangle with them, and was in high spirits, the return of his ID meant more than he anticipated, a symbolic and unexpected pardon, sign of better times coming. Officer Davis eyed the driver's license photo and Corbett, then laid the wallet on the counter. It was so fat my heart leapt, could some stalwart soul have returned it full. Corbett's smile blinded me, he counted 636 dollars right there infront of Officer Davis, and handed me 318. I took a local free paper on the way out, looking for rentals. One seemed to have our name on it, $40 a month, pets allowed, we drove right to a stately big old farm house. The landlord's housekeeper directed us into a nearby cow pasture. We tramped fresh-mown clover, stepping over cow-pies, to a man working on the engine of his John Deere tractor. And the snake bit its tail, circle complete, I was exactly where I should be, on the very spot in the entire universe, at precisely the right moment, and this was the only way I knew for sure, Jarl Sezby looked-up from his task, shaking his head, smiling big. I told the tale of Corbett's wallet, so like us finding his. He had sworn never rent to Hippies again, but the little house next to his was ours. We moved that afternoon, into a gas station and real estate office cobbled together and partially remodeled, caring about no thing more that the 72-inch perfect milk-white porcelain claw-footed bathtub, and being alone. I lit the candelabrum Gretchen gave us for Christmas, poured enough lavender bubble-bath in the running water, and we lingered in the voluptuous potion till all the hot was drawn. Gus nosing every crack and corner of the house, reporting in snorts and wags, every thing under his complete patrol.

Not two miles from the farm, compared to the tent and barn our humble home was grand. A long dirt driveway lead to the back door, the entrance inside through a windowless storage room stacked in sealed cardboard boxes, old plumbing fixtures, firewood, cobwebs, and things that sleep during the day, and in another door to a generous kitchen, fresh painted welfare-green, polyester lime Jell-O mixed with Cool Whip, so many low-rents were this color, it had to be a major mixing mistake sold on the cheap. Counter-tops and floor gray-speckled commercial linoleum, the sink had a wonderful large window looking South toward the milk barn, a droning old refrigerator stood a bit lopsided next to the oh-my-god gleaming extra-large extra-fancy brushed-stainless-steel gas stove and grill with two deluxe ovens, plainly for a restaurant. The real estate office porch now a dining room glassed-in on three sides, facing West across the grazing cow pasture to sunset, a king-size bed took most of the low-ceiling and yet to be painted bedroom. Ancient oil furnace filled one end of the long narrow living room, the front door at the other dropping-off four feet to the ground, no steps yet. Furniture, cupboards, closet, floors, everything but the windowless entry room immaculate and smelling clean. Corbett and my relationship was strained on many levels, but all tender little mercies returned to our life, intimate mornings lying in bed listening to crows talking, cows mooing, unhurried cups of coffee, uninterrupted conversation. I would take him to the farm at noon, some one brought him home by 7 or 8 or 9 or ten. So it was Gus and me, and my sewing machine on the dining room table, such excellent light in this room. I commenced the hunt for materials, finding the Arlington VFW Thrift Shop, a 2nd floor back-stairs walk-up hole-in-the-wall that needed paint, whose hand-written sign read, open Mondays 10AM to 4PM. I could not have imagined, fabrics to rival Monique and Loretta's, scrupulously gathered over lifetimes by consummate seamstresses whose daughters and sons plainly did not value the art, no matter how beautifully made, they did not sew, did not want to sew, had not the talent, and/or had been ridiculed wearing home-mades to school, and felt a real sense of release, and some guilt in getting rid of tell-tale reminders, but for a good cause, the VFW. Mondays I was waiting at ten sharp, and bought every sewing basket, carved crochet hook, pin cushion, thimble, bag of buttons and trim, every remnant piece and bolt of fabric, lace, embroidered napkin, tablecloth and handkerchief. Gus loved the familiar hum of my machine, one of few constants since he moved-in with us, lying content by my foot-peddle when not attending his vocation, policing the house for certain brazen field rodents who believed they held prior claim. Andrew and Jenn came for dinner one time. After, we lit cigars and walked West through fresh-baled alfalfa, leaned on the fence and waited for sun set, laughing, words now guarded, essentially empty, our bond fallen casualty to the battle, though Jennifer had finally warmed to Gus.

One whole flowing month the world was my way. Mid October Cyrene took me up on a-safe-place-to-land, moving her Self, her Son, a U-Haul load of stuff and Stanley into our long narrow living room. At the same time, unable to get on-tape what they did so well live, One Hand Clapping was falling apart, Ralph Gleason lost interest, Limey was too, the stipend he doled the Boys drying-up, Erik's abiding hype no longer enough to stoke the fire, Corbett and Lorenzo decided it was time to resurrect the duo, this time calling themselves the Socko Brothers, they began looking for work. And as life sometimes does, saying yes my dear you are going in the right direction, we gathered for Mom's birthday dinner at the Bleu Dolphin Restaurant, Dad and the Owner were acquainted from Synagogue, and he bragged-on Corbett, who was invited to audition at the baby grand, three songs and the Socko Brothers had a job, Tuesday through Saturday in Bellevue Washington. Gloria Burnett, the lounge manager and true music lover, made sure the Seattle Times critic knew there was talent in town.

After Dark by Ed Baker
   Almost all lounge groups play rock, and quite a few play standards, and

some play novelty tunes.

Then there are the Socko Brothers. They play rock, standards, originals, country, blues, barrel house boogie, and "Hand me down my walking cane".

The Socko Brothers are not brothers. They are Lorenzo Biancalana and Corbett Hawkins, Californians who were touring with One Hand Clapping until it disband recently in the Seattle area. The duo have been at the Bleu Dolphin in Bellevue ever since.

Rarely are they stumped in fielding requests for anything from "Rag Mop" to "Proud Mary" to a Hank Williams foot stomper.

The Socko Brothers seem to be having great fun. So do the customers who listen or dance, or try to stump the twosome with requests.

Stanley spent his time in Seattle trying to find a gig and place to live. We still clashed like bighorn sheep. But it was fun having Cyrene, for a week, then some fang-tooth Harpy took her, she started insisting Stan join the Socko Brothers. There was never talk of a job, only temporary place-to-land, Stan took Corbett aside assuring there was no illusions, after all he and Lorenzo were both drummers. Corbett approached Owner anyway, to hire Stan as a stand-up singer, Stan was a really good singer, but then so were Lorenzo and Corbett. Owner could not be impressed, even with rave Moby Grape magazine reviews and their celebrated record album laid on his desk, for unlike Gloria, he did not value talent, only profit, and saw no reason to pay another salary, even someone famous as Stan, when the Socko Brothers were packing the house every night. This was the proverbial straw, Cyrene disappeared completely into bitter Harpy, Corbett should have issued an ultimatum, hire Stan or quit, and since Owner was an acquaintance of Dad, this was somehow my fault. I knew she was scared, having been so sure life would become easy with Stan taking care of her and her Boy, but a musician's life was never secure no matter how famous, her expectations and rage had us sneaking around our own home, anything said or done twisted into justifiable retaliation, all past kindness forgotten. Four days holding our breath, no choice but to move-out, I started looking in the papers for place, maybe closer to Bellev-ue. Stan made earnest effort, willing to do any thing to get their life going, often apologizing for Harpy's maddness. I gained some respect for him as he tried many times explaining to her, there was never a promise of work, just a couch to sleep on till they got their legs, and she should be grateful. Harpy did not want explanation, only security. I felt for her Boy, and her, Stan had a wife and child not 12 miles from here, but she was fast becoming too callous to feel, I just wanted to go far away. Stanley delivered our reprieve, a friend in Seattle with an empty basement, they would move immediately. I wished them well on their way. Cyrene did not respond, biting acrimony following her out the door like a servile bitch. Corbett and I were not surprised how quickly the soft sweet rhapsody of our life again carried-on its singing.

Pacific Northwest Bell installed a phone, and I called Leda. Cyrene had been calling too, begging her move into a house with them, together they could afford the rent. Desperate to get away from her Mom, Leda said yes, and then panicking I would take this as betrayal, for Cyrene was actively slandering my name, tried assuring me we were true friends by blabbing a confidence "You know her Mom was homeless when she had Cy. They lived in San Jose shelters and on the street for ten years. Imagine. I'm sure that's why she freaked-out on you. Not having her own place and all…". I knew this was suppose to explain, even excuse the awful behavior, and it was persuasive, and I wanted to, but deep down a voice said the story was not a confidence really, but intended to be passed-on, and I just did not give a shit, we all have our bigger or smaller piles of crap, and my friendship and love could take just so many cuts, and then die of the wounds. In relation to my friends I knew my crimes, mainly a heartfelt duty to tell truth as I saw it, even when they did not want to hear. Everyone road their drama, most with manic highs, tragic lows, a bucking bronco that allowed almost zero focus on anyone but themselves, I was a fool to expect my motivations were seen. Anyway, the truth according to Shoshannah Leibofsky was often too heavy on an already over-loaded nervous system. I was learning to keep my mouth shut, sleeping dogs, unknowingly unconscious, if woken would surely snarl and bite. They wanted subterfuge, mendacity to support denial, their pain to terrible to face, and I did not blame them their slumber. Still I was tired of under-standing Cyrene. Yes I expected too much of my friends, and yes an unconscious complex had ahold of her, but she did not have to be so vicious, to me this was not due to circumstances as I was lead to believe, but to character. I knew Leda's Mom, and her need to get away, could hear the beseeching as she blabbed on "You know Brian got busted. I think he took the fall for Limey. And he skipped bail, got away to London. April thinks Limey gave him ten grand, a fake passport and ID. You know she lost custody of her Boy to her Parents. I feel really bad for her…". Waiting for an opening I made it easy "You know, it's fine with me that you get away from your Mom any way you can. And I really don't give a shit what Cyrene is saying about me. You be careful though, she can turn on you too".

Shopping Safeway for groceries, someone put a flyer for the annual Arlington VFW garage sale on the Bug's windshield, we decided to check-it-out. Finding a well wrought brass bird-cage, a portable electric heater, four gorgeously embroidered linen table cloths, three goose-down pillows, pea-coats just our sizes, and a 1940's tux jacket with silk faille shawl collar just Corbett's. Waiting in line to pay, an apple basket with a sign, free puppies. Corbett scooped the lone black poodle pup in one hand, dark eyes shining a mix of defiance and curiosity, no words necessary, she was coming home to Gus. Love at first sight, some one thinking Dog thoughts, nose to nose, better than the beach, Gus went a courting, showing off, sharing his know-how. And she was a precocious little sponge, learning to fix a penetrating stare when she wanted out, sitting close beside him, mimicking the precise angle of his head, supplicating eyes so irresistible, easily winning her way onto laps, couches, chairs, and the bed at night. Corbett nor I considered begging at the table noble enterprise for a Fur-heads, Gus knew he would eat from his own dish when we ate, still the smell of people food drove him crazy and he figured exactly how to wangle tidbits while I cooked. She stole all his move to great success. And they chased the other endlessly, chasing anything, dancing on their back legs play fighting, licking faces and other places, sleeping close. She was such a winsome urchin, long sweeping eyelashes, long tail, curly hair that kinked round her ears and face, she would be two-thirds of Gus full-grown. At first Corbett called her Gretta, thinking it sounded cute. Argus was sort of mine, I named him, this one sort of Corbett's, he had naming rights. I was always so pleased being named after my Father's Mother, Ashkenazi Jewish refugee, necessary Woman Warrior, died before I was here, I always felt I was given her spirit along with her name. And it wasn't just hers, but her Mother's Mother's, and no one knew before her, Jews are named for the last dead, I thought a name should be more than cute, I said nothing. Corbett shortly began calling her Gretel, which I found better. Then one very late night after a raucous show at the Bleu Dolphin, trying to unwind, drinking a beer and watching *Son of Kong* on TV, the big gorilla's scion looked so much like Gretel, he thought she needed a bigger name, Gretel became Gorilla, that sweetened to Grilla, which sounded right, Gus and Grilla. We had not fathomed how starved for companionship Gus was, when leaving him alone at home or in the car, even a small while, he was so all-over us on return, crying, frenetic, complaining, trying to never let us out of his company. Now with the lovely Grilla, he would greet us genuinely eager, but all that frantic desperation was gone, he had a life. We were simply surrogates, albeit good ones, still the secret knowledge Isis received in return for lying with the great angel Amnaël, *wheat creates wheat, and a man begets a man, and thus also gold will harvest gold, like produces like*, and later in the story of Noah, they went in pairs, not only to propagated the species, but the absolute necessity for communion, like needs like, face to face, no different from me and Corbett. Gus taught his beloved to sing the *Tennessee Waltz*. And she grew, such a wiggley-puppy I called her Little Fish, and so she became Grilla-Fish, now that was a name. And, she was smarter than Gus in some selfish ways. If she wanted something of his, a ball, a bone, a Milk-Bone, she would scamper from the room, Gus delighted, certain to give chase, she would race back and take what she wanted. Despicable little Bitch were she human, but in a Dog, I found selfish highly intelligent and entirely admirable.

Limey paid October rent on the farm before disappearing. November first the steadfast troop that was still One Hand Clapping moved into the Madrona Beach vacation cabins on Camano Island, 15 mile Northwest of us, they looked enough like loggers to pass on Camano for other than Hippy, and the off-season rate of forty-dollars a month all they could afford. The one room, wood-stove, no electricity log cabins were well compensated by free fire-wood, a daily bonanza on your own beach of clams and mussels for the picking, salty brisk air and breath-taking sunsets over the Straits of Juan de Fuca. Any work but music insufferable affront to their brittle egos, the Boys stayed home, digging shell-fish, stoking fires, babysitting, jamming, waiting-on the next big deal, haunting the Bleu Dolphin weekends, drinking on the Socko Brothers tab, never sitting-in. Marion and Colleen took minimum wage jobs at Twin City Food vegetable packing plant on the Island. Mid November Andrew and Jenn came by for one more dinner on their way South. He had written and gotten a grant to study Cuneiform at UC Santa Cruz, they would be living on campus. Never ever mentioning even a hint of this, still I knew there was more to Andrew than playing jug. Thanksgiving, temperature dipping below freezing, the oil furnace on all the way, no insulation, only half the long narrow living room was warm enough. I worried Gus and Grilla-Fish would tangle with the escalating population of rodents stealing in for warmth, and lose. The portable heater blew-out when I plugged it into the bathroom wall. The bedroom roof leaked. And, an unremitting sour ripe stink seemed to have direct route from the milk barn into the house. We'd grown beyond this humble.

Driving Highway 9 South through the Snohomish Valley to my Folks Thanksgiving dinner, feeling the peace here always got us wishing to move, this time Corbett swung-off the exit into Snohomish for a local paper. Only one place listed, rural farmhouse, senic view, wall-to-wall carpet, retired, no kids, sixty-dollars, pets okay, no address or phone number, just a post office box to send a letter, the top three would be contacted. Corbett sat down in the morning to apply, his occupation music teacher, mine seamstress, not retired but no kids. I went to Jarl for a letter of reference. Five shivering days, and congratulations, you are in the top three, call for an appointment. West off Highway 9 the Lowell-Larimer road hugged the South hill of the Snohomish Valley. Half-mile in, we had passed only three mailboxes and their weathered farm-houses, around a gentle bent, there it was, Rural Route One Box 106A painted in neat black letters on a new aluminum mailbox, its two-story old house painted welfare green. One-hundred yards more, Rural Route One Box 106, and up the driveway to a large modern rambler. Opening the door to Freaks, Landlady's eyes widening, and still she politely showed us the house. Front porch steps facing North, front door into an enormous living-room, two sweeping picture window looking North across the Valley to Mount Baker, Cas-

714

cade Mountains to the East. Kitchen big enough for a table and 4 chairs, a big window looking East. The room off the kitchen had the Northern view. Bathroom with tub and separate shower. New washer and dryer in the laundry room. And out the back door, a dilapidated little place used for storage, just like the one behind the Charles Street house, built to live in till the main house was ready. Pear, apple and plum trees filled the back land, thick pines and maples standing the slope. And there was a three bedroom upstairs, the largest with a walk-in closet, all boasting a fabulous panorama. This had been Landlady's parents' home till they died, she had raised three Babies here, all long fledged, her Husband build the new place next door, with a swimming pool, the reason for retired with no kids, she wanted no worry they could wander over and drown. To my absolute surprise, she offered us the place, we could move in day before Christmas. After signing an agreement, paying first last and one-hundred damage, and the receipt safely in my bag, I could not help my self "If you don't mind me asking, why did you rent to us". She looked me square "Well, my best asset has always been intuition, and I have an intuition". Then her eyes began to dance "And I happen to know Jarl Sezby".

Every work-night Lorenzo came by for Corbett, desperate to move from the Camano Island cabin, he pursued all possibility, no one would rent to a Long-hair. Our good news got no best wishes, only an urgent plea for Corbett to speak to Jarl. Who took Corbett's word without reservation. Lorenzo had the gas station real estate office shoved together for Christmas.

Morning before our move, I woke to that unmistakable hush, it was snowing. Corbett exhilarating as it piled, taking me back to my first time in Sugar Fairy Land. By noon the flat-white sky blew South, not a straight line anywhere on the downy landscape, we pulled-on our pea-coats. Running out infront of us, Gus and Grilla-Fish found themselves completely buried, yipping, squealing, biting the snow, they could not grasp how everything had changed and ran back in. Corbett and I built his first snowman, solid, fat, taller than me, pearlized chocolate-brown coat buttons eyes, wooden sock-darner nose, grin of black olives, our corn-cob dope pipe to puff-on, three yards of tie-dye Egyptian cotton wrapped round his neck, no hat, although Corbett did consider his mink-brown Stetson fedora with the black grosgrain ribbon hatband for a time. Then it was icicle wars, broken from the eaves, and raising snow forts, and arsenals of snowballs. Corbett totally creamed me, I thought with a bit too much zeal though I got my licks in. Soaked, exhausted, we all but poached ourselves in a hot bath, and crawled in bed early.

Braying choir, the house jostled from all sides, an eerie bristling sound woke us. Gus, Grilla-Fish would not jump down from the bed, barking cowards. Me too. While Corbett possessed this bold curiosity that some-times crossed into frivol, he was on his feet. I followed to the dining room, nervous Hounds on my heels, I had never seen them act like this, for some reason it made me smile. Luna was full, lighting the snow like a sound-stage, and the frantic brown eyes peering in the windows. Cows, lots of them, crowding the house, so much bigger up-close, bawling, disorien-tated, their fence downed in the snow. We started laughing and could not stop, living some Twilight Zone episode, none of us brave enough to venture through the massive creatures to tell Jarl, our phone already disconnected, we stayed-up and packed, fearing the house would not en-dure. Jarl arrived first light, annoyed we had not come for him, and totally amused by our cow-fears.

Chapter Twenty Nine

BECOMING DELICIOUS

Hard morning rain dissolving the snow, and then sunshine arcing a double rainbow, exposing what's just beneath the everyday, like the New Years Eve moonbow, it had us standing silent awe, another unmistakable magical exclamation pointing to what was coming. Loading the Bug, Lo-renzo rolled-in, equipment van half-full of his belongings, and our Bald-win. Corbett introduced him to Jarl, they shook on an arrangement, free rent and Lorenzo would fix up the place, he was a very good carpenter, I thought Jarl got the best of the deal. Ours was such a nice warm mid-dle-class house, Rural Route 1 Box 106A felt as if we had been admitted to The Club, so big, so many electric baseboard heaters, so overwhelmingly empty, no bed, no reason to use the upstairs master-bedroom, we would sleep on the front-room wall-to-wall. Unpacking, arranging kitchen and bathroom, Lorenzo showed with the piano, he and Corbett managed it to the spare-room off the kitchen, it was solid oak, really heavy, had been a school piano, the little wheels built into the bottom no longer rolled. We had nothing to eat or drink, Corbett offered "Pizza and beer on me". Renzo's laughed, or was it scoff "Thanks Hawk, but you know, The Wife and Kid, it's Christmas Eve". I just screamed deep inside that Corbett let this slide-by without even a slight twinge, didn't he understand how it insulted me, and right here in my own kitchen, no matter my feelings for Marion, it insulted her too, I swore on my life I would never be anyone's The Wife. Oh yes and The Holiday, it kind of slipped my mind, likely because I always felt so completely surrounded and brow-beaten by The Holiday. And then there were the Merrys, assuming every one is equally consumed with The Spirit. I had long-ago learned to just say thank you rather than explaining I do not celebrate, and sometimes oh Happy Chanukah to you too. Not one person, no matter how oh Happy Chanukah to you too they tried to seem, took this well. We made it to Olsen's grocery for staples and Coors before it closed for The Holiday. One small glass, and the cows, and moving caught me, I zipped our sleeping bags together on the well-padded wall-to-wall and laid down, Gus and Grilla-fish snuggling close to my shoulder, Corbett sat down close to the other, smoking our new brand of cigarettes, Merit Lights, he finished the beer.

Chirping hinges on the front door woke me, I knew at once it was too late, before I could breath, in swept the Hell-Serf, tall, pale, intense, and so stale, so hackneyed, I felt a flicker of contempt in my frozen fear. He glided caross the room as if on hidden wheels, bowing, flourishing the expected black silk cape lined in red, and kneeling sank those bulging fangs into my neck. I grabbed for hair, he jerked away, I grabbed ears, pulling his face to my mine, biting his disgusting nose, tasting blood. This foul beast was stunned, springing back with such elegance, flying-away with such momentum, sucking the door-slam behind him. The impact woke me, Morpheus lingering as I looked around, not sure, exactly where I was. Vampires, condemned till death to the Dark, and this made all the more terrible having been first born to Sol, for once you've seen the Light how great the Darkness. Epiphany stripped the veil of my fear, it was never the Dark, it was about losing the Light. Corbett softly snoring beside me, Gus and Grilla-Fish too, I remembered where I was, and needed to check the door, still locked. And then to the bathroom mirror, fumbling for an unfamiliar light switch, finding no mark on my neck or blood in my mouth. I lit a Merit, and gently nudged Corbett's shoulder till he grumbled "What". Listening to my dream, he wrapped tender arms and legs round me, and I knew at once it was too late, before I could breathe his grip tightened, and growling softly on the inhale he stole a taste of my neck. Jumping clean out of my wits, I shoved him and shot to my feet, every hair on me prickling. Their ruffs prickling too, and all the way down their backs, heads low, eyes burning, my trusty Hounds rumbled their intent. Corbett sat-up quickly and attempted to control his amusement "I'm sooo sorry Sweetheart, it was just a joke. A lame joke". I did not care, he knew my fears, it was not even a little funny, how dare he play-on them "God damn you. Just god damn you having fun at my expense. You gave me the creeps. How can I ever trust you again". Chastened and still amused he put his big tarantula hand over his big heart "I promise I will never trifle with your fears again". I lit another smoke and sat down facing him, my best friend who wasn't so trustworthy when drinking "Don't ever make me sorry that I tell you my secrets. Monsters have always laid-in-wait for me. Even when I was too little to remember, they lived in my room. No one saw them but me. I had to stay awake all night with the help of lights and my radio, till they were driven off by the morning light. They still wait for me, just beyond the corner of my eyes. But it's okay now, cause I understand the compensation, if they didn't want me, I wouldn't be worth getting. Being worth getting makes it better". Corbett asked one simple question "Is a vampire bite the worst thing that could ever happen to you". I nodded "Yeah, it would mean losing the light". He reasoned "Then the worst thing that could ever happen has just happened. So you have nothing more to fear". Now I was amused, for some where deep inside this made perfect sense, they never touched me till now, and this one, somehow so akin to Nick, I had bitten him back.

Landlady knocking after 9AM, we had no phone, Mom called her to please relay, they were coming over with the whole ball-of-wax. Sure of

718

well-meaning, I could not stop resentment flooding me. Fleeing Nick was good motive for going South, but there was also freedom from Parental prerogative, and moving North may have signaled green-light-go, Mom was not going to give us even 48 hours to make our place ours before making it hers.

Like fresh-baked bread, a warmth fragrance came in with their big loving smiles, arms lade in the whole-amazing-ball-of-wax. Dad had the baked ham, the bone-in kind, basted in Coka-Cola, with cloves and pineapple rounds and Maraschino cherries garnishing its perfectly browned crust, Mom the green beans, candied yams, and her home-made New York cheesecake, no sugar of course. And Chanukah gifts, and a two-foot tall live Blue Spruce Christmas tree in a green plastic pot. Corbett's eyes glittered like first snow, and I saw the wonderfulness of my Mom in them, her understanding Christmas had been one of those temporary respites that sustained his miserable childhood, and because he and I agreed on not making a big deal of religious rituals, I would never have known how much this meant to him. I spread a beautiful linen tablecloth on the front room rug where a dining table would have been, and lit the candelabrum. My Family never ate on the ground. Mom played good sport, but even with a velvet floor cushion under him, Dad eating on the floor was just plain awkward. No matter, Christmas dinner was perfect, even Mom let me off without a slice of pig's thigh. We all ignored the cheesecake's bitter Saccharin after-taste. And as it happened every time we saw them, marriage came up, when were we going to stop playing house. Corbett and I had agreed to let them speak their mind, and say no more than we'll think about it. This time Dad added a $1000 bribe to the already offered bedroom-set and kitchen-set of our choice. We promised to think about it. And opened Chanukah presents, chocolate gelt and a $50 Nordstroms gift certificate. With no repose but the floor, Mom and Dad bid us an early good-night. As I put left-overs away, Corbett eating another piece of ham demurred "So what do you think, should we get married, make a public commitment". I smiled "So you want me to be The Wife. I love you but no thanks. I won't ever be The Wife". Stung, he shot me a look "Shoshy I'm not one of those guys. I was only thinking out loud. My student loans, JCPenney account, the car payment, you know, it would be nice to have a bed off the floor and table to eat on". I was not persuaded "Me too. I just can't see why some authority other than you and me needs to have a say over us".

Such emphatic I won't ever, often a certain harbinger for I will, declaring seems so easy, almost without thinking, but in actuality never is. Our first mail on Rural Route 1 Box 106A came from Corbett's Parents, a seriously religious Christmas card with an offer of $1000 to get married, contingent of course on my conversion, something my Folks never asked for though I knew they wanted Corbett to. My voice echoed the walls of our big empty home "Why would I want to be anything but Jewish. They might as well ask me to rip my face off. Do they think Jewish is something you can just change like a dirty dish towel. It's in my blood. The audit Eddie did for me, I've always been a Jew, and that just fine with me. Can you just imagine me kneeling infront of that Jesus hanging on the cross, knowing he wasn't suppose to die. Can you just see me confessing sins to a priest who believes girls are second-class citizens. Imagine me believing in Hell, living in that kind of guilt and fear. No way. What I do here and now is the real deal for me, what really counts. It's simple, you need more credits than debits in this life to get out of here, that's it. My life's not a trial run for Heaven, oh yeah I forgot, go to Purgatory first, and then maybe the big reward, but only if you been properly humbled, you know, the on you knees kind, that's the way into your Parents' heaven, on your knees. No thank you, I don't want to go. Fuck them.". Corbett wisely let the storm blow itself out, and gently reminded "I'm on you side Shoshy. I know my Folks're energy vampires, masters at producing exactly this reaction. They've done it to me a million times. You don't want to give them what they want, do you". He used his radio DJ voice "Can't you just see tomorrow's headline. Jewish girl from Mercer Island, after taking LSD, joins the revolution, runs away with a rock'n roll keyboard player, finally sees the light, gives-up living in sin, converts to Catholicism and gets married". Corbett knew how to make me laugh, how to enervate the poison that came in the Christmas card. Like Ida Rose said, *one drop of love or levity would shake a million tons of evil to its very foundations.* It was time for a visit.

Day-breaking through the living room curtains, this was not a dream, my eyes wide open, watching as if through high-powered binoculars as

720

the ceiling gave-way and an enormous horse-shoe-shaped judge's bench came into focus, a floating parabola eons too big for any room, where countless former humans, most with their heads leaning toward another's, solemnly conferring, sitting in comfortable chairs around the curve and out far beyond what I could see. I was told this is where we go after death, to face the Crucible, which will hold each human accountable, not by God or Gods but by a host once human like you, they are called the Council of Essence, and Jesus the Jew was not the first to be seated. Their duty, to subject all who come before them to the Cosmic Crucible, that separates each human's golden untarnishable substance built on personal responsibility and integrity from the dross. And if gold is found, that individual personality will go on. And if not, their purified remains will be spread across the earth to fertilize humanity, finally resolving the reincarnation cycle. I understood reincarnation to be on-going, always realizing another flesh-bound walk in one form or another, again and again, the lack of character not being a finality. Once, in a far-ranging conversation with Ida Rose on reincarnation, she pointed-out that John D.Rockefeller Senior understood very well how to manipulate the process and come into his fortune time and again. And that after World War II and just before his death, General George Patton made known his still unwavering conviction that in his present incarnation he had failed to fulfill the role he came for, that after marching into Germany to defeat Hitler, he had pleaded with General Eisenhower to let him continue all the way to Moscow while he could, to vanquish the Russians once and for all, finally changing the course of history. Eisenhower said no. If this Council of Essence was the new criterion I had screamed in outrage for, and it was founded on conscious integrity, if Jesus was a standard illuminating these proceedings, and if Yahweh who according to Ida Rose was the best of the whole poor lot of Gods, yet could be so readily conned by Satan into a pissing match over Job, if He and the other Gods of that venerable ilk were no longer sovereign, and human dross instead of automatically manifesting its protean mutations again and again on earth, reeking havoc, was transubstantiated into nourishing humus, then I would gladly continue being one more *stalwart voice crying continually for justice and willing to accept the consequences.* Gradually, and with inconceivable speed the panorama withdrew and only the ceiling remained, my mind racing, quick, quick before reason rushes-in to qualify the impossible, I woke Corbett to tell. He had only one question "So who chooses these judges". As if being told, I knew "They choose themselves by what they do here. In a true Democracy, the rules are the same for all, each Justice has to stand before the crucible too. It's their own gold that make them eligible. It's not a permanent position, and there are so many, no one or group can hold sway".

Using the Holidays as good motive, I made Ida Rose a tie-dye silk-velvet shawl lined in liquid-gold silk, finished in a generous hand-tied gold fringe, it was gorgeous and I could hardly wait for her to have it. We were ready by 1PM for delivery when a timid hand knocked on our door. Katey stood on the porch gripping her little Boy's shoulder, cheekbone bruised and swollen, so very pregnant. She began apologizing "I got yer address from yer Mom. You said if I ever needed a place". I rushed to embrace her "I'm jus' glad we were here". She sighed and leaned against me "I wouldn't have but Willy knows where I go. I had no place else". Corbett squatted down face-to-face with the Boy, using his Popeye the Sailor Man voice "Hey thar matey. Ca'mon aboard, Gus 'n Grilla-Fish er waitin fer ya". Boy giggled "Grilla-Fish". Corbett nodded "Yep matey, that's er name har har". Boy searched his face "What's a Grilla-Fish". Corbett offered his hand "Let's go see". If Katey could find us, so could Willy. I hurried next door, to make sure it was okay with Landlady for friends to stay a while, and to call Mom, telling her absolutely do not give our address to anyone else. We carried-in her well planned ahead of time load of things, and Katey told the story. Willy had been busted, was out on bail waiting trial, drinking more and more, he began hitting her, though never threatening the Boy or her belly till now, accusing it wasn't his, that she was just a whore. She went to her Folks, but unwed and pregnant again, her Dad said get out, and her Mom did not dare a contrary word. I whispered "You want to call the police". She was adamant "No. Willy might find me from the report, find you". I snarled "I'm not afraid of Willy". She smiled for the first time "The trials next week. I'm pretty sure he'll go to jail right after, if he sticks around. It's my last two semesters of school I'm really worried about. It means my freedom, a good life for my Kids, and Willy's so mad they didn't arrest me too, he'd love nothing more than to ruin it for me somehow. School doesn't start for a while, but I need a permanent address to stay eligible for W.I.N., and get ready for this Baby". Gus and Grilla-Fish made Boy an honorary member of the pack, letting him play a bit too rough without consequences. And Corbett, his Grand Wizardness, using the same potent magic he conjures on stage, beguiled the wounded Little One, mimicking Donald Duck and Mickey Mouse and Porky Pig, anguish and confusion becoming gales of laughter, even Katey smiled. Still she was so pregnant I feared something could happen to the Baby "If you want I can take you to County Hospital". She shook her head emphatic "No. I'm okay. He only hit my face. I'm just tired and my feet are killing me". It was obvious she was sapped, while Corbett and the Youngling carried stuff upstairs, and pumped-up air mattresses she brought, I took her to the kitchen for chamomile tea, a thick ham sandwich and cheesecake. Grateful, ravenous, she ate standing at the counter, tears falling on the plate. I quietly gave her space, feeling the weight on her feet, wishing I had a chair to offer. And when the mattresses were ready, apologizing, she excused her self and the exhausted Boy upstairs. Lorenzo would come to get Corbett for work at 8PM, and I wanted to deliver the shawl, so I left a note, please eat whatever you want, the Dogs will deal with anyone uninvited, we would make the trip quick. Corbett drove to Seattle, and worried "Here we go again, people living with us". I nodded "Yeah, believe me Katey can be awful, but I know she won't turn into Cyrene". He got defensive "I'm not saying she shouldn't have come". I smiled "I know Babe. We'll give her some time to catch her breath, then help her find a place".

Ida Rose's Daughter, Son-in-Law and Grandson were there for the Holiday, and her Granddaughter and Husband from Alaska, and I felt a blushing embarrassment singe my cheeks, interrupting her Family. She was delighted "Oh wonderful, my little Lambs are here". Hurrying us in from the cold, into the living room festivities, where under the classic Christmas tree was a large package wrapped in silver foil, tied with big blue and white satin ribbons, with our names on it. So many more important people, I never imagined a present, my heart spilled all over me as Corbett undid the box, one-dozen beautifully sparkling Waterford crystal tumblers. I handed her the shawl, anxious, worrying while she unwrapped it, what was I thinking, would this woman even wear a tie-dyed shawl. Casting it around her shoulders, thrilled, her smile blazing "Oh Shoshannah, I would recognize your fine work anywhere. This must be the most exquisite gift anyone has ever made for me". I wanted to fly across the room and hug her, the shawl would have to do it for me "Thank you, I'm so glad you like it". At Ida Rose's behest, and over the worries of her Family, Tom had moved from his bachelor pad to the lovely light basement of the white brick house. As Principal Auditor, it was best to have him near. This was not mother-son, teacher-student, not renter-rentee, but a collaboration of fierce warriors and fast friends, and I liked him being there, with his formidable spirit, his youth, guarding her threshold. As we moved into the dining room, around the big mahogany table for egg-nog and slices of home-made Napoleon brandy fruitcake, I thought maybe I should introduce Leda to Tom, when we got some furniture, I would invite them to dinner. Granddaughter and her Spouse, the whole Family so close-mouthed at any mention of Ida Rose's work, I was hoping to talk about the Council of Essence, but did not. Corbett felt it too and gave me a let's go look. I nodded in the same imperceptible way Mom and Dad did with each other. Corbett invited them to the Bleu Dolphin to here him play, then gracefully excused us, he must get home and prepare for work. Tom and Ida Rose walked us to the door. She spoke softly "You are so wonderfully perceptive. My Family does not hold a great deal of stock in my work. I think they would rather I devote myself to them, be more of a Mother and Grandmother. I must admit to neglecting them some for my work. So I try not to say much when they are here". She took the top copy from a neat stack of papers on the hallway table "You kids should have this. I call it *The Great Enigma*. Information sifted from many audits. I have decided to include it in my new book *The Comedy and The Tragedy*, and have made photo copies for all my students". We thanked her. And then she spoke my favorite words, honey words, heroin words, hallelujah words, with long fingers that reach into the very fibers of my being "Come back soon Lambies".

Katey and Boy snoring upstairs, a note lay on our sleeping bags, Thank you, and don't worry, we will not over stay our welcome. Corbett filled two of our new tumbles with orange juice, he had time before going, we laid down and I read aloud.

THE GREAT ENIGMA
THE UNIVERSE IS ALIVE, EVERYTHING THAT HAPPENS IN OUR EXPERIENCE IS ULTIMATELY A REFLECTION OF SOME ASPECT THAT IS GERMANE TO THE UNIVERSE. AND OF COURSE, THERE IS NOTHING WITHIN OUR EXPERI-ENCE THAT ORIGINATES "OUTSIDE" THE UNIVERSE.
IN THE BEGINNING, THE UNIVERSE AS WE NOW SEE IT REFLECTED ON OUR EARTH, BEGAT AN ESSENCE, A FLAVOR, A TASTE OF SELF. IT BECAME APPRECIATIVE OF ITSELF. AND IN THIS APPRECIATION IT FORMED A TASTE, OR AN ESSENCE, OR A FLAVOR, OR A SUBSTANCE WHICH ALLOWED ALL THE WORLDS WITHIN WORLDS TO "PHE-NOMIFY", APPEAR OR BECOME.
THE UNIVERSE IN ITS EVOLVEMENT WAS BECOMING "FULL", AND IN ITS "MORE-FULLNESS" IT BEGAN TO MOVE IN-UP-AGAINST ITSELF AND THEN (*) SUDDENLY - "POOF" - A BUBBLE APPEARED - AN ENTITY BORN. THE COSMI-CAL FABRIC OF THE UNIVERSE, EVOLVING AS IT WAS AND IS, BEGAN TO BECOME CONVOLUTED AND WITH THE FIRST CONVOLUTION CAME A LITTLE BUBBLE, A LITTLE POCKET, A LITTLE SHAPE THAT DEVELOPED: A SELF-CON-TAINED SPACE, AND THIS WAS THE FIRST "CELL" OF CON-SCIOUSNESS WHICH THEN DEVELOPED INTO A GOD.
IT WAS A BUBBLE OF ETHER. IT WAS ACTUALLY THE FIRST FORMATION OF A CLOSED CIRCUIT, WHERE THE LINES OF INTELLIGENCE COULD COMMUNICATE WITH THEMSELVES IN WHAT WE TERM "SELF-CONSCIOUSNESS", AND IDEATION COULD DEVELOP AND BE SELF-CON-TAINED AND THEREFORE ABLE TO EXPAND ON AN INDI-VIDUAL BASIS WITH A FOCUS OF ITS OWN. NOW THIS WAS SOMEWHAT OF A SEPARATION FROM THE UNIVERSE-AS-A-WHOLE, THOUGH IT WAS DEPENDENT ON THE WHOLE. IT WAS ALSO DISTINCT FROM THE WHOLE IN THAT IT WAS

SELF-CONTAINED.

THEN THERE WERE "STARS" IN HEAVEN, A TERM SYMBOLICAL OF THE ESSENCE OF A CREATIVE POTENCY THAT THE GODS POSSESSED WITHIN THEMSELVES WHICH SOMETIMES TOOK THE FORM OF GREAT SHINING LIGHTS, REFLECTING THE RISE OF EACH GOD INTO ITS OWN GLORY TO EXPRESS THE "LIGHT" OF ITS OWN GROWTH.

THEN GRADUALLY AS PROCESS MOVED ON, THE GODS BEGAN TO OPPOSE ONE ANOTHER. THEY CEASED TO REGARD THOSE ASPECTS OF VIRILITY THEY FOUND IN ONE ANOTHER AS PHASES WHICH WERE TO BE RESPECTED. SOMEHOW THEY LOST THEIR SENSE OF COOPERATION AND THEY BEGAN TO FIGHT AMONG THEMSELVES.

ALL THE CAPACITIES THE GODS HAD, AND WITH WHICH THEY FOUGHT, WERE THEIR OWN CAPACITIES, AND AS ONE POTENCY CAME INTO ACTIVE ANTAGONISM AND STRUCK OUT IN OPPOSITION WITH ANOTHER'S POTENCY, THERE WAS A KIND OF THUNDER IN THE HEAVENS WHICH HAD NEVER BEEN THERE BEFORE. SPARKS WERE CREATED OF A NEW SUBSTANCE, WITH SOUND AND TEXTURE AND FEELING WHICH HAD NEVER BEEN HEARD OR SEEN BEFORE. THEY WERE THE CREATION OF THE LABORS OF BATTLE, WAR, AND OPPOSITION. FOR WHEN ONE CAPABILITY STRUCK AGAINST ANOTHER CAPABILITY, IT CREATED A "SHOCK" WAVE IN THE ETHER OF HEAVEN ITSELF.

THIS WAS THE BEGINNING OF A NEW "SOLID" LEVEL OF REALITY WHERE ONE CAPABILITY CLASHED WITH ANOTHER. THIS WAS A "SOLID" OPPOSITION WHICH GAVE BIRTH TO A DIFFERENT FORM OF MATERIAL THAN HAD EVER EXISTED BEFORE.

EVENTUALLY, ANTAGONIZING ELEMENTS STRIKING OUT WITH SUCH VIOLENT FORCE LEFT "SCARS" IN HEAVEN, AND OF COURSE, WHERE ONE HAD FORMED ANOTHER FOLLOWED MORE EASILY BECAUSE A PRECEDENT HAD BEEN SET. IT WAS AS THOUGH AT ONE POINT WHERE THE

POTENCY OF ONE GOD'S COURAGE STRUCK TO DESTROY OR CONFOUND THE CAPABILITY OF ANOTHER GOD'S POTENCY IT LEFT A SCAR, AN IMPRESSION IN HEAVEN. AT THAT POINT, WHERE TWO SYMBOLICAL SWORDS CLASHED, HEAVEN COULD NOT BE. IT PUT A HOLE IN THE FABRIC OF HEAVEN BECAUSE IN THAT PLACE HEAVEN COULD NOT BE.

THESE BECAME "NODULES" OR SMALL SPOTS THAT WERE STRIPPED OF PURE PRIMORDIAL LIFE-ENERGY, STRIPPED OF THE LIFE OF HEAVEN. AND YET, THEY GAVE BIRTH TO A NEW FORM OF LIFE WHICH INCORPORATED THE SYNTHESIS OF THE COMBINED OPPOSING POINTS OF VIEW WHICH STRANGELY, FORMED A NEW SYNTHESIS.

BUT BEING DEVOID OF THE LIFE OF HEAVEN, THE GODS FELL OUT OF THE HEAVEN INTO A SUBSTRATA, INTO THE BEGINNING OF ANOTHER DIMENSION, REFLECTED NOW IN WHAT WE DESCRIBE AS THE "PHYSICAL" UNIVERSE. THIS MAY HAVE BEEN REFERRED TO IN THE SOMEWHAT QUAINT AND SIMPLISTIC VERSION OF THE "FALL OF MAN" AS TOLD IN THE STORY OF ADAM AND EVE HAVING BEEN DRIVEN FROM THEIR GARDEN TO FEND FOR THEMSELVES BECAUSE THEY HAD TASTED OF THE "FRUIT OF THE TREE OF KNOWLEDGE OF 'GOOD' AND 'EVIL'". THEY SOUGHT "FREE WILL" TO EXPRESS THEIR OWN POTENTIALS. A NEW ERA IN COSMIC DEVELOPMENT.

ALL THIS WAS ACTUALLY GIVEN BIRTH BY THE WARRING GODS IN HEAVEN. THEY BROKE THROUGH THE VERY FABRIC OF HEAVEN ITSELF, PERHAPS BECAUSE THERE WAS A NEW NEED FOR A GREATER SYNTHESIS. UNFORTUNATELY, THIS WAS NOT BROUGHT ABOUT THROUGH "CONSCIENCE" AND SO HAD TO BE ACCOMPLISHED THROUGH "WILL", A PERSONAL DECISION.

THERE CAME A DAY AND AN AGE WHEN THE GODS THEMSELVES ACTUALLY DID REIGN IN THE HEAVENS, UNTIL THEY WERE "CAST OUT" BECAUSE OF THEIR REJEC-

TION OF A PART OF THEMSELVES WHICH THEY DID NOT UNDERSTAND. ASPECTS WHICH THEY DID NOT "LIKE", OF WHICH THEY DID NOT APPROVE, ASPECTS WHICH SEEMED TO THEM TO LEAD TO LIMITATION, WHICH POINTED TOWARD SELF-CORRECTION AND A NEED FOR SELF-RESPONSIBILITY, MOVING TOWARD THE IDEA THAT MISTAKES COULD BE MADE, THAT THE "SELF" WAS NOT PERFECT: IT WAS NOT "ALL-KNOWING", "ALL-POWERFUL", OR RIGHTEOUS, AND EVEN TO SUGGEST THAT THEY MIGHT BE REQUIRED TO DO CERTAIN THINGS THAT THEY MIGHT NOT WANT TO DO, OR LIKE TO DO. AN IN-TIMATION THAT THEY MIGHT HAVE TO CONSIDER AS-PECTS THAT WERE NOT IMMEDIATELY SELF-GRATIFYING, OR IMMEDIATELY REWARDING. ASPECTS THAT WOULD REQUIRE FORESIGHT, AND PLANNING, AND ORGANIZA-TION, WHICH TO THEM SEEMED APPALLING.

SO THESE POTENTIALS OF THREATS TO THEIR "FUN" AND "ENJOYMENT" CAUSED THEM TO BE CAST FROM HEAVEN. AND WHAT THEY REJECTED IN THEIR HEAVEN THEY THREW DOWN TO EARTH, AND WHERE THOSE UN-RESOLVED ASPECTS OF THEMSELVES CAME TO LIFE ON EARTH, THEY PRODUCED ELEMENTAL FORCES WHICH CONSUMED A PART OF THE BODY OF THE FABRIC OF THE LIFE-BLOOD, OR "JUICES" OF THE NATURAL FRUIT OF THE EARTH. THIS PLASMA BECAME THE KINGDOM OF EARTH LIFE, A GROPING, SENSE-BOUND, PARASITICAL BUT EVO-LUTIONARY WEB OF LIFE, EACH FACET WITH ITS OWN INTENSE, LUSTY APPETITE FOR THE ONGOING OF ITS OWN SPECIES THROUGH REPRODUCTION OF ITSELF. THIS TEEMING MINUTIA BECAME IN THE HINDU RELIGION THE MAZE - THE "MAYA" OF ILLUSION.

HERE MAY BE FOUND THE SUBSTANCE OF THE ALLE-GORY OF THE RAPE OF PERSEPHONE BY HADES-PLUTO-SA-TAN-THE DRAGON, HELL.

FOR HAVING BEEN CONFRONTED BY THESE "DANGERS"

TO THEIR FREEDOM, THE GODS MERELY WENT ON PLAY-ING GOD, REFUSING TO FACE OR ACCEPT THE PRESENCE IN THEMSELVES OF BLEMISH OR FAULT. THEY THREW SUCH INTRUSIONS AWAY, SWEPT THEM UNDER THE RUG, SO TO SPEAK, AND RATIONALIZED AWAY ANY UNPLEAS-ANTNESS, SEEKING TO SEPARATE THEMSELVES FROM THE NECESSITY FOR COMPUTING ANY TRUTH WHICH MIGHT HAVE SET THEM "FREE", AND THEREBY SEPARAT-ING THEMSELVES FROM ANY AVENUE OF SALVATION THE EARTH-LIFE MIGHT HAVE OFFERED. INSTEAD, THEY USH-ERED IN AN EPIC OF WARPED-EARTH-FABRIC WHEREIN THE NATURAL ELEMENTS OF LIFE BECAME PARASITICAL, FEEDING UPON ONE ANOTHER.

AND THE LONG LASTING EFFECTS OF THIS PATTERN IS EVIDENT AND, IN FACT, REMAIN DOMINANT THROUGH-OUT THE LIFE FORMS OF THE EARTH TODAY. IN THIS MI-ASMA OR MAZE, HUMAN BEINGS, HUMAN CONSCIOUS-NESS, AND THE HUMAN SPIRIT HAVE HAD TO DEVELOP. UP THROUGH THE NEGATIVES WHICH THE GODS HAD NEITHER THE COURAGE NOR THE INTEGRITY TO FACE WITHIN THEMSELVES.

THIS HAS BEEN THE GROUND WORK, THE FOUNDA-TION, THE SOIL IN WHICH THE HUMAN SPIRIT HAS HAD TO GROW AND WHICH IT HAD TO ABSORB FIRST, BEFORE IT COULD ATTEMPT TO RAISE ITSELF INTO A POSITION OF COMPETENCE TO HANDLE RESPONSIBILITY WITH TRUE APPRECIATION OF WHAT THAT MIGHT IMPLY: THE SUBTLE, AND SOMETIMES PAINFUL CHALLENGE OF FOL-LOWING TO COMPLETION ANY SMALL ENDEAVOR WHILE BEING CONCERNED WITH THE DANGERS OF PLAYING GOD.

FROM THE STAND POINT OF THIS WRITING, THE GODS NO LONGER HAVE POWER OVER THE PRINCIPLES THAT ARE EVOLVING ON EARTH, FOR THOSE PRINCIPLES HAVE PASSED OVER INTO THE DOMAIN OF THE HUMAN SPIR-

IT-MIND-BODY-CONSCIOUSNESS, MOVING HOPEFULLY TOWARD SOME WHOLESOMENESS WITH MOTIVATIONS HAVING CONTINUITY, CIRCULARITY, ROTATION, REVOLUTION, RETURN, CYCLES, SELF-REFLEXIVENESS, KNOWLEDGE, JUDGMENT, STABILITY, INTEGRITY, CONSTANCY, PURITY. THE ALTERNATIVE FOR MAN AND HIS EARTH MIGHT BE WAR, PESTILENCE, FAMINE, AND DEATH ALONG WITH THE OTHER PLANETS AND THEIR MOONS IN OUR SOLAR SYSTEM.

THE MIASMA REMAINS, BUT THE VIRTUES ARE, NEVERTHELESS, THE FLOWERING GEM STONES OF CONSCIOUSNESS, EVEN TO THE SMALL EXTENT THAT THEY MAY BE RECOGNIZED ON EARTH, WORKING IN SMALL FRAMES OF REFERENCE IN ISOLATED AREAS OF COMMUNICATION, PAINFULLY, SLOWLY, OR EVEN IN AGONY, THEY ARE WHAT HOLDS THE PLANET TOGETHER. WITHOUT THESE QUALITIES SYMBOLICALLY, THEORETICALLY AND IN ESSENCE THE VERY PLANET WOULD IMPLODE IN UPON ITSELF FOR LACK OF SIGNIFICANCE. PERHAPS THOSE ARE THE QUALITIES SPOKEN OF IN THE TEXT "YE ARE THE SALT OF THE EARTH. IF THE SALT HAVE LOST HIS SAVOUR, WHEREWITH SHALL IT BE SALTED?".

(*)NOTE: THE EXTENT OF THE INTRUSION AND THE ILL EFFECTS OF THE PRESENCE OF THE FALLEN GODS UPON THE EARTH WAS DESCRIBED IN THE BIBLE SCRIPTURE, NAMELY, IN GENESIS AND PARTICULARLY IN THE BOOK OF ENOCH, MUCH PRIZED BY THE EARLY CHURCH FATHERS: DELETED FROM THE BIBLE BY ONE OF THE EARLY CHURCH COUNCILS. FOUND IN ETHIOPIA IN 1773, WRITTEN IN A COMBINATION OF ARAMAIC AND HEBREW, LOST AGAIN AND FINALLY PUBLISHED FROM RESEARCH WITH HEAVY FOOTNOTES BY OXFORD UNIVERSITY PRESS IN 1912. THE PLATES OF THIS TEXT WERE DESTROYED IN THE BOMBING OF LONDON AND NOW CAN SCARCELY BE FOUND, BUT A QUOTATION FROM ENOCH READS AS FOL-

LOWS:

"...AND THEY (THE FALLEN GODS) BEGAN TO SIN AGAINST THE BIRDS, THE BEASTS, THE REPTILES, THE FISH AND TO DEVOUR ONE ANOTHER..."

"THE EARTH LAID ACCUSATION AGAINST THEM, AND AS MEN PERISHED THEY CRIED OUT AND THEIR CRY WENT UP TO HEAVEN"."

CHURCH COUNCILS HAVE DELETED OTHER BOOKS OF THE BIBLE TOO. THE PRAYER OF MANASSES. BEL AND THE DRAGON. THE BOOK OF ESDRAS. THE WISDOM OF SOLOMON. SIRACH. THE SONG OF THE CHILDREN. THE BOOK OF THE MACCABEES. BARUCH. THE HISTORY OF SUSANNA. THE BOOK OF JUDITH. AND THE BOOK OF TOBIT.

Lying silent for a while, Corbett spoke "Wow, creation by movement, that'll blow the roof off the Catholic Church". I giggled and rolled to face him "Every church. Ever since my Grampa died, I haven't thought much of God". After Lorenzo came for him, I read The Great Enigma again and wondered how this Girl of little promise could be so fortunate, so absolutely privileged to meet Ida Rose, and therefore get a long clear look at what most only see *though the glass darkly*, while her own Family seemed to hold her work in such disregard, which shed a measure of light on the price she paid for it, and allowed me to better understand my privilege came with a price too, an unconditional responsibility, an obligation to conduct my personal portion of this experiment in free will with all the courage, integrity, judgment and truth I could muster, and be ever vigilant for the heady feeling of great purpose and exclusive sense of destiny that so easily becomes smug pride, and vain inflation. I was also struck how The Great Enigma spoke to my vision of the Council of Essence, how erstwhile humans and not the Gods were in control there too. I saw implications, currents of this world-wide, in the Civil Rights movement, and the Women's Lib movement, which for me were both Human rights, and in the questioning of authority by a Flower-Generation, even the choice by some to stop eating animals, all were a heart-felt desire to move beyond the fallen Gods parasitical blood-letting.

A sound night sleep did Katey wonders, she was ready to find somewhere to live, starting with a trip into Snohomish for a local paper. I went, to use a pay phone and call Stanley for his now ex-wife's number. Pam lived not three miles North, in the country that small distance made us neighbors, and neighbors could presume on one another, she might know of a place since most of the good ones were often not in the paper. She had been scowling and chilly to me at her adoption celebration, but I always felt if circumstances had been different we would be friends. Now, she was not a rock star's The Wife and I was not a Groupie threatening what in retrospect was a very shaky marriage. And she sounded genuinely glad to hear from me, just so happened to have a nice little empty place at the back of her five-acre property, and would consider renting to the right person, thirty-dollars a month utilities included. After all the bad, Katey burst in tears, hardly able to wrap her mind around any good fortune. We went to look, one of those first-houses owners live-in while building the main one, however this was in splendid condition, and the only way-in, down a long driveway passed Pam and her Ol'man and two exceedingly protective full-grown German shepherds. Katey and Pam found much in common, their Kids bonded instantly, she felt safe, and could move-in tomorrow. Business done, we settled around the kitchen table, sipping tea, smoking, trading gossip. Delroy and his Wife split-up, he was giving her the California house and talking about moving to Seattle. Joey, Stan, and Cyrene had gone Born-Again.

New Years Eve at the Colonial Inn or the Bleu Dolphin the same, as 1973 rolled-in, the usual drunken desperation mounted. There were ten shots from well-wishers lined across the top of the Hammond for Corbett and Lorenzo, most Wild Turkey, most empty. When Corbett fingered the opening bars of *Flight of the Bumble Bee*, I thought what wonder-full nerve, this was a furious song even sober, but there was no risk he would not take on stage. As for me, the bartender Joni took pity, letting me take a stool behind the bar. Lorenzo dropped us home after 3AM. Too wired to sleep, sitting face-to-face on sleeping bags, Gus and Grilla-Fish curled in our laps, we ate scrambled eggs and toast and considered 1972. Our first New Year's Eve together at the Colonial, the moonbow over our bungalow on the cliffs of New Brighton Beach, Argus, the sweltering summer caravan North, sleeping on the floor at Limey's, Cannon Beach, camping in a MaryJane garden, losing our money, the barn, the 1972 psilocybin Hollywood smile, our money returned, the gas-station-real-estate-office, Cyrene's hysterics, One Hand Clapping's final clap, friends lost, Grilla-Fish found, Katey, Ida Rose, and how lovely, just us in such a nice warm bourgeoisie home.

Mid January Katey had a healthy eight-pound Girl. She'd became fast friend with Pam, who had been trying to get pregnant with her soon-to-be new Husband, thought Katey's fertility was good luck, and happily offered to baby-sit when she went back to school, her Parents had agreed to let her use their Seattle address so she could still qualify for the W.I.N. program. Willy was convicted and sent to McNeil Island Prison. And I never asked if Boy's father was Nick, though he looked a lot like him, which would explain why Katey had been so terribly angry with me. Corbett and Lorenzo continued to pack the Bleu Dolphin five night a week. And I ordered a phone installed, applied for a business license, and while searching Everett's thrift shops, found a seven-foot long mahogany library table with fine carved legs and three schoolhouse oak chairs, perfect for infront of the big kitchen window, two matching over-stuffed burgundy cut-velvet easy chairs for front room looking at the view, a four-poster bed-frame and new mattress and chest-of-drawers we moved into the upstairs master bedroom, and an oblong formica kitchen table and swivel chair perfect for my sewing machine, I set-up in the North facing upstairs bedrooms where the light was very good, and began to sew. My first call was Leda. Cyrene answered, self-satisfied surprised I did not know Leda moved home. Not ever wanting to speak to Leda's Mom again, Corbett phoned for me. Leda said she was there in church when Cy, Stan and Joey were baptized, saw them speak in tongues "It was so freaky, like they were invaded by this powerful demon. When it came my turn, I freaked and ran outside. No way I was gona let that in. Cy wouldn't look at me on the way home, like just seeing my face would contaminate her. I knew I had to go, decided to look in the morning, but soon as we got home she told me to get out right now, if there was no room in my heart for the Holy Spirit, it must already be full of the Devil. I was speechless, I still had two weeks rent paid, but the look in her eyes, she scared me, so I grabbed my stuff, called a cab and went to Mom's". I sympathized "Oh Honey-Pie, no matter how nice you were, she's so scared, so up and down. You did the best thing, just get away from her. Maybe Born-Again will help, give her something to hang her life on. She needs it. Look, let's don't talk about Cyrene anymore, give her any more of our time or energy, okay". Leda agreed. I gladly changed the channel "So my Pretty Girl with the electric blue eyes, I'd love you to meet a really cool friend of mine. His name's Tom and he lives in Ida Rose's downstairs and does most of her auditing". Leda giggled like a junior high school-girl "No way, being set up's so artificial. I'd be too embarrassed. But you could kept your promise and take me to meet Ida Rose". "God Leda, you and Gretchen used to set me up all the time, remember. Anyway, this isn't someone to just fuck for a night, it's someone to be friends with, someone to talk too. It's just meeting a nice person over dinner at a friend's house, that's all". Feigning reluctant she said yes. I'm sure because Tom was a way to Ida Rose. It wasn't that I wouldn't take her, every time I tried so far, had been the wrong timing.

Disillusioned Hippies, bitter Revolutionaries, desolate Druggies, lost FlowerChildren in droves were going Born Again. The latest trend with its own bumper-sticker *I Found It*. But *It* seemed more a lobotomy than a panacea, turning wounded seekers into living-dead, like those poor creatures in my dream walking the gulch. Born-Agains, Jesus Freaks, or as I called them, designer Christians, for I took born again from Ida Rose's audit the Legend to mean *returning to the catastrophe and revealing its lethal hold on the self*, not opening your soul to possession. These sorrow-full lambs who mourned the passing of the 60s, the death of a dream, a community where each individual could make a difference and not just live life in-line, these walking wounded felt abandoned, expelled from Eden, and craved what they were calling Sanctuary to fill the void. I had no problem understanding this, but every one of them sooner rather than later mouthed the same tired conviction, if you weren't one of them, if you didn't buy their brand of Jesus Incorporated, their way or no way, then you were not saved. And yet to a person they seemed blinded to the contradiction of this exclusivity, so incompatible with the inclusiveness of the early Christians and the 60s community they were aching to recreate. And as with any mental Golden Ghetto, they must give-up their personal power, their individuation, to an objective God, and therefore their free will, their sense of humor, their choice to grow and change, to be original, and vow to keep safe the all-mighty status quo, so they can be thought of as beyond suspicion, god-forbid being suspicious.

A rainy wonderful day, January 22, 1973, abortion became legal nation-wide with the Supreme Court decision called Roe verses Wade, it was already legal in Washington State. And Stan showed-up just after noon to proselytize, floating on Born-Again bliss, identifying completely with his sinless savior. I did not doubt his sincerity in wanting to share the joy. Happily he had no interest in me, a mere female, as he explained to Corbett "Your helpmate, don't worry, she'll go along once you take Jesus in your heart". Stan was already a serious chauvinist, how coincidentally convenient this latest *It* was so harmonious. And my darling Corbett, continually astonishing, leaned back in his schoolhouse chair at the library table, sipping coffee, relaxed, patient, listening to Stan's litany of goodness and rules, don'ts and do's, sins and rights, the same blissed-out smile on his face we had seen on other Designer Christian, what Corbett called glitter shock. And finally the ransom, Stan pressed "So Hawkman, if you want Jesus to come into your heart, if you want to be saved, get down on your knees with me now and pray". Corbett waited for silence to weigh, squaring his shoulders, straightening his back, fixing those crystal blue eyes on Stan, he spoke in a measured warm tone "First, I want to thank you for the sincere offer. You leave me no option but to reveal my self". He stood his full six-feet two-inches and seemed to fill the kitchen "You see Stan, I'm Jesus, and I don't want you or anyone on their knees". Corbett reached out his hand and smiled "Won't you follow me". Stan's eyes were glued to Corbett's, a terrible question burning, could this be true, then hands clapping over his ears, brain turning to scrambled eggs, he fled, Gus and Grilla-Fish on his heels. More amazed at how words so dramatically affect the nervous system than at Stan's expense, Corbett and I could not help laughing, for Stan was perfect fodder for this growing indiscriminate maw, vulnerable and guilty, desperate to conceal his ugly wounds in the seductive guise of sacrosanct beliefs and principles, that instead of relenting or sweetening him, fostered a spiritual arrogance, playing God just like the fallen ones, like Corbett's Folks, deciding who's in and who's not. We both felt truly sorry for him, his Band's manager had ruined their success, the expectations of a rock star had sucked all his juice, he was legitimately searching for Sanctuary, and found a fraud dressed in lamb's clothing. Months ago Corbett offered to take him to meet Ida Rose, Stan said no. Ida Rose often reminded her students, *Redemption is not vicarious. However religion at its best can provide a civilizing structure where there is none.* Maybe this was just what Stan and Cyrene needed, for he had shown himself a faithless partner, likely to betray her too, and though she emphatically maintained he would never do that to her, Pam and Goldie had to haunt some dark corner of her mind.

Lorenzo's marriage was rocky too, already confiding in Corbett he was considering separation, even divorce, and came an hour early for work to ask some questions about Ida Rose, someone he'd shown no interest in till now. Corbett tried explaining General Semantics best he could, how it helped him to understand how his mind worked, to begin grasping the subtle and not so influences, and consequently, to make better evaluations and choices. He offered to lend *A Challenge to Confusion*, and take him to meet her. Renzo's powerful arms folded tight over his barrel chest, jaw set as if comparison shopping a used car, confessing in a flat voice "Now I'm really confused, the bottom's falling out of my life, I'm scared of losing my Ol'lady and Kid, Stan and Joey want me to join their church and get Born-Again, and you think I should read a book and learn to be subtle". Corbett shook his head slowly side-to-side "No man. But those guys 're touting their thing as an instant cure, and I'm sorry but there's no such thing. You got to do the work your self, and that takes time. I know Ida Rose can help. Promise me you won't go Born-Again before you meet her". Lorenzo kept his eyes on his feet "I'll try man, really, but I'm drowning right now and gota do something.

Coming in the door after 3AM, Corbett's broad shoulders slumping, smelling of alcohol and smoke. He went to the frig for a beer, and sat down in the living room with me "Stan showed-up after the second set, you know apologizing for freaking out. But I knew he really came for Renzo. Part of their Born-Again thing is recruiting". He lit a smoke "We sat in a booth and he starts selling, hard. The instant Renzo bought I could feel it. Shit, after all these years playing together, I knew the first note of the

736

last set, this was it". Corbett swigged his beer "I know Renzo and Stan feel so shitty about themselves, like they've done so many bad things and the only way to stand the stink is give it up to Jesus. He's already done all the work for them, paid the price, this Born-Again thing's ready-made". He laughed in sudden epiphany "Shit they can't go see Ida Rose, and I know why, they're scared she can see right through them, like she's omniscient or psychic or something. They think she's some kind of parlor trick. I was blown away by her too".

Monday morning, Corbett still in bed reading the Sunday Post Intelligencer, Gus and Grilla-Fish with him. I was off to the Ave with three gowns, maybe the Arabesque was still there, maybe I could make my first lawful sale for No Bogus, the legal name of my first legitimate tax-paying business, I had crossed-over the dark-line and become one of the establishment. Getting less than I wanted, the one-hundred-dollar-bill still felt good in my pocket and I could not wait to get home and tell Corbett. Lorenzo's car was in our driveway on their day-off. He was sitting in the front room with Corbett, and from the queer electric-vibe I thought he must be peaking on acid. Turning his face to me, the glazed-smile of glitter shock, he announced too loud and too finally "Marion and I spoke in tongues yesterday. We took Jesus in our hearts as our personal savior". Gus and Grilla-Fish sat side-by-side directly infront of him glaring, neck muscles straining, Grilla growling a low steady rumble, seeing what she does that humans can not. My mind refused this impossibility, Renzo was renowned for his on-stage caricature of faith healers, his great gospel impressions, we roared countless times at those hilarious impersonations, I had to believe this was just the ultimate put-on "You're kidding me right". He lurched forward as if thrown, eyes boiling. I carefully drew away. Suddenly he smiled, only with his lips, leaning far back into the over-stuffed velvet chair, voice fatherly, liquid "No. Stan took us to Church. We found Sanctuary". I knew exactly what scared Leda about Cyrene, something else seemed in-control here, something volatile, hypnotic, freezing me in fear it might strike. Corbett was out of his chair standing between us "So, how'd it go with the gowns". Looking up into his beautiful face, I understood this was not my business "Great. Tell you about it later". I stole a quick look at Lorenzo and disappeared upstairs to my sewing room. Blaming him for buying-in didn't make any more sense than blaming Stan, for there were so many pretenders promising salvation, who understood as if by some predatory natural instinct that was miss-taken for wisdom, how to get you so high, tell you how special you are, and when you're in too far and have too much invested, a little yank and you're caught, the hook's in too deep, just like Scientology. I sat on the top stair listening to Lorenzo lay-out the advantages of joining up with the Illuminati. For this was also a Born-Again economic brotherhood, one hand washing the other, and since Corbett had always been the spiritual one in their group, he ought to share in the benefits too. First of course was the joy of speaking in God's secret tongue, and then the miraculously effort-less strength of conviction to give-up drugs, drinking, smoking, even Girls on the side, getting high on God instead. And there it was, the seductive siren calling from the depths of Renzo's soul, getting high on something besides drugs and Girls, he still needed a fix to mask his pain, for this was no cure, only temporary nostrum, and he did not know or maybe care it was not God but the feeling of possession, an expedient Demiurge conjured by the group and embodied in their charismatic Deacon. He would be lucky to ever think for himself again, for Designer Christians were not asked to think, Jesus Incorporated did that for them, they might as well be a jock or a pair of tits. Their task was to applaud and adore and bask in the glory of Jesus' immaculate salvation. Corbett said little for nearly an hour. Renzo's zeal finally exhausting into silence. Chairs springs creaking told me they'd risen. Corbett spoke tenderly to his friend "Thanks man. I can see what's happening to you, and I know you're sincere. Give me some time to think about this okay". Renzo's voice was bitten with disappointment "Sure Hawk, sure, that's all we're asking". Corbett said nothing. Lorenzo cleared his throat "Okay then, look man, see you tomorrow night for work. I'll be by for you".

Tuesday night Corbett came home hurting. Renzo had been completely possessed, between songs admonishing Regulars on their drinking and smoking. Thursday he never bothered showing-up. Corbett was not surprised, covering the night solo. Friday morning Stan called, offering to play drums, swearing to God he had no problem with clubs and booze. Corbett's voice was perfectly suited to rock'n roll, he could sing falsetto and scream with the best, finesse a love song, caress a ballad, cry the blues, still he thought of himself more a keyboard player than all-night lead singer, and, it was just easier to have another musician, so he said yes to Stan sitting-in, but only after his solemn pledge to keep Jesus out of it. I went Saturday night. Corbett and Stan plainly enjoyed playing together. The audience did not withhold their appreciation, especially an older good-looking man in an expensive suit, who seemed to know most everyone, buying round after round for the house. Joni explained he had been a big-time ex-basketball star, now a hometown has-been with a drinking problem, who opened a successful local car dealership, and though married with kids, came to the Dolphin with his latest blonde squeeze to dance, buying rounds not from any inherent generosity, but to seal all lips in complicity. Corbett played the familiar opening bars of Floyd Cramer's *Last Date*, using his radio DJ voice "Well folks, it's last call, so let's give our super-fine bartender Miss Joni Flame a big hand and a big tip. There no one like her". Everyone did as they were told. "And let's have another big hand for your fabulous hostess Miss Gloria Burnett". More clapping. "And for the great Stanley Malville on drums and vocals". The full-house whistled and cheered. "I'm Corbett Hawkins, and I want to thank you for coming tonight. We're here at the Blue Dolphin playing tunes every Tuesday though Saturday. So, thank you, good night, and drive safe". Mr. Has-Been tottered-up to the low stage, nearly losing his balance into the drums, taking a fat roll of bills from his pants pocket, he peeled-off a hundred and laid it on the Hammond "Aw, come on man, you see I got this beaudiful chick with me. Play one more so we can dance, you know *Mercy Mercy* by Cannonball Adderley. You know how it is man". Corbett smiled "Sure man, but how about a C-note for my partner here". Has-Been peeled another and laid it on Stan's snare.

It was near two when Joni coaxed Has-Been and his blonde into a waiting cab. Stan already went home. Corbett took the bar stool beside me "Wow, can you believe it, two C-note". He gave me his laughing "The second biggest tip I ever got". Pouring his tip jar on the bar, counting 106 dollars, not all paper "I was kidding when I asked him to give one to Stan. I still can't believe he did it". Joni counted her tips, 212 dollars and change, her second biggest night ever, she slide a twenty across the bar to Corbett

"Thanks as always my dear for your wonderful music". Lining three shot glasses on the bar, she poured Wild Turkey. We toasted Mr.Has-Been. She was pouring us another when Owner came in, never at work this late and already drinking, he took the seat next to Corbett, and tapping his fore-finger on the edge of the bar three times ordered "Dollface, my usual". Joni set up a glass and poured what we were drinking. He raised it to salute Corbett and leaned into his face "You my Boy are the one they come here to see. Far as I'm concerned, you have a job forever". He tossed the honey liquid down his throat "Ahhhuk". Joni hit him again. He held the glass up to show us the contents "But you see my Boy, we don't serve red wine here. Your drummers have attitude problems, and they got to go. You don't need 'em anyway". Corbett leaned back a bit "I see. Well, the Socko Brothers are definitely dead, I know that much. And I really don't want to do a single, I know that too. So I guess I'll thank you for the vote of confidence, and give my notice". Owner downed his shot and drilled Corbett with hard dark eyes "I do appreciate the courtesy, but I get fifty calls a day from bands begging to work for me. Notice ain't necessary".

Corbett sank into gloomy depression, mourning Renzo as if dead. Getting out of bed around eleven, every day he went to the liquor store, bought two quarts of Miller beer, and finished them off by 1PM. Stan called often, wanting to take him to church. On the morning of the 7th day Corbett had enough, drove to American Music, bought three reel-to-reel tapes for his Ampex and began recording. He realized it wasn't often the Hammond and Baldwin were home together. And he had enough of Stan, telling him he would rather go to Hell than get on his knees to whatever sucked the life out of his Friends. Not discouraged, or more likely not listening, Stan continued to phone. Corbett asked me to answer, saying he was not home. With considerable relish I gladly obliged.

> I used to have lots of friends
> We were all crazy and free
> Now I look in their eyes
> And they're not there
> Please don't go religious on me.

BECOMING DELICIOUS

Swallowing a spoon-full of salt would be awful, but that same salt mixed into a stew or pickles becomes delicious. Studying General Semantics lead Corbett and me further into Jung's work, and after reading his mind blowing *Answer to Job* out-loud to each other, we decided to try and claim our Demons, discover their real faces, integrate them if we could instead of pawning them off, projecting them onto the rich, the straits, the republicans, for when projected, Demons continue to operate from the new pretense, their real identity slipped down below the surface, into the underworld realm of the unconscious, taking a potent chunk of your life-energy and personality with them, and like fallen gods casting-off their negative prehensions because they did not want to bother doing the work, projections surreptitiously etch your face on the other, and you never suspect a Demon, infact you are absolutely positively, and if you're Stan and now Lorenzo, righteously sure your are absolutely right, because you're looking out for salvation instead of in, the Demon can not be you. Jung said, *withdrawing the projection is where knowledge begins.* That spoonful of salt, the stew, the pickles don't become delicious unless you add it, we were determined to claim our salt. Having Corbett home was wonder-full, while I played my sewing machine upstairs, he turned the room-off-the-kitchen into a music studio, and wrote, and composed, and recorded.

I Saw God

I saw God last night and didn't clap for him
Sometimes you have to be just as strong as the Devil
An everyone had a right to be there
There weren't no innocent bystanders
They put bloody Jesus up there for 2000 years
And it still ain't workin
Let's take him down
Let's take him down

I saw God last night I didn't scream for him
No new secret mysteries did he reveal
He said it's your problem now

And if you can solve it
Then you can be just as insecure as me

Don't look back – you could turn to salt
This is your life we're talking about
What you used to do is no longer an option

I saw God last night and didn't clap for him
He was singing that same old beautiful song
This time he was shaking hands with the Devil
And that bloody cross came tumbling down
So let's take him down
Let's give him a break
Let's take him down.

One of the abiding questions we tossed around, why were some people awake and some not. The answer evolved from just plain stupid, to just plain lazy, to bad luck, bad parents, bad breath, to they took a turn and just went the wrong way, to the thought that some people simply come in with something more, with their bulbs already lit.

She Musta Come in Lit

Here she comes scary as shit
Lookin around for a place to sit
Talkin to people she don't know
She musta come in lit
I think she musta come in lit

Ask her a question
She'll tell you no lies
A battered woman put the tears in my eyes
A red callus burns where the ring used to be
She musta come in lit
I think she musta come in lit

Well electric ice tea take her half way home
Till she try to stand up and walk to the phone
Stumble along she heads for the door
Now she's dancin alone on the bar room floor
Go babe

Well she still got the rhythm
It shakes up the floor
Don't you worry about her she never falls
She may be hurtin and she may cry
But she'll never give up until the day she dies
I think she came in lit

Well she still got the rhythm
It shakes up the floor
You can look in her eyes if you dare to see more
A flower-child she used to be
Yeah there once was a time she would love you for free

Now it's four letter words burnin off the walls
Don't you worry about her she never falls
She may be hurtin an she may cry
But she'll never give up until the day she dies
She musta come in lit
I think she came in lit.

Corbett won my heart all over with this tribute to strong women, and for breaking the silence of men beating on us, the only lyric I'd heard since the Beatles wrote, *I used to be cruel to my woman I beat her and kept her apart from the things that she loved. Man I was mean but I'm changing my scene and I'm doing the best that I can. And I've got to admit it's getting better.* Corbett's creative Genie thrilled mine, from years of sewing I understood every piece of fabric had its own inclination, that when I put my hand to it, I possess enough skill to fabricate a likely approximation of ingenuity, however, when inspired, my hands became merely the facilitator, helping the cloth's own natural bias to go where it wanted, somewhere ever-more satisfying and unexpected than plain skill. And I was making money, though not what I had in Santa Cruz, for my stuff was years ahead of even the hippest shops on the Ave. The current owner of Arabesque was from New York City, not unsophisticated, and bought every gown I brought in, because as she put it "They're a flawless meld of classic, romantic, and some fresh new wild element, unpredictable, young and free". I did not doubt her plaudits, but was only somewhat flattered, suspecting it more about wanting to be cutting-edge and feeling better about living in a small town, and her being so stoned all the time, than any patronizing of the Arts. Still with Corbett's regular monthly bills, I was not making enough to carry us for long. He knew, and on Valentine's Day asked me out on a date "Let's go into Seattle, take a look at the music scene. Maybe I can find a drummer and some where to play".

Pulling on our warm coats when Gus and Grilla-Fish raced to the front door barking mad. I opened a crack. There was Stanley, grinning as if he just had a jolly conversation with me "Hi, is Corbett home". Begrudging, I let him in. Gus and Grilla continued the alarm. Corbett shushed them, and put on a smile "Hey man, what's up". Stan smiled too "Look Hawk-man, I came to talk business. I'll be quick, I can see you're going out. You know the Grape has manager trouble, he's legally got us hog-tied, there's no money coming in, and I got bills to pay and babies to feed. I thought we made some pretty great music at the Blue Dolphin, and maybe we could do it again. And look, before you say no". He put both hand over his heart "I give you my word, on my honor I'll keep the Lord out of it". I did not want to go any where with this person, Corbett saw my eyes blazing and put his big soft tarantula on my shoulder "Sho, can I talk to you in the kitchen for a minute, please". I followed, silent, resentful, disappointed. Gus and Grilla kept their radar on Stan. Corbett stood tall, his face seemed far away from mine, he whispered "Stan knows his way around Seattle". I pouted defiantly "So do I". There was anxious in his voice "I know Sweetheart, but give me this okay". I knew he needed this and might even go without me "Okay". Corbett lightly kissed my lips "I'll make it up to you, promise".

We went with Stan, first to the Penthouse, which was closed for re-modeling. Next the Iron Horse, the cover for Dave Lewis more than we wanted to pay. Riding the elevator to the 11th floor of the Camlin Hotel, thinking what a bust, I found my self staring at a picture of the Gil Conte Trio, the group that played the Evergreen Hotel during Satsop Sky River. The Cloud Room's smoky bar had no cover, we took the only seats, a dark corner where two beautifully upholstered love-seats hugged a glass-topped coffee-table, and settled in for the last of the 2nd set. Corbett ordered Mai Tais. Stan a coke. We never got around to drinking, caught spellbound by Mr.Conte singing *The Lady is a Tramp*, becoming Frank Sinatra, not a physical parody or vocal imitation but the respectful essence, and Anthony Newley, *What Kind of Fool Am I*, and Tony Bennett delivering *San Francisco*, and then it was pure Gil, perched on a high leather bar stool, taking his own sweet-time lighting an enormous smelly cigar, just sitting there puffing, contemplating, as if alone in the room, the audience, including us waiting silent, riveted for what ever this Sicilian Lepreuchaun wanted to do to us. In a revealing show of ego, he directed our attention to the drummer, Kenny McDougald, who sang a singular rendition of *Blueberry Hill*, that would have made Fats Domino proud, taking a long tasty drum solo before the end, changing the tone of his tom by pressing the skin with his elbow, then as if his sticks were Fred Astaire tap-dancing the rim of his snare, he moved from behind the drums playing the crash cymbal stand, and gliding around the room using those sticks on tables, chairs, someone's glass, the round wooden edge of the bar, top of the pia-no, and playing the air he slipped in behind his kit, finishing the song with blackberry, orangeberry, purpleberry raspberry strawberry Overton Berry boysenberry blue blue blue blue blue blue blue blue blue blue blueberry hill. Set over.

The Trio's piano player quickly left the room. Gil, in a sharp black tux, could have been the adjoining four-star restaurant's maitre d' how he worked the crowd, greeting most by name, showing a couple of swells to a sofa close to the stage, making our table last, the only blue-jean Longhairs in the place, we had his interest. Stan offered to buy drinks. Gil sat down beside him and ordered Irish coffee, telling the waitress to bring a round for the table on him. Stan could not wait to vaunt his pedigree. Gil took a sip

"Gota say I'm sorry man. Haven't paid a whole lota 'ttention to rock'n roll since Bobby Darin. I'll sure make a point a listenin for Moby Grape now I met yous. Say, how bout sittin in a few tunes, show us your chops". Stan smiled satisfied "Sure man, love to". Corbett made a practice of leaving his braggadocio on stage, seldom mentioning what he did, normally I respected this, but found my self telling Gil what a great keyboard player he was. Kenny McDougald joined us. After introductions, Gil lit his half-gone cheroot, and eyeing Corbett leaned across the coffee-table offering him one "What you say big fella, can we see what yous got". Corbett took the cigar and smelled its length "Thanks man, but it's pretty obvious your key man's on shaky ground. I wouldn't want to horn in". Thoroughly charmed Gil smiled "Oh Mr.Billy Bright don' care. He's leavin us end a the month. Movin up to the big time, cruise ships. Booked a whole year's gig". Nodding, Corbett smiled "Then, let's go". Kenny stayed with me as the Boys took the stage. Gil called *Ace in the Hole, If I Ruled the World, Speak Softly Love.* I'd never heard Corbett play any of these, yet they rolled-off his big hands like old friends. Three songs enough for Stan, he stood to signal Gil. Who thanked him "Come on, let's here it for Mr.Stanley Malville, from the famous rock'n roll band Moby Grape". There was resounding applause and a two-finger whistle from a man at the bar "Yeah, you rock". Stan took a bow. Kenny politely excused him self to his station. And Billy no where to be seen, Gil called *Boulevard of Broken Dreams, Oh My Papa, Birth of the Blues.* Then making momentary eye contact with Kenny, just the slightest eyebrow raised, he climbed-up on his stool and addressed the audience "That's Mr.Corbett Hawkins on keys". Gil turned to Corby, and still talking into the mic "Kenny and I could sure use a talent like yous. Hows bout workin wid us kid". Corbett smiled, and with an inclination of his head accepted. Gil presented him like Odysseus returning from the Trojan War "Let's hear it for Sir Corbett Hawkins". Corbett took a modest bow, and the congregation came to its feet in full approval. Every big enough city has their own Gil Conte, beloved lounge singer, foremost talent, who instead of leaving to seek fortune and fame in Vegas or LA, where most end-up eeking a living in second-rate hotel lounges, drinking too much, their souls ground to indigestion being treated like a monkey every night if they're lucky enough to have a gig, had wisely chosen to stay in town, becoming a treasure. Kenny on the other hand happened to be one-of-a-kind. Add Corbett and the crowd knew they were getting something special, as he teased Gil musically like he used to Lorenzo, flying just beneath his voice, inconspicuously fortifying, provoking, exciting him to trust, to dare. Kenny had no trouble flying without a net. And Gil responded, singing the standards with the verve and honesty of the first time, ending the set with *My Way*, a standing prolonged ovation, and one encore of *The Second Time Around*. Kenny and Gil came with Corbett, Stan and I sat far from each other as two small sofas would allow. A satisfied flock filed by with approbations, while they discussed money, shook hands, and Gil ordered champagne. Such fortuitous turning of events, so entirely unexpected, I knew the Sweet Sisters were along for the ride, silently thanking them for my reprieve, I would not have to endure Stan on any regular basis. He and Corbett did not speak on the ride home, turning into our driveway after 3AM. Corbett broke the strained silence "Thanks man, I never would've known about the Camlin if you hadn't taken us". Struggling with the vanities Stan murmured "It's God's will". Corbett went on "I know things didn't work out like you wanted. I'm sorry man, but it was right there and I had to say yes. Those guys are great, but their act had gotten old and I can help em out". Stan choked on his words "It's God's will. Anyway, playing lounge music ain't my bag". I knew somehow Cyrene would make this all my fault.

Chapter Thirty

BRAIDED HEROS LOST TO THE SEA

Gil and Kenny met in 1962. Ken playing The House of Entertainment, known as the Hoe House, an after-hours club on 1st Avenue in downtown Seattle, with Overton Berry on keys and Bob Marshall on bass. Gil was headlining Frank Colacurcio's clubs the Diamond Horseshoe and the Wine Cellar at the Seattle Worlds Fair with Frankie Manfre and Toni Madofari. One late night Gil came by the Hoe House to catch this act he'd been hearing about, and when the Fair closed, teamed with Kenny and Bob and Overton for a juicy gig at the Roosevelt Hotel. Gil and Kenny remained solid over the years, with a succession of great piano players, who each went-off to do their own thing, Overton, Buddy Flame, Pete DeLaurenti, and now Billy Bright, and as consequence the act became an act, albeit a great act. With no time for rehearsing, Monday, Gil sent Corbett downtown to Brocklind's for a tuxedo, mandatory to play the Camlin, and to join Local 76, warning him "Be nice to those bums or they won't let yous work". Musicians Union Local 76 was run by two self-important thugs, operating a little fiefdom booking agency, where surprise surprise, only cronies got the gigs. Union dues were fifty to join and forty-two a month up-front, and if Corbett didn't pay every first-of-the-month he would be black-balled, never work in this town again, there were no other benefits. Tuesday morning Gil and Kenny came with a truck, for the Hammond, foot-peddle bass and Leslie speaker, Corbett would use the Cloud Room's Steinway. In the one week left on the Camiln contract, he re-arranged much of their material live on stage. By Saturday night, the New Gil Conte Trio sounded as if they had been together from the beginning, and were not so much of an act. Next was the Windjammer. And the music critics began to buzz.

Best Conte ever at the Windjammer

by Rambling Rhoads Dining and Entertainment

In any person's language, the current entertainment at Clark's Windjammer, on Shilshole Bay is great — "Socko" — powerful.

There is a three-fold reason for it. Corbett Hawkins — keyboards. Kenny McDougald — drums. And Gil Conte.

Corbett Hawkins *is about as versatile a keyboardist as one could desire. His rhythms are sure and certain in all styles of music that range from the 1920's and 1930's up to and including the latest rock hit. Plus Hawkins handles vocals too excellent effect.*

Master of rhythms, Kenny McDougald is also a master showman. While I was playing around with radio for the U.S. Air Force in Germany, McDougald was playing service clubs in the area. A powerful showman, he's not diminished in the intervening years.

Conte is singing better than ever. I arrived just in time to hear the closing phrases of the last song of the second set. I couldn't get into the Top Cabin fast enough. The New Gil Conte Trio had people waiting in line to sit in a cocktail lounge....

Kenny's name for Gil was Captain Video. Gil called Kenny Captain Soul. At first Corbett was the Kingfish, but soon Gil began calling him Geppetto. I never tired of going, fascinated watching these disparate elements coalesce, ones that never would anywhere but on stage. The next gig, Jack McGovern's on Lake Union. Gil and Kenny had worked for him before, there were hard feelings – he's a bum - a wino - scumbag - wants to get you on the cheap - doesn't wana pay. Corbett went into Jack's office to get his paycheck, and found him smoking a stogy, watching a wall of nine TV screens, peeping into every room.

Gil Conte Goes Back Home Again

by Walter Evans

Gil Conte opened this week at Jack McGovern's, his home for four-and-a-half years in the 1960's when it was Kim's Broiler. It was a homecoming that was pure dynamite for all concerned. It was like having years fall away from your life.

The room is bigger now, but that's okay, Conte's talent is big enough to fill it and then some. Although he did only a few old favorites from those days in the show that I caught, The New Gil Conte Trio did a lot of numbers that'll become new favorites for Conte fans.

The bigger stage gives him more room to move around, to let him express his zany brand of humor. (Wednesday night he crawled into the balcony to get a closer look at someone who was requesting a song).

And the bigger stage gives him a better chance to showcase his longtime side-kick, drummer Kenny McDougald. Kenny is a constant in the act, a talented musician, a peerless comedian and like Conte a master showman.

Along with those two members of the aggregation is an outstanding pianist Corbett Hawkins, the new kid. His addition to the act I'm sure will delight old Conte fans.

All I needed to make my grey hair turn black was Bob Marshall on the bass....

Walt Evans was right-on, Gil's fans totally embraced Corbett, including his biggest booster and adopted famiglia Frank Colacurcio. I knew him from newspapers and TV as Seattle's own Godfather, owning most of the topless joints, rumored to run girls from Alaska to Texas through his agency Talents West, and already indicted for racketeering by a Federal Grand Jury, for transporting illegal gambling equipment across state lines. After a triumphant week at McGoverns, Gil asked Corbett to meet him and Kenny downtown Seattle for lunch at the Firelite Room in the Moore Hotel, to talk some long term business. This was Frank's headquarters, he and some of his Goodfellas were eating lunch, watching the go-go dancers, and my coming with Corbett was plainly a serious breach of the rules. We stayed close together, took a booth and ordered the fish & chips. Gil slid in on Corbett's side and soon had his ear. Frank's expensive cologne could not dissemble the gamy scent of a dangerous predator, he moved in by me, and leaning too near offered "You want, I'll fix the topless contest tonight at the Bavarian Gardens in Bellevue. Make it easy for you getting into the clubs. A girl like you could make some real cash". He never would have propositioned The Wife, but the Girlfriend was just fine. And to my great surprise, I was so terribly insulted, yes because he saw me as a pair of tits, but equally that he thought I needed him to fix it. Stomach knotting, heeding the counsel, my body wisely feared this man, my mind warned do not be stupid Shoshy, you don't want to be anywhere near this guy's shit-list, so I smiled sugar "Thank you, but no". And then could not help my self, confronting his steely dark eyes "You wouldn't have to fix it for me to win". He smiled and went back to his lunch. I knew this guy, he was a Biker in a silk suit, same mind-set on women, and probably offered me because Corbett was such an asset for his friend Gil, and maybe to get something on me incase I over-heard something, I would keep my mouth shut, he did not need anything on me, I was convinced of his menace. And, who would have thought topless contests were rigged. As a 17 year-old Seafair Queen contestant, I could not have imagined the Pagent winner being picked before-hand. I thought of my first offer to become a professional pair-of-tits, how Mr.Bigger and Mr.Little from Playboy smelled just like Frank, how girls bodies were merchandise, even in the seemingly innocent business of beauty pagents. And now I knew for sure, had I taken the Bunny job, it would not have gotten me anywhere or anything, for even the local tit factory, even the Bavarian Gardens was rigged.

Lorenzo and Marion still looked like themselves, but soul snatchers had taken them. His anguished discontent had become pious virtue, her's dutiful Wife and Mother. And the economic reciprocity of the Saved began to flow, one of the Brotherhood owned a two-bedroom rental in the little community of Lowell, three miles West of us, no references were necessary they moved without bothering to notifying Jarl, he was not one of them. Lorenzo joined Stan and Joey in the Church Band, and with such heavy-weights there was talk of recording a Christian album. They constantly prevailed on Corbett to join-up and come play keys. Marion took a job as receptionist for another of the Brotherhood, Renzo stayed home with Baby. On most weekends he'd come by, no longer openly preaching, always pressing Corbett. A pane of glass stood between these old friends, who still loved each other, reminiscing now their only neutral conversation. And then Colleen inherited money from a rich Uncle, if anyone knew how much, none said. She wisely bought a house in North Lynnwood, ten-minutes from Lorenzo and Marion. Erik made plans for the rest, another album, Second Hand Clapping. On a sunny late March afternoon he made a rare visit, spinning the same old fame and fortune, hoping Corbett would go along for another ride. Erik was a sliver of steel wool I could not pluck from my paw, and yet if One Hand Clapping didn't play Sky River, and Gretchen hadn't come along, I might not have found Corbett. I wondered, was Erik some kind of karmic balance-due for some wicked thing I'd done in a past life, that I would gladly square to be rid of him. And yet, to his credit, when The Clap fell apart, it was his dream dying, and still he and Colleen never give way to the saccharine promise of Born-Again. And, from the way he mocked Stanley, Joey and Lorenzo as he offered Corbett a snort from a little brown vial of cocaine, he had no intention otherwise. Ted and Stoney came by McGoverns on their way home to California, to bid Corbett farewell. Having also resisted the Brotherhood, they were not willing to spend more of their lives on Erik's dream-scheme, despite the new money.

We celebrated Dad's 58th at McGoverns. Corbett arranged a VIP table front center. Laughing easily, Dad thoroughly enjoyed the privilege of being the notable piano player's almost Father-in-Law, and could not have been prouder if Corbett was his own. My Folks were fans of Gil back to the World's Fair. Dad especially understood how hard a person had to work and how talented they must be to reach this level of recognition in any town. Corbett joined us after the first-set. Dad patted his back "You're wonderful, just wonderful My Boy". Corbett's grin spread his whole face, a Father's praise such sweet balm to a wounded Boy. Dad went on "I hope you know, we think the world of you". He looked at Mom "And we've been talking it over, and want to make another offer. Five-thousand dollars". Mom waited for that to register "And that's not all. There'll be lots of presents from friends and family". Her face glowed "Your Grandmother has five sisters and two brothers, and your Grandfather five brothers and two sisters". Five-thousand-dollars was a king's ransom to them, and us, enough to rock my resolution, make me recall those weightless Mustang days before the yoke of debt. We could pay-off JCPenney, Smiths, student loans, the Bug, go on a honeymoon, and come home with money for a savings account, if I would only give-in to conscription, take my place among the world's legion bondservants. And oh those insidious happily-ever-after tales, so enticing, wrapped in blushing romance, ribboned in tradition, so antiquated, so unsuited to the life I wanted, and this very minute, they had my unwitting Parents bargaining their Daughter's dowry. I wanted to tear-out the rootstock and plant some weed "Okay, wait. I'm sorry but no amount a money's gona make me sign a marriage contract. Some idea dead men thought up to own the females, own the kids, no thank you". Dad grimaced as if slapped. I knew how my words must sound "I mean, that's not you Daddy. I know you have only the best in your heart. But could we please just drop this for now". Corbett excused himself without comment. Mom laughed defensively, something she did when not quite catching my meaning, and fell-back on her same old excuse for me "My Daughter, you've always been such a Little Mazik". Dad knew exactly what I meant "Shoshy, you can't single-handedly change society. Some traditions are so old, their sheer weight will squash you like a bug. Why would you want to make it harder on yourself than you have too. Starting out's hard enough. That's all we care about, you having a good life. Getting married can help". I wiggled in my chair, thrilled he so plainly liked Corbett "Daddy I know you're right, but as John Lennon says "*you may say I'm a dreamer, but I'm not the only one*". Can we please drop this for another time". Dad was invariably him self, and when he thought my head thick, felt compelled as my Parent to persevere "No. I don't understand, why do you want to bring trouble on yourself. There might be other ways of getting married that would satisfy you". Now I was mad "Dad, can you pleeeease just drop it, we're here to celebrate your birthday, okay". He gave me a tenacious smile "Yes, I'll drop it when you tell me you'll think again about getting married".

The second-set opened with *Happy Birthday to You*, swamping our differences as the crowd sang too. Dad basked in the attention. And on cue, the sugar free cheesecake I arranged for, with candles lit and bottle of Wibel Green Hungarian wine were delivered to our table. Only on occasion would Mom permit her diabetic one-and-only a little white wine. His eyes glittering, Dad blew-out candles, and like reigning royalty raised his glass to the room "L'chayim". And to Corbett, and me "Thank you Shoshannah for this wonderful birthday". It was the first time I understood how good being able to do something so grand for my Folks could makes me feel. The New Gil Conte Show closed in the accustomed ovations and encores. Standing in the parking lot saying good-nights, sky clearing, Mom pulled a folded note from her coat pocket, looked at it before handing to me "Here Shoshy. Your friend Jeffree Johnson called just as we were leaving, and per instructions, I did not give out your number. But I know how much you like these people and promised to make sure you got this". Looking at the paper, a phone number. Bonita-Kay's face shown in my mind like a harvest moon. I missed her. More than five years since we touched, happily my Folks still had their same phone number.

Bonita-Kay answered in familiar Southern lilt. So satisfying hearing her voice, in excitement we talked over each other. Jeffree had been promoted late '69 to the advertising firm's main office in Dallas. She found a house with property to expand raising her hounds, their prize-winning bloodline was growing sought after. And Jeffree's latest idea had been honored with a Clio Award, an Alka-Seltzer commercial he wrote and directed, called *The Unfinished Lunch*. Filmed in black & white, 1930's gangster movie genre, featuring George Raft and a troop of other known heavies, hundreds of men sitting at long tables in a prison cafeteria, tasting the food, it's garbage, and they begin banging their tin cups on the tables, all chanting to the banging, louder, louder, Alka-Seltzer, Alka-Seltzer, Alka-Seltzer, Alka-Seltzer. The acclaim brought him opportunity, to make a movie from a play he and Bonita-Kay wrote, about two Vietnam Vets returned from the war, unable to bear living among civilians or civilization, they move to the Northwest corner of Washington State, deep in the Hoh Rain Forest. Jeffree petitioned the parole board for many months, finally persuading them to sanction a short trip out-of-state. He would fly into Seatac day-after-tomorrow, to meet producers and backers and scout locations, and hoped to see me. I marveled at their using such a salty past, creatively transforming it to sweet success, like alchemists spinning gold from straw, and could not wait to see them, even for five minutes. Bonita-Kay's musical lilt resigned, she would love to see my face too but the parole board was not convinced of her need to go along, anyway she had obligations to her hounds, whom she loved more than most people, they needed her to sing to them every day. I bragged on Corbett. She was thrilled for me, agreeing with Dad I should find a way to marry that would not compromise my heart. Bitter-sweet gripped that heart on hearing of Josh and his great Wife and their twin little Girls. And Arthur, sculpting with a vengeance, being shown in the most influential local galleries, living with his 91 year old Grandmam, looking after her, planning on moving to New York City when probation was up, unless of course Grandmam still needed him. And they were saving every cent, planning on leaving Texas forever, maybe with Arthur. I told her some of Ida Rose, promising to give Jeffree copies of the audits, and thinking there might be another long interval, took the moment to thank her for being such a consequential teacher, when my journey could have taken me down any road, with anyone, how often things she shared with me, that did not seem like such big deals at the time, revealed their import later. I would get-it because she had so generously tipped me off. And how I felt certain had I not gone through Texas, I would not have found Corbett. She laughed, her experience had been the same, not until I went home did she appreciate what a fate-full hand I played in their life. Had I not come along with my healthy optimism for life's possibilities, they would still be on the run. With Bonita-Kay there were no games, no traps to avoid, no subterfuge obscuring intention, only the cost of long distance, we made pledges to never lose touch again.

Driving Corbett to work, I hurried to Seatac and Jeffree's arrival gate. Hardly recognizing him in a well-cut light-brown worsted suit, blue shirt, and rattle-snake cowboy boots, face clean-shaven, hair cut above the ears, carrying an armadillo-hide briefcase. Hugging him tight, no cologne to dissemble, I could breathe-in that ambrosia spirit, recalling who this person was and why I so dearly loved him. At arms-length, looking each other over in approval, he felt the need to explain his business clothes, necessary deference to the money-men. I took his free-hand walking to the airport coffee-shop. For him, Ida Rose's book and the audits, for me photos of Bonita-Kay and the hounds, from her with kisses. And he quietly revealed what she never would. The most destructive part of their probation forbid her singing where there might be drugs, including alcohol, killing the possibility of resuming her career. Soon after I left, she sank into dark depression. And yet, their lives grew in ways she never expected, his success, moving back to Dallas, the TV commercials, she began trusting in their future, climbing-up out of darkness, her Afghans indispensible. And now there was this movie offer, with prospects of her singing the sound track. Time flew, we took the escalator to baggage, where an expensive navy pin-stripe suit waited as Jeffree claimed his things. I offered to take them to McGoverns for drinks, food if they were hungry, hoping Jeffree and Corbett could meet. Mr.Pin-Stripe was in a mighty rush to get on the last Bainbridge Island ferry for the night, the Others had already checked into the Kalaloch Lodge out on the coast, there were some hours driving ahead, he already rented a car and wanted to go, maybe get some shut-eye before scouting locations in the morning light. Taking my face in his hands, Jeffree kissed cheeks and forehead, calling me his good luck charm. I burst in tears as he hurried away, watching his back till gone.

Cyrene and Marion became exclusive best Born-Again friends, so like the supercilious cliques of High School days. Not so Lorenzo and Stan, who almost daily called Corbett. They truly loved him, and hoped they ultimately saw a convert and keyboard player for their praise Jesus Band.

When Stan and Cy announced their wedding, he was invited and not me. I got the message, hopefully I was a passing thing, but Corbett had been such a good Christian Boy before me, maybe he would be again. Fortunately psychic poison follows predictable manners, rolling round-and-round in your brain, coming up again-and-again, occupying your mind with who sent it, spurring one-sided conversations with them. I knew this, and had a mantra to rout it from my head, I have nothing to say to you, I will not play your game, shut up, go away, shut the fuck up. Corbett's treacherous upbringing made him an expert on this kind of poisoning, music was his way of routing the venom, he wrote me a song to drown-out the conversations.

Together We Can

Now that I've got you
Sitting very close to me
When we grow up into the open
What do you think we will be
Where will be go
And what will we do
I know I love you
Together we will see it though

An I'm thinking about us
Just as we used to be
Where are the friends we once knew
Braided heroes lost to the sea
Where did they go
And what did they do
I know I love you
Together we can see it though

Cause we took the chance of life
Not knowing why
Only the young can be so free
We couldn't satisfy love easily
Ah but now face to face it's growing warm

Now that I got you
So close to me
Where are the places we're gona go
So many dreams we can see
Where will we go
Will they come true
I know I love you
Together we can see it though

We took the chance of life
Not knowing why
Only the young can be so free
We couldn't satisfy love easily
Ah but now face to face it's growing warm
Together we can see it though

Corbett's Parents sent an early Easter card, Christ on the cross, HE IS RISEN, and a note scolding us for living-in-sin, threatening perdition, and upping their ante another thousand-dollars to convert and marry. Tearing Jesus in-half, Corbett tossed the card and note in the garbage. That night as I stood over my sewing-table cutting a gown, poison rolling round and round, furious, having those one-way indignant conversations, no I would never even consider selling-out but I should for money, well fuck you, eat shit and die, and it was so unnerving, so bloody, for I was actually considering selling-out, as an artist. My creations were not selling so well, and I was torn, should I taint their as-yet unsullied honesty, make them more commercially suited to Seattle's provincial character. After all the persuasion went, this is a town that only four years ago changed the law allowing females to sit at the bar, where you still could not buy meat on Sunday, that arrests and prosecutes you for what you think, builds war machines, and there is no body-of-consumers impatient for my fearless fashion. As if standing in mid-air, my paradigm shifted from under me, I had to be care-full not to flinch or I would certainly fall, finding my self on the unexpected side of another point of view, maybe Dad was right, there might be another way of getting married that would satisfy me, Ida Rose was an ordained minister, I would ask her to do the deed.

When Corbett came home from work, I fixed his favorite grilled-cheese on rye with thin-sliced tomato, lots of mustard, and a tall glass of milk. While he ate, I proposed "Babe, I was thinking, you an me should get married". He choked, coughing, drinking half the milk, sputtering "April Fools right". I smiled "Nope, I mean it. Marriage won't change us. We don't have to do all the usual wedding stuff, you know, traditional vows, bridal registration, all that crap. We'll take the bribes, pay our bills, go down to New Brighton Beach for a walk, and come home with money in the bank, for our old age. Ida Rose can marry us, she's an ordained minister. What could be so bad". Mouth slightly agape, Corbett was speechless. I so loved being that unpredictable some one who could blow his mind, and grinning, sashayed over, took his big soft hand in mine and knelt on one knee "Corbett James Hawkins, will you marry me". His laugh began at the bottom of his belly, shaking his whole body. Gus and Grilla-Fish came running to see what the mischief. And I laughed too, for this was a crazy moment, in the spoon-fed fairy-tales of my childhood, I had just taken the boy's part, and now everyone would assume we sold-out for money, which to an extent was true, and worse, I would forfeit the immoral high ground to my Folks, Corbett's Folks, signaling an open door to visit more of their standards in our life. Tears welling in his increasingly solemn blue eyes, Corbett squared his shoulders and cleared his throat "Shoshannah Dvorah Leibofsky, it would be my honor to marry you". More thrilled that I could have ever imagined I stood "Okay Babe, we'll do it". He pulled me onto his lap "Ida Rose can marry us. What a great idea". Putting my arms round his neck I kissed his face all over "Yeah. I remember Tom saying she's an ordained minister. That should make it legit for everyone". He shook his head slow side-to-side and sniffed "Not for my Folks. They won't come unless it's Catholic, and that means you have to convert". I smiled without showing teeth "I'm sure my Folks wish you would convert too. Look, I'll promise if they come, I'll convert and get married in the church of their choice". Corbett looked worried "You will". I giggled "No Babe. It's a total lie, an it just might get them to come". His brows pinched, then relaxed "When you wana do the deed". He took a deep breathe and smiled "Get married". I kissed his lips and giggled softly "Soon as we can. Like the first Sunday in May. Celebrate Spring coming again. You now, rebirth, born again, it's perfect". Corbett hugged me tight "God I love you". I could not sleep for wiggling, marriage was a business contract that would legally make me Corbett's property, and the way he said yes made me yearn to be owned. He was restless too, wondering about this woman he thought he knew, who would go one way in such conviction and with the same confidence change her mind, someone willing to deceive his Folks, he murmured "You asleep". Spooning up-close he kissed my shoulder, and took a little nibble "So you want to be The Wife". I squirmed "Yeah, right. Don't expect me to wear a ring".

Only Gus demanding to go out got us up before noon. Deciding over coffee, with a month till the first Sunday of May, we better get on the wedding plans. First thing, ask Ida Rose would she do it. I wanted to in-person, calling, inviting her to McGoverns. Delighted to come hear Corbett perform, and at such a noted venue, she would make a hair appointment as soon as she hung up. I extended the invitation to Tom, thinking of asking Leda. He had to work till midnight, closing-up the gas station. I phoned Leda anyway. She had been hired on as bookkeeper for the Mercedes Benz dealership in Seattle, saving to move away from her Mom, had to be at work by 7AM tomorrow, and nothing would keep her away. We picked Ida Rose up at eight. She looked young and hip in cream-white wool slacks, matching cashmere cardigan, spun-silver hair, clip-on pearl earrings, black velvet flats, wrapped in the tie-dye shawl. And she was absolutely thrilled to hear of our wedding plans, and flattered we wanted her to marry us, sadly her ordination was legal only in Oregon, she could not do it. I sat in the back seat, crushed and confused, mind racing, who but Ida Rose could bless our union, now what, some rabbi, or priest, or judge who didn't know us or give a damn, how could that possibly be meaning-full, maybe we should take her to Oregon and do it there. Seeming undaunted Corbett asked did she think a priest might marry us without my converting, or a rabbi. Having heard of some very liberal priests in California performing mixed marriages, she suggest he call the local Ecumenical Council. I began to boil, no way a priest, Dad would never come and I would not do that to him, and then there were Halls and Arlene, nothing but conversion would satisfy them. I felt like a bone between dogs, then catching the tenor of Corbett's aim, I stood once-more in mid-air, paradigm shifting, and did not flinch, for he asked Ida Rose if she thought a rabbi might marry us, he did not care, only that we find someone of substance, some one we could respect. Solid ground, my fear this would set us against each other gone, for that was exactly what I wanted too, someone we could respect. Leda met us in the lobby. Having brought others to Ida Rose, and none but Corbett remaining, I realized I had been reluctant all along, for if Leda went the way of Nick and Ric, tonight might be the limit of our friendship. They enjoyed immediate rapport, and I smarted a bit from unexpected jealousy.

And Corbett, playing with such naked emotion and intensity, inspired Kenny and Gil beyond their customary heights to the most unpredictable and hilarious show I had ever seem them do. The week-night crowd, every chair full, stayed till the last note of the last set, wanting more, applauding three encores. Corbett had many of the cocktails fans sent to the stage delivered to our table, more than we cared to drink, although he drank too many him self. I drove, and he folded those long legs into the back seat of the Bug and dozed. Thinking his behavior rude, I apologized walking Ida Rose into her house. She was not offended "There's no need for apology Little One. That Sweet Lamb of yours worked awfully hard for us tonight, and I had a wonderful time". Tom sat at the big mahogany table drinking beer, raising his glass as we came in, words a bit slurry "Hi Big Mo. Can I get you one". Putting her handbag on the table "Yes dear, thank you". She left the room. Tommy still in his gas station overalls, grinning with all his white teeth "Hi purdy girl, how bout a cold brew". He was just drunk enough to be amenable "No thank you. But come to my house for dinner Sunday and meet Leda, a friend of mine, okay". Shaking his head no "I'd feel like a big fat dork. Whad's she look like". Laughing I took the chair by him "Beautiful Tom, absolutely beautiful inside and out. She has electric blue eyes. Anyway I just want you to be friends, nothing more". I could see his eager interest and pushed "You'll only feel like a dork for a minute. You'll get over it, and so will she". He scrunched his chin "Hum, electric blue eyes". I smiled to my self "Good, dinner's at six. And remember, just friends, someone to talk too, that's all okay". Ida Rose came back in her slippers "What a perfectly lovely evening. Thank you Shoshannah. And your friend Leda, I thought she was so bright". I twinkled at Tom "She'll be really tickled you think so". Ida Rose did not sit, waiting politely to walk me to the door. I shot to me feet "Corbett's in the car, I better go". She put a hand on my shoulder "I want you to know, I would have dearly loved to marry you two. Please don't let this stop you. I think you belong together". I wanted to hug her and scream and call the whole thing off, but this compelling desire that had its hook deep in my collective soul, this vestige Dad warned would squash me like a bug, was not going as planned, and would not go away. I felt overwhelmed, having no idea now what to do.

Leda called next morning, thanking me for introducing her to Ida Rose, she felt it was the most important thing that ever happened to her. And to tell me there were stories in the Times and Post-Intelligencer on the Seattle Seven. My concern for our friendship happily unwarranted, still I had to ask, did she think Ida Rose was evil, even a spec, even for one second. She laughed in surprise, unequivocally not, infact she had called around already, finding the downtown Seattle Fredrick & Nelson carried *The Pink Elephant: A Challenge to Confusion*, she would walk there on her lunch hour. I asked to buy me one too, and I would pay her if she came to Sunday dinner, 6PM, and oh yes, Tom was coming too. Giggling, she said yes. After breakfast I went into Snohomish for the newspapers.

U.S. Closes Books On Seattle 7' Case

The government quietly ended its case against seven young activists who were charged with conspiracy to damage federal property during a February 17, 1970, violent demonstration at the United States Courthouse in Seattle.

U.S. District Court Judge Russell Smith, assigned to the case after a mistrial and contempt-of-court charges against the Seattle group, has ordered the original conspiracy indictment be dismissed after a request that he do so from United Stated Attorney Stan Pitkin.

Pitkin's office would give no reason yesterday for the dismissal request.

The Seattle 7 were indicted by the Federal Grand Jury in April, 1970, after the Grand Jury began looking into some of the violent demonstrations then growing out of the anti-war movement. Trial on charges began November, 1970, before United Stated Judge George H.Boldt, who left the Federal bench the next year to head the Federal Pay Board. That trial ended in a mistrial after a series of courtroom disruptions by defendants and supporters.

Judge Boldt called a mistrial, found all Seven in contempt and denied bail, and the Seven spent 40 days in jail before the Ninth Circuit Court overturned the bail denial. Later the Ninth Circuit Court overturned one of Judge Boldt's contempt convictions, remanded the case for further action and recommended another judge hear the case if charges were refiled.

After the mistrial was declared, it was up to Pitkin, who personally prosecuted the case, to refile the original conspiracy charges.

Yesterday Pitkin made it official that he would not refile charges. Thus the government apparently has closed the books on the events of February 17, 1970.

<u>*Trial Papers Were Stolen Says Seattle 7 Attorney*</u>

One of the attorneys for the Seattle Seven said he believed his office had been burglarized twice before the trial.

Lee Holley, one of the four defense attorneys in the conspiracy case, said: "I know on two occasions before the trial, papers were missing from my office files. On one occasion I reported it to the Federal Bureau of Investigation. I couldn't prove it in a court of law but I felt I had been burglarized at least twice."

Holley's comments came in the wake of a Newsweek Magazine report that Senate investigators have been told by high administration officials that government operatives committed burglaries in connection with the prosecution of the Seattle case.

United States Attorney Stan Pitkin, asked to comment said "I'll be reading the papers like everyone else."

Throughout the trial the defendants complained their telephones were being "bugged", that the F.B.I. was following them and their houses were being rifled.

Carl Maxey another attorney for the defendants said: "If evidence comes out that there were burglaries, there will be lawsuits filed."

Well well well, here it was for all to see. Judge Boldt paid-off with a cushy federal job, and Pitkin quietly dropping charges, which made no sense on its own, but for the recent Washington Post explosion by Bob Woodward and Carl Bernstein, that in June of 1972 Nixon's brigands had also burglarized the Democratic Party's National Headquarters in a

Washington D.C. apartment-office complex called The Watergate. Nixon needed Pitkin home, for there was talk of hush-money and cover-up, and fingers pointing to Nixon as a common thief, who not five months ago was re-elected in a landslide, and was now being called Tricky Dick. I felt sanity completely restored, my constant companion paranoia had not been a delusion, more a wise fear, grounded in actual government sanctioned covert intelligence programs, CO-INTEL-PRO. Those times I had been followed, infiltrated, coerced, probed, trampled on and intimidated were not imagined. And how wink wink coincidental, the Seattle Seven had out-lived their usefulness as a diversion, just as Tricky Dick needed to fetch Pitbull to defend his master. Even the establishment press had softened toward us, for Americans yearned to reclaim their Daughter and Sons. Our public flogging was over, I no longer had to sympathetically feel the lash.

Thoughts turned affectionately to Keely, she had been a significant rabbit hole, our lives now ran in very different directions, near two-years since we had spoken, there was no better time. Justin's name was in the book, her's was not. She answered on the sixth ring. And after dulcet hellos and how are yous, I asked "Have you seen the papers". She sighed heavy "You mean the Seven. Look, I don't wana talk about it. Justin and me got married. I have the life I always wanted. We got custody of his Girls, even Sundance in February. You understand, with six Kids I need to be real conventional". Her pinched tone hurt, I played dumb "How are those precious Boys". "Fine" only just made it though her lips. But it did, telling me I was in control, for Keely never had the stuffing to say what she meant or she would have already excused herself off the phone, I could ask what I pleased "You have the best Kids. I miss 'em. How's their Dad". She bristled "Ric's still in Capetown, organizing against something called apartheid. Still smuggling bugs". I laughed "Still". She did too "Yeah, an makes good money. Sends me four-hundred a month". I recognized my old friend "Ric's a good head deep down". She sighed resignation "I can see the best and worst of him in the Boys". I had one more question "Speaking of the best, you ever hear from Miss Fetchin-Fine". Her voice tightened "No, not since her an Ava moved to San Diego with that poet, and left me holding the bag for rent. Look, I'd rather not be linked to the

MotherTruckers. Justin doesn't need to know all the details". My feeling abandoned was lightened by the truth, and because her focus was the Littles, likely Justin's influence, for she was a chameleon, always going along, even her politics had been for the most part Ric's, I did not resist "So be it my friend. Please say hello to the Boys for me, and Ric, please". I could hear the door close in her voice "I will, I will". And I let her go "Okay then, bye". Keely barely pushed bye over her lips. I could not tell if she was crying.

A six-pack of Coors under each arm, nervous as a cat on the Forth of July, Tom came to dinner an hour early. He and Corbett well into the beer when Leda knocked. Awkward embarrassment flushed their cheeks even before introduction, smoothing into comfortable conversation, they both knew Ida Rose. Over oven-roasted eggplant, Walla Walla Sweet onions, mushrooms, zucchini, plum tomatoes, and baby red potatoes drizzled in olive oil and sprinkled with fresh chopped basil, thin slices of mozzarella and parmigiano, and lots of crisp buttery garlic bread, Corbett leaked "Shoshy asked me to marry her. First Sunday in May. Pretty cool huh". His beery tongue could infuriated me, I was not ready for them to know, we had not talked our plans out beyond setting a date. Smiling, Leda prompted "So who's your maid-of-honor". I knew what she wanted, and had no desire for attendants "I really don't know what we're doing yet, maybe go to Las Vegas, one of those drive through Elvis chapels". Missing the sarcasm and smiling Corbett cooed "Doesn't matter Sweetheart, any way's fine with me". Drinking, he did not always keep the faith, and though always sorry afterwards, I choked on apologies and excuses. He had no idea the eons-old rituals and Parents and expectations that were coming for us, and I had no idea how much I had already planned "That's easy to say Babe. But we're in for a huge sticky tangle. This isn't just a party, we're saying personal stuff out-loud infront of witnesses. Maybe if we keep it simple, we can dodge some of it. Like invite close Friends and Family only. No one allowed coming to see the Hippy Freaks get hitched. And I don't want rings, they mean ownership. I could ask my Folks to have it at their place. Eliminate the complication of finding some where on short notice. Make say three-hundred-dollars the spending limit so it won't get big. And since Ida Rose can't marry us, I wana try an honor a promise I made my Grampa and get a rabbi". Charming and a little old-fashioned behind his big blue eyes and rock'n roll, Corbett's smile lit the room "That's all fine with me. I just want you to marry me. I'm with your Dad on this. And your Folks might even lay-off us". His smiled faded "But mine never will, if they come or not". I needed to say this "Can you just hear it if they don't. You know, all the whispering behind hands, what kind of Parents don't come to their own Son's wedding. No matter what the truth, they'll be called anti-Semitic. And the whispers will echo, oh poor Shoshannah, no doubt the hate seeped into the Son too. I will not have that shit staining the day. So I'm going to call your Mom, and promise if they come, I'll convert and have a church wedding next year. An you'll back me up, right". Corbett was already nodding "Yep I will. But they'll never forgive us when we don't do it". I shrugged "I don't care. You think they're ever going to forgive us anyway". He smiled "I hope not". Tom made a toast "Corbett, you're a lucky dog, mazel tov". Leda "To love, the most precious thing in the world". And since we had an audience, I raised my beer bottle and made Corbett swear "For the record, infront of these fine up-standing people, promise never to call me The Wife". Putting his big right hand over his big heart "I do, if you promise never to call me Hubby". My knight-in-shining-armor even tarnished with drink was irresistible, I put hand over heart "Promise". Oh shit, now it was real, now we had plans. Leda and Tom left before 8PM, saying she wanted to follow him home and ask Ida Rose to autograph her book before she went to bed. I only partly believed them. And though pleased they really liked each other, having deliberately mixed these mercurial entities, I felt burdened by the weight of responsibility that comes with playing god, interfering with the Sweet Sisters, vowing never ever to introduce anyone to anyone ever again.

Chapter Thirty One

VOYEURS VILIPENDS AND TARES

Stepping over this event horizon was unavoidable, early morning I walked around the house for a while before sitting down on the floor to call my Folks, asking Corbett to sit close and listen-in, I wanted him to understand what I meant by a sticky tangle. Mom answered "Hello Chicken Valley". I took a breath "Morning Mom. I know you're going to work, but could you get Dad on the other line for one minute. I have something to tell you. And don't worry, you'll like it". She sighed "Sure Honey, just a sec". Dad picked-up "Hi Shoshy. Everything okay". I told myself just say it "Corbett and I are getting married on May 6th at your place. It's a Sunday". Dad's voice was smiling "Ohhh. I always knew you were a smart girl. And I want you to know I'll be proud to have Corbett as my son-in-law". Mom's voice not so smiling "My Little Girl getting married. You know I think the world of Corbett too. But with our huge Family, and your friends, and ours, how can I possibly plan a wedding by May 6. It's what, a month away". Ever since I could remember my Folks participated in this social ritual with all their Friends and Family, inviting each other to brit milahs, bar mitzvahs, confirmations, graduations, showers, weddings. Anyone getting an invitation was obliged to send a gift even if they could not come. Mom and Dad's largess had been sincere, and with the expectation that when it came to their children, the generosity would be reciprocated. However to keep the deal, I would have to invite them all, and though all might not come, some would "Mom, please listen to me. I know it's not much time, and you probably have always seen my wedding as big so we can get all the presents, but that whole thing's your bargain not mine. Corbett and I only want people who care we're getting married. No voyeurs or we won't do it". Dad huffed "Shoshannah, this is blackmail. I'm kind of disappointed in you". I would not be shamed "You're right Daddy, but I never intended on getting married anyway. This is all I can handle. I'm not trying to be mean, but we could just as well elope to Vegas". Dad tried getting around me "Now Shoshy, you're not thinking clear. It's my job as your Father to pay for the wedding, and I'm proud I can afford a big one". I was pretty sure Dad would take this tack, and knew more than anything they wanted to be there to see me say I do, it was my trump "Corbett and I want to keep it small, round 40 people in all. And to make sure, you can't spent more then three-hundred-dollars, period, for everything". Conjuring Cronus the Terrible who devoured his own children, he tried "You're going to humiliate your Mother and me, make us look like pikers. Everyone will talk". I giggled at his trick "Daddy, I've seen behind the Wizard's curtain. You can't make me, so just be nice okay. People are going to talk anyway. Catholic and Jew, Hippies, Longhairs. I know what you an Mom want, but this is what we want. Can you see that". To my surprise Dad conceded, at least to my ears "Yes, you're right, they're already talking. We'll do it your way, here, three-hundred-dollars, and not a penny more". I knew how to win Mom too "Come on Mom, pleeease say yes. Just think, you and Granny can cook all your specialties. It'll be real geschmak and haimish". Usually amused at me speaking Yiddish, she could not hide her indignation "There's not enough time to do it right. A lot of people are going to be mad at me. I don't like it". Dad interrupted "Honey, we have to get to work". I knew he wanted to talk before she said more, I hoped Corbett took notice. And though this was not over, for now anyway I was satisfied "Thank you. An don't worry Mom, it'll be great, you'll see. I'll call you tonight".

Corbett lit a smoke, and one for me "Wow, your Folks are so cool. You can actually argue with them and they don't try to kill you. I had no idea there was so much to getting married". I nodded "Yeah. I'm the Girl, this is the first wedding, and the only one they'll have any say over. They probably had plans since I was born. Weddings 're an old program that runs deep. We need to stick together tight and stay awake, know when to stand firm and when we have ta give in. And we need to talk about every thing before we say anything". Making the sign of the cross, he mouthed cross-my-heart-and-hope-to-die. I handed him the phone smiling "You'll need the protection. It's your turn. Call your Folks and I'll listen". Arlene answered "Hello". Corbett cleared his sung-out throat "Hi Mom, it's Corbett". She went strait for that throat "It's been a while since we heard from you. What's wrong". The deep and bloody guilt-wound had scabbed over a bit and he did not flinch "Mom, Shoshy and I are getting married on

May 6th. It's a Sunday, and we sure would like you and Dad to come". She gasped "Is she pregnant". I stuck my middle finger against the phone. Corbett laughed "No Mom, we're getting married, like you been asking us to. Will you come". Her voice iced "Corbett, you know your Father doesn't have vacation until August". I turned the mouthpiece to me "Hi. Mrs.Hawkins, it's Shoshannah. If you come to our wedding, I'll convert. I'll go to the St.Monica's and study, and soon as I'm baptized and take communion, we'll get married again, at your church if you like". Corbett turned the phone to him "How 'bout it Mom". She did not defrost "Well it's on a Sunday. I think your Father could arrange one day off". I knew when a fish bit and took the mouth-piece "There's a real nice Travel Lodge on Mercer Island. I'll be glad to book you a room". She was all business "Thank you. Let's see the calendar here. Come in Saturday, leave Monday. We'll need the nights of the 5th and 6th". Corbett smiled at me, turning the phone to him "Thanks Mom. Just let me know when your flight arrives. I'll come pick you up". Her words struck hard "No, your Father and I will take a cab. Just send me confirmation on the room". She hung-up. And we laid on the floor quiet, looking-up, Gus and Grilla-Fish sniffing us, wondering. I knew Corbett felt the blow, climbed on-top of him, pinning his shoulders to the rug "We won Babe. We won. And I don't care what your Folks reason for coming, or how they get here. I just want it all smooth on the surface. Just for one day, an we'll never give 'em another chance to hurt us again". I waited till he left for McGoverns and called Mom back. Her whole tone had changed "Your Father and I had time to talked, and May 6th is perfect". I smiled to my self "I love you Mom, thanks. Okay, so Corbett's Folks are coming up. They're booked in at the Travel Lodge on the Island, the nights of the 5th and 6th". She was delighted "Great Honey, they'll be close by. We can take them to dinner Saturday night, to McGoverns. You too of course. We can listen to Corbett play. All get a chance to know each other". She fizzed "After all we're going to be machetayneste and machuten. We have lots to talk about". Supposing Corbett's Parents were like her and Dad, she could not imagine in her sweet and somewhat artless soul how cruel they could be. I wanted to trim expectations so reality would not be so harsh "Mom, they might be too tired". Exasperated, she quipped "We'll all be tired from working, but they have to eat don't they".

Such hopes and dreams are a Daughter's wedding, and no matter how I struggled to make it mine, the juggernaut was rolling, insisting, crushing, and I did not ultimately matter. All I really wanted was to take Corbett and Ida Rose and elope to Oregon. He said he would do what ever made me happy. Which at first lightened my load, and then not when I realized he had just waived all responsibility to me. Infact no one but me seemed bothered by the sticky tangle, the unquestioned, universal wedding precepts, marked-out in exhausting detail. As I stood at my sewing table drawing a wedding-dress, I had to wonder why it felt like life and death, why wasn't I like the countless willing girls before me, every detail already planned, even to the names of my kids. I couldn't be the only one to ever feel this way. And yet there was no evidence, for the fairy-tale always ended in happily-ever-after, and Mothers are never heard telling their Daughters just because I did it doesn't mean you have to. Even in the last minute they could say, to hell with what everyone thinks, do what's in you heart. Once I signed the marriage contract, could I salvage integrity from the pyre of my self-respect. And still, I could see my self a blushing Bride, in an antique-white heavy satin wrap-skirt, cut on the bias to give it the necessary curve, flaring like a blossom at the hem. I wanted to look like an up-side-down calla lily, a bodice of green raw-silk, very-fitted with long full sleeves, Monique and Loretta's carved crystal buttons closing the cuffs and front. I would make Corbett a matching satin shirt. Knowing exactly what I needed, I planned on a quick hunt for fabric, and alone. Mom absolutely insisted on taking the day-off, after all I was her only Girl, she wanted to be involved in every detail, instructing, meet her for lunch at Clark's Crabapple in Bellevue, and she would take me shopping. The meal was too much food, and too long, and the tangle flared at the fabric store. I found just the satin to hold the lily's shape, and just the new-leaf-green raw silk. Mom was horrified "I will not buy that for you. It's not proper for a Bride. You should be in pure white, with lots of lace and tulle". She took me by the arm to bridal whites. I wanted to wrench away and scream, leave me alone, I'm not six-years old, I know how to dress my self, I've always known how to dress my self even when you didn't think so, and I never liked the way you dressed me, well almost never, and I don't give a shit what's proper, and I want to buy the fabric myself anyway. I stood infront of the ubiquitous froth of cloth muttering "I'm not a sacrificial virgin. I'm not even a virgin. Who are you trying to kid Mom". She glared as if I was six and making an embarrassing fuss in public "How can you do this to me. You have to wear white Shoshannah. You just don't understand the rules. I'll be a laughing stock. My friends 'll never stop talking behind my back". Sticky sticky tangle, this was about her not me. I did not care what her friends thought. I did not want them at the wedding, or most of mine for that matter. But her life was dictated by what Family, friends, neighbors, even strangers thought of her and her actions. Everyone's persuasions matter before mine. And if I said Mom don't you see how selfish you're being, doesn't what I want count too. I knew she would not understand, and turn to that usual response when she wanted the last word with me, I couldn't possibly understand how a Mother feels until I have Children of my own. I did not want to fight her, it was her battle not mine, and I was the only one who knew it was going on, the only one who could or would give-up "So what's new. They talk about me behind your back anyway". She ignored me, selecting a blinding-blue-white satin polyester, pushing "This will make a beautiful dress". Mom did not sew, this fabric had a cold-blue undertone, was too thin, more for a blouse, and ugg, polyester, and I was about to educate her when every cell in me relaxed, as if I had just done smack, my ego relinquishing its fists. I understood why Corbett had wisely waived this fight, it was not his, it was not worth the sticky, and it was not mine. No longer caring what I wore, I took the bolt of fabric from her hands "Okay Mom, this'll work". She gave me a quizzical look "Thank you Shoshannah".

We went next to the print shop. Invitations ordered today could not be ready for two weeks. Here was a chance to do one thing my way "Mom, Corbett an I planned on making them ourselves". Her eyes blazed in frustration "No, it's not right. Invitations have to be printed, and should have been sent months ago. They're your first impression and they're already late". I followed her toward the car, to likely another print shop, reasoning softly "Mom, it's the only way they'll get out in the next few days". She stopped "So what do you want me to do". We were standing infront of Newberry's five-and-dime-store. I pulled her inside, collecting colored construction-paper, calligraphy pens, sealing wax, and a seal of hearts entwined. Mom warned "People will be insulted to get such an invitation. They'll think your wedding is a joke". I decided to take a chance "Mom, what's really on your mind". Her eyes welled, and the story tumbled "Your Father and I married in such a hurry. It was war time, and he was waiting for orders to be shipped out. We were so in love, and I wasn't sure he'd come back. There was no time, and less money. I wore my best suit. You Father looked so handsome in his uniform. And the Rabbi came to my Gramma Monya's house. Relatives, friends, everyone pitched in their ration stamps, and cooked, and brought wine and flowers. We had a feast. But I always felt cheated. And when I first saw your little shayna punim, I never wanted you to feel that way". I had tears too "I love you Mom. An I promise I don't feel cheated. Your marriage turned out great, right. The kind of wedding doesn't matter, only the love". She knew where I was going and gave me a look "Love takes you through the years, but this isn't war time". I smiled, it was, Vietnam war-time "If it was good enough for you and Dad, it's good enough for me and Corbett". These were the abracadabra words, the haunted look of long held disappointment fell away, her voice low and calm "I never wanted my Little Girl to feel that way. Your Father and I just want you to be happy". Ah ha, Mom had picked the color of her bridesmaids' dresses and the names of her children long before meeting Dad, and never imagined I had not. I thought she should not live through me, and marry Dad again just the way she always dreamed, bridesmaids dresses and all. I said none of it "A small three-hundred-dollar wedding 'll make me happy". She sighed, emotionally exhausted "Okay Honey". Somehow I did not believer her, as we sat on the bench outside Newberrys, puffing Benson & Hedges from her gold lamé cigarette case, watching people walk by. When smokes were butts, she turned to me "We still have to find a photographer". I wanted to go home "Mom, that'll cost at least a hundred bucks. Can Dad take the pictures. He's always been the one recording our lives". Tired in her voice, she smile at the thought of him "Your Father is a wonderful photographer. He knows just when to click the button. And maybe your Little Brother will take some, he's got a good eye too". Opening her wallet, she handed me two tens "Here, this is for stamps". I never felt totally comfortable taking money from Mom, often there were strings "Thanks. Now I better get home and start working on those invitations, and the dress". Such is the labyrinth of animus and affection with Mother and Daughter.

Corbett had a grace-full steady hand writing invitations. I folded, sealed and addressed. And we disputed debated wrangled discussed stonewalled bristled compromised and laughed over who to invite. Corbett wanted Erik, contending they had a long history together. I had a longer history with him, but only wanted those who had our happiness at heart. Erik certainly did not. Colleen was first to hear about my falling inlove, and though she had never been so very friendly, I'd come to see this might be her natural disposition, and had sentimental feelings. Then momentarily outside my subjectivity, realizing Corbett's experience with Erik was so very different from mine, I said yes, hoping he would see our legal union as a personal defeat and not come anyway. Corbett wanted Stanley for similar reason, which meant Cyrene. I ranted and railed and reluctantly gave-in, convinced she would not come either. Same for Joey. The Others were easy, Ida Rose, Tommy, Leda, Rachel, Katey, Gil and his Girlfriend, Kenny and his Wife, Lorenzo and Marion, Delroy, and Frank and Amber who made it possible for us to have our Seacliff Beach bungalow. And immediate Families, Paul and Angela, Maggie and Diego, knowing none could afford the trip. Forty-two including Gus, Grilla-Fish, and us. After the post office, I phoned Mom to let her know invitations were in the mail, who was invited, and who was likely to come so she could plan the food. A deafening silence as I read the list. She warned in a tight growl "The rest of your Family's going to be terribly hurt you left them out". I had already invited more than comfortable with "Mom, you know and I know they'd only be coming to see the Freak show". She balled-me-out "You're such a stinker. And you're wrong. All your Aunties and Uncles love you. They ate you up when you were little, and they all want to be there. Your Grandmother is going to bite my head off. At least let me invite her Sisters, and the Girls I play cards with". Her tone softened "Just think of the gelt you'll be missing out on". I held fast "No Mom. You know if you invite one you have to invite them all". Her voice so pinched it hardly squeaked out "Have it your way".

I hated the fabric and it hated me, pretentious unyielding polyester, when pressed it smelled like burnt gasoline, and would not completely flatten or forgive an unintended crease. I cut the sleeves too short, sewed the bodice seams inside-out, finishing with a tight zigzag before noticing. The more I fought, the more it tangled. I needed help and knew Rachel was the person. Having seen her last night in one of those vivid dream, though not in-person for more than five years, I phoned her Folks, finding her living with them. Her small voice quivered with emotion "Course I'll come. Tomorrow around eleven. Funny thing is, I've been thinking about you".

Opening the front door I was thrown on my heels, though she wore thick wool slacks and bulky fisherman-knit cardigan over a heavy cashmere turtleneck, Rachel was maybe 80 pounds, her face a raw-boned skull. I could not hide my shock and looked down, noting a second pair of pants and a third peeking from under her cuffs. Avoiding my eyes too, she stepped forward for a hug. Her breath burned of a body consuming itself. And I could hardly feel her embrace, did not return it for fear of crushing her ribs, wishing this too was a dream. Because of sick upon ill, Rachel had always been thin. We were the same height, shoe and glove size, and me never more than ten-pounds heavier, but in an unrelenting and as far as I was concerned one-sided rivalry, she rarely missed a chance to point-out or demonstrate how dainty she was. But this was concentration camp thin, we were the right age to have died there, I had to wonder was this some past engram pathologically playing itself out, or some just plain weakness because her Mother was experimented on. We met far too young to know or talk about what was inside, through the years this had not significantly deepened, I felt still bound by those polite parameters from speaking the obvious, and took her into the kitchen to meet Corbett.

Eating breakfast, he froze in position, then quickly offered her his plate of toast and jam. She stepped back raising hands as if to protect her face "No thank you, I've eaten". And then dismissing him entirely turned to me "Let's go look at your dress". I gave him a see-ya-later look, and smiled at Rachel "I'm so glad you're here. Come on. Every time I put my hand to this material something goes wrong. It hates me and I hate it". She followed upstairs, standing at the top to recoup. And bearing no antagonism for the fabric, her fingers commanded it, lengthening the sleeves with

Monique and Loretta's lace, effortlessly taking the bodice apart, fitting it on me, mentioning how it would be much too big for her. She could still make me feel terrible, perhaps because she felt so terrible, people treat you like they feel, but the enormous mouth in my head was screaming, too big compared to what, you, what a preposterous fucking competition, had nothing changed in the five years we hadn't seen each other. I kept my lips shut tight, resolving if we were to continue a relationship it would have to somehow grow-up. As if looking for some jealousy or maybe regret from me, she spilled having run into and fallen for a high school boy-friend of mine, Larry Marklund. When I genuinely congratulated her on picking one of the nice ones, her tone was acid "But I would never marry Goyim, and neither should you. Just think, they might have been Nazis in their last life". And there is was, what she came to really say. A bitter paranoia had always been eating her, justifiably based on endless mercy-less persecution. I'd read about the Inquisitions, seen too many films on death camps, heard the first-hand stories of twelve-year-old Frieda being hidden by Russian soldiers under the floor-boards of their barracks for three-and-a-half years, and the farmer who dug-out his barn floor to make a room, hiding Rose and other children four years. And I felt the outrage of the virulent hatred in my own life. But what struck me was how extreme it had become in Rachel, and getting worse, and how just like her Folks she sounded, making me even more grateful to mine for limiting the legacy of this legitimate fear. And I was unable to look away from the wormy blue veins and boney knuckles bulging her papery translucent emaciated hands, surprised to find them so beauty-full. And I think because I just listened and did not respond, she opened "What I have, it's called Crohn's disease. The walls of my intestines scar, and narrow. It hurts to eat anything, and sometimes they stick together and nothing can get through. I've had five operations, removing sections of the intestines. My Doctors wants me to have another one soon. A big one, to cut out all the ulcers and scarring. And if I need it, some of my colon, maybe a lot of it. That means a colostomy, wearing a shit bag for the rest of my life. I just can't. Anyway, my Folks think the operation will kill me and have forbidden it". Her eyes were so terribly sad "But the way things're going, Crohns 'll kill me anyway". Till this moment I thought we had time to work-on a difficult friendship, I no longer cared about polite parameters, and spoke the obvious "Well then what choice do you have but cut all the bad stuff out". Her doe eyes were fully dilated from Talwin, a pain medication she took too often, and gave an accusing look "My Parents are my only comfort and support. I can't go against their wishes".

Two more days in unbearable pain, Rachel went into surgery at Group Health Hospital, where my Grampa died. I sat in the waiting room with her Mom and Dad, who held me in snarling contempt, as if this was all my doing, but then since the beginning, they pointed the bad-influence finger in my direction, blaming me for any trouble Rachel got herself into, and she let them without a word. Having my character so maligned had hurt like crazy, and my younger days' inclination for heated defense only seemed to reinforce their conviction, so I held steady without a word, now, when we should be comforting, there was too much history. And so we waited, reading 1968 Sunset magazines and Ladies Home Journals, pacing the beige hallways, smoking cigarettes, feeding vending machines, surreptitiously eyeing one another. Three PM the Rabbi came for a comfort visit. Listening to his compassionate ministrations, I thought he sounded broad-minded, even reasonable. When Mom excused herself to the ladies-room, and Dad to a necessary business phone call, I approached "Hi Rabbi. I'm Shoshannah Leibofsky. You probably know my Folks, they go to your synagogue". He nodded smiling "Yes. And how come I haven't seen you there". I did not bother an answer "Rachel and I have been friends since we were little. I met her in Sunday School. I know you're here for her Parents today, but I was hoping to ask you a question. See I promised my Grampa to be married by a rabbi, and I was wondering if you would marry Corbett and me". He tilted his head slightly "Corbett. Is that a Jewish name". I nodded "You're right, he Catholic. But he doesn't go to church anymore". Rabbi leaned forward "Does he believe in Jesus Christ as his personal savior". I bit my lip "Well, I'm not exactly sure what that means, but I think so". Folding arms firmly across his chest, his too small JCPenney suit-jacket not quite letting him comfortably complete the job, he slowly leaned back "I have to say no. I couldn't possibly marry you. But you might try calling Rabbi Singer". I could feel Rachel's Father behind me. He sat next to Rabbi and glared my way, folding arms cross his chest, his cashmere suit jacket allowing easy movement. My neon face gave the wrong impression, fuck you, just fuck you so loud in my head I thought hospital security would arrest me for public profanity. Far as I was concerned every fiber of my being was as Jewish and good as theirs, these righteous old men might believe they are entitled by God, that He gave them jurisdiction over me, how could they know I'd called-out Yahweh in His own house, and no longer feared their judgmental human posturing. Trying to relax I walked across the room and took a seat where the tropical fish-tank hid most of me, giving my full attention to the one with iridescent blue lips, gliding along the glass. The I Ching counsels, act like water. I never understood what that meant till now, floating, peace-full, and spilling into each empty fissure and cleft, filling it up no matter what and moving to the next, I became liquid, and in this filling, oppression had no place to leave its poison. Near 4PM Doctor came in with news, the five-hour operation was a success, he did not have to remove as much of her colon as originally thought, no need for a colostomy. Rachel's Mother came apart, bawling, giggling, thanking God, demanding to see her. Doc dissuaded, please go home, get some sleep, give your Daughter the night. Rabbi echoed. But she was Mother, and she would tantrum till she got her way, and Dad did not stop her. These selfish vindictive children passing themselves off as adults exhausted the last of me, I went home. Nothing could have taken my joy, for there was still time now for me and Rachel to try and know the other, beneath the surface.

I telephoned her room after noon. Words barely audible in slow-morphine, she claimed to feel better than before the operation, though the drug didn't really kill the pain, only made her feel as if it was happening to someone else. Hearing her brave little voice gave me an idea. I asked could she be on her feet in 25 days, standing as my maid-of-honor. Thrilled as a gutted and sewn person could be, she would make it her goal to be there. My next call, Rabbi Singer. Known as the liberal one in the Northwest, if any would marry us it was him. I waited nervous, every time the receptionist came on the line asking did I want to leave a message or keep holding, answering a cheerful "Hold please". The near fifteen-minutes I practiced how to win him. Rabbi said "Hello". Best-laid plans blanking, I spilled my promise to Grampa, Corbett's religion, and petitioned "Will you marry us Rabbi". Listening quietly, he began to laugh as a loving parent does a child's illogical logic "I'm sorry, but no Rabbi I know of will do what you are asking. Your Grandfather wanted you to marry a Jew, that's why he made you promise". Thanking him for the insight I hung-up, smiling to my self how even at the end Grampa was sharp. I felt him close and said out-loud "Well, I tried my best". Some where over seven years the pain and anger of his death had become less constant, I did not always need them to feel him near, there were times like this when all I felt was his warmth and love. Ida Rose had suggested the Ecumenical Council of Seattle. I looked them up, thinking okay then maybe a Priest, it would make some people happy. The Father asked, did I believe in Jesus Christ as my personal savior. I said I wasn't exactly sure what that meant, but I didn't think so. His decreed "Then you're going to hell and I can't marry you". I hung up immediately, hoping to avoid some of the concussion, ran up-stairs, and under the covers with Corbett, tucking in-close to the comfort of his great-heart, affording me some refuge as Ida Rose predicted he would. And then I began giggling, that frothy brook of reprieve from guillotine condemnation, I was free, no Rabbi, no Priest. Our quandary remained, but without such a sticky tangle, hallelujah praise the lord. Corbett proposed a Justice of the Peace. It did not matter to me if a Witch Doctor married us now, infact I would have preferred one to an innocuous Justice of the Peace. Calling my Dad later for advice, I could just see the broad smile on his face. He recommended Justice Solie Ringold, the first Jewish Supreme Court Judge in Washington State, founding member of the American Civil Liberties Union Washington State Chapter, and King County Superior Court trial Judge, being called a flaming liberal, and often under-fire from Republicans, someone Dad knew many years and highly respected "In my eyes Shoshy, he's as good as a Rabbi". This Judge was the genuine juice, having the kind of courage I would be honored to stand infront of. I called the Courthouse, ah the Courthouse, and was told by his bailiff getting an appointment with this Judge ordinarily took weeks, but there was a cancellation for tomorrow at 2PM. Considering the other calls, this one went so well I could not help but think it was the Sweet Sisters.

Corbett believed in mentally planning ahead for a parking-space, visualizing it on the way, a spot would be waiting when he got there. It often was, this one half-a-block from the Courthouse. A showy April day, sparkling clean from early morning rain, cumulus clouds sailing the sunny blue sky, snow-capped Olympic mountains verging West, and a reliable salt-breeze gusting-up from Elliott Bay, Seattle deluxe. We shared the same buoyant mood hand-in-hand along 3rd Avenue. Corbett possessed by John Wayne. And me imploring oh please oh please be good in the Judge's chambers or he'll think we're too weird, when I saw Penny walking toward us. Having lost touch when Nick and me moved in together, I hesitated to complicate our day as she passed without seeming to notice. But I loved this old Friend and called her name. Looking, eyes panicking, she froze. I pulled Corbett to meet her. She would not look at or speak to him, only me. Second-speak, I could smell Nick on her, and wished I kept my tongue, knowing anything I said would get to him "We're on the way to see a Judge about getting married". Suddenly I was her long-lost Best Friend, she flung greedy arms around me "I'm so glad for you little Shoshy. Nick and I are back together you know". Every shade of emotion shot through me, jealousy compassion anger fear relief, sadness winning, for Penny had been innocent prey to a Father's sexual nightmare and Mother's preoccupied looking away. Nick would be sure to consume any scrap of self-esteem she needed to get away from him again. I returned her embrace and hushed "If you ever get loose of him and want to talk, call my Mom, she'll know where I am". She clung, let me go, stole a peek of Corbett, and gushed "Nick's been diagnosed schizophrenic you know. He got five years for the Sky River bust. Served six months. He had to get you know a legit job on parole. Union Pacific hired him on their maintenance crew. Then he had an accident coupling cars, terrible you know, crushed his left hand. He moved in with me to heal. And then got busted carrying his Kabar into a club. So stupid. Parole was clear about weapons you know. So he went back in for a year, an busted his right hand in a fight. He went home you know when he got out, to live with his Folks. His hands're ruined. Can't play anymore. Really fucked him up bad you know…". Way more than I wanted in my head, I knew nothing about schizophrenia beyond how it was pronounced, and could not fathom anything worse than losing his music, which had always been the best part of him, the only part

I missed. The phone calls, the sightings, it was him stalking me, and I felt powerfully unnerved he could find me on this of all days though Penny. I cut her off "Sorry. We're going to be late for our appointment. It was good seeing you". She seemed anxious to get away from me too "Yeah you know, it was good seeing you too". I took Corbett's hand as we scaled the Courthouse stairs, and turned to watch her cross James Street, thinking there but for the Sweet Sisters grace go I.

Walking though the revolving doors, I had never actually been inside the Courthouse, and flashed-back to the sound of breaking glass, FBI informant Horace L.Parker, running from the Pigs, and here I was getting married. We were shown into the Judge's chambers. He asked fondly after my Father as we sat, and explained that he took the responsibility of marriage seriously, and wanted to interview us before making a decision. Corbett winked at me as if to say relax, leaned back in his chair, crossing those long legs. I was so taken with the principled ethics and charisma of this Man, so urgently wanted him to be the one to marry us, and it was not a done deal, I never imagine he might say no, sitting bolt up-right in my chair, hands folded in lap, legs crossed at the ankles, I was ready for the test. We talked an hour, about hopes, dreams, aspirations, beliefs, heroes, families. Judge excused him self to the bookshelves, selecting a thin volume, opening as he crossed the room, sitting quietly in his high-backed leather chair, considering the pages. Then with a smile and nod, he suggested as part of the ceremony he could read from *The Prophet* by Kahlil Gibran. My jaw and shoulders relaxed completely, he was going to do it, and with my Grampa's blessing, for the last thing I read to him before he died was this book. Corbett asked what he had in mind. The Judge read aloud.

ON MARRIAGE
YOU WERE BORN TODAY, AND TOGETHER YOU SHALL BE FOREV-
ERMORE.
YOU SHALL BE TOGETHER WHEN THE WHITE WINGS OF DEATH
SCATTER
YOUR DAYS.
AY, YOU SHALL BE TOGETHER EVEN IN THE SILENT MEMORY OF
GOD.

BUT LET THERE BE SPACES IN YOUR TOGETHERNESS.
LOVE ONE ANOTHER, BUT MAKE NOT A BOND OF LOVE:
LET IT RATHER BE A MOVING SEA BETWEEN THE SHORES OF
YOUR SOULS.
FILL EACH OTHERS CUP BUT DRINK NOT FROM ONE CUP.
GIVE ONE ANOTHER OF YOUR BREAD BUT EAT NOT FROM THE
SAME LOAF.
SING AND DANCE TOGETHER AND BE JOYOUS, BUT LET EACH
ONE OF
YOU BE ALONE.
EVEN AS THE STRINGS OF A LUTE ARE ALONE THOUGH THEY
QUIVER WITH THE SAME MUSIC.
GIVE YOUR HEARTS, BUT NOT INTO EACH OTHERS KEEPING.
FOR ONLY THE HAND OF LIFE CAN CONTAIN YOUR HEART.
AND STAND TOGETHER YET NOT TOO NEAR TOGETHER.
FOR THE PILLARS OF THE TEMPLE STAND APART.
AND THE OAK TREE AND THE CYPRESS GROW NOT IN EACH
OTHERS SHADOW.

The designation Judge was not misplaced on this one. Corbett's shining smile told me he felt the same. Still, I had one little sticky, in the love honor and obey department, obey must be left out. Judge glanced at Corbett, who nodded almost imperceptibly. This inferential exchange made the Furies gallop though me, broadsword drawn, I had not asked would he leave out obey, but most plainly that he must, there was no need for Corbett's approval. Tyranny, dictators, religion, mother, traffic signals all might share a sentence with obey, not me. It seemed no matter how wise or liberal the authority, patriarchy considered me less than a whole person, men wink-nod have the real say. I was getting-up to wag my tongue, knowing he could find his schedule already filled. The Judge stood too, as if hearing my head, he assured me there was no problem with my request, then walked to the chambers door, called his Bailiff, and asked about the date. Corbett took my hand, squeezing gently as we waited on the Judge's back, whispering he did not want to obey either. The Judge's calendar was open, yes to a 4PM ceremony, he bid us good day, there was another waiting for his time. Major tangle unwound, I felt really great that a green-eyed possessive dictatorial rabbi-priest God would not be attending our nuptials.

Corbett rarely showed teeth smiling, because of shameless amalgam fillings. But riding home in the Bug there they were for all to see. I teased "It's not too late. You sure about this". John Wayne "Sure am little lady". The thought of marrying Mr. Wayne struck me hilarious, still I had deep-rooted anxiety "Do you think maybe it'll ruin everything. It's no ones business how I feel about you. Especially since most will be coming just to see the Freak show". Mr. Wayne put a tarantula hand on my thigh "Why little lady, I think you have a case of stage fright". Seeing I did not think him funny anymore Corbett found his own voice "Don't worry Sweetheart. It's like getting ready for a big gig. I have to remind myself it's not fear but thrill". My thoughts went to an unwieldy leather suitcase, sun setting over the Pacific, and me weightless and carefree, sitting on the fender of a brand-new Mustang at the precipice of Highway One, as Gretchen Fetchin-Fine, Leda with the Electric Blue Eyes, Amaru, Keely, and the sixteen-year-old Boy who rode us to Santa Cruz in his birthday car wend their way down to the shore. I could vividly recall how alone I felt, no one to talk too, resigned to solitary, thinking I had loved once and lost and would never love again, and was okay with it. Putting my hand on Corbett's, I said what I had been wanting to for more than a year "Promise me. You'll stop drinking before you're thirty". He simply said "Promise".

Mom was in her glory, every day after work cooking and cooking and freezing. We talked nightly around 8PM. She called it the progress report, and was always busy making something while filling me in on every detail, shopping for ingredients, plans for chopped liver, how well blintzes hold-up in the freezer, what Granny was cooking, so much food. I did not ordinarily talk to her but once a week, and began to dread the nightly accounting, feeling more and more my life was no longer mine, finally finding some gumption "Maybe we could talk every other night". Mother's rule went like this, any further debate will be taken as impertinent, no argument, effectively cutting-off any discussion "Don't be ridiculous Shoshannah, there's too much to plan and do". But I dared "You know it's funny Mom, I remember Family dinners and cocktail parties with more than 40 people that took just a couple days to get ready". She closed the door "Your wedding is not a cocktail party". Three nights had passed without her call, Corbett's and my life almost usual, but now I had to tell her about the Judge. Answering on the 8th ring, her voice flat "I'm kind of busy making sweet'n sour porcupine meatballs". I swallowed a raging tirade, aren't you suppose to be an adult too Mom, why make it so hard, and just incase you forgot, I'm a vegetarian and can not stomach the nightly reckoning of dead animal parts being chopped fried boiled and baked in my name, saying what I always do "Sorry Mom. I know you're busy. I'll be quick. Judge Ringold said he would marry us". She never held any animus on my capitulation, indifference left her voice, something heavy and taut remained "That's wonderful news Shoshy. I know your Father'll be so happy to hear". I presumed "You have a hard day at work". Taking a long drag on her cigarette she sighed on the exhale "No, that's not it. Your Grandmother's taken it upon herself to invite all her Sisters and Brothers, and your Grandfather's Sisters and Brothers, and Spouses, and first cousins". I felt run-over "Oh no Mom. All those people watching us say private stuff to each other, whispering behind their hands. Where's the good in that". Mom tried to move on "What's done is done. Anyway, they'll be lots of good food with all your Aunties cooking too". Platitudes never suited me "Yeah and how about all that lots of good food. I couldn't figure out why you and Granny were cooking so much. You knew all along didn't you. She's your Mother, you had to know she'd do this". Mom pleaded innocent "No, honest. I only found out yesterday. Anyway, what do you want me to do, uninvited them". I was white-hot, mostly at my self for tipping the first domino to begin with "Yeah, I do". She sniffed "I can't do that. Anyway, what's a few more, it won't matter one way or another. They're your Family, they love you". A few more won't matter crushed my brain "Mom, I gota go". She readily agreed "Sure Honey. And don't worry, everything's going to be fine". Leaving for McGoverns, Corbett wrapped me in his arms "The wedding's already been corrupted. My Folks're coming. So your Mom's kind of right, what difference does it make if more come. Let it go Shoshy. Nothing anyone says or does will spoil our love". Kissing me, he went his way. And I stood at the front window watching long after the Bug disappeared, all this don't worry shit from everyone, I hated him for being so sensitive and yet disengaged, so withy and knowing when it came to my Folks. Reaching my fists high above my head, opening them to the sky, symbolically surrendering, I called Mom back "I'm not mad at you. And I won't bring this up to Granny if you make her stop inviting right now. She's still up, call her now, okay". Mom swore "Soon as we hang-up. But your Grandmother doesn't listen to me, and I can't guarantee what she's done since yesterday, or what she'll do no matter what I say". I was calmly amused, well well so your Mother doesn't listen to you either, and heard my voice acquiesce as from a tremendous distance "That's all I can ask Mom, thanks". I had been sucked over the event horizon, falling though empty-space without the feeling of falling, no time, no gravity, no landmarks, no me, nothing but velocity.

Fifty-four hours and counting, my dress, a well done undiluted homage to my Mother, ideal wedding cake figurine, when I modeled for Corbett, he said I was divine. His antique-white satin shirt with generous flowing sleeves and ruffled cuffs fastened in the brass-and-pink-jade links I bought in San Francisco's Chinatown, his regulation 13 button U.S.Navy wool bell-bottoms that lace-up the back, his psychedelic paisley bow-tie and cummerbund made from a length of Monique and Loretta's silk I had been saving for the right occasion, his 1940's wool tux-jacket with shawl-collar found along with Grilla-Fish, and dusky blue-suede cowboy boots more fairly spoke to his romantic rebel spirit. I grumbled half in-fun, how no one leaned on him to wear what they wanted. Just before noon, Lorenzo came by, peace offering to sing at our wedding. Their long friendship badly bruised, had been built on solid ground and looked like it would survive Designer Christian. We had not given a thought to music, and the tickle on Corbett's face said reservations were not allowed. Sounding awfully like my Mom I did anyway "But it's only two days away. I just can't handle any more stuff". Corbett cocked his head at me "What do you mean". Why he would question me infront of anyone on such well-known circumstances, I was shaken, his standing-us-apart so near the deed "You know Mom's got every detail planned and probably set up already". I turned to Lorenzo "I'm really sorry, but bringing in sound equipment will just freak her out. I can't tangle with her anymore, I just lose". Renzo grinned "How 'bout I sing a cappella". Corbett raised his brows at me "Any objections". This was an olive branch Corby wanted, they made such music together, its demise more unbearable than either were willing to admit, and me saving what hide I had left was just not worth it. Grinning with all my teeth, opening my hands "Nope, not if it's *Great Balls of Fire*". Always the one to sing this song, Corbett was delighted "Good call Sweetheart, I love it". Renzo cleared his throat, took a deep bow, and belted a gospely version "Well well well now, take me to synogogue America. *You shake my nerves and you rattle my brain. Too much love drives a man insane. You broke my wheel, but what a thrill. Goodness gracious great balls of fire*". Gus and Grilla-Fish had joined in. Pure-glee lit Corbett's eyes, he clapped Renzo on the back "That's it man, I couldn't a done better". I was clapping too, and mulling how to break this to Mom.

Dad wanted in on the preparations, asking please meet him at Pike Place Market after 1PM, together we would buy the flowers and cake. Friday always busy, lunch-rush was over for Chicken Valley's daily standing-in-line-fifteen-deep waiting for the chicken to come out of the broaster customers, buying it before it ever made it into the showcase, Mom could handle the place for a while. I had come-up with no better way than helium-enthusiasm to break the sticky "So, great news. Lorenzo's going to sing the wedding march Sunday". Mom fired "What. Are you meshuggeneh. There's no time for changes". I still felt ground under-foot "No problem Mom, he's going to sing a cappella". She took a step toward me, always an advantage, she was two-inches taller "And exactly what wedding march is he going to sing a cappella". Ground gave-way, I was standing on tiptoes "*Great Balls of Fire* by Jerry Lee Lewis". She seemed to get bigger, madder, and hurt, pointing a sharp finger at my nose, shaking so fast it blurred "Shoshannah Leibofsky, how can you be like this. It's your wedding, not some keg party. Lorenzo can sing *Sunrise Sunset* from Fiddler on the Roof or nothing, and that's final". I forced my hands open, telling myself, it's only a song, it's only a stupid song "Okay Mom, okay, if Lorenzo knows it. But he's going to sing, cause it means a lot to Corbett". Hanging his knee length white cotton butcher's coat on a hook by the walk-in freezer, Dad pulled-on a grey wool newsboy cap he'd taken to since hair began thinning, the alpaca vest Mom knit him, and kissed her on the mouth. Exchanging their confidential little look, and that last necessary embrace always before parting, he motioned to me with such love in his eyes, making solid ground again under my feet "Come on Shoshy, let's go". Walking Pike Street to the flower-shop, he put a Father's hand on my shoulder "You know your Mother's heart is always in the right place. And I happen to agree with her, *Sunrise Sunset* is a good choice". The only sticky he had asked me for, I could only say "Okay Daddy. *Sunrise Sunset*". A fragrant-medley beckoned us in the Florist's door, he called Dad by his first name, and brought the wedding catalog. We stood side-by-side at the counter, thumbing, each bouquet beautiful in its way. Near the end one call to me, a demure cluster of seven pale-pink rosebuds held in fragrant lavender, tied in white velvet, $7.50. My Dad enjoyed nothing more than having money to spend on his Loved Ones, he turned back to the most extravagant, encouraging me pick one of them. But the innocent little nosegay alone had spoken my name. I selected a simple white daisy tied in white velvet for Corbett's lapel, the same for Dad and Halls, three yellow roses in full-bloom for Mom, Arlene and Rachel, a daisy for Gus, pink rosebud for Grilla-Fish, and daisy table arrangements, $45.00 total, delivered tomorrow after work. Dad said nothing, paying in cash, stooped shoulders bearing the degradation of looking cheap infront of a fellow businessman. I sorely regretted having been the cause. At the bakery, Owner called Dad by his first name. There were two full shelves of ornaments, all prissy little brides in gowns much like mine, standing by their square-jawed groom's side, all looking remarkably like Tara and Will, I was happy to do without. Dad plucked a white heart with two sparkling bells from the top shelf and placed it in my hands. And I counseled his eyes as we turned the catalog pages, letting him pick what I picked, a cake more expensive than all the flowers, his proud shoulders and high head all I wanted. It would be delivered Sunday. We walked to the Athenian Cafe, upstairs at the Public Market, sitting across from each other in the small wooden booth as we had so many times, over-looking the sun-gilded bay, ferry-boats coming and going, I did not resist sharing a bucket of steamed clams with drawn-butter and French bread, small talking, sipping clam nectar, enjoying each others company. The last time I would be my Daddy's Little Girl.

Saturday morning mail, our living room filling with gifts and gelt, we had shunned the rules and still the not invited generously reciprocated Mom and Dad's years of giving. Corbett took a call from Erik before going to pick-up his tux jacket from the cleaners, some equivocal Family emergency, they could not make it to the wedding. I was de-lighted. And Leda called with tidings "I was totally surprised to hear from Cyrene last night. She wanted you to know quote, the cheap invitation was such a deliberate slap in the face, they would not be coming to your wedding. I told her everyone got the same. She called me a liar. I'm really sorry, I shouldn't be passing this garbage on". Stung as Cyrene had intended, I took a breath "Wow, no honey. You did fine. It's always been about her. She sure gives me way more credit than I deserve for being mean". And then giggling as the irony dawned "But then maybe not. I did get exactly what I wanted. She can't say I didn't invite her, and won't be coming. So ha ha ha". And, Ida Rose called "I must fly to Alaska in just a few hours. Tom's taking me to the airport. My Granddaughter delivered her Baby late last night, cesarean. I simply must go. I'm so sorry to miss your wedding. I know you understand". Without her depth, her blessing, the day would be an act of tradition, attended mostly by voyeurs vilipends and tares, I held my tears "Course I do. Are they okay". Ida Rose sounded in a hurry "She tells me she is, but I must go see for myself. I hope you know Lamby, how I would love to witness your marriage. I will keep your darling faces in my thoughts tomorrow". Phone still at my ear, I sank to the floor, glad it was there, too numb to cry, talking to the dial-tone "Oh well, what the hell, Sister Fate can be so cruel, *don't be cruel to a heart that's true*, ha, guess some would say the worst already happened so there's nothing more to worry about, all wrapped-up, tied round my neck, put out the trash, close the lights, nail down the fucking coffin lid". I began to sing "Well you can't get to heaven with a can of beans on your head". Gus and Grilla-Fish climbed into my lap, burrowing cold noses under my hands, looking up at me with those knowing eyes. I was grateful for their solid diversion, soon running a bath for them. Since I began using baby shampoo that did not sting their eyes, they began to fancy the soapy if-sometimes-too-personal rub-down.

May 6, 1973, Corbett and I lay quiet holding hands, Grilla-Fish and Gus circling the bed, suspicious our being awake in the young of the day. We showered, and took them and wedding costumes to Mercer Island by 10AM. Dad raising the huppa in the living room. *The Voice of Mirth, and the Voice of Gladness, the Voice of the Bridegroom, and the Voice of the Bride* from Jeremiah embroidered in Hebrew and English across the blue and white silk canopy. Mom spreading freshly-ironed lace and linen tablecloths, flowers were everywhere, lots more than I ordered, the house smelled wonderful. Having brought my magic teapot, I put it on the boil. As she complained her disappointment to Corbett "I wanted to do the right thing, and called your Mother yesterday morning before we left for work, to find out what time they were coming in. I offered to pick them up at the airport, and take us all to dinner. A chance to get to know each other before the big day. And I'm sorry, but your Mother's really good at the brush-off. They would be much too tired, couldn't possibly put me to all that trouble, and would take a cab. She even refused to let me pick them up today for godsake. Right here on the Island, one mile and she'd rather take a cab. Couldn't they put out just a little effort". The corners of Corbett's blue eyes cringing at the thought of his Folks, how their tangle preceded them, how the sticky was stuck to him too. It was not right, making Corbett responsible for his Parents' actions when nothing could be done, when she refused her own Mothers. How could he explain these people were not human but minor Lords of Form with no real feelings. Knowing him, knowing he would not, I stepped in-between the growing silence "Mom, don't take it personal. Halls and Arlene are just spoil-sports. You know, cold fish". A naïve optimist, Mom harbored the old fairy-tale, and would try and try to make it come out as written, believing if she just went at it hard enough, was just so very nice, sheer willingness would make it happily-ever-after. Behavior Halls and Arlene saw as pushy Jew. She lit a smoke, stress deeply creasing her brow, tensing neck and shoulders "Well I don't think it's right". Sticky as this was, it justified the Janus-face promise I'd made to get them here, and the show would go on, and Corbett would escape the worst whisperings "Mom, what's right for you isn't what's right for them. I gave up on them already. It'll save you an Dad years of tsuris if you do too. You have to get baptized and take Jesus Christ in your heart as your personal savior. That's it, or you can't get to heaven. And they don't care about anyone who won't be there with them, and never will". Eyes glazing-over from more than she wanted to know, Mom blew a puff of smoke at my face "I can't even imagine people so cold toward their own Son's wedding. But they're Corbett's parents Shoshannah, you can't give up on them". I signed "Yes Mother". Hesitating, Corbett offered "My Parents aren't like you guys". Loading film in his cameras, Dad harmonized "You're right about that My Boy". Corbett grinned bashfully. My Father claiming him had begun to sweeten a terrible nagging privation, of which I had no experience and little power to affect. Dad had a jerk for a Dad too, and understood exactly, Corbett needed a Father's loving approval, and gave it to him freely.

Mom stacked Connie Francis, West Side Story, Mario Lanza and Ray Charles on the record player, I made ice tea, and we went to work singing the songs and setting-up. The bar on a long table in the rec room, with local prize-winning Chateau Ste.Michelle wines, and bottles of good scotch, rum, bourbon, vodka and gin Dad had bought in Reno, waiting in a dark closet ten years now, aging, likely for this purpose since they were not drinkers. And because the day was glorious sunshine and spring flowers, champagne, cognac and cigars went to the backyard gazebo. Every cherished bowl, dish and platter, cup, snifter, jigger and glass, every candlestick, fork and serving spoon from Mom and Granny's sterling silver and crystal collections had been washed and polished and waited its fill. Leaving space for the cake, sweets went on the dining-room table and sideboard, Boehm's chocolates from Issaquah, Jordan almonds, honey-sesame candy, marzipan, halvah, coconut macaroons, apricot strudel, apple strudel, peanut-butter fudge. In the family room, one table for roasted goose and capon, smoked turkey, sesame-honey chicken wings, chicken livers wrapped in oh my god bacon, home-made pickled peppers, sweet and dill pickles, green and black olives. Another with jumbo prawns, crab-filled mushroom caps, oysters on the half-shell, paper-thin lox, smoked salmon, and caviar. A third, little loaves of sliced caraway-rye, bagels and challah, crackers, hard and soft cheese, porcupine meatballs, pickled herring, chopped herring, chopped liver, pot-la-john, platters of fancy-cut vegetables, a parade of dips. We worked with one-mind, till knocking on the door, the cake delivery. A magnificent three-tiered lemon-curd-filling pound-cake with boiled white frosting, lavished in pink rosebuds and daisies, leaning seriously to the side. I love the leaning, it made such perfect sense.

Rachel arrived, her steady recovery had not surprised the doctors, and absolutely astonished her Parents. Having already gained 7 pounds, she felt stronger than in years, and by coming, was taking some autonomy from their clutches. Mom asked for her coat, catching her breath. Rachel's bare arms spindling as wrists, her sharp-boned hips slashing at the long teal-blue rayon designer dress, and yet she mustered a typical come-on-you-know-I-look-like-a-Vogue-model smile. Which at this point of my own insanity granted such comfort and perspective, for here and very much alive was that familiar rivaling vanity of hers, where even emaciation was not too thin, that for better or worse near-death had not managed to defeat, and just when I most needed to know some thing even this frail could survive the juggernaut. She set her lumbering shoulder bag on the floor unzipped, it was full of jumbo rollers. I carried it to the bathroom, where we'd spent countless Junior High School hours smoothing our locks, confident her capable fingers would once again make the most of mine. Using every roller and pin, she tied my head in a big challis scarf. And having given me all she had, I took her to my bedroom, and gave her to Morpheus. Granny and her Sisters came in two cars, with all their delicacies, gefilte fish, brisket, sweet and savory kugels, blintzes, potato knishes, cheese boyos, lemon bars, mandelbroit, biscochos, and cookies. And they took-over, covering every surface with their celebrated specialties. And Mom, having never really wanted me in her kitchen, had no choice but yield into their capable hands. Leda came, an impressionist's pastel-floating-dream-garden in a flowered long ball-gown and broad-brim yellow ribbon hat. She came to do my make-up, and deliver a pink rosebud garland for my hair from Ida Rose. I found my self in tears placing it safely in the back of the refrigerator for now, Leda with the Electric Blue Eyes, one of the MotherTruckers had remained true. Katey came to paint my nails. Irish-white freckled skin and waist-long red hair outstanding contrast to her long forest-green velvet empire gown. The Baby was healthy and happy, both Kids spending the evening with Pam, she had one more school semester, Willy had not found her. Again my eyes filled, there were four of us, and I marveled how Katey, Leda, Rachel, never having met, each came early, some kind of cosmic organization at work here, calling my Bosom Girls to prepare the Bride for sacrifice. Oh shit, I'm the Bride, the first of us to marry.

Before the scarlet nail polish dried completely, Mom knocked on the bathroom door, summoning me. With her already, Corbett gave me worried eyes as we followed down the hall to their bedroom. Dad waiting by the window, gazing out, Mona Lisa smile on his face, a small red leather ring box in each hand. He lit-up on seeing us, and without prelude, gave one to me, and one to Corbett. I instantly knew he made us rings, and still could not have expected those rose-gold guards with Burmese ruby all the way around, and the 24 carat gold band with five channel-set brilliant-cut blue-white diamonds, flawless, one-half carat each. My heart ached, for I had desperately wanted to spare the third finger of my left hand a permanent metal halter, even these, ever before of my eyes, swearing publicly I am The Wife. And if I took them with the idea of wearing only when Mom and Dad were around, and forgot even one time, there would be those questions, so where are your rings, aren't they comfortable, don't you like them, did you lose them. I knew my Folks, they never took theirs off even to chop chickens or sleep, and would so delight in seeing these on my hand, they could not help but notice, and any dissembling now or later would leave a stink, eventually causing the same hurt as saying no thank you now. They stood so wide-open, and I was so grateful it was them who raise me, so loved how Dad still called Mom his Girlfriend, I would keep my qualms forever sweet and simply kvelled. Corbett opened his box, a wide gold band also channel-set in five flawless blue-whites, one-carat total. He was overwhelmed, and wrapped his arms around Dad and kissed him on the cheek. I did too Mom. We all shook-off some nerves.

Yellow Cab brought the Hawkins, their white clean good and oh so very tolerant faces firmly fixed. A tumbler of rum and coke in hand, Corbett introduced them around. Duplicitous as it was, I knew having them here today meant symbolically more than he wanted to admit, and would shush most of the whispers, about them and him anyway. Trickle became a tide, Grampa's five younger Brothers, each resembling him in an unexpectedly satisfying way, each prospering, sporting expensive watches, new spring suits and comb-overs, followed by their short dark curly-haired wives, every finger wrist neck and earlobe spangled in jewels. And

Granny's Sisters' Husbands, even more prosperous, yet not so showy or chauvinistic, which I attributed partly to character, but more to my five Aunties, whose love and allegiance to each other made them formidable MotherTruckers in their own right. And my grown cousins came, most not seen since we were small. The kibitzing and noshing, clucking and purring, I felt a clown in jumbo rollers, and went to the bathroom to take them down. Mom opened the door, asking me please stay out of sight till the ceremony begins. Here was the final sticky, and I could not swallow it, every insensitive unthinking impertinence rose-up for redress, and my poor Mom standing there target. Happily Katey and Leda flew-in carrying the rosebud garland, and Mom went away smiling. Yawning, stretching, Rachel joined us, having a measure of herself again and a clever idea, using my own hair to invisibly fasten the pink halo to my head, the same color as Ida Rose's aura, the color of love. I sat on the toilet seat as her deft fingers threaded one hair and another using a big-eyed needle. Not since working for Boeing had I been this polished, and I could not help railing at the Golden Ghost, lurking, enjoying Herself way too much, that shallow little Sylph who still owned some of me, though she had no right to even one crumb, for I had ventured way too much cultivating her mediocrity into an original, and yet here I sat in the line of human tradition. The touch of Leda dabbing gloss on my lips dispelled the Revenant, she had done a splendid job keeping tinctures and creams under-stated, her tender care sweet as honey, and yet having worn no paint since traveling to the Haight with Casey, I felt stagey and neon. I thanked her without reservation. Rachel too. And Katey, who having seen Delroy and Corbett sipping cognac, puffing cigars in the gazebo, confessed to a blushing crush on Delroy, she was twitching to meet him. Rachel too. I had forgotten he was a genuine rock-god, and bid Leda please do the honors, I would catch up with them later.

Mom's directive rolled round my head, hot breath debating, no, I will not remain hidden. I did not fear some big bad omen if the bride is seen before the ceremony. Staying close to the walls, care-full to elude her notice, bystanding my own wedding, watching, Dad welcome the Judge, Rachel and Katey compete for Delroy's attention, Renzo arrive without Marion, hollow-eyed, unsteady, the exaltation of speaking in tongues, the free floating high of giving all his shit over to Jesus, the blinding ecstasy of glitter shock had gone its way, leaving the same-old life and problems festering from neglect, they had separated, and early this morning she took the Baby and the train home to Mom. Corbett asked him to stand as best man. Renzo's face brightened, it was just the boost he needed to reclaim a bit of self-worth. Re-minding me of the first time I saw them, on stage at the Gate of Horn with Delroy. Even then I could see Lorenzo rode Corbett's coat-tails, and in the dynamic of the moment it was still true. Somewhere in this life or past, some essential part of Renzo had been stolen, and till it was named and claimed, would actively continue to leave him powerless, needing somebody or some program to name and claim him.

Mom made her entrance in a beautiful sleeveless knee-length navy raw-silk sheath dress, narrow black patent-leather belt and sling-back pumps. Dad a brown and mauve pin-striped suit, pale pink shirt, paisley tie, brown alligator loafers, new wire-rimmed glasses, and mutton-chops to rival Elvis. But they could have worn their peel and it would not matter, the proud blazing from their eyes was all anyone could see. Little Brother arrive with his Fiancée. She seemed someone I could have as my first legal Sister, but she was the oldest of five Girls, would probably never understand how much just one could mean to me. Big Brother and Marlee swaggered in soon after. Ambitiously sun-tan, reeking of estrogen and testosterone, his starched white shirt unbuttoned to far, sharks tooth dangling from a gold chain, she wore a black satin spaghetti-strap mini-dress, red high heels, and the tallest beehive hairdo I had ever seen. Though Marlee did not resemble Gretchen, there were shades of Fetchin-Fine in her, Daddy's Little Girl shades, especially in the way her dewy skin and pouty mouth made her seem in constant cum. And Big, a highly varnished expert in flaunting the moment no matter where by displaying sexual prowess, did not disappoint, announcing his intention to whisk Marlee to Vegas soon and tie-the-knot, and then grabbing, pressing her full-on against his body, knee spreading her thighs, ramming his tongue down her throat, which she expertly relaxed to avoid gagging. Big was so like Nick, he thought the way to a woman's heart was his dick. I knew, even if they made it legal, anyone who would marry Big had too little self-respect to be a real Sister of mine. When I stamped and addressed their invitation, we decided not to send it. Mom asked them anyway.

House and yard percolating, counting me and the Furheads, 106. In the mix, Leda and Tom only had eyes for the other. Kenny, Gil, Stan, Renzo and Corbett standing camaraderie at the bar, oh shit Stan, meaning Cyrene. I glided the walls, finding her belly-up to the seafood buffet with Corbett's Mother, noting how energy vampires were drawn together, and musicians, and all the pockets of guests. Cyrene had a gold hoop impaling her right nostril, I had only seen this in National Geographic Magazine, and though it did compliment her broad proboscis by distraction, such a titillating ornament seemed wholly incongruous and far too provocative on so humble a Bible-Thumper. She saw me, our eyes locked, and I felt Granny's hand clamp on my elbow, pointing to Cyrene with her chin, growling "Who's the Shiksa in white. Has she no manners. Kineahora, you should be the only one in white today. Something must be wrong with her head". Though a pierced snout seemed defiant, I knew Cyrene accommodated the never-agreed-to-rules far more than me, her wearing white was not innocent, and yet I did not care "Yeah Granny, there really is something wrong with her head, so please don't make a big deal over it". Granny obeyed the rules too, and their violation mattered terribly to her, she charged across the room to avenge this mocking trespass of her Granddaughter's special day. I could not make out words, the gestures were unmistakable, and as the house hushed to an audience, Granny grew louder "You could be a pretty girl if you didn't disfigure your punim like that". Having met her match Cyrene was speechless. My dear Granny had given voice to what was surely on most minds, the chasm of intractable culture clashing, the rank and nettle when Straits and FlowerChildren occupy the same space, I was beginning to enjoy my self.

Gus, Grilla-Fish, Corbett and me took quiet shelter in my bedroom. Corby looked so handsome in his tux, my heart thundered as I pinned the single daisy to his lapel. Gus and Grilla were our Flower-Dogs. Having made them satin collars, Grilla's trimmed in lace, I safety-pinned on the boutonnieres, and tied them round their necks, they did not resist. Corbett offered me his cognac. I gulped it "Thanks Babe. You know, it's just too weird losing my name. How would you feel giving up yours. It's like giving up your identity". John Wayne "Well little lady, it sure ain't fair. But if you have your way, this will change soon". I smiled "How about now, today. I'm just learning who I am, and don't want to be called someone else. I hope this doesn't hurt your feelings, but I think your Father's a jerk and don't want to carry his name. It's your name too, I know, and I hope you understand, I like my name and can't see any reason I should lose it cause of some ceremony". Corbett always managed to amaze me "I don't mind at all Sweetheart. I think my Father's a jerk too, maybe I should change my name to yours. Do you think I could get away with being a Leibofsky". "No Babe, you're way too tall". He put his arms around me "We'll sign the marriage license as we please, an no one will know". I mused "Or understand. Maybe we should a done this on acid". He hugged me tighter "It's already such a trip, I feel like I'm on acid anyway". I suddenly understood, he was feeling the velocity too.

Rachel Katey and Leda knocked on the door, anxious, the ceremony would start soon. I looked up at Corbett. He touched my cheek, using Bogart's tender voice *"Here's looking at you kid"*. And left with Gus and Grilla-Fish. My Waiting Ladies had come to dress me, all but Rachel proclaiming hearty approval of Hubby to be. And when properly trussed, they left me too. My gown a wilted lily was lovely. Mom's borrowed antique cameo necklace just the touch. Hair and make-up exactly right, nails long and red. My new white peau de soie pumps soft and not too heeled. I pulled the blue garter up my thigh, it would be publicly stripped later, the symbolic taking of my virginity, I would not resist. Picking up the bouquet, I stood looking in the full-length mirror on the back of my bedroom door. I was still that same girl who grew-up in the Golden Ghetto, and she had the same hopes and dreams, but I'd become more, having struggled with God, trusted the Sweet Sisters Fate, found a teacher, some real Friends, and some one to talk too, who knew this lonely girl of little promise no one else really saw, and loved her. My life was full, and if I had dreamed of a wedding this was just fine, but I never spent one minute in this room thinking about getting married. Soon it would be my turn, and I took commitment seriously. Some girl-friends of mine had confessed to knowing days before or on their wedding day they did not love their husband-to-be, and going through with it anyway. This was not my problem, and it wasn't really the rituals and sticky tangle, I was terrified it would tame me. I went to the open window, inhaling the cooling air, and with a long shiny thumb nail unscrewed the screen, having snuck-out this window many times, I considered it now. But Corbett was already standing in the living room under the huppa, I could almost hear him breathing, waiting for it to start. My beautiful Mother waited with tears of joy in her eyes for her beloved Golden Girl to wed. Dad stood right outside my door, so chesty he might burst, waiting for it to start so he could walk his Little Girl and give her away. Renzo began *Is this the little girl I carried. Is this the little boy at play.* Dad knocked. And I took a simple last glance in the mirror to make sure I looked perfect.

www.ingramcontent.com/pod-product-compliance
Lightning Source LLC
Chambersburg PA
CBHW070728120726
47910CB00001B/13